OATHBOUND

Also by Tracy Deonn

Legendborn
Bloodmarked

OATHBOUND

TRACY DEONN

SIMON & SCHUSTER

London New York Amsterdam/Antwerp Sydney/Melbourne Toronto New Delhi

First published in Great Britain in 2025 by Simon & Schuster UK Ltd

1 3 5 7 9 10 8 6 4 2

Simon & Schuster UK Ltd
1st Floor, 222 Gray's Inn Road
London WC1X 8HB

www.simonandschuster.co.uk
www.simonandschuster.com.au
www.simonandschuster.co.in

Simon & Schuster Australia, Sydney
Simon & Schuster India, New Delhi

The authorised representative in the EEA is Simon & Schuster Netherlands BV,
Herculesplein 96, 3584 AA Utrecht, Netherlands. info@simonandschuster.nl

A CIP catalogue record for this book
is available from the British Library.

HB ISBN 978-1-3985-3143-7
TPB ISBN 978-1-3985-3145-1
eBook ISBN 978-1-3985-3144-4
eAudio ISBN 978-1-3985-4154-2

Printed and Bound in the UK using 100% Renewable Electricity
at CPI Group (UK) Ltd

MIX
Paper | Supporting
responsible forestry
FSC® C171272
www.fsc.org

For the girls who face the unknown . . . and leap anyway

PROLOGUE

WHAT MUST BE DONE

I

THE SHADOW KING could destroy me.

I can feel it. When the ancient demon's magic swallows us both, I sense my own ruin, but there is nothing I can do to stop it.

His swirling black wisps tighten like a fist around my rib cage, then . . . *pain*. Squeezing, crushing, breath-stealing pain.

On the grassy hill above the Northern Chapter's Keep, his myrrh-and-sap-scented smoke turns opaque, obscuring my view of Nick running to stop us. The King's magic billows, until all I can see is Nick's aether armor glinting in the sun. His outstretched hand. His blue eyes burning for battle. My final memory of the Keep is Nick, fighting to keep me safe.

There have been so many fights and losses, just to *keep me safe*.

Volition, a haven destroyed because I took shelter on its ancestral grounds. Lu, Hazel, and Mariah's Rootcrafter refuge, compromised because they offered me sanctuary. Alice, in a coma after I struck her down in the throes of possession. Selwyn, succumbed to demonia after consuming my power to bring me back to myself. And Nick, risking his life by returning to the very same Order that sent Merlin assassins to kill him. Too many fights. Too many losses.

The King grasps my hand.

"I'm sorry," I say to Nick, to everyone, to myself.

I avoided Nick before I climbed the hill because if anyone could stop me from leaving, it would be him. Nick's eyes see too much, too clearly, and always have. He would offer understanding when I don't want to be understood.

Not for this.

I whisper, "Please know that I—"

Then, we are traveling through shadows.

Blackness surrounds us in thick, inky streams. My body *knows* we are moving. I feel the leaps across space. Sometimes, when slivers open wide enough in the whirling dark, I glimpse visions of terrifying places—blackened fields burning under a darkened sky, miles and miles of gravestones at night, the deepest parts of the ocean—before the cyclone closes again. My stomach lurches when the world reappears, and twists when it is gone.

This is what it means to travel through shadows, I think—before I begin to suffocate.

In this here-and-there vortex, there is no air. I wonder if I might die before I've even begun this new life.

No.

The thought sharpens my oxygen-deprived mind. I clench the hard hilt of Excalibur to my side.

I will not *die here.*

How much time has passed? Seconds? Minutes? I don't know.

Then suddenly, without warning, we land.

My knees buckle, hitting cold white marble. My grip loosens; Excalibur clatters to the floor. The sharp scent of cleaning supplies catches in the back of my throat, and I cough. Wheeze out a curse. Gasp for air. Try to get my bearings.

We are in a long, empty, windowless corridor inside a building I don't recognize. Coughing still, I raise my watery vision to the mass of smoke before me. Where a face might be are obsidian eyes with shining crimson centers. A demon so strong that this close, even his casual scrutiny sears my skin.

The Shadow King, inhuman.

While he observes the messy humanity of me panting and clammy on the floor, I notice a tendril of dusk has wrapped itself around the security camera mounted on the wall behind him, blocking the lens. Wherever we are, the Shadow King has already ensured that our presence will go undetected.

The black cloud draws my attention again. It churns slowly, then melts, then hardens into the familiar, solid form of Erebus Varelian, Mage Seneschal at Arms of the High Council of the Order of the Round Table.

Erebus watches me with a single brow raised and both hands clasped at his belt. His eyes are now those of a middle-aged Merlin's: heart-blood red with human black pupils. His thick raven hair is perfectly combed back in the Mageguard undercut, and a dark overcoat lies flat on his shoulders, draping down his torso to his knees.

This is the man who fooled the world's most powerful and ancient secret society into believing he was one of them, for who knows how long. Even now the Order believes Erebus to be their highest-ranked, most loyal Merlin soldier. Only he and I know the truth—that he is the Order's greatest enemy. And only *we* know that I, the Order's own Crown Scion and king, have left the Round Table to become his pupil.

My next inhale is a shaky one. *What have I done?*

"Can you walk?" When Erebus speaks, his voice is low and unimpressed. The deferential respect he showed when we first met is absent.

"Why did you," I croak, "take me before I could—"

"And what would you have said to Nicholas Davis," Erebus murmurs, his expression unreadable, "had I not traveled you away?"

My mind flashes to those final images again. Nick's armor. His hand. His eyes. His fingertips straining to meet mine. Our call and response, left unfinished. I grit my teeth. "None of your business."

Erebus's brow lifts. "Then I was right to remove you when I did."

"What does *that* mean?"

"If Nicholas Davis had touched you, he would not have let you go." Erebus's lips purse. "He will be a nuisance enough as it is."

Fear is a quiet, cold trickle inside my chest. The High Council of Regents wants Nick dead because they can't control him; my absence won't change that. I rise to my feet. "Nuisance?"

Something cruel flickers through the Seneschal's gaze. "Once he recovers from the shock of your disappearance, whom do you think Nicholas will pursue first? You . . . or Selwyn?"

My stomach dips. I don't have an answer, but I know I don't *want* Nick to look for me.

Erebus chuckles at my silence. "In either case, the boy will be chasing ghosts: I will ensure that no one finds you, and Selwyn is a lost cause."

That quiet fear doubles. I asked Erebus to take Sel to his mother in the hope that she could reverse his descent into demonia, but even the king of demons could not guarantee that Natasia Kane could save her son. Sel trusted me to control Arthur, and because I trusted *myself* in a moment when I shouldn't have, he sacrificed his humanity to save me.

My breath hitches and my eyes burn. It's done. It's all *done*, and nothing can change it.

I swallow hard and meet Erebus's gaze with a fierce one of my own. "I think Nick will pursue *you*. He saw you, after all. Saw *Erebus* take me away."

Erebus's facial features fade in his brown skin until they become gray mist. Until he is not Erebus, not the King, not *anyone*, exactly. A shadow in the shape of a man.

"Did he, now?"

My heart stutters at the reminder that Erebus is a face the King *chooses*.

I wasn't looking at the Shadow King in that final moment on the hill; I was looking at Nick. The King can mimic the identity of an endless number of murdered victims. Unlike part-demon, part-human cambions, full demons like him don't *possess* humanity; they steal it. They kill us, then wear us. Like clothing.

Bile rises in my throat. "If Nick saw you like this, then who does he think I left with?"

"No one, I suppose. Or anyone." The King's body shudders. Now in place of Erebus's figure is a tall, narrow-faced person I don't recognize, with pale, freckled skin and gray-and-brown-streaked hair.

Fear and horror take a back seat to the anger that roils up from my gut. "Do you even remember the name of the human whose face you're wearing?"

"His name was not important," he replies in this new body's voice. Without another word, the Shadow King turns on his heel to stride down the corridor in long, swift steps. When he is not waving gloomy wisps at cameras ahead of him, his hands are shoved into deep pockets.

I scramble after him, grasping Excalibur to carefully rest it at my hip, pointing the blade down and back. I really should have found a scabbard before leaving. "Where are we?"

Erebus the Seneschal would have answered his Crown Scion's question, but this demon is not that Erebus, and I am not his Crown Scion. Those were just the masks we wore—and his always fit better than mine.

I am the Bloodcrafted descendant of King Arthur. I am a Rootcrafter and Legendborn, or I *was* before I deserted both groups. Now I am the Shadow King's bloodmarked *investment*. I am a power source that I've asked him to teach and help grow, even as he plans to use my power to eventually help him triumph over the Order we both despise. With him, I will become a weapon—one he will wield when I am strong enough.

I have a feeling the Shadow King won't let me forget that in leaving with him, I chose *this* identity—that of a weapon—above all others.

The King's demon feet make no sound, but my human ones do. The soft brown boots Greer found and left in my room at Northern create a shuffling noise as my strides lengthen to keep up with his. Greer had also left a pair of loose jeans and a band T-shirt; their clothes, I think. I wonder if I'll be able to find more wherever we end up, or if this will be it. Perhaps I should have packed a bag and not just a sword.

Ahead, the Shadow King turns a sharp left and pushes through a door. I follow, struck mid-thought by the brightly lit room we've just entered—and its contents.

On either side of the King's direct path through the room lie Egyptian sarcophagi behind large glass display cases. With a flick of his wrist, the King obscures the cameras mounted evenly along the high ceiling. I call out to him. "Where—"

The King's new voice reaches me as he walks. "The British Museum."

"In *London?*" I squeak.

When I look at the sarcophagus in front of me with fresh eyes, a quiet sense of injustice creeps through the dissipating fog of surprise. According to the white placard at the base of the case, I'm looking at a young woman who lived in Thebes in 800 BCE. The beige, yellow, and red paint illustrate her face across the wooden casket—and I'm reminded sharply of another young woman who would not wake. Alice. I breathe through the clawing memory, the guilt. Shuttle them both away.

This shouldn't be her resting place, I think. *Not stuck here behind glass in collectors' hands. This isn't where her people imagined she'd be.* My fingertips itch to touch the sarcophagus to see if the girl's spirit lies awake inside. It's a Medium's instinct. One I'm not even sure I can act on after what I've done to my ancestral stream—

The King clears his throat by a door at the far end of the gallery. I shift the heavy length of Excalibur to my other hip and jog to join him. The door is labeled CURATORS ONLY. When I reach his side, he holds out a hand. For a moment, I am confused.

"The sword, Briana."

I grasp the hilt in my fist. "It's mine."

It's the wrong thing to say.

He hisses, lips pulling back. "You have no *authority* here, girl." His voice turns harsh and otherworldly. "No court of children to kneel for you, no Regents to scramble over your lineage. You are not the *Crown Scion* in *my* presence. And if I choose, I will take the sword Caledfwlch by *force.*"

A raw, primordial terror streaks through me. Every instinct inside me screams that the Shadow King is far, far more powerful than the Merlin he pretends to be. That he is far stronger even than the goruchel mimic demons the Legendborn Order most fears. That his true demonic nature is unknowable and hidden and older than the oldest mountains. He just whisked me across the planet, bending space and light and matter to his will . . . but I chose this. I can't let him bend me, too.

"I need it——" I begin.

"For what reason?" he snaps.

Strength. Power. Control. They are what I need more than anything. They will make the running worth it. And now that I have reforged Excalibur, it is more my weapon than ever.

"For training." I lift my chin, set my jaw. "As Erebus, you train Merlins and command the Mageguard. As the Shadow King, you've seen every Camlann, every demon uprising, and every Legendborn victory. As the Hunter, you've watched every woman in my family since Vera. You know what we're capable of."

"All true."

"You agreed to teach me," I say. "And I'm ready to learn. We have a bargain."

The corners of his lips curl upward. "An *unregulated* bargain."

I narrow my eyes. An unregulated bargain, made without a third-party broker, is something I am very familiar with. "It may have been unregulated, but I made my terms clear."

"*Your* terms were clear." His face shifts to Erebus's once more. "But mine were not."

My breath catches.

"Did Valechaz never explain the anatomy of a demon bargain to you?" He circles me slowly, expression amused, and tuts softly. "That is unfortunate."

The furnace in my chest opens without my permission. My root, rising to meet a threat. "Valec taught me plenty," I respond. "Unregulated bargains make it easy for demons to claim whatever they wish from a human, but I told you *exactly* what I'd be willing to do and what I needed from you. I agreed to go with you and stay by your side if you took Sel to his mother. Our bargain is negotiated and complete."

He continues as if I'd never spoken.

"For each demand made in a bargain, the opposing party has the right to make a demand in return. As a broker of repute, Valechaz regulates such bargains to ensure that every demand has been addressed and accepted, thus allowing the bargainers to close on equal footing. This regulation *is* critical, because unless and until *every* demand is addressed and accepted, the bargain cannot be closed at all."

My heart freezes in my chest. "Meaning?"

"Meaning the party who has yet to state their requirements at the time of closing walks away with an open, unfulfilled debt." He smiles. "An 'I owe you,' if you will."

"No." Fear kicks my heart into a sprint. "I . . . we——"

"You said you would go with me and stay by my side if I performed a single favor, and yet you made not one but *two* demands of me, Briana." He holds one finger up. "The first, that I take Selwyn to his mother. You said, 'If you take him to her, I will go with you.'"

I glower at him. "I know what I said——"

"But do you *remember* what you said?" His voice turns derisive. "What you demanded *before* you asked me to transport one Kane to another?"

"What other——"

"You demanded my *knowledge*. You want to learn strength, power, and control. 'Only a king may teach a king.'"

Blood drains from my face. Pools in my stomach in a dizzyingly cold vortex.

"Two demands, and only one fulfilled. You owe me, Briana." His smile spreads. "We are as good as Oathbound, you and I."

"No, I . . . I . . ." I flounder.

"*Yes.*"

"It was . . . a bargain——"

"What is a bargain if not an oath? And what is an oath if not a promise with a price? Call these what you will. All are cut from the same cloth—a cloth woven of intention, will, and sacrifice. Your power is bound by my bloodmark. Your death is bound to my triumph. And *you* are bound to me by your very own words." The Shadow King drops both hands into his pockets. "If I am not able to name my return for educating and training you, then we are out of balance, and the deal can be struck in its entirety."

"Then don't teach me! I'll . . . I'll learn on my own," I say, even as I don't mean it. Even as I know *he* knows I don't mean it. That I *can't* learn on my own. That I've already tried—and failed.

Instead of saying what we both know to be true, his voice grows quiet. A whispered threat. "You do not wish to see what happens when you break a fair bargain with a demon, Briana Matthews."

My chest heaves as I search for the cold disconnect I'd found on the hill at Northern. The confidence. I can't find it. "This isn't *fair*—"

"It *will* be fair when your debt is paid. If it is not, you will be in breach, and your breach will earn my vengeance *tenfold*." He steps closer, fangs glinting in the light. "First, I will see to it that Selwyn Kane dies. Next, a Mageguard will slit Alice Chen's throat while she sleeps. And *Erebus* will be certain to carry out the Regents' plan to murder Nicholas Davis."

Each threat wraps my throat. I can't breathe. Can't finish a single thought, ears *ringing*—

He leans in to whisper the next words: "Or perhaps I will simply suggest to Aldrich that if we wish to draw you out from wherever you've run away to, perhaps your father, Edwin's, life is not the too risky leverage I once thought it to be. . . ."

I suck in a breath. My father is innocent in all this. He knows nothing about who I really am. "What. Do. You. *Want*."

All humor leaves his face. "Something that will cost you dearly to surrender. A price that I will reveal when the time is right, and not before."

I shut my eyes. Living in unknowable debt to the Shadow King, for as long as he wishes, is worse than destruction.

"In the meantime," he murmurs, "you *will* give me Excalibur of your own volition."

There is no other choice.

Abruptly, I think of Nick again. He'd blood walked with me to the sixth-century origins of Legendborn power. Together, we'd watched the original Merlin cast the Spell of Eternity upon the original knights of the Round Table, initiating the cycle that allowed those knights' descendants—their Scions—to inherit their ancestors' magical gifts from one generation to the next. The core of the Spell is tied to my life as the Scion of Arthur, and being born the Scion of Arthur is what allowed me to pull Excalibur from its stone. After everything we've witnessed together, I wonder what Nick would say about me handing the symbol of the Order to its greatest enemy. Would he understand? Or would he want me to fight to keep it? Fight to make the blade my own?

Finally, I raise Excalibur by its hilt. An offering.

The King tugs the sword from my grip, and a high-pitched, metallic whine zips through my mind when it leaves my fingers. My eyes snap open. I have heard Excalibur's war cry, but nothing so mournful as this.

As the King hefts the blade beneath his arm, his Erebus identity melts away until he is the freckled nameless man once more. He knocks twice on the door behind him.

After a moment, a muffled voice responds, growing louder as its speaker approaches. "When will you interns *learn*?" The door cracks open to reveal a narrow-shouldered white man in a pale blue button-down. "If you continue to disturb me, I'll—"

"You'll what, Agaraz?" the Shadow King challenges in a low, crackling voice.

The man's eyes widen. "Sire!" He drops to one knee. "I did not recognize—I was not expecting you."

"Rise," the King commands. Agaraz moves to his feet in a smooth, single motion, as if his limbs are attached to strings that have been pulled all at once. Goruchel. The third I've met after Rhaz and Kizia. At my gasp, Agaraz's head whips around, his gaze burning my cheeks. He tilts his head curiously before he inhales, slow and intentional, in my direction. The King releases a long-suffering sigh. "I need your assistance with a blade."

"Yes, of course, sire." Agaraz's eyes are drawn to Excalibur as the King walks past him into a dim room lit by a banker's lamp on a wooden desk. Before Agaraz moves to follow, his gaze finds me again. The open hunger on the goruchel's face startles me. The door closes shut.

I listen for voices behind the door but hear nothing. Even if Excalibur remains here in the museum, that doesn't mean I can get to it. Are we staying here or returning to the States? If we return, how would I travel this far on my own?

My hands begin to shake as the threats the King so quickly offered settle deeper beneath my skin. I thought we were on equal footing of a sort, but I have already been outmaneuvered. My eyes are hot with sudden, embarrassed tears. Why did I think I could outsmart an ancient demon older than the Order itself?

Valec would have instantly known that my bargain with the King was incomplete. Alice would have stopped us to ask questions. But Valec isn't here right now, and Alice isn't even *conscious*. And Selwyn . . . Sel would have physically torn me away before negotiations ever began.

What have you done? I flinch at the memory of Sel's last words to me.

His contempt joins my own. *What* have *I done?*

My breath speeds. With each exhale, a wisp of red root flows from my mouth, floating toward the ceiling before it dissipates. I have breathed fire before, but this feels like breathing misery instead.

Abruptly, the door opens, and the King returns empty-handed. He pauses, nose raised to the air. The red root is gone, but I'm sure the scent of it remains.

"You already took one of my weapons. Will you take my root now too?" I ask. "Lock me away by keeping me weak?"

The King looks pointedly at the museum exhibits behind me before returning my gaze. "Greedy men collect what they cannot understand, and weak men destroy what they cannot control. A man who is both will attempt to recreate that which is beyond his comprehension, obliterating the original in the process."

I remember the dead girl in the sarcophagus and eye him warily. "What do demons do?"

"I will build you into a girl whom no one can destroy. You won't need a weapon. You'll become one." The King wraps his fist around my elbow, squeezing tight, cloaking us in the tendrils of his power.

"Deep breath, Briana."

I do as I'm told, and we slip through space once more.

II

THIS TIME WHEN we travel, each leap to a new shadowy location is accompanied by a squeezing sensation. As if my very atoms are being forced into new spaces, pressing me into something too tight, too dangerous. I see ruins under a moonlit sky, the thickest underbrush of a towering forest, the arctic under never-ending night.

When we land, I collapse to my knees once more, but this time on a foyer floor laid with red brick. We are surrounded by white plastered walls. To my left, a small entryway table is tucked below a gilded mirror. Ahead is a living room where brown wingback chairs sit on a thick, expensive-looking rug set before a stone fireplace. Wherever we are, afternoon light filters in through the stained-glass window in the heavy oak front door behind me to create a collage of color. The foyer walls are bathed in deep goldens, warm blues, and burnt sienna nearing orange. It was the end of the day in London, so maybe we are back on the East Coast? And Excalibur is thousands of miles away.

The Shadow King moves around to block my view into the rest of the home——the large living space, the hallways to my left and right.

I stand, exasperated. "*Now* where are we?"

As if in answer, his body changes shape again, to Erebus once more. "This is Erebus's home."

I hate myself for finding this face, this voice, the barest hint of comfortable. I tell myself it's because I know Erebus, but that's not really true, is it? "What I know" feels like sand sifting through open fingers.

"Did you murder him, too?"

"Yes."

"How long have you been impersonating this Merlin named Erebus? How long have you been living his life?" I ask.

"Long enough," he replies.

I stare at him, gathering my thoughts. "Erebus" is the nickname that Natasia Kane gave him at the Merlin academy . . . but was that nickname earned by the *demon* who stands beside me now, or is it yet another story stolen from the Merlin boy whose life had been cut short? "How long did the academy's instructors unknowingly teach and train humanity's greatest threat?"

His mouth twitches in a small, appreciative smile. "You are asking good questions, Briana."

"I don't want your approval," I spit back.

"Nor will you easily earn it. Wait here." After drawing the flickering darkness toward him, Erebus disappears in a gust of smoke.

He could be across the world again for all I know. In another country, several time zones away, or even back with the Regents, pretending to be their Seneschal.

After a moment, the room's shadows relax and melt back into place, taking the shapes of their parent objects until they are still. The only thing moving in this entire room is my chest, rising up and down with my jagged breaths.

I don't know how long I stand there waiting for Erebus to return. Long enough that the light changes around me, making new shapes against the plastered walls. Long enough for the faint ticking of a grandfather clock standing tall in a corner to grow loud in my ears. Long enough for regret and uncertainty to make themselves known in my chest. For me to wonder if, in choosing my own fate, I have doomed myself to a worse one.

How long have I been waiting again? I check the clock. Too long.

I take a step forward, half expecting my new mentor to reappear at my elbow at the unauthorized exploratory movement. He does not. I take another step, then another, until I am standing in the center of the living room and able to examine the details of the home more thoroughly.

For the home of a demon king, it is all rather . . . innocuous: High archways lead from the main space to other halls and rooms. A partially enclosed kitchen sits to the left. Brown built-in shelves on either side of the fireplace hold five rows of leather-bound books that remind me of the rare book collection at the Lodge library, except these look like they are better cared for. There are no picture frames of people, but the home does not feel abandoned. The mantel is spotless, without a speck of dust, and the lampshades are equally clean.

Is this where Erebus will leave me until he decides I am ready to be trained? For how long, I wonder? Days? Weeks? *Months?* Mild panic sets in, enough that I mistake the tingling sensation at the nape of my neck for nerves instead of what it truly is.

When the sensation doubles, any doubt is erased.

I am being watched by a demon.

I inhale silently. Shove the panic aside and prepare for a fight. Rather than allowing my breath to become shallow, I take in steady, long draws of oxygen to fuel my muscles and brain. Feel the familiar heat of my root deep behind my sternum. Feel Arthur's strength in my body and remember that it's mine, not his.

My eyes dart to the hearth near my left foot. That wrought iron fireplace poker will do.

Slowly, I pivot on my heel to face the room—and come face-to-face with a Black girl my age with long, thick twists down her back. She wears a thin-strapped black tank top, tight black jeans, elbow-length fingerless fishnet gloves, and a Cheshire smile. Her makeup looks fresh. Dark, smoky eye shadow and liner, deep eggplant lipstick, a soft pink blush on high, warm brown cheek-bones. She could be equally at home at a coffee shop or a concert. Hers is the dynamic type of beauty that's equally as powerful at rest as it is in motion.

And everything about her posture—her flexed fingers, her eager grin—feels poised for a fight.

Her eyes are a deep human brown, so at first, I question my own senses, my own paranoia. Then that smile widens, and her irises flash red before flickering back to brown. Then I know—she is not a goruchel demon, whose eyes are either deep red or the eye color of the human body they've taken. Not a *mostly* human Merlin with a golden or ochre gaze, but a balanced cambion with human and demon parentage like Valechaz. Which means she could be my age . . . or she could be hundreds of years old.

Perhaps traveling with the king of demons himself has made me immune to regular fear, because a balanced cambion should *terrify* me. Instead, I feel cold, like when I left Alice. Like when I stood on the hill at the Keep. Like there is nothing this moment can take from me that I have not already given up.

The cold is what I need right now.

"Who are you?" I ask as I edge closer to the fireplace.

"I'm Zoelle," she purrs. "Who are *you*?"

The iron poker is at my hip. Blood walking through left-handed Arthur's memories has made *my* left hand more adept than it used to be, enough that I'll be able to grab the iron with confidence. Which means my right will be for wielding root. That will have to work, because I don't plan on letting Zoelle get close. If she gets her hands on me, I won't beat her by grappling; cambions are too strong.

I try one more maneuver before this gets ugly. "Erebus brought me here. He won't want me harmed."

"He did, did he?" Zoelle looks me over once, up and down, eyes landing on my sternum. "Brought you here with all *that* power?" She grins. "I bet it's delicious."

"You *really* didn't have to say that," I reply with a grimace.

"Why not?" Her eyes sparkle. "Is it true?"

Instead of answering, I fling my palm outward, firing root flame in a short blast.

She flattens to the ground. "Hey!"

I use the distraction to grab the iron—but before I can swing it, a green fireball appears, cracking open in front of my face, startling me back.

That was an aether bomb. I never even saw her forge it.

I need more room.

I dash in front of the fireplace—and Zoelle's hand shoots out to wrap around my ankle. She yanks me down. When I hit the ground, the pointy end of the fallen iron poker grazes my cheek.

A few inches over, and it'd have punctured my right eye.

I growl, twist, then thrust my flaming palm in her face. She screams.

While she writhes, I pop up. I need to get outside. *Now.*

I sprint across the floor. Aim for the back doors. Abruptly, a body blurs between me and the exit, stopping me short.

"Where you goin'?" a deep voice asks.

I blink, certain I'm seeing things. The cambion in front of me looks just like Zoelle—no, not *just* like, *almost* like. In place of long twists, he has black hair shorn close to his scalp. Same eyes. Same slim, tall figure, but he's wearing a long-sleeved navy T-shirt rolled up at the elbows and a pair of dark pants over red Chucks. If Zoelle is coffee shop or concert, this newcomer is mostly coffee shop, with a crooked grin and eager, searching eyes. Where Zoelle is kinetic, this person is measured energy. A steady, hot drip of power, rather than the bright spark of Zoelle's attention, lashes my skin as he examines me. But that doesn't mean he's not dangerous.

Behind me, a burst of laughter. I whip around to see Zoelle grinning with her arms crossed in front of her chest. Her left cheek is already healing, the raw red of the burn turning deep pink.

"I'm Elijah. Who are you?" I jump at the deep voice too close to my ear.

I backtrack, keeping both of them in my sights. "You're—"

"Twins," Zoelle calls. "He's my annoying-ass brother."

"And she's my stubborn, devious sister," Elijah says. "And you are . . . ?"

"Not interested," I hiss, dashing around Elijah toward the door.

Elijah laughs and grasps my arm, squeezing. "Don't run! It only makes us wanna chase you!" I jerk back from his grip instinctively, and having seen Valec's strength, I half expect to hear and *feel* my bone breaking in his hold. Neither happens, and not for Elijah's lack of trying.

So they're balanced cambions, but they're not as strong as Valec? Are they as strong as Sel? I tug again, and Elijah's fingers slip an inch.

"We just want a taste." When Elijah releases me to sling an arm over my shoulder as if we're friends, I realize something critical: no matter how they compare to a Merlin, they aren't as well *trained* as Merlins.

A Merlin would never make the mistake of letting me go.

"Not gonna happen." I grab Elijah's forearm with both hands and yank down and in—fast, before he can react—curling my spine and pushing both hips back into his torso as I pull. He flips over my shoulder in a perfect arc, crashing into the glass coffee table and sending shards everywhere.

For a second, we all freeze. Zoelle's mouth falls open. Then, Elijah's shocked expression melts into one of fury. Before he can push to standing amid the sea of broken glass, his sister's laughter reaches us.

Our heads jerk in her direction, where she's holding her sides, eyes sparkling red and black.

"Jah!" Zoelle gasps. "Your ass went *flying!*"

"Zoeeee . . . ," Elijah growls. In a blink, he's up on his feet and in front of me, a snarl marring his brown face as he stands in the epicenter of the exploded glass table.

He extends a hand to call aether, and a green cloud swarms around his fist— only for Zoelle to command it to her outstretched palm, turning it into a solid, shining bat—

"*What is going on?*" Erebus's voice booms from the foyer, cracking against my ears.

In a blink, Zoelle and Elijah are kneeling with their heads bowed. Erebus stands over them, his eyes blazing red.

Elijah's voice is a furious mutter from his sister's side. "We didn't—"

"You *did*," Erebus corrects. Elijah goes silent. "Because when I left Briana here, she was alone. Explain yourselves."

"She——" Zoelle begins.

"Explain *yourselves*, not her. *Now*."

The twins flinch at Erebus's tone as the room darkens around us. Even light flees in the Shadow King's presence. The shadows themselves grow bolder.

"We thought she was an offering." Zoelle's voice comes through a pair of clenched teeth. "Tribute."

The midnight gloom behind Erebus clings to his back, then flares out like wings, painting the room in shades of gray and black. "If she was tribute, her power would be *mine* to consume. Not yours."

"Yes, sire," Elijah mutters. "We apologize."

"Zoelle?" Erebus's voice takes on the echoing, otherworldly quality from before. A voice that invades your mind from the inside out.

Zoelle's eyes squeeze shut in a pained grimace, as if she's resisting the impulse to reply.

"Zoe!" Elijah chastises.

In the end, his sister's voice is curt and sharp. "I apologize."

Appeased, Erebus draws his power inward until he is shaped like a man once more.

"To your feet," he orders. The twins rise, their heads still bowed.

Erebus doesn't seem surprised at their behavior; in fact, he seems bored of it.

"Who are they?" I ask Erebus.

He looks at the pair for a long moment, considering. "My wards."

I sputter, "Your *wards*? Like your kids?"

Elijah opens his mouth—to protest or correct me—but one look from Erebus silences him. Zoelle—Zoe—shoots me a brief death glare before bowing her head again too.

Erebus notices it all. "I had hoped to return before the twins did so I could make proper introductions, but I was waylaid by the Regents. However, this unanticipated moment provides us with a reminder of the work we need to do, Briana."

"What *work?*" Zoelle spits. "Who is this girl if not an offering?"

"The two of you say that you do not want to be treated like children. That you wish to earn my trust." The twins' heads jerk up. Erebus has their full attention now. "You claim that you are ready for more responsibility. Perhaps Briana here presents a solution."

"I don't like the sound of that," I mutter. The three of them turn to me as one.

Erebus crosses his arms. "Your first lesson begins now, Briana Matthews."

"And that is?"

"Calling on your power is not enough; you must also learn how to *seal* it." He points at my chest. "It appears that both Zoe and Elijah here sensed it right away. Just as Agaraz did earlier at the museum. This is unacceptable. You must be able to close it so tightly that no demon or cambion can detect it. So that no magical being who meets you thinks of you as anything other than a human girl."

I look at the twins, then remember Agaraz's lingering gaze. His hunger. "Why?"

"Because if you don't, you'll be devoured or destroyed before your real training can begin. I cannot and will not be with you every moment of every day. Nor do I control every demon and cambion on this plane."

Now that's *curious.* Even the king of demons has his limits? I search Erebus's face for any sign of his feelings about this fact, but his expression gives me nothing.

"Fine." I nod, conceding the point. "How do I learn how to seal my power?"

He strides across the room to the back doors and slides one open, gesturing through it to the forest beyond the yard. To the trees and bushes in the distance and the rolling hills that seem to go for miles. A gust of winter wind blasts through the opening—and I am the only one in the room who shivers. "With a ten-minute head start."

"A game?" Elijah cracks his knuckles. "Hide-and-seek?"

"Indeed."

"Do we get to eat her if we catch her?" Zoelle asks, eyes steady on me.

Erebus hums. "Catch her using *only* your aether sense, and I'll consider it."

"What?" My heart leaps into my throat. No way he'd let another demon consume my root.

But the vengeful glint in Elijah's eyes says that he can't wait to take me down a notch. Beside him, Zoelle bares her fangs as she pulls her twists up in a ponytail. "Let's go," she says with a smirk.

Erebus points toward the grandfather clock. "Ten minutes, Briana—"

I'm sprinting before he finishes his sentence.

Out the doors, down the steps, across the patio, and into the trees as fast as my legs will take me. My arms pump at my sides; my thighs burn as I dash over the ground, kicking up pine needles as I go.

If this is the first lesson, then I have no choice but to master it. And the next one. And the one after that. I have no choice, because there *is* no choice.

I will learn everything I can from the Shadow King, because only *he* can teach me what I need to know.

Once I am strong enough, once I am powerful enough, and once I have total control, it won't matter what I face next. It won't matter whether my opponent is human or demon, cambion or spirit, Morgaine or Regent . . . because no matter who they are, I will never let them hurt me again.

III

TEN MINUTES. *TEN minutes.*

My eyes bounce around the terrain, seeking a hiding place, while my mind debates whether I can hide at all.

Zoelle and Elijah don't appear to be trained for combat, but that doesn't mean they'll be easily outwitted or outfought. I've faced demons made of stone and demons made of decaying moss and fully corporeal hellfoxes. I've fought against a goruchel ranked higher than his elemental and animal isel brethren— and won. But if there's one thing I know about the world of demons, it's that they are *all* unpredictable chaos creatures.

As I trot, my feet crunch over leaves until I slip on a rocky patch, twisting *into* the fall at the last second so that I don't break an ankle. I land in a huff, pop back to my feet. Turn to scan the ground back the way I came.

How many minutes have passed? Three? Maybe four?

And I still don't have a plan.

The wind slices through my thin shirt and pants, whipping my curls around my face. Wherever we are, it's bitterly cold. Colder here in November than in Chapel Hill or back home in Bentonville. The mountains, maybe? I glance up. Beneath these skeletal trees, that cold will set into my limbs quickly, making my joints too stiff to run or fight. *Can't stay here. Can't stay put.* I pick up the pace and settle into a quick jog.

What do I know? I think. *And, more importantly, how can I use what I know about my opponents?*

I tick off the details: The twins are cambions. They are preternaturally fast and strong. They possess fast metabolisms; they heal quick. Their senses of smell and hearing are heightened, but Erebus restricted the twins to using only their aether sense to find me. Don't know how they'll avoid using their *other* supernatural senses . . . unless he mesmers them, blanketing their eyes and ears. The same was done to *me* months ago in the forest behind the Lodge, on the night of the First Oath, when Sel temporarily took my sight.

At the thought of Sel, my chest clenches. A wisp of root slips from between my lips—deep bloodred power floating away like mist overhead. *Shit.* I clap a hand over my mouth as it drifts higher. A piece of me, dancing and fading into the air. *Not good,* I think, not *good.* I'm supposed to be sealing my power, not letting it loose!

I sprint away from the residual, pressing my lips tight together as I put some distance between my power and my body.

Around me, the land shifts dramatically. A hundred yards to my right, hills rise like great hulking shadows. A couple hundred to my left, the land drops off into nothing. Wherever we are, a hint of a mountain range peeks through the trees in the distance. The earth is a collection of dead and dying plants, everything dry and crisp and loud beneath my feet. In the silence, every twig echoes like a gunshot in my ears. Every gasp of breath grinds like a bone saw.

Think, Bree!

If Valec—at the thought of Valec, another lick of flame rises from my mouth. I run faster to escape it. *If* he *were hunting me, where would I hide?*

Somewhere high, so I could see him coming.

Somewhere so obvious that he might miss me.

Somewhere that would keep me from being cornered if I needed to fight. *There.*

A large brown barn sits at the foot of a tall hill with a small field of grass and gravel near its entrance. I speed toward it.

There are two large doors in the front that I avoid entirely. Instead, I head toward the gently sloping hill thirty feet or so behind the barn, scrabbling to find foot- and handholds up the incline. The barn is too easy to get trapped in, but *behind* the barn and up the hill that overlooks it? A good spot to see the twins enter the clearing and hopefully high enough that any more leaking root floats up toward the clouds before they sense it.

I reach the top and flatten myself among tall, mostly dead switchgrass just as I hear a voice ring out, echoing against the trees and landscape.

"Brianaaaaaa. Where are youuuuuu?" Zoe. Laughter in her voice. I hear a low rumble—Elijah—then she laughs again before she speaks. "Elijah thinks you're going to make this easy for us, but I think you might actually be clever!" A pause. "Are you clever, Briana?"

I close my eyes and focus on the root inside my chest. What did Erebus say? Seal it, so that I don't appear to be anything other than a human girl. I've spent so long trying to *open* my furnace on purpose, but now that I've found out how to use it, I have no idea how to close its doors. Now that I am without the protection of the Legendborn and Mageguard, it's like I've been left alone with uncontrollable weaponry. A bomb with no off button. A flamethrower with a stuck trigger.

The power that felt like freedom a day ago can just as easily cause my downfall. Blood in the water, drawing ravenous sharks.

And no one here to protect me.

Just like that, I'm back in my memory—Nick's face at Northern, his hand outstretched, his fingertips. *Nick*—another flare of power leaps from my lips like an angry flame.

"Oh-ho!" Zoe calls. "What was *that*?"

Shit. I squeeze my eyes shut. *Stop! Don't think of Nick. Don't think of anyone. Don't*—

Don't be stubborn about it, just smile and eat the cake. Alice's words.

The smell of freshly baked cake in my memory mingles with the rubbery scent of a single birthday balloon. I grit my teeth—root rises from between them. *Don't think of Alice. If you think of Alice, you'll think of—*

As long as you're all right, kid. Long as you're safe. My father's care.

My father, burying his concern when I lie to him—again—and tell him there's no need to worry. When there are so *very* many reasons to worry. Pain so sharp, I gasp—and root streams from my lips.

Goddamnit.

"Briana!" Zoe again. "Girl, you're truly god-*awful* at hiding! May as well be sending up fireworks! Fourth of July–ass . . ." Snickering laughter from both twins now.

Elijah calls to me next. "Where'd you get that red aether from anyway? Does it run out after a while? Like a rechargeable battery?"

"Do you plug yourself into the wall?" Zoe shouts.

"Did you steal it? Or bargain for it?" Elijah asks, and he sounds genuinely curious. "Wait . . . are you a warlock?"

"Ooh, gross, Elijah. They *stink*. Bree's power smells *good*."

I hold my breath, as if that will help anything, and flatten myself farther into the earth.

I reach for the mental image I once used to protect myself—the imaginary wall of steel and brick that I brought with me to Carolina. The mile-high barrier with no seams or fissures. That wall used to keep me safe from my fresh grief, used to keep my After-Bree self contained. But the wall doesn't work here. Not anymore. Red root bursts from my mouth. I suck it back, mouth bright with it, try to swallow it down—

"There you are!" Zoe's voice reaches me from the bottom of the hill. I don't dare move in case she's bluffing, trying to draw me out.

The tall grasses at my elbows bend all at once under a strong whoosh, my only warning before I feel a pair of hands underneath each elbow, lifting me up like I weigh no more than paper.

I bare my teeth as both twins grin, their hands tight on my arms.

"There she is." Zoe's eyes narrow, and now that I'm up close, I can see the effect of Erebus's power on their senses. Thin layers of black smoke coat their faces, writhing and swirling in the air like masks made of aether. Beneath the layer, her eyes flash red. "Where's that power?"

Show me that power, little girl. A demon's threat.

A flash of a memory ricochets through my entire body. Kizia, the goruchel assassin, sent to ambush me at a Legendborn safe house. Her claws digging into the flesh of my throat. Root rises from my breath.

Even my enemies trigger this messiness, this lack of control.

Zoe chuckles. "Oh, this is gonna be good, Jah—"

I hear Zoe's voice, but all I *see* is Kizia. Even with the twin cambions threatening me in the here and now, I am in the past.

I remember the uchel I fought in the woods during the first Oath. The stone creature who tumbled me around in an armored car like it was a toy. Even Selwyn, who threatened my life more than once before my lineage was revealed. I remember the Regents, who thought I was too much to live a free life, but never enough to be their king.

Even though I've run away from the Order, I am still the same Onceborn-raised teenage girl held at the mercy of a snarling, laughing opponent.

Still. After *everything.*

Three months ago, I saw a demon at a quarry when I wasn't supposed to . . . and everything has been breathless and relentless from that second onward. Six months ago, my mother was still alive and I didn't know what death looked like.

Now I know what it *sounds* like.

I know its smell. Its taste. The weight of it in Rhaz's body pierced by my sword. The deep, thunderous crack of snapped bone. Now I know what my own body looks like when it is torn open. I've seen my inner flesh—shiny, wet, vulnerable. I understand how deeply pain can course, what it feels like when nerves scream and muscles rip. I want to sob aloud—*I don't want to know these things.* But I do. *I do.*

And I have had *enough.*

Completely unaware of the vortex of grief and rage building inside me, Zoe shakes her head at her brother, face amused. "Can't believe the King's going to let us have a taste—"

"*Shut.*" My vision flashes red. "*Up.*"

Zoe's eyes snap to mine. "Excuse me?"

"You want my power? Take it." With a twin on each arm, I open my palms— and release root like a volcano beneath their chins.

Flames engulf their heads in a satisfying whoosh.

They scream and release me, stumbling back. With their attention on their pain, I take the advantage.

I drive into Elijah's chest with my shoulder, grunting with the effort. He makes an "oomph" sound and flies up—hanging in the air—before dropping down the hill. He tumbles down and out of sight.

Zoe emits a low growl. I turn—

But she's caught on to the fact that my hands are my greatest weapon.

In a blur of motion, she speeds out of range.

She stands twenty feet away, chest heaving, and wipes the back of her hand against a singed cheek, drawing smudged makeup across her temple like a purple gash. "So it's like that, huh?"

"Yeah, it's like that." I glance down at her brother where he lies still at the base of the hill. "Hope he didn't hit his head."

Zoe blurs forward, coming at me with a wild, untrained swing.

I dance back, reflexes moving my body on instinct—and her clenched fist skims the air in front of my nose.

We pause again, sizing each other up.

"How fast can you heal?" I taunt. "Faster than you punch, I hope."

"Shut up!" Zoe darts forward. She swings again—and I duck, grateful for my time under Gillian Hanover's tutelage. Grateful even for my enemies. For Vaughn and Rhaz and every isel who taught me to move before they strike.

She stumbles over a clump of grass and soil, recovering instantly, but still—I see it.

That tumble rattled her.

I wonder if . . .

I dart forward, a feint. She *steps* away instead of running.

My guess was right. Her caution makes her slow—even on the defense.

Now every time Zoe advances, I dodge more than easily. Every time she huffs in frustration, I smirk.

My footwork is better than hers. I know it. She knows it—and it's making her angry. Her anger makes her sloppy.

"Careful, *Zoe*," I say. "Don't trip again. Might twist an ankle."

She hisses but does not attack. Wary enough not to take my bait a second time.

"I've fought hellfoxes faster than you," I poke. "And they were one foot in the grave as it was."

That works.

She swings slowly, angrily. I duck under, pivot in. Hit her with a closed-fist rib shot before spinning away. Not my best work. Probably only half of my inherited strength, but it's enough to send her staggering, hand clasped to one side.

Fear makes its first appearance on her face.

I skip backward, careful not to veer too close to the edge. Glance down to see Elijah, moaning and shifting onto his side. He'll be up soon.

Zoe tries to rattle me. "Gonna drain you dry, baby girl."

I snort. "Why? You don't need aether to survive. You don't need human pain, either. You don't need to feed like a demon at all."

When she grins, her fangs become visible between the deep purple of her lips. "Sure, me and Elijah don't need to feed like full demons, but aether and messy misery sure are fun to chase."

"So you're just greedy." I duck as her fist swings over my head. "Untrained, slow, and greedy. Why does Erebus even bother with you?"

Her eyes widen. "You little—"

Too easy. I take the opening I've been waiting for and rush her, counting on the unexpected move to catch her off guard. It works.

Sort of.

She grabs at my shoulders, tips us back, and we go tumbling down the hill.

A rock jabs into my lower back, and something tears a long, angry stripe down my upper arm. We end up falling right at Elijah's feet.

Recovered from his fall, Elijah grasps me by the collar with both hands, dragging me up to my toes, teeth bared as he lifts me. I kick out and land a blow against his shin. His grip loosens, but Zoe grabs my shirt, dragging me over to her instead. She raises me higher, grip like iron. "This game isn't fun anymore."

"Oh, really?" I chuckle between gasps. "I'm having a great time."

"I could snap your neck right now." Zoe seethes.

"*Zoe!*" Elijah calls. "She's not worth it!" He glances furtively over his shoulder, scanning for Erebus, I'm sure. I don't know where he is either, but I *do* know one thing about the King. One very important detail.

"You *could* kill me, sure," I mutter. "But you won't, because your *sire* would never allow it. You know that, and I know that." I strain forward until our noses touch. "Don't we, *Zoelle?*"

Fury robs her of her voice. Instead of responding, she growls—then launches me backward into the sky.

I don't even have time to brace for my collision with the heavy wooden doors—but it's a collision that never comes. Instead of smashing into the barn, my spine smacks *hard* into what feels like a thick concrete wall. The air around me flashes bright green-white. My skull cracks against it too, and black spots dance across my vision.

Whatever this glowing wall is, it's not only solid; it feels *alive*. My entire body is held against it, as if magnetized to its buzzing surface, for the span of a heartbeat. My mind blanks, no words, no thought—instead, I feel a deep, stomach-roiling, primordial terror. And a desperate, answering need to walk, no, *run away*.

Runaway—leavethisplace—neverevercomehereagain—runaway—

When the wall finally drops me, electricity zips through my torso and limbs, numbing the impact of the sharp gravel on my cheek. I land in a heap, face down, gasping and stunned at the emotions in my gut.

A strong hand pulls me half up by the back of my shirt. I'm being dragged, limbs limp at my sides, through the gravel and back toward the grass. For a disorienting, confusing moment, I feel relief. So much relief that I'm being pulled away from the barn, that my body is moving in the right direction, even if I'm not running to get there.

The hand flips me over roughly. I blink against the shining sun and bright gray winter sky, the view going watery. "What . . . ?" I croak. "What was that?"

I don't get an answer, but my mind conjures it up anyway. A ward? A barrier? But it felt *alive*. Wards and barriers don't feel like that.

Both twins crouch over me, their faces appearing on either side overhead as they block out the sun.

It's too familiar. I've been here before, at the mercy of cambions. Root rises from my body in a pale red mist.

"Ha!" Zoe smiles down at me. "No wonder the old man's trying to train you. Every low-ranked demon in the county would come running your way if they knew how much juice you had."

I surge upward, snarling to meet her, but my own muscles thwart the attempt, still weak from the barn's magic. The twins each press a hand down on my shoulder until I give up and collapse.

"We caught her . . . ," Elijah begins, eyeing me warily. "So . . ."

"So we win!" Zoe's grin is slightly feral. "We get to taste her power."

"He said he'd *consider* letting us consume her," Elijah corrects. He looks around again. "Consideration is *not* permission. We should wait for him. . . ."

"Elijahhhhh," Zoe whines. "Stop being a demon king's pet."

Elijah scoffs. "I am not—"

I writhe beneath their grips. The compulsion to run away from the barn claws at the inside of my mind. As I fight against them, my root blooms, and both twins' attention snaps back to me.

"Nah . . . ," she says in a rough, low voice, eyes flaring red. "I don't feel like waiting."

When Zoe leans close to my face, it only takes a second for her brother's hesitation to fade. Together, they inhale over my throat in a single movement, my red flames swirling toward their faces—

And then, just as in sync, they both rear back with identical howls of pain.

Any thought of the barn fades in the face of something I had forgotten in all this. Something completely out of my control.

The angry awakening of my bloodmark.

IV

ELIJAH GASPS AND gags, spitting on the ground. "What *is* this?"

I sit up with a groan, holding my head with both hands, vision still swimming. But at least the strange magic of the barn seems to have left my system; I don't feel like running away.

"Gahtdamnit!" A gargled shout from Zoe draws my focus. To my left, she claws at her face and tongue. She curses at me, eyes watering. "What did you do?"

"Nothing," I respond. "I didn't do a damn thing, believe me."

"Then why does this fugging *burn*—"

"You have always been too eager, Zoelle." Erebus's voice is mild and unamused. All three of us turn to see him standing ten feet from where the twins remain on the ground, grimacing in pain. "Too impatient."

Zoe fixes me with a glare. "Gonna tear your throat out—"

"No, you will not." Erebus blurs between us.

"Why?" Zoe shouts. "She burned us!"

"Briana did not burn you," Erebus corrects. "Her power did, without her control."

I blow a rough breath from my nose as conflicting emotions rise within me. Frustration at myself for forgetting my bloodmark and begrudging gratitude for its existence.

Erebus tuts. "I never guaranteed that you could consume Briana's power."

Elijah groans in his sister's direction. "Told you."

Erebus nods, pride glimmering in his red eyes. "Good ear, Elijah."

He plays word games, even with them, I think.

"A good ear for trickery and misdirection doesn't make this . . . *discomfort* go away, sire."

"No," Erebus replies. "I had hoped your logical mind would prevent you from following your sister into a bad decision." The King turns to me. "This is always the way with them, Briana. Zoe rushes, Elijah follows. They are driven by hungers of different stripes."

When his brow lifts, frustration and humiliation wash over me—and I realize that he set us all up. Me *and* the twins. "You knew I'd fail to hide my power," I say, climbing to my feet.

Erebus's chin dips. "I am a teacher, Briana. I know my pupils well."

I bristle at what feels like an audacious inclusion of *me* as one of his "pupils" but then shove it away. Indignation has gotten me far, but I suspect it won't help me here, not while I am indebted to the Shadow King in more than one way. His education is what I wanted, I remind myself. This is what I bargained for.

"You knew the twins would try to consume my magic no matter what, and what would happen to them if they did."

Zoe jumps to her feet in a blur. "Wait, what?"

"That power belongs to her, but it's somehow connected to you, isn't it?" Elijah guesses. He sits back on his knees and drags a hand across his mouth, head tilting in thought as he stares at Erebus.

Erebus nods. "What you experienced was her magic triggered by my bloodmark."

"What the hell is a bloodmark?" Zoe asks. Erebus shoots her a chastising glare, and she swallows, bowing her head with gritted teeth.

"Sire?" Elijah stands, solemn expression and presence adding silent support to his sister's question.

Even though Valechaz explained to me what a bloodmark is, I find myself eager to hear the ancient demon king's explanation myself, straight from his mouth. While I am the ninth descendant in my maternal bloodline to bear his mark, I am the only one who ever learned that it even exists—and who applied it in the first place.

"Before demon contracts were written and signed in blood, we had bloodmarks," Erebus explains. "A bloodmark has two purposes: it permanently binds a human to their agreed-upon debt, enforcing that they will pay when the time comes, and it marks for other demons that the bounty that human possesses is already claimed and cannot be bargained away to another. In this case, I marked Briana's ancestor but have not yet taken my payment, so she was born with my mark, having inherited it from her maternal bloodline."

"A simple 'hands-off' sign seems like it would suffice," Elijah grumbles.

"Briana's source of power is truly unique on this plane," Erebus continues. "An unending furnace Bloodcrafted into her body via an unregulated bargain made between her ancestor Vera and the spirits of the dead to whom Vera pleaded for aid. Unbeknownst to Vera, I joined that open plea to stake my claim on the furnace within a future daughter in exchange for providing a measure of protection to her descendants. When someone attempts to consume Briana's magic forcibly, my bloodmark flares her power to life, burning the thief away."

The twins stare at me with new eyes, and the concentrated sensation of the eyes of two cambions and the Shadow King scalds my skin. Makes it crawl.

For a moment, I feel like the dead Theban girl in the museum. A prize collected by hungry hands, a valuable artifact that had once been a whole person. A girl who had once been alive, now trapped behind glass in a land and time she never could have imagined.

Zoe's cheeks flush a deep reddish brown. "You could have just told us—"

"No." Erebus's eyes swivel to hers. "You, in particular, learn things the hard way, Zoelle."

Zoe winces.

I hate that, even in my own waning discomfort, I am suddenly eager to learn more. The past half hour of running and fighting seems a minimal price for the knowledge I might gain in return. This education *is* valuable. *Is* worth a price. I *need* what the Legendborn and Rootcrafters couldn't teach me. What my own ancestors could not or would not teach me. I need what Vera did not and could not know. The Shadow King is a demon who is equally incentivized to both make me stronger *and* prevent my death at the hands of anyone else. A demon who, I must begrudgingly admit, appears willing to teach.

Erebus surveys the twins, his gaze casting farther to include me. "Inquiries?"

Elijah raises a hand. "What would have happened if we had kept going?"

"Too vague," Erebus corrects. "*Specificity,* Elijah."

Elijah huffs, then studies me in a way that makes my skin itch. "If Zoe and I had persisted past the painful effects of the bloodmark and continued to feed on Briana's power, would we have died?"

Erebus answers, "Remember that order favors balance. As you both are the product of a human-and-demon union, you are balanced beings, well suited to live on this human plane. If you had managed to endure the pain of my mark and truly consume Briana's power, that power would simply intoxicate you. Beyond that point, however, it would lead to certain death."

"So we could have accidentally *ended* ourselves?" Zoe exclaims, throwing her hands up. "And you let us walk right into it? Come *on*, old man . . . !"

"I knew you'd stop, Zoelle," Erebus adds, *almost* gently. I wonder again what his relationship is to these two. Why they're with him. How they're so familiar and, at times, casual with the king of demons.

"And what if we were full demons?" Elijah presses. "What would have happened then?"

Erebus lifts a shoulder. "A full demon strong enough to bear the searing pain of the mark would gain unimaginable power. Which is why Briana's power must be guarded."

I have my own question to ask. "And how about an imbalanced cambion?"

Like a Merlin, I think. *Like Selwyn.*

The twins exchange a puzzled glance at my interjection. Erebus pivots slowly to face me. When his eyes meet mine, I know immediately that he is thinking of Selwyn too.

"An example?" he murmurs.

He's going to force me to ask. "What would happen to a Merlin who attempted to consume my power?"

Erebus's mouth twitches at my omission of Sel's name, but he answers the question anyway.

"Chaos favors imbalance, and the Order's Merlins are mostly human. Their fate would be worse by far than the fate of a full demon *or* balanced cambion."

"Worse than *dying*?" Zoe exclaims in disbelief.

"There are many fates worse than death, Zoelle," replies Erebus warmly. "Shall I list them?"

Zoe grimaces. "Nah, I'm good."

Elijah shakes his head. "No, thank you."

"Yes," I say. "Tell me what's worse than death."

"What the hell, new girl?" Zoe hisses. She looks at me with horror while her brother studies me with sharp interest. I ignore them both.

I couldn't say goodbye to Nick. I can't say goodbye to Sel. I don't know how to let go of the two people who blood walked their way into a nightmare and refused to let *me* go. Refused to let *me* fall. Root burns against the back of my teeth, fighting to get out.

Erebus and I hold a silent gaze. "You know, Briana."

"Tell me *anyway*," I insist.

"He is *gone*," Erebus snaps in a low voice. "Better to accept this now than to pine for the impossible."

"Who—" Elijah begins.

"Tell me how," I say, voice tight, fists tight on my thighs. "Tell me why."

Erebus's eyes narrow. "If an imbalanced cambion were to wield your power, say by creating a construct with it, they'd first become intoxicated. Deeply so. Slurring, disorientation, a lowering of inhibitions." He looks at me pointedly, and I know why.

When we were on the run, I'd invited Sel to forge my root so that we could create a barrier against Erebus together. While it burned Erebus, it didn't burn Sel. But it did leave him aether-drunk and delirious.

"However," Erebus continues, "simply wielding your power is nothing compared to consuming it. If a Merlin's gradual turn toward their demon nature is a slow descent, then the absorption of your power is an accelerated, fathomless plummet. Any Merlin who feeds on your power"—he pauses, with intention—"*whomever they are*, would be wholly consumed by the raw instincts of demonia. Permanently altered to feed without reason or logic. A Merlin cambion in demonia has lost their humanity forever. They will crave aether and human pain, like all demons do."

I swallow and look away. I know that's the Order's version of demonia. That Sel's humanity is allegedly gone. But I still don't believe it. I *can't* believe it.

"Briana," Erebus continues, stepping closer as his voice drops. "Wherever he is, *if* he is even capable of thinking of you, Selwyn is ravenous for more than your misery. If you were to face him, you would meet a demon driven to find out not only how much pain your human body can endure before it dies, but how much pain you can endure and *still live*."

"His mother descended, and she retained her humanity."

"His mother is singular, among both Merlins and demons. A once-in-a-lifetime scholar and sorceress," Erebus says. "What you say is possible, but *she* had time to plan for her descent. Her son had none."

I wince, remembering the way Sel's body curled away from me and Nick. I remember his inability to speak. I remember not even *recognizing* him. But now, a horrible new puzzle piece slides into place in my mind: that Sel continued to consume my root even through the pain caused by Erebus's bloodmark.

"He felt the bloodmark . . . ," I whisper. "And he still didn't stop trying to save me."

"He doomed himself," Erebus says. "He knew what would follow."

"What's more human than sacrifice?" I snap.

Erebus's eyes narrow.

"What's more human than risking what you have and what you are for someone else?" My voice breaks. When I exhale, a curl of thick, rich red root floats out of my mouth and rises into the air above me.

Zoe covers her nose just to avoid the scent of my power—and my fresh misery.

Erebus glares at me. "Enough," he says, voice like venom. "Leave us."

"Why?" Zoe asks. Both twins turn to him with wide eyes.

"Your lesson is complete, and I won't repeat myself," says Erebus. "I need to speak with Briana alone."

The twins exchange a glance and come to some understanding, then turn together and drift back through the woods toward the house, their silent cambion feet leaving no sound to follow.

I CAN'T HEAR the twins' sulking trek back to the house, but Erebus can; his head tilts in the familiar listening gesture of demonkind while I wait. After a moment, his attention turns back to me to study my raised chin and stony jaw.

"It should go without saying that there is much that you should not reveal to the twins or to any other demon we may come across in our time together."

"Why did you let them attack me?"

"To teach you a lesson. You failed."

"No one has ever trained me to use root," I protest. "Why did you put me in a *position* to fail?"

"Because you needed to understand what will happen if you reveal your root by accident. If you do not *learn* to seal it away."

I let his sentences roll around in my mind. I can listen for the tricks, just as Elijah did. Finally, I observe: "You don't call my power 'root' in front of them."

"I do not." In his face there is a silent invitation to keep going, keep pushing.

Unlike the Erebus I know from the Council, *this* Erebus wants me to keep asking questions.

"What other secrets do you keep from the twins?"

"More than I keep from you."

"Such as?"

"Where you come from. What title you used to hold. That you are Legendborn. If they, or any demon, were to find out that Arthur Pendragon's blood runs through your veins, they would kill you without hesitation."

"Same story everywhere," I groan. "I've been running from demons since *before* I pulled Excalibur, you know, and I'm not dead yet."

He counters me in three sentences: "You have often had the benefit of comrades who fight for or with you. You have mostly run from lesser demon isels. You are still human and easy to kill."

I fire back with three of my own: "Demons of every class are always trying to kill me. I'm here to make sure they don't succeed. You're going to teach me how."

Erebus studies me again, like he is searching for something beneath my skin. Sifting for some detail that I possess and that he cannot ascertain. He blows a slow breath through his nose before he speaks again.

"To demonkind, the earthly plane is an environment rich with food but hostile. The Order, the Legendborn, and its Merlins are our natural-born enemies. You have fought lesser demons who can barely function beyond their dual hungers for aether and human emotions, but you do not truly know the type of demons whose company *I* keep. Not isel, not uchel, but goruchel. These greatest demons have their own hierarchy, their own rules, their own goals."

"I *know* that—"

"The Scion of Arthur is a glorious prize to a goruchel," he says, speaking over me. "Striking you down could lead to an endless, unchallenged feast for all eternity—and total command over their lesser brethren. This plane would become ours." He steps forward, eyes gleaming. "To a goruchel, your death is a holy aspiration."

I shudder and resist the urge to back away. Erebus himself can't harm me, but the look in his eyes reminds me that even if my joining him has slowed the march to slaughter, I am still on that path. One foot in front of the other, on the way to my death no matter what. And once they kill me, they destroy the Round Table's might, and once the Legendborn are gone for good, the demons will feed endlessly. Own the human plane as much as they own the demon one.

Erebus's voice is low with displeasure. "You are not as you once were, when we first met at the Southern Chapter. You are fractured."

"Well, I was thrown out of my own body and nearly trapped in Arthur's nightmare," I say, crossing my arms over my chest. "That changes a person."

"No, that is not the cause." He steps closer. "This loss of control, this *seepage* of your power . . . This is new."

Erebus pulls his right glove off with his teeth and, without warning, thrusts his palm toward my sternum, a foot away from my chest.

I choke out a cry as my body reacts on its own, lifting me up on my toes. "What are you—"

"Silence," he murmurs, eyes lidded. Each time his fingers twitch in the air, my bloodmark twinges in my chest, growing hotter and brighter.

"Let me go!"

"Not yet," Erebus says, eyes snapping open and flaring bright. With a twist of his wrist, something *inside* the bloodmark snaps painfully—I gasp. A flood of ancient magic fills my nose: myrrh, oud, saps, and incense. Then, he releases me.

I stumble to the ground, clutching my chest, and watch in horror as the branching bloodmark spreads underneath my T-shirt and out to my biceps and down my arm. When I meet Erebus's eyes, they are pulsing in time with my mark, bright red and eager. "What did you do?"

"I altered the mark's spellcraft," he says, winding his wrist in one hand before he returns it to his glove. "It will still notify me if you are in mortal danger so that I may protect you if I am near. It will still call on your root if anyone attempts to consume it, but if I am to build your strength, then I need to be able to *monitor* that strength. Now I can."

He clenches his fist suddenly, and the mark shines, pulsing painfully in my chest, making me gasp once more before it fades again.

"What?" I gasp, rubbing at my sternum. "You can—"

"Sense the level of your root at any time I wish, and at any distance? Call on my mark and hear its answer?" Erebus says with a nod. "Yes."

My nose wrinkles at the prospect of Erebus checking in on my power levels like a battery he's charging. I suppose Zoe was right.

He blows out a frustrated breath. "I still do not understand your newfound lack of *control*. It began at the museum and has worsened with every hour that passes. If you continue like this, you'll drain yourself to incapacitation within the day. You have already grown weaker."

That alarms me. I don't want to be drained here, among enemies.

"This lack of control will get you killed before you're of any use to me."

"I won't—"

"Silence!" Erebus's voice grows loud, like splitting boulders or thunderous waves. "*Something* is generating dire emotions within you in layers so rich that, together with your root, your uncontrolled humanity floods this clearing *and* my senses. Even now, you radiate a cocktail of suffering so thick that you could draw a passing demon to my home with a stiff wind."

As I watch, the black of his pupils bleeds away, leaving only glowing red in its place. Erebus—no, he's the Shadow King now—seems to grow in size, black mist lifting from his shoulders. His fury lashes against my skin, shadows wildly spiraling away from his dark coat, then dissolving before my eyes.

"It is unacceptable."

I shrink back, reminding myself, again, that he himself can't feed from me . . . but it doesn't make me feel any safer. "I can't . . . I can't stop it—"

His voice is a deadly whisper. "You are the girl who faced the High Council of Regents, whose mind survived a mesmer by the Seneschal Tacitus himself. You are the girl who fought the Pendragon back into his own dimensional prison. What unsettles *that* girl? That you so easily lose grip of the very same power you fought tooth and nail to harness?"

"I . . . ," I stammer, not sure what to say. That when I think of certain people, I lose control? Even if I can say that much, I don't know *why* it's happening now, like this—

His next question slices through me. "Will you never truly claim that which you have inherited?"

My silence is met by his low cackle in the darkness. The Shadow King's laugh ricochets all around me now, bouncing against my ears, breaking against my face, buffeting me from every direction.

"Don't toy with me," I warn. "That's what Arthur did."

He spreads his hands. "Arthur Pendragon manipulated you, took advantage of your ignorance, and throttled your power for his own gain. Unlike Arthur, I care whether you live or die. I *need* you to become powerful."

"You are just another ancient king who wants to use me!"

"And *you* are a seventeen-year-old girl, a sovereign in her own right, who wishes to use yet *another* ancient king!" he retorts. The King's eyes begin to smoke like hot coals. "This is what leaders do, child. Find each other and wring out what only their equal can provide. Remember that *you* called for me. I was there when the first shadows fell. I was there when humans stumbled their way into consciousness. I was there when the moon and stars were the only lights in the darkness. I know the magic you are so desperate to wield, because I was there to see its first wielder. Human hearts are truly simple things to grasp. And you wear yours on your sleeve, Briana Matthews." His voice dips. "Just as your mother did."

At the mention of my mother, at the reminder that *he* knew who she was when even *she* didn't—a Scion of Arthur, a wielder of Bloodcraft—a coiled thread of root escapes from my mouth.

"Is *that* it?" the King asks. "Is it the thought of your mother that drives your guilt, your shame, and your fear? That loosens your grip on your own power?"

I glower at him. "*Don't* talk about her."

"Let us experiment." He steps back. "Forge a construct."

When I hesitate, he scoffs. "By the age of five, every Merlin can forge a simple construct. Selwyn Kane forged one at three."

I clench my jaw, unable to fight the surge of root that leaves my body at the thought of Selwyn. Not just the thought of Selwyn but the image of Selwyn as a child. Before Erebus and the Order and his Oath—before his innocence was ground down and out. "I am *not* a Merlin."

"No," Erebus admits. "You could become something much, *much* more powerful than a Merlin, if you wanted to."

"I want to."

"Then consider this your second lesson, since you failed so horribly at the first."

My fists ball at my sides. "Most teachers would go back over the material before setting their student up for another failing grade."

"I am not most teachers," he snaps. "Forge a simple construct."

Fine.

I call on the aether in the air the way that the Legendborn do, and create a shining blue-silver longsword.

The King tsks. "Your affinity for aether allows you to forge Arthur's sword and armor, but your *root* is more flexible than that. Forge something to *stop* me, not stab me."

I release the blue-silver sword. Let it go to dust. Call up the root furnace in my chest, open it wide, let the red flames race and lick down my biceps to my forearms and to my hands until the color is reflected in the King's dark eyes. But I cannot command it into a shape. I grit my teeth and envision a gauntlet. A small sphere. A blade—anything.

He glares at me. "Fight for yourself, Briana."

My eyes *burn*. "I am!"

"No, you aren't." He paces away, hands resting against his spine. "Why did you call for my aid? What do you wish to become?"

I release my root in frustration. "I told you!"

"Strength, power, and control are what you wish to *possess*, girl!" the King shouts, coming to a stop. "Not what you wish to *become*."

The King can't read my mind, but his words pluck at my unspoken ones. Tears of anger streak down my face, because he's right. Those are things I want, not who I want to be.

What *do* I wish to become?

Here, in the presence of the demon who took advantage of her bargain with our ancestors, Vera's voice returns to me: *You are the one who decides now how to keep our Line alive, Briana Matthews.*

But Vera doesn't understand that this world has curdled her amazing gift into a curse. After eight generations of fear and soul-tearing grief, of our mothers dying when we needed them most, of losing the knowledge that could have connected us to one another and to Vera herself . . . the old violence hasn't died; it has simply found new life. Our bodies break down like clockwork, our mothers die early, our daughters die young, then it begins anew.

Our cycle is death and confusion—and I have not learned enough to break it. But I will.

My gaze rises to fix on the King's.

He nods slowly. "Tell me."

"I will fulfill Vera's wish. I *will* honor her sacrifice. But if neither she nor my other ancestors can teach me how, then I must become something they never could." I gasp twice, then swipe my tongue over my chapped lips. Hoarse words burst from my chest before I can second-guess them. "I must become untouchable."

The King's eyes glisten like rubies. "Because . . . ?"

"Because my enemies are everywhere." I feel my lips pull back, as if *I* am a demon catching a scent on the wind. As if *I* am a monster, snarling at the world. "And if they are everywhere, then I will become something they cannot reach."

The King presses again. "More."

"If my opponents are relentless," I say, "then I will become unstoppable."

"And?"

My words speed up with my breath. "And if they want my power and body and suffering for their own ends, then I will become impervious."

"To what end?" he asks quietly. "All of this . . . to what end?"

"So that . . ." I grimace. "So that my power, and my pain, belong . . . to me."

He nods slowly, stepping closer until his gaze turns dizzying. "And what are you willing to do in order to become these things?"

I don't answer him out loud, but my reply appears in my mind, bright and steady as the sun.

Anything.

I'm willing to do anything.

Anything.

"I see the answer in your eyes," the King murmurs. "Now I understand what must be done."

The world turns black, swallowing me whole.

VI

I WAKE UP in a strange room, on a strange bed, with my cheek pressed into a faded gray comforter.

Somehow, a day has passed since my first training session with Erebus. The last thing I remember was facing him alone, and the darkness that followed.

Early morning sun casts itself through a pair of black-framed, stained-glass arches directly in my line of sight. Through my half-opened eyes, the multi-colored panes seem to wink and shimmer.

I roll over with a groan. The room around me is plain and small. Wide-planked wooden floors. White plastered walls with a couple of framed landscape paintings. A small antique writing desk sits in a corner with a heavy, gilded mirror leaning against the wall beside it. A rug beneath the bed in tight red and gold and green patterns. A pocket door leading to what looks like a tiny closet. The twin four-poster bed beneath me takes up the entire wall opposite the dark wooden door. I could cross the entire room in six steps, tops. It is the most guest bedroom-y guest bedroom I've ever seen.

The twisting, tugging sensation of hunger clears my head some and heightens my awareness of my body. I wiggle my toes in my socks and feel that my boots are gone. I can tell by the way the fabric digs into my hips that I am still in the same borrowed jeans I put on when I left Northern. Just like I'm still in my borrowed T-shirt. The clothes that . . .

I blink.

The clothes that . . .

Blink again.

The clothes . . . *someone* . . . gave me.

I shove up on my elbows, brows drawn tight as I stare at the pillow, searching my memories. Someone gave me these clothes—I'm sure of it—but I *don't* know their name.

My stomach growls, but my hunger is accompanied by something heavy and unsettling.

I shuffle into the tiny attached bathroom, only big enough to fit a toilet and a small sink, and relieve myself while I put my thoughts in order.

As I make my way back to the bed and lie down, my mind is clear, and my thoughts feel ordered, and yet I still can't think of the name of the person whose clothes I'm wearing. But I used to know their name, I'm sure of it. I knew it yesterday, but today . . . don't.

Alarm and unease rattle through me now, growing stronger with every breath as I search my memory. Where that someone, that person, lives in my mind is simply a shapeless gray mass bathed in mist. No name. No face. No body. No distinguishing features. I don't know their personality, their smile, or how we know each other.

It's like they never existed.

No. There's . . . *something.*

When I think of them, I feel a single clear emotion: gratitude.

That makes sense; if this person gave me clothing to wear, they must be a friend. And if they gave me these clothes recently, before I left Northern, then they must be Legendborn.

But everything else about them is gray mist and shadows.

I mentally walk through yesterday again, retracing my steps. I woke up. I put on these borrowed clothes. I went to the hill at Northern. I burned my ancestral stream, restored Excalibur, called for Erebus. I bargained with him. He took someone away—

Wait. Who was *that* someone?

When I focus my inner eye toward this second person, I come up blank again. Like everything I know about them has been removed from my mind.

They are a gray, identity-less figure.

No. There's more. Even if I couldn't identify this second person in a lineup, an emotion rises within me at the thought of them. I squeeze my eyes shut, reaching for it, then I feel it: guilt. An immense, immeasurable, consuming guilt.

Beyond that, I don't know anything more about them.

What happened after Erebus took that person away?

There was a third person who ran after me just before we left. They were chasing me, trying to stop me from leaving.

Again, no details. Gray mist and shadows. And again, there's a single emotion. It is muted loss and deep pain, together. It is . . . longing.

If this third person was running to keep me from leaving, then they must have wanted me to stay. I longed for this person . . . and yet I ran from them?

Confusion floods me.

I think frantically about anyone else, other friends and other people I know, but everywhere I look in my old life, there are blanks. Gray, misty faces and bodies. Nameless companions and friends and even enemies. All gone.

If there are emotions attached to these people, I can't immediately locate them. Not when my heart is starting to race with apprehension and worry.

Let's start with the basics.

I remember my mother. All of her. Every moment and detail. I see her clearly. Feel dozens of emotions over time, all attached to her.

My heart stretches toward hope—but when I think of my father, there is another blank.

I know the last time I saw him we were at Waffle House. The emotion I feel about him? Regret.

Dread pools in my belly. People can't just be wiped off the board and erased from my history, can they? Not without . . . magic.

Like a mesmer.

Erebus *mesmered* me.

I groan and sit up, swinging my legs over the side of the bed. *Of course.* How could I be so gullible? So silly to think that he'd actually help me, when all he's really done is take my sword, remind me that I am in his debt for an indeterminate amount of time, let his cambion wards attack me, and now manipulate my memories?

There's a deep bruise on my knee from when I fell at the museum. I press my fingers into it—hard. The pain lights up my senses and makes my eyes water. I wait for the familiar burning away of a mesmer cloaking my mind—but it never comes.

I press the bruise again, even harder, apologizing silently to my battered body—but it doesn't work.

The apprehension in my chest blooms to full-blown panic.

"Erebus!"

I storm through the house—every room is empty. Then, I'm back outside, running toward the field by the barn.

When I reach the field, Erebus is manipulating two green-silver hellhounds against the twins. They are each fighting one, dodging and rolling to avoid the quick attacks of his large constructs.

"What the hell did you do to me?" I shout.

Erebus's eyes widen, and he tilts his head. His constructs fade. "What are you experiencing?"

The question takes me aback. "Your mesmer?" I say. "Obviously."

"Answer the question." His eyes glance back and forth between mine, as if digging into my mind. "Tell me what you are *experiencing*."

I spread my hands wide. "I'm missing people! Missing my friends!"

He waits. Watches. Does not repeat himself again.

"Did you hit your head, new girl?" Zoe asks. Her eyes flick to the barn. "Against the barrier?"

"No, I didn't hit my head," I snap. "He took them away! I don't know, or don't remember them."

Elijah steps closer, watching us warily but still giving us a wide berth. "Your memories are gone, or your friends are gone?" I shoot him a glare, but he only shrugs. "Just asking. For clarification."

"My friends are gone," I say with a huff.

"Entirely?" Elijah asks. "You still *know* they're your friends, so obviously—"

"No, not entirely!" I shout. "But they're just . . . blanks in my head. I don't know anyone I used to know. Can't see names or faces."

"Fascinating," Erebus says mildly. "Does this affect only your friends?"

"Stop pretending you don't know what you did," I say, pacing away. "I should have known—"

"Be explicit," Erebus says. "Tell me more."

"You did something to them!" I whirl back. "That's it, isn't it? You did something to my friends. You did something to my dad."

Erebus sighs, shoving both hands in his pockets. "I did nothing to your friends and father. They are all as you left them. Where you left them. In whatever state you left them."

I don't miss the emphasis on those words. "I thought you couldn't hurt me—"

"Through my fulfillment of my bargain with Vera, I can't physically harm you by my own hand, it's true," he replies. "And I did not do so here."

"So, you *did* do something," I accuse. "Some sort of . . . super mesmer?"

"There's no such thing as a 'super mesmer,'" Elijah interjects, rolling his eyes.

I whirl on him, and he puts his hands up, stepping back. I glare at Erebus. "I can break a mesmer, you know."

"You can break a mesmer?" Zoe asks.

"She can. *If* it was a mesmer, she *could* break it," Erebus says. "But you have already tried that and failed, haven't you?"

"Yes," I admit.

"I did not manipulate your mind," he says. "I gave you what you needed to meet your own objectives. The loss of your 'memories' of other people, if that is indeed what you're experiencing, is unexpected—even to me."

That worries me. Erebus did something, *gave* me something, but didn't anticipate this result? I swallow. "Whatever you did, *reverse it*."

His hands spread wide. "I cannot." We hold each other's gaze for a long moment, and I haltingly, frustratingly, almost believe him.

"Then tell *me* how to reverse it."

"You cannot either."

I feel my heart racing beneath my rib cage. Anger turns to panic under my skin, in my lungs. "Well, who can?"

He shakes his head slowly. "No one can."

"I don't believe you."

"He doesn't lie," Zoe says confidently. "Not to us."

"How would you know?" I pace, filled with the sudden urge to hit something. To strike out. To tear and to rip. "You don't know how much he lies. How much his entire *life* is a lie."

"Watch your mouth, new girl!" Elijah steps forward.

I sneer at him. "You really think I care to watch my mouth right now?"

"Zoe is not wrong," Erebus says calmly. I turn back at that and see him glance at both Zoe and Elijah in turn. "I will offer you the same agreement that I have offered the twins. In your time with me, however long that lasts, while I will not always tell you all that I know—and I know that neither will you—if you ask me a question, what I do say will be the truth."

"Lies of omission are still lies," I say.

"I won't argue with that," he replies evenly. "But what are your other options?"

"Go back to—"

"Go back where?" he asks, eyes glinting. "And to whom?"

I hesitate.

"If you remained as you were yesterday," Erebus says, "that question would have resulted in a stream of your magic spilling out, unbidden."

I open my mouth. Close it. He's right. "But——"

"Now that your emotions are not muddying the waters of control, let us see what you can do." He raises his hand, thumb and forefinger poised together. "Step back, Zoe and Elijah."

The twins take a large step back in unison on either side of us, out of the pounded earth and gravel and into the scraggly weeds at the edge of the field.

Erebus snaps his fingers, and the world turns dark.

Overhead, a black aether dome bleeds around us, curving into the earth until we are trapped within a massive glass marble.

At first, the inside of Erebus's barrier is silent. Then, a hot wind picks up, as if we are in an open desert at midday instead of a barrier made of night. "What is this?"

"What all aether workings are." The voice that reaches me feels as though it is being whispered at the curve of my ear. I shudder away, but Erebus is fifteen feet in front of me—and his mouth has not moved. "My intention, made manifest." Sweat drips down my spine. A flash of silver lightning streaks across the false sky, white and blinding. "The twins cannot see or hear us. We can speak plainly."

"Then speak plainly," I shoot back. "Tell me what is happening to me, or I'm leaving."

"Even if you were not in my debt, you don't *know* the people you left behind. If you return to them, how do you think they will feel when you suddenly reappear and don't know a single thing about them? When you know everything about yourself and your own history? When you remember the Christmas gift you received when you were nine and the grade you earned in your English class months ago and your last very good meal? How do you think they'll feel when you remember everything about yourself, but not them?"

My jaw tenses. I don't know how he knows, but he's right; I know all of those things.

"You said it yourself," Erebus begins, musing aloud, "you are *missing* people. To you, they have been erased. But to *them*, would it not appear as though you simply . . . forgot them?"

My body grows chilled. "I didn't—I would *never* forget them—"

"Do they know that? You did, after all, volunteer to leave them," he says idly. "Is it not possible that your friends and family might feel as though they weren't important enough details in your life for you to hold on to?"

"Stop," I say. "They'll understand when I tell them what happened."

Erebus continues as if I'd never spoken. "What *will* happen when you don't recognize your own father's face? Or recognize the boy you last kissed? Or know the name of the best friend you sent into a coma?"

My father, missing from my reality.

The boy I last kissed? Missing.

The best friend that I sent into a coma—abruptly, the last moment I shared with this nameless girl returns. She was lying in a bed, weakened, breathing magic. Then an emotion rises: worry. So, so much worry.

"I—"

"What of the Merlin boy who sacrificed his humanity to save you?" Erebus prompts, voice quiet and curious—and knowing. "And whom you then sent away?"

I suck in a breath. I remember that someone sacrificed themselves to save me. That person was a Merlin boy? And *he* was the person I sent away at Northern?

Guilt still rises within me when I think of the boy, but with this added information from Erebus, guilt not only rises but it takes me over in a crushing wave. So deep, it could swallow me into its ocean. So heavy, it threatens to drag me beneath its depths and never let me go. The type of guilt that claws at my heart from the inside out, threatening to shred it open.

"What of the boy you ran from who only wanted to keep you safe and close?"

The boy I ran from, the boy I longed for, wanted me safe . . . wanted me close. The confusion there is enough to choke my voice away.

Gratitude. Longing. Regret. Worry. Guilt.

What can I possibly do with these remnants? What can I possibly expect to take back to those five people who elicit these emotions, much less anyone else in my life? If I returned, why would they accept me back at all?

Especially when I look at them as though they are strangers?

"Some oaths, Briana," Erebus murmurs, "we make to ourselves. And to no one else."

As he speaks, the emotions that felt unmanageable begin to recede. A thunderstorm waning. A wave pulling back out to the sea. I can breathe again. "What is happening to me?"

"Do you know what oaths you have made to yourself? What commitments you have made, in the silent parts of your being?" Erebus continues speaking. "Have you ever been asked, by anyone? I know it cannot be to win a war that doesn't belong to you or to defeat Arthur Pendragon's ghost. Is it revenge?"

"No . . . I . . ."

"The Order has taken so much from you, girl." Erebus steps closer. "From you, your mother, your maternal line. Arthur himself took you over without your consent, spoke through you, fought through you, *destroyed* through you. Is revenge so difficult to imagine?"

"No, but—"

"But?"

"I told you what I wanted to become."

He nods. "Indeed you did. You want your power and your pain to belong to you. That is your intention. And so our lessons continue. Forge a construct."

I sputter. "You know I can't—"

"*Forge a construct.*" He raises a hand overhead, fingers like claws to the sky, like his crown—demanding the very stars down to his fingertips. "I will strike you with my power in ten seconds unless you can create a construct to stop me."

I stumble back, eyes above, where the darkened sky has started to churn into swirling black clouds. "No, stop!"

"Aim your intention outward!"

Panicked, I reach for my root—and my fists ignite. Not red but a deep, dark purple.

"Make your mind a void!"

Lightning gathers, splitting the sky—

"Channel an intention into a single word. A single desire!"

His lightning cracks down, aimed right at my skull— I find a word. Utter it like a weapon.

"Protect!"

The lightning lands like a bomb. My ears pop. Dust and stone blast up from my feet, clogging my nose and mouth. I am nearly blown to my knees, but I fasten my feet to the ground, bracing for impact . . . but it never comes.

"Open your eyes, Briana."

My eyes open to slivers.

I expect destruction, but the world has gone quiet. Gone still. And I am standing in the center of a crackling, glowing purple sphere embedded a foot deep into the ground—and fed by the power at my fists.

This sphere is not an accident, not a hastily cast shield, a roar of root from my mouth, or a burst of flames from my hands, but a perfectly constructed dome.

The bomb wasn't the King's lightning. The bomb was . . . me. My barrier, erupting into place to protect me. He didn't break me.

I broke the earth.

Erebus's own casting, the dark marble, is already fading. It is nothing but crystallized pieces, sparking down to the earth around us. The twins stand beneath the shower, jaws dropped and eyes wide.

A laugh bubbles up from my throat.

I let it out. Let myself hear my own adrenaline-fueled wonder.

I meet Erebus's burning crimson eyes through my glowing shield. "Congratulations are in order."

"For passing your lesson?"

"Not my lesson. Yours," he murmurs. "You became untouchable."

Erebus and I, the Shadow King and the former Crown Scion of Arthur, face each other through a shield of magic made possible only through our collaboration. Through my decisions and his own.

I gave you what you needed to meet your own objectives.

I have no words . . . but I grant him a nod.

He looks up. "One word to take it down."

I consider, then speak. "Collapse."

My barrier falls.

As my very first construct fades away, it reveals the barn, the winter trees, and the late-morning sky overhead, all in utter clarity.

My new mentor crosses his arms over his chest. "Now," he says, "we are ready to begin."

PART ONE

UNTOUCHABLE

William

SOMETIMES "TOO LATE" is a matter of seconds.

By the time I arrive at the top of the hill, heart pounding and breathless, Bree and the stranger are nowhere to be seen—and Nick stands alone. While I am winded from our sprint, chest rising and falling with every full breath, he is deadly still. His gauntlet-clad forearm and bare palm remain outstretched in the empty air, frozen in his attempt to grasp Bree before she disappeared. Before us, the woods ahead are empty. Tall oaks stand sentinel while short shrubs sway in the breeze. Even the ground is undisturbed, without a trail to follow.

Too late.

A matter of *seconds*.

My panted question breaks the silence. "Where . . . did they go?"

Nick does not answer.

It had all happened so quickly: Sel, in his anger and frustration, had been breaking furniture in his room all morning, so when it went eerily silent, Larkin, Nick, and I rushed inside—and found him gone. Disappeared from within his locked, warded, and guarded room. Panicked, we looked for Bree next.

When we found her beside a strange figure at the top of the hill at Northern, Nick and I were standing shoulder to shoulder. We ran to her together, but he outpaced me quickly, faster as a Scion of Lancelot than I could ever be as a Scion of Gawain, calling aether to his body as he moved.

In a single heartbeat, silver-blue magic surrounded him. In *two* heartbeats, crystalline armor had snapped into place, shining and ready for battle, at his legs, across his torso, down his arms. It was an impressive feat—only Merlins can call and forge aether that effectively while so preoccupied.

But it was too late. By seconds.

"Where did they go, Nick?" Again, Nick does not respond. It is only then that I notice he is not looking in the forest as I am. Instead, his eyes are trained on the wisp of black smoke writhing between his fingertips like a thin, dark snake.

That wisp is aether. Black aether.

Aether can be many colors. Silver-blue, green, gold, Bree's own crimson. Aether is never, ever black. And yet this aether moves like a shadow come to life. Like the air itself has been cursed. We watch together as the wind catches the strands, spinning them upward until they dissipate.

Fear for Bree courses through me so wholly that I feel my breath shake with it. She's suffered so much, but she has always had people with her. She had us.

Now she's alone.

When Nick releases his hand to his side, he does not acknowledge my presence. Does not meet my eyes. My healer's attention immediately shifts from concern for Bree and Sel to the Scion in front of me. I swallow my fear and draw on the calm I reserve for moments like this.

"Nick. Hey, look at me." I wave my hand before him, but his blue eyes are unseeing, unblinking. *Awake but unresponsive. Catatonia?*

My fingers itch for a penlight to check his pupils.

Nick's aether armor shudders once, like an image losing focus and then regaining it, but it does not dissolve. Armor retention is a common threat response when Legendborn are overwhelmed. Their bodies in fight or flight keep their defenses in place. It's a subconscious, magical protective mechanism that tells me something crucial: Nick is still "in" the battle. His mind is buried in some unreachable place.

Recognition drops like a boulder in my stomach.

I've seen this response within Nick before. I know where it comes from. How he hides it. How, in a matter of seconds, he has been thrust back into a time and place where no one else can follow.

"William!" Larkin's bellow reaches us from the bottom of the hill. I jump at the sudden sound—Nick doesn't.

Larkin speeds toward us, auburn hair tousled by the wind, Scottish burr thick under stress. "I've looked everywhere. There's no trace of Kane. Did y'find Bree?"

"No," I say, watching Nick carefully. "But—"

Larkin's sharp inhale cuts me off. "But Bree *was* here. Her scent is fresh." His amber eyes narrow before they follow the same path mine did: left, right, to the woods, across the ground. He inhales again, sharply. "Someone else was here too. Their scent is faint, barely there . . . but it smells like . . . like . . ."

Abruptly, his spine straightens like a dagger, and he whirls around, mage flame lifting the edges of his hair. "What the hell happened here, Scions? Why does it smell like Shadowborn?"

"Larkin." I keep my voice even, watching Nick's breath quicken. "If it was a demon—"

"There is no 'if'! I *know* what a demon smells like!" Larkin's palms flare to life with magic. Mage flame whips up around his wrists. A Merlin, on alert. "Bree is—"

"*Gone.*" Nick's voice is a hoarse, angry whisper behind me, but I can't suppress the relief I feel at hearing it. "She's gone, William."

"I know," I say. Nick's sympathetic nervous system is running the show right now. A storm, brewing over sea. I keep my voice even and steady. Offer a rescue buoy. "We'll find her."

"She was just—I'd almost—" Nick releases a frustrated breath and blinks hard, like he's waking up from anesthesia. "They're *both* . . . gone."

"And we'll *find* them both." I fold every ounce of confidence I have into my voice, hoping it surrounds Nick and grounds him. "We'll get them back."

"How, exactly?" Larkin demands. His agitation breaks any calm I might have transmitted, jarring Nick where he stands.

I take a deep breath and remind myself that cambions, even trained Merlins, can be erratic in a crisis. "Larkin, control yourself—"

"They've left no trace!" Larkin exclaims, eyes wild. "They've—"

"Stop." Nick's command is quiet but firm. Larkin stills immediately, as do I. "Panicking won't help us and won't help them."

Larkin's flames recede as he eyes Nick warily. "Scion Davis? Are you . . . ?"

"I'm fine."

While Nick's eyes are on Larkin's face, my healer's gaze is on *him*. The pulse in his throat is slowing down. He's coming back to us, to the here and now, but I've learned not to believe anyone who, without prompting, declares that they are "fine." Sel says this constantly. Bree, far too much for my liking. Nick? "Fine" was the word he uttered in a relentless stream right before he publicly renounced his title and left the chapter.

Nick has always *said* he is fine, but Nick has never *been* fine.

"Nick—"

"I'm *fine*." Nick's attention is on Larkin. "What do we know?"

"Not enough." Larkin doesn't miss a beat, a Merlin pursuing his quarry. "Few clues. Too many questions."

"Then we tackle each question one at a time." In Nick's reply, in his sharp gaze, and in his quick recovery from his shock, I am reminded of the leadership for which he was trained. It's kicking in now, clearing his head as he draws on drilled protocols and old memories. I have seen enough injured warriors in my infirmary to know that those drilled protocols are protective in moments like these. "We do a threat assessment. Now, while everything is fresh."

I want to press Nick again. Ask him to pause. I am itching to offer him respite, if not healing. Space, if not clarity. But Larkin continues before I can put the right words together to stop what Nick has started.

"Right." Larkin nods, gathering himself. "First threat, first question. Were

Kane and the Crown Scion taken by the same demon? Or two demons working together?"

Nick's reply is swift. "We should assume it's one. If the man we saw can teleport, then taking Sel one moment and Bree the next would be possible. Easy, even."

"Powerful demons don't like working together. An alliance between two goruchel of that level would be atypical. Against what we know and what we've been taught."

"We left 'typical' behind a long time ago," I say.

"Yes." Nick glances at me, then his eyes fasten onto Larkin. "And the last three months have proven that we won't get far if we only rely on what we've been taught. Does the stranger's scent tell you anything else?"

Larkin sniffs the air again. "No. S'nothing like I've encountered before."

Nick's jaw flexes. "What about Sel's room? Is there an aether residual there, too? It might linger longer inside—"

"The room's a dead end." Larkin throws up a frustrated hand. "Kane forged so many weapons trying to escape, it was like an aether bomb had gone off. We wasted time searching for him when a greater demon was after Bree—"

"Searching for Sel was *not* a waste of time," Nick says in a low voice. "He isn't expendable. Neither is Bree."

"Briana Matthews is the Crown Scion and Awakened King of the Round Table, Davis," Larkin snaps, eyes flashing. "She's as irreplaceable as they come. We should have been guarding her. *I* should have been guarding her!"

"The wards around the Keep were breached," I protest, shaking my head. "We had every reason to believe Bree was protected within them. This isn't your fault, Larkin."

"I am her *Kingsmage*," Larkin growls. "This is exactly my fault!"

"You are *not* Bree's Kingsmage." Nick's voice is steady and clear. When Larkin whirls on Nick, Nick doesn't flinch. Instead, he raises his chin, his frame and height made even more commanding by his shining armor. "No matter how much you may want the title, Guard Douglas, it is not yours."

Larkin's face flushes red. "With all due respect, Scion Davis—"

"Now would be a good time to remember that you are speaking to someone who has actually *taken* the Kingsmage Oath." Nick's voice is not laced with venom; instead, all I hear is a solemn weariness—and a biting clarity. "I've lived nearly half my life bonded to a Kingsmage. You and Bree *are not* bound, and that matters here. If you were, you would have felt her mortal fear. Since you aren't, we have no evidence as to whether her life was or *is* at risk, only guesses."

Larkin does not hear Nick's weariness, only the pointed critique. His face flames further as he jabs a finger at the empty spot before the woods. "The Crown Scion has been taken *hostage* by a demon of *unknown* origin. A demon who can disappear into thin air. She could be dead. The war could already be lost." His eyes flash. "I won't stand here and be insulted—"

"Then stand here and *use your mind* instead, Mageguard," Nick snaps. When he raises his right hand and glowing aether gauntlet, the light bounces off his skin, casting one side of his face in icy-blue brightness and the other in shadow. "My armor is still active. My inheritance is *alive* within me. Which means—"

"Bree's alive," I whisper, relief flooding through me. I stare at my own glowing dagger of Gawain. "Nick's right. My dagger hasn't dusted. If the Awakened Scion of Arthur dies by a Shadowborn hand, all the Legendborn inheritances—all our abilities and magic—would disappear with her."

And never return. This silent truth is one we are all thinking but dare not say aloud. Larkin presses his lips into a thin line. "Forgive me, Scion Davis. I should have remembered—"

"It's forgiven," Nick interrupts, lowering his arm and gauntlet. "But keep thinking. We need to be smart about this. Determine what action to take and take it quickly. Bree's alive. What else does that mean?"

"If she's . . ." I swallow around the lump in my throat. Nick nods, encouraging me to continue my train of thought. "If she's not dead by now . . . then the demon who took her doesn't mean to kill her."

"We can't know that," Larkin argues.

"I think we can." Nick's jaw clenches. "Think of how knowledgeable this demon must be to know for a fact that the Crown Scion was on this property.

Think of how powerful he must be to breach the protective wards of a Legend-born chapter. Think of how *strong* he must be to handle Selwyn Kane in his current state. Do you *really* think a demon with that profile would hesitate for a single second to kill Briana Matthews if all he wanted was to end the Lines and win the war?"

"No," Larkin admits. "He'd have killed her immediately. On sight. Her blood would be at our feet."

I check my watch. "And they've been gone going on ten minutes now."

Larkin's eyes widen. "He . . . wants her for something."

"No." Nick's gaze darkens. "He doesn't just want her; he *needs* her. Isolated from us and at a location he controls. The question is . . . for what?"

"And why take Selwyn?" I ask. "He's a handful right now, more than. Aggressive, violent, likely starving for every negative emotion within reach. Given that Selwyn is in full demonia, whatever inhibitions he normally places on his rage will be gone now."

Larkin raises a brow. "You speak as though Kane is a *reserved* personality to begin with."

"Selwyn manages himself as best he can," I say, feeling my defenses rise.

"When he's able to, yes," Nick murmurs, eyes going distant. "But right now? Sel is uncontrollable."

"And even more powerful now that he has descended," Larkin mutters. "Based on how he trashed his room, his aether abilities and spellwork haven't diminished at all."

Nick taps his thigh in thought, eyes scanning the Keep in the distance. "Somehow, I doubt the demon took Sel for his aether abilities. Why bother with a Merlin, even one of Sel's caliber, when you're powerful enough to walk through wards and teleport? No. He took Sel for another reason—and likely took him somewhere else. Separated them."

Larkin frowns. "How can you—?"

"Because Sel wasn't standing here with Bree and the demon," Nick explains, gesturing toward the place that Bree stood. "And I don't believe for a second that this demon was too weak to transport them simultaneously; Sel disappeared first because Sel was his first trip. Then the demon came back for Bree. Wherever Sel and Bree are, they aren't together."

"There's a small mercy." Larkin breathes a sigh of quiet relief.

"Excuse me?" Nick says, voice a warning. "Why is that better? Sel could protect Bree—"

"'Could' is the operative word." Larkin purses his lips. "I'm not as close to Kane as you or Will are, but I know Kane isn't himself. There's no telling how he'd react to Bree right now. If he'd see her as food or . . ."

Nick's eyes narrow. "Or what?"

"Or blame her for his descent," Lark says. "Attack her in revenge, even cause her pain on purpose—"

"Sel wouldn't do that," I interject. I may not know what a descended cambion looks like up close, but I refuse to believe Sel capable of that level of cruelty. I can't believe it. I *won't* believe it.

Hesitation crosses Larkin's face, but only briefly. "The Selwyn you know is gone, Scions. This is where my distance from the situation is a benefit. I know that—"

"You don't know Sel." Nick's jaw clenches. "He sacrificed his humanity to bring Bree home."

"Exactly my point!" Larkin snaps, fangs flashing. "Kane sacrificed his humanity, and now that humanity is *gone*. His reasoning is different now, his faculties altered. If he's not careful, he could get himself killed, either by a goruchel who sees him as a threat, this demon who kidnapped him, even another Merlin—"

Nick is steadfast. "Impossible. Sel would—"

His sentence is cut off with a gasp. He falls to his knees without warning, landing roughly on both palms with his head bowed.

"Nick!" I lurch forward instinctively, wondering if I have missed an injury. Hoping it's not Sel and the end of their Kingsmage bond. Praying that Sel's not dead, wondering what that would do to Nick—

Beside me, Lark has forged an aether axe. "Is it the Shadowborn?" His eyes dart from Nick to the land around us, senses on alert. "I don't sense anything—"

"Are you hurt?" I grasp at Nick's shoulder, pulling at a pauldron, but he wrenches away.

"Don't touch me!" he hisses.

I step back, shoving down the bloom of guilt at touching him without his consent. "Tell us what's happening."

Nick shakes his head, fingers digging into the dark brown loam. "Nnnnnngh . . ." His groan is low and guttural. A shout, trapped behind his teeth like he's trying to hold it back. "Just . . . ," he grits out. "Need . . . a minute—" His torso trembles under the force of some wave that has taken him over. Some invisible wound that I cannot see or stop.

After a long moment of shaking, rattling breaths, Nick leans back on his knees. I gasp at the mix of emotions on his flushed face. Pain, I expect. Frustration, sure. But in the set of his jaw, his brow, I see something else—a potent rage. Then, as fast as it appeared, it recedes—and Nick begins to laugh. Gasping, full-bodied laughter emerges hoarse from his battered throat . . . and I have no idea how to respond.

Larkin looks at me in horror. "What the fu—"

"Sel." Nick's dancing blue eyes meet mine, crinkling with unbridled joy in the corners. "He's . . . not dead."

Relief floods me. "The Kingsmage Oath and bond are still active," I breathe, half to myself and half to Larkin. "Sel's alive."

"Sel's not . . . only . . . alive. He's . . . murderous." Nick pants, smiling, both hands on his knees. "He wants *someone* dead. Don't know who . . . but I can feel it, bright and clear: Sel wants to tear a body apart, limb from limb." He huffs a laugh, dark amusement making his features glitter. "Slowly."

"Your mortal fear and Selwyn's murderous intent," I murmur, remembering that I've seen this before but from the other side of the equation. When Bree, Alice, and I were outside the Crossroads Lounge in Georgia, Sel too had doubled over from the barrage of Nick's side of the bond. "I truly wish the bond gave you access to more than one emotion each."

"One is plenty, believe me." Nick shakes his head. "I'd hate to be the person in Sel's sights right now."

"Aye." Larkin eyes Nick as he recovers. "Whoever that poor soul is, they aren't long for this world."

I realize this is the first time Larkin has witnessed the Kingsmage Oath exact its price from its Oathbound. Nick was right to remind him of what he's missing, and I'm suddenly grateful that wherever Bree is, at least she won't feel Larkin's anger.

Larkin watches Nick for a moment longer. "You seem awfully delighted by Kane's appetite for dismemberment."

"I am." Nick nods and pushes to his feet with a small, delirious grin. "Because now we know they're okay, both Bree *and* Sel."

"'Okay' is relative," Larkin cautions. "'Okay' is not the same as 'safe.'"

"No, it's not." Nick's eyes flash to mine, and I don't like what I see there.

"Nick?" I ask cautiously. "What are you thinking?"

He glances away. Runs his tongue over his bottom lip.

Larkin's brows furrow. "Scion Davis?"

After a beat, Nick inhales, drawing his shoulders back until he stands at his full height. When he releases a long, slow breath, his armor fades, then disappears entirely, revealing his loose navy shirt and jeans—and a still-bandaged left hand. I recognize the injury immediately: it's his half of the matching shallow cuts that he and Sel made on themselves in order to blood walk to Bree.

I haven't had a chance to heal it yet.

When Nick turns, there is something in the set of his jaw and shoulders that I have never seen before: cold authority.

"Hand me your phone, Guard Douglas."

Larkin startles. "What?"

"Your phone." Nick points his chin at Larkin's jacket, voice mild. "The one you keep in your breast pocket. The one you used to call the Lieges when you and the others were at Volition. I assume you have other numbers saved?"

Larkin's hand flies to his breast pocket. "Yes. What other numbers?"

Nick levels his gaze at Larkin. "That's an order, Guard Douglas."

Larkin hesitates only for a millisecond before he unlocks the phone with a swipe of his thumb and passes it to Nick.

"Nick?" I ask.

Nick's jaw remains tight. "This must be done, William."

"What must be done?"

Nick navigates Larkin's phone history and hits a call button. When a voice answers, his face shifts into a charming smirk. "Regent Cestra. Been a while."

Larkin and I both lunge toward the phone, but Nick dips his shoulder, side-stepping the two of us smoothly. Cestra manages a muffled, shocked response from the other end of the line before he replies. "Yes, this is Scion Davis."

I reach for Nick again, but this time, Larkin holds me back. He's listening to his Regent's low, angry voice. Cestra never rescinded the kill order on Nick's life, which means Nick has just called the exact person who sent her world-class assassins after him.

And yet, Nick chuckles, eyes sparkling. "What the hell do *I* want? Well"— Nick tucks one hand under his elbow—"the Council and I have much to discuss, wouldn't you agree?"

The long vowels, the near-rhetorical questioning . . . when I recognize the familiar speech pattern and who it reminds me of—Lord Davis, Nick's father— my jaw hardens. There's a pause as Cestra sputters. I wonder if she hears the late Viceroy Davis in his son's voice too. If it unsettles her like it does me.

"I cannae believe this," Larkin mutters. "Cannae *believe* this right now—" He thrusts his hands through his hair and begins to pace back and forth.

"No, I don't think I *will* 'listen here,'" Nick says brightly. "In fact, I think *you* will listen to what *I* have to say. Every single word."

Cestra says something sharp in retort, a shouted phrase that sounds like an affronted "Why would I do that?"

"Because," Nick says, his warm drawl dripping with molasses and knowing, "I am speaking to you and, through you, the High Council of Regents. As the Awakened Scion of the Line of Lancelot, second-ranked knight of the Round Table, and first blade to the king, I invoke curia conventus."

I freeze, and Larkin sputters a curse of disbelief. At the sound of Cestra's shocked gasp, Nick's smirk grows and twists.

I rack my brain for the rules of a curia, but it's been ages since I've even *heard* of one. It's archaic. Unheard of—

"You're familiar with the term, are you not?" Nick continues. A pause. "You are? Excellent. Then we understand each other. You, the other Regents, and your Seneschals have no choice but to comply. I summon you to a formal audience here at the Northern Keep in three days' time." His smile is a quick and sharp blade against the warmth of his face, turning it cold. "In the meantime, why don't you have Mageguard Douglas and the Merlin posted here at the Keep arrest me?"

Beside me, Larkin chokes. I suck in a breath just in time to hear the piercing tone of Cestra's voice.

"Why would you arrest me? Aside from the fact that we both know you'd sleep better at night if I was captured?" Nick asks. "Or, better yet, if I was dead?"

Her voice grows clearer through the speaker. "Scion Davis, we'd never——"

Nick laughs, voice low and taunting. "Come on, Regent Cestra. Just arrest me. You know you want to."

She begins to respond, but he cuts her off. "All right, fine, we'll set aside your not-so-secret plan to kill and replace me with the next eligible Scion of Lancelot for the moment. Even without that diabolical chess move, I think you—and your Mageguard—will likely want to arrest me for something else. A crime no one can contest, much less me, since I'm prepared to confess to it."

"And what crime is that?" Cestra asks.

Nick holds my gaze as he answers, voice steady and clear. "The murder of your Mageguard Maxwell Zhao."

2

William

THE NORTHERN CHAPTER'S Keep, with its isolation from nearby Charlottesville and its looming dark gray Gothic architecture, has always seemed unnecessarily intimidating to me. Perhaps it is my quiet, small-town, Southern sensibilities.

It certainly doesn't help that the Keep has its own prison.

Nick is being held there, and even though he can't receive visitors, I have come to lay eyes on his chosen lodgings.

The prison tower is a tall, narrow, four-sided structure sitting apart from the main two-story residential building. The single wooden door is dark brown with black hardware and a heavy metal lock. *At least this prison looks like what it is,* I think. Not like the Institute, where the Regents held me and Bree captive. *That* looked like a modern business conference center. Sterile, bright, and clean but torturous all the same.

I wish that I was not watching yet another friend be confined by the same Order we were born into serving. I wish that wherever Bree is now, she's comfortable. What has it come to that I can imagine our enemies treating our king better than our leadership would?

An extra ward surrounds the tower. When I press my hand against the magic, it lights up, blue-white and electric . . . then dread fills my belly, deep and thick and heavy. Misery roils like magma behind my chest. I retract my hand immediately—and the ward goes quiet and invisible once again.

This is an affective ward. Selwyn doesn't cast them at our chapter, but I know why the Northern Chapter's Merlin does.

These wards are not cast for barrier protection or used as a simple deterrent, but as a severe punishment to anyone—human or demon—who manages to touch its surface.

The Southern Chapter is the oldest home of the Order. It was designed to house the Line of Arthur, which means it is protected not only by the Kingsmage but by the Scion of Gawain, too. Other chapters can't afford for their prisoners to escape or for their members to get injured unexpectedly.

Up here, they must heal the long way . . . or not at all.

It is not fair for me to judge the tactics of our fellow Table members, especially when those tactics have been employed, in part, because I am not present in their ranks. But I find judgment in my heart anyway.

Even now, the ward leaves my fingertips stinging in pain. Touching it only for a second left a sharp, layered aftertaste in my mouth—the coppery taste of fear and the bitterness of bile and torment.

How many innocents have touched this ward by accident? How many live safe within these walls, but do so in fear?

My silent inquiries are cut short when I hear a familiar voice. "William!"

Samira Miller and Risa, the dark-haired Merlin of the Keep, walk toward me. Samira waves and I wave back. Both, I notice, take a wide berth around Risa's affective ward.

Samira, like many Lieges, wears tactical gear. Today she bears a Bedivere pin on her collar. "Liege Miller. Merlin Takada."

"Call me Samira, Will." Samira's easy smile broadens across her warm brown face.

Every time I see her or any Liege up close, I am taken aback at the contrast between their faces and bodies and their prematurely gray hair. The visible cost of wielding Legendborn powers—and a reminder that the Abatement is waiting for them.

"Scion Sitterson." Risa's low voice is polite. She is muscled, thin, and dressed in typical Merlin black and silver. She looks toward the tower, then back to me. "Scion Davis can't receive visitors."

"I know. I wouldn't expect such a kindness when imprisonment is so objectively inhumane." I pause, making sure my gaze locks on hers before I continue. "I merely came to see where he was being held."

Risa's eyes narrow. "You needn't worry about Scion Davis. We are treating him well, with respect and civility—"

"Worry how?" I inquire.

She frowns, her dark brows drawing tight. "I admit my wards around the Keep were compromised by the teleporting demon that took both former Kingsmage Kane and Crown Scion Matthews, but I've reinforced them. The affective wards around the tower alone are now two layers deep and three times as painful; I laced the first one with doubt and the next with terror. Whoever this mysterious demon is, I don't think he could break through to get Scion Davis in the night—"

Samira steps in. "I think Scion Sitterson knows that Scion Davis is *physically* safe, Merlin Takada. He is not questioning your abilities. The Line of Gawain are healers, so the nature of their concerns are often"—she pauses, smiling in my direction—"multifaceted."

It is a gracious clarification on my behalf, and yet it rubs me the wrong way. We don't *know* what this mysterious demon can do. Any worries I have are *more* than merited. And Nick's imprisonment is inhumane no matter what.

"I see," Risa says.

Samira crosses her arms. "While there have been no more signs of this demon, there have been more sightings of Gate openings. Isel attacks on humans are picking up. The most recent sightings are in Georgia. You may think about taking some of your own chapter back home, Will."

"We aren't leaving before Nick's curia," I say sharply. "Out of the question. And what if Bree comes back? Or Sel? We should be here in case they return."

"It's been twenty-four hours. . . ."

"And every Legendborn still has their powers," I counter, flashing a gauntlet onto my forearm with a squeeze of my fist. I release it just as quickly. "Bree's still alive. She could escape. Make her way back here."

"With respect, Scion Sitterson, I doubt any demon that's strong enough to break past my wards would also be weak enough to let someone as untrained as the Crown Scion escape," Risa says with a helpless shrug.

"With respect, Merlin Takada, you don't know Bree Matthews," I counter bitingly.

"Okay, okay, let's take a beat here. . . ." Samira holds up both her hands to calm us. "Let me speak to Scion Sitterson alone, please. Risa, see if you can get an ETA on the arrival of the Mageguard. We need to keep prepping for the Regents' arrival, even if we are shorthanded."

Risa bristles. "Of course, Liege Miller. I need to patrol the perimeter as well." She checks the sun's position in the sky. "Mageguard Douglas will just be getting off the night shift."

"Good idea," Samira says smoothly. Risa nods to her and runs off into the distance, her body a dark blur.

"Forgive her; she is young," Samira murmurs once she is out of earshot. "She was posted to the second most important chapter in the Order at sixteen."

"We're all *young*, Samira," I say with a sigh. "Even you. But Merlins grow up faster than even Legendborn, and cambions always seem their age and many others. Eternal, even in their youth."

"Hard to imagine that such a sweet girl like Risa can make such devastating enchantments," Samira murmurs as she comes to stand beside me, gesturing toward the hidden ward. "I expect the wards here and in Georgia to be more severe, but that doesn't mean I'm ever ready for the hit when I accidentally glance off one. Even as a young Squire, I hated passing nearby. We had a Page without the Sight fall into an affective once. She never really recovered."

"They're indiscriminate." I grimace, my stomach twisting. "I can't condone these."

"There's a lot going on around here that any reasonable person would not condone." She nods toward the way that Risa has disappeared. "Nice show of temper just then, by the way. If I didn't know you, I'd almost believe you really are *that* irritated with Risa. Made it easy for me to get rid of her."

"I appreciate the assist," I say. "As for the temper, well, perhaps Selwyn has rubbed off on me."

"A healer with a snarky streak? Fantastic." She laughs and turns to face me, arms crossed over her chest. "Gillian said you want to speak with me alone?"

"I do." I can't help but smile at the glint of mischief in her dark brown eyes. "I have a favor to ask."

"Scion Sitterson," Samira drawls. "This 'favor' already sounds like something ill advised, against the rules, and potentially dangerous."

"All three, I'm afraid."

Samira grins. "What do you need?"

SIXTY-TWO HOURS

AFTER BRIANA MATTHEWS DISAPPEARED

Mariah

"MY DADDY WOULD be rollin' in his grave if he knew where we was headed right now." Aunt Lu scowls at Valec from the back seat of his expensive SUV.

"Wudn't he cremated?" I ask, barely holding back a smile.

"Hush, Mariah," Lu snaps. I grin wide and settle deeper into the heated leather of the front passenger seat.

"It's a fair question." At the steering wheel beside me, Valec chuckles, a flash of white teeth against his brown skin in the dim cabin. There aren't any streetlights on this back road. He glances at Aunt Lu in the rearview mirror. "You got ole Ephraim in an urn on your and Hazel's mantel; don't lie."

Lu's ready for him. "You can bite your tongue too, Valechaz."

"Sure I can," Valec drawls. "Right after I remind you that I was there when Ephraim was born, so I sure as hell remember where y'all put him when he died."

"Valec," I ask, "why're you always reminding people you know where the bodies are buried?"

He frowns as if I'm not making sense. "Exactly *because* I know where the bodies are buried?"

"And cremated, apparently," Lu murmurs.

"That too," Valec says. He glances at Lu again. "You cold, Lucille? Take advantage of the heated seats, niece. Not like I bought 'em for me."

"I know, I know." Lucille pokes at the button on the rear door. It's a rare moment when Lucille actually lets Valec treat her like *he's* the elder and *she's* the one who needs caring for. She grumbles at him all she likes, but he's the only family member that she lets dote on her. She'll never admit it, but I always notice. So does her wife, my Aunt Hazel. And, as evidenced by his wink at me after Lucille turns on her heated seat, so does Valec.

"You gonna make me hit the button, Riah? It's your body heat droppin', not mine." He takes one look at me and punches the heater on my side of the car to high.

"Yeah, yeah." I pull both hands out of my down coat's pockets and hold them out to the vent with palms open. My fingers tremble a bit. Curling them into fists helps them feel steady, but when I open both hands again, the tremors remain. I stuff them back in my pockets.

I study Valec in the dim light of the dashboard. I haven't seen him in a couple weeks. Not since we left my Aunt Hazel's house in the country. Today he's dressed in a more subdued version of his normal Crossroads Lounge attire: heather-gray slacks and a matching vest, a deep yellow-ochre dress shirt rolled up at the elbows, and slick but functional black boots. His dark curls are freshly washed and gelled. His cheeks are the same deep warm brown, his eyes a brown deeper still, and his fangs peek out from below his top lip.

To anyone from the normal human world, Valechaz looks like a nineteen-year-old boy dressed in expensive, old-school, classy attire, out for a late-night ride with some family members. Instead, he's a two-hundred-and-five-year-old half-human, half-demon cambion driving a twenty-year-old Medium and her aura-reading Grand Dame aunt across state lines for reasons no human could follow.

Valec glances at me while I study him. "All good there, Riah?"

I look back out the front windshield. It's a moonless night. With only Valec's headlights to guide us, the solid white lane marking down the middle of the road feels like it could go on forever. "We've been on the road for six hours. I think I passed 'all good' two hours ago."

"Almost there."

"Just feels like we're driving straight into the lion's den, that's all," I say.

"Naw, these are just the cubs," Valec murmurs. "The real lions don't show up 'til tomorrow. We got time to get in and get out."

"But Legendborn are still gonna be there," I insist. "They still got three Merlins on the property. Selwyn—"

Valec nods. "The girl they got stationed up at this chapter, and—"

"That Mageguard boy who was at Volition," Lu adds from the back. "The one they left behind when the rest ran off."

I scowl at the mental image of the retreating Merlins and the Council members, Erebus and Cestra. Any satisfaction I had at their departure was lost in the outrage that they'd dared violate Volition in the first place. That they'd taken Bree. And even all that had been put on the back burner in place of the immediate concern for Alice's and Sel's unconscious bodies under our care.

"'Course the guard ran off," Valec mutters. "Once their superiors were gone, why stick around? Especially after the ancestors broke the earth. Cowards. Wish I'd been there to break *them*."

"That many Merlins? The Mageguard?" I frown. "They mighta killed you."

"They mighta *tried*, y'mean." Valec chuckles low beside me and turns away from the road so I can see his eyes flash red. "I'm more demon than all the Mageguard combined, baby cousin."

I roll my eyes, and he laughs. Valec and me aren't blood related, but we *are* family. Technically. My second Aunt Lu's grandparents on her momma's side are descended from Valec's human half-sibling . . . or something. I narrow my eyes at Valec and try to imagine him going up against that many Merlins at once. I've never seen him fight, but my Aunt Lu says he ain't nothing to mess with in a brawl. Guess having two hundred years under your belt and being half-demon will give you an edge over even Order-trained Mageguard. He'd handed Selwyn

Kane his ass once, I've been told. Sorta wish I'd seen that, to be honest.

"And what about . . ." Valec runs his tongue over his teeth. He isn't one to hesitate over his words, ever. Valec is, in general, smooth as hot maple syrup. Even when he's outta his depth, he's comfortable . . . but the next words take a minute. By the end of that minute, I already know who he's thinking about.

Bree.

"What about the powerhouse?" he asks.

"You know everything we know," Lu says from the back seat. "Which ain't much. The Merlins ambushed Volition. That Cestra woman manacled Bree, and that's why the ancestors broke the earth—"

"I *know* why the ancestors did what they did, Lucille." There's a tic in Valec's jaw. He understands what fueled the ancestors' rage better than anyone. He lived through enslavement. Lived past it. He's a walking memory, and sometimes I forget.

Lucille's apologies are rare, but she offers one now. "Apologies, Uncle," she says quietly. "Didn't mean to offend."

"Accepted," Valec replies with a tight smile. "I understand why Volition looks like it got hit by an earthquake. What I *don't* understand is what happened after. Cestra and Erebus cuffed her, their own *king?*"

"Yes, but she wasn't *just* Bree when they took her. It was Bree . . ." I pause, knowing that the Rootcrafter way would be to honor the living spirit that embodied my friend, but Arthur Pendragon is not a spirit who deserves my respect. "And Arthur."

His brow lifts. "Bree and Arthur."

I nod. "Possession. Total. After she let him in, she didn't come back."

"The Order couldn't have exorcised her," he says.

"No, they could not," Aunt Lu says. "Still not sure where Arthur sent her, to be honest. Somewhere deep. Somewhere a Medium can't bring herself back from."

"Bree fought him," Valec says. His voice holds something like faith. "I know she did."

I shake my head. "You weren't there. You didn't see what I saw as a Medium.

That spirit is old and *strong*," I say, and remember the silver curls at Bree's temple. Arthur's touch, with her all the time. "Arthur had already claimed her as his. *Been* claiming her, at every blood walk."

"Mariah's right. Arthur was one sonofabitch spirit." Lucille tuts. "Still not sure how those boys got Bree back. A Legendborn Kingsmage and a Scion with no exorcism experience?"

Valec's jaw works back and forth. "Those boys mighta helped break Arthur's hold on Bree, wherever she was, but they didn't bring her back. I know that, and I wudn't even there. Don't need the whole story to know that girl brought *herself* back—and them, too." His eyes narrow as he peers out into the darkness. "Here's our turn."

He flips on the left-turn signal, and we ease down a single-lane paved road marked PRIVATE DRIVE. A few low security lights stand between trimmed hedges on either side of the road, but they're only enough to illuminate the dense pine trees that rise directly above us.

"A Merlin's ward," Lu warns. "I can feel it."

"Mm-hmm, and I can See it." Valec slows to a stop and puts the car in park. He points from one side of the windshield to the other. "It's faint, but there. Runnin' all the way around the grounds, I bet. We'll avoid it. Stay on the outside."

Valec's Sight is better than both of ours given that he's half-demon, but Aunt Lu can *feel* the ward in a way I can't. As an aura reader, she's more sensitive to living magic. That's what a ward or barrier is: a bit of the caster tucked into the layer of magic itself. The Volition barrier is more my territory than hers. Mediums are better with the true dead and the magic *they* create.

Valec checks his golden pocket watch and nods. "Almost time." He cuts the engine. "We'll walk the rest of the way."

I scowl. "It's freezing out here."

"Extra coats in the back." Valec opens the door to walk around to the back of the car, and I stubbornly hunker down in my seat and wait for him to reappear. He shows up with not only a couple of long winter coats for us to switch into but gloves and a pair of thick hats. Aunt Lu and I tug on our new attire as Valec paces out to the front of the car, listening for things we can't hear and watching for things we can't see.

When we come around, the crunch of our footsteps breaks the silence. Valec's feet make no sound as he walks toward us and offers his arm to Aunt Lu. She slaps at him playfully. "I can walk on my own, thank you."

Valec doesn't look put out or surprised. Normally, he'd shoot back a wry comment about them both getting old, but the humor is gone from his face. As he hands us both flashlights, his eyes flicker red the way an animal's might in the darkness. "Let me walk out front. Keep your beams pointed toward the ground no matter what."

We do as he says. This type of environment—deep woods, pitch-black, cold as hell—is best navigated by a cambion. I don't feel fear, exactly. Valec would protect us with extreme prejudice, but I'm not used to physical confrontations. At all. Most Mediums don't see a lot of action, so to speak. Our powers aren't as flashy as other branches of root. I've never even thrown a punch, much less fought a demon.

Not all of us are Bree Matthews.

Most Mediums don't get to speak so directly to their own ancestors the way Bree has. We glean from them, we interpret, we imagine what they might want or need. Bree got to plead with her ancestors for aid during the revival at Volition, and it was hard not to envy her for the sustained contact. Bree's ancestor Vera may not have given Bree the assistance with her abilities that Bree had asked for, but at least she'd given her some direction and made it clear that Bree is meant to be her family's chosen one.

It's not like I want to *be* Bree, but . . . sometimes, I wonder what it'd be like to not only *have* a plan but *be* the plan. Because that's what Bree is—the end result of her ancestor's bargain, a bloodmarked walking time bomb, the tip of the spear. Bree isn't the thought; she's the action. It just seems like no matter what Bree's facing, she can barrel through it. Bree Matthews was born to be one of one. The right person at the right time to make the right choices.

The rest of us will just have to figure it out on our own. Get ready for our moment so we can move when it comes. Add the pieces up and hope they'll fit.

"Come on," Valec calls as he leads us into the darkness. The road is smooth beneath our feet, illuminated by the twin yellow-white cones of light from our flashlights. My ears aren't as good as a cambion's, but I'm listening for . . .

something. Anything. It only takes a couple minutes before Valec pauses. "Over there." He points and changes direction, sensing something that we can't, because he guides us off the road and into the woods proper. Our steps are louder here, crunching on dead twigs and crackling leaves. Something about the forest throws the sound every which way—I know our footfalls belong to us, but the trees send the crashing echoes right back at me, making the forest feel fuller than it is. More dangerous.

I step on a pine cone and roll my ankle—Valec is at my side before I stumble. I didn't even see him move. "Careful."

I nod as he rights me, squeezing my elbow before he moves back into position at the front.

I can't smell magic signatures the way Bree can, but I wonder if she'd be able to scent the pale golden wisps of magic that start to gather around Valec's wrists.

I begin to ask him what's got him gathering root when I see two glowing green lights about fifty feet away and coming closer. They are evenly spaced apart, about head height—and flickering.

My heart thuds against my ribs. "What the hell is—"

"Easy, Riah," Valec murmurs. "He's right where he said he'd be."

I squint and step forward to stand at Valec's side. Now I can hear the footsteps, steady and slow. And the flickering lights grow closer still and then flicker twice in quick succession—like a blink. As the lights come closer, I realize they're eyes, and attached to the person we came here to meet.

"Scion Sitterson," Valec says.

"Hello, Valechaz." William Sitterson, the Legendborn healer boy with the gentle smile, appears out of the darkness, just barely lit by our lowered flashlights. The blazing emerald of his eyes moves over each of us. The glow is bright enough to tint his pale cheeks a faint neon green. "Mariah. Lucille. Thank you for coming."

He nods at each of us in turn but does not extend his hand in welcome, because in his arms, cradled close to his chest, lies the sleeping form of Alice Chen.

4

Mariah

I SAW ALICE only a few days ago, and she looked just like this. Still. Limp. Dead to the world.

Someone—William, I'm guessing—has cleaned and dressed Bree's best friend in soft sweatpants and shoes, a matching coat. Even pulled a warm wool hat over her black hair.

Above her breaths are silent, steady swirls of Legendborn aether—silvery and blue and thin. They rise in a slow rhythm from her nose, up and up, then dissipate into the darkness. Up, up, then gone again.

"Ho-ly shiiiiit," Valec whispers.

"What in the world—" I say, blinking. "Don't tell me she's breathing magic."

"I didn't mean to—" William says, frowning. "I don't know—"

"Tchht." Aunt Lu sucks her teeth, and William gives up his explaining. "Let me get a look at her." Aunt Lu and I both move as if to walk past Valec, but Valec holds his arm out first.

"You expectin' company?" Valec asks, eyes scanning the woods beyond William's shoulder.

"No."

"Sure 'bout that?" Valec frowns. "If I know Kane, he'll be here in a flash—"

"Sel's gone," William interrupts.

"Gone?" Valec's eyes narrow. "Whatchu mean, 'gone'?"

"I mean, gone," William says, impatient. "There are only two Merlins on-site right now, and they're using wards to secure the perimeter and patrolling the buildings themselves. I slipped out when they changed shifts. We've got fifteen, maybe twenty minutes."

Valec looks like he might push the topic of Kane further but then thinks better of it. "You right. Time is tight." He drops his arm, and Aunt Lu huffs at him before proceeding forward as if she hadn't been stopped at all.

As she gazes down at Alice, Lu holds her flashlight between her teeth and mutters around the plastic. "I know you asked for Hazel, but she couldn't make the drive. She's setting things up back at the house. She's the diagnostician. I'm a nurse at best." She makes a soft, dissatisfied sound as she slips a hand under Alice's bangs to feel her forehead. "Cold as ice. Her life aura is faint, barely there."

"Yes," William says, brows drawn tight. "Her temperatures trend cool. Heart rhythm is steady, breath regular. Pupils are dilated and reactive to light, but she's unresponsive to other stimuli. I worried about starvation and dehydration. Started searching for supplies to give her an IV or a tube, but she's not deteriorating like one would expect. No bedsores that I can see, no sign of clotting. No need to eat or drink. I don't understand it and neither would a human hospital. It's a coma as far as I can tell, but nothing like how they describe it in textbooks. I don't think she can sense what's happening around her. It's like she's . . . frozen in a kind of stasis. Maybe the aether I gave her is keeping her this way?" His mouth twists in frustration. "Because the magic from her breath *is* aether. From my casting. But Onceborn human bodies aren't meant to absorb aether, so I just . . . I don't know."

"What about her parents?" I ask. "The busy-with-classes excuse has gotta be wearing thin. . . ."

William nods. "I'm sure it is. The Lieges watching her parents are watching Bree's dad too. They're loyal to Bree, but there are protocols for this kind of thing. Processes I can't stop once . . ." He shrugs helplessly.

"Once some innocent person runs afoul of the Order of the Round Table?" Valec supplies, eyes cold. "Yeah, I've heard about your so-called *protocols*."

"Their parents won't be harmed," William confirms. "That's all I know."

Lu drapes Alice's hand back over her stomach with a frown. "That number Samira gave us for you works? Hazel can call you to ask more questions about Alice here?"

"Yes, of course." William frowns down at Alice. "I've done everything I can, magically or otherwise. Healed the broken bones, the internal bleeding, but . . . I . . ." He winces. Swallows. "This is beyond me. Dr. Hazel's the only other provider I trust."

"She gets a lot of that," Lu says with not a small amount of pride in her voice over her wife's accomplishments. "And it takes some strength to acknowledge your own limitations."

"Yes, well." William grimaces. "My limitations are an ever-growing list."

I step forward and take a peek at Alice's face. Her dark brows are tensed together, like she's having a bad dream. I grasp her hand—and feel a tiny jolt zip from her cool fingers into my palm. William notices my reaction immediately, gaze sharpening on my face. "What happened? Did you feel something from her?"

"I'm no healer or doctor or anything." I give him a small, soft smile and shrug. "But I can sense it when death knows someone well." I look back down at Alice. "Feels like . . . like she came close."

William swallows audibly. "Yes." His glowing eyes seem to pulse, then grow brighter. "She did."

"Your . . . um, eyes?" I finally ask.

William's mouth twists, and his cheeks flush. "Scion of Gawain. Strength at noon and midnight." He looks back at Lucille. "I didn't want to meet you out here without my full abilities and defenses. Just in case."

"Just in case what, exactly?" Lucille pulls her hand back from Alice.

"In case I needed to fight." William purses his lips and then kneels with

Alice's body close so that he can set her on the ground in a sitting position. He glances up at me and Aunt Lu. "Could you . . . ?" Aunt Lu darts forward to hold her in place, kneeling so that the unconscious girl's upper half is resting against her shoulder. William murmurs his thanks, then stands, flexing his now-free hands as he joins Valec in looking out at the woods. "I asked to meet you here because it's beyond the last protection ward. I don't expect Shadowborn, but after what happened to Bree and Selwyn, I can't be sure."

I find myself searching the woods too, wary of a demon appearing from the shadows. "What exactly happened to Bree and Kane?" I ask, tension darting up my spine. If we *were* attacked right now by some demon, what would I do? What *could* I do? "I was there when Samira called Aunt Lu, and she didn't really say."

"And I *wasn't* there," Valec says in a dry voice. "So why don't you tell me fresh?"

William swipes his tongue over his lips. "A little over two days ago, Selwyn was in a locked and warded room. He had descended by then, and we were monitoring him." Valec makes a small sound at that but doesn't interrupt. "When we went to check on Sel, the room was empty. We ran to find Bree and we saw her outside with . . . a figure."

"A figure?" Valec asks.

"What kinda figure?" Aunt Lu says.

William's mouth draws down at the corners. "We couldn't see his face. It happened so fast. By the time I got there, Bree and the figure were gone. Disappeared."

"Just disappeared?" I say, frowning. I look at Valec. "Like Louis, the bouncer at Crossroads?"

Valec's arms cross over his chest, and his dark brows furrow. "Louis is a warlock. A human who bargained for his power. The uchel demon he made a deal with could make short jumps, tiny distances. Never heard of another demon who could teleport for real." Valec eyes William, back to the matter at hand. "No clues left behind?"

"Not really." William's jaw tenses. "Bit of aether."

"Color?"

"Black. Like smoke. Nothing I've ever seen before."

A muscle beside Valec's eye twitches. To anyone else, Valec's expression wouldn't appear changed from a moment ago, but Lu and I know what he looks like when a thought has taken hold. When I blink, the twitch is gone, and Valec's expression is back to dry and critical. "A mystery, then."

The subtle finality of Valec's words may have worked on a stranger, but William Sitterson is observant. His own glowing green eyes narrow slightly. "You've heard of this demon before, haven't you?"

"Now why would you say that?" Valec asks blithely. "You think I had something to do with Briana's kidnapping?"

"No." William tilts his head. "But . . . I think you might know who took her."

Valec smiles. "Look here, Scion, you can't accuse me of knowing every other demon just because I'm part demon myself." He presses a hand to his chest in mock offense, but there's something there in the effort. A straining at the corners of his eyes. I worry that if I can see it, William can see it too.

"Valec," William presses.

"The stereotyping?" Valec tsks. "When will we, as a society, move beyond our petty prejudices—"

"*Valec,*" William snaps. This healer can see through Valec's deflection.

Valec's face goes dangerously still. "William."

William steps closer to him, voice low. "Bree and Sel are my *friends.* They are in *danger.* And I can tell you know who took them. Who was it? Someone you work with, someone you've heard of, someone you—" Abruptly, William stops himself, eyes growing wide. "Wait . . . wait . . . Why didn't I think of this before?"

"Think of what?" Valec asks, voice stony. "Why don't you share with the class?"

At my knee, Aunt Lu has gone still as well. I glance between both Valec and Lu and wonder what I'm missing. I feel more left out than ever, but I bite my tongue because it's clear William is close to uncovering something that my family does not want to divulge.

"The . . ." William's eyes dart back and forth as he searches his own memory.

When he finds his target, his green eyes flash bright. "The Hunter."

I stiffen. The Hunter is a Rootcrafter boogeyman. *Our* boogeyman. Not a phrase we ever hear outsiders use, and the only reason William knows that demon's name is because Aunt Lu told Bree and her friends—including William—that there are rumors that he is active again. Our monster, on the prowl.

Valec makes a final attempt at ignorance. "What's the Hunter?"

"You're trying to distract me," William murmurs, looking from Lu to Valec. "You both know who he is. *You* told us about him. The ancient, power-hungry demon you asked Bree to fight when she gained control of her powers. The one who hunts Rootcrafters for their power. Valec discovered his bloodmark on Bree's body and said he'd find her one day, that he's *owed* something from her." William steps forward. "It was him, wasn't it? The Hunter found her and took her."

Valec releases something internally—the tension gone—and sighs heavily, then glances down at Alice as if she's suddenly caught his attention. "This here is a big favor you're asking of us, Scion," Valec says. "Taking Alice Chen into our fold. Looking for a cure for her condition . . ."

William blinks. "Yes, I know, but the Hunter—"

"Now make no mistake, I *like* Chen." Valec steps close to William, one hand tucked in his vest pocket. "Chen is Bree's people and so are we, so that's why we're here tonight . . . but if we take Alice Chen for safekeeping, I need you to understand that as a gift given to *her and Bree*, not to you or the Order."

William blinks again, confusion crossing his face as he processes what Valec's said—and the questions Valec is so clearly sidestepping. "I understand. It's a lot to ask; I just . . ." William frowns. "Valec, are you threatening to go back on your word?"

"Naw," Valec says with a small, noncommittal shrug. "But why should we take her? Remind me again."

"Because she deserves to be safe," William insists. "And I can't keep her safe here. Not anymore." His eyes are so green that even his pupils are the color of dark, wet seaweed. "I'm willing to promise you something. Anything. A bargain or an exchange or—"

When Valec holds up a hand, his eyes flash a deep red before returning to brown. And that's how I know that this Legendborn Scion has walked directly into Valec's trap.

"Bargains bind both ways," Valec intones. "They require formal demands and equal exchanges. An official contract. I'm not prepared to tie myself to you, but I *am* prepared to say that you *owe me*, healer. You okay to leave it there?"

William is smart enough not to agree right away to something so broad and open-ended. But when he looks down at Alice, his light brown brows furrow over his eyes, as if the very sight of her healed but unconscious body upends his reasoning. He looks back up, jaw set. "I'll need assurances. Nothing that harms anyone else, physically or emotionally."

Valec's mind is quick, especially when it comes to deal terms. "'Nothing that harms anyone *else*, physically or emotionally.' But harm to yourself is acceptable?"

William lifts his chin. "You heard what I said."

"And I heard what you *didn't* say." Valec huffs a laugh that holds a hint of admiration. "Real *Scion of Gawain* of you, healer. Just because those are your terms, and they're terms I respect, I'll add in a bonus: I won't ask you for anything that could harm *you*, either. How 'bout that?"

William nods. "Agreed."

"Agreed." Valec extends his hand with a smile, an offering to shake on it.

The moment William's hand meets Valec's, Valec grasps it tight—and the green in William's eyes goes dim.

Valec steps closer, his voice a low, hypnotic whisper. "You're a very smart boy, William Sitterson. And I truly wish you had not remembered what I told you about the Hunter and bloodmarks. Hell, I wish I hadn't let that slip in front of a Legendborn Scion at all, so believe it or not, this is on me, not you. All the same"—his voice takes on a resonant tone, the vibrations making my teeth clench even though the magic isn't directed my way—"I need you to forget what you just said about the Hunter, Scion, and everything you heard me and Lu say that night at Crossroads about who that demon is and who he hunts for power. Can you do that?"

This is mesmer, I think. I'm sure of it. I've never seen a Merlin do it, but this is what Aunt Lu warns me against when she tells the stories about Merlins hunting Rootcrafters down. What they do to "rogue" aether users like us. But those are Merlins. Valec is *not* a Merlin . . . and yet . . .

William's brows draw inward like he wants to fight Valec's suggestion, but his voice is calm when he answers, "Yes."

"And . . ." Valec's next words are uttered in a tight voice through labored breathing. This magic is costing him something; it's not without work. Not without focus. "And I need you to forget that the Hunter is the caster of Briana Matthews's bloodmark. Can you do that?"

William nods dreamily. "Yes, of course."

Satisfied, Valec slowly withdraws his palm. His chest is heaving in deep breaths, the muscles in his jaw flexing as he pants. "Thanks, Scion."

William blinks once, twice, then shakes his head. He clears his throat. "What was I saying? Sorry."

"Not to worry," Valec reassures him. "We'll take Alice. You agreed that you'd owe me one, with reassurances, and we shook on it."

"Right." William nods, that memory still solid in his mind, it seems. He notes Valec's breathlessness. "Are you all right?"

Valec nods tightly. Lu ducks her head and turns away. Their guilt is evident, and I feel it myself. It's painful to watch William ask if Valec is all right after being mesmered by him. Anger seeps in at the edges of my mind; William is a good person, and Valec violated his own code by taking away a memory without his consent.

"Yes, Valec," I ask, "*are* you all right?"

Valec's eyes shoot to mine. He answers William while glaring at me. "Perfectly peachy."

William is uncertain but insistent. "And you'll keep Alice safe? From anyone who might come for her?"

"Yes, of course. Like she's one of our own," Valec states. Before he can speak again, his head jerks up and over William's shoulder. He hisses, lips drawing back to reveal his fangs as his voice drops to a lower register. "We got company."

Now my heart is racing, because I see the filaments of golden root filling the air around Valec's body. William pivots in the same direction as Valec, eyes alert and body taut as a wire. The Scion stands at Valec's side, both palms extended as blue-white aether swirls into his palms. Even Aunt Lu has shifted so that she is between the forest and Alice, hand outstretched.

They'd all reacted *instantly*, moving to face the unknown. Shame washes over me at my paralysis. I'm standing still, empty-handed with shallow breaths and wide eyes, while everyone else is readying for a fight.

"William, get back!" An accented voice breaks the silence as the newcomer makes himself known, blurring in front of William to face off against us.

It's the Mageguard boy that Cestra and Erebus left behind at Volition, Larkin. He is wearing much the same outfit as I'd seen him in a few days ago: all-black gear with silver lining, black boots, and a black hooded tunic. In his palms are twin tornadoes of churning aether that only grow brighter when his eyes take in the scene fully—me, Lu and Alice on the ground, William—then fixate on Valec. "Don't move, any of you."

"Larkin, no—" William says. "It's not what you think."

Larkin growls at Valec. "What are you doing here?"

"William invited us. Take it up with him," Valec says lazily.

Larkin's eyes skip over to me and Lu again, but his body doesn't release any of its tension. "Everyone else here I recognize," Larkin says, fingers twitching at his sides. "But I don't believe we've met."

Valec grins, root flaring along his forearms in a low, thin layer. "You'd remember if we did."

"William," Larkin repeats. "Explain."

William douses his aether before he answers, but Larkin's is still crackling at his fists. "Alice needs more help than I can offer, and she can't be here when the Regents arrive tomorrow. Nick may be protected for now with the curia ritual, but Alice has no such protection; I called in a favor to get her out of harm's way."

"You called a goruchel to our grounds?!" Larkin exclaims. "What were you thinkin'?"

Valec clears his throat and raises one glowing hand. "Not a goruchel, thanks. Balanced cambion here. Valechaz is the name."

Larkin's eyes narrow. "I've heard of you. You're that power broker from Georgia."

"Infamous among the Mageguard?" Valec's smile grows wide. "I'm flattered."

"Don't be. We let you run your business because you stay out of ours," Larkin responds.

Valec's smile disappears. "That a threat?"

"Not a threat," Larkin says. "A reminder."

Valec runs a tongue beneath his right fang. "S'pose you have to drop those *reminders* here and there nowadays, huh? With y'all being spread so thin."

Larkin stiffens, and Valec's smile returns. Some unspoken thing passes between them, followed by a challenge to see who will address that thing first. Larkin breaks before Valec does. "If you know something, I suggest you say something."

"You the TSA now too?" Valec drawls. "And here I thought y'all were just cops."

Aether sparks around Larkin's fingertips. "I'm not joking with you, broker—"

"Okay, okay." Valec laughs. "Stand down, Homeland Security."

William steps in between them. "Larkin, stop. This isn't a fight. This is a rescue—for Alice. You know what the Regents will do if they return to find the girl they'd already mesmered once back among the Legendborn. And not just that, but in some sort of magical coma that even *I* don't understand."

Larkin makes a frustrated sound. "I can't believe you did this behind my back. You could have told me—"

"And take away your plausible deniability?" William counters. "I didn't want to rope you into something else you'd have to lie about."

"Well, he's gonna have to lie about it now," Aunt Lu mutters.

"Yes," Larkin agrees, "I will. But at least I would've known the truth. I would have noticed Chen was gone tomorrow, Will, and what then?"

"I would have told you after the fact," William says, "that I called in a favor. And kept Valec's, Mariah's, and Lu's names out of it to protect *them* from the Order."

"Thanks for that," Lu says.

I sigh. "Thanks for the attempt, anyway. Now this Mageguard knows Root-crafters were here. Which means the Regents could find out."

"Nah. He won't say a word about us," Valec says, "will you, Scotsman?"

Larkin ignores Valec—but also doesn't correct him. Instead, he faces William—and douses the flames at his hands. "So you still would have lied to me, by omission?"

"Alice is my *patient*," William states. "I have to do what's best for her."

"The way you talk, *everyone* is your patient!" Larkin says, shaking his head.

"Maybe they are!" William snaps. He runs a hand through his hair, frustration visible on his features. "I didn't keep this from you to hurt you—"

"No, you kept it from me because you don't trust me," Larkin says sharply.

Aunt Lu's eyes widen, and Valec whistles. "*This* just took a turn." He releases his own root finally and puts his hands up. "We've got to get back on the road if we want to get home before dawn. I'm gonna suggest we three leave with Chen right about now so y'all can continue this lovers' quarrel in private."

"We're not lovers," both boys say, and even Aunt Lu shakes her head in amusement.

Valec blinks. "Sure." He turns to me. "Mariah, Lu, let's go." With easy grace, Valec bends over to lift Alice into his arms. He maneuvers her like she weighs nothing. Holds Bree's best friend like precious cargo.

"Wait." William steps forward and presses a gentle hand to Alice's brow. He tugs her hat back down around her ears and adjusts her collar. "Please have Hazel call me with any questions. Or text. I'll get back to her as soon as I'm able."

Lu stands, grasping my shoulder in one hand. "Will do."

William takes a step back as if that's the only way he'll allow himself to let us go. *Alice is my* patient. "Thanks, Will," I say softly as the others turn toward the car. "For getting her out of harm's way."

He nods and says one last thing before we leave. "If you hear from Bree or Sel, or if they find you . . ."

"We'll let you know," I say, even though it feels like something I can't promise. I wave and join Lu and Valec on the trek through the woods, flicking my flashlight on to help guide my steps. I hear William's footsteps and Larkin's voice as they begin to walk away in the opposite direction.

The three of us don't say a word until Alice is settled in the back seat with her head in Lu's lap and her legs bent against the backrest and the doors are closed. We don't even say a word until we get back on the main road. It's only then that Lu speaks.

"I thought only Merlins could mesmer folks, Valechaz," she says quietly.

"That's what they think too," Valec replies.

"How did you—" I ask, but Valec shakes his head.

"Long story and not urgent," he says. "I'll tell you later."

"No, you'll tell me now," I say. "You took William's memories, Valechaz. You did something against his consent. You never do that kind of thing. How *could* you—"

"I didn't enjoy it, Riah!" Valec snaps. His fingers tighten on the wheel. "I'll apologize to Will and restore his memories when this blows over. I'll explain—"

"When what blows over?" I demand, not letting him finish. "Explain what?"

"You really think it could be the Hunter that took Bree and the Kingsmage?" Aunt Lu asks.

Valec nods. "I do."

"Why didn't you want William to know that?" I shrug. "Wouldn't it be good for the Legendborn to know too? They have the firepower to go after him."

"They *think* they do," Valec says, voice tight, "but they don't. I erased Will's memory because if the Order realizes that the Hunter took Bree, their king, they will mobilize to go after her. If not on order from the Regents, then those kids will set off on a rogue mission. You saw the healer's integrity back there? Between him and that Scion of Lancelot, they'd come up with a plan to go after the Hunter some kinda way. And we can't afford to let them do that, because that demon is a goddamned apex predator, and if the Order figures that out, they'll do what every human does when they meet a monster they can't beat."

"Which is . . . ?" I whisper.

"Go after its prey." Valec glances at me before looking back at the road. "Seek out the monster's food source, either to eliminate them or use them as bait to back the monster into a corner." He jerks a thumb behind him. "You heard Will. He was halfway down the road to that conclusion already, asking us what we knew. He has no idea what demon he's messing with and no idea what our people have done for generations to try to *survive* that demon."

A silent dread fills my stomach at the same time that I'm awash with relief at Valec's understanding of the situation. "And the Hunter needs . . ."

"Aether." Lu shudders. "Lots of it. And human beings. Demons need both to exist on this plane, and as old and powerful as he is, he's the most ravenous of them all."

Valec nods. "*Particularly* for those human beings who can tap into a near-limitless pipeline of root when they commune with their ancestors."

"Rootcrafters," I whisper. "If the Order finds out that the Hunter stole their king, they'll eventually come after Rootcrafters to draw him out, because we're his prey."

Lu curses low under her breath. "That was quick thinking, Valechaz, to protect us all."

"They already came for Volition," Valec says. "And you heard the Mageguard—they've been waiting for an excuse to come after me. After us. We can't hand them that opportunity."

My throat tightens. "But what about Bree?"

"Bree agreed to take the Hunter on if she could, on our behalf," Aunt Lu reminds us. "Maybe she went with him voluntarily?"

Valec shakes his head. "She said she'd do that once we helped her get control of her abilities. She doesn't have control yet. And even if she did, goin' anywhere with the greater demon who bloodmarked you is a fool's errand. Goin' somewhere voluntarily with *the Hunter* is a death wish. Bree's smarter than that."

"Maybe she went for another reason," I say, suddenly indignant—and angry. "That doesn't mean he should take her power. Kill her and get stronger and come back for us with no one powerful enough to stop him. And I don't like Sel, but . . . why would the Hunter take *him*? What's he planning? We shoulda used Will's insight to find out more. The Legendborn—"

"No." Valec's thumbs drum on the steering wheel.

"Valec!" I cry. "We can't just let Bree die! She's . . . she's . . ." The chosen one. The plan. The action.

"I won't let the powerhouse die."

"How?" I ask.

I look between him and Lu, who are already eyeing each other in the rearview. After some silent understanding passes between them, Valec nods.

"Well, baby niece," Valec says with a determined look, "that's the thing. If *anyone*'s going after the powerhouse, Kane, and the Hunter . . . it's gonna be me."

5

FORTY-EIGHT HOURS

AFTER SELWYN KANE APPEARED

Natasia

AUDIO LOG—ENTRY #1

My son is with me. After thirteen years, *my son is with me. Here, in my home.*

But Selwyn is not awake—nor is he at rest. Erebus said he was forced to put my son under in order to control him, and after two days, I understand why.

Selwyn has been unconscious since the moment he appeared in my living room, but his mind and body have been increasingly fighting some invisible battle. Sweat streams from his face and body now, soaking the bedsheets beneath him. He thrashes danger-ously, and has already left a fist-size dent in my guest bedroom wall. His black-tipped claws curl and unfurl, slicing his own palms open until they heal again. His brows are drawn tight in focus, in rage. I speak to him, but he cannot hear me. His sounds are unintelligible growls and groans, no words that I can discern. My son is boiling over with silent fury while fighting an opponent that I cannot see . . . and all I can do is wait as Erebus's sleeping spellcraft continues to wears off.

If Selwyn is like this while unconscious, then what destruction had he sought while awake? I may never know. Erebus claimed that he is in demonia, but it is too soon, he is too young, this is too violent a fall——

I have already worn a path in my living room rug from pacing back and forth. I've been living mostly on adrenaline and caffeine—a bad combination.

Maybe my own emotional state is why I reached for this audio recorder to begin a new file of notes and observations—to give myself the refuge of scholarly distance. Anything is better than the silence and agony of the past two days—and I can't keep pacing and worrying. The rug won't survive.

So. [Slow exhale.] Notes and observations. Let me begin:

Even in Selwyn's current state, he is a marvel. Tall. Strong. Hair as raven black as my own. Even though he is unconscious, I can sense that his affinity for aether is precise and powerful—that he is powerful. In his calloused hands and athletic build, I see that he has learned much. Seen much. Fought much. But there are other details that I did not expect:

At some point, he began to collect tattoos. Tattoos! *We both bear the mark of the Merlin, but he has expanded on our shared symbol, inscribing his own story on his skin in curving lines of ink. And his ears! They are pierced with thick-gauged black rubber plugs. How is he old enough to have tattoos and piercings? Did he get them on his own? Did he go with friends? Does he have a partner? Someone who adores him and someone whom he adores equally? Do they know of his current condition? Are they worried?*

As I hold vigil at his bedside, my mind swims with relentless questions. Old ones mixed with new. And with those questions, the familiar guilt of leaving him behind turns it all . . . messy. And hard.

The last time I truly spent time with my son, he was five years old. He was curious. Bright. Talkative. The boy Selwyn was when the Regents took me away has been gone for some time now. I do not know if that boy will ever return. If it is his demonia that has placed that childlike self forever out of reach, or if the Order wrung that innocence out of him years ago . . .

Perhaps I should leave the speculation to another time. Another recording.

Selwyn was born a Merlin, but like all Merlins, he was born with a splintered self. From birth, the slivered, small parts of us that are demon, the parts of us that are not quite alive the way that humans are alive on this plane, live at the corners of our minds, testing their boundaries, pushing at our consciousnesses. Our demons are hungry, gnawing, persistent—and patient. Because one day, after enough time, they will make themselves known. Just as Selwyn's demon has made itself known—far earlier in his life than I would have ever expected.

I am glad that I am the one holding vigil at his bedside, rather than a human friend and rather than his bonded, Nicholas. I imagine he might frighten a human right now, including the Legendborn Scions and Squires under his supervision. It is better that they do not see him like this. As he is now, when he wakes, his eyes will only see the emotions that his body and mind now hunger for. I can only hope that he will know me as I am: his mother . . . and the woman who abandoned him for reasons he can't understand.

The Order does not recognize Merlins who descend. To them, we are both the "succumbed." To them, we are lost souls.

They are wrong.

Unlike the society that orchestrated both his and my own conceptions, ensuring our strength and power only to discard us later, I hope that Selwyn will recognize me in the same way that I will recognize him—in full.

But that is not why I have started this recording. [Audible sigh.]

I keep losing my train of thought. What kind of scientist am I? What kind of scholar?

I ask that . . . and yet perhaps I should give myself grace. If Faye were here, she would remind me that I am not just a scientist. Not just a scholar. Not even just a Merlin. She would remind me that I am all those things—and also a mother.

And so, here are the details of the moment that my son returned to me, to the best of my memory:

I keep a cabin by the ley line that runs through the Appalachian Mountains. It is the same line that runs through the Cambrians in Wales, and so makes for fruitful study of Gates. As with every other hideout, I don't stay here long, keeping visits brief so as not to become too relaxed in any given location. I send Faye letters to—ahem. Sorry, when Faye was alive, I sent encoded letters to alert her of when I might visit. And when we saw each other, briefly, over the years, we both understood why I could not share the locations of my residences. And in the months since her . . . her passing, I have moved five times, perhaps due to some paranoia on my part after risking exposure to Faye's daughter while in the fresh throes of my grief. That paranoia was only doubled when I felt Martin Davis die through our Kingsmage bond. After Martin died, I went out of my way to see no one and be seen by no one. I have been more than careful. Greater than cautious.

I say all of this to explain that there is, simply and factually, no explanation as to how Erebus Varelian could have been made aware of my current location.

The only way that Erebus could have found me so urgently and immediately is if he has been watching me, consistently, for some time—and that I simply cannot fathom. He is a Mage Seneschal, and I am, in the eyes of the Order, a criminal behind bars. If Erebus has been watching me, then he must be aware that I escaped from the depths of the Order's most notorious Shadowhold—and yet he's chosen not to pursue me or return me to that prison. Why?

And how did he appear to teleport with Selwyn in his arms directly into my living room? The only beings that have such powers are demons, and even they can only use them over short distances and to places they have been before.

[A pause.]

I worry that my old friend has been left much too alone in his research, or that perhaps he is working with the Scion of Mordred, who is known to dabble in less-than-ethical demon experimentation. The pact magic that warlocks use has ill effects on the human bearer and has long been considered not only unsavory among the Merlins of the Order but dangerous. Has Erebus been experimenting with pact magic on himself? At the academy, he was secretive and sometimes displayed a lack of care for others, but his distaste for warlock practices was as strong as any other Merlin's. But that was nearly thirty years ago now. We have all changed, I'm sure—

I digress.

The details, Natasia . . . recount the details. The facts.

Two days ago, Erebus Varelian, the Mage Seneschal at Arms, appeared in my living room, holding my unconscious son in his arms. My first instinct, my immediate fear, was that Selwyn had been killed in battle. I have not felt fear like that . . . in a long time.

Erebus said, "He is alive. Be calm." Short but appreciated.

Selwyn was freshly unconscious then. Limp and unresponsive. And, upon closer inspection, deeply subsumed by demonia. Dark veins line his wrists and arms, and his claws end in black points, indicative of the change in his blood. His skin is flush, and his fangs have grown past his bottom lip. The tops of his ears now end in slight points.

Erebus, for his part, appeared preoccupied and irritated. He made to leave soon after depositing my son on the floor in front of me. Before he could do so, I asked what happened.

Erebus replied, "I was forced to render him unconscious, lest he continue to fight me. He will remain so for perhaps a day or two, so you will have some time to prepare for his awakening. Be warned, he is dangerous. Even to you."

"How did this happen? His Kingsmage bond to Nicholas should have protected him——"

"Selwyn has been separated from his bonded for some time. His descent was slow and manageable until recently."

When I asked what happened recently, Erebus appeared . . . frustrated. Angry. "Selwyn consumed power that did not belong to him."

I did not and do not know what he meant by this sentence. As a Merlin, Selwyn shouldn't have been consuming anyone's power.

Instead of explaining further, Erebus asked, "Will Selwyn's father come looking for him?"

Of course a Mage Seneschal would want to know if a human man would be searching for his son, causing trouble with the Code of Secrecy, getting in the way of things. I let him know that Selwyn's father would not be looking for him. While my son has inherited his father's general insouciance, sarcasm, and good looks, Selwyn's quick sense of duty to others comes entirely from me. Besides, he was raised more by the academy and the Davises than his father.

Again, I digress——

Erebus paused, then said, "I do not presume to know what news you gather from the world of the Order, but if you have not heard——"

"You let them put me away, Erebus," I interrupted, suddenly angry for myself and my son. "You didn't stop them."

"I was not yet a Seneschal. And even if I had been, I could not intervene" is all he said. All he said twenty-five years ago and all he said two days ago. All he has ever said to explain his inactions when he could have spoken up on my behalf.

"*You could have vouched for me,*" *I said.* "*You knew I'd never have opened those Gates.*"

He grew cold. And just as before, he only repeated, "*I could not intervene.*"

At that, Erebus turned to leave, but before doing so, he offered a note of discouragement that I only repeat here so that the record is whole. He said, "*It is too late for Selwyn, Natasia. Even for someone as knowledgeable and adept as you.*"

Perhaps he meant this parting message as a type of comfort. A kindness given to an old friend for whom you still hold some measure of regard. As Erebus is not a parent himself, perhaps his words were an attempt to show sympathy to a mother in crisis. I do not know Erebus's reasoning for giving that precise warning to me—and I do not care.

Without hesitation, I made my position clear: "*Selwyn is my son, Erebus. It is never too late.*"

SEVENTY-TWO HOURS

AFTER BRIANA MATTHEWS DISAPPEARED

William

"WHAT'S THAT KID thinking, calling a curia?" Gillian groans.

The meeting hall at the Keep is set apart from the main residential building by a long outdoor walkway. Gillian met me at my temporary room at dawn, and our journey to the hall has taken us past a covered koi pond, an empty gazebo sitting on stone pavers on the left, and an herb garden beneath iron arbors on the right. We take several more steps together, our dress shoes clacking on the path beneath our feet, before I reply.

"I have asked myself this several times," I say. "The curia allows him to be granted a single boon from the Regents. They have made it clear they will kill him to move on to the next eligible Scion of Lancelot. Maybe he'll ask them to withdraw the assassination Order they've given the Mageguard?"

"That seems too obvious," Gill says.

I sigh. "I thought the same. He would still be under suspicion. He would still be watched closely—and they still would not trust him. He renounced his title once; he could do so again. Especially after his father's betrayals."

"What else could it be?"

"A search for Bree or Sel?" I suggest.

"Also obvious," Gill replies. "And he'd have to choose one or the other. Those are two requests, not one."

I fear she's right. We walk silently for a moment before I raise another thought I've had in the days since Nick's self-requested imprisonment. "Did you know that when Bree first entered the Squires' tournament, it was because Nick told her that if she became Legendborn, she could call a curia?"

Gill stops walking and turns to me, eyes wide. An early morning breeze caught between the buildings lifts her dark hair. "He *didn't*."

I raise my hands. "Unconfirmed by Nick, but I think I'm right. I remember Bree telling me she infiltrated the Order to find out what happened to her mother. She wanted to know if the Regents were behind it. If they had answers." I cast my gaze ahead at our destination in the distance—the meeting hall that will hold all former and current Legendborn still on-site. "I think even then, Nick had the idea of a curia in his mind, but as a strategy to help Bree, not himself."

"So he's had this loophole in his back pocket for a long time, then." Gill curses beneath her breath and starts walking, and I follow. "Still, calling one for himself is a gambit right now. It forces the Regents into a corner, and they don't like being cornered."

A voice calls to us from the grass beside us. "It depends on what he asks for, doesn't it?"

I smile at Samira's approach and nod as she joins us on the path. Like us, she's wearing more formal attire today; she's in a dark blue pantsuit with the one-winged falcon sigil of Bedivere set in a silver clasp at the top of a bolo tie of purple cord. Gillian's Line of Kay umber necktie is held in place by a clip in the crossed keys of the Line's sigil, and it rests over her dark gray sports jacket and slacks.

"Whatever he demands," Samira adds, "the Regents must grant his request."

"A fact that they truly appreciate, I'm sure," Gillian says dryly. She turns to Samira abruptly, then glances back at me. "Everything okay with our sleeping Vassal?"

"She's well over state lines by now," I answer. A smile tugs at my mouth. "Sleeping Vassal" isn't a bad code for Alice. I had mocked up paperwork to make her a Vassal of the Line of Gawain, after all. "The handoff went as well as can be expected."

Samira stuffs her hands in her pockets. "Got an earful from Lucille about Larkin's surprise appearance."

"It was handled," I say slowly.

Samira sniffs. "Larkin was furious, you mean."

"Yes." I pull at my tie. "But watching them take her was a worthwhile relief."

We reach the outer door of the round meeting hall building. When the three of us approach, the two Mageguard standing on either side of internal double oak doors straighten. They are in the usual Mageguard uniform: black pants and combat boots, a black sweater and a heavy black cloak and cowl with fingerless leather gloves. One looks to be young, fifteen at most. Her deep yellow eyes widen as she takes in our group's colors and sigils.

"Scion Sitterson," the young Guard says, dipping her head in acknowledgment to greet me first. "Lieges Hanover and Miller." When we greet her in return, her eyes widen like saucers.

Abruptly, the young Mageguard's companion, an older Merlin, clears his throat. The young Guard snaps to attention before they both open the doors behind them and allow us to pass.

The rotunda behind those large doors feels sacred. It's certainly big enough and grand enough to appear like a historic church. A cathedral complete with stained-glass windows that send splintered rainbows of light onto its worn wooden floor. When I was a small child, I thought what we did, the fighting and the hunting, *was* a religious calling. An objective good in service to the Shadow-born holy war. But now . . .

The double doors close behind us, muffling the sound of chirping birds outside and enclosing us in solemn silence. We walk down the long, empty aisle, past rows and rows of empty pews. Beneath our feet, the hewn stone path slopes gently downward, as if to reach the center of the room is to descend to some great and terrible core.

"The Merlin at the door is too young to be a Guard," Samira says quietly, eyes scanning the empty rafters, the pews, the brightly lit platform at the end of the room. "Takes at least three years of solo fieldwork and two recommendations from Master Merlins before the Mageguard will even consider adding a new Merlin to their units."

"Times have changed." Gill's voice is somber, distracted.

"Have they?" Samira muses.

"What're you thinkin', Sam?" Gill asks warily.

A beat passes between them. Then—"G'on ahead, William," Samira says with a smile that barely turns her lips. "We're gonna take a seat in the upper level. Gill and I will see you after the ceremony."

While we were always going to part ways to find separate seating in the rotunda, Samira's comments feel abrupt. As former Legendborn, Lieges are allowed to attend the curia, but they can only observe the proceedings and are not allowed to participate.

Gill doesn't address her fellow Liege's odd redirection and simply turns to me with a wry grin. "See you later, Will."

They know something—or at least suspect it—but aren't sharing.

Lieges keep their own counsel, so there's no pressing them for more. Especially not here and now. Instead, I salute them both. Together, they turn to walk down an empty pew until they disappear into the candlelit darkness toward the balcony stairs. As I stare after them, though, a small bubble of dread builds behind my sternum.

I gaze up at the balcony and see the silhouettes of more Lieges, scattered in groups around the upper level of the rotunda. I can't see their faces or bodies, but I know what I would see if I could: premature silver streaks and salt-and-pepper hair, missing digits or limbs aided by prosthetics like Gillian's, scars from wounds that healed the long way. The Lieges' bodies bear the physical costs of their longevity, their successes, their failures. And today, they will be hidden from the eyes of the three human Regents who lead the Council. Their injuries and disabilities will be tucked away and their voices silenced from impacting any of the proceedings.

The sudden anger that slices through me is enough to take my breath away—and enough to take me back to the dying words of Jonas, a Liege who violated his Oaths and who was willing to sacrifice his life to end the cycle.

I watched her die, felt her anger, her fear. . . . The Legendborn cycle saves human lives while destroying them in the same breath.

How many Lieges have witnessed the Order's corruption and, like Gill and Samira, chosen the path of resistance . . . and how many have seen the evil up close and, like Jonas, chosen the side of the monsters?

"William?" Greer's voice is at my elbow.

I turn away from the balcony of Lieges, the ghosts and shadowed faces. "Hey, Greer."

Greer has also been gifted a tie, this one with a golden clip. On a dark gray suit, the tawny yellow of the Line of Owain is a bright slash down their chest. Their blond hair has been combed down and left in a loose, low ponytail at the nape of their neck. They jerk a thumb over their shoulder at the section of pews closest to the round stage. "We're over here."

A curia conventus is a closed ritual. Not quite a trial, but a hearing of sorts between the Order's highest-ranked parties. Only the Legendborn, Lieges, and the Council will be admitted today—along with a limited number of Mageguard for the Council's protection.

We pass the small section designated for the Lines of the Western chapter and dip our chins in acknowledgment. Out of us all, they keep mostly to themselves unless the need is dire.

As I walk with Greer to the Southern Chapter's section of the pews, I wave to our friends. Greer's Scion, Pete, has saved a seat for them. Next to Pete is Beau, our fallen Scion of Bors's younger sibling and replacement. Felicity, our Scion of Lamorak, pats the empty wooden space beside her with a smile.

As I take my seat, I find myself seeking out the auburn undercut and amber gaze of someone who is not yet here.

The seating in the circular meeting hall is arranged to represent the cardinal directions and chapters. Northern, Southern, and Western each have their own sections, and in the east is a large, empty dais with six seats prepared for the

Council's three Regents and paired Mage Seneschals. When the time comes, Nick will take the stage at the center of the room.

Already seated is the Western Chapter, whose four Scions I identify by color. The aquamarine of the Line of Erec, the currant wine red of the Line of Caradoc, the midnight black of the Line of Mordred, and the stone gray of the Line of Geraint.

The doors at the top of the hall creak open to admit the Northern Chapter Scions of Kay and Bedivere, a younger cousin of Gill's named Alex, a girl named Hannah—and the former and mistaken Scion of Lancelot, Donovan Reynolds.

Donovan's lazy smirk is permanently sprawled across his mouth. His broad shoulders pull at the black sweater he wears over a pair of gray slacks, and his shiny shoes click loudly over the stone floor. He is built like an athlete, he walks like a wealthy prince, and he wields the type of openly handsome face that one hopes belongs to an equally kind heart.

Unfortunately, that hope would be mistaken.

Donovan and I met a decade ago, when we were both nine years old, at one of the training courses for eligible Scions. He'd been devastatingly good with one sword. With two, he was exemplary. In all things, he was brutal and cruel.

He would have made a terrifying Scion of Lancelot.

"What is *he* doing here?" A quiet voice at my shoulder interrupts my thoughts. I turn to face Felicity, who is dressed similarly to me: gray slacks, a dress shirt. On her right arm, she wears two matching red leather cuffs bearing the griffin of Lamorak. Her cuff and the cuff of her fallen Squire, Russ.

"I don't know," I reply. "Now that Nick's true lineage has been revealed, we know Donovan was never the Scion of Lancelot or Legendborn. His title should be stripped, and he shouldn't be admitted to the curia."

She groans and pushes her wavy curls back behind her shoulders. "*Some* people can still bend the rules however they like."

A grumble of agreement from the others of our chapter flows down the pew in a wave. I don't speak aloud my own worry about Donovan's presence: that it serves as a reminder that none of our titles, our powers, are truly safe. That the Regents could kill any one of us to replace us with a more agreeable Scion who will behave in their image, just as they are threatening to do with Nick.

"Just making sure I'm following: We have no clue how Nick is gonna play this thing?" Greer asks.

"Correct," I say, and they grimace. "My best guesses are demands that would understandably save his own life. Possibly permission to search for Bree or Sel, maybe a request for resources to pursue them. Maybe a preemptive request to drop any charges for killing Maxwell Zhao. Zhao was a highly ranked Mage-guard and one of Erebus's favorite soldiers. Loyal, strong, and valuable as a Merlin who had grown in power but not yet showed signs of demonia."

Pete nods. "Zhao was well-known, but if what I'm hearing is true, the Regents ordered him to murder Nick in cold blood. Even after Nick's father got caught in the line of fire, Erebus still didn't call Zhao off. Nick killed Zhao in self-defense!"

I don't disagree. I catch another bit of movement at the back doors. Tor and Sarah enter, standing together but not quite as close as in times past. They take a seat two rows up from us in the Southern section, pointedly not looking or speaking to each other.

"Trouble in paradise," Greer murmurs. "Wonder how Tor is holding up— not that I give a damn."

"Who cares," Felicity says, her English accent elevating her vowels as her eyes darken. "Tor plotted with the Regents against Bree, lied about where William and Bree were when they were *being held captive*, and when the Morgaines reached out to give the Legendborn information we needed, she ratted us all out. As far as I'm concerned, you're either with us or against us, and Victoria chose her side, so she can *rot* in it."

"Felicity . . . ," I say warningly, wondering how we'll ever gather the Table when the grudges run so deep. When Bree is gone and we're so very fractured.

She challenges me with a single lifted brow. "Yes?"

I don't have a proper chastisement for her. I find I don't feel like keeping the peace as I might have done a year ago. "Nevermind."

Suddenly, our ears pop. The other Scions and Squires stop speaking and moving; they feel it too.

An aether barrier is being forged nearby.

"The Mageguard?" Greer asks.

I nod. I glance up at the exposed trusses and the ceiling cast in shadows, shivering at the sensation of aether overhead. Of the remaining Southern Legendborn, my aether sense is the sharpest. Has to be, to track aether's path through an injured body. "They're casting a barrier ward to protect the building while the Regents are here."

Without preamble, a door behind the stage opens, and Erebus Varelian walks through the closed curtain in a plain black suit. I can't help but shudder as his red eyes cast over the room. When they land on the Southern Chapter, his lips purse, but he says nothing.

A small group of Mageguard in formal black cloaks enter behind him, fanning out and down to stand guard around the stage, facing the audience.

Somewhere in that group might be Larkin. We have not spoken since he found me and the Rootcrafters in the woods and discovered my plan to send Alice away.

I hope he's not expecting an apology.

The other Regents enter in a steady stream. First, Erebus's own Regent of Shadows, Cestra. The Mage Seneschal of Mesmer, Tacitus, and his assigned Regent of Light, Gabriel, arrive next. Then Serren, the oft-silent Mage Seneschal of Constructs, and the High Regent himself, Lord Regent Aldrich, enter last, both in slacks and button-down shirts. All but the Lord Regent take their seats.

I have never seen the Regents dressed quite so informally. Perhaps the confrontation with the Morgaines and Legendborn has altered their pomp and circumstance. Or perhaps they have realized that there is no formal attire that can assuage the distrust they've sown between our two groups.

"Well," Lord Regent Aldrich says as he paces to the edge of the stage with one hand in his pocket. "I call to order this so-called *curia conventus*." His mouth cuts against and around the words as if he despises them. "We are all here on the demanded day, summoned per the requirements of the ritual." Aldrich spreads his hands wide. "Where is our guest?"

"Perhaps Davis used the delay of this meeting to configure an escape plan from his tower prison," Regent Gabriel drawls from his chair.

"Escape is impossible," Erebus calls out. "I trained Merlin Takada myself. Her affective wards are enough to incapacitate even a Mage Seneschal. Nicholas Davis could not make it past her wards without his brain turning to mush."

"And yet only a *Davis* would be arrogant enough to try," Cestra says with a snide laugh.

I lose track of their words, their voices. Suddenly, all I can see and hear is their cruelty. These two—Regent Cestra and her Seneschal—held both me and Bree captive for days. Forced me to do things I never thought myself capable of. Forced me to become a person who would hurt my friend when the choice was either harm or something worse.

I am the Awakened Scion of Gawain, and they threw my training—and my calling—back in my face.

"But Nicholas *isn't* a Davis, not in truth." The words are out of my mouth before I can call them back. Beside me, my friends' heads whip in my direction. Greer grins, delighted by my impudence even as I am vaguely shocked by it. Shocked even more when I keep speaking. "He's a Reynolds, as we now all know. As *you* all know. More importantly, he is your Scion of Lancelot—and you will treat his curia with respect."

Lord Regent Aldrich begins to respond, but Cestra beats him to it. "Have something to say, Scion Sitterson?"

"I have much to say." I stand before I can convince myself not to. My hands rest atop the back of the pew before me, and I notice that my fingers are trembling. It seems even my own body can't square my behavior with my instincts. Or maybe it is the brainwashing of the Order, its last veil crumbling to ash as I face my former captors.

Whatever this force is that keeps me talking, it reminds me of Bree. Sharply, desperately, and wholly of *Bree*. Her bravery, always laced with her fear. If Bree can stand against them, then I must stand too.

"I have much to say," I repeat. "For now I would simply like the record to reflect *the facts* before we begin." I drag my gaze purposefully to Donovan

Reynolds and his permanent, unearned smirk. "Nicholas Davis is a Reynolds by blood, and the Awakened and rightful Scion of Lancelot. Whatever 'arrogance' he possesses is made of the same material as the Line of Lancelot's famous stubborn streak and swift ingenuity."

I trace the sneer on Cestra's face with my eyes. Her long, shiny nails and smooth cuticles. The hands in her lap, resting gently without the hard-earned calluses of a warrior.

Cestra's expression darkens. "Your point, Scion Sitterson?"

"My point is that as a child of Tristan, even *you* were taught to revere these traits—though you were never Called to battle to witness their necessity." Her eyes widen at my words, but I can't stop them. "My *point* is that you mock the very values that keep you relevant—and you should hold your tongue in gratitude."

William

THE ROTUNDA IS so silent, a dropped pin could be heard.

My own *breathing* can be heard.

But Cestra's anger and embarrassment are *satisfyingly* on display. Her face flushes red, the blood vessels in her neck and face responding to her nervous system, which is responding to my insult. Her nails curl into the ends of the wood chair beneath her hands. She cannot even muster a false, polite smile.

When Cestra does and says nothing, indeed, when the Lord Regent does and says *nothing*, Felicity emits a low, curious hum beside me. I wonder if she has landed on the same conclusion that I have: the Table's rebellion with the Morgaines must have struck a nerve. That is the only explanation for my open insult to go unchecked. "Your point is well made, Scion Sitterson." Lord Regent Aldrich clears his throat. "Of course we should honor Nicholas Davis's true lineage."

"Like you honored *Bree Matthews's* true lineage?" Greer asks with a scoff. I raise a brow at them, and they look up at me, grinning. My interruption emboldened them to make their own, and something like pride grows roots in my chest.

Aldrich tenses. "This convening is not about Bree Matthews, Squire Taylor."

"How could it be?" Erebus says. "When she is nowhere to be found?"

"Does that mean you've been looking for Bree and Sel?" I voice the question we all have.

"With every resource available to us—and some we do not have to spare," Erebus returns. His brows draw together tightly. "It is just as you, Scion Davis, and Guard Douglas reported: There is no trace left behind, no sign of them anywhere. They have both vanished."

"How do two people just vanish into thin air?" Hannah, the Scion of Bedivere, asks hotly from her seat. "And what is the Council doing about it?"

Shh-shh-shh-shh. The whispering sound of thumbs brushed over fingers fills the space—a nonverbal sign of approval from the other Scions and Squires in the room and even from the Lieges up above, whose spoken voices are not welcome here. Table members, both former and current, are listening. The Council's eyes follow the sound of our dissatisfaction and distrust as it bounces around the room. *Shh-shh-shh-shh.*

"This Council is responding accordingly, Scion Mather," Aldrich says, "to an unprecedented set of circumstances."

"*Several* unprecedented circumstances, in fact," Seneschal Serren adds, voice loud enough to carry through the space easily. "The Order has no record of a demon who is powerful enough to materialize and dematerialize in and out of several layers of wards. Not even a goruchel can do such things, nor a Merlin of any level."

I glance at Greer, then Felicity, who gaze back at me with wide eyes.

They truly have no idea where Bree and Sel are, and no leads on the demon who took them.

"Perhaps your records are incomplete," I begin cautiously, thinking not just of Nick but of Valec and Mariah, of Volition—and of Bree. "It would not be the first time the Order fell short in documenting the truth of our world."

"Merlins make it our business to know demons, Scion Sitterson," Erebus says haughtily, sitting back in his chair. "As cambions, we understand the nature of Shadowborn better than any human. Our demonology records are both extensive and exhaustive. If this *being* has existed on our plane before now, it likely makes a habit of eliminating any witnesses in order to cover its tracks." His red eyes bore into mine, cold and detached. "You three should consider yourselves lucky to be alive. If this mystery demon had possessed other impulses, I am certain that you would be dead and that we would be welcoming your bloodline replacements to the fold at this very moment. Be grateful it seems to have had other priorities."

I swallow. Erebus is right; that demon could have easily killed us had he wanted to.

Had we gotten in his way.

"This is some sort of super-goruchel, then?" Alex, the Scion of Kay, stands.

"We do not believe this novel demon can be understood within our existing classifications," Seneschal Tacitus adds in a gravelly voice. "This monster is beyond 'uchel' and 'goruchel.' There is no scale for power of this kind, no reference for black aether as described by Scions Sitterson and Davis. It is in a new league, Scion Hanover."

"A league we are ill-equipped to pursue." Erebus temples his fingers. "This so-called teleportation ability you witnessed is no doubt a mere taste of what this demon is capable of. It is not hyperbole to consider that the true depth of its powers is beyond our knowledge."

Aldrich continues, his voice slowly growing in intensity. "While this Council and the Legendborn have had our . . . differences, it would be irresponsible for me to not make this clear: This new demon, wherever it is, is a danger to us all. Legendborn, Liege, Regent, Merlin, and Onceborn alike. Its very existence threatens *everything* this Order has built. Make no mistake, the kidnapping of Briana Matthews and Selwyn Kane is a sign that *this* Camlann, however it may have begun, will end like none other before."

The room quiets all over again. A knock interrupts the moment.

"Come," Regent Cestra calls. The double doors at the back of the rotunda open, and the light from the outer hall spills down the center aisle in an arc of white.

I immediately recognize the first two Mageguard to enter. Guard Olsen, one of the first Mageguard to arrive at the Southern Chapter, gazes straight ahead, and beside her walks Larkin.

As he approaches, I half expect Larkin to look my way. Then, I remember that the Council is watching and they still don't know that his true allegiance is to Bree. If he shows any real expression in my direction, it might blow his cover, so I only allow myself a single glance.

It is, to my odd sense of dismay and frustration, more than enough.

Today, Larkin is in his dress grays. Silver-threaded slacks, a cross-buckled dark stone-gray jacket with a generous cowl, and an extra pair of silver aether-conducting rings on each hand. His Mageguard undercut is freshly touched up, and his hair lies slick in a thick wave, away from his face. *He is handsome when he is focused*, I realize, then swallow at the surge of unasked-for heat around my collar.

Finally, Nick enters. I have not seen him in three days, but aside from a shadow beneath each of his eyes, his pallor and demeanor are much the same as they were when he first called Cestra and asked to be arrested. His left hand is mostly healed and without a bandage, and today he wears dark pants and an unbuttoned charcoal-gray vest over a navy dress shirt rolled up at the elbows.

However, unlike that morning on the hill, when Nick was moving freely, his gait today is guided by two other Mageguard behind him. Nearly as tall as he is and flanking him on either side, they push him forward with a heavy gloved hand at each shoulder. It is only when the group clears our row that I see the thick black iron bands around Nick's wrists.

"Fuck," Greer curses under their breath. "Are those what I think they are?"

"Yes," I reply lowly. "Cyffion gwacter. 'Void cuffs.'"

I've only ever seen the cuffs on Selwyn, as they are typically forged for Merlins. Designed to block their cambion ability to sense, call, or forge aether. Even then, Selwyn's cuffs were unchained, allowing him individual use of his hands. Nick's restraints are connected by a heavy length of iron links, leaving his arms partially immobilized along his torso, palms facing inward.

As he passes our row, Nick's blue eyes find mine, his expression both amused and alert, before his gaze returns to the stage ahead.

"Mageguard plus void cuffs? What exactly do they think Nick's gonna do here?" Greer hisses. "Attack the Council with aether swords drawn?"

"Well," I reply, "I'd say that's *exactly* what they're worried about."

No one here but Erebus saw Nick attack Maxwell Zhao, so perhaps we cannot fathom the violence our friend is capable of. I turn back to find the Seneschal regarding Nick's approach with watchful, sharp eyes and don't have to guess whether Erebus is the Merlin who bespelled Nick's cuffs—which means he is the only person other than Bree who can break them.

"Thank you for gathering on such short notice, High Council," Nick calls out in a loud voice.

As he is brought to a halt before the stage, the humor on his face matches the blatant taunt of his next words. "I cannot truthfully say it is good to see you. I could lie, if you prefer?" His eyes brighten, almost hopeful. "Or you could lie? It would be like old times."

Aldrich stands with one hand in his pocket, pointedly ignoring Nick's jabs. "It is not like we have a choice in being here, Scion Davis." He waves the Guards guiding Nick forward, and they walk him up the stairs to the stage. At a second gesture the guards retreat, leaving Nick alone. Even cuffed, his body and face are relaxed, his shoulders loose.

Nick raises both linked hands to Erebus. "No chance you'd be willing to remove these?"

"I'm afraid not, Scion Davis." Erebus sits back. "You have proven yourself to be a threat to my Mageguard."

Nick drops his arms. "Thought you might say that." He shrugs a single shoulder, the action lifting his lowered wrists at an angle. On anyone else the movement would be impossibly awkward; on Nick, it is effortless. "And I can't exactly deny your reasoning."

"I am glad you agree," Erebus says dryly.

"Oh, I'm sure there's much upon which we agree, the Council and I."

Nick pivots so that we can all see him clearly. He scans the small group of gathered Legendborn first, pausing on Donovan, then casts his gaze upward to the silent and shadowed Lieges tucked away and hidden on the balcony above— as if he can see them clearly too.

I frown. Only a Merlin can see in the dark.

Nick circles back to the Council. "And there is much upon which we disagree."

"You drew on old Order traditions to bring us here today, Scion Davis," Aldrich says, walking back to take his seat in the line of six chairs at the rear of the stage. "And yet you stand before us a self-proclaimed criminal. What do you have to say for yourself?"

Nick smiles softly. Then, in a resonant voice that carries, he recites: "Y cyngor, wedi'i alw ynghyd, i glywed gorchymyn. Y cyngor, wedi'i alw ynghyd, i ganiatáu cais."

The Council, gathered, to receive a demand. The Council, gathered, to grant a bid.

"Llw o gefnogaeth i'r Chwedlanedig, yn addawedig. Llw o wasanaeth i'r Chwedlanedig, iddo'n rhwym."

An Oath of Support to the Legendborn, pledged. An Oath of Service to the Legendborn, bound.

Aldrich's jaw works back and forth. "I am aware of our commitment."

"Thought you might be," Nick drawls, turning, "as answering a Legendborn call for a curia and granting their formal request is the only Oath the Council ever swears to the Round Table. The only promise that ties you to *our* demands, rather than the other way around. And, like any other Oath, if you do not fulfill it as sworn—you'll die a long, burning, painful death."

The room shifts uncomfortably, clothes sliding across wood and coughs interrupting the silence. Beside me, Greer makes a surprised sound. It seems they did not know that at the center of the curia conventus lies an unbreakable Oath the Regents cannot avoid. Only the oldest Scion families even teach this ancient truth—and it's why the Regents themselves never discuss it.

"We of the Council do not need to be reminded—in detail—of the consequences of a broken Oath," Aldrich says with barely contained disgust. "Make your request and make it quick so that we may get back to the *real* business of running this order."

Nick spreads his hands wide within their cuffs. "I assure you my request is in alignment with the Order's objectives."

"We will be the judge of that." Cestra sits back, crossing her legs. "State your demand."

Nick's relaxed expression does not falter. "As Scion of Lancelot, second-ranked to the Round Table, I wish to be granted a formal knight's quest."

I shift in my seat. It makes sense that Nick wants to search for Bree, but formal knight's quests are archaic, outdated journeys. I've never even heard of a modern Scion seeking one. And, by the looks on the Regents' faces, this is not what they were expecting at all.

"Let me guess," Regent Gabriel says with an eye roll. "You wish to search for Briana Matthews? Or Selwyn Kane? You cannot seek both."

"No." Nick's voice does not waver. "I cannot seek both, nor do I wish to."

No?

"No?" Cestra leans forward in her chair. *"No?"*

"He said no, my Regent," Erebus murmurs in a low voice.

"What else, then?" Cestra scoffs. "Don't tell me you seek a Grail quest."

Nick smirks, eyes crinkling at the corners. "What I desire is not a fiction made up by Councils past, I assure you. Unlike the Holy Grail, what I wish to pursue is real."

Cestra huffs. "Then what or whom is your objective for this so-called quest?"

I suck in a silent breath. If not Bree or Sel, then who? His mother, Anna?

Nick levels his gaze at the Regents. "I will pursue the Morgaines who conspired with the Round Table and who attacked the Council at the Keep's fields."

Low murmurs bloom across the hall. Beside me, both Greer's and Felicity's jaws drop.

"He can't be serious," Pete whispers.

Apparently a similar thought has crossed the Council's mind, as the six of them exchange uneasy, uncertain glances.

Shadowborn demons are the Order's primary enemy, but we are taught that the elusive Line of Morgaine comes in a close second. Though they were never cambions, the Morgaines were once considered a sect of Merlins themselves.

They even used the same title and fulfilled similar needs in the hierarchy of the Order, working with cambion Merlins to hunt demons and protect humans. But in the 1400s, there was a splinter. A break in ranks over how the Regents at the time ran the society. According to the stories, the Morgaines who called themselves Merlins turned on their fellow sorcerers, turned on the Regents and Legendborn, and eventually abandoned their adopted title in favor of referring to themselves solely as "Morgaines," then disappeared.

Until they recently revealed themselves to the current Legendborn Scions and Squires to expose the Council's lies and hidden agenda—including the truth of my and Bree's imprisonments and the Regents' plan to usurp the Round Table's power.

Given that the Morgaines are the root of the wedge of distrust between the Legendborn and the Council, I am certain the Regents and their Mage Seneschals would love nothing more than to hunt the Morgaines down and squash the splinter cell for good. But why would Nick?

Lord Regent Aldrich clears his throat and recovers first. "Scion Davis, you came before this body five years ago as a twelve-year-old boy to renounce your title as Scion of Arthur, mistaken as that lineage may have been. You have made your disrespect for our Order and this governing body *appallingly* clear. Are we to believe you despise the Morgaines, our enemies, so deeply?"

Nick releases a low chuckle. "To be perfectly honest with you, I don't give a damn about the Morgaines. Particularly as they sent the goruchel Rhaz to end my life a few months ago under the impression of said mistaken lineage."

"Then why pursue them?" Cestra asks.

"I grow weary of the games you play. We are at war. Humans are dying and new enemies have made themselves known. I cannot live as a hunted man, nor can I fight as one, wondering when your next assassin will make an attempt on my life," Nick says. "I seek a formal knight's quest to hunt the Morgaines, your enemies, on your behalf and on the behalf of this court and Table. Let me show you my loyalty."

"This is no simple boon you ask for, Davis," Cestra states, sitting back with a glower. "A formal quest grants the endowed knight a reprieve from court and military responsibilities—and clemency from any assigned punishments—for as long as their journey requires."

Nick tilts his head, a flicker of mock surprise on his brow. "Is that so?"

And understanding dawns.

Nick planned all of this. In those swift seconds after Sel and Bree disappeared, Nick conceived of everything that led to this moment.

The call for a curia ensured that he would be granted an audience by the Council with the Legendborn and Lieges present as witnesses, making whatever happened during the ritual unavoidably public.

But Nick knew the Regents would love nothing more than to replace him with the next eligible heir in his Line, and if they had killed him before today, his death would have stopped the curia before it started. So he taunted Cestra into arresting him, knowing it would lead to his imprisonment—and that the tower and its ward would keep him safe from any further assassination attempts.

And today Nick used his deep knowledge of the Order's own history to demand a formal knight's quest, an obscure, archaic journey that would not only force the Regents to remove the kill order on his head, but require them to let him roam free.

With a single phone call, Nick Davis manipulated the entire Council of Regents into sending him on a fully sanctioned, unsupervised mission that could take weeks, months, or even years to complete. And no matter how much the Council hates the trap Nick set for them, they can't refuse him—or they'll die.

It's not just quick, strategic thinking; it's genius. Terrifying, brutal, ruthless genius.

Nick's drawl turns syrupy. His words sticky. "Have I displeased you, Council? Upset you? I assure you that was not my intention."

While the rest of the Council undoubtedly processes how a seventeen-year-old has just outmaneuvered them, Erebus recovers first. He alone seems unsurprised by Nick's feat. "I find many of your intentions hard to believe, Scion of Lancelot. Are we to assume that you were not aware that once you are operating under the aegis of a curia-granted knight's quest, this Council cannot pursue you for new crimes or otherwise attempt to harm you, without also risking the wrath of our Oath to the Legendborn?"

Nick's eyes sparkle. "Yes, that is what you are to assume. And as for your Oath, well . . . the Line is Law."

Erebus releases a sigh. "A frustratingly clever loophole, Scion Davis. I am impressed."

Nick bows his head. "Thank you."

"We have no choice but to grant you this boon, Scion Davis." Aldrich inhales sharply. "The loophole you have so *clearly* exploited makes it so. But that does not mean we have to grant you your quest immediately. You will submit to our questions first—for the sake of the Order."

"Of course," Nick says.

"Why the Morgaines?" Aldrich asks.

"You know the answer to that question better than anyone." Nick jerks a chin at the Mageguard in the room. "You're already running short on Merlins."

Another silence floods the room, but this time, the Regents look rattled. Erebus and Cestra exchange silent, weighted looks that tell me that something *else* is running in the undercurrent of this exchange—something about which Nick has a clear and unexpected grasp. This time, the Mageguard share wary glances too. Then I think of Gill's face, and Samira's, and the young Merlin too young to be a Mageguard. . . .

"What do you mean?" Hannah the Scion stands. "What's happening with the Merlins?"

Across the room, Larkin's jaw is clenched tight, not with surprise but with resignation. What had Valec said to him last night about the Order's presence in the world? *S'pose you have to drop those reminders here and there nowadays, huh? With y'all being spread so thin.* My fingers tense on the pew. Valec *knew* the Merlin forces were thinning. And Larkin knew too.

Aldrich clears his throat again. "I don't know what you are referring—"

"In my time on the run, the Morgaines sought me out," Nick reveals. "They knew *many* things about the Order from their years of silent observation.

Their leader, Ava, sought to seduce me to their interests. She spoke of a plan to weaken the Order by killing off its Merlin army."

Feet scuff the balcony floor overhead—the Lieges, shifting in place in response to this news.

"Don't like that," Greer mumbles. "What does he mean she 'seduced' him—"

"Hush," I admonish Greer, although I have the same question myself.

"I was not taught to believe the Morgaines could become strong enough to kill Merlins," Nick says, eyes narrowing at the Council, "but it appears they are succeeding. We cannot win this war without Merlin support, and we all know it."

"As the Scion of Lancelot, you make a good target for Ava," Erebus murmurs, lifting a shoulder. "Perhaps her so-called plan was just lies to invite your betrayal of the Order. A world-weary Lancelot ready to turn against his upbringing would make a fine prize for our enemies."

Nick huffs a laugh. "Perhaps. But you Seneschals should see your Regents right now. . . ." He raises his cuffed wrists to point with both hands, sweeping slow across the line of Regents. "Those looks of dread on their very human faces are a dead giveaway that her plan *is* working. Merlins are being murdered, aren't they?"

I swallow thickly, wrapping my head around something that seems impossible. A thinning Merlin army is quite possibly one of the Council's worst nightmares, and with good reason. The Legendborn can't cover nearly the same territory that Merlins can. There are only twenty-six of us, even when the Table is at full power. There must be at least a thousand Merlins in active service, maybe more—or there were.

Aldrich's face reddens before he sputters back to life. "How exactly do you plan on stopping the Morgaines?"

"Ava hates the Order and knows that I have every reason to hate it too." Nick's words hit the ear like treason. "In other words, she will believe the enemy of her enemy is her friend."

"Then what?" Regent Gabriel says, waving a hand as if to say, *Go on*. "Will you kill her?"

"If you like." Nick's voice betrays nothing.

I stiffen. Try my best to read Nick's expression for more hesitation or distaste, even duplicity—but his face is blank and emotionless.

Killing Ava is murder, no matter how many Merlins she herself has killed and no matter how many goruchel she once sent to kill Nick. That the Legendborn world traffics in so much death that its Council openly speaks of murdering an enemy, without worry about censure or consequences, doesn't surprise me as much as it should. It is Nick's true willingness to commit that murder that I care about—and I find I cannot read him at all.

I search Nick's face for remnants of the boy I grew up with. That boy is still there in his stature, in his hair and eyes, even in the noble lift of his chin. But the boy I grew up with is not who Nick has become. *This* Nick, the one with the hard glint in his blue eyes, the one in void cuffs, the one who casually agrees to kill an enemy, is not someone I recognize. I feel a surge of guilt for not seeing the emergence of *him*—and an answering wave of determination to untangle this newcomer from my friend.

Erebus taps his chair impatiently. "You may be successful in killing one of our greatest enemies, but that does not mean you can be trusted. You have already killed one of our own."

"Maxwell Zhao was attempting to kill *me*. Am I not 'one of our own'?" Nick counters, something sharp in his voice. "Under your orders, Zhao threw an aether spear aimed at my heart, and my father died from the blow instead."

"I am aware of the events, Scion Davis." Erebus sighs. "But how can we be certain—"

"Be certain of *this*," Nick says, taking a slow step toward the seated Council. "I have never hidden my distaste for your methods, but I do believe in the Order's core mission as it was taught to me and my fellow Scions. I believe in using our inheritances to fight demonkind and to protect Onceborn lives." As he speaks, Nick takes another step, then another, until one boot rests on the stairs ascending the dais where the Council sits. "Do you also believe in these things, High Regent?"

The powder-keg tension of the room twists further. Aldrich's eyes narrow a fraction. "I do."

Nick's smile is sharp and quick. "Then have we reached an accord? Will you grant me this quest so that I may leave a free knight?"

Aldrich taps his fingers on his armrest. "You have not provided sufficient reasoning to this Council as to why you would not immediately seek either Briana Matthews or your Kingsmage and defect from the Round Table in the process."

A long pause.

"I think we both know Selwyn Kane is gone," Nick says quietly. "In spirit, if not in body."

My stomach drops. Has Nick truly given up on Selwyn? That can't be possible. I know what the Order has taught us about demonia and I know that Selwyn's progression toward *something* is real, but I refuse to believe that he is truly out of our reach. And the Nick I grew up with, the Nick I saw in the moments after Bree and Sel disappeared, would never take the Order's word about demonia at face value. He's lying. He *must* be lying—

"I agree that Kane is a lost cause." Erebus tilts his head. "And what of Briana?"

Nick steps back. "Six months ago, this Council and its mission would have deemed Briana Matthews a Onceborn. An ignorant innocent at best, an expendable nuisance at worst. I myself sponsored her entry into our Order—a decision that will haunt me for the rest of my days." A pause. "In the months since the revelation of Briana's true lineages—being born of not one Line of power but two—she was lied to and deceived, drugged, imprisoned, tortured, and possessed by the malevolent spirit we Scions were raised to worship. And every act against her was not committed by demonkind enemies, but by the very Order that should be *kneeling at her feet*. This Council sought to *break* Briana Matthews . . . and found it could not. I think you are fortunate that she has not sought vengeance against you. As are we all."

Nick raises his eyes to Lord Regent Aldrich, finality written on his face.

"To answer your question, I will not pursue Bree, because even if she is with an enemy, I know that she will survive—which is a far better fate than what awaits her here."

A long silence fills the rotunda.

Aldrich's mouth is a pursed line. His next words break the silence like stones thrown in a still pond. "You dance with treason today, Scion Davis."

"If treason is truth, then perhaps I do. Or perhaps I merely tire of your version of loyalty." Nick levels his gaze, hard and flinty, at the older man. "I was raised by my father under the Order's philosophies. I heard him speak daily of the rights and access he deserved and that he claimed I was owed. You have made me parentless twice over, Regents. I am an orphan of your Court. I have lived beneath your violence; I have seen what you seek to hide, not just here but everywhere. And in my time away from this court, I have seen and felt your truths more clearly than ever."

"What truths?"

"Your supremacy," Nick says, brows tight. "Your misogyny. Your racism. Your cowardice."

Aldrich snarls. "Scion Davis—"

"I only state out loud that which you enact in plain sight. That which we can *all* see, if we can stand to bear witness." Nick seethes. "Will you punish me for doing so? Your *chosen son?*"

The Regents are silent.

"Briana Matthews cannot be the only voice that speaks against you." Nick's face turns derisive. A bright fury, rising beneath his skin. "Not when she bears our burdens for us and goes so unprotected. Not when you erase her humanity to guard your own power and protect your own whiteness."

Aldrich and Gabriel both sputter, while Cestra's face turns red. The High Regent shoots to his feet. "Scion Davis—!"

"I'm not done!" Nick roars back. "And I wasn't just talking to you." Nick turns to the room, to the other Scions and Squires, to the Lieges up above.

"We have to know these sins. We have to name them. Not only in Bree's presence"—at this, Nick looks at the Southern Chapter, at me—"but in her absence, too."

William

A FULL-CHESTED WAVE of immobilizing shame swamps me.

Did I ever name the forces that Bree faced? Did I ever call them what they were, full voiced in front of her? Or did I hope that she would understand that I knew them? Did I hope she would *know* my heart without seeing me declare it before others?

I drop my head. If I cannot recall the facts of my own words, then I cannot expect her to.

Have I ever even considered who Bree might be outside of the Order's sins? Who she could become without our casual violence? I find I want to meet that girl and get to know her. But as long as I remain part of the Order as it exists now . . . I don't think I ever will.

Aldrich sighs, sitting back. "Your comments have been noted."

Nick's expression turns thunderous. "That's all you have to say, isn't it?"

"Your words were very moving, I'm sure"—Aldrich waves a hand—"to *someone*."

"I can only hope," replies Nick, shaking his head in disbelief. "Bree truly is better off with a demon. But at this point, I almost pity her captor."

"And why is that?" Erebus asks in a bored tone.

"Because"—Nick gazes at the Seneschal with not a small amount of pleasure—"no one dead or alive can control Briana Matthews."

"Is that so?" Erebus asks, brow arched.

"Woe betide the human or demon who tries. Briana belongs to no one but herself. I know that better than anyone. Now grant my quest."

"We are aware of your romantic relationship." Cestra rolls her eyes. "You know the rules of intimacy between Scions, Davis. The Lines cannot, must not—"

"I am aware of the *activities* that 'cannot, must not' take place between Scions, Regent Cestra," Nick scoffs, shaking his head. "These questions are distractions. Delays to the inevitable outcome you are Oathbound to provide. I have told you my objectives. Grant me my quest *now*."

Aldrich looks to his left, then to his right, waiting for other inquiries or protests.

Cestra raises her hand, and her eyes glitter as she speaks. "As I recall, a *traditional* quest allows for two companions. A second-in-command and an attendant guardian—"

"I won't need any companions," Nick replies shortly.

"But we *must* follow tradition," Cestra retorts. "It's only fair."

My body moves again without my permission. Suddenly, I am standing with one hand raised. "I volunteer as quest second."

Nick's head whips to me. "I reject your aid—"

"I will join Scion Davis's quest," I say louder, without meeting his gaze.

"A team will only slow me down and make trouble with the Morgaines!" Nick turns back to the Regents. "Scion Sitterson is a healer needed by the rest of the Table—"

"Scion Sitterson's request is approved, per tradition," Cestra says with a smile. "Who will be your champion?"

"I volunteer as quest champion." I recognize Larkin's voice even before he steps forward. "I will protect Scion Davis in the field and report back to the Council as necessary. Confirm success when the Morgaine is eliminated."

"I reject this," Nick protests. "I did *not* request companions. Ava will never trust me with a Merlin in tow—and she is *killing* Merlins. You did catch that, right?"

"You drew on the old traditions first, Scion Davis," Aldrich says sagely, his eyes sparkling. "You cannot abandon them now." The Lord Regent nods to both me and Larkin. "As quest second and champion, you will aid Scion Davis in pursuing his quest objective to kill the Morgaine leader Ava. And in the meantime, you will monitor his progress to ensure that he remains active toward his goals. We will expect regular updates to that effect."

Larkin nods, face a blank, obedient mask. "Of course, Lord Regent."

"If you do not report back as commanded or it is discovered that you permitted Scion Davis to abandon his stated quest, then he will be considered a traitor and his quest will be void and forfeit," Cestra says smugly, "along with all of your lives."

Nick glares at me. Imploring me to step away. Pleading with me to withdraw my bid.

My throat constricts, but Larkin and I answer in unison. "We understand."

"Then I am satisfied," Cestra states primly.

"As am I," Gabriel says.

"I am *not!*" Nick shouts.

"I am satisfied as well," Aldrich says with a nod. "Scion Davis, your quest is granted."

Nick looks as if he might protest but suppresses the urge to do so. It does not take a strategic genius to know that he is caught—he either takes his boon as it is offered, or they further delay the inevitable. Or question his motives entirely.

A final, silent exhale of acceptance rattles through him.

Good.

Nick's fists close in their cuffs as he dips his head. "Thank you, Regents and Seneschals. Consider my curia concluded and my—"

"*No!*"

Whatever Nick may have said next is lost beneath the sudden roar of a single Mageguard—and the whistling sound of an aether dagger being thrown straight at Nick's back.

"Nick!" I shout.

Nick whips around at my warning—and just barely catches the hilt between both palms, halting the flying blade point at his chest. A small circle of blood blooms at his sternum, staining the center of his blue shirt a deep grayish purple.

A fraction of a second later and he'd be dead.

Deeply pierced hearts are beyond even my abilities. Fortunately, this wound appears shallow—the blood spreads without spilling.

A heartbeat of silence passes—before the powder keg of the room finally erupts.

Flashes of silver-blue aether in the dimly lit space temporarily blind me as the Mageguard arm themselves at once. Angry Legendborn storm over pews and run toward the stage, shouting.

Onstage, Nick searches for his assailant as he flips the blade around in his chained hands, arming himself with the dagger that nearly killed him. Behind him, each of the three Seneschals has cast a two-person barrier over himself and his Regent.

I am running without thinking, in motion beside Greer, armor flowing up my elbows to my shoulders—

Out of the corner of my eye, movement.

In the deepest shadow to my right, tucked beneath a balcony, a cloaked figure sprints forward—a Mageguard?

They rush the stage in a streak of black and silver. Leap high over their fellow Guards—

And are in front of Nick in a blink, sure-footed and steady.

With a smack, the figure clasps their hands together. A shining, solid blue dome surrounds the stage—trapping a handcuffed Nick inside with a raging Merlin.

"Regents!" Gill's voice roars from the balcony, barely audible over the din. "Stop this!"

The figure throws their hood and cloak onto the wooden floor, revealing a dark-haired Merlin in his mid-twenties with pale skin. Like the other guards, he is in dress grays, but his undercut lies disheveled across his brow, half falling into his deep orange eyes.

"Thompson, stand down!" Erebus shouts at his Guard, but the Merlin doesn't respond. Instead, he extends a hand toward Nick to recall his blade from Nick's right fist. Nick struggles to hold it—but the blade flies back to its forger, landing neatly in the newcomer's hand.

"Thompson!" Erebus commands. "Now!"

Thompson turns the dagger in his fist over once. Twice. "I can't let him walk, sir! Not after what he did!"

Nick slides a foot back for better balance. "I have no fight with you, Guard Thompson. And I am cuffed—this won't be a fair battle."

By now, all the Scions and Squires are on their feet at ground level, spread out around the dome, shouting for the barrier to come down.

"You don't *deserve* a fair fight." Aether swirls around both of Thompson's wrists. "You killed Max."

Nick eyes the magic growing at the Merlin's sides. "I think we've already covered that."

"Stop this!" Samira calls.

Instead of intervening, the Regents remain silent. Erebus is the only member of the Council who takes action. He steps outside of his own protective casting to hold a palm toward Thompson's barrier, silently calling it to himself to dissolve it—but is arrested by a bolt of aether knocking his arm sideways.

At the far end of the dais, Serren lowers his hand. The two Seneschals glare at each other, a meeting of wills.

Understanding freezes my feet to the floor.

The Council can't harm Nick now that they've granted his quest, but a Mageguard can—and the Oath of protection the guards take is sworn only to the king. If Thompson wants to kill Nick, he can, and no Oath will stop him.

Serren doesn't seem to care if Nick dies—but Erebus Varelian, for all his faults, *does*.

Before the other Seneschal can react, Erebus raises one hand, twisting it in the air—and the void cuffs around Nick's hands clatter to the floor.

Serren rolls his eyes but does not respond.

I step forward, moving toward the stage myself, to stop Thompson, to help Nick—and am halted by the steel grip of Gillian Hanover at my elbow.

My eyes widen in alarm. "Gill—"

"No." Gillian's sharp eyes dart between the Seneschals; the Mageguard that surround us, waiting for an order; the Regents, who are unmoved; and the circling figures of Nick and Thompson. "Too many variables."

I shake her hand from my arm. "But Nick is injured—"

"Which is why he needs to focus," Gill states.

Thompson's roar draws our attention back to the stage.

"He was a good soldier!" He circles Nick. "A good man!"

"If you say so." Nick carefully crosses one foot over the other while watching the aether surrounding Thompson's arms. He does not forge the ball of aether in his palm; he simply holds it ready. "My father died on Zhao's spear, so forgive me if I have my doubts."

With another roar, Thompson darts forward. Forms a longsword as he moves.

Nick calls a blade to life in an instant—they meet in the middle, their swords sparking—

Nick and the Merlin backpedal at nearly the same pace.

A beat.

They flash together again in a blur of streaming aether, swords clanging as they cross. Both wield their blades in nearly the same manner, until Thompson shouts—and his blades melt into snakelike whips, curling around Nick's weapon.

This time, when Thompson darts back, he takes Nick's sword with him.

Nick releases his constructs—and his blade sparks to dust within the Merlin's grasp.

Without Nick's weapon in their writhing grasp, Thompson's snake constructs begin to shift, change shape into something new—

But Nick is already moving—nearly a blur himself as he rushes across the stage.

He takes a flying leap at a shocked Thompson, swinging his right fist back— to land a hard, crunching blow to the Merlin's nose.

No Merlin expects a fistfight—not with a slower, weaker human.

And while Nick is not as strong as a cambion, his Line of Lancelot speed gives him an advantage—and Thompson wasn't ready.

The Merlin's head snaps back—his face an explosion of blood—as Nick lands, rolling out of range.

Nick springs to his feet. Thompson groans, both hands coming to his face.

Merlins are extremely durable, and they heal quickly—but a broken nose is a broken nose. A high-value hit against a more agile opponent.

Nick speeds back to the other side of the dome, his chest rising and falling beneath his bloodied shirt. He shakes out the hand that has a deep red bruise blossoming along its knuckles.

Thompson flashes bloodstained teeth and takes a new stance at the far side of the circle.

"Stand down!" Nick says.

"That punch was a lucky shot!" Thompson replies, voice angry and nasal.

"I've already admitted to murdering Zhao. I can't take it back—"

"Max was following orders!" Thompson shouts. "He didn't have a choice. And your father was a traitor!"

"I won't argue that, but—" Nick's eyes flicker in surprise, stopping him halfway through his sentence. "Oh. *Oh*." His eyes widen. "This isn't new anger; you've been *nursing* it."

Thompson claps his now trembling hands together, growing another ferocious ball of swirling aether between his palms. "Shut up."

"I see now." Nick's brows draw tight. "Max wasn't just a 'good' man; he was *your* man."

"Yes," Thompson growls, forging a long, narrow weapon.

Nick watches the older man carefully, understanding growing in his eyes. "You loved him."

Thompson's face darkens. "And you *killed* him."

"I did." Nick forges a sword, the blade extending slow and steady until it shines. "I am sorry for my part in your loss. I wish I could change it, but I can't. And I don't blame you for wanting revenge."

"I don't give a damn what you're sorry for, Scion!"

"We both paid a price that day, Guard Thompson," Nick says solemnly. Sadness clouds his features as he raises his sword with both hands, leveling it at Thompson. "Take care that you do not pay another now, at the end of my blade. I am not here for you."

"But *I* am here for *you*." Thompson's aether staff is heavy now, with solid round ends the size of my fist. *Thud!* He slams it on the floor of the stage, and sparks fly from the impact. "I'm ready, Scion."

"This can end," Nick says, circling again with his blade at the ready.

"You started this," Thompson sneers, twirling the staff in one hand. As it circles, aether flames spill out from the ends, making a heavy *whoosh-whoosh-whoosh* sound that fills the meeting room.

Nick dips his chin. "I know."

Thompson lunges forward, extending his arm, but Nick is already dodging. Nick drops his blade. Slides beneath the rotating staff—and sweeps Thompson's legs out from beneath him.

The next seconds are a blur.

Thompson hits the stage back-first, already moving into a kip-up, pressing down to flip forward—but Nick is waiting.

He sends a roundhouse to Thompson's face at breakneck speed—kicking the Merlin out of the air and back down to the floor before he ever gets the chance to land.

Thompson's body skids across the wooden stage until he comes to a stop.

The Mageguard lies unconscious, splayed awkwardly. His weapon dissipates.

The room is silent once again.

I know Nick was taught by Gillian as a child and that he grew up sparring with Selwyn, but I sometimes forget what that combination of training looks like in a life-or-death battle. Lessons from an experienced Liege of Kay made Nick dangerous, but endless bouts with a young Kingsmage made him nearly unstoppable. Now, with Lancelot's speed, Nick is truly deadly, even against an adult Merlin and trained Mageguard like Thompson.

Beside me, Gill's eyes are bright with knowing pride because throughout the entire fight, she knew something that I didn't:

Nick had been holding back.

9

Natasia

AUDIO LOG—ENTRY #2

Selwyn woke up twelve days ago.

I have been a poor scientist. In an ideal world, for both Selwyn's records and my own, I would have documented the moment of his awakening and the days since then with several audio log entries and observations, but there are intentions and there is reality . . . and it seems I am forever caught between the two. And so, with regret, this is only audio log number two.

I am recording this second entry a mile or so away from the cabin so as to save Selwyn from the understandably awkward experience of hearing himself being described by his mother. I think he's showering now, and will be for at least the next ten minutes, so I will make this quick.

That first moment of seeing him stir froze the breath in my lungs. The time spent waiting for him to open his eyes was . . . interminable. [Quiet laugh.] *My heartbeat thrummed in my chest, nearly as fast as a human being's. No doubt that my appearance would have been alarming had someone else been there to see me. When my demon rises, my eyes turn a deep red. The tips of my ears grow to points. My fangs drop. My emotions, briefly, feel out of my control.*

My son is in front of me, and soon he will wake, and we will speak to each other once again, *I thought. I was thrilled near to tears.*

Then, his eyes fluttered open—and the golden gaze I had last seen years ago was gone, replaced by a deep heart-blood crimson. He blurred to a crouch on the bed, snarling, fingers curled to call for aether, ready for a fight.

I did not flinch or move from my seat at his bedside; I know from experience that Selwyn's predator senses are especially attuned to the behaviors and movements of prey, and such movement on my part would have encouraged him to strike.

I believe his demonia-heightened senses detected that I was not a foe before his conscious mind did, buried as it was, because his eyes quickly left me to scan the room for other threats. His nose raised to the air, taking in information about the home, the building. His fingers twitched at his sides.

I held my breath and held still, and waited for his eyes to return to me. A moment passed, and then they did.

When Selwyn truly saw me for the first time, his snarl faded. His eyes widened.

I knew the exact moment he recognized me as his mother, because when he did, confusion and hurt mingled on his features until they settled into disgust . . . and then fury.

I cannot blame him for this cocktail of emotions. I have, unfortunately, earned them.

His jaw tightened to iron, and he remained in his crouch. Still alert. Still on edge. I gave him a moment. To speak. To ask me questions. To do anything. I would give this boy, my son, anything at all. Anything.

But instead . . . he said nothing. He stared at me. Taking in, I assume, what thirteen years has done to my features. His eyes lingered on the gray at my temples, just beginning its trek down my long black hair.

I kept my voice low. Remained still. "The gray started a few years ago. Seems to be gaining speed these days."

His eyes, sharp and narrowed, flicked to mine. He seemed to understand me.

"I probably have a few more lines on my face than the last time you saw me too."

I didn't move my body but let my gaze fall to my own hands—silver rings, long fingers. "My wounds don't heal quite as quickly as they used to, so I have a few more scars here and there." When I looked up, his eyes were on my hands, cataloging the thin twin slashes that twist from my knuckles, around my wrist, and down my forearm. "Hellsnake fangs," I explained, and held my hand up slowly—but not slowly enough. His lips pulled back and a low growl began in his chest. I assured him quickly, "I won't hurt you."

His snarl remained.

I lowered my hand again, and his face relaxed.

"I'd never hurt you, Selwyn," I said.

One of his thick brows rose. Disbelief?

"Not physically, ever," I said. "I . . . I know I've hurt you in other ways. . . ."

He seemed to ignore my gesture, my bid. Instead, his eyes dropped back down to my hand, expression turned curious.

Okay, I thought. He wants to know about my injuries, not my feelings. We can do that.

"I found a clutch of hellsnake eggs in South Dakota one winter," I explained. "Their mother had been attacking local residents at night, and the Merlin assigned to that region had already been called in to eliminate her. But they were young. Didn't know enough to go searching for her nest."

He blew out a quick breath. Annoyance?

"Agreed," I said. "A lot of the younger Merlins aren't trained the way I was. The way I trained you."

When I looked back up, the curiosity in his eyes was gone. They had turned cold. Unfeeling. Hostile.

"I'd like to explain——" I started, and he looked down at his own hands, as if seeing them for the first time. I didn't get insulted; instead, I followed his attention.

I know, after all, what it feels like to witness your body become something you yourself do not recognize.

I watched Selwyn study his open hands where they rested, palms facing down on his lap: the elongated, darkened nails. The black veins lining his fingers, running up the back of his knuckles, past his wrists to his forearms.

I attempted to offer him some information. Empathy. "You'll find that when you—"

He rolled his wrists over so that his palms faced up—and tiny sparks of green aether erupted along his palms. He hissed.

"You'll find that when you call aether now, it will manifest as green mage flame. Your constructs will also be green. I know this is alarming to see—"

Selwyn's low growl interrupted me as he twisted his hands back, quieting the aether in them until the room was dark again.

I waited. I was not sure if his warning growl was for me and for what I was saying when he'd rather have not been distracted, or for what his body and magic had become.

He repeated the movement. Rolling his wrists, tucking his fists inward, then spreading his fingers up and out. Bright silver-green aether erupted at his palms again, but this time, he curled his hands in as if to harness the flames and make them his.

"Selwyn—" I tried again, but he only snarled.

After several more minutes of this, he seemed satisfied. Then, he placed his palms in his lap and closed his eyes.

I don't think I've ever felt so dismissed.

[Long sigh.]

And it's been like that every day for the past twelve days. He has not spoken to me once, even though I try a different tactic each day to encourage him to do so. Demonia does not affect language centers, so I have ruled out that he cannot speak and have had to accept that he . . . simply chooses not to. Based on his visceral and clear responses to my attempts at reconciliation—his facial reactions are very expressive, as they have always been—I can safely guess that not only is he choosing not to speak; he's choosing specifically not to speak to me.

Our history is . . . complicated. Unfortunate. And entirely my fault.

In these days of one-sided silence between us, I have made sure to bring back new clothing in his size, supply him with toiletries, and prepare a variety of foods. His body is still mostly human, so he must eat to sustain himself—even if demonia will soon surface other hungers. Thankfully, I am not the worst cook: I've been feeding him, and he's been eating. He explores my home. Rests. Observes. He doesn't leave the house. Often doesn't leave his room. I think he is waiting to decide how to proceed, or perhaps he senses that I am waiting to decide when to proceed to the next steps of his recovery, if he is agreeable to them.

Selwyn does not experiment with his new green aether abilities beyond testing them quietly in his palm. He does not call much more than a handful of flames. He does not forge constructs. He simply twists his wrists around to call the green aether, as if familiarizing himself with his newfound power.

Alone in my prison cell at the Shadowhold, I did much the same when my called aether turned the green color of a true Shadowborn. I tested my abilities. I tested myself. I sought the boundaries between my Merlin selfhood, my humanity, and my suddenly strong inner demon.

I had no one to speak to in those early weeks. I had always thought that if I had been able to share that time with someone else, a friendly face, my transformation might not have felt as bad. I wanted to speak to someone who did not judge me for a descent that was not my fault or for a crime I did not commit. Someone like Faye, who I did not get to say goodbye to before the Regents locked me away.

Faye would not have judged me or scorned me. Faye would have met me where I was and done everything in her power to see if she could help.

Perhaps I could not record another entry in this log because these days have been so hard on me, and in so many ways. As a fellow Merlin, as a mother, and as someone who has also been made to suffer at the hands of the Order.

I find myself thinking again and again of my dear friend and what she would do.

It is painfully easy to remember Faye's face—to see her wide smile and too-clever brown eyes—but doing so gives rise to my grief once more.

It has been months since her death, and I cannot seem to shake the despair I feel from failing her. At not being there to stop the car and stop the inevitable.

Faye never seemed to fear her own death. She spoke about it as if it were a force coming for her, even as a young girl in her late teens. In those days, I felt invincible. I didn't understand how much time she spent thinking of her own absence. How so often, when a strange silence fell upon her, it was death that consumed her thoughts.

I never thought that I would share a similar fate as my son.

I am eternally relieved that the same won't be true for Faye and her daughter.

I wonder what Bree is facing now. I hope she is home safe with her father and that they are able to offer comfort to each other. Whatever grief I feel is likely a hundred-fold worse for Faye's daughter and widower.

I am grateful, once again, for Faye's wisdom in testing Bree for Rootcraft early and confirming that her abilities had skipped her daughter.

This world of Legendborn and Shadowborn, of ancient wars and betrayals, of the Round Table and the Shadow Court, is no place for a child. Not my own and certainly not Faye's.

In all of this, I can at least find some solace in knowing that Bree Matthews will be free to live her life without the chaos we call the Order.

10

TWO MONTHS

AFTER BRIANA MATTHEWS DISAPPEARED

Mariah

THE NEW YEAR has come and gone. The Appalachian Mountains have already seen a few fleeting rounds of snow. The new semester at Carolina is underway, my junior year of college is halfway over . . . and Alice Chen *still* hasn't woken up.

I visit my aunts' house every weekend, and Bree's best friend is the same as she was the weekend before, lying in the guest room where she and Bree had once slept while on the run from the Order. Alice doesn't weaken or wither like a regular coma patient would—her body doesn't seem to need sustenance or water. Now, leaning against the doorway early on a Saturday morning, I wonder if this is it for Alice. If this is her life now.

The girl I met was observant, quick-witted, and suspicious in all the best ways. She knew Bree better than anyone but didn't hesitate to question Bree's new reality. I got the feeling, sometimes, that Alice was making up for lost time. . . . Not sure whether that time had been lost between them in the past, or if it was time she anticipated losing with her friend in the future. The Alice

Chen I met was smart enough to know that Bree's life had an expiration date but wise enough not to remind her best friend of that fact on the regular. Not that Bree needed reminding.

In the past two months, I've wondered if the ticking clock of Bree Matthews's life is something Bree herself is thinking about while in the clutches of the Hunter. If my friend is counting her remaining time on this planet in months and years instead of decades. Sometimes I wonder if the next time I see Bree again, she'll be dead. If death is the price of being the right chosen one at the right time.

I'm a Medium. We're no strangers to death. People think death is a dark, dormant thing, like the earth in the middle of winter. And it's true, death *can* feel dim, but when you grow up around Rootcrafters, you know that ain't always the way. Around *us*, death can be bright. At least to me.

I can sense death and, with an offering and a boost from my ancestors, guide others to their loved ones. And I know what a body feels like when it's no longer in use.

I worry sometimes if I touch Alice Chen, that's what I'll feel—a body no longer in use. The last time I touched her, I felt that she had come close to death—and skirted it. Call me superstitious, but I worry that if I touch her now, I might remind death that it missed her the first time, and it'll come back for a second try.

Aunt Hazel and Aunt Lu worry Alice might slip away too. Before they head to their bedroom at night, they poke their heads in the room to make sure she's still breathing. Her aether breath is easy to spot. It's so bright, the glowing wisps illuminate the entire guest room. Little, rhythmic blooms of light in the darkness that remind us she's with us but not the same.

Wherever Bree is, I like to think she'd be comforted to know that we've got Alice under our roof. Wherever Bree is, I hope she's still breathing too.

Still, I find myself anxiously twisting a braid near my collarbone as I stare at Bree's best friend. Alice Chen isn't dead . . . but what she *is* can't be good.

A quiet curse from behind me interrupts my thoughts. Aunt Hazel never curses, not really, but when she does, it's the softest thing you've ever heard.

Halfway to a blessing, almost, in that you're just happy she cared enough to curse you in the first place. If a curse can sound like love, Aunt Hazel has found the way to do it, but usually, the only folks I hear her cussing about are the administrators at the university where she's tenured.

I close the door to Alice's room behind me and join my aunt in the kitchen. "Aunt Hazel, who you cussin' at today?"

"Nobody," she says with a sigh. She stands in the middle of an explosion of herbs and mortars and pestles and jarred preserves. Every surface of her kitchen is covered with ingredients for tinctures and salves and poultices and teas, half of which we haven't used, just in case they interact with another. There are a few brass focal items, small leather mojo bags with charm-strung strings pulling them tight, and a couple strips of beaded leather piled in a mixing bowl. "Myself, mostly."

I pick up a jar of feathery-looking pale green leaves. "Well, I don't like that. You're doing the best you can."

Over the past month, Hazel has been doing everything I've ever seen an herbalist do to cure Alice and then some. She's not a Wildcrafter, a Rootcrafter who can manipulate plant energy to heal, among other things, but a Magnifier. As a Magnifier, she specializes in connecting folks to their own life force, their own vitality. But on top of that she's gotten skilled at creating small treatments and tiny cures. For one reason or another, her kitchen is drenched with golden magic by most evenings, sparkling in the air as Hazel works.

My Aunt Hazel is a bit famous. She's a molecular biology professor at the University of Georgia to the nonmagical crowd and the most powerful herbalist and Magnifier in the area to every Rootcrafter in the Southeastern territory. Hazel brews teas and tinctures from every herb in her garden, plus some she's asked me and Valec to deliver when we're out of the house. I come back from school to help her in her cozy kitchen, which is part lab and part altar at this point. Each corner and nook of her glass-front cabinet is stuffed with dried green and brown and gray herbs—angelica and basil, celandine and clove, fleawort and feverfew for protection, healing, cleansing, circulation.

She's applied so many poultices to Alice's inner wrists, ankles, and throat that the guest room is flooded with the scent of the earth and growing things.

And still Alice sleeps.

Hazel's brown face folds into a gentle smile, and she walks over to let me give her a much-needed hug. "Thank you for being here, Mariah."

I wrap an arm around my aunt's small shoulders and feel a pang at how narrow they've gotten over the years. I hate recognizing that the women who helped raise me are aging, even though I know to age is an honor. I just wish it didn't remind me that time is passing. "Of course, Auntie." I pull her against me, and she runs her fingers loosely through the braids down my back, patting my spine here and there as she goes.

"You know," Hazel says after a quiet moment, "some of these aren't for Alice."

I frown and pull away from her. "What do you mean?" I look at the handful of things cooling on her stove in small pots or covered jars, sides still foggy from their heated liquid contents. Wonder which one of these was brewed for someone else in the community, or as a reinforcing tincture for her wife's aura readings, or . . .

Hazel pats my hand and holds it in her own as she comes around to face me. "Look closely."

I stare down at the table until I see it—a leather pouch hidden by a few scraps of dried thyme. "Is that—"

"Mm-hmm," Hazel hums, and picks up the pouch. "Lu left it with me for a cleansing. After I'm done with it in here, I'll let the moon and some black tourmaline do the rest. Set it out in the yard overnight."

I hesitate, fingers itching to touch the leather. "Can I . . . ?"

Hazel tugs open the straps around the worn leather bag. "Palms."

I present both palms, cupped together, over the table and hold my breath when Hazel spills the talisman of the Grand Dame into my waiting hands. It sends an electric bolt from my hands, up my elbows, to the base of my skull, just like it did the first time I held it.

We call the stone at the center "the Heart."

My Aunt Lu wears the Heart only for special occasions, not for her regular aura work at the Crossroads. Ceremonial stuff, home blessings, new births, that type of thing—and any time she has to face another Dame from another territory. Anyone from any Rootcrafter community can recognize a Dame by her energy, her glow, but if that isn't enough, this talisman'll do the trick.

Aunt Lu's Heart is a large stone set in a dark gold disc about three inches in diameter. Every Dame talisman has a stone for protection and strength, two pillars of Rootcrafter practices everywhere. But lots of stones and herbs and materials can represent those pillars. It's the center stone the reminds us of what the ancestor who set the piece had in their heart at the time of the setting. In this case, Lu's Heart is a smooth brown onyx—for grounding, regeneration, and, most importantly, intuition.

"'Intuition is just a fancy word for gut instincts,'" I murmur, remembering what Lu told me the first time she showed me the Heart.

"'And instinct is blood knowledge,'" Hazel finishes with a smile. "'Knowledge from your bones, passed down through time.'"

I hold the Heart up between my forefinger and thumb. "Don't tell me she preaches about this thing to you, too."

Hazel chuckles. "She used that line on our first date."

I roll my eyes. "Using root to catch a pretty girl's attention?" I pass my thumb over the stone—cold and still and quiet. "Sounds like Aunt Lu."

Hazel bumps my shoulder. "I'll tell her you said that." She holds her palm up, and I pass the Heart back. She slips the Heart back into its pouch. "I've been thinking . . . ," she begins.

"Uh-oh," I say reflexively, smirking.

"Hush." She grins. "I've been thinking about what we can do for Alice, since nothing else I've tried has worked." She peers up at me with curious eyes. "Thinking it might be something *you* need to do instead."

I blink, startled. "What can I do for her? I'm no healer. I deal with folks who're already dead, and Alice is still alive."

Hazel presses her lips into a thin line. "Thing is—"

The crunch of gravel interrupts her, and we both glance at the front door. "Expecting somebody, Aunt Hazel?" The heavy thump of bass coming from the car in the driveway is too crisp and precise. "Valechaz?"

"He said he'd stop by." Hazel frowns. "Listen, Mariah, I do want to try something with you. With the herbs?"

"Hold that thought." I squeeze Hazel's hand before walking to the glass front door to see an expensive-looking SUV roll to a stop in the driveway.

Valec steps out of the car in glistening leather boots, wearing a pair of deep burgundy slacks and a matching jacket. He's on the phone, talking to someone while nodding. He glances up at me through the glass, and something in his expression gives me pause. I feel my brows tighten, and he looks away, turning so that his voice is even more muffled while he faces back toward the driveway. He's a *hiding* type of man today, I see.

Hazel hums behind me. "That boy is up to something."

"You read my mind."

Valec has been digging into his *particularly* underground network for the past few weeks to look for a lead on Bree. Asking about the Hunter without alarming the local population of magic users is easier said than done, though. If someone hasn't heard of the Hunter, then hearing about him from Valec draws suspicion. If they *do* know who he is, then they know plenty enough to fear any mention of his name. I wonder if Valec's found something concrete that we can use.

While I'm waiting for Valec to end his call and come inside, another car rounds the corner. I know without seeing the driver who it is, and from Valec's audible groan, so does he. The way the driver pulls in, the way he takes the turn at the end of the drive . . . Only one family member drives like that.

"Aunt Hazel!" I call. "Emil's here, and he's pissed!"

Hazel's head appears from around the kitchen corner. "He better not bring mess to my house."

"Looks like he tryin' to," I mutter.

We got a lot of family in this area. There's Harper and Birdie Wyatt, play cousins who I used to ride to elementary school with. Gail and Ernestine Blevins, sisters who can sing like nobody's business and who used to always get the soprano solos in the youth choir at Clarion Baptist. And then there's my first cousin Emil.

The second car, a red SUV with a restaurant logo on the side, slams to a stop right by Valec, making the cambion jump out of the way. When the door opens, a tall, chestnut-brown-skinned man emerges wearing jeans and a light black jacket. Emil nods at me, then clears his throat. Valec says, "I gotta go," and hangs up, slipping his phone into his breast pocket. "Hello to you too, Emil."

"Valechaz." Emil is an Earthmover. He's older than me by a decade and nice enough, but like a lot of folks in the family, a little standoffish with Valechaz.

Valec dips his chin cordially. "How's the restaurant?"

Emil lifts a shoulder. "It's the slow season." Emil owns a soul food joint in downtown Clayton. Caters some too. His greens are the only greens other than my Aunt Hazel's that Auntie Lu will touch; it's the turkey neck he simmers right there with 'em for hours.

I open the door and step out onto the porch just in time to see Emil fix Valec with a glare. "What are you doing here, Valechaz?"

Valec crosses his arms over his chest. "Visiting my niece-in-law. How 'bout you?"

"Need a mojo bag," Emil mutters. "A blessing. Not something you use down at the Lounge, I expect."

"We use blessings just like anybody else. Different kinds for different folks," Valec replies. "You seem agitated, Emil. What's your problem?"

Emil slams the door. "You know damn well that you shouldn't bring your business into their home."

"I don't bring Crossroads business into *anybody's* home." Valec leans back against the door of his car, voice taking on that slow quality that sounds like he's being casual—but means the exact opposite. "And if I did, why would that be a problem?"

"Cuz it's winter. The veil is thin. The highway between the dead and the living is too open." Emil circles his car to face Valec, dragging his hand through the air as he goes. Golden root trails from his fingertips, leaving a long stream of five threads floating in the air behind him. Emil must have called on an ancestor recently if he's able to manipulate root that easily. Twine it around his fingers like a glowing ribbon. "And you don't need to be around all that root."

"I'm a cambion. Half human." Valec sighs loudly through his nose. "I don't go 'round *consuming* root, Emil. I don't go after it like the greater demons, because I don't need it to survive. Don't know how many times I have to tell you this—"

"But you can still *crave* it," Emil counters. "You could go over the edge, and then what?"

Valec straightens, and a scowl mars his expression. "I'm not some Shadowborn animal out of control." He nods at Emil's still-glowing hand. "All that root you're swimming in? I See it everywhere, all the time. All that root you're accusing *me* of being hungry for"—he points at the gold in the air, fangs showing as he lowers his voice dangerously—"*that* root? That's your ancestors *giving* you access to it. Which means that's *my* ancestors and *my* descendants being real generous by powering you up. *My* people, long before they were yours, you arrogant, ignorant *child*."

Emil clenches his fist, and the root goes with it. "You know who else're your people? That demon who hunts Rootcrafters for sport and food."

Valec rolls his eyes. "I ain't the Hunter, man."

"Don't 'man' me," Emil snaps. "There have been disappearances."

Valec's brows draw tight. "What disappearances?"

"Whatcha talking about, Emil?" I call out.

"Rootcrafter girls gone missing," he says loudly. "Didn't make the news."

"Never does," Valec says. "Which girls?"

"A Wyatt girl. Shieldmaker." He glances up to me. "A Richardson, about Mariah's age. Wayfinder. Another girl from a state over. Her daddy came by the restaurant asking if we'd heard anything."

"Her branch?" I ask quietly.

"Wildcrafter."

Valec's eyes slide to mine, and I know he's thinking the same thing as me. The same thing I say next. "Three different branches of root. Different levels of power. Different types of offerings made, different ancestors, different families."

"Mm-hmm." Emil nods, and his attention returns to Valec.

"Any of them make it back?" Valec asks. "Sometimes, they—"

"Still missing." A pause. "Don't suppose you know anything about all this?"

"I heard the Hunter was afoot months ago. Sent out warnings to the community but"—Valec bares his teeth—"didn't know he'd already been taking folks. Like he's powering up for something big—or draining himself quick on something bigger. I'll check with my network. Thanks for letting me know—"

"How do we know it ain't *you?*" Emil says, pointing.

Valec rolls his eyes. "What am *I* gonna do with Rootcrafters? I got plenty of my own power. 'Sides, I been saving 'Crafters on our railroad, moving 'Crafters from station to station, since before your grandaddy could blow a spit bubble. It ain't me, Emil."

Emil steps closer to Valec until he's well within striking distance for a human, much less a cambion. Valec's fingers twitch at his sides. "Was all that rescuing done before or after you used to . . . indulge?"

Valec goes stone-still—like the air has frozen in his lungs.

"Emil Verne Richardson!" Aunt Hazel's voice is shaking as she pushes around me to stand at the railing on the porch. Her fingers clench the wood so tightly, her brown knuckles turn pale.

Emil gives Valec a final smirk before turning away and walking toward the porch. "I'm sorry you had to see that, Auntie."

"I'm not," Hazel spits. Her shoulders tremble with the effort of staying upright, and I step forward to place a hand against her back. "I'm glad I saw just how nasty and mean-spirited you can be. You will get *off* my property. Right now."

Emil flinches. "*Auntie—*"

"No, sir," Hazel says. She glares at him and points one finger over his shoulder, back to his car. "You ain't bringing all that ugly into *my* house. We got a girl here, resting. This is a place of healing, and you are poisoning my well."

Emil's eyes flutter at Hazel's voice, lower and more stern than I've ever heard it. Of my two aunts, Lu is the one likely to bite someone's head off, but Emil has crossed a line today. I spread my hand out over Hazel's spine, pressing my fortitude right into her if she needs it. Just like she does to me when I need it.

Sometimes you need another voice to press itself into you and remind you that you're right to say the scary thing, even if that scary thing is absolutely true.

"Go." Hazel's tone brooks no argument.

"But—"

"*Go*, Emil," I echo my aunt, stepping forward to be level with her. "And don't come back 'til we send for you."

The Grand Dame community is a matriarchal one; Emil is outnumbered and outgunned, and he knows it. He still looks like he's eaten a rotten grape, though. He swallows and nods once to signal his understanding, then bows his head before turning on his heel and getting back into his car. He reverses, gravel kicking dirt in Valechaz's face, and pulls a three-point turn in the driveway before speeding off.

We wait a long moment before Valec moves, blowing out a puff of air in a long stream.

"You didn't have to say all that on my account, Hazel." He turns slowly to look at us up on the porch, skin pulled tight around his deep brown eyes. "I had him on the ropes."

Hazel releases her own ragged breath, the tension flooding out of her back beneath my fingers. "I know you did."

Valec pushes off the car door smoothly to walk in our direction. When he reaches the step, he comes to a stop and wraps a hand around Hazel's elbow wordlessly. She leans forward to drop a kiss on his forehead, lingering to press her love in good. "Come on, now. You're all right."

Valec smiles and straightens, releasing her. "I know I am." His eyes sparkle, but the light is duller than usual. "Thank you, anyway."

Hazel waves her hand at him and shuffles back inside. "Interrupted my brewing," she says without an ounce of irritation.

Valec and I watch her go inside. The glass door bounces against the doorjamb in the quiet morning. I pull my sweater around my shoulders and shiver in the January mountain air. I turn back to find Valec studying me. Waiting, I suspect.

So I just ask it right out. "What'd Emil mean by that? You . . . 'indulging'?"

Valec sniffs, shoving his hands in both his pockets, searching for the words as his gaze sweeps around the porch, the yard, the sky overhead. "I been around a long time, Riah."

"Yeah, I know," I mutter.

"Long enough to have made plenty of mistakes." He shrugs. "Long enough to realize I need to make amends for them too."

"Is that what you do at the Lounge when you broker all those deals between humans and demons?" I ask quietly. "You makin' amends?"

"It's a start."

I release a low laugh, part confusion and part awe. "You been running the Lounge for over eighty years."

Valec holds my gaze for a beat. "Like I said, baby cousin. It's a start."

11

Mariah

HAZEL GATHERS US all in Alice's room, to my surprise. "Thank you for coming, Valechaz. I need both of y'all for this experiment."

"Experiment? I thought you came to visit Aunt Hazel," I say to Valec.

He tucks his chin as he regards Hazel. "That's what I was told. You keepin' secrets, Hazel?"

"It's no secret; it's just . . . an experiment. I have a theory. Theories require testin'," Hazel says, sitting at the foot of Alice's bed, settling in like she's at a lectern and not resting on a quilt in a country home. She looks between us where we stand in the doorway and waves us inside.

Valec eases forward, brow pinched. "What can I do? I'm no healer."

"No." She taps her own nose softly. "But you can pick up on things that I can't."

"Like?"

Hazel beckons Valec over. "Can you get close enough to Alice to check something for me? Kneel down?"

Valec eases to his knees on the floor in a liquid motion, shuffling forward to sit by Alice's bedside. "Sure, Hazel, but—"

"Let me know what you scent from her skin."

Valec and I exchange confused glances. I shrug, and he looks back. "All right." He gently lifts Alice's arm from where it rests across her belly and brings her limp hand to his face. He raises his eyes to Hazel, and she nods encouragingly before he dips his nose to the back of Alice's hand. He closes his eyes and inhales—and his spine stiffens immediately. His eyes snap open, red and bright, jaw slack. "She's . . . she's not all the way here, Hazel."

Hazel nods. "Thought as much."

"Wait," I say. "What does that mean, 'she's not all the way here'?"

Valec takes another long draw of Alice's hand and then nods, placing it on the bed at her hip. "She's alive but . . . not. She doesn't smell like decay; it's more like . . . she's not quite living, not quite dead. I don't understand."

"I think Ms. Chen is caught," Hazel says slowly. "Close to death but not in its clutches. That is why my acquired skill with herbs and tinctures and even my entire branch of Magnifier root are not effective."

"You can't help her, because your branch of root focuses on the life force of the living, the *truly* living." Valec stands gracefully, tapping his chin. "Makes sense—you can't really treat me or other demons. Too much death in us."

"You're not dead," I protest. "I *know* what death feels like."

Valec smiles, a note of appreciation mixed with reassurance on his brow. "I hold more death in my makeup than most, but you're right that I'm not dead. Not at my core. Goruchel, on the other hand? They're a form of undead. It's why they have to steal the life from the humans they impersonate. Full demons are not of the plane of the living."

"My theory is that Alice is trapped between two worlds," Hazel adds with a sigh, "and that she might smell like a goruchel in that way, even though she is human. My diagnosis is that she is in limbo."

"Isn't that what all comas are?" I ask tentatively.

"No," Hazel says. "A healer like William would identify this as a coma, but someone who works with the dead the way we do would know the difference. Which is where you come in, Mariah."

"Me?"

"Yes," Hazel says. "A Medium walks the path between the living and the dead. She bridges the two naturally. She can see the connections. *You* can see them. A rare gift."

I gape at her, my mouth opening and closing. Mediums are rare Rootcrafters but not unheard of. *Bree Matthews* is a rare Medium, special even among Mediums. What I do lets me connect other living people to death, not connect people in limbo to *themselves*.

I feel inadequate and bare beneath Hazel's gaze.

"I don't know, Auntie," I whisper. "Bree can actually walk the ancestral plane and talk to the dead—"

"The powerhouse ain't here, Riah." At the mention of Bree's name, Valec's jaw clenched, and he turned away. "And Alice ain't dead."

"Mariah." Hazel shakes her head. "Alice needs our help *now*, baby. I don't know what's happening to her life force, but what little I have sensed has grown weaker since we took her in. You can see the connections between *others'* lives and their brushes with death. We need *your* specialty here, Mariah, not Bree's."

I shake my head slowly. "I don't know. . . ."

Hazel purses her lips. "It's up to you, of course."

"No, it ain't!" Valec interjects, scoffing. His eyes are still crimson, flashing against his brown skin. "We all agreed to take Alice in for her sake, but we did it for Bree, too, who might be facing the Hunter right now. All on her own. Facing *our* biggest threat, next to the Order itself. Might even be foolishly thinking she can win against him, because we"—he swallows, shaking his head—"because *I* told her about him. And me and Lu asked her to take on our boogeyman."

Hazel sighs. "Bree inherited great power, but she also inherited a haunting—several, really. From Arthur, the Order, the Hunter. And she inherited her own maternal ancestors' well-founded fears about them all. Her path was always going to intersect with the Hunter's, Valechaz. . . ."

"Bree would do this for one of us. You know she would!" He thrusts a hand toward the sleeping girl. "Helping Alice is . . . is . . . *balance*—"

"Valechaz! You forget yourself!" Hazel says sharply. "No 'Crafter has to do a single thing against her will."

Valec bows his head, his red eyes shifting to brown and back, then brown again.

"No, he's . . . he's right," I say quietly. "Bree would do it for any one of us, without question."

A smirk tugs at Valec's lips, barely visible beneath his bowed head. "Damn straight she would."

I push my glasses up on my nose and take a breath. "What do you need me to do?"

Hazel studies me for a moment, then nods and stands. She wipes her hands on her apron and heads for the door and the kitchen beyond. "I got something for you to drink."

"I can do that," I say to her as much as to myself. Valec tilts his head to eye me. "I can drink something; that's easy—"

"It's not gonna taste good," Hazel shouts back. "Gonna be pretty bad, in fact."

"Oh." I frown. "Well, that's okay—"

"Valec, move the second bed close to Alice for me, please!"

I blink as Valec blurs into motion. "The bed?" I call to Hazel, concerned. "Why do you need *a bed*?"

"Don't need to know the plan to know the extra bed's not for her," Valec says as he gets both hands up under the twin bed frame and lifts it easily, setting it down beside Alice like it weighs nothing. "It's for you."

The forest is filled with ancient trees. They tower over me, their canopy higher than my eyes can see and dense enough that light from the full moon has to claw its way down to the earth. The ground ahead of me is bathed in shimmering blue, gray, and silver, like the sheen of oil atop Hazel's root-enhanced tea.

The effects of Hazel's tea had hit me before I could properly settle onto the covers of the bed beside Alice's sleeping body. I'd fallen after the third sip and felt Valec catch me and lower me to the mattress. Thank goodness for cambion speed.

Pungent, rich flavors. Earth and fire and air elemental scents. The taste of the tea lives at the back of my throat and floods my nostrils, even here—cinnamon for a power boost, cypress for its ties to the dead, sweet cicely for spiritual connection, patchouli and parsley to strengthen my own Medium abilities.

When I look down at myself, I am wearing a heavy black gown with a tight bodice that I'd normally never pick out for myself. Definitely not something in my closet. Black boots strapped against my shins feel like leather cages around my legs. But I march forward, compelled to move ahead. I move as one does in the unknown dark, swiftly toward the light and away from the shadows.

A small hill sits up ahead in a clearing. Crowded at its base are wild, curving roots that arc like black snakes, twisting up and around themselves as if to restrain the hill from growing any wider or higher. I look to the left for a path around the curled mass and, seeing none, walk quickly to the right.

Nothing there either.

I'll have to climb the twisted mass to move forward. And forward is the only option. I can't turn back. Something deep inside stops me from even turning my head to look over my shoulder. So. *Forward.* I lift a heeled boot toward the first thick briars rising from the ground and hear the crunch of dead leaves as I step.

It is as if that first step triggers a release from the forest, as if the dark woods have been waiting.

"Wind" is really not the best word for what surrounds me now, whipping the skirts of my dress and pressing the thick fabric against the backs of my thighs. It picks up behind me too, blowing my braids across my eyes. This force isn't wind at all but a powerful mist, damp and black and reeking of mold. The darkness soaks me, plastering my hair against my cheeks and throat.

I scramble forward frantically, clawing at the brambles, but the heels on the ridiculous boots slip through the open gaps. The thicker roots make for easy handholds, but moving quickly means they tear the palms of my hands. The higher I climb, the greater the swirling force at my back bites at my spine and neck. The stench makes me dizzy.

In the distance, a howl pierces the air.

It begins as a single high-pitched call that sounds nearly like laughter. The sound whips around my head in stereo, starting from the right, crossing my face, and continuing around my left shoulder, then fading. On the second pass, the laughing sound seeps into my body like water into a sponge, settling into the deep space behind my heart, quickening my breath.

Then the sound doubles. And triples. A pack of hounds is near.

I make it to the top of the hill and have just caught my balance when the dark mist circles me again, rotating in faster and tighter rings—and I recognize it for what it is.

This is Alice's death. Howling at my back. Clamoring for my attention. Seducing me away from the light.

Valec didn't smell decay on Alice in the real world, but it is here. Cloying and thick and eager.

Then, I see Alice.

She is dressed as I saw her when we were last at Volition. Jeans, a longsleeved shirt, her iron knuckles looped around her right hand. But there are shadowy figures around her, and her left hand is held high, a small black device clenched in her fist.

The figures around her are still, like statues—mid-step, mid-flight, and mid-strike. It's only when I recognize those figures for who they are—the Mageguard—that I understand what I'm seeing.

Alice isn't just frozen in stasis in the real world. She's frozen here, too, in a *moment* from the battle at Volition.

I clamber down the hill, holding my skirts up high, and shout for her. "Alice!"

She doesn't move.

"Alice!" I try again. I reach the bottom of the hill, breathless, still yelling for her attention, but she does not respond to my voice.

This is not my ancestral plane or Alice's, not a place where she is in communion with her ancestors, but a precipice. A type of purgatory. Half in, half out, like Valec said.

By the time I reach the level ground of Volition, I see Bree-Arthur in their own fighting stance. Bree's face, a grim and determined expression, and aether armor are all in full color, and so is Selwyn Kane, caught leaping in the air. The people we harbored at Volition are drenched in color while the Mageguard are a dark, muted gray and indistinguishable from one another. Even the leader of the Mageguard, Erebus Varelian, Selwyn's opponent, is nothing but a dark shadow against the early morning light of this captured moment.

The hounds outside the valley yip and howl. They sound as if they're circling. Or waiting.

"Alice?" I whisper. Her eyelids flutter, and she squeezes the black device. The sound of it reanimates the shadowed Merlins. The supersonic weapon Alice had held that day lasted ten seconds, but here it lasts twice as long.

The pain drives all but Erebus to the ground, just as it did that day. Selwyn has fallen, curled into a ball with his hands clasped to his bleeding ears. Alice tosses the weapon and jerks forward, moving as if through thick, invisible liquid, each step silent as she approaches Selwyn's prone body. Behind her, I see the Volition barrier open—and see my own image step through. See my mouth wide and shouting at her.

I remember what I'd said in those frantic seconds. *Hurry. Hurry!*

Alice heaves Selwyn up. He's too heavy.

Erebus trains his sights on them both.

I watch myself watch it all, as helpless now as I was then.

Bree-Arthur dashes forward to intercept Erebus's attack, punching him into the shining Volition barrier. Bree-Arthur stands panting, watching their foe fall to the earth.

I know what happens next.

Alice reaches for her friend, relief written on her face—and Bree-Arthur reacts without looking, throwing Alice into the van.

The sound echoes here—the crack and crunch of bone hitting metal.

"ALICE!" Bree-Arthur yells, and the echo goes on and on and on. Spiraling high in this valley that Alice has created, louder and louder—

Until the scene resets.

Alice stands in the middle of the fray, hand held high, eyes darting over the scene. This time, she triggers the sonic weapon and runs as it blares. The Merlins go down. Selwyn, on the ground. Erebus sees her, moves before Bree-Arthur can react, conjures a blade that slices her belly open.

The scene resets.

Alice stands before the barrier, hesitating. Eyes moving as if calculating her odds. Like the memory of this moment is a chessboard, and she is devising a new strategy before she ever moves her pieces.

My heart twists.

I don't know if any Medium has ever witnessed someone negotiate their own death.

"Oh, Alice . . ."

At my quiet whisper, Alice's eyes turn to meet mine. Her dark eyes are red-rimmed and frustrated. She shakes her head. Her voice reaches me through gritted teeth. "One more time."

I don't know what to say. Don't know how to tell her that it's already happened. That the only way forward is to leave.

She looks back at the scene. "One more time—"

And I am thrown back into my body.

Mariah

I GASP AWAKE. It must be night now. The lamplit guest room replaces the forest trees. Beneath me is the well-worn quilt that always drapes this bed. Beside me, in the next bed over, is Alice Chen, her skin wan and thin. She inhales deeply, a shudder wracks her body, and then she lets the breath go. A wisp of silver-blue aether rises from her mouth, illuminating the darkened room.

"It didn't work," I rasp, my voice barely a whisper. But aside from Alice, the room is empty. No one is there to answer. Instead, I hear raised muffled voices from the other side of the closed door.

I move to sit up, stand, make my way over to the door—and the world blurs. Not sure whether that's the aftereffect of finding Alice in the place between life and death . . . or the aftereffect of Hazel's awful tea. My mouth tastes like I just licked the floor of the Crossroads Lounge. Not a clean section either—somewhere sticky and dusty that never sees daylight.

"Are you out of your mind?" My Aunt Lu's screech straightens my spine, sets my ears to attention, and clears the lingering mist from my thoughts. She must have gotten home while I slept, but the only person she speaks to like that is Valec—

"Lucille . . ." I hear Valec's low voice in response. He follows her name with a couple of sentences I can't quite make out, but said in that drawl he uses on new customers at the Lounge—the human ones with deep pockets who want to be charmed by a cambion. Evidently Aunt Lu knows that voice too and doesn't like it one bit.

"Don't you dare try to butter me up about this, Valechaz!" Aunt Lu says sharply. "It won't work on me. I am not a customer! Or one of your little friends."

Valec snorts. "Lu, come on."

"No."

"It's not even right away. I gotta set it up, so give me a few weeks to confirm. Then, it's just one night, a few hours. Three, tops—"

"No!"

My Aunt Lu and Valec are more alike than not. They bicker all the time. Argue over how things are run at the Lounge. Argue over what services to offer. Nothing they don't get over the next day. But Valec's not giving up. "Come on, now. I'll do all the talking! You know I will—"

"You're gonna have to find another way." I can just imagine my Aunt Lu shaking her head. "It's bad enough you're considering going there yourself. What if—"

Going where? I shift to sit upright, but the dizziness falls over me again like two heavy hands pushing my shoulders back into the mattress. What are they even talking about?

"I'll be all right, Lu," Valec says in a low voice. "You know I'm fine."

"Now!" Lu corrects. "You're fine *now*! *Right* now."

Valec's voice is stilted. Hollow. "You sound like Emil."

"Emil don't like you because Emil don't know any better," Lu corrects. "Right at this moment? I don't like you because I know you plenty."

"Aw, Lu—"

"Don't 'aw, Lu' me, Valechaz. That's my final answer."

"Lucille . . . ," Valec protests. I hear my Aunt Lu's house shoes shuffle across the floor, pass the guest room door, and then on to the bedroom.

A beat of silence.

"Hazel."

It's not until Valec voices her name that I realize my Aunt Hazel was still out-side in the kitchen. Had she, like me, just been listening? Or did this argument, whatever it's about, involve her, too? "She's set on this," Hazel says with a sigh. "She's not gonna budge."

"Talk to her?"

"Not this time, Valechaz. This is between y'all, not me."

Silence again. Hazel's step is lighter than Lu's, so her feet are a whisper. If I know her, she's probably moved over to give Valec a hug before bidding him good night. The mumbled "Thanks, Hazel" from Valec confirms my guess.

"Check on Mariah before you go, please," Hazel says. "She was still under about a half hour ago, but she should be coming up soon. Come get me if she doesn't wake in an hour."

"Yes, ma'am," Valec mutters.

A few seconds later, I hear Hazel and Lu's bedroom door open and close again. My mental clock is a bit off, but based on the quiet outside the window, I'd guess it's close to ten p.m. and past their bedtime.

I swallow, waiting, then realize that I won't hear a thing unless Valec decides to make some noise. Cambion feet and all. I can't quite move yet, but I don't need to move to get his attention; all I have to do is murmur, "I'm awake."

A second later and he's at the door, opening it without knocking. "Hey, there." He flows into the room, shutting the door behind him with a whisper of a click. The usual evening cloud of golden aether has swirled inside, gathered around his ankles and knees—drawn to him without his needing to call it close. "How do you feel?"

"Wrecked," I answer. Valec sits on the edge of my bed, between me and Alice.

He puts a warm hand against my forehead, and I brush it away. "You run so hot, how can you even tell if I'm feverish?"

He chuckles. "More worried you'd be cold than hot. That tea knocked you right out, sent you to sleep in a strange way. Your lips turned blue."

I bring a hand up to my mouth and frown. "Oh." I try to sit up a third time, and he blurs to my side before I can move.

"Easy." He helps me lean against the headboard.

I blink, expecting fatigue to draw me back to horizontal, but I don't feel tired. I feel restless. Disturbed. Worried.

"What'd you see in there?"

I try to put my experience with Alice into words but struggle to. After a moment, I ask him a question instead of trying to answer his. "Why're you fighting with Lu?"

He raises a brow. "You first."

I try again. "Alice is in there," I whisper, "still alive."

"Doing what?"

I remember the hounds, the forest, the woods. Bree-Arthur. "Running through the scenario where she was hurt over and over again."

"Why?"

I look up at him. "I think . . . she's trying to figure out if she could have changed something?"

Valec releases a sigh. "That type of thinking won't get you far. A person could get lost in it. Never come out."

I look back at Alice. Watch another swirl of smoky mage flame climb to the ceiling from her parted lips. "I don't know how long she'll last, but I think . . . I think she's running out of time. Death is ready for her. It just doesn't have her yet."

Valec's eyes narrow. "Suppose we should call William?"

"No," I say, straightening. "She's still fighting it. The clock is ticking, but Alice Chen has found a way to slow it down."

Valec cracks a smile. "Powerhouse's clever friend. Smart girl. Observant girl. I don't doubt that she's found a way to hold death at bay."

Valec taps his fore and middle fingers against his thigh as if he's thinking about something.

"You gonna tell me now?" I ask.

"How much did you hear?"

"Enough to know you want Lu to do something she doesn't wanna do, and Hazel doesn't think she'll budge on it. And something about you going somewhere dangerous."

Valec tilts his head back and forth in a gentle protest. "Not dangerous to me, personally. Probably."

"Valec." I thump his shoulder. "What the hell does that mean?"

"I'd never let anything happen to Lu," he says cryptically. "But it's not the best sort of . . . context."

I don't like the way he keeps tapping his fingers on his thigh. "What's going on? Does this have to do with Bree?"

"Yep." Valec tongues a fang. "I got an idea, but it's not a good one. It's a bad one, in fact." He runs a hand down his face. "But if it works, it'll get us some answers and quick."

"*Valec,*" I repeat.

"No." He groans. "This is too risky. Lu's right to wanna skin me for asking her this." He stands up. Walks away. "*I* should skin me, to be honest—"

"Valec!" I whisper-shout. "Tell me."

He paces back to me and swipes his tongue over his lower lip. "There's a . . . place. A spot where demons gather. If I go on my own, I'll look like a threat. If I go with the Grand Dame, it's more . . . political. Like an ambassador paying another country a visit."

I straighten. "What kinda place? Where is it?"

He holds a hand up as if to say, *Slow down*. "Like I said, it's just a lead. Bringing her in is dangerous, but if I don't, *I* won't be able to step a foot in the door."

"Whose door?" I ask, impatient.

Valec fixes me with a long stare, mouth twisting sourly. "You ever heard of Nightshades?"

I squint. "The fruits?"

He glares at me. "No, Riah, not the damn fruits. Goruchel. Powerful ones. Members of the Shadow Court."

The hairs on the back of my neck rise. "You told us about that at the Lounge. You said they're locked away on the other side."

He winces. "I said it was a *rumor*, which it is—"

"They're not locked away?" My eyes widen. "You said—"

"I said 'allegedly'!" He raises his hands in defense. "That gets me off the hook, I think—"

"Valechaz!" I screech.

"You sound just like your auntie." He turns away with a grimace. "I don't need to get yelled at by two generations in one night. Come on, now—"

"The court of demons is real?"

"Of course it's real!" He thrusts a hand out, sputtering. "I couldn't confirm the truth with a damn Merlin sitting in the room, Mariah! It's always better to let the Order think they know everything; you know that."

"Not if it means we're all gonna get eaten!" I hiss.

Valec scoffs. "The Nightshades of the Shadow Court found a way out hundreds of years ago, most of them, but without leadership they scattered. Legend has it that long ago they had a king who united them, but he perished at the hands of the original Merlin. After that, some went renegade. Rebelled against the Court. If any Shades wanted to eat 'all' of humanity, they'd have already figured out a way to do it. That's not what they're up to."

"Well, what are they up to, then?"

His head tilts back and forth again. "Various . . . things."

"Sounds like illegal things. Dangerous things," I say, crossing my arms.

"I prefer to stay out of their way, let's just say that. But they know things too. Things I *can't* know. They each have little fiefdoms nowadays. Mini courts of their own. There's one who . . ." He stills, then shuts his eyes. "I can't ask for help at a distance. You have to go there. Pay tribute on a certain day of the month when they're open to supplicants."

Valec doesn't get nervous. I've never seen him fidget or stutter. But something about Bree being gone has set him on edge . . . and now this Shadow Court business has him looking apprehensive and unmoored in a way that I've never witnessed.

"And if Lu goes there, it'll make it safer?"

Valec opens his eyes. "If *I* want to walk back out alive, then, yeah, I need the

Grand Dame. A party a Shade won't cross, whose presence erases the chance that my move is a territorial one. Ensures I appear as benign as possible."

Aunt Lu is hard-headed. If stubborn had levels, she'd be an eleven out of ten.

I glance at Alice and remember her repeated efforts to change her fate, even at death's door. Alice, who wasn't born into magic the way Bree and I were, and who, by sheer will, is keeping herself tethered to the world of the living. She's an eleven out of ten too.

I gnaw on my lip for a moment, an idea and a decision both floating before my eyes. Swirling together, weaving in and out of each other's tendrils like the golden aether mist still writhing around Valec's legs.

"What's that look on your face?" Valec asks. "I don't know if I like it."

I don't answer him. Instead, I stare at the door and imagine the kitchen counter on the other side where Hazel has been working for eight weeks straight to heal a girl she barely knows, because it's the right thing to do. Because she's stubborn as hell too.

The women around me are all in the business of throwing themselves at the wall, again and again, until it breaks—or molds itself in their images. It's a type of impatient living that I've never dared try.

Bree Matthews doesn't wait until she's ready to act, and her ancestors believe in her. They have faith in her. Maybe I shouldn't wait either.

Maybe it's not about having the answer, but making yourself the answer.

"Not having a plan but *becoming* the plan," I murmur.

"Say what?" Valec asks.

"Has Aunt Lu ever been to this fief before?" I ask.

Valec tosses his head a little, jarred at my sharp turn. "No, she's never been. And you heard her. She never will. It was a long shot to even ask."

"So they don't know what the Grand Dame of the Southeastern territory looks like," I say, keeping my voice curious and light.

Valec blinks. "What? No, they don't . . ." He follows my gaze to the door and the kitchen beyond—and to the onyx talisman quietly resting on the counter-top in its bag. *"No."*

"You said a few weeks to confirm a date, right?"

Valec turns back to me. "No."

I wiggle my toes experimentally, stretch my arms overhead. "I'll test it first. Make sure I'm good to bear it, of course, but I think I will be because Aunt Lu and I are blood related—"

"Mariah," Valec interrupts. "No."

I grin, abruptly thrilled at our switch in roles. "Valec. Yes."

"But—"

"You said Bree would do it for us," I counter, and his mouth snaps shut. "You're right. Bree Matthews would walk into a den of vipers if she thought she could save her friends."

"No offense, baby cousin," Valec says through gritted teeth, "but Bree Matthews can *handle* a den of vipers. You *can't*."

"Yes, I can," I argue, crossing my arms over my chest again, "if I'm the Grand Dame."

Natasia

AUDIO LOG—ENTRY #32

The original Merlin, a balanced cambion born from an incubus-and-human union, was also a demonologist and scholar. By all accounts, he was gifted with a keen sense of curiosity and a drive to enrich and enhance his natural abilities.

Over Merlin's long lifetime, he gained for himself three sorcerer abilities that did not seem to exist in other cambions of that era, those being the abilities to create constructs, cast mesmers, and deepen his natural affinities for aether.

Merlin was able to teach his human mage apprentice, the young Morgaine and half sister of Arthur, how to create constructs, but the other two abilities seemed beyond her reach and tied to his demonic heritage. While it is said that Morgaine could not wield all three abilities, Merlin's children could. And so he created his own version of the Legendborn Spell of Eternity to enshrine these abilities into his descendants' bloodlines, creating thousands of Merlins since who are born sorcerers, including myself and my son.

As imbalanced cambions with only slivers of demonic heritage, the descendants of Merlin appear human until we reach the age of seven and grow increasingly richer in our demonic traits as we grow older. Our strength and speed manifest first, alongside our heightened senses. Our connection to aether, what some call "aether sense," grows deeper with every year, just as every year our humanity seemingly slips away.

In addition to embedding his three unique sorcerer abilities within his version of the Spell, Merlin embedded what he believed was a therapeutic measure for his descendants——the practice of magical Oaths.

When we Merlins administer and act in service to our Oaths to the Order, it slows our inevitable descents into demonia. The Oaths tie us to humanity on a cellular level, which counteracts our increasingly otherworldly natures. As long as we are in service, we are in control, but demonia, or "succumbing to the blood," as the Order calls it, is still expected to be every Merlin's eventual fate.

In my research, I have found that while it is true that the hierarchy of needs of an imbalanced cambion shifts toward baser demonic instincts——the hunger for negative human emotions, such as anger, fear, remorse, et cetera——I do not believe this so-called descent is inevitable.

Over the centuries, the Order has applied a layer of what I might call religious moral values to the progressive stages of an imbalanced cambion's "demonic" development. This externally applied ideology has made Merlin's descendants mutual participants in their own Oathings——and in their own eventual incarceration. We may progress in a way that the Order does not deem suitable, and certainly we may progress in a way that could harm the human beings around us if we are not properly supported, but what if we cast this progression as a naturally occurring development rather than a "succumbing"? What if "succumbing" is the language of those who most benefit from our ignorance about our own natures? I posit that even the term "demonic" is value neutral. I do not believe an overabundance of desires, impulses, and hungers is inherently immoral, but I do believe those drives do not fit the Order's grand design.

When studying balanced cambions, those beings born directly from concubi-human unions, what I have found most evident is that the more they embrace their demon natures, the more they eventually and truly exhibit the "balance" for which they are named.

Using Faye Matthews's generously shared knowledge of herbs and plants, I was eventually able to devise an experiment to prove my theory over many years of study and research. The result of this experiment was a . . . treatment? No. No, that's not the right word. That's what the Order would use to pathologize us. My experiment was . . . [A groan.] *An intervention? Yes. An intervention. One that was successfully self-administered amid my own so-called descent, and it has allowed me to maintain my humanity and my demonic strengths well into my fourth decade.*

However . . . when I attempt these same applications with my son, Selwyn . . . I . . . [Clears throat.] *I have found that when I attempt to assist my son—*

"It doesn't fucking work."

I release the button of my recorder, dropping it, and turn to Selwyn in a blur.

He sits on his bed in the back bedroom of my cabin, leaning against the wall in the darkness. It is past three a.m. "Selwyn, I . . . I'm sorry, I thought you were resting."

His eyes blink back at me from across the building, two red orbs glowing in the shadows. He does not respond. That, I expect. What surprises me most, and what has left me in shock now, is that he spoke at all.

I frown. "Is that *really* the first thing you say to me in *two* months? 'It doesn't fucking work'?"

The cabin is pitch-black. We can both see in the darkness, so I know he knows that I can see the glint of his fangs. A sardonic, sour grin in the night.

"Back to not talking?" I ask.

He slides down farther on his bed.

He has been drinking the herbal tonics after I explain what they are and what they should do. He seems emotionally stabilized by them, but his physical condition remains the same. The tonics should have reversed some of his hungers and their accompanying physical transformations so that we can attempt the next steps together. So that he can think as clearly as he needs to in order to make informed decisions about how to proceed.

But the tonics are *not* working—and his hungers and physical changes only continue to become more severe. It does not matter how much I feed him now; if his system wants to consume human pain instead, his body will continue to adapt to make that more possible. Soon, human food will not be enough.

He'll get stronger. He'll get faster. He'll be able to scent human misery from a distance—and manipulate a human in order to make their emotions worse. I am fortunate that so far, he hasn't seemed interested in leaving the house.

I've warded the perimeter so that no one can find us here, but not warded it to prevent his escape. I won't do that unless he proves to me that he needs to be restricted for his own safety—or for the safety of others. And even then . . . I hesitate.

I have been imprisoned. I do not wish to imprison my own son.

"I thought at first that speaking was painful, or that you'd been injured in some way," I say. "I was worried that Erebus had hurt you. Then I realized you were *choosing* silence."

His voice comes to me through the darkness, dry and bored. "I don't have anything to say to you."

I sigh. My eyes trail over the makeshift lab I have created in my dining room. "The tonics are not working yet, but that does not mean the Regents are right about us."

Sel stares, unmoved.

"If you heard me earlier, then you know I do not believe what the Regents believe. What Erebus believes." I pause, frowning. "Do you?"

This time, my son's silence is its own answer.

"You may think yourself to be the proof of their knowledge, but you are also proof of my negligence. I should have taught you what I suspected long before I left."

"I was five years old when they told me my mother died," Selwyn states, his voice a crackle of electric anger. "I grew up thinking you were killed on a mission. I thought you were *dead*."

My throat constricts. I knew this, but hearing it from him is another thing entirely. "I'm sorry. Your pain must have been . . . immense."

"And my father was so foolishly, hopelessly, *stubbornly* in love with you that he decided to get remarried—to his own grief."

I knew this, too, and it makes my heart clench. "He is a good man, and he deserves help."

"Did you know that at the academy I was *proud* that you had fallen in battle? That you had gone out fighting like some legendary warrior?" He huffs sourly. "But that was a lie, and I was a gullible little boy soldier."

"If I had told you more, taught you more—"

He scoffs. "Stop wishing for an imaginary son. He is not here. I am."

"I know that—"

"Maybe this imaginary son who knew how to resist his demonia—"

"Your demonia is *not* a failing to surpass—"

"Maybe the son who could resist his demonia is the son you didn't leave behind!" Selwyn snaps. "As it is, it is your *absence* that I have learned to overcome, Mother. You left. My demon didn't."

We stare at each other for a long, painful moment.

"You're right, Selwyn," I whisper. "I wasn't there for you, in many ways. But I am here now. You're right that my tonics aren't working as I'd hoped. But I am a sample of one. How things progressed for me is not necessarily how they will progress for you."

He stands in a blur of movement and is at the living room entrance in a second. His eyes narrow on my face, and if I were a different person, I might be frightened by his cold, stony glare. "Is that based on science or a wish?"

I'm the one who taught him that look in the first place, so it doesn't work at all.

"I have been doing other research, you know," I say idly, gesturing with my chin over to my desk and piles of papers and notes. "During the day, when I go out, I have been working the contacts in my . . . less savory networks to learn as much as I can about Martin Davis's death and the circumstances of your separation from Nicholas. If you're up to talking, perhaps you can fill me in? That might help me understand exactly what occurred to your Kingsmage Oath, how it happened, when it happened. It would be helpful to know if there are other variables at play here."

He leans against the doorjamb and waves his hand in an invitational half circle, as if to say, *Tell me what you've learned.*

I resent how much of my attitude this boy has inherited. Was I this arrogant?

I answer him anyway. "Well, I have learned that in my . . ." *In my grief.* That's what I want to say. In my terrible, harrowing, haunting grief for my friend, who I have missed so much of the last seven months.

I think of Faye. Her accident. The hospital. And then, her daughter. Young, in shock, and so very lost.

The last thing I want is for Faye's daughter to be caught up in the Order's interminable, vicious, ruthless war.

Selwyn clears his throat—shaking me from my thoughts.

"S-sorry," I stammer, frowning, "just lost my train of thought. What was I saying? Oh . . . I . . . um, as I have gone digging, I realized that I have missed much in the last seven months. I felt Martin's death but assumed that it was either by natural causes or because he had finally found a way to earn the valor he so desperately wanted. I had no idea that he had kidnapped his own son, that the Lines had been called, that Nicholas pulled Excalibur—"

"Nicholas did not pull Excalibur from its stone."

I blink up at him. "Excuse me?"

"You heard me."

He sighs, turning against the doorjamb to rest the top of his spine against it. He leans back, head against the wood, eyes closed. He snaps his green aether into existence in his palm, clawing the magic, feeling its shape, then releasing it.

"Selwyn—"

"Nicholas was never in line to be king," he mutters without looking at me. "And neither was his father."

I shake my head. "No, that's . . . that's not possible—"

One of his glowing red eyes peeks open. "We were, both of us, bonded to impostors. Unwitting impostors, but impostors all the same. And we've both suffered for their lies. Like mother, like son." He shifts, heading back to his room and away from our conversation.

"Wait!" I say, stepping forward. Resisting the urge to grab my son's shoulder, twist him around, demand more. "Who . . . who is the Scion of Arthur, then, if it's not Nick?"

He pauses. Turns his head over his shoulder, just far enough that I see the slow elongation of his mouth exposing a single fang to my view. It is a quiet, knowing gesture. One meant to mock and taunt me for what I do not know. For what I've missed.

But my son's smile stops my indignation short and steals the breath from my lungs, because it is not a smile I thought I would ever see on his face.

It is the smile of a starving dreamer, savoring an image he will not share.

It is the smile of a hunter, imagining his prey.

The taunting grin of a prowling demon who doesn't care for the kill, but craves the pursuit.

Does the very *thought* of this Scion of Arthur, this innocent person Called into our world's most powerful title, elicit such a . . . hungry response in him?

I find myself suddenly worried about this individual and what my son wishes to do with them once they are reunited. Does he want to serve them, protect them, *worship* them . . . or devour them whole?

Without another word, Selwyn turns and walks into his room, slamming the door shut behind him.

PART TWO

UNSTOPPABLE

14

Bree

THERE'S A DEMON flying above the businesswoman's head.

The woman is tall, white, dark-haired. Dressed in a long winter coat over a blue pantsuit with a nice bag on her shoulder. And she's talking on her earbuds, preoccupied by a phone call as she walks through downtown Asheville. She seems irritated, which I'm sure the demon loves. Its teeth gleam a bright green in the twilight. Its disproportionately wide mouth is open in an O shape as it sucks on her low, brewing anger while its black-tipped claws swipe at her hair.

An imp, playing with its food.

I'm so focused on following the streaming green aether flowing from its silver iridescent wings that I stumble over a raised brick in the Pack Square Park walking path and nearly face-plant down the middle. As it is, my low "humph" is enough to make her pause, start to pivot—and barely miss me as I dive behind a low stone pillar with a lamp on top.

I suck in my breath and release it silently while I wait for her to turn back and carry on the way she was going through the quickly darkening park.

It takes a second, but then she's moving again. I peek up and around the lamp to find the isel fluttering around her shoulders. It's gotten her scent now and will probably linger around her for days, feeding on the negative emotions she's carrying like an invisible parasite and amplifying them however it can to capture an easy meal.

"You gonna let it get away, or . . . ?" a smug, low voice says over my left shoulder. I jerk my elbow back, but Elijah is much too fast. I knew I wouldn't hit him anyway.

It's the thought that counts.

"*No*. I'm just not exactly sure how to"—I flap my hand, as if that'll help explain—"hunt a lesser demon *while* it's feeding off a moving human being."

Zoe appears at my other side, crouched low so I can see her face. "She's distracted. Typical human. Once she pauses, burn the crap out of it."

"What do you mean, 'typical human'?" I retort. "I'm human. *You're* half human."

"Yeah, exactly," Elijah says, pointing toward the other end of the park. "We just distracted *you*—and now she's crossing the street and getting away."

"Shit." I spring up from my hiding place and jog-walk as fast as I can through the park so I don't draw too much attention to myself. By the time I catch up to the woman, she's across the street and passing a Starbucks. While I'm loosely following her, debating what to do next, she stops in front of the window display of a local witchy-themed crafts store selling handmade candles, wooden carvings, and an assortment of large, colorful crystals.

Elijah catches up to me easily—then he elbows me in the ribs.

Right.

Erebus's deep voice echoes inside my ears. *Your Bloodcraft comes from within you. Your furnace lives inside you. But your targets are real, so you must make your power real. Externalize that which is internal. Force it out with your will, then shape it with your focus.*

Cut, I think. And the hidden root in my hand takes the shape of a small throwing-knife with a slim handle, perfectly balanced in my palm.

I tug the knife slowly out of my pocket, more so that the movement does not catch the businesswoman's attention; it's not like she or any other nonmagical human can see the magical weapon anyway.

I glance down at the tiny, near-translucent, deep-purple blade in my fist and feel a rush of satisfaction at the shape I've been able to create just by imagining what I *need* my power to do. Not for the first time, I wonder if this is how Merlins feel, with their steady access to aether all the time. Their ability to create anything they can imagine.

My little knife is not a solid construct—otherwise, it'd be visible to everyone on the street—but it's solid enough that a demon will feel it. Elijah, sensing the creation of my blade, shifts aside so I have room to throw it—and checks for any watching humans before I do. After a moment, he nods. *All clear.*

The woman shifts too—to face away from me. I lift the blade in my palm, drawing my hand back at shoulder-height.

With a flick of my wrist, I let it fly. It hits the imp in the chest, burying itself right to the hilt.

The lesser demon falls off her shoulder immediately, and the woman tilts forward when it drops, as if she's just lost some of her steam. She blinks, suddenly confused. She probably feels lighter, or at least less irritated.

She's lucky the only demon that found her tonight was an imp. Its Gate is probably nearby, as imps are too weak to fly far from their entry points into our world. Most of the Shadowborn that cross are invisible and incorporeal, and most are lesser demons with one of two things on their underdeveloped minds: aether to fortify their bodies or human energy to clarify their minds. Imps are annoying, but like every full demon, they are ruthless, relentless, and hungry.

Always hungry.

The businesswoman blinks again. "What just . . . ?" she asks no one in particular.

Elijah has already slipped around to block her view of me, making it appear as though we are deep in conversation. Still, I chance a quick peek around him to find the lesser demon writhing on the ground. It'll dust soon, invisible to any passersby. For now, though, it's dying.

I watch it squirm and shift—and remember another scene like this one, except it was someone else standing over a demon he'd pinned. Someone else cornering and interrogating a demon while I hid and watched from behind a tree. I remember that the screams of that isel haunted me for *hours* afterward, but I can't remember the face of its killer.

After a moment, the woman continues her phone call and her walk along the street—and Elijah nods. "Well done."

A rare compliment, but I'll take it. "Thanks."

"Night's not over." He points with his chin back down toward the park where Zoe's waiting for us against a low wall. "Let's go."

February is cold in Asheville, but at least it's not currently *freezing*. There's no snow on the ground, and the wind is calm. The streets are busy enough that we have to weave in and out of other people—couples and groups—as they cross the park to seek out warm restaurants and bars for the night.

It's my first night hunting with the twins. I've been training with Erebus for months, though, and he finally ordered them to take me out to practice forging and using weapons in public without drawing any attention to myself. There are humans everywhere, and so far, we've killed five lesser demons—two imps, one too big and scaly to be called a squirrel, one that looked like a glowing rat, and another that had leatherlike wings like a bat.

As if reviewing our progress, Zoe hums. "With the imp, that makes five. I say we go for one more, then call it a night. Bree can spot a lesser, kill it, and do so stealthily. We could get a slice of pizza and head back in time to catch *Real Housewives*."

Elijah snorts. "Living with the king of all demons and you spend your time watching *Real Housewives*."

Zoe shrugs. "He's not home until tomorrow. You can't be the teacher's pet when the teacher isn't home, Jah."

Elijah's jaw drops. "I am *not*—"

"You *so* are!" Zoe exclaims. She turns back, smirking, affecting her brother's lower voice near perfectly. "'Can you tell me what the Court was like before Arthur, sire? What trials do the Mageguard need to pass before they are initiated? At the academy, when do Merlins—'"

"Shut up!" Elijah claps a hand over his sister's mouth.

Zoe continues, muffled, until she yanks his hand down. "'Please, sire, tell me about the good old days, when demons roamed the earth freely—'"

"*Zoe!*" Elijah snaps, eyes flashing a burning red. He glances over my head and back up the street, where a few people are headed our way from deeper downtown. "Keep your mouth shut."

Zoe sidesteps her brother and swings around, letting her long twists swing with her. "Not like they'd believe anything we say. If I say the word 'demons,' these humans will probably think it's a metaphor. Like, my haunted feelings about my past or whatever." She rolls her eyes, unbothered. "They don't care if we kill them; they don't even know they exist."

I speak up abruptly. "Why *do* you bother killing the demons that feed off humans?" It's a question I've had for a while. The Legendborn kill demons because they want to protect humanity, but Zoe—and to some degree, Elijah—don't seem all that interested in protecting other people. "Since you don't like humans."

Zoe lifts a feathered brow. "Because killing demons reminds the lesser ones who outranks them. Helping the humans is just a necessary byproduct."

"When you say you outrank them . . ." When Elijah eyes me warningly, I hesitate, uncertain how to proceed. This seems to be a touchy subject for the twins . . . their family and where they come from. They aren't from the South, that much I can tell—or at least, they weren't raised here. No accents, no drawl. And from what I've gleaned from grocery expeditions over the past three months, the twins have *no* appreciation for Southern breakfast food. They don't glance twice at grits, never ask about hash browns, and don't crave biscuits. That last one is a shame, really. When it comes to who they are beyond being wards of the Shadow King, they don't ask me questions, and I don't ask them. It makes hiding that I'm the Scion of Arthur a lot easier, which is a relief. Makes conversations like this tricky, though. "Do you mean as in . . . cambions?"

Elijah turns away. "Yeah, let's say that."

I wonder if I've met a balanced cambion like the twins. If I have, I can't remember.

"But what about goruchel?" I say, keeping my voice low. "Do you kill them?"

"We could," Elijah says, but he doesn't sound confident. He's scarily good at manipulating aether, but I've never seen him draw on it the way Zoe can. "If we were ordered to, that is."

"And we could do it without relying on a damn *bloodmark*," Zoe says pointedly. When she grimaces, her fangs flash in the light of a nearby coffee shop's window, nearly glistening like the imp's. "We'd kill one for real. Cuz *we* have the stomach for it."

This time, it's my turn to lift a brow. "I've killed a goruchel. I have the stomach for it."

"When I say 'kill,' I mean up close, Bree," Zoe says smugly. "Not throwing some dagger or blasting them from far away—"

"I drove a blade through a greater demon's chest," I say evenly, "and then watched it scream and bleed out until it died. That close enough for you?"

The twins pause at that, eyeing me with near-identical suspicion. Around us, the early evening has gone quiet as the streets empty, so we no longer have an audience. I let them survey me, let them try to suss out whether I'm lying.

Erebus may have removed my knowledge of the living, but he hasn't taken away my memories of the dead. I remember killing Rhaz—and I remember it well.

After a moment, Zoe stands back with a quiet "Huh."

Elijah takes a second longer than his sister to make up his mind, but he doesn't give me the satisfaction of acknowledging what he's decided either way. "Whatever." He sniffs and turns on his heel on the sidewalk, heading south toward the Whole Foods off Broadway Street.

Zoe catches up to Elijah and slings an arm over his shoulder while they talk. Probably about me. Probably about Erebus. Probably about how much of an annoyance I am. How much attention the King gives me. Not that I care.

However, I have no choice but to follow. The twins and I are, unfortunately, stuck together. At least in public. And none of us is happy about it. When we're outside the house, I have to be chaperoned by them. For a while, they just left me behind to avoid having to let me tag along everywhere. Tonight started out interesting, but I can tell they'd rather not be on Bree duty.

A couple passes us by. A dark-haired girl and her tall boyfriend, bundled up in matching North Face jackets. I don't recognize either of them—I never ever recognize *anyone*, anymore—but something about how she curls into him and the way his arm hangs heavy around her shoulders makes my heart twinge with envy. I don't know this couple, but the connection they have feels like something I *might* have had, once. Like something I *could* have—or should.

With whom? I have no idea.

This happens sometimes. I see a glimpse of some stranger, feel something familiar, and get a hunch that there's a *person* behind that familiar feeling . . . then the hunch fades to nothing.

Over the past three months, I've uncovered more about the knowledge gap that Erebus created within me. Even though he still won't answer any direct questions about what he did, he has experimented with me to help us both understand how it works.

We confirmed that Erebus was right that first morning: there is a difference between "memories" and "knowledge."

I don't lack memories—what I lack is *information*.

My own personal history is complete. Those memories are crystal clear, but it's as if I have lived my entire life with nameless, faceless ghosts.

I know my past, but I don't know the *people* from my past.

I remember the conversations I've had with others, but I don't know with whom I was speaking. I remember the things I've *done*; I just don't know the people who were with me when I did them. There are gray, misty spaces where their faces and bodies should be, blanks where their names and backgrounds should be, and only silence where I might recall their voices. I can make guesses about these people I no longer know, but that's all they are: guesses. The facts have been erased and the people have gone missing.

Like an afterimage burned into my mind or a resonant echo, the only detail I've retained about the people in my life is a single emotional remnant from the memories of our last encounters. For each person I've managed to conjure so far, that single emotion resonates so loudly and clearly that it has now taken the place of their identity. The father who makes me feel regret. The Merlin boy who makes me feel guilty. The chasing boy who makes me feel longing. The best friend who makes me feel worried. The *many* people who leave me feeling helpless, who must be my enemies. And the list goes on. . . .

Out of every living person in my previous life, the only people who have not been erased in full are the goruchel demons I've fought. Erebus believes I have retained them because demons are a type of undead people, while everyone else that is missing is alive. Perhaps that's true. I still remember my own mother. I remember murdered boys named Russ, Whitty, and Fitz. I remember a man named Martin Davis, who was murdered in front of me. Of all things, the *violence* is clear—

Like someone using his aether blades to slice another person's head off.

The thought pops into my mind without warning, and I trip over my feet, stumbling.

The twins glance backward, alerted by the sound. Elijah keeps walking. Zoe scowls at me as she backpedals. "Can't even walk right."

I ignore her to chase the memory down. Who killed a person like that? I try to imagine the killer's face but can't. They could be someone whose emotional resonance I've already recalled—or they might be someone else entirely.

But I know the killer's victim, and I know I *despised* him. His name was Maxwell Zhao.

A deep buzzing sound interrupts my thoughts. Elijah reaches into his pocket and pulls out his phone. "Zoe." His sister stops, giving me enough time to catch up to them. Elijah shows his sister the screen on his phone, tilting it so that I can't read what's on it. "Contact wants to meet up tonight. At the Rat."

The Rat, short for the Ratskellion, is a café and bar downtown. The twins frequent it and other places for their *assignments* and have never taken me. So far, these assignments are the only thing that Erebus has strictly forbidden me from attending. Every time the twins are away from the house and I ask him about these outings, he shuts me down. Changes the subject. And the twins seem to enjoy that there is something *they* are permitted to do and know about that I can't—which only makes me want to know more.

Zoe reads the text on the screen. "Thought he'd be dropping by *tomorrow*?"

"Apparently he's headed there tonight." Elijah pockets his phone. "We gotta go. Both of us, or he won't take us seriously."

They look at me, heads tilting the same exact way. Mouths frowning the same exact annoyed and frustrated way. I feel like a container of leftovers in the fridge. A mystery of unknown and undesirable origin. Something they know they need to discard.

"I could go with you," I offer, taking care not to be too eager or too excited by the prospect. Instead I match their energy with my own affected boredom. "I won't get in the way."

Zoe and Elijah tilt their heads to the other side, this time with expressions of near disgust.

"Nah."

"Nope."

"To which part?" I exclaim.

"Any part." Zoe scoffs. "You'll be too obvious, and the old man doesn't want you at the Rat."

"I won't be obvious," I counter. "I'll just sit there until y'all are done. Or sit somewhere else, if that's better. Or stand in a corner."

"None of those is a legitimate option." Elijah sighs heavily and scratches the back of his head, turning to his sister. "If the contact's gonna be there, we need to get her home. Come on."

Before he can turn away, his phone buzzes again. He checks the lock screen and curses.

"Shit. Says if we're not there in an hour, he's leaving—and taking his lead with him."

"Who does this guy think he is?"

"He's someone with intel, and he knows we're people who need that intel."

Intel? I resist the urge to ask more questions. I've come up with half a dozen likely reasons for the twins' trips to the Rat. The more time I spend with the King, the more I realize that, after fifteen hundred years of planning revenge on Arthur Pendragon's secret society, he has more irons in more fires than I can possibly count. Plans upon plans, machinations upon strategies. As many objectives as he has identities, probably . . . which is to say, a lot. But what does he trust the twins to pursue in his absence, and why are they the ones who chase intel instead of him doing so himself?

"An hour is tight," Elijah says with a groan. "We can't get Bree home and get back in time."

Zoe continues to talk about me as if I'm not there. "Maybe she can get back on her own?"

"The old man'll skin us alive if his precious project makes a run for it."

"If she runs, we'll chase her, simple as that—"

"I won't *run*." I cross my arms over my chest. "Not like I'd get far anyway without an ID or a phone or *actual* money. I'm here because I want to be, remember?"

It's true. I may not remember the people I left behind, but I remember why I'm with Erebus and the twins. I'm getting stronger every day, gaining better control every day. I'm well on my way to being able to fight my own battles—finally.

The twins exchange glances. Then, like they are prone to do, they share a swift conversation that I'm extremely in earshot of but not invited to.

"If she gets hurt, it's both our asses," Elijah mutters.

"She's annoying as hell but mildly capable."

I huff. "I kicked your entire ass the first day we met, Zoe."

Zoe rolls her eyes. "She doesn't follow directions. Not unless the old man gives them."

"I can *hear* you!"

"It's not ideal." Elijah studies me. "*She's* not ideal, not for a contact like this."

"But we can't miss the meeting either," Zoe insists. "The old man'll hate that, too."

"And *I'll* hate that. I worked hard for this one. We need the lead. Can't lose it."

It sounds like a debate, but none of this is necessarily conducive to my joining them. Usually their banter leads up to a joke at my expense, which is so very typical of the twins. They like to watch me squirm. A demon thing, I think.

I don't know what this "lead" is, but I've heard Elijah mention it before. He's always on the phone and stepping out. Always digging through the internet on his laptop while Zoe watches TV, absentmindedly typing with one hand and scanning search results and forums with the other. He walks around on his phone in the kitchen, twirling a pen that he stuffs in his mouth when he needs both hands to text. They're hunting for someone or something.

"Well?" I demand.

The twins look at each other for another beat, exchanging some silent communication that's not meant for me, before Elijah sighs and looks away. "Fine," he says to no one.

"Fine," Zoe says to me. She steps forward and taps my nose with a fingertip, borrowing Erebus's deep tones and enunciation. *"Behave, Briana."*

"Personal space, please." I jerk my head away from her finger and its sparkly green nail.

Elijah turns back the way we've come. "Let's go, *pet*."

The Ratskellion is tucked down a handful of worn stone steps with a winter-snow-battered door. Its dingy windows are so desperately in need of cleaning that the panes are dirty-dishwater brown. It's early enough on a Friday that the crowd will probably be a blend of patrons, half café regulars drinking coffee on laptops and half bar patrons getting an early start on the evening.

What I do not expect from the Rat, however, is for the name of the bar to be scrawled in bright green aether, wavering and hovering a few inches above the door like living neon.

Whoever cast this sign, they meant for it to be seen by someone with the Sight. There's only a tiny brass plate visible to the human eye. Foot traffic would pass this place by and assume it's abandoned or condemned unless they happened to actually witness someone walk in or out.

"Those steps look hazardous," I mumble, staring warily at the steep but dry steps. Black ice is a thing, I've discovered, this far up in the mountains. The twins check the street for onlookers, then leap down the ten-foot flight. I step down a bit more carefully. I may be strong, and I could make that jump as easily as the twins, but I don't heal overnight like they do.

At the low landing, the door swings inward at Elijah's touch. As I pass underneath the floating Ratskellion sign behind Zoe, I feel the brush of magic against my skin. When the door closes behind us, we step inside a long, dimly lit, empty gray hallway. I take a second step, and my feet find something sticky on the floor. And the hallway smells like fruit that has just turned. I gag involuntarily and cover my nose. The twins turn back and frown.

"Stinks," I explain.

Elijah's eyes narrow as he steps closer. "The owner here is a human who keeps his hands dirty in the demon world. He's loyal to the old man. Lets us do business on the premises as long as we blend in with the locals. It's the only neutral territory some of my contacts will accept. Don't disrespect anyone you don't know, don't make a scene, and don't raise your voice. In fact, don't say anything to anybody."

I drop my hand. Breathe through my nose. Smile without teeth. "Fine."

"And keep that furnace of yours locked up tight," Zoe says as Elijah moves toward the second door at the end of the hall. "Our contact is a goruchel, but there may be others inside."

"I have it under control," I insist. And I do.

"Good," Elijah calls back, "because the old man will tear our ears off with his bare hands if some random shadow asshole gets even half a mouthful of you."

"Don't say it like that," I mutter. Beside me, Zoe snickers. "My *power* does those things, or is those things, or—whatever. My power is not *me*. I don't know everything, but I know that much. I know *myself* just fine."

Zoe shrugs easily. "Your power, you, they're one and the same. We may know ourselves best, but we *don't* always know what we're capable of doing— or becoming."

I pause at that. I don't think I've ever heard Zoe get . . . philosophical. Before I can ask what she means, exactly, Elijah tugs the door at the end open with a final warning. "In here, Bree has no power. In here, you're a normal human girl."

It's been months since I've been the Scion of Arthur—to the court I can't claim, to Erebus, even to myself. Months since I've been a Medium; the grave-yards nearby are dirt and stone and shrubs to me now, nothing more. I've only been Bree, and my only power has been my Bloodcraft. But here I'm none of those things at all.

I close my eyes as I let that thought settle into my bones and veins and lungs. Inhale. *Normal*. Exhale. *Human*. Inhale. *Girl*.

I breathe out again, this time with my low belly only, pushing quietly until all the air leaves my lungs, holding my upper body still . . . then draw in through my nose while I imagine closing all my root inside an iron-encased box.

When I open my eyes again, I follow the twins into the Rat as a normal human girl.

15

"WELCOME TO THE Rat," a voice announces.

A human man—or at least a man who appears to be human—sits on a stool at the bottom of another set of stairs. He turns a toothpick over in his mouth as he stares down at a Rubik's Cube in his palms, turning the sides this way and that. His pale skin is ruddy from too much sun, and the color stretches all the way up his temples and across his bald head.

Behind and above him, the din of early evening casual drinkers is broken by the occasional loud voice. A smattering of laughter from a group I can't see. Steady bass thumps at us from the speakers within. The mixed scent of clove cigarettes and old leather hangs heavily in the air. Somewhere deeper in the room, a cue ball breaks a rack on a pool table.

After being cooped up for so long, I'm somehow disappointed. "*This* is the Rat?"

I can *feel* Elijah rolling his eyes from four feet away. "Ignore her, Tyson."

Tyson pockets the Rubik's Cube he was fiddling with before he looks up and fixes me with a sharp gaze. "How old are you?"

"Seventeen." I know I look younger than the twins, who are also seventeen, but not *that* much younger.

"You can't drink here."

"I won't."

"What's up with your hair?" Tyson asks, pointing at my temple, where my lock of Arthur-touched silver hair stretches down in one of the two long braids down my back.

"Rude. What's up with *your* hair?" I ask in return.

Tyson blinks, then chuckles as he runs a hand over his extremely bald head. "Old age, kid. Lived a lot of lives."

"Funny story," I say with a smirk. "So have I."

"She's cool, Tyson," Zoe interjects. "Mostly."

Tyson regards the twins. "Y'all here for business?"

"Yes," Elijah answers without looking up from his phone. "Party of three."

Tyson points his toothpick at me. "Her too?"

Elijah looks up to Tyson, then to me. "Party of three, *plus a guest*," he corrects between clenched, unhappy teeth. "Meeting somebody, so we'd like to go ahead and get seated."

"Y'all can go on in," Tyson says, "but your guest here, Ms. I'm Seventeen, will need to pay for entrance if she's on the premises for business."

"I don't have any money." I jerk a chin at the twins. "My friends can pay it."

"Folks who do business at the Rat don't pay in money, kid," Tyson says with an eye roll. "They pay in collateral. If your *business* here goes south, we keep your collateral. If all goes well, you get it back. So, hand over somethin' of value. Somethin' you're gonna want back."

I hesitate. "I don't—"

"Nice bracelet you got there."

The man raises a brow at the golden charm bracelet on my wrist. My mother's. A gift from someone I know and love and *remember*. The warm brown skin of her face, her dark hair, and wide smile are all clear in my mind's eye. Her big laugh, easy to hear. And this charm bracelet is the only thing I possess that once belonged to her. "You can't have my bracelet."

Tyson shrugs. "The necklace, then?"

I resist the urge to touch the Pendragon coin at the end of my necklace where it lies hidden beneath my T-shirt. I used to use this coin, and my mother's bracelet, to perform blood walks, but that Medium ability is lost to me now, and there is no bringing it back. Like the bracelet, I know the necklace was a gift too—even if I don't know the person who gave it to me.

Well, my *mind* doesn't know them . . . but my body does.

When I touch this coin, electricity zips along my skin, as if my nerves recall the sensation that person's fingers left behind when they closed the heavy silver clasp around my neck. My heart pounds and blood rushes in my ears. My veins brighten and come *alive.* "You can't have that, either," I say finally.

Tyson stands up from his chair. He's broader across the shoulders and biceps than I realized. "Then you gotta leave—"

"Wait." I peek into the venue beyond him, weighing my desire to go inside with the twins against holding on to a necklace given to me by someone I don't even *know.* It's not a hard decision. Still—"I get it back, right?"

Tyson holds out his hand. "If you *act* right."

I hand it to him with a deep scowl. Without a word, he reaches into the stand by his stool, producing a metal lockbox. After placing the necklace inside, he hands me a key. Once Tyson tosses the box back onto the hidden shelf, he waves a hand for us to follow him into the bar.

The rock music in the background isn't blaring, but it gets louder the second we cross the threshold, and the space opens up to a half-filled room of couches and coffee tables, booths, and bistro tables, all lit by a scattered collection of mismatched lamps and wall sconces.

It's not until I find myself looking for aether shots and glowing eyes that I realize I'm comparing this first glance of the Rat to my experience at a very different kind of venue down in Georgia, the Crossroads Lounge. I was there with other people, and the owner there was . . . Blank gray mist. Again.

Tyson jerks a thumb behind him before he leaves. "Your usual table is reserved."

Elijah dips his chin. "Thanks."

Zoe grips my elbow tightly. "Hey, that hurts," I whisper, irritated, and glance down at her hand. "I could probably break your bones too, remember? That what you want?"

"No one's breaking anyone's bones," Elijah hisses.

"Stay close," Zoe murmurs, but she's not even looking at me as she speaks. She and Elijah are both moving through the room, weaving in between patrons with me in tow, but their eyes are everywhere. She scans the left side of the room while Elijah searches the right, both their noses raised to the air.

They're looking for a cambion—or a goruchel demon. Someone who could *appear* human but who is not human at all.

My own nose is assaulted by the sharp, pungent smell of hoppy beer and freshly ground coffee beans. There are two women in black leather playing chess at a corner table, a group of four college-aged kids laughing at the pool table, high schoolers studying on the couches, and a few older guys sitting at the bar proper watching the local news on a small, mounted flat-screen.

Everyone here looks human, at least to my eyes.

I can't help but wonder if I'll see anyone I know. Or rather, I wonder if anyone I know will see *me*. Erebus and I discovered pretty early on that no matter how many facts he shares from my past life to prompt me, I can't fill in the blanks of my missing people. Older memories don't help me fill in the blanks either. Even if I had multiple encounters with the people in my past, I can't use those memories to connect the dots today. If I saw someone I once knew here in the Rat, it would be like meeting them for the first time all over again, no matter how well *they* know *me*.

From my perspective, we'll be starting fresh.

From theirs . . . I'll have forgotten them.

The twins seem to decide there are no goruchel present—or at least no threats. Zoe leads me to a deeply shadowed, round booth at the back of the room that sits two steps higher than the rest of the floor. A plastic RESERVED FOR VIPS sign rests atop the table.

Elijah moves up the two steps and slides into the booth until he sits with a clear view of the entrance. Zoe nudges my lower back with her fingers. "Get in."

I don't miss that she's pushing me into the booth in such a way that traps me between her and her brother. Not a fan of *that*. I slide into the booth, stopping a foot from Elijah, and Zoe slides in behind me so that I have a twin on either side.

"Can't believe you gave up your little trophy," Zoe says.

"Tyson doesn't know it's a trophy," I reply.

Elijah studies me with hard eyes. "You ever going to explain how exactly you got the Scion of Arthur's necklace?"

"I took it from him," I lie smoothly. "In a fight. It's mine, fair and square."

Zoe grins. "And I bet he just *hates* that. I heard the Scion of Arthur is a white boy raised with a silver spoon in his mouth. Bet he never expected a Black girl like you to show up and hand him his ass."

I keep my breathing even. Keep my heart rate steady. The twins know the King works among the Regents of the Order as Erebus. They know about the Legendborn and the Spell of Eternity. What they can't ever know is that the Scion of Arthur whose life holds that spell together sleeps down the hall from them each night.

My thoughts turn to the nameless, faceless boy who the twins think is their greatest enemy. "That Scion of Arthur kid never saw me coming."

Zoe sits back in the booth. "Gotta say, every time I hear this story, I get a little less mad about the old man bringing you into the fold."

"While *I* only get a little more curious," Elijah says sharply. "The Order's not known for being kind to rogues."

"They weren't kind to me," I say with finality.

Elijah studies me a beat longer, then turns to his sister. "Speaking of rogues, I'm doing a little extra recon myself these days. Keeping an eye on the rogue network. Tracking rumors about the Order, other Shadowborn, that kinda thing. You think the King'll appreciate it?"

"He should," Zoe says with a proud smile. "You work hard."

I perk up. "What're you hearing?"

Elijah eyes me. "That's need-to-know information between me and the old man. Got it?"

"Got it," I say, raising my hands.

Just as Elijah settles back in his seat, a broad-shouldered, middle-aged white man approaches with three glasses of ice water. Even though the Rat feels run-down, this man does not. His jacket and watch look expensive. "Elijah, Zoelle. Haven't seen either of you in a while."

"Haven't had cause," Elijah murmurs, sliding one glass to his sister, another to me, and the last toward himself. "How are things, Syd?"

Syd rests his fingertips on the table. "Slower in the winter. You know how it goes."

"Winter gets like that," Elijah answers, and extends his hand to Syd.

Syd returns the handshake, but it takes a beat too long—something I can't see is passed between Elijah and the older man. Cash, maybe? "Appreciate your business," Syd replies with a smile. *So he's* the owner, *I think. The human who lets the twins do business on the premises.*

"Thanks, Syd," Zoe says, then snaps her teeth at him—a sharp clacking sound with her fangs meeting in the middle. Syd's eyes grow wide before he turns around to leave.

"Zoe . . . ," Elijah warns.

"Let me have my fun." She sips her ice water demurely.

"Why are y'all VIPs here?" I ask, eyeing the sign. "Does Syd work for the King like you do?"

Suddenly Elijah bares his teeth. "We don't just 'work for the King,' pet project."

Zoe lays a hand on Elijah's arm. "What my brother means to say is that we don't have to prove our loyalty to the old man."

"Why not?" The twins share a doubtful glance. "Come *on*, y'all. Who am I gonna tell? I literally don't *know* anyone."

Elijah sighs and waves a hand. "Just tell her."

Zoe leans in close, eyes sparkling. "Our father's a Nightshade."

She clearly expects me to have a big reaction. "Is that . . . important?"

They both groan. Elijah drags his drink over and chugs it, laughing. "She really *doesn't* know enough to be dangerous."

Zoe recovers with a shake of her head. "Okay, so you know the Shadow Court, right?"

I nod. "Yep, got that part."

"Well, the Court was made of the King's Nightshades, the original demon leaders of the Shadowborn army. When the Order took the King's crown, they thought it would kill them—and it nearly did. The Shades scattered and the Round Table chased them to the other side, where they were eventually trapped. For a while, anyway," she concludes.

"So the Shades aren't trapped anymore?" I ask.

She rolls her eyes. "Obviously not, since our father's a Nightshade and we're half human."

My confusion must show on my face.

Zoe laughs into her hand. "You don't actually understand how cambions are made, do you?"

"I know how babies are made!" I say hotly.

Elijah leans forward. "It's like this: demons can reproduce with other demons on the demon plane, but they *can't* reproduce with one another once they cross over here."

"Why not?" I ask.

He taps the table with a fingertip. "Because this is the plane of the living. When demonkind cross over, every demon, greater or lesser, becomes too undead to create life here, except for one exception—concubi."

"Like the original Merlin's father?" That was one of the first understandings I gained about the nature of the Order's cambion soldiers—that the original Merlin was the child of an incubus and a human woman.

"Exactly." Elijah nods. "Concubi and those descended from concubi are the only demon class that can procreate on the plane of the living, and even then, they can only do so with human beings. Every cambion you know can trace their bloodline to a concubi, including me and Zoe."

"Because your father is . . . ?" I prompt.

"An incubus," Zoe says, then scowls at me. "Don't make it weird."

I raise my hands. "Not making it weird."

"Anyway," Zoe speaks around the water straw in her mouth, slurping between words, "our dad is one of the original Shades, which is why the King took us in. Our parents are off on other official missions for the Court. That's why we aren't in the same league as other supplicants like Syd, not even close."

"Do you miss them?" The question falls from my mouth before I can stop it. "Your parents, I mean."

"Um, yeah?" Zoe says, as if it should be obvious. Then she pauses. Considers. "Don't you miss the people you left behind?"

I shift in my seat. Erebus's taunts have dug deep under my skin over the past three months. I don't know the people I'm missing, and if I return, they'll figure that out right away. But it's the lingering emotions that have made themselves at home in my heart—the guilt, the worry, the regret—that make me question whether they'd even *want* me back. Whatever our relationships were, they've all lost so much already. Wouldn't I just make it worse if I appeared out of nowhere one day, showing them that they've lost me, too?

That we've lost each other?

Finally, I say, "How can you *miss* something that feels like it was never really there?"

Zoe whistles. "If that ain't a word. Some folks are dead to me, too, even though they're still alive."

"I knew you could grieve dead people," I whisper. "Guess I didn't realize you could grieve living people too."

"Sure can," Zoe says.

I recognize something familiar in her dark eyes. A haunting. "What happened . . . with your people?"

Zoe's face sours. "Our parents are cool, but let's just say *all* demons are easier than *most* humans. With demons, it's about strength and presence—or if you're entertaining enough to not need either. Hierarchies aren't set in stone, but you always know where you stand. Rules can change. It's not like that with humans."

I shake my head. "What do you—"

"Demons," Zoe says lowly, "don't care whether Elijah and I were born fraternal or identical. Demons don't ask about this." She gestures to the rounded shape of her throat. "Humans, on the other hand, are nosy about all the wrong shit and ask all the wrong questions. Human beings deny other human beings' humanity and call *that* power."

I find my own face twisting, mirroring her expression. I've never seen the twins interact with anyone other than Erebus, but of course that doesn't mean they don't run into people when they leave the house for their usual errands—for grocery shopping, for putting gas in the old truck the King lets them drive. I'm not there to see people treat Zoe any differently than they might treat me, but I don't have to see it to believe her. To believe that when she's just being herself, people try to punish her into their too-small boxes of gender.

Elijah nudges his sister in the shoulder, a comfort. I don't know her well enough to let my support be silent, so I speak it instead.

"That's really shitty, Zoe," I say. "You don't deserve that."

"Yeah, it's shitty." She tips her water back, the ice clinking against the sides of the glass. "Waste of everyone's time and energy, especially mine. Waste of humanity's time on this planet too, since they get such a short run of it."

A memory comes to me, then. Two angry people at a gas station. I remember wondering why I'd ever fight to save them. Then, a second memory—someone who accused me of being undeserving across a dinner table at the Legendborn Lodge. A person who later attacked me when I was vulnerable.

Cowardice and bigotry don't have to have faces. Their actions speak loudly enough.

"Maybe humans like that deserve to be fed on by lesser demons," I murmur.

"Damn." Zoe drops her glass and raises a brow. "Bree, are you secretly . . . ruthless?"

Am I? I wonder. "I know the parts of humanity that bother me."

Zoe regards me appreciatively. "I eff with that."

Across the table, Elijah nods in agreement. The three of us let our new allegiance—and old anger—work its way through us. The anger goes from hot, to warm, to cool and steady.

"You said humans ask the wrong questions," I say. "What kinda questions do demons ask?"

"Saucy ones." Zoe laughs again, and I am relieved that the sound is only slightly dimmed from our discussion. Not as light and loud as before, but a laugh all the same.

"She means they're nosy in different ways," Elijah clarifies, although the brown skin of his cheeks flushes a deeper color.

"Nosy how . . . ?" I ask, then nearly regret it. Something about the glint in Zoe's eye tells me I'm wading into territory that she had *hoped* to get into and just hadn't yet found the opportunity.

Her eyes sparkle. "The first day you got here, you and the old man argued about some Merlin boy who sacrificed himself for you, so what's the drama there? Was it romantic? And is there more where that came from?"

I gape at her. "Those are three *very* nosy questions."

"I can count," Zoe replies. "Answer."

"I can't. He won't say anything else about that boy. I've asked."

"Boring," Zoe complains. She gestures at the younger kids nearby. "Same topic, different question. Who are you into?"

It's my turn to flush. "Who am I into, like . . . romantically?"

"Sure," she says with a shrug. "If you're into that."

"I know I'm into that," I confirm, then search my mind for more clues.

At first, all that comes to me is the longing. The deep *want* of the boy I left behind.

Then, I remember the sizzling sensation when I touch the Pendragon coin, and I wonder if he's the one who stamped that memory onto my skin.

"Boys," I say quietly. "I know that much."

"So"—Zoe looks out into the now busier main room of the Rat—"you're into boy people?"

I follow her gaze to the high schoolers on the couch, deep in conversation, then look out beyond them. There are more people here now, some my age and some a bit older. It looks like a dance at the local high school must have gotten out—there's a small group in formal wear. I watch the shifting colors of long gowns under lamplight and study the clean lines of rented tuxedos and shiny lapels. "I think . . . ," I say, watching the crowd with new eyes, "I'm into . . . *people* people."

I feel both twins' eyes on my skin in a bright, quick scald. When I turn, they're both staring.

"Interesting," Zoe murmurs.

"Can I ask . . . who you're into?" I try to shift the focus off me. "Either of you?"

They answer at the same time.

Zoe says, "Depends," as Elijah mutters, "Girls," and looks away.

Zoe fixes her brother with a glare. "*Mostly* girls."

"Yeah, yeah." The corner of his mouth quirks. "Mostly girls."

"Oh." Their expressions are challenging and expectant and curious. My cheeks grow heated for reasons I can't name. A tiny fissure of uncertainty opens inside me. It must show on my face.

"You know yourself, right?" Zoe asks quickly, voice firm. "You know your own shit?"

"Yeah," I answer, "I do."

She gives me a sharp nod. "Then that's all there is to it."

With her answer, that new fissure of uncertainty begins to close.

I sit with that for a moment. In the past three months, I haven't deeply wanted *anything* other than to become stronger under Erebus's tutelage. Untouchable, unstoppable, impervious. But now, with the twins looking at me, making me feel both bare *and* bold, I'm reminded that *this* is okay too.

The world is here, around and between us, and we're allowed to live in it. We're allowed to figure out what we want from our time on the planet—and who. Or at least, we should be.

"Depends" and "mostly girls."

There's so much *space* there. Those answers give the twins possibilities, even within certainty. They allow other people to surprise them. Hell, those answers allow the twins to surprise *themselves*. A type of freedom, I think, toward a full life. My answer—"*people* people"—grants me a free and full life too, in all its certainty and possibilities.

When I look up at the twins, they smile—and I smile back. Two hours ago, they annoyed the crap out of me, but now, I feel like we're a unit. Banded together by honest answers and real shit and this little circle of freedom we've given each other.

Zoe waggles her fingers at my forehead. "You love making things complicated in your head. I see the wheels spinning. You ever have any fun in there?"

A laugh bubbles up before I can tamp it down.

"See, there you go!" Zoe grins.

"That laugh was accidental. It wasn't for you," I say, fighting a smile. I move to stand up as best I can. "Shoo. I gotta go to the bathroom."

Elijah grasps my forearm. "You can't go alone," he repeats. "It's not safe."

"I'll be fine," I answer, and shoo Zoe again. "I just need a minute for . . . things."

"What things?" Zoe stands next to the booth while I step down to the floor level.

"Menstrual things," I state.

"Ah. Legit," Zoe agrees, and points the way. "Make it quick, Ruthless Bree."

I weave through the crowd toward the metal sign that says BATHROOMS to the right of the bar. There are two doors, and each has a block figure with a left leg and body in a dress and a right leg and body without, and a GENDER NEUTRAL sign beneath the figures. I pick the door on the right and find the small, three-stalled bathroom slightly dingy but empty.

I didn't lie. I *do* need to fish out a tampon from the back pocket of my jeans before walking into a stall, but I take a moment to stare in the mirror over the sinks first. Something I find myself doing more and more of lately.

My hair has gotten longer. The ends need trimming. For the first time, maybe because of our conversation at the table and the something-like-friendship this outing seems to have sparked, I consider asking Zoe if she might help me. Her twists are shiny and healthy, and we use mostly similar products, but I don't trust myself to cut all the curls. The one errant curl at my right temple has gotten longer too—its roots growing out shiny and silver over time instead of dark brown like the rest. The mark of Arthur, unavoidable and permanent. I try to work it more deeply into the long braid over my shoulder. Hide it.

My face has gotten leaner, even though I'm eating more than I did while on the run from the Order. My cheekbones are sharper somehow, while my hips have filled out, gotten firmer. Curves and muscle, rearranging themselves around my body in response to the demands of Erebus's training. I turn this way and that in the water-spotted mirror and decide that I like this version of me. I look . . . strong. Powerful. Competent. I wonder what the people I don't know would think of me now if they saw me, and feel a pang of remorse.

I don't need anyone else to validate how I feel about myself, how I've grown, and who I'm becoming . . . but that doesn't mean I don't want it. Don't secretly wish for it. For them.

A few minutes later, I'm drying my hands off at the sink inside one of the tiny single stalls when I hear the door slam open. For a second, I'm certain it's Zoe coming to yell at me for taking too long, and I even open my mouth to call for her before another voice interrupts me.

"Get in, get out, *that's it!*" the voice orders, pitched low so as not to carry but filled with sharp annoyance. Bright irritation twisted with desperation.

My inner alarms go off.

I leap up on the toilet seat, landing silently with one foot on each side of the lid. I rest my palms on the metal walls for balance. Take a deep breath. Become still as a statue.

"No funny business, or I'll make you regret it—"

"I'm going!" a younger voice says, voice breaking. "Please, I just—" Then, a smack—fist against skin—and a body hits the floor. Slides halfway under my stall.

A Black girl, with dark curls like mine and a brown face twisted in fear.

A bruise is already forming on her cheek.

She looks up at me from the floor with wide, frightened, light-filled, golden eyes—and the rich, warm scent of root magic fills my senses.

THIS GIRL *KNOWS*. Somehow, in the span of a heartbeat, she knows that I can See her golden root.

It is the deep color of sunset, and it seeps out of her eyes in wisps of curling smoke. She has no pupils or irises. There is only the gold of her power.

And I know exactly what that power is and where it comes from.

Her head moves left—what might be the beginning of a headshake—and then she is dragged away, under the door, across the tile, and back out to the open bathroom.

I'm on the floor and opening the stall door in a blink. "What's going on?" I shout.

The scene before me is harrowing. The girl is on her back on the floor struggling against a stronger, older white man. He has both her feet in his hands as she kicks at him, but she's much too small to do damage. When I yell, the man drops the girl's feet and stands to face me, and she crabwalks away with tears streaming down her face.

"I'd walk away if I were you," he growls. "Walk out the door. You never saw this."

"Unlikely." I let my eyes fill with the rage, the disgust, that this man rightfully deserves. "You're the one who should walk away."

The man is a few inches taller than me but much broader. He wears jeans and a loose black denim jacket, unbuttoned to reveal a tight-fitting burgundy T-shirt over a firm chest and trim waist. A fighter, or an athlete, or just someone who lifts a lot of heavy weights. Whatever he is, he's no slouch.

But neither am I.

I let the furnace in my chest creak open, invite the flames to rise, keep it faint, so faint that the King might not sense it—

"Stop!" the girl shouts—but her scream is not directed at the man; it's directed at me. She scrambles to her knees, facing me. "Stop! Don't."

I blink, taken aback and not sure what she's even asking me *not* to do, until I realize that her eyes are glued to my chest and filled with fear not for herself but for me.

Like I can See her root, she can See mine.

"What are you—".

"Don't," she says again, voice hardening. "He's not *hurting* me, not like that. He just wants my root. It's okay, please. I'll be okay—"

"Not like that" does very little to assuage my fears.

"I don't care what he wants!" I say.

"Things were going just fine before you showed up," the man says, eerily calm. His pale face breaks into a slow, greasy-feeling smile. The hairs on the back of my neck rise. His hands are empty, his posture loose, no tension in his neck or legs. Just because he's not preparing for an attack doesn't mean he won't if he gets close enough. "Me and girlie here were just taking a potty break." A lie. He doesn't even try to sell it.

My eyes narrow. "She can go to the bathroom on her own, I suspect."

The man advances a step toward the girl. I step closer too, pivoting so that my shoulder is in his path.

"Walk away from me," I advise.

He smirks. "Why don't *you* walk away from *me*?"

"I'm not turning my back on a girl who is very *obviously* being attacked, kidnapped, or—"

The girl, to my surprise, pushes to her feet and shakes her head for real this time. A full back-and-forth, with her curls bouncing around her face. "Please just stop. . . . It's better if you don't." At the last word, "don't," she gestures with her chin toward my chest—where my root furnace is still slightly cracked open. Not enough to visibly leak anything or even be detectable by the twins, but my greatest weapon is at the ready for my call.

For his part, the man doesn't seem to know what she's looking at—his eyes are dancing between her face and mine, a slight frown of confusion drawing his brows together.

He doesn't know what she's talking about. He can't sense my root.

So he's human, then.

To my shock, the girl slides closer to the man, teeth clenched in a tight jaw and eyes cast to the floor. "I don't want you to get caught up in this."

"Good advice," the man says, smiling again. His hands are behind his back, working something out from beneath his jacket and untucking it from his waistband. If it's a gun, I'm screwed. Arthur's strength makes me faster than I would be otherwise, but I'm not faster than a bullet.

Thankfully, he doesn't pull out a gun. Instead, he brings out a switchblade.

I nearly laugh out loud.

I can cast and forge a blade of root twice that size if I want to. One solid enough that even this human man could see it. But a weapon that well-constructed would absolutely draw any nearby demon or cambion's attention to us. Is *that* what the girl is worried about?

Before I can wonder any further, the man speaks a garbled, guttural word—and the switchblade in his hand erupts in green mage flame, elongating until it's the shape of a longsword. It burns a bright, sickly green-yellow at the tip—and is so foul-smelling that I nearly gag as I reel backward in shock.

His mouth curls and warps around words no human should ever speak. The sound lands so unnaturally on my ear, so jarringly not of this plane, that everything, *everything* inside me tells me to run.

The man grins. "Not so mouthy now, are you?"

The blade is not yet solid, but it's gaining shape. He notices me watching it as it goes from air and flame to a deep crystalline solid. I know what magic looks like, but I don't understand what I'm looking at *right now*.

A fully corporeal, forged aether weapon. Not the bright green of the twins' power, but the pale vomit-colored green of a full demon. But this man isn't a demon . . . is he?

He chuckles, breaking my concentration. "See that, do you?"

I blink. A *normal human girl* couldn't See this. *Shouldn't* See this. My cover is blown.

I open my mouth, close it. "I—"

"No!" The girl rushes between us, arms spread wide, partially blocking the man's view of me, placing her chest directly in the path of his glowing blade. "Leave her alone!"

Suddenly, the answer rings clear in my mind: this man is a warlock.

A human who has bargained directly with a demon for temporary power, and at some cost he likely doesn't comprehend. The types of humans who know about demons and make pacts with them are either very rich, or very foolish, or both—and all are greedy.

I wonder which one this man is.

"You can See this, girlie. You know what it is." He holds the blade high, and I wonder if he even knows what he's holding. If it matters. If all he wants is violence. "If you don't want to watch this girl get sliced in half, you'll shut up and let us walk out of here." His voice wavers slightly—and I can tell by the way the muscles in her back tense that the tip of the blade is pressing tightly against her chest.

Foolish and greedy—and desperate.

That last one is what makes my entire body freeze.

I'd rather fight a demon in a bathroom than a human man with malicious intent.

But before I can open my furnace further, the girl speaks, voice resigned. "If you fight her, you'll draw attention to all of us. You want root, not some random human girl who just happens to have the Sight. Let's go."

This warlock might be foolish and greedy, but he wants an easy answer, and this girl just gave him one. He looks at me, glances at the door, where voices have gotten louder—and the bar is filling up—then at her, then me again. "Don't follow us."

"She won't follow." The girl glares at me over her shoulder, eyes wide and serious.

And with that, the girl turns. His blade follows, shining bright against her sweater. She backpedals slowly toward the door, and the man goes with her while her shining golden eyes hold me still, sending a message I can't miss. *Don't follow us. Please just stay there and let us go—let me go.*

As soon as her back hits the door, she turns to grasp the handle. While she pulls it open, the man flips around, blade pointed directly at me now, the green magic dancing across the ceiling. His message is clear too. *Make one wrong move, and she gets cut wide open.*

They're too far away for me to reach them quickly. His blade, even if it wasn't enchanted, will meet her body before I can stop it.

My feet are frozen to the floor. My chest is heaving, taking shallow, frantic breaths as everything in me fights the scene before me without moving.

Then I blink.

And they're gone, the door swinging shut behind them.

I race toward the door, heart pounding. It's only by instinct that my root furnace closes itself tight in my chest again before I burst out into the hallway.

The crowd has gotten thicker, the music louder—or my senses are too flooded as I whip my head around, searching for them.

Cold wind slices into my body from my left—there! A door to the outside. I push between a couple talking in the back hall that runs behind the bar, ignore their shouts of indignation, and race toward the door, hitting it shoulder-first before it can close and latch.

But the warlock and the Rootcrafter are gone. Outside, fluffy snow has started to fall. The landing ends in a black iron railing directly in front of me, offering two directions down to the empty parking lot: a loading ramp on one side and stairs on the other. A scuffle breaks the quiet from somewhere straight ahead—an engine starting.

I dart to the icy black railing, place both hands on it, grip it tight, ready to launch myself over the side—

"What the hell are you doing, Bree?!" A strong hand yanks me backward by the collar, tearing my hands from the metal railing, and lifts me up in the air. I twist in their grip, see Zoe's flashing red eyes.

"Zoe—" The fabric cuts into my neck, choking me. Tires squeal behind me. A car getting away. *No, no—*

"We trusted you!" Zoe cries. "You *told us* you wouldn't run—"

"There was—" I gasp out, scrabbling at my collar, toes dragging on the concrete. "A girl. A girl in trouble."

"What?" Zoe blinks, the angry crimson bleeding from her eyes to reveal a concerned brown.

"In the bathroom," I repeat. "She needs help—"

"Which way did they go?" Zoe drops me to my feet and strides forward, searching the lot for herself. On high alert, eyes bright and fingers flexing at her sides. Her head whips around. "Which way, Bree?!"

"I didn't see." I rush beside her. "I came out here and the lot was empty, but I heard tires—"

She raises her nose to the air. "Yeah, I can smell them too. They peeled outta here real quick. I smell fear. Anger. And—wait—" Abruptly, she blurs closer to me, tugging me close enough to bury her nose against my jacket before nearly tossing me into the railing. "Gross!" She snarls. "You smell like *warlock*. What—"

"I told you, she's in trouble!" I say, rubbing my neck where my collar had been yanked tight. "There was a girl in the bathroom with a warlock. He was kidnapping her for something. Her power, I think. She told me to back off, but we have to go after them—"

"We . . . we can't," Zoe says, growing suddenly still.

"What do you mean? We gotta follow them—"

"How would we?" She jerks a chin out at the lot, where flakes are starting to come down more heavily. "Whoever you saw is long gone by now and traveling by car. The snow's coming down, and it's only gonna get worse. Besides, even if we could go after them and you fire up your power, they'll wanna grab your ass too! Then what? Warlocks don't work alone; there'll be at least two more with him, with who knows what borrowed magic."

"But—"

"And shit's going down right now, right here!" She jerks a thumb behind her. "Regazel just showed up, and it looks *really* bad that I left the meeting to go find you. There're protocols with demons, Bree, serious ones—"

"Zoe!" I cry. "The girl—"

"Is gone!" Zoe says, waving her hand. "Also . . ." She shrugs, voice too light, too dismissive. "Sketchy stuff goes down at the Rat; you know that."

"'Sketchy stuff'?" I exclaim. I stare at her like I don't know who she is. "This wasn't sketchy; this was *wrong*—"

"You said yourself this girl told you to back off, right?" Zoe says, advancing on me. "She knows more about her situation than you do—"

"She was a Rootcrafter!" I say.

Zoe's gaze heats my skin. "What do you know about Rootcrafters?"

I gape at her. "Don't worry about what I know. What do *you* know about Rootcrafters?"

Zoe holds my gaze, fiery and red, and opens her mouth to bare her fangs. A gesture that stopped scaring me ages ago.

"What do you know, Zoe?" I ask again, unmoved.

Zoe closes her mouth with a snap and backs off. "Ancestral magic users have the strongest access to aether—to root—than any other humans. Rootcrafters, especially. And their emotions can . . . can be richer, too. So greater demons prefer to feed on them." She looks away. "Let's go back inside—"

The only demon I know of who feeds on Rootcrafter power is the Hunter. The Shadow King. Erebus. A chill falls over my body, deeper and colder than anything the winter mountains could send my way. "Greater demons, plural, or just one?"

Zoe stares at me, something in her eyes warring. Then, abruptly, the fight I see within her is over. "Let's go back inside, Bree."

"Answer the question."

"No."

"Are the Rootcrafters okay?" I ask. "Will she be okay if he feeds on her?"

Zoe looks away. "Physically, yes, but . . . spiritually? Her magic? I don't . . . I don't know," she mutters, turning back to the door. "Elijah is expecting us. Please, let's—"

Her magic. Rootcrafters' magic is what ties them to their communities, their families. It connects them to one another, even before an ancestor is ever called upon. And Rootcrafters' innate branch of power—their personal magic—is what their ancestors enhance. But unlike my own body, Bloodcrafted to hold limitless ancestral root, the average 'Crafter is only meant to borrow power from their ancestors for a short time.

I don't have to think long to see what the danger is: The King is beyond ancient and beyond powerful. If he feeds on that Rootcrafter girl mid-working, drawing everything he can from her with his vast appetite, her personal branch of power will likely give out before her ancestors' root will. And if her personal branch of power breaks . . . she'll be cut off from who she is.

Disconnected from her own family and severed from her community.

A type of death.

I grasp Zoe's arm. "Where does he feed on them?"

"I don't know! He doesn't tell anyone how he feeds, when he feeds—" Zoe throws up her hands, a nervous, thin laugh escaping her. It's the kind of quick laugh you hear when someone doesn't want something to be true. When they've decided to turn away from the hard thing in favor of easy ignorance, and the laugh helps to paint the world over. "He needs to consume aether and human energy just like any other demon, but he doesn't need to feed as often as other demons. Maybe it's not even him!"

"Does he hire warlocks?" I ask, and she shudders like she always does at the very mention of the pact magic users. I remember one of my mysterious *someones* having a similar reaction to a warlock at the Crossroads Lounge. Warlock pact magic is not very popular among cambions—even the King himself openly despises warlocks. I can't imagine why he'd work with one, unless . . . "Does he hire them because the warlocks are human, so they can get to other humans more easily, go undetected—"

Zoe scoffs. "You know we can't even bear to be in the same room as pact magic. It's so *bitter* and sort of rotten and—"

"Is it *him,* Zoe?" I ask.

Zoe blurs toward me, mouth twisting in a scowl an inch from my face. "You ran away with a *demon*, Bree. Not just any demon but *the King*. What did you expect to see when you were with him?"

In the quiet between us, something deep and terrifying opens up inside me. A silent scream tears at my guts, my heart, my lungs. I don't have an answer for her, and she knows it.

Her eyes soften infinitesimally. "I'm sorry about the girl you saw. I know you want to help her, save her and her magic. I—I want to save her too. Wish we could," she says, "but we really need to get back inside. We can't lose this lead or the old man. He'll . . . he'll get mad at us. Punish *us*. Me and Elijah. Okay?"

I blink at her, the storm inside my heart churning so deeply I'm nauseated. "Punish you?"

Zoe nods, eyes skittering away from mine. "There are things you don't know . . . about me and Elijah. It's a trial situation, and if we mess it up—"

"What will he do to you and Elijah?"

"Please, Bree?" Zoe says quietly, voice wavering. "Can we go? I have to be there with Elijah, and you—you can't be out here alone."

I don't answer. I don't even feel it when she tugs on my jacket the first time. She tugs again, and my eyes find her, dazed from all I've learned in the last few minutes. Worried for the strange girl. Worried for Zoe. Even worried for Elijah.

"You gotta take this off," she mumbles. "The smell . . . it's too strong."

I let her take the jacket off me. She carefully folds it inside out and stuffs it under her arm. "Come on. I'll tuck it behind the bar before we head back to the table."

As I follow her back inside, all I can think is that she's right: I chose to be in the Shadow King's circle. And Zoe and Elijah did too. And we keep choosing.

But that girl in the bathroom didn't choose her fate; she resigned herself to it. And tried to save me, a stranger, in the process.

17

I CAN IMMEDIATELY tell that the man sitting at the far end of the booth is a goruchel. A full-blooded demon, wearing the skin of a man he killed. A mimic whose eyes scorch my skin in only the way that Shadowborn attention can.

I've become somewhat desensitized to the twins' gazes by now, but it's been a while since I've felt the angry attention of a full demon. It doesn't erase my apprehension—and fear—for the Rootcrafter girl I'd just seen in the bathroom, but it grounds me back in my own body at least for the moment.

"Who the hell is this?" the man asks as I slide across the booth to sit beside Elijah. Zoe moves in next to me, and the three of us make a tight arc opposite our guest.

"We're watching over her"—Elijah shoots me an unreadable expression as he sips what appears to be something dark brown and alcoholic—"for *him*."

The man's eyes widen at that. He draws his own liquor closer, clutching it tightly. "You mean you two are actually in touch with . . ." He gestures with one hand. "Him?"

Elijah's eyes haven't left my face, the only indication that he has any emotion whatsoever about my presence. "Yes, Regazel." Elijah's eyes flicker red, then brown as he turns to face the man across from him, drumming his fingers on the table in what I know to be a tell. He's irritated. "But you aren't here to impress him. You're here to impress *us*. Now that we're all in attendance, what have you brought as tribute?"

"A valuable trophy." Regazel produces a small velvet box. "I hope this will suffice."

Trophy. That's what Elijah had called my necklace. Does that word mean more here than what I'd first realized? Zoe said there were "protocols" with demons. Is this one of them?

I can't help but think of the Rootcrafter girl and the warlock who wanted her for her power. Would he bring her as tribute to some demon employer? Was that demon employer the King? My confusion and anger mingle into a toxic knot strong enough that Zoe kicks me under the table and shoots me a glare with a message. *Calm down.*

Elijah drags the box across the table and flicks it open. Within it lies a single deep-golden-colored coin. "What is it?"

"A coin from a bank robbery in the seventies, tainted with human greed." Regazel gestures at it. "Give it a whiff yourself."

Elijah lowers his head and inhales, long and slow. His eyes flash red, and he swipes a tongue over his lower lip. "Smells weak, but good."

"Smells even better if you actually *need* that humanity." Regazel tilts his head, looking between both twins. "But you don't need it at all, do ya?"

Zoe takes the box for herself. "No, we don't."

Something ugly passes through Regazel's eyes. "Must be convenient. Never starving." His lips pull back. "How easy it is for you balanced cambions. All the perks of demonia and none of the drawbacks."

Elijah's eyes slide to Regazel's. "You *would* think that, wouldn't you?"

Zoe snaps the box shut, sliding it under the table and into a pocket. "Your tribute is accepted, Regazel. We'll hear you out as official representatives of the King, but you still have to prove your worth and loyalty to him, or else we'll end this little interview that you insisted on having a day early, for some reason."

"Call me Reggie," the man says, glancing at me. "I can speak freely in front of her?"

Zoe snaps at him. "Don't look at her. Look at us."

Elijah sighs, long and deep. Almost bored, even though he was so visibly anxious about making this meeting less than an hour ago. "Tell us what you have to offer, or we're out of here. So far, all you've said is that you've faced off against a Merlin and won."

I hold perfectly still, unsure how to play this game of politics, of urgency and patience, of inviting the other party to show their hand without showing one's own hand at all. All I want to do is chase after the kidnapped girl, but the quick burn of Reggie's eyes on my face lets me know that while the demon's still playing the game, he's growing tired of it. An explosion is under the surface.

Reggie clasps his hands together. "Sent 'im packing, yeah."

Zoe leans back. "You got lucky, so what? Maybe if you'd killed one, I'd be impressed."

Reggie takes a loud sip of his beverage. "Y'have any idea how *hard* it is to kill a Merlin?"

"We've heard," Elijah responds smoothly. "Tell us something new."

"I got your *something new*." Reggie leans in close, expression turning sly. "Have you heard that someone is taking Merlins out? I bet that's some intel the King wants."

For the second time tonight, alarm bells ring in my head. I know Merlins. I may not know their faces or names, but I know their strength, their speed, their skill with aether. Sitting here in the bar, I can see their features and techniques behind my eyes. Golden irises, amber, deep orange. Fangs both beautiful and frightening. Bright flashes of silver-blue and blue-silver . . . quarterstaffs and scythes and mage flame tornadoes.

What of the Merlin boy who sacrificed his humanity to save you?

Wherever he is, wherever I sent him, I don't want him to die.

My technique for sealing my root is good, but something about my body must have changed at the memory of this Merlin I know—my scent, my heartbeat—because Elijah's eyes dance over my cheeks and the bridge of my nose. By the time I look up, he's looking at Reggie again.

Zoe turns to Reggie. "What do you mean, 'taking them out'?"

Reggie lifts a lazy shoulder. "Deading them. One by one. Eliminating the Order's perfect soldiers. Real methodical-like."

"I don't see what that has to do with us, and it's not why we agreed to meet." Elijah's face tightens. "That better not be your intel, or we're leaving."

Reggie waves a hand. "Nah, consider that a freebie. A demon-to-cambion courtesy, if you will. Maybe you're protected by the old man, but Merlins give us all equal trouble. Want us all equally dead. They don't check to see how much demon you are when they're running you through with an aether spear, kid."

Elijah's eyes narrow at the word "kid." "Thanks for the tip. But the old man is looking to retake the Court, not entertain a woulda-coulda-shoulda goruchel who's gone soft for human food and drink." Elijah raises a brow as Reggie finishes off his beverage.

Reggie's deep red eyes darken further at Elijah's insult—and stay that way. "Watch your tongue, crossroads child."

"What did you just call me?" Elijah snaps, fangs glinting.

"You heard me," Reggie snaps back. "I was on this plane killing humans for sport before you were a bad idea in your father's ballsa—"

Zoe's hands shoot across the table to grasp Reggie's throat. She squeezes hard enough for a human to choke, but Reggie merely grins. "Be very careful what you say about our father—and my brother. It's not nice to call people names, Regazel."

"You've gone and upset my sister," Elijah purrs. He leans forward on one elbow, tilting his head at Reggie. His eyes flick up to the bartender, Syd, who is watching our table as he dries a glass. "Zoe here is going to let you go. And when she does, tell us what you have to offer, or this meeting is over."

After a beat, Reggie withdraws his smile and gives a shallow nod.

Zoe releases his neck, and he rubs lightly at the imprint of her nails. "I heard the . . . *the old man*," he tries the phrase out, "is looking for something."

On either side of me, the twins grow still. Then, Elijah taps his glass once.

"He is. Has been. Are you suggesting you know where that something is?"

Reggie leans in. "I know who has a lead."

"You *know who has a lead*? I thought you *were* the lead." Zoe scowls and stands up. "Let's go, Elijah."

"No, no, wait," Reggie hisses, waving her back into her seat and glancing at the full bar behind us. "This is legit. It's a member of the Shadow Court, one of the King's own precious Shades who's gone rebel."

Elijah and Zoe stare at each other in silence. Elijah turns back to Reggie. "A Nightshade has the crown?"

"No," Reggie says, voice irritated. "A Shade has a *lead* on the crown. Aren't you listening? Approach her and she'll tell you. Probably."

"You're wasting our time." Zoe leans forward, baring her teeth. "The rebel Shades won't rejoin the Court if the King isn't *wearing* the crown. They won't even take a meeting with us as his emissaries. They're all mini-sovereigns of their own fiefdoms now. Approaching one empty-handed is an insult and a death wish, even for us—that demon, whoever they are, will ship us back to the King in body bags just to send a message."

"Then don't approach her empty-handed," Reggie says. "Bring tribute."

Zoe rolls her eyes. "You're full of bullshit. The crown has been lost for centuries. Even the King can't sense its location."

"Not lost," Reggie says. *"Hidden."*

"By the Morgaines, yes, we know." Elijah sighs. "The Morgaines enchanted the crown to be undetectable by any demon, including the King himself, its original forger and only bearer. I find it *very* difficult to believe that the Line of Morgaine suddenly, after fifteen hundred years of keeping both the crown and themselves concealed and untraceable, decided to change their tune and trot the crown out for public display."

A memory rises in my mind. Arthur's dreamscape. The King's crown behind an aether cage, like an artifact in a museum. Brief snatches of conversation between the original Morgaine and her half brother: *This crown is not unlike your Caledfwlch. It's . . . tied to you. Connected. That's why no one else can wield it in battle* but *you. An aether weapon.*

Just as I am connected to Excalibur, the King is connected to his crown. Our weapons are alive. *Is that why the King took Excalibur from me?* I think. *Because he knows what it means to lose our living weapons?*

Reggie beams. "That's the thing—they *didn't* trot it out. It was *stolen* from them."

Elijah's smile drops. "Say that again?"

"Word is, the Morgaines got overconfident and lax. Thought their secrecy and *special enchantments* would protect them forever, but times change." Reggie lifts a shoulder. "They've been making deals with a few demons lately—warlocks too. Seems they linked up with the wrong one. A warlock who didn't share their commitment to keeping the crown locked up. He snagged it and ran."

A warlock stole the King's crown? I just saw a warlock stealing a whole human being. Clearly these pact magic users keep themselves busy, but was this thief working for demons—or against them?

Zoe raises both brows at her brother, encouraging him, but Elijah does not appear to be moved. Not yet, anyway.

"The Morgaines didn't want one of the King's loyal demon servants to be able to return his crown to him in the event that its location was ever found, so they *also* enchanted it to be untouchable by demon hands," Elijah says. "Which means that, unlike a demon, a warlock *could* actually touch the King's crown without erupting in flames. But the rest of the story's a stretch, Reggie."

Reggie snarls. "I didn't come here to lie! I'm telling you, the crown is on the move!"

"On the move where?" Zoe demands. "Does this rebel Nightshade with a lead know where the warlock thief scuttled off to? A lot of good that does us. Only a Morgaine can remove a Morgaine spell, and they'll never help a Shade *or* the King. The crown could be sitting on this table right now and the King still couldn't touch it."

Reggie lowers his voice. "I've been working for this Shade for years and I want *out*. She ain't interested in going back under the boot of the King. She was never gonna tell anyone on his side that the crown resurfaced, but I overheard her talking to someone about it on the phone! She wanted to keep it secret, used code words, but I know who Shades mean when they call someone 'the old man.' I knew the crown she was talking about belonged to the King." He points to himself. "And I contacted you because I knew *you'd* want to know!"

The words leave me in a rush, my curiosity too much. "Which Nightshade has it?"

Zoe claps her hand over my mouth. "Don't answer that, Reggie!"

"Goddamnit, Bree," Elijah groans, squeezing his eyes shut.

Reggie grins. "But one of your party has asked for the name, Zoelle."

"She's *not* a member of our party," Zoe hisses. "She doesn't count."

Reggie's eyes sparkle with dark mirth. "She's at the bargaining table. She asked for the information. I am now free to give it, and if I do, that binds you to my demand in return."

My eyes widen. "M'sorry!"

Elijah groans. "Fine. The name will prove your loyalty to the cause. Name your demand."

"If the King retakes the Court, then I want in on the blessing," Reggie says.

"We can't make the King do anything," Elijah says.

"Then commit to making a case on my behalf."

Zoe and Elijah exchange glances. Finally, Zoe releases me and nods. "We'll commit to making the case for your blessing. Give us the name of the Shade."

Reggie sits back. "Daeza."

Zoe curses immediately. Elijah drops his head into his hands. "Couldn't have been any of the others?"

Reggie shrugs. "I didn't say it'd be easy."

Zoe curses again and glares at Reggie. "Daeza would throw you in the ring if she found out you were sharing her business."

"She already did." His eyes darken. "Why do you think I'm ratting her out to you? She needs to learn a lesson about treating her people like crap."

Elijah heaves a sigh. "If we can get in to see Daeza, if we can convince her to talk to us, *if* the lead on the crown checks out and we get it back, then we'll make sure you get prioritized when the time comes."

Zoe shakes her head and waves a hand. "That's a lot of *ifs*, Reggie. Don't know why you bother."

Reggie taps a finger on his glass. "You're too young to realize this, kid, but when you live as long as we can, you hedge your bets in every direction . . . and wait. I've given you three the name. Pay Daeza a visit or not. Your call."

After that, Reggie slides out from the booth—not before his eyes turn back to a dull brown—and the twins watch him go for a beat before turning their burning gazes on me.

"Sorry," I say, shrinking back into my seat.

Elijah springs to his feet in a blur. Using cambion speed in public, even in a dark corner of a human bar, tells me exactly how frustrated he is with me. "Home. Now."

Five minutes later, we're back out on the nearly empty sidewalk, walking home under the glistening light of snowfall and streetlights.

"So . . . ," I drop the Pendragon coin necklace back into place on my chest beneath my reacquired coat. "Daeza?"

Elijah and Zoe flank me, and neither one of them answers right away.

"Sounds like the King's been searching for a needle in a haystack for hundreds of years." I grimace. "Gotta be frustrating."

Silence, made worse by the quiet stillness that only snowfall can bring.

"Can't touch his own crown even if he finds it," I murmur. "That's wild. Morgaine magic sounds pretty intense."

"Morgaine enchantments are the most powerful concealments in history," Elijah mutters. "After the Order excised them, they went into hiding and perfected their spellcraft. The Morgaines themselves are untraceable when they want to be and so are their constructs, and anything those constructs are forged to occlude."

I pull my coat hood up higher, wincing at the pungent scent of the warlock's magic. "Can't he just forge another crown back in the demon dimension?"

"The King can't *go* back to the demon dimension!" Elijah whips around. "When Arthur Pendragon and Merlin took his crown, they did so with the intention to kill him, and it nearly worked. He eventually regained most of his lost power, but he can't return to his domain unless he bears the crown. He needs it to cross over; there is no passage back without it."

I stop on the pavement. "The King is . . . trapped here?"

"*Arthur and the Round Table* trapped him here. And in doing so, they denied the other world its king and denied the King his Court—but they guaranteed his revenge." Elijah turns around. "And I'm going to help him get it."

I don't know what to think of this revelation about the King, but I know one thing: it explains his potent anger and his single-minded focus to punish and destroy the Table. Not only did the original Round Table take his crown, depowering him near to death, but in the wake of that theft, his loyal subjects scattered and splintered, and he was blocked from returning to his own kingdom. No wonder he hates not just Arthur Pendragon, but his entire legacy. His entire bloodline. Including the blood that runs through my veins.

Sometimes when Erebus looks at me, I catch a flicker of dark humor and satisfaction pass across his features. Is it because he sees me, and our training together, as the poetic justice within his revenge? A phrase from my ancestor Vera appears bright in my mind: *wound turned weapon.*

"Does he—" I begin, but a bright red glow from my chest cuts me off. Each twin grabs one of my arms and blurs me into a nearby alley. We only barely make it into the deep, cold shadows between two buildings before my blood-mark fully awakens and begins to pulse.

The mark flares first at my sternum, bright enough to glow through three layers of material. It spills outward, liquid fire making furious branches down my ribs and up my collarbone, spreading over my shoulders, and forking into crimson lines across my biceps and forearms.

The twins stand back from me, eyes wide, having released me just in time not to be affected by the bloodmark's burn.

"Goddamn, that's bright," Zoe whispers, shielding her eyes.

Elijah edges closer, drawn to the pulsing red glow by an inch, then two. "Is he—"

"Calling me?" I mutter, watching the bloodmark rise in time with my heartbeat. "Yes."

Ever since the King reset his connection to his bloodmark, when it comes alive it brings with it his aether signature: myrrh, oud, saps, and incense. I associate those scents with Erebus's signature, but other times the magic of my mark smells—charred. Spices heated far too long to be pleasurable. An ancient scent that was once rich and full, now burnt to ashes. *That* scent I associate with his true form—not Erebus, the Shadow King.

"Does it hurt?" Elijah asks.

"No, it's . . ." I purse my lips, shame flooding me at once.

Elijah's eyes flicker up to mine, for once the red in them coming not from his own power but mine. "It's what?"

I take a beat to find the words until they spill out of my mouth in an angry stream. "It's a reminder, okay? That while he isn't the *source* of my power, he's forever linked to it, and I'm forever linked to him."

Elijah watches me closely, as if he can see that there's more that I'm not saying. "He do this often?"

The power begins to fade, finally, casting the alleyway in a softer red light. "Some times more than others, never predictable. Just often enough that I don't forget that I'm not *entirely* in control here," I say with a sour smile. "It's an unnecessary display of power, if you ask me."

"Every display of power is necessary," Elijah counters without ire. He steps back as the power dims. "But that one's particularly . . ."

"Creepy?" Zoe suggests.

"Annoying?" I offer.

"Conspicuous," says Elijah with a frustrated huff. "Imagine if he'd done that while you were at the Rat?"

"I wasn't supposed to *be* at the Rat, remember?" I say. "I was supposed to be safe at home, tucked away and hidden by his wards."

"Ugh, don't remind us," Zoe says, turning to walk back to the sidewalk. "Let's go."

By the time we get back to Erebus's historic Tudor home, it's snowing in earnest. Fat, wide flakes fall into Zoe's hair and across Elijah's dark knit cap. I know they're littering my two braids too. I shiver and wrap my hoodie tighter around my hands, more focused on my chilly fingers than where I'm going, so I bump into Elijah's back at the front step of the house where he's stopped.

"What're you doing?" I mutter. "Let's get inside, I'm cold."

Elijah turns back to me and eyes me up and down. "Why does your coat smell like warlock?"

I falter. Zoe doesn't help. "There was a Rootcrafter girl in the bathroom with a warlock. I tried to stop him from taking her away, but I . . . I couldn't. They escaped. Zoe—"

"Found her looking like a lost puppy," Zoe interrupts quickly, rolling her eyes. "Don't think Bree's ever encountered a warlock before, but I explained what their deal is. How gross pact magic smells."

Elijah sighs. "Didn't think Syd would entertain warlocks, but he did say business was slow. Must have let them in the back way. Offered the Rat up as a pit stop for a handsome fee, I'm sure. Rootcrafter power is hard to come by."

"You know about the Rootcrafters and the King?" I ask.

Elijah tilts his head at me. "The greater the demon, the greater the hunger." The wind shifts, and Elijah scowls, covering his nose. "You're gonna have to take that coat off. Leave it outside or, better yet, burn it. The old man hates that scent even more than we do and if he smells it on you, he'll know we took you somewhere we shouldn't have."

"He's right," Zoe answers. "Take it off."

The snow's really coming down now. "Out here?" I squeak.

Elijah's brows rise. "That's the point."

This is the first time I've ever felt the closeness of a shared secret with the twins, and I don't want to jeopardize the tentative peace with them over something that costs me nothing except a coat I found in the back of Zoe's closet.

I take the coat off and ask a question while I have their attention. "Won't the Rootcrafters' families call the police about their disappearances?"

"It won't matter if they do," Zoe says.

"Why?" I ask. "Does the King have contacts with the local police the way the Order does?"

"How do you know so much about the Order?"

"He told me," I say, carefully holding the coat out to Zoe, who snatches it between two nails, then blurs off into the woods. To bury it, I suppose. "But what happens when the 'Crafters get reported missing?"

"The amount that anyone cares about a missing person report depends entirely on who's gone missing," Elijah drawls.

My teeth are chattering, but I ignore them as I follow him to the front door. "You mean . . ."

"You know exactly what I mean," Elijah calls over his shoulder as he unlocks the front door. "Whether your abduction ends up on the news depends on who deems your unexplained absence newsworthy. Rootcrafters are Black. Rootcrafter girls, specifically, make a good target, because a missing Black girl won't raise the alarm bells the way a missing white girl would."

"You don't think it's messed up that he's taking advantage of human bigotry and apathy?"

"I tend to be more furious at humanity for cultivating and perpetuating said bigotry and apathy," Elijah says with an air of finality, "so, no."

In this moment, I find I don't have a counterargument for him.

All the same, as I lie awake in bed that night, I think about that girl and the iron in her voice when she told the warlock that I wouldn't follow her. The certainty that I'd choose myself and forget about her, and I wonder what kind of person I'd be if I let this go—as Zoe and Elijah seem capable of doing.

I may not know the people in my life, but I know myself.

I won't be able to let this go.

18

EREBUS RETURNS EARLY the next morning as the three of us are in the kitchen, hunched sleepily over our respective breakfasts.

He materializes in the foyer, out of sight, but we can hear his arrival. The small pop of air molecules being shoved aside by atoms suddenly filling the space, the whoosh and crackle of shadow magic surrounding his body. After months in this house, I can easily imagine the way he materializes out of the smoke. Often, he is already moving, wisps of gray and black trailing behind him as he departs one location and arrives at another.

The twins scramble up from their barstools to greet him. I don't bother. I hear his voice, distant before it gets far: "Back to your food." They return to their seats without a word.

I don't miss Elijah's eyes flashing crimson when they pass over me, sparking against my skin. He glances down at my uninterrupted meal of toast and a fried egg over medium as I cut into my yolk. I know he and Zoe resent that Erebus doesn't require me to stand or bow in his presence the way he expects the twins to. Elijah had asked about it within days of my arrival, and neither Erebus nor I gave him an explanation. Erebus simply told Elijah that it "was not his concern." After our adventure at the Rat last night, however, I find myself feeling chagrin.

I send Elijah an apologetic glance, and he sighs, nodding back. Apology accepted, I hope.

I glimpse Erebus's profile as he passes the kitchen archway and goes upstairs. Even in that quick passage, I try to catalog as much as I can about his movement, his general countenance. Gauge if he is well-rested or fatigued.

These slight shifts in his demeanor are the only details that suggest weakness in the most powerful demon in the world, and today, they are details that I cling to.

I have learned that shadow traveling is an energetically expensive ability and one that only he can do. And yet rarely does Erebus appear out of a shadow walk looking weakened. Today, there's light discoloration beneath his eyes. Skin drawn too tight over high cheekbones and chapped lips. Beneath his long coat, his shoulders are carried high and tense, and I'm reminded of a wild predator with haunches raised. He *is* run-down, then. Low on energy.

Hungry.

I grip my spoon tightly enough that it bends.

"Whoa, can you stop destroying the utensils?" Zoe's voice interrupts my thinking, and I blink up at her.

"What?" She points down at the spoon in my hand, bent backward into a U shape. "Oh. Sorry." I try to bend it back, but the dip in the middle seems here to stay. I'm usually better about my strength, but I must've gotten carried away.

"Uh-huh." Zoe moves to the sink to rinse out her cereal bowl. As she rinses her dish, I fall into another swirl of thoughts about my mentor.

The Shadow King seems to have no equal. He is his own kind of greater demon, maybe the oldest, and possesses abilities I didn't think possible. And yet he is not invulnerable. I don't know how much he consumes of either humanity or aether, but it must be a great amount for him to continue as he is.

The greater the demon, the greater the hunger, Elijah said.

I consider, for a brief moment, whether there is a way I could give *my* power to him so that he stops going after the Rootcrafters . . . but dismiss that fairly quickly. He has never once consumed my power in our time together or seemed interested in trying. He says he won't do that until I am at my strongest.

I move to clean my own dish, and Zoe shifts to the side at the sink. My mind is turning over everything I know again and again, searching for a way to stop him from feeding. And then, a way to rescue the girl I saw, who may or may not be his next victim.

The plate snaps in half in my hands.

"Oh," I mumble.

"That one's a goner." Zoe takes the broken pieces out of my hands and drops them into the trash.

"Briana!" Erebus calls from another room.

By the time I walk slowly to the kitchen entrance, Erebus has already descended the steps. He stands in the living room, rising wisps of anger radiating from his shoulders, telegraphing his mood.

After the initial shock of Erebus's sharp baritone, my body responds just as I've trained it to when in the presence of my mentor, my bloodmark holder, and my fellow king: with even breaths. I will my heart to slow from its racing pace. I imagine the rushing blood in my veins turning sluggish. Slow belly breath out, pushing down all the adrenaline and jitters, because I have nothing to fear.

I have had to adapt. Although Erebus has not fed on my negative emotions, he can detect them the way a hungry animal can smell a warm meal nearby. He knows when I am upset, and I have learned to bury those emotions down deep in his presence, lest they betray me.

It doesn't matter what Erebus does or how many masks he wears; he is an ancient demon of near-limitless power—and like every other full-blooded demon, it is not in his nature to be generous, kind, or humane. Closing myself off has helped me survive.

"Yes, Erebus?" I ask as I enter the room.

It doesn't matter that I've lived in his home for months. It doesn't matter that I've seen him eat like a human being, rest like a human being, even drive a car like a human being. I remind myself every day that a well-decorated, comfortable home is part of his mask. Wearing finely tailored clothing is part of his mask. Even his niceties are part of his mask.

He holds out his arm. An invitation that I, as always, have no choice but to accept.

It surprises me that he shadow walks us both to our training location, but then I realize that it's not the usual spaces: his wooded backyard or the basement beneath his home. Today, we stand before a clearing where a single gray warehouse sits in the middle of a gravel driveway.

"We are just outside of town." Erebus answers my unspoken question.

Without needing to ask me to follow, he begins walking toward the warehouse. "The original Erebus's family, the Varelians, own this property. There's no one around, but as your magic can be quite bright and potent, it will be better to fight inside the training center."

"You were Erebus yesterday," I comment.

A few steps ahead of me, he pauses and turns, waiting for me to catch up. "Yes."

I pull a hair tie out of my back pocket and begin to twist my twin braids into a bun, away from my neck. Not for the first time since I've come to live at Erebus's home, I consider what his time with the Regents must be like. The Order stripped him of his every power fifteen hundred years ago. Brought him low. And the Morgaines, who were part of the Order before they themselves were exiled, ensured that he could not even begin to claw his way back to the power he once held. I know from experience that demon and cambion natures are passionate—and sometimes temperamental and violent. How can he sit at Cestra's side while actively plotting her downfall? How can he uphold the Order's mission, knowing all the while that it is *his* mission to destroy it— forever? The depths of his ancient patience and simmering rage are difficult for me to fathom, or maybe I just don't want to.

Erebus tilts his head curiously at my thoughtful silence. "Really? No questions? No request for details about my time with the Council or Legendborn?"

I finish tying up my hair. "You don't answer any questions about my life from before."

He dips his head. "This is true. And yet I am left to wonder if you are not asking because you know I won't answer, or if you are not asking because you are no longer curious."

"What's the difference?"

His eyes narrow slightly, and his lips draw back in slight displeasure and impatience, as if I am a student who has disappointed him. "The difference is *you*, Briana. And what you want. Are you no longer curious about your past?"

I think of the girl's face beneath the bathroom stall door. Her eyes widened with fear, then narrowed with determination when she ordered me not to follow. I can still call up the stench of her captor and the sparkling triumph in his eyes as she went willingly with him. Is she held somewhere, now, at knifepoint until Erebus leaves to consume the root flowing through her?

"Not particularly," I say, and feel the truth of it in my bones.

His deep red irises seem to bore a hole through my face.

"I see." He pauses. "But you are curious about something else."

No reason to lie. "Are you hunting Rootcrafters?"

If he is surprised by the question, he doesn't show it. "Not currently."

"Have you fed from them?"

"You know I have."

I grind my teeth. "Recently?"

"No."

"Would you hire a warlock to hunt them down for you?"

At this, his mouth twists. "No. I have not, nor will I ever, hire pact magic mercenaries to do what I could easily do myself, and have done since before humanity *invented the wheel*."

"Tell me how you really feel," I say dryly.

"Warlocks are an abomination and a stain on the worldly activities of demonkind."

I huff. "I didn't mean that literally."

"Then I hope my answers suffice," Erebus says as he walks away.

I don't know if I can believe him. I never know. But I follow him anyway.

The wind whips around us, sending the long-faded leaves of oaks and maples swirling in circles among the remnants of hay in front of the warehouse. The building itself seems well taken care of, and the painted exterior is a dark charcoal. Too fresh to have been left to bleach and crack in the dry winter sun.

I wonder if the Varelian family still cares for this place, or if Erebus himself pays to have staff tend to it to keep up appearances.

Again, he seems to read my mind. "The Varelians are all long gone now, but their funds help keep the place running. I have taken young Merlins from the academy here from time to time, for a change in scenery and cooler weather when the Asheville summers grow too hot for their comfort."

My hip tingles with the memory of heated fingers pressed against my skin through a borrowed dress. Scorching palms beneath my thighs, bark scraping my spine, lips hot and burning. "Because Merlin bodies run hot," I reply automatically.

"Hm." Erebus turns to me, eyes sharp. "And how would you know that? What Merlin bodies have you had such close contact with that you know of their core temperature?"

I blink. Those hands, those fingers . . . the trails of heat . . . they were from a Merlin. A flush seeps through my neck and cheeks.

When I don't respond, Erebus rolls his eyes and shudders. "Teenagers are the same in every era of time. Unrelentingly driven by their hormones and libidos. I don't need to be told what happened in order to infer it."

I scowl. "I'm *not* talking to you about my hormones or any . . . happenings."

"I have trained teenaged Merlins for long enough not to *want* to ask you about any happenings either," Erebus says with a groan. "But I can't help wondering: What exactly were you thinking with him, Briana? Truly, you can do better. He was a waste of talent."

I don't have to know this boy to hear the cruelty of Erebus's words. "Don't say that about him. About anyone."

"If you prefer."

Then, it's my turn to stop. "Are you saying I was *with* the Merlin boy?"

"To my torment, yes," Erebus mutters, distaste evident in his deep red irises. "You were entangled with the very same reckless, arrogant Merlin boy who sacrificed himself for you." He pauses as if considering, then releases a new detail that he has not yet shared. "He was a Kingsmage."

My throat sticks. *He was a Kingsmage.* "I didn't know that. . . ."

"And what does that knowledge change?"

I exhale sharply. "Now I know he was a guardian as well as my friend, as well as—" I gaze around the winter landscape, heart speeding up. "He was important. To more than just me."

"And now he is gone," Erebus states. "Sent away to his mother, to suffer."

I feel as though I've been physically struck. The guilt comes in new waves, reaches deeper and wider. The Merlin boy was a Kingsmage, which means he is missed in more ways than one. Not just by me or his friends or the Scion of Arthur he was mistakenly bonded to, but from his own duties. From himself. Just like I've gone missing from *myself.*

And I was a part of that.

Sent away to his mother, to suffer.

But there are other things I know: I know the Order can be wrong, and I know their own knowledge is incomplete. I know there was a Kingsmage who somehow retained their humanity against all odds and in secret. Which means there's a very good chance that this boy *isn't* missing forever.

That he's not really gone—just absent.

He was a Kingsmage. Erebus has told me too much. Words meant to amplify my guilt have found a way to transform it. Hope sparks inside the wave, a tiny beacon of defiance.

Erebus mistakes my silence for sorrow.

"In your own words, you left the Order because they asked far too much of you. They wanted your suffering. Their demands of you were unfair for a teenage girl, a grieving girl." He sighs, long and deep. "I do not wish to bring up topics that pain you."

"Then why do you?"

"Because I want you at your strongest." His face betrays nothing.

I eye his placid face, his dark, fathomless eyes. "Why should I believe you? Why should I believe *anything* you say?"

"You have asked me this many times," he replies. "And I will say again, I will not lie if you ask me a question directly. Beyond that, you must rely on your other senses, your other knowledge, in order to determine whether you can trust me. This is true in every case. With every opponent."

"*Are* you my opponent?"

His mouth quirks. "That, also, is up to you. But I would not advise you to consider me one. Even you cannot fight a mountain, or bring down the wind, or stop the sea."

"Bold words."

"I have earned them." Erebus looks up at the sky for a moment, watching the clouds pass. "Do you know what a quest is, Briana?"

"Something a knight goes on to save a maiden. Slay a monster. Retrieve a treasure. Like an adventure, but with a purpose."

He tsks. "Knights have staked a claim on the term, it's true, but they don't own the very idea of a quest. Anyone can embark on one. Try again."

I huff. "A quest . . . is a long journey that someone goes on to search for something."

He hums. "Better. Nearly every culture on the planet has produced a quest story, although they may call these journeys by different names. While the purpose of a quest is often defined as an external achievement—slay the dragon, save the maiden—the true end product is not external but internal." He looks at me. "The beginning of a quest is often loss. A great and necessary loss, to spark the first step down the road unknown."

"Are the missing people in my life a necessary loss?" My voice comes out too hot, too angry, but Erebus does not comment on it.

"You've gotten stronger in your time here," Erebus observes. "They were holding you back."

I consider his comment and the conversation that led us here. Lies and truths. Enemies and mentors. Maidens and dragons and demons, and who gets to slay them.

My mouth moves faster than my brain. "Is the crown *your* great and neces-sary loss?"

He stills. A flicker of fury crosses his face, followed by the vibrating shim-mer of grief—too quick to hold, too quick to catch. For most people, anyway. I recognize that sequence of expressions because I have felt them cross my own face. And shuttered them away like him too.

"My crown is none of your concern." With a wave of his hand, a ward around the warehouse ripples in a thick wave of magic, then disappears.

In a few steps, we cross the previously warded gravel and stand before the heavy wooden beam that lies over the doors, barring us entry until one of us raises it.

I haven't hit something in a couple of days, and I'm feeling . . . antsy.

A tiny figment of a warning runs up my spine before we step inside. I don't know what it's warning me against, exactly, except that it's something about Erebus today. Something that I need to be watchful of. Something more dan-gerous than normal, more treacherous. When I realize what it is, I turn to him. "You're upsetting me. On purpose."

"Am I?" His eyes study me. Without warning, he grasps my right wrist.

"What——" I protest, but before I can say more, my chest burns to life under his scrutiny. My bloodmark, blooming in jagged vines, hot and bright from my chest, down my forearms, to my wrists, and right to his hand. Oud and incense.

He hums quietly and releases me. "You seem strong today. Steady."

"I could have told you that." I rub the bones of my wrist and thumb, delayed indignation from last night's surprise bloodmark calling coloring my voice. "You don't have to keep activating it."

"Forgive an old man his paranoia. The Morgaines have magicked my crown so that it does not return an answer when I call. With your bloodmark, at least, I can keep an eye on my investment," he says. "Each time I call it, I can feel that you are gaining power."

I scowl.

"After you," he says, and gestures for me to enter the darkened warehouse.

He navigates to the left-hand side of the dusty space, hitting a light switch that I can't see. At once, a series of sconces embedded in the walls around the three levels of the warehouse begin to light up, traveling around us until the entire space is lit in a warm, golden glow.

The warehouse itself is massive and modern. The floor is laid with the same sort of bouncy black training surface I've seen in the Lodge. There are even three concentric circles, just as there were for the Page bouts in the Squire tournament at the Southern Chapter. The walls are reinforced, and the surface has been fitted with a variety of handholds, long spikes, and curved metal hooks. There are even hanging lengths of rope attached to heavy metal rings in the ceiling that I can imagine Merlin trainees using to swing from one end of the room to the other.

I wonder if Erebus brought the Merlin boy here at one point, or if he left the academy to join his Kingsmage post and missed out on training at the Varelian compound. I wonder if the boy even remembers his training, or if his past has faded away beneath the . . . cravings. He is missing, and so am I. Missing people, missing ourselves.

I swallow, blinking hard against the heat of unexpected tears in my eyes. My voice comes as if it's from far away. "Have you brought the twins here?"

Erebus is watching me take in the space with unreadable eyes. "No."

"Why not?"

"Because they lack focus."

I blink, thinking of Zoe's mercurial demeanor and Elijah's laser focus on their missions for his king. "You could train them more often. They told me about being children of one of your Nightshades—"

"Children born from Shades are rare assets," Erebus says curtly. "For now, I am training them to be emissaries. My eyes and ears. To negotiate on my behalf. Balanced cambions who can walk between the demon and human worlds are too useful to lose in a back-alley scuffle."

Now I think of the frustration of Elijah and the impetuous nature of his sister. How powerful they could become if they were given a real chance. "You train me. The twins could train with us—"

"The twins have not experienced what you have." Erebus's eyes narrow. "You have walked with death in ways they have not, and I find that makes your potential, your hunger, *sharper*. In all things. And, of course, I need your strength to increase my own; the twins cannot offer me what you will at your peak."

I don't know how to respond to that, so I don't. I walk to the center of the room, and something about the look on Erebus's face sends my heart pounding.

The tone in the room has shifted.

This is the knife's edge that I walk. Seeking—and gaining—information and perspective while living with the danger of the King.

Biding my time until he makes me strong enough to escape him.

Breathe in, breathe out. "Shall we, *old man?*" I ask.

When I look at Erebus again, he allows himself a small smile. "Let us begin."

19

"LOOK ALIVE, BRIANA!"

One of the three aether foxes Erebus has forged yowls from its low position in front of me, another paws at the earthen floor to my left, and the third hisses from my right.

I take a deep belly breath and exhale my furnace open, feel the flames roll beneath the surface of my skin, and expand into my limbs and fingers. Pressing against the limits of my body, ready to be released.

My right foot slides back once, then again, to create space between me and the living constructs. Each fox has paws the size of my face. Each has scales lining its massive back. And each is made of crystalline aether, but their aether is not the same.

Because the Shadow King commands not one form of power but three.

The first fox construct shines in silver-blue like a Merlin's construct.

The second is green-yellow, like the aether of an isel or goruchel.

The third is barely a fox shape at all—made of the nearly formless obsidian-black smoke that is unique to its caster.

The silver-blue hellfox tenses, preparing to leap—

Defend.

A deep purple crystal shield springs into place just as the fox swipes the air in front of my nose. Its nails scrape down the hardened root, dragging sparks in their wake.

I jump back, taking the shield with me—and the fox screeches in failure.

The other two foxes, one on my left and one on my right, make low, chittering sounds. They tense together—

I release the shield. Raise both hands with fingers wide.

Protect. A round dome, sized to fit me, shining and solid.

The foxes crash into my barrier, paws and limbs meeting its walls.

Their bodies crumple. Slide.

"Very good, Briana. Your barrier holds."

The three foxes recover. Grow still.

"For now."

That is my only warning. The foxes spring—

With a snap of his fingers, Erebus transforms the creatures in midair from foxes into towering bears with beady eyes and dripping fangs—and much more power behind their attacks.

Their heavy paws strike—and my dome dents.

I send more power surging into my construct—but the bears' paws are too heavy, and the walls crush inward. "They're going to break it!" I shout.

"Then stop them," Erebus replies calmly.

"I can't attack and defend at once!"

"Then learn," he insists.

I grit my teeth and draw up even more power from within my chest, sending it through my arms, down my elbows, into my wrists, and out from my fingertips. The rush of root flows into layers behind the first barrier, flexing and adjusting behind the dents to reinforce them.

The bears circle me on the ground, roaring as they search for weak spots in my sphere.

"Good," Erebus calls. "A second layer working beneath the first. Repairing it." I can just make out his dark figure as he watches from the shadows. "Now, how long can you keep that up?"

"What?" I exclaim.

He is already turning from me and pacing toward the entrance to the warehouse.

"I've given a bit of my own will to the constructs. A sliver of independence so that they can function without my supervision. They will keep going until they reach you—or until I return." He taps his watch. "Merlins aged eight or nine can last as long as an hour. Kingsmages, when pushed, can hold a simple protective construct like this in place for up to six hours before they break."

He looks up at me before he exits.

"Let's see where you fall, Briana Matthews."

Then, he's gone, leaving the heavy doors to bang shut behind him.

"Erebus!" I call over the sound of the roaring constructs. "Wait!"

My dome has been up for a few minutes at most now, but it's already straining me. There's sweat at the back of my neck, in between my shoulder blades, running down the Pendragon necklace.

I try to tune out the animals' sounds, the dull thuds of heavy, padded paws striking against the structure around me. I close my eyes and focus on the furnace in my chest, drawing another round of flame out the way one might scoop out fresh, hot coals to deliver them to an empty hearth. I send a fresh wave of flames down my limbs to my hands, plenty to apply another layer to the construct—but at my fingertips, the magic stutters and sparks out.

Not from a loss of power, but from a loss of focus.

From broken attention.

From Erebus, upsetting me on purpose and rattling me before we even entered the barn.

For so long, I had no command over my root. Now, I can control it, but my mind and heart interrupt that control.

Erebus's creatures seem to sense my desperation, my thinning application of root, and growl more fiercely.

I don't know how long I keep drawing more from a well that is so deep that I cannot sense its end.

Time loses meaning—I can only follow the rhythm of protection.

Draw root up, breathe it out. Send it to reinforce the layers.

Draw root up, squeeze it out. Flood it into the claw marks.

Draw root up, force it out. Harden it into the gouges.

In the end, I become a ball on the floor, the dome small and tight around my heels and shoulders, barely covering my head.

The roaring has gotten closer—the constructs bellowing as they near their prey.

My teeth clatter a rapid tattoo, rattling my jaw. I curl tighter, a fine tremor working its way up my spine, growing, until I begin to convulse on the floor.

There is one more well I can draw from, and I do it just before my root shield collapses—Arthur's armor. A fixed construct that draws from the ambient aether in the air rather than the furnace inside me, and one I can call on with ease now. His armor snaps into place around me, helm and all, just as the bears' blows break through the shield and onto my body.

But even the armor has a time limit.

I feel it fading, denting, and crumbling.

I smell the bears' hot and hungry breaths as they heave and roar—

They're going to shred me to pieces.

I've been gouged open before. My wet muscles split wide to the forest air, parts of me exposed that should never be.

The first bear's strike rips my forearm open—and I scream.

The second set of claws tears my hand down to the bone—and I whimper.

The third bear digs two claws into the tops of my thighs—and drags them to my knees.

This is not how I'm supposed to die, alone in a warehouse at the mercy of creatures that aren't even real—

Then, they stop.

And the pain disappears.

My heart thunders, a train of blood in my ears—until I hear a quiet sound.

A slow, steady clap of hands.

I take two shuddering breaths and open my eyes a sliver—to see a pair of shiny dress shoes about a foot in front of my face. I drag my eyes up to find Erebus standing over me with a pleased expression on his face, one hand holding a bronze stopwatch.

"Take a guess at how long your constructs lasted."

"I . . ." I gaze down at my body, still curled in a ball, and find that I am not lying in a pool of my own blood, and the bears are nowhere to be found. I am uninjured, entirely. "What . . . what happened?"

"How long, Briana?"

I struggle to follow his words, reconciling them with what I'd just experienced. How long had I lasted? "I don't know. I don't—"

He shows me the digital screen of the bronze stopwatch. "Four hours and twenty-seven minutes."

"What?" As I push myself to my elbows, I feel the echoes of the attacking bear claws all over my body. The cognitive dissonance of feeling wounded but not seeing any wounds.

"Not as long as a Kingsmage, but that's to be expected. This is still a very, very impressive time for a first effort."

I can barely keep up with what he's saying. I blink once, then twice, staring at my forearms and fingers, my thighs, where I'm sure deep gashes should sit. They are phantom wounds, but . . . "It felt so real."

"A mesmer," Erebus explains, waving a hand. "An illusion. One I implanted into the creatures to activate upon your failing reserves. You believed it was happening, and your brain supplied the rest of the experience."

"They were slicing me open. . . ."

"An illusion," he repeats. He does not offer his hand to help me stand, so I am left to make it to my feet without him. "You will always think it's real, no matter how many times we do this, because the human brain has a survival instinct gained from believing that the hidden thing in the dark is truly there. It benefits you to believe that you are being attacked."

"It *benefits* me?" I gasp.

"Yes. You are well on your way to becoming unstoppable." He steps back and snaps his fingers, this time bringing three wolves to life. "Again."

Becoming unstoppable. One of the goals I stated on my first day with him. It sounds right. Sounds good. But . . . my throat constricts. Can I do this again?

Before me, the wolves await their creator's command, tails swaying softly in anticipation. There is no ire to them. No bite or rage.

And yet just looking at the creatures sparks a tremor in my hands.

Erebus moves on to his next inquiry, fine-tuning his lesson as he manipulates his constructs. "You only drew on Arthur's power at the very end. Why?"

"I don't need Arthur," I say, voice cracking. The floor swims before me, rippling even though my feet are still. "Don't want him."

"Understandable, given your history. But perhaps you should call on your other ancestors directly this round," he says as he feeds power into the wolves. "The ones who tapped into your power could—"

"I can't," I say quietly.

He straightens and drops his hands. "Why not?"

Realization hits me a moment too late. My mouth opens—and I shut it tight.

His eyes narrow in suspicion.

"You do not speak of your maternal ancestors. I thought that perhaps you had been weakened after your possession by Arthur at Volition, but now I see something in your eyes. A secrecy that I do not like." He steps closer. "Call on them. Now."

"No," I say, and look away.

"Now, Briana. You are a powerful Medium, if untrained." He casts and forges a small knife in an instant and tosses it my way. I catch it in the air. "Use your blood and call on them."

"I can't."

He goes still. "Can't . . . or won't, Briana?"

"Can't," I answer, finally glaring at him. "I . . . burned my ancestral stream."

The warehouse is silent around us. My heart pounds in my chest.

His stillness should scare me, but I only feel numb. "When?"

"Right before I used my power to call to you at the Northern Chapter."

His eyes flare red. "And that means . . . ?"

"That I can't speak to Vera or Arthur or anyone, even if I wanted to. I can't blood walk through their memories. I can't ask for help. And they can't possess me or demand things of me that I cannot give."

The blade dissolves in my hand.

"Which means you cannot search Arthur's, or indeed *any* of the previous Scions of Arthur's, memories, can you?" he asks, his voice deadly quiet. "You cannot invite a possession?"

"No," I say. "Why would I want to? You saw what happened with Arthur. He took me over completely. I couldn't fight him on my own. If I try again, he might never let me go!"

"Silence!" he snarls.

My mouth snaps shut, but my trembling fingers curl into fists.

"Why would *I* want you to be possessed again? The answer is simple." He leans close. "Because the Morgaines stole my crown and hid it *and themselves* for centuries, but *one* of your Scion ancestors could be the key to finding the crown and a Morgaine who can unlock it at long last."

"You wanted me to ask one of Arthur's other descendants to tell you about the Morgaines?" I shake my head in confusion. "There's no guarantee they'd help me—"

"They will if I threaten the end of their bloodline," Erebus growls.

Dread spirals in my belly.

"But only a descendant vessel and Medium with *full control* over her abilities can resist the possession of an ancient spirit. You were not yet powerful enough to do this at Volition, and even though you have shown much progress with me, you still cannot control the spirits you would call. You need more training to make it possible, more time. But because you, in your childish *tantrum*, burned away your ability to commune with any spirits *at all* . . . then it sounds like we shall never find out what type of Medium you could become."

"I . . ." I find I can't say I am sorry, exactly. "I didn't know."

He stares at me for a long, long moment.

Then, he walks away, flicking his wrist at the wolves. *"Again."*

"No."

He twists back to me in a blur. "What did you say?"

"I said, *no*," I repeat quietly. I point back with a shaking hand to where I'd lain curled on the training floor, weathering his siege. "That was . . . awful. It was . . . *torture*." My eyes burn at the corners. "I never want to do that again. Never."

His red, burning eyes turn cold. "Are you defying me, Briana?"

I swallow hard. "If the illusion is so consuming that I can't convince myself I'm safe, then I'm *not* safe. And I can't trust you to end the attack, because ending the attack isn't what you want."

His jaw clenches. "Are you quitting? Running?"

"I guess I am," I say.

"You are made of tougher mettle than this," he insists.

"Maybe I'm not!" I shout. In the ensuing silence, a new thought chills me. "Will you force me to keep going? Threaten me with the debt I owe you?"

A pause.

"No. Not yet."

I know better than to let myself feel relieved. "Not yet" still means "someday." He grows so still, he becomes a shadow himself. When he speaks, it's not Erebus's voice that reaches me, but the King's. "Shadows are birthed from both light *and* darkness, Briana Matthews."

"I'm not a shadow." I shake my head. "Take me back."

After a long moment, the King waves the wolves away and steps closer, black threads already pulling toward us both. "If you prefer."

20

THE NEXT MORNING when I come downstairs, Erebus is in the kitchen and the pallor is gone from his olive skin. His high cheekbones are brushed with a dusty pink, the whites of his eyes bright as he informs Elijah of his plans for the day.

I don't need to wonder why his demeanor has changed. Why he appears so rested and replenished.

Aether and humanity, those are what all demons need, and sometime overnight after he returned me to his home, Erebus consumed one or the other—or both.

The memory of the Rootcrafter girl arrests me where I stand, hovering in the archway between the main living room and the kitchen. I wonder if he fed on her. Or if by some chance, she made it out alive. Then I wonder if I'm just kidding myself the same way Zoe's laugh fuels her own denial of what the Shadow King is capable of.

I watch Elijah and Erebus talk, hear Zoe clink around in the kitchen as she prepares her own breakfast, and realize that I can't laugh this away. I can't wish apart the truth, because even if I don't remember who my people are, I know how I *feel*—and I know what I know.

I know what the King did to me yesterday, all in the name of *training*. It doesn't matter that I want to become unstoppable—a relentless force that can't be denied—if those are his methods for transforming me. I will become unstoppable on my own if I must, in my own way.

"Briana." Erebus's low voice calls to me.

My head snaps up. "What?"

"Come here, please."

I walk into the kitchen. Both twins eye me carefully as I approach. In his chair at the counter with a mug of coffee in hand, Erebus narrows his eyes and wrinkles his nose. "Why are you . . . leaking guilt and anger? Is this because of how we left our session?"

As he speaks, I scent the tiniest hint of brightness from his breath. Magic— that does not belong to him. Too lively to belong to a demon or a goruchel. Too familiar to be aether.

I scented the same magic in the dimly lit, dirty bathroom at the Rat. The recognition strikes me so swiftly, I have to steel myself not to respond to it.

If I only suspected it before, then I know it now.

Root. He has recently fed on *root*. Not just any root, but the root that belongs to the kidnapped girl.

"Briana? I asked you a question."

I blink back to the room, to the sensation of sparkling red eyes glancing across my skin. To the eyes of the twins on me, waiting for me to respond.

I affect a bored eye roll. "Yes," I lie. "I'm still mad about our session."

"I feared as much." He sighs. "It is true that one route to my objectives has closed, but I have spent fifteen hundred years creating and attempting new strategies when previous ones did not come to fruition. Your failure will not deter me from retaking my Court and crown."

I feel reckless, so I speak recklessly too. "*My* failure? *You're* the one who has been plotting and planning for fifteen hundred years with nothing to show for it."

Silence. Erebus's red irises flicker to black, his usual black pupils shift to crimson—and then his eyes return to normal. The only hint that I have enraged him.

As we hold each other's gaze, I wonder what I could say to make him even angrier. Maybe even enough to lose his human form entirely. I wonder what I could get away with when he is, technically, bound to protect me.

"You'll watch your tongue around a sovereign," Elijah bites out, jumping to his feet.

"I do not need a defender, Elijah," Erebus says without looking away from me.

Elijah's jaw drops at his guardian's measured response. "Sire, she speaks to you like you're a common Shadow—"

"Briana is not my subject," Erebus cuts him off smoothly, and this time, his eyes do flash at his ward. "I do not demand her obedience as I would a subject. As I demand it of you and your sister."

"And why is that?" Elijah says, thrusting a hand out to himself and his sister. "We are balanced cambions. True hybrids. Rarer than rare. She is what, exactly? A walking battery? So what? We have served you for *five years* without complaint—"

"I would call this outburst a complaint, wouldn't you?" Erebus stares at Elijah, whose face is twisted in unreleased rage. "Your father has served me for nearly twenty centuries. That is the sole reason I took you and your sister in when you needed shelter. You have proven your value over time, Elijah, but do not overstep generosity extended to you not of your own earning. You are a child. You and your sister are mere blinks in the eternal eye of time."

"And Bree isn't?" Elijah challenges.

"Briana is a once-in-a-millennium confluence of events. Irreplaceable and invaluable. You are her opposite in every way."

Silence falls again in a room that is now filled with shadow. At Elijah's side, a fine tremor has set in across Zoe's narrow shoulders. Her brother's eyes are glassy with emotion but burning with every response he visibly holds back.

I don't have any love for the twins, but Elijah's face, its mixture of shame and anger, sends a sharp stab of pain through my chest. A familiar pain, for another person who did not deserve Erebus's ire. And Zoe's frustration, bottled and held as she somehow avoids that same ire but watches her brother receive it all . . . it is familiar too.

And how I feel now, the sudden desire to protect them both . . . reminds me of . . . *me*.

The me from before.

"Leave them alone," I command. The three of them look at me at once.

Erebus blinks. "Is that an order?"

"Yes, it is"—I raise my chin—"and I suggest you take it."

"Stay out of this, Bree!" Zoe pleads.

Erebus watches me, eyes curious. "Let her speak. Tell me why I should follow your orders, Briana."

I look to Elijah. "Because Elijah is loyal. He and Zoe have a lead on your crown and should be rewarded for their work, not insulted for their dedication. Be a leader, not a tyrant."

Zoe's brows shoot up. Erebus looks between his wards. "What lead? Speak."

Elijah's mouth works open and closed for a moment before he recovers. "I did not—" He blinks at me. "The lead is not substantiated. A contact, Regazel, he . . . he told us that a member of your Court knows where it is."

Erebus goes very, very still. "One of my Shades has the crown?"

Elijah stiffens. "No, sire. But one knows where it is."

"Which?"

Elijah hesitates. "Daeza."

The King's expression darkens as he speaks, but this time, the ire is turned inward. "Another dead end, then."

"We're not sure," Zoe whispers. "We were going to ask to visit Daeza—"

"That won't be necessary."

Elijah begins to protest, but Erebus shakes his head. "Of all my Shades, Daeza is the *least* likely to let slip any information about the crown's whereabouts, if she even knows such a fact; its return to me would put an end to her empire of"—his face twists in irritation—"earthly delights. If Daeza knows where the crown is, she'll never risk *my* discovering it. She would kill you both as my emissaries for even asking."

"If Zoe and I have suitable tribute," Elijah begins, "we can visit. Investigate for ourselves."

"No." Erebus's tone is final.

"We won't make any promises to her, no bargains—" Elijah adds.

"*No.*" Erebus draws up to his full height. "If Daeza, by some miracle, does not kill you the moment you set foot in her domain, sending my emissaries to a Shade of the Court based on *hearsay* will make me appear desperate before my own subjects, when many already disparage me without the power of the crown and have abandoned their fealty for centuries."

Elijah frowns. "But—"

"This discussion is *over*, Elijah," Erebus says. "Briana, you are to train on your own for the day. Stay within the wards."

"Where are you going?" I ask.

"There are pressing matters that I must attend to with the Order and Council. Trouble brews where I cannot afford for it to grow."

"What kind of trouble?"

His gaze flickers to me. "The kind that sees too much."

With that, he gives us all a hard look before closing his eyes and disappearing in a cloud of billowing dark smoke.

Elijah growls deep in the back of his throat and speeds to the back door, a blur in bright green. He's on the other side and into the woods before Zoe or I say a word.

She collapses onto the stool at the countertop and leans her head back, groaning. "Ughhhhhh, that was not good."

I sigh. "I thought he would *want* to hear about the meeting with Regazel. . . ."

"Not like that." Her head pops back up. "Elijah wanted to get the details straight before he brought the intel to the old man. Like he said, it's all hearsay at this point. All of those 'ifs' I mentioned, remember?"

I wince. "So I made it worse?"

"Sure did." She shifts forward, dropping her elbows on her knees, and her eyes soften. "But I appreciate you trying to help us out. Elijah does too, even if he's too proud to say it."

"I won't expect a thank-you."

"You shouldn't," she says. "He wants to earn a place on the old man's Court, to be on equal footing with our father."

"Is that even possible?"

She lifts a shoulder. "Maybe. Our place here is an experiment. To see if a balanced cambion born from a Shade can become as strong as a Shade themself. The alternative is . . ." She shudders. "Being out in the world of humans on our own. Neither of us wants that. Our mom's side of the family doesn't know about the demon world. They don't understand us."

"Sorry to hear that." And I am.

Her eyes dart up to mine. "We don't miss what we never had, yeah?"

I smile. "True. I was just going to say, *they're* missing out. You and Elijah aren't . . . awful."

"Thanks." She huffs a laugh, then pauses, gazing toward the yard. "Sucks that we got banned from even *trying* to go to Daeza's, though, cuz I was thinking last night that it'd be great if we could save the girl you saw the other night, or save another one like her. Maybe even save a *lot* of girls like her."

"You *do* want to save her!" I cry, my heart expanding with warmth for her. "I *knew* it." I don't know if I'm too late to save the Rootcrafter from the bathroom, but I've got to try. And with Zoe's help . . .

She rolls her eyes. "Don't be annoying. Of course I want to save her. Elijah and I need to stay in the old man's good graces, but I'm not *heartless*." She looks out the window again. "Another circumstance, another day, that girl that night coulda been you . . . coulda been *me*. And who would come looking for us? Who would fight a human, much less a demon, to save us?"

"Yeah." I inhale sharply, then release a slow breath. "Who."

Not for the first time, I wonder if those people who I can't remember, the ones Erebus says treated me badly, might be wondering where I am. Wondering if I'm okay. Looking for me.

I had called the girl's potential losses and disconnections from her community "a type of death."

Does that mean I've died a type of death too?

I turn Zoe's comments over and over in my mind, considering what it means to go missing and then be sought, be severed, then connected, but my mind catches on one sentence. *Maybe even save a* lot *of girls like her.*

"Wait." I hold up a hand. "What does our visiting Daeza or finding the crown have to do with saving other Rootcrafters?"

She lifts a brow. "Do you even know *why* he wants the crown?"

"I know it's an aether weapon, like Arthur's Excalibur. The crown aided him in battle. Made him strong. Helped him lead his Court, his armies. And that he needs it to go back to the other side."

Her grin spreads, slow and devilish. "I love it when I know something you don't."

I roll my eyes. "It's not a competition."

"Of course it is, but anyway," she says, "Excalibur's like . . . a fancy sword. The crown is better." Zoe's eyes dance, brightening in her face. "*Much* better."

My heart picks up. "Say more."

We find Elijah in the clearing in front of the barn. He is sitting a few feet from the ward, staring sullenly at the glimmering surface.

"What's a tribute?" I stop at his side and stare down at him. Behind me, Zoe watches with curious eyes.

Elijah glances up at me, then away. "What do you want?"

"What's a tribute?" I repeat.

He leans back on his hands in the gravel, stretching his neck in the sun. "It's an offering made from one leader to another or from one supplicant to a sovereign. It signifies respect, serves as a physical manifestation of your humility, and is a required precursor to a request. The Shades who hold territories allow new supplicants, new requests, every month."

"What's the best tribute for a Shade?"

Elijah rolls his eyes in my direction without moving. "The Nightshades are nearly as old as the King himself. Old enough to be their own lords. They are proud and stubborn and ruthless and *hungry*. The only tribute that means anything to them is something that makes you seem worth their while. Something as old as they are or close to it. Ancient artifacts made by human hands, with human pain laced into the object. A blade from the Crusades with bloodstains in the engraved hilt. A wine chalice used by a Roman magistrate who dictated whether a gladiator lived or died. The older and more pain-soaked the artifact, the more they can consume from it to hold them over between feedings."

I nod. "Okay, and where do you get something like that?"

"The King keeps a collection." Elijah moves like liquid, pushing to his feet and brushing gravel dust off from his hands. He jerks toward the red barn. "In there."

Zoe's jaw drops. "Excuse me? How do you know that?"

"I guess it could be something other than artifacts," he says sullenly. "What-ever it is, he's hiding something from us."

I step back and eye the barn beyond the ward. "And all we have to do is get inside his collection and take one of those tributes, and Daeza will speak to us? Tell us who has the King's crown?"

Elijah scoffs. "Sure, if you can snag a tribute savory enough for Daeza, then we might be able to waltz right into her lair without getting our heads cut off. But the King is right—she has incentive to keep the crown from him. So your idea is *totally* great, except for the fact that it's impossible. This ward is impenetrable."

I tilt my head at the ward now, tracking its shimmer shape. "Says you."

"Says the Shadow King," Zoe corrects.

Indignation is a ripple of heat beneath my skin. "I can bring it down."

"Bullshit." Elijah scoffs. "I can't do it, and neither can Zoe. Even if you, by some miracle, had the raw power to do it, which I highly doubt, you'd have to push past the emotional bombardment. It's an affective ward. Not just a barrier, but a form of psychological torture."

I close my eyes, opening the furnace in my chest with a slow, steady inhale. It rises up in my throat, steam in my mouth. Yesterday's session didn't dampen its flames at all. Flames leak from my mouth—but only because I've called them to be ready.

When I speak, my voice is a low whisper. "I am aware."

"You're not hearing me," Elijah says. "The affective layer is *thick* in this thing.

It was laid by the king of demons himself. He's been consuming human fear for *centuries*. He knows *exactly* how to break someone with it."

"But does he know how to break me?" I say, and, with a deep breath—I thrust my palm into the Shadow King's ward.

The blowback is immediate.

Just as before, the ward injects sensation into my body broad enough to feel like a physical impact, sharp enough to command all my attention, and specific enough to become words, become thought.

RunawayrunawayrunawaygogoleaveleaveLEAVEorelse—

I press against the ward, leaning my whole body weight against that single point of contact, stamping myself on the King's barrier. An attack, in the exact shape of my hand. I curl my fingers against the heavy surface. The ward heaves against me, rolling like thick rubber under my palm.

LeaveleaveleaveNOWrunawayorelse—

It's like it knows that I am here, boldly attempting to breach it, and it's fighting back.

I bury its unspoken words down within me, fold them in, gather them. It is like swallowing glass. A thousand shining slivers injecting themselves into my lungs.

I raise both hands against it now, jaw set. "Come on . . . ," I mutter through gritted teeth. *"Come on!"*

The King's ward flares at the contact, pressing back.

RunawayrunawayrunawayGONOWorelse—RUNSTOPFLEE—

The ward throws images into my mind—a single figure, then three, then five, then ten.

People I *should* know, but don't.

The ward slices them down, their gray misty bodies falling in halves, then quarters.

"That *would* work," I say with a mocking grin, "if I knew who they were."

But the ward has given me an idea.

Words are powerful, but images are stronger. Words are effective, but they come to an end.

My power doesn't end. My power is always.

I stop using commands, and think of images instead. What do I wish to become?

I inhale—and root erupts from my chest, flowing down my arms in a rush of scaled armor, covering my arms in glistening purple plates. The points of my fingertips become long, blood-purple claws, carving into the ward.

I laugh. This feels like stretching after a long season of smallness.

Growth after the stalemate of a forced winter.

Breathing after being told to hold my breath.

The ward is fully lit now, a visible dome of aether arcing and lashing into the air. It blows my loose curls up and back. Whips the strands at my cheeks.

Distantly, I hear the twins shouting to stop.

But I don't want to. I don't *need* to.

And I don't have to.

Erebus may not like the idea of my attacking his ward, but he can't complain about me becoming unstoppable on my own terms.

In the heat and smoke flowing from my nose and mouth, I am a steam engine, roaring.

A dragon, unfurling her wings.

Then, with a final shudder, the ward shatters.

Countless shards burst into the sky overhead, raining down onto my hair and skin in glittering silver-green specks.

What remains of the King's ward floats down over my chest and arms. I flip my claw-tipped, root-armored fingers over to watch the construct's dust settle in my palms.

When I turn, breathless, to face the twins, their eyes are everywhere—on the scaled armor gauntlets that extend up my shoulders, the starlike dust in my hair and on my face, and the sparkling air around me.

Elijah's mouth works open and closed, his eyelids fluttering in disbelief. "How . . . ?"

"It tried to break me," I say quietly, my voice coming from far away. "But I broke it."

"The ward showed you something, didn't it?" Elijah says, gazing at me curiously. "What did you see?"

I take a deep breath, closing my root furnace for now. "It showed me the people I used to know, then it killed them."

Zoe rears back. "That's *fucked*."

"Yes." The purple scales break apart on my hands and arms, but rather than falling, the shining dust particles disappear beneath my skin. Returning to me. "But it didn't work."

"Why not?" Zoe asks.

"Because," I murmur, "once you lose everyone . . . fear loses its advantage."

Zoe looks at me strangely, with a flicker of apprehension.

"What?" I ask.

She averts her gaze. "You, uh . . . you sound like the old man."

I hear it too. I *do* sound like the King, even though I still feel like myself. *I will build you into a girl whom no one can destroy.*

Elijah shakes his head. "You're lying. You've got to have felt *something*. Fear, terror, *something*." He closes the distance between us in a single, long-legged stride and, before I can react, he grasps my elbows, inhaling deeply against my throat.

"Well?" I challenge.

He steps away with a furrowed brow while my skin prickles where he touched me. I've never seen Elijah take a deliberate sniff of the negative human emotions full demons crave, much less take one from *me*.

Zoe eyes her brother. "What did you smell?"

Elijah's eyes flit to Zoe and back. After a beat, he says, "Power."

I don't know how to respond to that.

I jerk my head toward the closed doors of the unwarded barn. "Come on. Let's go find something old and painful for Daeza."

THREE MONTHS

AFTER SELWYN KANE APPEARED

Natasia

AUDIO LOG—ENTRY #101

My son's last escape was two days ago. The one before that, five days ago.

The intervals between these disappearing acts are getting shorter, not longer. The amount of time it takes for me to locate him in the mountains is getting longer, not shorter.

I am loath to admit that I have had to resort to containment.

My only comfort is that when I find him, he returns willingly. When I ask him to go back inside the wards I've now cast around his room, he enters without a fight.

But I cannot ignore these facts:

First: If Selwyn wants to leave my home, he will find a way. It is only by his choice that he stays.

Second: The trails of blood that lead me to him are sometimes black and sometimes red . . . but they never belong to him.

Third: When my son was a child, I was more powerful than him in every way.

I am no longer certain that this is true.

22

William

THERE IS ONE argument that has not waned in the months since we left the Keep. So, as Larkin and I walk through the parking lot that surrounds the highway motel we've stopped at for the night, I am not surprised when it comes up again.

Nick has just disappeared into the woods behind the motel. He informed us that this is one of the places his father and Isaac used as a hideout while they were on the run. I can see why; the motel desk agent's security and identification practices at check-in were . . . laxer than most.

We're here because Nick is retracing his steps, hoping to better understand the Morgaines' preferred territories. As with the Legendborn who met with the Morgaines behind the Regents' backs, he was never given a way to contact them.

Apparently, Ava and her group find you . . . not the other way around.

After nearly three months of being on this quest without being sought out by the Morgaines, I'm starting to doubt whether Nick's approach will work. Whether having Larkin with us, even if he often hangs back to let Nick search on his own, is the hindrance that Nick said it would be at his curia.

"The Morgaines were rumored to have mesmered Lieges before they splintered off, you know," Larkin says as he walks the mostly empty lot. He has already assessed that there are six other guests here, total. "What if the rumors were true and they can mesmer Legendborn as well? Davis's mind could be manipulated as we speak, and we wouldn't know. They aren't to be trusted."

"Neither are the Regents, Larkin." I reply with my rote response at this point. "If that was the basis for not trusting someone, we shouldn't have trusted Sel, either. He mesmered Bree. Repeatedly."

Larkin purses his lips. "He shouldnae have done that."

"That story about the Morgaines is the tale that we cannot trust, because we cannot trust the tellers." I shake my head. "I believe Nick has a plan."

"Do you believe he'll tell you what that plan is?" Larkin asks. "It's been months. He could be buying himself time. This whole endeavor may be his way of running from accountability and saving his own skin. But if he doesn't go through with killing Ava, it puts all our lives on the line."

"And yet you joined the quest just as I did," I counter. "And did not abandon it when Cestra made her threats clear."

"I joined the quest *because* you did," Larkin says quietly. "And did not abandon it for the same reason."

We walk silently for a few more minutes. A strip mall of restaurants is just up ahead.

This is where the argument usually pauses. Where I set aside Larkin's concern for me, in particular, and remind myself that he is a Mageguard assigned to protect the king, and Bree's intended Kingsmage. That he does not favor me out of the Legendborn or put my safety above the other Scions'.

But it has been months of this argument and months of my setting these thoughts aside. The road has been long. The days longer. And when Nick is on his own, retracing his steps from his time alone in the mountains, he cannot take us with him for fear of us being spotted and attacked by the very Morgaines he seeks out. It means that Larkin and I have spent more time with each other than I had anticipated.

"The Merlin scouts from yesterday haven't returned," Larkin says, jarring me out of my thoughts. "I think we'll not see them for another few days at least."

Nick and I weren't surprised when, two weeks after we left the Keep, Larkin alerted us that he'd detected a pair of Merlins following us from a restaurant in South Carolina. He checks in regularly with the Regents, sharing our location and progress with them in a weekly text, but it was to be expected that they would send their own eyes and ears eventually. So far, the Merlins haven't contacted us or made themselves visible—at least to me and Nick.

"And they're still not aware you've spotted them?" I ask.

He responds with wordless indignation and bright insult.

I raise my hands. "Apologies. I should have known better than to ask."

"I was set to be Bree's Kingsmage, remember?"

I chuckle. "Yes, I remember."

He shakes his head in mock annoyance as he continues to scan the parking lot. "To answer yer question, no, they don't realize I've spotted them. That's half on arrogance and half on youth. Their surveillance skills are fine, but they aren't Mageguard trained and they're still growing into their heightened senses. The Council probably can't afford to send stronger soldiers just to watch us wander around in circles. But if the Regents get antsy one day, or something changes, we should expect a stronger show of force than a couple of wee scouts. They may want to see a dead Morgaine sooner rather than later and challenge Davis on his approach if the trail runs dry."

"I see," I say. "I suppose if he *is* successful, they'll want proof of that too."

He peers at me. "Will you be able to stomach that?"

I lift a shoulder. "Maybe it won't happen. Maybe it's all a ruse."

"And if it's not? Are you really prepared to watch yer friend murder someone? Not a kill made in self-defense, but one committed with intention?"

I answer honestly. "I don't know."

As I watch Larkin's sharp eyes scan the forest around us, his ringed fingers twitching anxiously in the ready position for calling aether, I wonder if he, too, has grown tired of our familiar argument, or if he is waiting for me to push it forward.

"Why is that, exactly?" I ask abruptly.

"Why is what?" Larkin's golden eyes flick to mine, then back to the trees overhead, the long driveway to the parking lot, the glowing windows of occupied rooms. In the months since we left the Keep, his hair has grown long. The shaved sides are hidden by the dark auburn locks that fall past his ears and frame his temples. I have tried not to notice, but after three months, I find I am too tired to keep trying.

"Why *am* I the reason you raised your hand?" I ask. "You don't approve of my defiance of the Regents, nor do you approve of Nick's methods. You have your own duties and responsibilities. There are parties searching for Bree; you could have joined them instead of going on this journey, which, after three months, may turn out to become a fool's errand or, as you said, Nick's attempt to buy himself time."

Larkin's silent steps keep moving at a steady pace, but I see the flush working up from beneath the loose collar of his black shirt. See his Adam's apple move once as he swallows. "You shouldn't be on your own. Erebus held you captive once," he says. "I worry he might do it again."

"Ah," I say quietly, nodding. "That is a *fair* concern." Even I hear the dissatisfaction laced through my comment, but I don't know what to do with it.

Larkin, however, seems to have some ideas.

He stops abruptly, turning to me, dark brows scrunched together. I stop as well. "'A fair concern'?" He drags a hand over his face. "I cannae believe you just said that. As if I was reminding you to check the mail before you left the house or . . . asking if we have enough milk left in the fridge. Jaysuz."

Now I am at a loss. "I'm not—"

"Your own capture, your potential *recapture*, by one of the most powerful Merlins on the planet is not a 'fair concern,' William," he says, laughing hollowly. "It's an injustice and a . . . a . . . *danger!*"

I nod silently. "Yes, you're right. If the Scion of Gawain—"

"You are not *just* the Scion of Gawain!" Larkin interrupts. He huffs in frustration, his cheeks blowing outward. "For God's sake, you are a person. A good person who has sacrificed any semblance of a normal life to protect others!"

"I haven't sacrificed more than any other Scion," I say. "I don't think I've sacrificed more than you—"

"Because you do it *quietly*," Larkin insists, expression pained as he closes the distance between us. "In tiny ways. *Hidden* ways. You put yourself aside when someone else is hurt, which is fine, you're a healer. But you don't put yourself center again after! You don't talk about your own losses. Three of your friends have been kidnapped in the last six months, and you never bring it up. Legend-born were *killed* in the battle of the ogof, and you don't mention it. You lost your *bonded Squire*, and you never talk about it. I *know* you broke up with your Onceborn boyfriend to protect him from harm, for the sake of the Order, and you *never talk about it*."

I blink at him, taken aback by his outburst. "How do you know about Dylan?" is all I can seem to manage.

"Not the point!" Larkin throws up a hand. "The point is that *you*, William, never treat *yourself* like a patient. You tell the others this all the time, but you deserve protection too. You deserve someone looking out for you, too. Do you not realize that?"

I gape at him, flushing hot and cold with emotions I can't fully process.

"No, you don't," Larkin says, shaking his head. "You don't realize it at all. 'Medice, cura te ipsum,' goddamnit!"

I pause to translate. "'Physician, heal thyself'?"

"Aye," he snaps frustratedly. "Best to hear it in two languages. Maybe then, it'll stick!"

"Larkin, I . . ."

He shakes his head again. *"Lark."*

"What?"

"We've been traveling together long enough for you to call me by my preferred name." He runs a hand through his hair, fingers lifting the thick shock of it up and back until his ears and temple lie exposed. "'S Lark."

I close my mouth, then nod. "Yes, of course. Lark. You call me William, after all."

"You told me I could," Lark says quietly.

"I did." We were on the Liege's plane after Larkin—*Lark*—brought Sel to us, unconscious but alive so that we could escape the imprisonment of the Regents.

"I think that . . . duty is a complicated thing," I begin slowly. "Duty is something that is easy for us in the Order to identify with since we are born into our roles and titles. My sense of duty is defined by my role to protect others. I don't . . . I don't think of myself as the 'protected.'"

Lark sends me a searing look. "I've noticed."

I grant him a smile. Then decide that my silent question is worth asking aloud. "Did you come here to protect Nick's quest as his champion . . . or to protect me?"

Lark's shoulders rise with a sigh, then drop. "I don't know that I'll answer that straightaway. I know it's not kind to answer a question with a question, but I wonder sometimes if you are here to protect Scion Davis as the Scion of Gawain might . . . or if you are William, here to protect Nick's secrets?"

This time, I am the one who has to look away. "I am a healer," I murmur. "I respect healer-patient confidentiality. I know better than anyone that people sometimes must keep their own confidence. To keep secrets, as you call them. I trust that Nick has reasons to be . . ."

"Evasive?" Lark offers. "Consistently and unnervingly evasive to any direct questions that we ask about his plan with the Morgaines?"

"There are plenty of reasons to keep secrets," I say with a bitter smile. "I trust Nick to know when to share his thoughts."

"And what if *I* don't?" Lark sighs. "What if he does something while we're out here that I can't stand by and watch happen?"

"On whose orders would you be acting?" I ask, suddenly seeing something in Larkin's eyes that looks too *much* like duty and not enough like care. "Not mine, as Nick's healer—"

"Is Nick your patient too, then?" Lark shoots back. "Does *he* know that?"

"Yes. And no."

Lark takes a breath as if to steady himself. "Is everyone always your patient?"

This argument again. "No," I reply. "But Nick is. Ever since—"

"Ever since when?" Lark steps closer.

I halt him with a hand. "It's not my story to share."

"William." Lark catches my wrist in his hand—warm palm enveloping it whole. "I need to understand why *you're* willing to put yourself in harm's way because of him." His mouth quirks into a sad, quick smile. "I need to understand why *I'm* still allowing you to put yourself in harm's way."

My breath catches. "I'm not sure I can help you with . . . that second 'why.'"

His eyes flicker between mine like gold at the bottom of a wishing well. What has now become a familiar heat begins to spark and spread behind my sternum. When Lark speaks again, his voice is like hot honey—and I am reminded that all cambions are attractive. It's in their genetics. Their very DNA. "All right, Scion. We won't talk about that second 'why.'"

And if Larkin Douglas happens to be the most alluring cambion I've ever met, well, that might just be due to our proximity.

His hand tightens, then he releases me. "But you'll tell me about the first?"

Why am I putting myself in harm's way for Nick? I think about Lark's question before I answer. Really think. And, not for the first time, *remember.*

"It's . . . about . . . ," I begin, "the night that Bree pulled Excalibur from its stone."

Lark points me toward a wrought iron metal bench set among overgrown weeds in the green space at the back of the motel. Once there, he falls into it, somehow both effortless and easy in the same joint-freezing winter air that has me pulling my Gawain-green scarf up to my ears.

"I'm listening," he says. "And I won't repeat anything you say. I swear it."

It's a quiet vow. One that I usually make to my patients and friends, not the other way around. "That's my line," I say, shifting against the metal seat.

"Tch," Lark says, voice fond. "You're stalling."

"A bit," I admit, then swallow. Then, I begin.

"The night Bree became the Crown Scion, after the battle had been won, she lost consciousness in the cave. She was exhausted in every way. Sel carried her through the tunnels from the ogof back to the Lodge, and after I healed her injuries and cleared her from the infirmary, we settled her in Nick's bedroom so that she could recover in peace. Nick stayed with her on his own while I went back downstairs and spoke with Alice. I was so worried about Bree that it wasn't until I returned to his room to check on her that I realized that Nick wasn't okay either and maybe never had been. . . ."

"She has so much to learn now," Nick said, his eyes distant and mind traveling as he rubbed slow, small, gentle circles into the back of Bree's hand.

"I know."

A pause. A refocused gaze on me. "Not all of it good, William."

"No," I replied, "not all of it good."

"I told her. . . ." Nick's voice drifted off. "I told her I hated Arthur. Told her what happened to my mother. How Arthur destroyed my family. She held all of that with me, for me . . . and now Arthur will find a way to take things from her, too."

"We'll help her, Nick," I whispered. "You know we will. You can help her."

"I can't protect her from Arthur," Nick said, voice hard. "We can't protect her from everything that will change around her the second she wakes up."

BANG! An exterior door slammed open below—and we both jumped. Two voices reached us from the open foyer down the hall: Sel, back from reinforcing his wards and speaking to Greer.

I said, "Now would be a great time for Selwyn to not slam every door he closes."

I turned back to Nick, half a smile pulling my face—to find him standing between Bree and the door, shining aether armor wrapping his chest and forearms, eyes blazing and teeth bared. Two longswords had materialized in his fists.

Nick looked . . . lethal. The expression on his face reminded me that he had been trained to enter the war only when it is most dire. Unlike the rest of us, Nick was raised not to fight Camlann, but to end it.

"Nick, it was just Sel." He didn't respond to me, so I stepped—slowly—into his field of vision. "We're safe. Bree's safe."

After a long moment, he blinked, shuddering back to the present moment. The fight left his eyes.

"I—right. Sorry," he said, releasing his armor. The sword returned to crystalline dust, then disappeared. He turned back to a sleeping, silent Bree. "I just thought . . . You know."

"Your nervous system is still primed for a fight. Understandable after tonight, but not necessary any longer. The danger has passed."

But the line of tension didn't leave his shoulders. He pulled back a curtain at the window near the headboard, peeking outside as if to check to make sure the grounds were clear.

I tried to change the subject. "For someone who never expected to be Called by Lancelot, you forged his weapon and armor impressively quickly just now."

He shrugged. "Arthur's and Lancelot's armor and weapons aren't that different."

"No," I conceded. "But you've been training to inherit Arthur's abilities, to forge his armor and longsword. Not Lancelot's."

Nick's smile was sharp and quick. "I know that better than anyone, my friend."

I pressed him further. "Nick, no Legendborn Scion in existence has ever had to master the abilities of an unexpected knight's spirit. Without warning, you've inherited abilities you've never studied or considered, but you've also been Lancelot's true Scion your whole life. After a lifetime of preparation to be the Scion of Arthur, there are bound to be unexpected consequences—"

"You are right on that point, Will," Nick said, his jaw tight. "I have been preparing for my entire life. Maybe not to become Lancelot's Scion but to be a Scion. Other than that, everything you've just said applies to Bree, too. She's never studied Arthur's abilities. She doesn't know what to expect either."

"But your father—"

"My father never let me forget what I would have to become one day 'without warning.' How good I had to be. How much control I'd need. How I couldn't fail, not with Camlann attached to my Calling. Why do you think he forced me to train with Sel near daily? Forced us to spar against each other until we were both bruised and bloody?"

That surprised me. "But the Kingsmage Oath—"

Nick scoffed. "Sel can hit me if it's done in the name of 'training,' William, you know that. He can do more than hit me if he's been brainwashed to believe that hitting me is for my own good, or praised for 'preparing' his Scion for battle. My father knew the way to Sel's heart—and fists—was to tell him that sometimes, protection looked *like violence. That was the only language Sel knew for a while. Until I renounced my title and we both learned better."*

I had never heard Nick speak this way. Never heard anyone else describe their own training in these terms, much less that of the boy who would be king. I was speechless.

But Nick wasn't done.

It seemed that some great, invisible dam had been broken that night. That after his father's open betrayal, the battle, and the deaths of our fellow Legendborn, something in Nick had come unraveled——or he'd finally allowed his grip on it to loosen.

He saw the look on my face and laughed——a hollow, aching sound. "You look horrified."

"I am horrified," I'd said.

He turned back to the window, voice mild as he searched the grounds and trees. "Wait until you hear about the broken bones."

My stomach churned. "Bones?"

He waves a hand. "Not from Sel, don't worry. Some injuries were too severe for him to risk inflicting on me, so Dad left those lessons for the Lieges. Not Gill but . . . others. Lieges who were bitter about losing their inheritances. When they left our house, they'd leave me behind with broken bones, black eyes, cracked ribs." He turned back to the room then, eyes wild with memory. "Internal bleeding, a concussion or two. Or five. Honestly, I lost track."

I questioned his reporting. Out of ignorance, but still.

"Nick," I said cautiously, "I've treated you dozens of times over the years and never seen signs of those injuries, never seen scars. Concussions are serious, traumatic injuries, and repeated ones leave devastating effects. I would have sensed old fractures. . . ."

Nick only waved his hand, dismissive. "Your cousin Reese made sure everything was healed up before the next training session. Made it like the injuries never happened."

Two sentences said with a wave of hand. But they stopped my heart. Froze it in my chest.

My cousin Reese was my mentor. The Scion of Gawain two Callings before my own. He taught me everything I knew about caring for patients, about calling swyns to heal. Reese taught me how to set a bone when I was nine, well before I was eligible to inherit Gawain's gifts.

I'm ashamed to say I didn't believe it.

I didn't believe him.

"Nick . . . no." *I'd shaken my head.* "That can't be right. Reese was a healer."

Nick had laughed then, full voiced. "You think I don't know that? Reese Sitterson *was at my house every week for a year before my mother tried to put a stop to my father's 'training.' Before she took me, and the Regents took her. Your cousin was a real stand-up guy who was happy to do the former Scion of Arthur's bidding. Ole Reese'd be there at our doorstep to heal me as soon as my dad called him, but he never said a word to stop the injuries in the first place."*

"But Scions of Gawain are——"

"People, William," *Nick had replied.* "People."

"But Reese . . ."

Nick went still. All humor gone. "You don't believe me?"

I stared at him. In minutes, he'd thrown into question everything I'd been taught since I was a child. How could Reese have shown me the proper way to bandage wounds while using his inheritance to heal injuries that never should have happened in the first place? But Reese also taught me to read my patients' expressions. To listen to their voices for hidden signs of pain.

Nick's face and voice were filled with anguish. His features were open and honest. As he said, Reese's healings would have left no trace, even to me. Nick knew that without evidence of his injuries, some people would never *believe him.*

"I believe you," *I said. Then I repeated it so he understood.* "I believe you, Nick. About everything."

Nick swallowed audibly, then looked away. "Thanks."

My fury at Reese took hold then. I frantically rifled back through every memory of healing Nick that I ever had. Whether I'd missed something in evaluating him, whether he'd had other symptoms from head injuries I knew nothing about. Memory loss, aphasia, headaches——

"I got checked out by a doctor eventually," *Nick murmured as if reading my mind.* "They took scans. X-rays. Did some tests. They didn't find anything, so it's all healed."

It's all healed. I didn't need to see the scans to know that's not true.

"It doesn't matter what your title was going to be, Nick," *I'd said.* "You were a child and there's no excuse for what he did to you. What they did."

Nick's spine stiffened. "I know."

I felt like it wasn't enough, so I kept talking. I shouldn't have. He'd shown me he was vulnerable, and I should have paid attention. Instead, I said, "Nick, you cannot—"

"I cannot what?" he asked, brow raised in a manner that was unerringly like his Kingsmage's. "I cannot *what*, William?"

I should have stopped talking.

"You cannot act like the revelations of tonight affect only Bree and not you. It's clear you—"

"You think I don't know how much this affects me?" Nick retorted. "Affects every-one?"

I should have noticed that he was in distress and stopped talking.

"I'm not talking about everyone. I'm talking about you—"

"Tonight isn't about *me!*" He gestured to Bree, his eyes wide and stricken. "It's about her! It has to be! This is a curse, William. She could die—"

"Yes, but—"

"Bree is the innocent here. She wasn't born bathed in this . . . this Scion-violence-and-bloodshed bullshit. It could poison her—Arthur could poison her—and I won't have it." Nick shook his head, eyes shining and defiant. "I can't allow it. She deserves more than us. She deserves better!"

"Is everything all right?"

The door behind us opened, and we both turned to see Selwyn walk through. He was still in his short sleeves, with wounds around his arms and chest from the goruchel and the demons afterward. All injuries that I couldn't heal because he is a Merlin.

His sharp eyes missed nothing—my stance facing Nick, the tension in Nick's shoulders and body, Bree resting under the sheets. Selwyn closed the door softly behind him.

"I heard raised voices." Knowing Sel, he heard more than raised voices. He likely heard most of our conversation. Sel's eyes found Bree again, then me, and remained there. "I believe it was you who told me that patients require peace and quiet to recover, William."

My head bowed at his silent admonishment. Shame coated me. "Yes, that was me."

"Nicholas," Sel asked, voice even, "are you all right?"

Nick's teeth had ground together. "I'm fine. . . ."

Sel moved past me toward his charge, swift and steady, to wrap his hand around Nick's elbow. Nick faced me as Sel faced the window.

When Sel leaned close, bringing his mouth to Nick's ear, I saw the way that Nick's shoulders rose to his ears, then dipped, relaxing at Sel's touch. I saw the way he shuddered, the anguish still there, working through him.

I couldn't hear the words the Kingsmage whispered to his Scion. All I could witness was how those words washed over Nick, making his eyelids flutter. All I could do was observe as Nick nodded and finally, slowly unclenched his jaw.

I heard Nick's first deep ragged breath. I heard him murmur, "I know." And when Selwyn spoke again, Nick shook his head. "I'm sorry——"

"Do not apologize." Sel's grip tightened until Nick met his Kingsmage's eyes. Something silent and deep passed between them. An understanding. A grace.

Only Selwyn had seen what Martin Davis had done to his son. Only Selwyn had born witness to Nick's recovery from injuries healed the slow way . . . and the fast way, from my cousin's swyns. And, as a child himself, only Selwyn had had his Oath so contorted that he could be used to batter the very Scion he was sworn to protect.

They had become weapons, against themselves and each other.

And I never knew.

Nick brought his empty palm to cover Sel's at his elbow, squeezing Sel's fingers once. After another moment, Sel nodded—and let Nick go to sit back against the windowsill, eyes stony.

"Thank you for your assistance, William," Sel said as he turned to face me, voice firm and formal. "But I have it from here."

"Bree needs——"

"I have them both," Sel said, his golden eyes hardening, "and you have done enough. Please leave."

I opened my mouth, closed it. Then pursed my lips, fighting indignation I didn't earn.

I dipped my chin toward him, a second apology, and looked around his shoulder to where Bree slept. "Let me know if Bree's status changes."

Sel stepped between us then, blocking my view of both my patients. "If you are needed, I will come find you." There was no rancor in his voice. No recrimination. For that, I am still grateful.

I began to say something else—to thank him, maybe, for taking care of Nick and Bree, but Sel had already turned away. His Kingsmage gaze shifted between Bree, his new king, and Nick, his old one. His liege and his bonded.

And I realized that I had nothing else to offer there. That I had done enough.

That Selwyn had them both.

When I finish my story, Lark's face is troubled. "William," he says hesitantly. "You didn't know. Even if you *had* known, Nick's father would have denied it; that's why he had your cousin heal the wounds before others could see—"

My fists are balled at my thighs. "But other people knew! Adults knew, or at least they had to have suspected. And they looked the other way because a powerful man bade them to."

"William—"

"*Reese* knew," I whisper, my voice tight with anger. "And I trusted Reese. He taught me everything I know about being the Scion of Gawain, but he never told me about Martin Davis. Never told me he was making house calls to heal wounds that our own Order membership had inflicted on our child king. The night that Bree's and Nick's true lineages were revealed, I thought I was pushing Nick forward, helping him, when all I did was take him back to some of the worst moments in his life. I didn't believe him immediately, like I should have. I should have thought of the swyns, how they accelerate healing."

Lark swallows. "I read the reports; this conversation with Davis happened the same night your bonded Squire perished, Will. I know about the agony. What happened to Whitlock—"

"Whitty," I correct, even as the pain swells in my chest. "His name was *Whitty*."

"Whitty," Lark says, nodding. "What I mean to say is—"

"I told you this story because you should know that Nick understands the Order, and what it's capable of, more deeply than most Scions," I finally say. "Nick has been forced to consider its tyranny over its own members, its children, the Merlins, over Bree. Nick takes *that* part of our war, the silent part that no one speaks about at curias or funerals or dinner parties, perhaps more seriously than even the war against the Shadowborn. You asked why I am here? I am here because I believe in Nick. I won't make the same mistake twice."

To that, Lark has nothing to say.

We go back to waiting for Nick in silence—and I fear that is how we will remain. That this memory that does not belong to me, that I should not have shared, will create a wedge between Lark and Nick when I would have preferred to create understanding. I am abruptly worried that I told Nick's story for all the wrong reasons. That I didn't tell it for Nick at all, but for myself.

Lark's voice, when it comes, is low and contemplative. "Merlins have our own burdens, but I've been a Guard long enough to see that suffering takes many shapes. And Davis isn't the only Scion who needs and deserves healing from what the Order's done to him. From what he has endured in its name."

My voice cracks when I answer. "Oh?"

"Aye," he says quietly, and drops his left knee until it knocks against my right—as warm and certain and solid as his voice in the night. "You do too, Will. You do too."

23

Mariah

"OKAY, RIAH," VALECHAZ says, backing away with both hands up. "When you're ready . . ."

I swallow and look at the leather satchel in my palm that holds the Heart. For a stone and bits of metal, it feels much heavier than it should be, but perhaps that's just my guilt weighing me down. Like the stone knows that I'm not supposed to put it on.

Like the Heart itself knows that this big, bold idea was a mistake.

"We can always give it back," Valec says.

I shoot him a frown and a glare. "Too late for that. We already swiped it."

I look up at the balcony around the empty Crossroads Lounge. Valec cleared the place out, not just for customers and potential clients but staff too. There are printed signs outside the door that say CLOSED FOR HEALTH INSPECTION in Valec's scrawled handwriting; it's sort of adorable, but also very necessary.

Whatever happens when I put on my Aunt Lu's necklace is not something that should be witnessed.

"Okay," Valec says, then repeats it for good measure. "Okay."

The stage lights are on overhead, the heat of them already generating a bit of sweat on my upper lip. I gesture at him with my empty hand, shooing him farther away—and brushing back my fear. Be the answer, be the plan.

I remember Alice fighting her own death, and take a deep breath. "Step back more. Just in case."

Valec puts his hands on his hips. "Mariah Rochelle. There ain't nothing you can do that's gonna hurt me. You haven't even put the damn necklace on yet."

I groan. "We don't *know* what it's gonna do, is my point! You ever see a Medium wear the Heart of a Grand Dame?"

He scratches at his chin, eyes narrowed. "Well, no. But it's an amplifier. What's the worst it can do to you?" He waggles his fingers. "Ooooh, spooky. You see ghosts. Now, you see *more* ghosts."

I roll my eyes but smile. I know he's just trying to calm my nerves. Calm *both* our nerves.

The reality is, the amplifier of a Grand Dame doesn't come with a manual. It's charmed and recharmed and soaked in soil at plantation sites like Volition overnight, when the moon is full and round in the sky. It's a shortcut for a Dame to wear when she can't make an offering for root, and it's passed down from one Dame to another. It usually stays in families that have held it the most, but like anything, it can hop to a descendant the ancestors decide is worthy.

If I put it on, my Aunt Lu will still be the Grand Dame of our territory, but given that I'm related to her, it should work on me, too.

"Should" being the critical word.

"You gonna put it on, or . . . ?" Valec prompts.

I scowl at him and pour the necklace out of its pouch into my palm. Again, I am hit by an overwhelming sense of age and weight. I smell Hazel's kitchen and gardens all over the thing—and Valec must too, because he wrinkles his nose as he stares at the obsidian under the yellow stage lights.

I toss the pouch to him, and he catches it easily, snatching it out of the air and tucking it in his back pocket.

In my palm, the stone is cool and black and still. I untangle the soft leather cord and unclasp it, taking a deep breath before drawing it up over my braids and clasping it closed again. After I pull my braids through and feel the stone settle over my shirt . . . I wait.

"Is that it?" Valec calls.

I frown. "You tell me. Is it supposed to do something right away?"

Valec tilts his head. "Technically, this gets transitioned to a new Dame with a full ceremony. Maybe we're lucky and it'll lie dormant the whole time we're there?"

"Maybe." It's possible that's what'll happen, but we don't know. We decided that the Shade we're meeting at their monthly appeal won't know the full nature of a Dame's Heart. Valec guesses that just the appearance of a Dame at their lair will be enough for them to hear us out. That, plus some sorta gift Valec is securing.

I allow myself a tentative smile. "Listen," I say, clapping my hands together, "I'm not mad—" A beat after my hands meet, the world turns bright gold. I hear Valec shout and my knees hit the stage. Then, darkness.

"Mariah!" A hot hand gently taps my cheek. "Mariah, come on, baby cousin. . . ." Another tap.

I bat the hand away. "Stahh—"

"Oh, thank everything holy and unholy," Valec breathes. I hear a long huff and crack my eye open to see him resting back on his heels. "Phew. You scared me."

I am lying on my back on the Crossroads stage. That thought alone—all the things that happen on this stage on a regular business night—sends me shuddering up to a seated position.

Bad idea. The world blurs.

"Whoa, whoa." Valec rushes over to steady my shoulder. "Don't sit up quick like that!"

"I'm fine." I bat his hand away again, but this time, I look at it closely—and see a faint gray-black . . . shadow beneath his brown skin. Or, it's *like* a shadow, but it's also like a light? Like something that glows but . . . dark? I grab at his hand, and he yelps in surprise.

"What're you—"

"Hold still." I turn his hand over in my palm, see the light there beneath his fingers, turn it back, and see it again. Use my fingers to trace up the veins of his brown arm to his exposed forearm and elbow. "Oh my God."

"What?" Valec says, peering down at me. "What do you see?"

"I'm not . . . not sure," I say. But it's a lie.

And Valec can hear it in my voice. "Spit it out, Riah. You can't scare me."

I drop his hand and look up at his face, seeing the light there, too. "I . . ."

He raises a brow. "What? I can handle it."

"Well," I say, voice cracking, "I'm not sure *I* can."

"Mariah."

I squint, then breathe out a slow breath. "You know how you joked about me seeing dead people?"

"Uh-huh . . ." Valec shifts back onto his heels, leaning slightly away from me. "I'm not dead."

"No, but you're sort of . . . *half* undead," I say cautiously, "aren't you?"

Valec blinks. "Oh, shit."

FOUR MONTHS

AFTER SELWYN KANE APPEARED

Natasia

AUDIO LOG—ENTRY #126

Nothing is going as I have hoped, but at least Selwyn no longer wishes to escape. Or, at the very least, he has stopped attempting to escape. The way he prowls behind the dense ward enclosure I have cast and the calculating clarity I occasionally glimpse in his eyes make me wonder if he is simply waiting. Waiting until the day I don't come after him. Waiting until he has enough information. Waiting until my ward lapses and he doesn't have to make any effort to escape.

I'm not even completely sure how he's escaping the wards in the first place.

It is the clarity that I find most distressing. He should be succumbing to his cravings in such a way that he cannot hold on to reason. I remember the hunger for humanity that my mind didn't need and the craving for aether that my body did not require. I was a cambion driven by the appetites of demonia, not necessity.

But I did not care.

Faye's Wildcrafted tonics were the only way I finally found my path back from the hungers. But they aren't working on my son. And if they don't work, then I can't ask—or expect—him to be able to face himself and make the choice to rise from his so-called descent.

I am at a loss. I may need to tap networks I would rather not use. Ones I do not especially care to expose myself to—

The sound of another barrier breaking interrupts my thoughts. I am on my feet, my logbook cast aside, blurring back into the spare bedroom to find Selwyn standing behind my mostly intact ward.

Selwyn's red eyes stand out against the electric-blue grid of the barrier, a pair of glowing irises above a fang-tipped smile. The ward has a single fist-shaped hole in it.

I glance down. He is holding his right hand in his left, the long black claws cradling smoking knuckles.

The ward is already repairing itself. "Are you hurt?"

Selwyn tips his head to the left, watching me curiously. "Are you hurt?" I repeat, stepping closer.

He raises his right hand, palm facing in, to eye level. What were likely third-degree burns have already healed to second. Dark black edges disappear before my eyes to be replaced with deep red and purple wounds with bright, shiny pink centers. As I watch, even those begin to heal smooth. I release a breath.

"Good," I say. He drops his hand and shoots me a sardonic glare, as if mocking my concern.

"Yes, I know you heal quickly—maybe even more quickly now than before—but I am your mother, and I get to be concerned when you're wounded."

He lifts a dark brow, casting his eyes over the glowing gridded ward, to where it penetrates even through the ceiling and—to our eyes, if not to a human's—extends overhead to surround the room in a bright cube. When my gaze rests back on my son's face, the message I find there is clear without a single word: *What kind of mother traps her son in a cage?*

I flinch, nodding. "I know how it looks. How it feels, even. But I can't risk you getting taken down by a Merlin or a goruchel in the state you're in." I cross my arms over my chest. "Are you going to tell me whose blood I keep finding in the woods? And why the trails lead to you, when you're feral and wild?"

His mouth quirks, as if "feral" and "wild" are compliments.

"*Selwyn.*" I make an attempt at a stern, motherly voice.

His frown and short, soundless laugh make it clear how unsuccessful *that* was. He shakes his head, humor fully at my expense, eyes brightening.

Nice try, Mother.

I find I don't care if his humor is at my expense. It warms my heart to see my son *laughing* at anything. "You used to do that with me, remember?"

His chin tips up. *Do what?*

"Laugh."

He paces up the cage and back, dragging his nails along the bars, ignoring me.

"I'm keeping you here because I just got you back in my life," I call. "I'm not going to let yours be taken away because you aren't your . . . normal delightful self."

He sighs and blurs to his bed. On the other side of the ward, there is a small fridge for food and supplies, a door to a bathroom and shower, a television set, books. The best I could do without knowing exactly what my son likes to do. Guilt takes a hold of my stomach, twisting it.

I don't know what my son likes to do.

I wrap my sweater around my shoulders and sigh. "I thought I could help you in a week or two. I've done everything I can, gone through all the old journals I have here. Everything I used for myself I've now tried on you, Selwyn, and—" My eyes burn. I rub the heels of my palms over them and groan. "And I'm out of ideas."

He leans back on the bed with both elbows behind him, body loose in a half lounge. He tosses up one hand as if to say, *Oh well.*

"You aren't the only stubborn one in this house," I bite back, "so don't give up on me. I'm not giving up on you."

He makes a *very* rude gesture.

"That's . . . that's fair," I mutter. "I wasn't there when you needed me to be. Believe me, I would have been if I thought I'd be able to see you and get out alive."

He sits up then, elbows on his knees, giving me his full attention. Lifts a hand again. *So you didn't even try?*

"After I escaped, I tried so, so many times," I murmur. "Martin—" I look away, down, feel an old rage clawing its way up my throat at the very mention of Martin Davis. I rub at my chest, at the memory of the searing pain I'd felt the day Martin died, grateful that the bond had not flared fresh and bright for me as it must have done for Isaac Sorenson. While a single Kingsmage cannot be bonded to two people, one Scion can be bonded to two Kingsmages. "The last time I tried to see you, I got close to the house in Chapel Hill, and it happened to be a day when Isaac was visiting."

Selwyn's expression doesn't change, but the lines around his eyes tighten. He knew Isaac. Knew what the Master Merlin was capable of, because he was Selwyn's teacher.

"Isaac caught my scent. Found me quick. Nearly tore me apart while Martin watched," I whisper. "My left shoulder was hanging on by . . . well . . . 'threads' would be a generous word."

Selwyn's mouth purses into a line. His eyes darken, and his fist clenches.

"They, of all people, kept the secret that I had escaped. I suppose Erebus kept it too. Maybe the three of them knew that I'd never do anything to endanger you, and so let me go." I pause. "They were right, in the end. But I . . . over-corrected."

He rolls his eyes.

"Sel, you were *so* small. Only eleven years old," I explain. "They told me the next time I tried to see you, it'd be *your* turn to lose an arm—this time in front of me."

Selwyn's lips curl back in a snarl, black-tipped fangs glinting. I feel my own mouth opening, an answering snarl leaking from my lips. Then I cover my mouth, flushing. Like mother like son, I suppose. I cough once and nod.

"Yes. Agreed. They were both . . . true monsters." I fix him with a gaze. "More monstrous than you or I could ever be. I'm so, so sorry they let you think anything otherwise."

His gaze flows away from me to the ground, to the wall, to the ceiling. He leans back with a deep sigh. A half-raised shoulder. *It is what it is.*

"Please be patient with me," I say, stepping close to the ward. "Let me keep trying, Sel."

His eyes return to mine. He watches me for a long moment. After a beat, he shrugs. *Fine. You can keep trying.*

I breathe a sigh of relief.

Then, while still holding my gaze, he taps twice on his wrist.

But the clock is ticking.

25

Bree

DAEZA'S CLUB IS a large building that sits across from the French Broad River near downtown Asheville. There's a bouncer standing in a cone-shaped pool of light at the entrance underneath a bright sign that says ECLIPSE.

"He's human," Elijah observes. His eyes scan the group of people who walk down the sidewalk, laughing and talking with raised voices. "But we shouldn't let our guard down."

I let my left fingers fall down to my thigh, where a black-hilted dagger rests in a leather-strapped thigh holster. My own root dagger would feel more secure in my hand, but this one—from Zoe's collection—feels good enough.

When we reach the club doors, the bouncer looks up. "Tribute?"

I nod. "We have one."

The bouncer narrows his eyes. "What's on offer? Humanity or aether?"

"Humanity," Elijah supplies. "But we're not showing you that. Daeza's eyes only."

The bouncer rolls his eyes and opens the door. "Your funeral if it doesn't work out."

A wall of sound meets us—shouting, growls, rock music. When we slip in behind Elijah, Zoe hisses, "That was easy!"

"Zoe . . . ," I say, staring at the scene before us, "the front door is the least of our problems."

Before us is a brightly lit, massive room of multiple levels. In the center is a three-story silver barbed-wire cage.

And in that cage are two fully corporeal uchel, fighting to the death.

It takes Elijah several attempts to find somebody who looks like they actually work at Eclipse. We end up in a back corner in line behind a group of grungy-looking warlocks holding wads of cash. When it's our turn at the caged window, another warlock who appears to be a bookie greets us with a bored expression.

"Current fight's bets are closed. Next fight is at eleven thirty." He points to a whiteboard hanging over the window. "Combatants are listed above. Place your bet."

Elijah is supposed to take the lead here, given his familiarity with this part of the demon underground, but his eyes grow wide at the scene before him, and he hesitates for a beat too long.

I step forward. "We're not here to bet. We're here to see Daeza."

The bookie's eyes travel up and down me, then look over the twins. "Got tribute?"

"Yes," I answer simply.

The bookie doesn't bother asking what it is. He turns over his shoulder and shouts at someone we can't see. Another warlock steps out from a side door and gestures over his shoulder for us to follow.

Someone in the cage match hits the ground with so much force, the floor shakes—and shakes again when the crowd boos.

The warlock leads us down a dingy hallway with sputtering lightbulbs hanging overhead, then opens a door to reveal a much smaller but more refined dimly lit space with golden tile floors, a teak bench, and dark cherrywood columns. It just fits the four of us standing side by side.

"Wait here. She's finishing up with our first supplicant of the night." The warlock approaches a single door on the opposite wall and knocks three times in a rapid pattern, then twice. Without waiting to be admitted, he cracks the door, barely revealing another larger space similar in design to this one, before slipping inside. The door makes a muffled *whoomp* sound when it closes, and our ears pop.

The room gets stuffy quickly. Especially with the heat rolling off Elijah's nervous skin and reflecting off the soundproof paneling on the walls and ceiling. Soundproofing in the antechamber and its door? Daeza must not want any prying ears to hear what goes on back here.

Elijah paces stiffly in the tight space. "I choked," he mutters. "Just . . . froze."

"We don't usually have to pretend to be something we're not," Zoe says quietly. "Not anymore."

Elijah presses his lips into a line. "We're bad liars, you mean."

"I always was," Zoe says softly. "You, too."

"But not Bree." Elijah looks at me. "Lies fall from your lips so easily, it's actually kind of scary."

I cross my arms. "The truth is valuable too. I just don't need it here."

"Spoken like a demon," Elijah mutters. "At least it sounds like we're early. Maybe she'll be in a good mood."

The door opens again, and the warlock pokes his head inside. "This is wrapping up. Who's your rep?"

Elijah raises his hand. "I am."

"State your case well, present your tribute, and Daeza will consider your request." Elijah tugs down on his jacket and nods. The warlock disappears.

A moment later, the door opens again, and Daeza's prior supplicant walks out.

The woman is preoccupied when she exits, her eyes unfocused. It gives me a chance to look at her before she sees me. She is tall and lithe with long black hair and pale skin. Even without seeing her eyes, I suspect that she is a Merlin.

I suck in a quiet breath—the sound loud in this enclosed space—and her head whips around to find me. Her eyes are a deep, rich gold and framed by dark lashes.

She blinks at me, jaw slightly slack, eyes widening every second. Her gaze leaves behind sprinkled, hot embers as it trails over my face. Across my eyes and brow, along the shape of my jaw, over my mouth, my cheekbones, my hair. She is frozen, breath held.

"Do I know you?" I blurt.

The woman's brows tighten, mouth working open and closed before she gathers herself. "No," she says in a low, curious voice. She says the word nearly like a question, but edging toward a statement, if a cautious one. "No, I don't think so."

"Uh," Zoe says, looking between us. "You sure? Because you're looking at her like you know her."

The Merlin woman's eyes slide to Zoe—assessing, analytical—then slide back to me. "I don't." She steps closer to me, eyes boring into mine like she's searching for something. I see the moment when she finds it, whatever she's looking for inside me. "Oh."

I rear back. "'Oh,' what?"

She tilts her head, murmuring, "I've never seen anything like that before. What *have* you gotten yourself into?"

"Excuse me?"

Zoe scowls. "Who are you—"

The woman turns to Zoe abruptly. "Can you keep her safe?"

Zoe seems to detect that something else is going on here. Something that could be important. She shifts her weight. "Yeah?"

"*Will you* keep her safe?" asks the woman. She turns to Elijah, too, who is staring at her, wide-eyed and curious.

Zoe looks to me and then back at her. "Yes."

Elijah's mouth gapes. "Do you know Bree?"

Without answering him, the woman's gaze turns inward once again. Preoccupied, like she was when she entered the waiting room. "I can't stay." She looks at me. "This is impossible."

"What is?" I ask.

"Looking out for you both at the same time," she says. "I can't be everywhere at once."

"Um . . ." I wrap my arms around myself. "Okay?"

She looks as if she might reach for me but catches herself before her hand can move. "You look like her."

Zoe's had enough. "Bree, what the hell is this white lady talking about?"

"I've got to go." The woman gives me one last look, as if to memorize my features, and steps around me, giving me as wide a berth as possible so that no parts of our bodies touch. She opens the door we used to enter and closes it quickly behind her.

"What was that?" Zoe asks.

I shake my head, dazed. Merlins don't work with demons. "Don't know."

And I don't.

Just then, the warlock opens the door and beckons us through. "Daeza will see your party now."

I don't know how many people Daeza has killed in her time on this plane, but one of them must have been a young, light-brown-skinned girl with pink hair, no more than twenty, because that's how she looks right now. In a pair of flowy pants, a dark brown corset jacket, and hair pulled to the side in a thick braid.

Aside from the teak throne she is perched on, one leg crossed over the other, I'd have never known that she was over a thousand years old just by looking at her.

Unless I'd seen her eyes.

Like the Shadow King's eyes, they are deep red. And when they find me as we walk inside the room, they feel hot on my skin, like a poker digging deep to get at my insides.

"Tribute?" Daeza asks in a low voice.

Elijah nods. "Yep. Yes." He steps forward and produces a large wooden box.

Daeza does not budge from her throne. She points to the floor, and Elijah places it down, then moves back. After admitting us, the warlock went back to the main area of the club, leaving us with Daeza and a human attendant at her side.

With a snap of her fingers, Daeza signals the human attendant, who bends at the knee to remove the heavy-locking mechanism from the box. Once it opens, he examines it, then calls back to his leader, "It's a reliquary, my Shade." The man looks up at the three of us. "Origin and age?"

"France," Elijah replies. "Eleventh century."

Daeza's brows lift. "Impressive. Bring it here."

The attendant picks up the bronze box and carefully presents it to Daeza, who takes it from his grasp with careless fingers in turn. She leans forward and takes a deep breath over the box. "A relic is inside," she murmurs. "Royal, not religious, by the scent. At least a dozen colonial blood gems set within that probably meant something to the humans who made this. And"—she takes another breath—"were painful losses to those from whom the stones were taken." When she opens her eyes, they glow bright red. "Humanity at its worst. Delicious."

"It pleases you?" the attendant asks.

"Yes. Toss the metal but research the item and repatriate the stones," she says with a wave. "I've taken my fill. I don't need that type of energy in my home."

The attendant nods and rushes away, leaving us alone.

"Well done," she murmurs. "You've proven that you deserve to live long enough to ask me something."

"Er, thank you?" I reply. Elijah shoots me a glare, but Daeza chuckles.

"Who are you?" she asks.

This is where things get . . . tricky. "My name is Bree."

Daeza blinks. "I don't care about your name, child. Who do you represent?"

Tricky again. Elijah clears his throat. "My employer sends me out for certain intel. One of my informants tells me that you might know of the location of something we need."

"Vague." Daeza makes a *hmm* sound and sits back. She taps her fingers on the armrest and looks at each of us, one at a time. "An evasion."

Zoe steps forward. "We just need information. We heard you have that information."

Daeza ignores her. "You say you are supplicants, but I've never seen you before. You bring an ancient tribute of a kind most goruchel could never procure, and you aren't human"—she points at the two cambions beside me—"even if *she* is."

"We never said we were human," Elijah replies.

"You're balanced cambions. Rare these days." Daeza's eyes darken. "Who is your Shadowborn parent?"

"We don't know," Zoe says.

Daeza smirks. "Yes, you do. Tell me. And don't lie to me again." She looks at Elijah. "You're quite bad at it."

Zoe rolls her eyes. "We're just nervous. We——"

"We are the children of Ozyrus," Elijah says loudly.

Daeza speeds off her throne and blurs to us in a blink, raising Elijah off the ground in a single motion, her hand on his throat. "In that case, I have to kill you after all."

"Elijah!" Zoe runs to Daeza, who kicks her in the chest——sending her flying back to the other side of the room to hit the wall with a loud grunt.

"Let him go!" I step back, opening my palms.

Daeza looks at me. "Why?"

"We brought you tribute; you're supposed to hear us out!" I shout.

She shrugs. "Rules can change."

"These rules should stick. It's better for your health," I snap.

She grins wide, black-tipped fangs long in her mouth. "Oh, you're a mouthy little human!" She drops Elijah, then steps back to regard us both. "I'll let you live a little longer just to see what else you might say."

Elijah rolls to his feet, voice hoarse. "You'd be smart to keep your hands off all of us."

Daeza throws her head back to laugh. "You certainly are the progeny of Ozyrus! Arrogant, just as he is. Speaking of, seen your father lately?"

"No," Zoe grits out, making her way back over to us as she rubs a bruised hip.

"Mm." Daeza turns to walk away, back up to her throne. "Me neither. Ozyrus and I had a falling-out."

"So I've heard. If you kill us, I have a feeling he won't be happy about that," Elijah replies.

"No, I suppose not." Daeza settles back on her throne, this time leaning forward with both elbows on her knees. "Now why would Ozyrus's offspring bring tribute to me?"

"We heard you know where the King's crown is." Elijah takes a bold step closer to Daeza to make his case. "We bring tribute so that you may understand how badly we would like to find it and so that you will tell us where it is."

Daeza raises both brows. "Ozyrus turned on the old man?" She cackles. "Fucking finally."

We don't respond. She thinks the twins' father sent them here for the crown?

"You know, I am glad for Ozyrus," Daeza says. "Being a Nightshade to a king without his crown is not being a Nightshade at all. Without that crown, the King is as bound to feeding from humans and scrounging for aether as we all are."

I bite my tongue so that I don't make a sound. This is what Zoe told me that morning at Erebus's house. The real reason I broke into the King's warded barn: if he gets the crown, he won't have to feed any longer. He'll stop hunting Rootcrafters. It won't stop him from seeking his revenge on Arthur, but this? This is something that has to end. And if we get it to him in time, maybe we can save the girl from the bathroom.

"If you don't want to be on his Court," I begin, "why don't you just go back to the other side? You won't need to feed there."

Daeza laughs again. "I hate being hungry all the time, but I like the chaos here. I *like* the humans. They are awful, messy creatures, and their every negative whim and motivation tastes delectable." She waves her hand at the building around her. "Plus, I have my freedom. I've *built* my freedom."

"So you won't tell us where the crown is, I'm guessing," I say, frustrated.

"No." She smirks. "I'm going to kill you in a few minutes, before the other supplicants arrive."

"Before you do that," I warn her, "you should know we aren't here for Ozyrus."

Zoe grabs my arm. "Bree . . . bad idea . . ."

"Bree!" Elijah warns.

I pull my arm free and walk forward. "You should know who we really work for."

Daeza considers this. "Who?"

"The King himself," I say.

Daeza's face stills. "The old man needs more than the crown to win the Court back. He knows it too. The Merlins and the Table are too strong, the Order too widespread, too tapped into the human network. The Scion of Arthur is afoot."

"He has more ammunition than you think. A weapon the other side doesn't have."

"And what would that weapon be, little human?"

I inhale and exhale, letting purple root spill from my mouth and palms. It spreads along the floor not like flames but like smoke. Rolling, creeping smoke that crawls toward her feet—like a shadow. "Me."

Daeza's eyes widen as my root flows across the floor of her chamber and up her steps, stretching toward her ankles. She backs away. "What is this?"

With a snap of my wrist, the purple smoke turns to flame, then solid bands. They wrap around her chest and arms, holding her up in the air as she held Elijah.

Daeza screams, fighting against the restraints and cursing, but she can't break free. "Let me go! Now!"

"Tell us where the crown is, Daeza." My band of root tightens. "Then we'll leave you alone."

She growls low in her throat before she answers. "Another Shade has it," she gasps. "Mikaelaz."

"Mikaelaz?" Elijah says slowly behind me. "As in, Mikael, the broker?"

Daeza nods stiffly, growling between jagged breaths. "Yes. But he—he hates the old man—even more than—than I do."

I freeze at this revelation. I knew a broker once. Not this one. Another.

And that is the exact moment when the Shadow King *pulls* on my bloodmark.

The crimson light glows under my shirt, but this time, a burning sensation takes me down to the floor. I grunt, collapsing. Zoe catches me, barely, before my skull tips backward on the tile.

"The actual worst timing," Zoe mutters.

The King's burnt ember signature fills my nose. Spices, charred and furious. I speak between gritted teeth. "Feels like the old man finally discovered his broken ward." I wince at the light, turning my eyes away. "Took him long enough."

Daeza stands at her throne, shaking off her restraints until they fall into loose sparks, dissipating on the steps. "That's a bloodmark," she declares, staring at me as I writhe on the floor. Her eyes flash to Elijah. "Whose?"

"It's his." Elijah swallows. "The King's."

Daeza's eyes dart from me to Elijah, then back. "She really is his weapon, then," she says, half to herself. She gnaws on her lower lip. "Her power, it belongs to him?"

"As good as," Elijah says.

Daeza's eyes grow wild for a moment. "With her, and the children of Ozyrus, and the crown . . ." She paces away, nodding to herself excitedly now as I groan. The mark begins to die down but still shines bright beneath my clothing. She paces back to us, a sly smile on her face. "I'll help get you to Mikael. Help you get the old man his crown."

"Why?" I croak, pushing to my feet.

Daeza grins, red eyes bright. "Because if he has *you* on his side, we might be able to take the Table. End the Legendborn bloodlines by killing this new Scion of Arthur, once and for all."

"Yes," I say with a steady voice, even though my heart is racing. "That's the plan. Kill the Scion of Arthur, once and for all."

The King calls on my bloodmark three more times before we make it back to the house. It leaves a constant, low-level burn against my skin, even when it finally dies down and turns invisible again.

As soon as we step through the wards and into the house, the heat of his anger scalds my cheeks.

He is pacing the floor half as Erebus, half as the Shadow King, and fully made of fury. "Where were you three?" he says, snarling at us all as we stand in the foyer. "And why is my ward destroyed?"

I don't bother to equivocate. "We know who has your crown."

His eyes widen, then flash to Zoe and Elijah on either side of me, who are struggling to contain their excitement while still showing the proper decorum of bowed heads. "Elijah? Zoelle?"

"It's true," Elijah says, breathless. "We defied your wishes, but—"

"You went to Daeza?" Erebus's nostrils flare wide in his anger. "I explicitly told you—"

"It was my idea," I interrupt. "I broke the affective ward. I took a tribute from your collection. I told the twins I wanted to go to Daeza to confirm what we'd heard, and now we know where the crown is."

Erebus seems torn between a desire to discipline us for everything I've just shared and the ancient, eternal wish to retrieve his precious crown. I sort of enjoy the turmoil and half-hide the smile from my face.

"Don't enjoy this too much, Briana," Erebus snaps. "The crown is still at large."

Silence. We just need to wait. Then—

"Well?" he demands. "Where is it?"

"Mikaelaz holds it, sire," Elijah says.

"Another of my rogue Shades." He turns away with a groan. "And yet between Mikaelaz and Daeza, he is the worse of the two. Mikael brokers with humans for . . . any number of riches. Every Nightshade has specific appetites and preferred feeding grounds. They manufacture the environments that will best attract the prey they desire. Daeza surrounds herself with chance and chaos, which invites a certain type of clientele to her business. Mikael, however, thrives where there is both human devotion and human greed. He pretends to be one of them, but remains elusive in order to foster allure and aspiration. He flaunts his wealth and access to rare artifacts, but only enough to nurture his followers' elitism and hunger for exclusivity. He knows how to lure in a particular kind of human and, with them, particular kinds of emotions." The disdain is evident on the King's face. "All is a game with him. Always has been."

"Mikael's estate is not far," Elijah says eagerly, his eyes bright. "He is hosting some sort of party. Daeza says he'll auction off the crown to a crowd of wealthy bidders—"

"Oh, I'm sure he will," Erebus says, the last of the fury—against us, anyway—flowing out of him. "Mikael is deeply enamored with pomp and circumstance. One of his so-called Collectors' Galas will make a perfect opportunity for him to dress up his human followers and toy with them like dolls. Ferreting my crown away to the private collection of a greedy human buyer at an auction would keep it out of my hands *and* allow Mikael to continue his . . . enterprise." He pauses, shaking his head. "But we cannot trust the source of this information. Disloyal Shades like Daeza or Mikael would never help me seek the crown or its disenchantment—"

"Daeza was swayed to your cause," I offer mildly. "She is willing to help us get into Mikael's auction."

Erebus turns to me, eyes narrowing. "Swayed? How? Speak plainly."

I cross my arms. "I gave her a taste of what *I* can do. What *you* can do with me at your side."

"You revealed your power in front of a *Shade*, in a lair full of demons?" he hisses.

"Her chamber was warded to contain anything that happened inside it," I counter. "I made my point, and she saw the bloodmark, realized it was yours, and didn't even bother to try and feed from me. Now, she believes that you have a chance of winning the war with or without the crown. I'd call that teamwork."

Erebus takes a deep breath, then scowls, turning away. "I am displeased."

I roll my eyes. "Do you want your crown or not?"

Beside me, the twins hold their breaths.

Erebus turns back to us. "I cannot confront Mikael. He will have the crown moved as soon as he senses my presence."

"We'll go, sire," Elijah says. "Daeza says she can get an invitation for two. Zoelle and I will take the mission—"

"No," Erebus cuts him off. "It is too dangerous."

"I know the rules of an auction!" Elijah protests.

"Rules can *change!*" Erebus reminds him.

Silence. Erebus's stony gaze is on us all. Then—

"Briana and Zoelle will go. You will stay here, Elijah."

"What?" Zoe exclaims. "Why?"

"Three reasons," Erebus replies. "First, Briana is somewhat protected by my bloodmark in the house of a Shade—they would think twice before attempting to pursue her power, as Daeza did. Second, Zoelle, should the rules change, your casting and forging abilities are stronger than Elijah's—"

"Elijah has to go," I protest. "It was his work that led us to Reggie in the first place—"

"And the third reason," Erebus continues, "is that I would like collateral."

"Collateral?" Zoe cries. "For what?"

Erebus's eyes slide to Elijah. "Care to hazard a guess, Elijah?"

Elijah's hands are fisted tight at his sides. "If Bree does not return safely . . ."

"I will ensure that Elijah's time here will come to an end," Erebus finishes coldly, "in one way or another."

A beat of horrifying silence as his words settle across both twins. I feel my chest tighten like one of the bands I used against Daeza is around me instead, squeezing the breath out of me.

"No!" Zoe hisses. "You can't—"

"I can."

"Our father—"

"Understood the risks of leaving his children with me."

As I listen to her shout and rail against her mentor, her guardian, and her king, I feel nothing but an icy resolve wrap my heart. As the King calmly refutes her every suggestion and as Elijah turns to stomp up the stairs, that ice hardens. When his door slams in the distance, shaking the entire house, I don't even jump.

All I can do is watch Erebus, watch the Shadow King, and think of his downfall. Not my escape or my own power, but the end of him and the end of the suffering he causes so easily, so swiftly.

Like the pain of others is nothing.

First, I decide, I'll find the crown. Next, I'll save the kidnapped girl and any other Rootcrafters he could hunt.

Then, I'm going to kill the Shadow King.

26

Mariah

"IF SOMETHING GOES wrong," Valec says, "your aunts are gonna kill me."

"Yeah, they will."

"You're heartless. Please don't die, is what I'm trying to say." He pulls into the lot across from the club, Eclipse, with fingers tight on the steering wheel.

"Worse comes to worst, I pretend to be a wayward, desperate potential human client looking to make a deal with a warlock. Lord knows I've seen plenty of those hanging out at the Lounge all these years." I smile to set him at ease, but it doesn't work so well when your companion can hear your heart racing.

He taps his ear. "I know you're nervous. I *hoped* you'd be. This ain't some small mission. It's a big deal."

"Yeah." I can feel the Heart pulsing near my ribs. I wasn't exactly sure what to wear to a demon's club, but I figured every cambion I've ever met is always dressed to the nines, as Aunt Hazel would say. So I did too. I picked a dress cut low enough that the Heart of the Grand Dame lies prominently beneath my collarbone. The stone is warm tonight, like it knows we're using it. "Aunt Lu never said this thing was like wearing a hot piece o' coal around your neck. Never burns, but feels like it could."

Valec sighs, heavy and long. "Don't try anything with that. Don't let them know—"

"Valec!" I hiss. "We've talked about all this before. I can do this. I'm no Bree, but—"

"Hey," he interrupts, tapping my knee. "Not everyone needs to be Bree. Half the time, I'm not even sure *Bree* needs to be Bree." He shakes his head. "This ain't a Bree Matthews–ass mission. You can't go in and blow the place up, then apologize later."

I grin. "That is *definitely* a Bree Matthews–ass mission."

"We still don't know what this thing does on a Medium, okay?" He points to the Heart, where it rests on a chain around my neck. "Just let me do the talking. There are rules here, but rules can change. Don't accept any offers, no bargains, no favors."

"Got it." I grasp the door handle and take a deep breath.

"This is a bad idea," Valec says, shaking his head and cutting the engine. "But leggo."

Daeza sniffs at the small wooden box in her hands. "Anger. Potent."

Valec nods, hands loose in the pockets of his slacks. "Politician."

"Ah," she says. "That's why it's so sweet."

"Yeah," he drawls. "They get so mad when things don't go their way."

"I used to keep one on call"—she hands the box to her attendant—"until he died."

I blink, trying to remain cool. But Valec and Daeza both tilt their heads at my suddenly rapid heartbeat.

"Heart attack," she says, sweeping her long skirt over her thighs before crossing her legs. "Not my fault. Or was it? Who can say, when a human is filled with that much spite?"

I have to work hard to pay attention to what Daeza says, because when I look at her, all I can see are the parts of her that are undead. The nonliving energy writhing inside her is so active, it makes her skin look nearly translucent—at least to me.

"Is the tribute of value to you?" Valec asks.

"Oh yes, I accept it," Daeza replies, "but I have to say I almost didn't need it when I heard it was *you* who had come calling."

Valec dips his chin, all charm. "You flatter."

"No," Daeza states, "I'm just being honest. What would bring the great Valechaz to my doorstep? I haven't seen you in over seventy years, pup."

Valec's smile is tight. "Only a Nightshade can get away with calling *me* a pup."

"I can get away with quite a lot, as you know."

"Yes, ma'am."

Daeza tosses her head. "Don't try that charm on me, cambion. I know your games. I helped *invent* some of those games."

"Not mine, I'm afraid," Valec purrs back. "Mine are all homegrown."

Daeza taps her chin. "Tell me, Shadeling, did you ever find out who sired you?"

I stifle a gasp. Valec's the child of a Nightshade? Beside me, Valec's spine stiffens. "I never looked."

"Not in two hundred years?" Daeza whistles. "That's some impressive restraint. Why not?"

"What kinda father leaves a woman and infant in enslavement?" Valec returns, eyes flashing. "Not one I'd like to know."

"Fair." She stands, pacing in front of her throne with her hands resting at her stomach, fingers steepled outward. "I must say that tonight's requests have been . . . interesting."

I shift on my heels, from one side to another. At my chest, the Heart burns. Daeza has power, and it's roiling under her skin, but so is a deep, dark spectre. Unlike the lines I can see on Valechaz, what I see on Daeza *churns*. A shadow become restless.

"Your attendant said we are the last supplicants of the night." Valec glances at me.

Daeza gestures to the room vaguely. "We have entertained more visitors than usual. Too many bodies, too many disappointing requests. You are the third Shadeling to pay me a visit tonight, if you would believe it."

I look down to where Daeza's eyes have fallen—and immediately regret it. There's blood splattered on the floor. Bright red—fresh. Deep, dark red—dried. And a generous collection of greenish black—demon blood too. Valec's eyes have followed mine, although I'm certain he smelled the blood before I did. "Is that so? Three in one night? Can't help but notice there's a lot of blood on the ground."

"Occupational hazard. Now"—Daeza stops pacing, her skirts flowing around her ankles and heels—"what do *you* need of me, Valechaz, son of no one?"

"Son of Pearl," Valec corrects sharply. "A good woman who had a good name. A name worth knowin'."

Daeza dips her head. "Son of Pearl. My apologies."

"Daeza, Nightshade of the Court, I come to you—"

She holds up a hand. "Wait."

Valec closes his mouth, jaw tensing. "Yes?"

"Grand Dame of the Southeastern territory." She points to me. "Why don't *you* state Valechaz's request?"

"Now, Daeza, *I* called the audience. I brought the Dame here to make sure you knew I came in peace. You know Dames don't intervene in demon business, don't tangle with our disputes—"

"I know what a Grand Dame does," Daeza says. "And I won't do anything to cross one. I know the rules."

Rules can change.

Behind my back, my hands tense. At my chest, the Heart pulses, beating in counterpoint to my own. I see Daeza's inner shadow swirl beneath her skin, a strange, bright darkness, and my fingers twitch.

"It is because I know what a Grand Dame stands for that I ask yours to state your case. I know it will not be twisted by your trickster tongue. And I will find it entertaining. A good way to end a rather eventful night."

Valec bares his teeth. "No—"

Daeza is a blur between blinks, rushing to Valechaz until their noses nearly touch. He does not move, does not breathe. "Let her speak," Daeza says quietly. She smiles. "Or else."

Valec's own smile is slow and easy. "As you wish, Shade."

Her eyes slide to mine. I swallow, my throat dry as saltines. "We seek the demon we know as the Hunter. The one demons call the Great Devourer."

Daeza's head tilts. "Very interesting."

"Does that mean you'll point us in his direction?"

"He is impossible to find," Daeza says. "Always in a new form, a new face. He uses emissaries, these days."

"Where can we find them?"

Her smile spreads. "Now *that* I can help you with. I happen to know of an event where two of his emissaries will be in attendance in one week's time."

"Really?" Valec glances at me in surprise, then back to her. "What's the catch?"

"Well, for one," Daeza says, "you can't attend."

Valec takes a deep breath. "Let me guess. Is this event hosted by another broker?"

"Bingo," Daeza replies, nodding. "Another Shade, in fact. Mikaelaz'll think you're there to poach his clients, and you'll end up with a turf war on your hands. Lots of dead people, and I don't think you'll win."

Valec grits his teeth. "Then I suppose we've reached a dead end. We thank you for your—"

She wags her finger. "Not so fast. Just because *you* can't go doesn't mean your little Grand Dame impersonator can't."

My jaw drops. Valec freezes. "Daeza—"

She rolls her eyes. "Did you think I was born yesterday, Valechaz? That girl isn't the Grand Dame of your territory no more than I'm an actual twenty-year-old girl from Texas."

I blink, looking down at her body. "You're . . ."

"Wearing the *skin* of a twenty-year-old girl from Texas, darling," Daeza purrs. "Just like you're wearing the Heart of the Dame to help with *your* disguise."

Valec blurs in front of me, arm outstretched, but Daeza waves him away.

"Stand down, cambion. Let me finish. *You* can't go to the auction, but she can. And since she's so eager to go undercover to places she *really* shouldn't, I'll even offer your little *faux Dame* here a fake identity that'll get her into the auction with zero issues. I just so happen to have one invite left. Think you can pretend to be a buyer for an art gallery?"

I can already see the fight brewing behind Valec's tight jaw. "Thank you for your offer, but we can't—"

"I accept!" I say. "I'll do it."

"You did *not* just say that, Mariah. . . ." Valec drops his head in his hands.

"Delicious!" Daeza claps. "I'll get the paperwork started."

"You seem eager to help, Shade," Valec mumbles tiredly as he looks up. "A bit *too* eager."

Daeza strides back to her throne. "I am a very old demon, Valechaz. I get bored easily. But this will be fun."

"Fun for who?" Valec mutters.

"Me, of course." Back in her seat, Daeza crosses one leg over the other as she gives Valec a final appraising look. "It's good to have you back, Valechaz."

Valec's fingers twitch at his sides. "I'm not back, Daeza."

She smirks. "We'll see."

Natasia

WHEN I RETURN to the cabin from Daeza's club, I walk straight to Selwyn's room. "Well, that was an almighty failure."

He is sitting cross-legged on his bed behind the ward, eyes closed in what I can only guess to be meditation. Something I taught him long ago, when he was young. A way to focus his energies, contain his turmoil, and find his calm *between* battles—not just within them.

The current ward is a multilayered wall of two-inch-wide bars of pure crystalline aether, crafted so densely that it will burn through skin. Before I left for Daeza's, I wryly suggested to my son that he consider using an aether weapon to break this ward down if he felt so inclined to run away today, rather than his bare fist. I am pleased to see that he decided to stay put.

"Selwyn?" I call.

One red eye peeks open, and his silent, annoyed response is as clear as if he'd spoken it aloud. *I heard you.* His eye closes.

I take a seat on the other side of today's ward creation. "Back to not speaking to me?" I ask. Sel had inquired about the ward as I cast it this morning, and his curiosity about my methods of barrier construction had given me a small morsel of hope that we might be on the way to repair.

He responds to my question by, well, not speaking. Both eyes remain shut.

It seems that our healing, like many processes, will not be linear. Time for a new strategy.

"You are an impertinent piece of work, Selwyn Emrys," I say, half-exasperated and half-amused. I let sarcasm crawl into my voice. "I'm sure your friends enjoy that trait of yours so very much."

The edge of his mouth kicks up in a manner that tells me his friends do *not*, in fact, enjoy this aspect of his personality.

"Unless they have grown accustomed to it," I muse aloud, "and give you back as good as you give."

Both eyes open at that, narrowed and cutting. Caustic indignation rolls off him.

"So there *is* someone in your life who doesn't put up with your more *pleasant* qualities?" I say, smirking. "Excellent. That person must irritate you greatly; I adore them already."

He rolls his eyes.

"Is it Nicholas Davis, I wonder?"

He frowns. Huffs.

"No, I don't think so," I say. "You and Nicholas may bicker and fight, test each other's boundaries and the limits of the Kingsmage Oath, as I did with Martin. But our bonds tie us to our bonded as if they were the opposite sides of our coins. We may dislike them, but before my descent, Martin was a part of me. Acrimony like that has deep roots, but rarely grows new shoots. Your current irritation feels bright and fresh, so it must belong to someone else, not Nick." I pause. "This new Scion of Arthur, perhaps?"

My ears are sharp, so I hear it: an increase in his heart rate. And my eyes are sharp, so I see it: his pupils blowing wide. His body responding even if his voice does not, as if he can't help himself.

I make my tone as casual as possible: "Could it be that the mere *thought* of this new Scion of Arthur sparks such frustration in you? Such dissatisfaction? Do they bring about feelings in you that you wish they could not? Feelings you can't control?"

Selwyn's face grows still. Expressionless. Emotionless. The way that a goruchel can sometimes void their features of any humanity on purpose, to chill their prey. It is my son's way of telling me to stop my continued inquiries about this new and unexpected Scion of Arthur. And it is a clue that I am close to unlocking that which he has kept guarded.

I soften my approach. "You have not told me any more about this new wielder of Caledfwlch. I cannot imagine the conflicting feelings you must have about a Crown Scion to whom you are not bonded . . . whom you cannot protect as you were trained to protect."

His fingers twitch on his knees, the silver rings flickering in agitation. *Bingo.* Now it's time for a more *direct* approach.

"I may be the only person on the planet who can understand what you're going through, Selwyn. I know what it means to be betrayed by what we were taught and even by the Kingsmage Oath itself and what it stands for. I know what it feels like to be held by an Oath that you can no longer serve. Please," I say, lowering my head to catch his eyes, "tell me what has been happening in your life and with this new Scion. I want—I *wish* to help you."

While his face does not change, his eyelids flutter infinitesimally. He turns his head away, any softening in him hardening with the movement.

I sit there for a moment, hoping for an acknowledgment that I am not owed. It does not come. *Nonlinear healing it is, then.* I sigh.

"In other news, I visited a rather . . . unsavory demon today. She could not help me." As I adjust my seat, crossing one booted foot over my knee, the AC clicks on overhead, blowing my hair forward—

Then Sel is at the ward, a low growl rising in his throat. *"Where is she?"*

I did not even see him move. "Sel, what—"

When he inhales deeply, I realize that he has scented something. I sniff the air myself and cannot detect anything but Daeza's club on my skin, my clothes, my hair. Then I look up—and realize that it was the AC turning on that carried my scent to him. That he is picking up on some fragrance, or catching some tiny hint of aether, that even I cannot detect.

"I smell her on you." His voice has shifted into a guttural rasp that I've never heard from him before.

Does he mean Daeza? That is the only aether I can detect. "The demon I met is not a typical demon—"

He ignores me, pressing his face into the glowing bars—and letting them burn his skin. *"I feel her on you."*

The descent of his voice into a lower register—and the scent of his singeing flesh—stun me so wholly that my reaction is delayed. Then I am on my feet, heart racing. "Step back from the ward, Sel—"

"Where. Is. She."

"Do you mean the demon?" I ask. "Sel, she's not safe—"

Selwyn shuts his eyes, inhaling again. I watch in horror as my son presses harder into the ward, pursuing the scent I've carried with me. As he lets the densely cast bars burn *deeper* into his cheekbones, inviting my magic to sear through his muscles, to hit bone. Like a wild animal willing to sacrifice his flesh to get free.

My hands are already moving, pulling the ward down in frantic swipes. "Stop!" I've never seen my son like this, not once in these four months under the same roof. Is this the Selwyn that I have been tracking in the woods? The one that leaves trails of blood in his wake?

"What is this?" He murmurs against the bars as if drunk, as if he can't feel the pain at all. *"If scent can be sound, if sound can be feeling, if feelings can become instinct . . . then that is what I am experiencing. And I want more . . . more . . ."* Eyes still closed, he drags a clawed hand down the remaining ward, slicing through it like a hot knife through butter as he mumbles, *"I want to chase it all down. Fold myself into it. Dig in—and never let go."*

"Let me take down the ward!" I shake my head, panic cracking my voice. I groan and *pull* at the air with both hands, finally dropping the entire thing. I screech at him where he stands, eyes blinking open, face striped bright red and glistening raw. "What the hell are you thinking?"

Sel steps across the sparkling remnants of the barrier, unhearing. *"Where is she, Mother?"*

"Who?"

His eyes fasten to mine. The open muscle beneath them is already stitching itself back together.

"Where is Bree?"

I blink, his words settling in beneath my shock. "How—how do you know Bree?"

Selwyn chuckles darkly. As he speaks, green flames rise along his shoulders, lifting his hair. *"She is my Scion of Arthur."*

"Your—" I stumble backward, shaking my head. "No, that's . . . Bree can't be."

"Oh, but she is." Sel prowls toward me. *"Briana is mine. My Scion. My sovereign. My king,"* Selwyn utters, lip curling. *"Just as her mother was yours."*

Faye.

My vision clouds with memories, colliding behind my eyes. Faye's wide smile. Her big laugh. Her dignity. Her integrity. The power I'd never seen before, never thought possible—

"No." I shake my head again. "Faye was . . ."

"A Scion of Arthur," Selwyn says. *"The* true *Scion you should have been bonded to. Just as Briana is who should have been bonded to me."*

"Faye . . ." It seems all I can do is speak my friend's name.

And remember.

The way Faye drifted toward the Bell Tower without thinking when she walked idly across campus. Her tendency to settle there, studying beneath its tall shadow—unknowingly drawn to the exact place on campus that sits above Excalibur's resting place in the ogof below.

The way Faye charged into the fray to protect innocents, risking her own secrets.

The bright bloodred burn of her power, uncontrolled and beautiful.

The way she led, both by example and by word.

I remember it all.

And in my bones, in my heart, I know that what my son says is true.

"*Faye Matthews didn't know, of course.*" Selwyn answers my question before I ask it. "*She died without knowing. It was her daughter Bree's fate to uncover that truth. Bree's fate to wield the blade. Bree's fate to meet the cycle . . . and to bring the Regents to their knees.*"

"Bree is a *child*," I insist. "She wasn't raised for this war."

"*No. She wasn't,*" he says, eyes turned inward and savoring. "*But you* truly *haven't lived until you've seen her fight it.*"

"What does that mean?" I ask, alarmed.

"*She is Bloodcrafted,*" Selwyn says. "*Like her mother before her.*"

Faye's red root blazes behind my eyes. "No, Bree didn't inherit it," I say, stammering. "Faye checked; she made sure—"

But then I remember the hidden memory she'd asked me to implant into her child's mind. An insurance policy. A "just in case."

I think of Bree, who looks so very much like her mother. Bree, who should have been at home with her father tonight, not at a Nightshade's club accompanied by balanced cambions. Bree shouldn't have remembered me, given that the last time I encountered her I mesmered both her and her father, but her uncertainty and hesitation when prompted by the cambion girl worries me still.

And now I know that whatever has happened to Bree, she has been tampered with by a force beyond my own understanding.

A force who likely knows that Bree Matthews, like her mother, wields a furnace of unending, world-changing, Bloodcrafted power.

Knowing both what has come to pass and what is yet to come, I look upon my son and see him with new eyes—the demon glow of his irises, the elongated fangs, and the tipped ears beneath his hair. The black veins lining his pale forearms and the black-tipped claws at his fingertips. The hunger that could never, ever seem to be sated and only grew.

"It was Bree's power, wasn't it?" I whisper. "You consumed it, and it tipped you over into demonia. Devouring Bree's power is what made you like this."

Sel grins. "*Ding-ding-ding. You win a prize.*"

Horror makes my heart race. Not for myself and, for the first time in months, not for my son—but for Bree. Bree is an unwitting, untrained Scion of

Arthur without a Kingsmage—and my son wants to be with her. Or feed from her. Or both. And she has no idea that the path he's on seems resistant to my interventions.

"*Tell me where she is,*" Selwyn says, fingers flexing at his sides.

There is an agony in seeing him like this, knowing that I cannot help him pursue what he wants, but it is even more painful knowing that what he wants is Bree—and that I can't let him have her.

"No." I shake my head slowly. "You aren't in a state to go to her."

Sel tilts his head, drawing another deep breath as he steps closer. "*Her scent is not . . . right. What have you done?*"

I raise both hands, backing away. "I didn't do anything to her. I only saw her by accident, pure accident—"

He growls again. "*Something is* wrong *with her.*"

"I know. But you can't fix it, and neither can I."

He blinks, clarity returning to his gaze briefly before he shakes it away, his long hair falling over his eyes. He bears down on me again. "*Where—*"

"I don't know how to find her, and if I did, I wouldn't tell you. Selwyn. . . . You're not yourself in full."

"*And how would you know what I'm like?*" he sneers. "*You haven't exactly been around to find out who I am, have you?*"

His words knife through me, but I breathe them away. Set them aside for now.

"*I'm very much myself, Mother.*" He bares his teeth. "*Maybe I'm finally myself.*"

"No—"

"*I've allowed you to keep me here, but no longer.*" His right palm falls open, aether gathering in a tiny ball. "*I need to capture a king.*"

I stiffen, every hair on the back of my neck standing.

My son is calling aether against me in my own home. "*Please* don't make me do this. Let me help you—"

"*Tell me where Bree was and then tell me where she is now. You must know. After all, you kept such good tabs on her and her mother*"—his smile turns cruel—"*Faye.*"

My vision turns black and red, the room fogging up with my own grief, as sharp as ever. It is the taunt in Selwyn's voice that clears my mind. The thought of Faye Matthews—the brilliant, beautiful girl who should have been my Scion of Arthur and king—that finally, finally turns my palm open.

I hear my own voice, low and quiet. "Be very careful what you say next."

"What I *say next? About* your *Scion of Arthur?"* His aether extends into a long blue-silver staff. *"The one who died on your watch?"*

Shame nearly arrests me, but I do not let it.

"Do not speak about Faye Matthews." I call and forge my own aether staff to match his and make a silent promise that I will never forge a weapon against him that he does not forge first. Never call on enough aether to do harm, only enough to match his. "This is about *Bree.* She needs help, Selwyn. Help that you and I cannot give. You *crave* her, which means you cannot be the one to heal her."

Hesitation flickers across his face, then dies. *"I do not care."*

"You are not what Bree needs right now," I state. "She needs *refuge.* You will only make things worse."

"I do not care!" he roars.

"Yes, you do; you've just forgotten. Your care is *buried,*" I answer, raising my staff as he raises his. "You need to care again, or I can't let you pass."

"I don't need *to do anything!"* he snarls, stepping forward. *"I only need* her."

When we clash, staffs sparking against each other, I barely feel it.

All I can think is that I was meant to be Faye's Kingsmage. Her protector. Her guardian.

In the end, I failed to save her, but I will not fail to save her daughter.

I was a Kingsmage then, and I will be a Kingsmage now.

I will protect the Scion of Arthur against all threats—even if that threat is my son.

28

William

THE MORGAINES FIND us before we find them.

Lark and I are leaning against the side of our vehicle in the parking lot of another motel as the sun nears its zenith overhead, waiting for Nick to return from his scouting. This time, we have looped back into North Carolina, just across the border from Tennessee. Beside me, Lark reads a message on his phone, then curses.

"They found another Merlin body three days ago," he mutters. "Said he was ambushed on a patrol—magical death confirmed." With a taut expression on his face, he shoves his phone back in his pocket.

Not for the first time, I wonder if he might have been safer at the Keep. Whoever's hunting Merlins might isolate him while he is in the field with me and Nick, or when he is up at night patrolling. And because he is a Merlin, I can't heal him.

This thought has crept into my consciousness with increasing frequency lately. It is a concern I always had with Selwyn, but Selwyn rejected all caution as a matter of course, and unlike humans, Merlins heal injuries quickly without much intervention. And yet . . . the very image of Lark being wounded drives an impotent sort of terror through my heart.

If my worry keeps me close to his side a bit more frequently as every week passes, then I think that's more than fair. If he notices my proximity, my tendency to walk closer to him than I do to Nick, which I *know* he does, he does not comment on it.

In fact, he seems to encourage it. Even now.

As if seeking comfort, or offering it, he slides closer to me against the side of the car until our hips touch.

We are interrupted by Nick's tall figure striding back into the parking lot. He approaches us deep in thought with a frown on his face, and we both straighten to greet him.

Abruptly, Lark grows stiff beside me. Across the lot, Nick has frozen too. Then, I see her.

A girl is leaning against another SUV parked twenty feet away near the tree line.

Ava the Morgaine and I have never met, so I don't recognize her at all, but Nick clearly does—and so does Lark. But even I can tell that the confident smirk on the girl's face as she studies us is too knowing, too clever, to belong to a Onceborn.

She is South Asian, with light bronze skin and short, thick brown hair. She is a few inches shorter than me, built like an athlete. Broad-shouldered, muscular arms, and completely stunning. High cheekbones and long lashes frame her dark eyes. She's half model, half Marine. Black combat boots and fitted cargo pants and a fur-collared bomber jacket. Someone who could kick your ass and look absolutely perfect while doing it.

"You're looking for me," the girl says. "Why?"

Lark blurs in front of me in a blink. Nick turns on his heel and allows a gauntlet and the hilt of a blade to spring to life in his hand.

Nick's face, like all of ours, is worn from travel. Blond stubble on his cheeks and along his jaw, hair shaggy under his wool cap. Long days on the road will do that to you. "Stand down," he orders Lark. "It's her."

"Davis?" Lark asks, palm tipped up. "Is—"

"Nice to see you again," Nick says. He squints at her face, and I'm surprised it takes me as long as it does to see what *he* sees. "You're injured."

She's holding one arm awkwardly at her side. Fair bit of bruising on her fingers.

Ava sniffs. "Found a group of fresh Shadowborn, newly crossed. Caught them unawares, but they were big enough to do some damage."

I notice how stiffly she holds her shoulder. She's acting tough, but she's in pain. "Do you want me to heal that for you?" I ask before thinking twice about it.

She smiles condescendingly. "Let me guess. Scion of Gawain?"

I dip my chin in acknowledgment. "We haven't met yet, but, yes. My name is William."

"And who's the Merlin lapdog?"

Lark's smile is all fang. "Aren't you cordial." His eyes are already searching the parking lot shadows, glancing beside her car, back toward the main office. "Bring any rude friends?"

Ava smiles. "Wouldn't tell you if I did. We know how to hide from your kind."

"How long have you known I've been looking for you?" Nick asks, stepping forward.

The minute Nick moves, Lark shakes his head. "Snipers in the trees," he warns Nick. Nick holds.

Ava shrugs. "We've been following you a few weeks now. Wanted to see if the Regents sent you to flush us out."

"They haven't," Nick replies. "I asked for a quest to find you myself." He nods to me and Lark. "Will and Lark are backing me up; that's it."

"You expect me to believe the Regents would let two Scions go for a three-month-long *walk?*"

"You've been watching us for longer than a few weeks, then," Nick replies, raising a brow.

Her smile falls, and a scowl replaces it. "Caught me in a lie. Don't you feel clever?"

"I'm a good listener," Nick says.

Ava kicks one leg over the other. "You went back to where we found you last year in Sapphire Valley. You didn't think we were there just for fun, did you?"

"I assumed you were there following me, my father, and Isaac," Nick said.

"Yeah, like I said, we weren't there for fun." She smiles. "It's cute you thought you could just seek us out whenever you like, Scion. Maybe this is news to you, but we don't give a damn about your title and rank. We don't come running just because you go looking."

Nick spreads his arms wide. "And yet here you are."

Ava narrows her eyes at him but does not respond to his comment. Instead, she says, "Surprised your Scion of Arthur isn't with you. You two seemed rather close."

"She's missing," Nick replies, face placid. "But I bet you knew that, too."

"Heard rumors," Ava answers. "Either that, or the Order locked her up again."

"That was only me this time, I'm afraid."

"Hope she's all right, wherever she is, and that she stays hidden, for her sake. Wouldn't want to accidentally kill her."

Lark huffs. "Nick, let's ask her about the Merlins and quick. The rest of this conversation might make me *accidentally* forge a weapon."

"Big talk from an Oathbound cambion. How's that going, by the way? Protecting these two Scions is enough, right?" Ava holds her fingers up in front of her mouth like fangs. "Or are you turning *fangy* sometime soon?" She laughs, and Lark glowers.

"Davis . . . ," Lark warns. "I'm ready to wrap this up."

"Ignore them," Nick says sharply. "This is my quest, not theirs." He steps forward again, this time with both hands raised. Ava allows him to approach and doesn't budge from where she leans on the car door. "Let's talk."

Ava looks at him. "*Talk?* We hired a goruchel to assassinate you. You know that, right?"

"Unsuccessfully." Nick's teeth flash white, all charm. "I'm hard to kill."

"Apparently," Ava murmurs. "And you know that if your girlfriend were here right now, we'd be trying to kill her again too, right?"

Nick drops his hands and smiles. "Well, for one, she's not my girlfriend. And, two, Bree's even harder to kill than I am, so I think you'd have a fight on your hands."

"Ha!" Ava says, standing up straight and, to my dismay, looking genuinely delighted by her banter with Nick. "I look forward to another assassination attempt. Successful, this time."

Nick dips his head in a half bow. "I look forward to thwarting you."

"All right, I'll bite." She puts her hands on her hips and looks us over. "What do you want?"

"Like I said, I want to talk," Nick replies. "Just you and me. You can take me captive, if you like—we can do this on your terms, whatever you want. I'll go to one of your safe houses, of which I'm sure you have many. Surround me with your fellow Morgaines." To my shock, he puts his hands out. "I'll even let you void cuff me."

Lark looks like his eyes might bug right out of his head. "Davis! This wasn't the plan."

Ava raises a brow, looking between them both. "The void cuff offer is tempting, but no. Why are you being so . . . agreeable and self-sacrificing, Davis? You were born to be a king, not a pauper."

Nick's eyes sparkle. "I could play hard to get. I just thought this would be more efficient. Pauper or king, take your pick."

"Oh, you are *funny*." Her mouth quirks. "But I don't trust you. Didn't then, don't now."

"I get that a lot."

"What do you want to talk about?"

"That's my business. Could be yours, too." Nick's eyes slide to Lark, then back. "But it's not theirs." His eyes flit up to the trees. "And it's not your soldiers' business either."

Ava crosses her arms. "I am intrigued, but I still don't trust you."

"The feeling is mutual." He grins. "And I'm not offended."

She signals with a flick of her wrist, and the trees above us shudder, then go still. The Morgaines, retreating.

"We'll be in touch." And with that, Ava begins to fade into the darkness. "Probably."

"Name your price," Nick says, following her. "If you want money——"

"No, rich boy, I don't want your *money*," Ava says, face twisted with disgust.

Then, as if the thought has tripped an idea in her mind, she begins to slowly smile. She studies Nick in a way that makes me uncomfortable, and I'm not even subject to her scrutiny. She takes in his longer-than-usual blond hair, the light growth of facial hair down his cheeks and across his jaw, his broad shoulders and height. Nick shifts under her gaze, as uncertain as I am about the gears he sees turning behind the young woman's gaze.

"You *are* a rich boy, though, aren't you?" Ava murmurs.

"What are you talking about?" Lark interjects. "What does——"

"My family has money, yes," Nick says. He tilts his head. "How much do you want?"

"How much do you have?"

Nick's brow rises. "Plenty. Add a lot more. Then plenty again. Times five."

She grins, wide and genuine. "I *like* that answer."

Nick considers her. "You've never struck me as the type of person who cares about cash."

"I'm not," Ava says. "But I know people who do. People with things I want."

Nick hums. "And yet you aren't looking at me like I'm a bank."

"No, I am not." Ava's grin spreads. "I'm looking at you very, very differently than I was a few moments ago, though."

"Aw, shucks," Nick drawls, voice tinged with sarcasm. "You'll make a guy blush."

"You *are* a rich boy," Ava repeats, "but more importantly, you look the part."

"Which part?"

Ava releases her arms. "Here's the deal. You say you want to talk to me, but that's just code for *asking me* for something. Something you don't want to say in front of your fellow Order boys here"—she gestures to us—"which means you want information that's important and secret and, I'd wager, valuable. Information that you seem very certain I can give you."

Nick nods. "I'm one hundred percent certain you can."

"My information isn't free."

"We've addressed that."

"I'll give you what you want, Nick Davis."

"But?"

"But you're gonna have to do something for *me* first. Something you're good at. Look and act very, *very* rich." But Ava is already melting back into the shadows beneath the trees. "I'll find you when it's time. See ya later."

"Wait!" Nick darts closer to her.

I'm running forward before I can stop myself, forging a dagger. Lark is already a blur ahead of me, but we both stop short when Ava's fists erupt in crosshatched silver-blue magic.

Her face is twisted in rage in her aether's light. "*I knew it——*"

"No, wait!" Nick holds his hands wide, empty, powerless. "I'm unarmed!"

"No Awakened Legendborn, no Scion of goddamned *Lancelot* is *ever* 'unarmed,' Davis!" Ava hisses. "Do you think I'm a fool?"

"Wait," Nick repeats. "Just . . . just wait." He glances back at us, then to her. "Please."

The pleading stops her. Stops us all.

Nick swipes a tongue over his lower lip. "Give me five minutes to talk to my companions. Then . . . I'd appreciate it if you brought me with you to do this favor now, not later."

Ava appears intrigued. She nods once but does not put her aether away.

Nick backpedals slowly, keeping his hands visible, and swings out so that he doesn't turn his back directly to her. With a short jerk of his head, he turns away from the Morgaine and to us, waving us over.

We approach him warily, keeping Ava in our sights while stepping closer.

"Nick," I whisper urgently, "what are you doing? Are you . . . ?" I swallow, unsure of how much Ava is listening, and try to communicate what I'm asking with my eyes. *Are you really going to go with her to kill her?* Out loud, I say, "Doing a favor for the Morgaines was not part of the plan."

"None of this is the plan, William," Nick says. "Neither of you was supposed to come."

"Nick, you can't do this alone."

"That's the thing, I *have* to do this alone. I can't tell you why, and don't ask me to . . . because I'll have to lie." Nick smiles, shaking his head. "More than I already have."

Lark is watching Ava, but his eyes meet mine in a look that says, *I told you so*.

The truth of the situation finally settles deep in my gut. A pain so sharp, it takes my breath away. "Do you not trust me?" I ask.

Nick's face softens. "Other people need you, Will. The people in the Order who are only doing as they've been raised to do, still following the mission. A mission you still believe in. It's not right to allow the Scion of Gawain to abandon his post—that alone should tell you how corrupt the Regents are."

"Nick—"

"You have to go, William." Nick claps a hand on my shoulder. "You and Lark both."

The shock nearly rocks me backward. "No, the quest . . ."

"Tell them I attacked you," Nick says. "Tell them I chose to abandon the quest."

"What *is* your quest, Nick?" I demand. "Your real one?"

Nick squeezes my shoulder and releases it. "Something greater than the Grail." He looks to Lark. "Get him home safely?"

"No, I'm not—"

To my shock, Lark lays his hand on my arm. "Will do."

My heart leaps against my rib cage, panic settling in. Realizing that I am outnumbered, that Lark will drag me away when Nick leaves, and that I won't be able to stop him. I glance up—it is near noon, but not near enough. I need to buy time. "Nick, you're my friend."

"And you are mine," Nick says. He glances up too, his expression mild and amused. "Larkin, it is too close to noon for my liking. If you don't get him away now, he'll beat both of us to a pulp—lovingly, of course—and we'll have to have this fight all over again later."

Lark looks between Nick and me to Ava, who has been listening intently. Back to me. "Is that an order, Scion Davis?"

Nick's smile is tight. Sad. "Yes. Take William away, please."

Lark has me over his shoulder in a blur across the parking lot before I can call aether to stop him. I'm shouting, pounding on his back, clawing at his shirt before he puts me down unceremoniously—two hundred feet away from Nick and Ava. "Lark!"

Lark shakes his head, his arm wrapped around mine. "Will, we have to let him go—"

"No, we don't!" I pull forward, but his strength is too great. Nick and Ava are speaking in quick tones. She still seems to be fighting with him, but he is shaking his head, refuting her.

I call aether to my free palm, and Lark's hand tightens on my elbow. "Will . . . ," he says, eyeing my gauntlet and newly formed dagger. "Will . . . don't do this."

"Let me go," I growl.

"William." Lark glances overhead. "Please."

I feel my eyes burn; the world begins to turn green. "Larkin, I am *warning* you—"

Lark steps closer, whispering, "Sweetheart . . . honey."

My breath turns shaky, rattling in my chest. He's never called me those things before.

Lark taps his forehead gently against mine. His slides his hand down to wrap around my wrist as his voice turns soft. "You don't want to hurt me, and I don't want to hurt you. We have to go. . . ."

"No, we don't—"

"God, you're stubborn," he chuckles, "but so am I."

Just when I am beginning to wonder if he's right, if I need to let Nick go, let my friend, my patient go . . . the world explodes around us.

29

William

THE CAR BESIDE us blows apart in a blast of heat and silver-blue light that sends us flying backward. Lark and I land at the same time, but he recovers first—pulling me to my feet as an aether bolt zips by us both.

We turn to see two Mageguard spill into the lot from the far side of the forest, fighting two Morgaines. Our own vehicle is still in one piece—for now.

"Shite," Lark curses.

Our attention snaps to Nick and Ava, who appear just as shocked as we are at the appearance of the Mageguard.

"Go!" Lark shouts, waving at Nick. "Cestra must have sent them! Run, now!"

Ava's eyes dart around the scene, from her two Morgaine companions to the Mageguard in full tactical gear to me and Lark across the lot and back to Nick, who is shouting for us to run.

But when Ava sprints into the forest, Nick hesitates.

In a moment, I know what he's thinking. That there was a time, not that long ago, when he ran from Bree and Sel. I see it in the set of his jaw and the flash of his armor as he builds it around his body. I know this Nick—and *this* Nick will risk his mission, whatever that mission is, to save his friends. To save us. And I know, in that exact moment, that I can't let him do that.

That I have to trust him.

"Nick!" I scream over the fray of the Guards and Morgaines. "Go!"

Nick freezes mid-step, shock clear across his features.

"Go!" I say again, waving him away. "We'll cover you!"

Nick opens his mouth to argue—just as the sun reaches its zenith overhead.

We look up with shared understanding. When our eyes meet again, Nick nods, dips his chin in thanks, and disappears into the woods in a flash of aether.

I lift my face to the sky to meet the cool, familiar power of Gawain. As it always does, wherever my inheritance touches me, only a calm, certain clarity is left behind.

The world turns pale green in my sight.

Lark is watching and waiting. "You ready?"

I spread my fingers wide, then ball them tight, feeling the familiar strength in them once more. When I open my hands, Gawain's twin daggers appear in my palms.

I nod to Lark and step forward. "Let's go."

The power of Gawain makes me a healer, but there are times when healing is simply not enough. For me, those times are noon and midnight.

Our unspoken first objective is to subdue the Mageguard.

Not because we want the Morgaines to win but because we want Nick to get his chance.

As soon as the Morgaines realize that we're attacking our own, they drift away from the fight and melt into the woods in silence—no doubt to avoid the risk of the tide turning against them.

Once we're left to focus on the two Guards, we knock the first one out easily—and discover the second is someone we know.

"Thompson," Lark growls, his hands still alight with aether. "Should have known Cestra would send you."

Thompson, the Mageguard Nick defeated at his curia, scowls up at us from where he had been knocked to the ground. Beside him lies the other Guard—a young one—unconscious and sprawled awkwardly in the gravel.

"You're just gonna let the Morgaines get away, Douglas?"

"Nick's quest is to hunt Ava," I say. "Not random Morgaines. Explain why you attacked her companions just as he was making strides toward his goal. Were you trying to sabotage him?"

Thompson eyes me warily, the green power of Gawain enough to make even a seasoned Mageguard apprehensive. I'm stronger than he is right now by many orders of magnitude—and he knows it. Even if he could break out of the quick-chained cuffs that Lark forged around his wrists, he'd have to get past me to escape.

"Answer the Scion's question, Thompson," Lark snaps. "We're in the field, and in the field, the Legendborn outrank us both."

"The Mageguard aren't Oathed to protect the Legendborn," Thompson retorts.

"Doesn't mean you don't have to answer his questions," Lark replies with a smile.

Thompson shakes his head. "I don't have to answer to anyone but the Regents. I'm here on Regent business, not Legendborn business."

"So the Regents sent you to sabotage Nick?" I ask.

"Davis thinks he's so clever," Thompson says with a sneer. "But the Regents are always two steps ahead. No one trusts him to complete the mission, which is why they sent me."

"But you didn't attack when we first encountered Ava," Lark says, looking at the destruction around the lot. "You waited until her subordinates peeled off from the group." He jerks a chin at the tree line where they'd first emerged. "Why?"

Thompson smirks. "No reason."

Lark kneels before him. "I think there's a reason. And I think Will and I are gonna—"

"No, we aren't," I mutter, flipping my dagger to catch it overhand. I lunge before Thompson can get to his feet, striking his temple with a short, quick blow.

He falls face-forward onto the pavement.

Lark's jaw drops. "What did you just do?"

"They don't teach temple blows at the academy?" I murmur.

Lark gapes at me. "Of course they do!"

"It was a precision tap," I say, kneeling beside Thompson's hip, "with enough force to knock him out but not do any serious damage."

He looks down at his fellow Mageguard. "I was interrogating him."

I shake my head. "No, you weren't. He was toying with you. Buying time, likely, until reinforcements show up or until Gawain's power times out. He wasn't going to give us anything more than he already had."

"So, you just . . . knocked him out because you got tired of hearing him talk?"

"No, but that was a bonus." I shift Thompson to the side slightly and start pulling at his black outercoat. "Help me get his jacket off."

Lark kneels but complies. "I have no idea what you're doing right now and no idea why you're doing it."

"And yet you're following my instructions," I say wryly.

"I'm questioning my life choices, is what I'm doin'," he mutters. "Here, turn him over, get this sleeve, then the next."

We work together quickly to take the Merlin's jacket off. Lark sits back on his heels as I rifle through the pockets.

"Here we go," I say as I dig around the inner left breast pocket. After a moment, I pull out a zippered-shut, semihard case about the size of my hand.

"What is that?" Lark asks.

"Let's see."

I unzip the case, laying both sides open and down on the pavement between us. I recognize its contents immediately: two capped syringes, snug in their molded compartments.

"Syringes?"

I nod. "Not just syringes, but syringes meant to travel."

Lark peers closer. "They're empty."

"These aren't used to inject solutions *into* someone; they're used to draw samples away." I look up and around the lot. "Wherever the guards parked, there are likely labeled vials and a cooler inside the vehicle for safer, longer transport."

Lark picks up one of the syringes carefully, avoiding the capped end. "There are labels."

I pick up the other—and my blood chills. "'Morgaine S1—Enthralled.'"

"Mine says 'Morgaine S2—Out of thrall.'"

"Sample one, sample two. Possibly labeled to avoid contamination," I murmur. We stare at each other. "Thompson wasn't following us to find Ava; he was following us to find a Morgaine . . . perhaps any Morgaine. Or two."

"But what does it mean to be 'Enthralled' or 'Out of thrall'?"

I frown, thinking. "No clue. It sounds like a state of being like Bree's possession. Or maybe . . . maybe like her blood walks?"

Lark places the syringe back in the case. "But Bree can't control her possessions. You couldn't expect to catch her in one state or the other."

"No," I say, churning over the ideas. "If the Regents sent Thompson and his companion into the field to take these specific samples, they'd do so with the assumption that the guards could find a Morgaine or two in both of these magical states. Not happenstance, but expectation. And these labels indicate confidence and knowledge in the Morgaines' abilities."

I place the syringe in my hand back in its place and pick the case up, zipping it before I pocket it myself. "We need to get on the road." I'm already walking toward the car. At my side, Lark is pulling out his keys.

"You're going to confront the Regents?" he asks. "We don't know where they are right now, Will. They don't stay in one place long, and they usually don't travel together. They could be at the Keep, the Institute, Pembray, or somewhere up North or West. They could be back in Cardiff, for all we know."

"Toss me the keys," I order as I get to the driver's side. Lark throws them over the top of the SUV into my waiting hand. "I know where we need to go."

We climb into the car together, and I'm starting the engine and peeling back out of the parking spot as my mind races.

"Where?" Lark asks.

I pause, both hands on the wheel, and nod to myself. Circumstances have changed and, apparently, I have changed with them, because I am already steeling myself to return to a place I swore I would never set foot in again.

"The Institute. We need to go back to the Institute."

30

FOUR MONTHS AND ONE WEEK

AFTER BRIANA MATTHEWS DISAPPEARED

Bree

"ELIJAH THINKS WE can do this," I say out loud, for both our sakes.

"Not true." Zoe scrolls through her phone in the back seat of our human driver's black SUV. "Elijah doesn't think anyone can do *anything* right without him."

Our driver is too busy nodding along to his music to be paying attention to us, but I keep my voice low anyway. "I don't know why he's so worried," I mutter. "We're gonna be fine."

Zoe eyes me warily. "We're gonna be *something*, Bree, but I don't know if it's fine."

We arrive at Mikael's Gilded Age mansion, the Penumbra Estate, in the early evening. By the time our car joins the line of vehicles waiting to get into Mikael's, I've seen enough of the other guests at the mansion entrance to be extra grateful for Zoe's efforts on my appearance in the bathroom at Erebus's home.

Zoe's full glam will help us fit in with the youngest attendees in formal wear exiting their limos and high-end black electric vehicles. The rest of the guests could be in their thirties or forties, and many are much older. Actual established wealthy people who own actual businesses and corporations, unlike us.

"'People are coming from all over the country,'" Zoe quotes from Elijah's texts. "'Make a good impression. Get in and out quick. Don't get caught. I mean it, Z.'" She rolls her eyes. "He's *so* annoying."

"You have the invitation?"

"You're almost as bad as he is. You've already asked me that three times," Zoe mutters. She digs around in her bag before handing me a heavy black paper envelope previously sealed by an embellished fleur-de-lis stamped into glowing green wax. I open the envelope to tug the heavy cardstock invitation into view, taking one more look at our names for the night.

Tonight, I'm Vivienne Keaton and Zoe is Tamar Keaton. Allegedly both women are real heiresses based somewhere in New York, and Daeza's staff made sure to get their names on Mikael's invite list. I hand the invitation back to Zoe, and she secures it in her small overnight bag along with her clothing, a change of shoes, and her medications.

We'd both protested bringing more than a cute clutch to tonight's events, but Erebus insisted. When Zoe asked why, he'd only intoned, "Rules can change."

My own overnight bag contains a skirt and a pair of slacks, one casual black dress, and a pair of low heels. When I nervously sift through it all again, I barely recognize my own hand—I'd borrowed one of Zoe's burgundy nail polishes to match my dress.

I examine the rest of my appearance in the handheld mirror I stuffed into my purse. To fit the occasion, Zoe's given me the most dramatic smoky eye I've ever seen outside of a magazine or social media. Full, deep red lips. Blush I don't remember her applying. Brows brushed and arched.

"I look like I could walk a red carpet," I murmur, still in shock.

She chuckles. "That was the point." Then, she leans close to me, whispering, "Listen, girl, you look like a freshman in college on a good day. But tonight, you need to look *worldly*. Sorta evil, ridiculously rich, and like nobody, *nobody* can fuck with you."

I grin slow. "Oh, that's good."

"Exactly." She pats my shoulder and sits back in her seat. "Now think that about twenty times in the next five minutes so it actually shows up on your face, please. You're good at lying. Don't stop now."

"Here okay?" The driver slows at the curb behind three other cars dropping off attendees.

"Yep, this is great," Zoe confirms. As the driver rolls to a stop, Zoe pulls out a thin eye mask and hands it to me, then pulls out another for herself.

Mikael's gala auctions aren't very . . . legal. Politicians, celebrities, and public figures could be in attendance—and would lose their status if they were revealed to be attending something so unsavory. As such, masquerade masks are required for all gala guests before they can enter the building.

Our masks are both black lace filigree, delicate but snug. They cover the bridges of our noses, our eyebrows, and the very tops of our cheekbones, leaving our eyes, cheeks, and mouths exposed. The lace on my mask climbs to a pointed, flame-shaped crest in the center of my forehead, while Zoe's design sprawls wide to curl and twist down her temples. When she finishes securing her mask in place, she harrumphs at the way its hidden band interferes with her carefully crafted two-strand twists.

When I look in my hand mirror again, a memory flares bright behind my eyes: checking my appearance in a dingy bar bathroom. The girl with reddish-gold root the color of a sunset. A reminder that we're here to play a role so that we can return the King's crown. Not because he deserves it, not because it was taken from him, but because when it's back on his head, he'll stop hunting. And maybe, just maybe, we can save the missing girl who tried to save me.

Zoe steps out first, then straightens her dress and adjusts her bag. Her golden gown looks absolutely stunning on her—long and fitting, flaring over her slim hips and shapely legs with a slit up the side showing off a long stretch of brown thigh. She looks like a model.

When I stand at the curb, I smooth my hands over the wine-red velvet and bead-and-lace detailing of my own gown. The dress dips into a low V neckline in the front while its straps expose my upper back beneath my partial updo and loose curls. Like Zoe's, my gown has a high slit on one side that reveals the length of my right leg. The dress makes me feel powerful . . . but so does the dagger strapped to my left thigh and hidden under the heavy material.

Zoe holds a hand out, and I take it, grateful for her support as I walk in my new heels. Together, we start up the sidewalk, joining the flow and laughter of wealthy people attending a party at a demon's estate.

Nobody can fuck with me.

Mikael's mansion is gorgeous—and massive. The stone building extends wide on either side but it's also four stories tall and topped by pointed spires. While we wait in line to be admitted by his security, I catch glimpses of the interior through the large windows over the double entry doors. A three-tiered chandelier hangs in the enormous two-story foyer, casting a sparkling glow over dark walls lined with gold crown molding and wainscoting.

The estate feels like something out of a European Gothic fantasy. It is extraordinary, ostentatious, and a show of not just money but of power. Over people, over the imagination, over the very idea of what "progress" should look like.

Nothing about the building feels like a warm home. Instead, everything is a declaration. A challenge. A dare to cross the ideals of its owner and, for some, an invitation to join his inner circle.

No wonder Mikael and his enterprises annoy Erebus. The Shadow King is power incarnate with very little need to show it, while Mikael, one of his Shades, plays with humanity's ambitions by living loudly on riches they could never hope to attain in a single lifetime.

As the line inches forward, I assess the other auction attendees—and realize that I don't feel any cambion or demon eyes on me at all.

In the end, goruchel align themselves with power, Elijah had said with a shrug during our prep session in Erebus's living room last night. *But Mikael is unusual, even for a Shade. He isn't known for letting other demons close. In fact, he doesn't keep goruchel on-site at all; he doesn't trust them not to turn on him when they're unsatisfied, like Regazel did with Daeza.*

The only magical beings on Mikael's staff are warlocks. Humans who offered their servitude to the broker in exchange for longer-term, more substantial demon abilities. Ones they wouldn't have to give up right away.

"We're up," Zoe murmurs between the tight lips of her smile. Tonight, she has her most human face on. While a warlock couldn't detect a balanced cambion on her best behavior, it's better to play it safe. Brown eyes only, no superspeed, no hyperagility or strength. Just a normal, human young woman with her normal, human sister, playing dress-up for a night at an auction.

I step up to greet the two bulky men at the door, both in tuxes, both too wide and tall to be *only* human. Warlocks, for sure. Their faces are fully exposed. No masks in sight. I suppose Mikael's staff have the Shade's protection if their identities are ever exposed, but gala guests can't guarantee the same.

"Invitation?" The pale-skinned, freckled warlock on my right holds out his hand, eyes skimming over Zoe's face and down her dress to her exposed leg.

Ew, I think.

"Right here," Zoe says, fishing the envelope out of her bag and handing it over for the both of us. The man examines the thick paper with eyes that flash green.

Elijah's voice comes back to me: *Mikael's gala invitation is sealed by aether-infused wax stamped with an event-specific symbol. Like a temporary password, the aether glow will fade and the symbol will expire so that the invitation can't be reused at next year's gala. Mikael may prefer to spend his time with humans, but only a greater demon could apply this kind of seal and even then, they'd have to know this year's design. Either he trusts some of his fellow demons, like Daeza, to send human guests his way . . . or Daeza's spies are as good as she claims. What matters is that the identities Daeza gave you are far less important than the seal. The seal is the real ticket to entry, and someone with the Sight will have to verify it before they let you in.*

The guards don't know what the guests look like, and even if they did, everyone's wearing masks. They don't even bother checking our names against a list. The name isn't critical—the seal is. And Mikael's human guests will never be the wiser.

After a second of examination, the man approves the seal and hands the invite back to Zoe, eyes already over her shoulder to the next guest as he speaks. "Keep your invite on you at all times. Stay together at all times."

"No problem," Zoe says, and it feels to me that she's more than caught up in her role as a rich human socialite. She's on her tiptoes looking past the bouncer. "Is that a Mugler?" she asks, peering around the bicep of the guard.

"A what?" the guard asks.

She smirks back at him. "Designer, honey."

He grunts, and waves us in. "Welcome to the Collectors' Gala."

Zoe links arms with me as we cross the threshold, shuddering against me in what looks like a show of excitement but is actually a genuine response to the rippling of a ward down our backs.

"Damn," she mutters under her breath. "That feels nasty."

"Mm-hmm." We keep our eyes ahead, taking in the walls of the enormous foyer. Mikael has a taste for fine art; the burgundy walls are lined with paintings in gilded frames. Elijah guessed there'd be a ward. I keep my voice so quiet, barely a whisper of breath between my lips, so that only Zoe can hear. "Whatever it's meant to catch, it didn't stop us."

We pause beside a painting. Her arm, pressed against mine, is covered with goose bumps. "You okay?" I ask.

"Yeah, 'course." She nods. "I don't get nervous."

"Right. 'Course." I hide my smile as I look up. The painting we've stopped beneath depicts a pale woman being tempted to a bedroom by a red-eyed, horned beast.

As I turn, I catch a glimpse of myself in a wall mirror over a gray-streaked marble console table and barely recognize the person staring back at me—she looks older. Deadly, strong, and like she might be a monster herself. I give her a smile and turn back to Zoe to ask her if we should move to the ballroom with the other guests, but I never get the question out.

A rush of heat from the doorway hits us both where we stand while the humans around us continue to chat and mingle.

"Hey! Stop!" A man is being held in the tight grip of one of the security guards—because he tripped the ward.

Zoe and I watch as the iridescent shimmer of the ward jumps and dances around the doorway like a lake beneath a rain shower.

The shouting man catches the attention of several guests, but before anyone can do more than whisper with eyes wide, a pale white woman with hair the golden color of Zoe's dress walks across the tile floor with swift steps, dispersing the crowd around the door with a glance.

"Step inside, please," the woman orders. The guard who greeted us guides the struggling man into the foyer. The woman beckons them to follow her past the admitted guests and down a narrow hallway off to the side until the man's raised voice is muffled from earshot.

Human earshot, anyway.

I glance at Zoe, and she narrows her eyes, listening. After a beat, she starts whispering for my ears only. "The man is saying he knows Mikael. That he's an old friend." She tilts her head again when the voices raise. "The woman who walked up is saying that he can take it up with Mikael himself?" She shrugs.

"She must be Bianca," I murmur.

"Yes."

Bianca is human—and Mikael's second-in-command and captain of his warlock security team. A warlock herself, Bianca has been granted status from Mikael in return for her role in his empire. What powers she possesses seem to be a mystery to most; Elijah himself didn't know.

"Let's go," I say. "When Bianca comes back, she'll notice anyone who's still standing around."

Zoe nods, and we drift up the grand staircase to the massive ballroom on the second floor. Tonight's event is both a gala and an auction, with bidding happening throughout and between schmoozing, dinner, and drinking. Dozens of small white cloth–covered tables take up most of the ballroom. Those tables are set up in a wide half circle around an open stretch of shining hardwood floors that create a sort of stage, with a raised podium in the middle. Larger round tables covered in black cloths with hurricane glass candles illuminate the empty corners of the room left dim by the chandelier overhead.

Those placing bids will sit at the white tables closest to the center stage, while other guests will sit at the back, watching the auction for entertainment. For now, the room is a loud, buzzy mixture of jazz music played over speakers and guests talking and mingling.

We pick up a few passed appetizers from staff in black and emerald, and look for a pair of empty seats close to the exit.

"There," Zoe murmurs, spotting a large round table in a corner that will work for our mission. The table has four open seats and three older, well-dressed couples who seem very preoccupied chatting among themselves. "Save my seat while I get in position." I nod silently and we split up. She moves toward the far wall while I stride to my own objective.

The room is so loud and the couples are so engrossed in their conversations—and what looks to be their second round of drinks—that they barely glance up when I approach. Perfect. I set my small bag down on an empty seat for Zoe while I drop quietly into my own chair.

The woman beside me is speaking with a gentleman in a tuxedo. Their masquerade masks match too—solid black satin covering their upper faces with wide holes for their eyes. I wonder what their "normal" day jobs are, or if they even have any. If buying and selling rare objects is just their very expensive hobby.

When the gentleman beside her excuses himself to head to the bar, the woman seems to notice me for the first time. Long earrings ending in pear-shaped rubies catch the light when she turns and smiles warmly beneath her mask. "Are you a new Collector?" she asks in a low voice.

"Yes." I return her smile. Smooth and easy, not too eager. "This is my first gala."

"Welcome." She leans close, pressing thin fingers into the black cloth between us. "Have you heard about the finale?"

"S-sorry?" I stammer.

"The grand finale," she says, raising her hand in the air to give the words an added flourish. "Allegedly, Mikael has something that is truly one of a kind. Unique in this world"—she leans closer—"and in the *other* world too."

It's just as Elijah said: *Word on the street is that Mikael's followers believe the supernatural exists, but they don't know any of the real details. They think he's a regular human being who just so happens to have access to the occasional magical object. Keeps them hungry to know more, collect more. Drives the prices of his auctions up too.*

Still, as I consider this woman and her gentleman partner, I can't help but think of Erebus's words to me at the museum: *Greedy men collect what they cannot understand.*

I raise my brows high and widen my eyes beneath the mask. "I didn't hear that, no . . ." I lower my voice to a purr to match hers. "You must be in the inner circle."

She flushes pink below her mask. "Well, I can't say *exactly* how I found out, but let's just say that we often make it to the third round in auctions like these." She waves her paper invite. "Mikael knows us by name."

"Ah." I nod but don't truly know what she means. Grand finale? The Shadow King's crown fits the description the woman shared, but what if it's *not* the item she means? "Since this is my first gala, I'm not planning to bid on anything. I'll just watch."

The woman nods sagely. "Good for you. It's best to get experience before you jump in the deep end." She pats my hand and goes back to her drink.

I can't help but wonder what this woman would say if I told her that the *real* reason I won't be bidding on an artifact is because I'm here to steal one instead.

The lights overhead dim twice, signaling that the auction will begin soon. I find Zoe exactly where she's supposed to be, chatting with a server near the exit that should be closest to the ballroom-level elevator. We make eye contact before she glances away, nodding without looking. That nod tells me what I need to know: that the elevator is indeed nearby and should be ready for me when the time is right. Just then, Bianca the warlock security captain strides in from the foyer with another warlock guard beside her, whispering something in his ear as they cross the room. The man caught by the ward is nowhere to be seen.

I check in with Zoe again, and again, she nods; she's seen them too. Bianca and the other warlock are moving toward the same elevator, which goes down to the basement, where Elijah told us the auction items are held in secure storage. If they linger there, then our mission is over before it's even begun.

A server stops by the table to offer us champagne in crystal flutes. His body and tray momentarily obstruct my view of both Zoe and Bianca, and I stifle a groan beneath a stiff smile.

I pass on the champagne he offers and as he moves on to the woman beside me, my sight line returns. I'm relieved to see that both Bianca and the warlock are gone, but I don't know for certain whether the path to the elevator is clear. Zoe and her chatty server, however, are still near the far wall. She laughs at a joke the server makes and crosses her arms over her chest. After she makes a quick scan of the room, she taps her fingers twice on one elbow. *All clear.*

Ten minutes later, the first object is rolled out onstage from behind a curtain. It's a shining, restored sextant from the early 1800s and the Napoleonic Wars, supposedly held by Napoleon himself.

The bidding starts at a half million dollars and quickly escalates—which is my cue to get moving. I start to excuse myself from the table, but it's unnecessary. The other couples at the table are too engrossed in the swiftly moving bids popping up across the room.

Before I slip away from the ballroom, I glance over my shoulder to see Zoe still playing her part. Her gaze flicks to me, then to the rest of the room, then back. *Go.* I dip around the corner and walk swiftly to the elevator.

Everything is in motion.

THE NEXT TIME I see Elijah, I'll have to thank him for the near-militant way he forced me to memorize this section of Mikael's estate. Luckily for us, since it's a historic building, its floor plan was easily accessible on the internet.

Here's the deal, Elijah had said, *this house is so big, they measure the interior in acres, not square feet. There are four floors above ground level, with over fifty guest rooms, twenty-five bathrooms, an amphitheater to seat one hundred, and the two-story grand ballroom where the Collectors' Gala will be held. Out back, there's gardens and a hedge maze and beyond those, the mountains and a lake. If things go sideways, the most straightforward exit is the front door, but if you make a run for it that way, Mikael's warlock enforcers will definitely be waiting for you. So, my advice? Don't let things go sideways.*

I don't plan on going sideways, out back, or any other direction tonight. I only need to go one way—down.

The elevator sound is still ringing in my ears when the basement doors open. From where I stand pressed flat against the control-panel wall, I can just glimpse in my handheld mirror what lies beyond the open doors: a long concrete hallway covered by a heavy red-and-gold runner. Warm pools of light cast upward on the walls by lit iron sconces. High ceilings lost to shadow and—there!—security cameras.

Just as I've done with the cameras in the elevator, I drop my hand low and out of sight to send a spool of purple smoke into the hall. Using my mirror to guide me, I draw my dispersed root up by my fingertips, then give it a little push. My power moves lazily but steadily up the walls to wrap itself around the lenses of the cameras, just as I'd seen Erebus do at the British Museum so many months ago.

Satisfaction spreads through me at the thought of using the King's own techniques to steal his crown—not to help him but to thwart him.

Still, it's Erebus's guidance that echoes inside my mind now: *Fortunately for all demons, aether sense is not an ability that warlocks can acquire via pact magic; it is too innate to share or transfer. As for Mikael? After living almost entirely among human beings for hundreds of years, Mikael's original demonic nature has been altered. His ability to detect humanity's worst instincts has sharpened impressively, but at great cost. Aether no longer sustains his physical form, so he must fortify himself almost entirely off human energy. And as aether no longer feeds him, his own aether sense has grown dull. Use your power sparingly, Briana, but know that as long as you do so out of sight, neither Mikael's warlock guards nor Mikael himself will be able to trace your magical signature back to you.*

I snap the mirror shut and shove it down into my bra beneath my dress. Now that the cameras are adequately obscured, I know I have limited time. Ten minutes, max, if Mikael and Bianca have someone monitoring them. Hopefully, with dinner service beginning shortly, a room of unpowered human guests upstairs, and all the aether invitations getting strictly vetted at the door, there won't be a reason to check the cameras more than once every half hour.

I'll just have to hope I'm at the start of one of those half-hour windows, rather than at the end.

Sticking to the thick runner to dampen the sound of my heels on the floor, I enter the hallway and jog quickly past the rooms on either side until the hall comes to a darkened T. I stop before the branch—and peer silently around one corner.

Down the short hall to the right there is a single guard on his phone standing in front of the storage room holding the rest of the auction items—and the crown. I slip back around the corner and out of sight. The guard is definitely another warlock; Mikael would put someone in place who could protect the supernatural auction items using supernatural means, not a human with only human strength and human combat skills.

Consider this part of your mission a test, Erebus said. *Focus on your objective. Devise a plan. Make quick work of an unknown magical opponent. Be untouchable, unstoppable—*

Impervious.

Knocking the guard out won't be hard. Dragging him into one of the empty rooms I've passed—and locking it behind me—can be done quickly. Removing his earpiece and phone and any other means he may have of contacting the rest of the security team can be done within seconds. But all of that takes focus and precision.

I take a deep, steadying breath as I slide down the wall to drop softly on the carpet. The warlock won't expect someone to come at him from below his eyeline. A bolt of root to his knees oughta do it.

Of course, I don't know what type of demon ability he's acquired—could be physical, like size or strength, or control over aether. *No, too many options.* I don't have enough time to get lost in scenarios I can't fully anticipate.

Deep breaths.

One . . . two . . .

I settle low into my squat, balancing on—and cursing—my heels.

Three.

I launch myself across the opening on the floor, skidding in my dress, palm outstretched, root streaming—

The guard's head rises, mouth opening to shout—then gasping in pain when he's struck across both knees.

He crumples. Before he hits the ground, I widen my fingers. The root expands—enclosing him in an iridescent sphere, just like the ones I've created to protect myself.

He falls against the side of the sphere with a dull thud. His hands scrabble against the sides, slipping as he attempts to climb the concave structure—and he screams. Oh, he *screams*.

But no one can hear him.

His fists grow larger. He pounds against my barrier, but it does not break. Cannot break.

I push myself to my feet and walk toward him, a satisfied smile curving my lips. As I get closer, I widen my hands again—and the thuds grow quieter and quieter as I thicken the barrier. He can't see me, but I can just make out the glow of his eyes. His irises are green with fury, and I imagine what I would look like to him if he *could* see me.

A young brown-skinned girl in a long formal gown, striding toward him with her palms out wide. A girl with deep purple magic flowing from her hands to feed the structure encasing him. A girl raising that sphere into the air, levitating him from the ground. A girl trained by the deepest Shadow himself, her teeth bared in an electric grin.

"This construct—to contain and protect—was the first thing I learned to truly forge for myself," I murmur. He stills, eyes searching, straining to hear me. "It can't be cracked, certainly not by a human playing with Shadowborn powers. Certainly not by *you*."

The warlock snarls and shouts, then begins to cough as he runs out of air. His face turns red, then a deep purple.

Oh, shit.

Hand outstretched behind me, I half-jog, half-drag the construct and warlock within it back down the hall toward an empty room before he can suffocate. Inside the sphere, the green glow dims, then blinks out—his eyes rolling back in his head. I curse again—collapse the barrier.

Catch him before he falls. Grunt at the weight. I'm strong, but he's *heavy*. And sweaty. And a couple hundred pounds of pact-magic muscle.

I stagger with the warlock into the room and shove him onto a dusty, cloth-covered couch. When I drop him, a hot breath rattles out of his lungs. I press my ear to his mouth and chest. He's breathing. His heart's beating. He's alive but out.

"Whew," I whisper, relief mixing in to sour my triumph. This'll have to be good enough. I gather up his earpiece and phone from his jacket pocket and, running across the hall, shove them into another dusty storage room and close that door behind me too, then hurry back to the door he'd been guarding.

The door opens with a swift punch to the keypad. I enter as quietly as I can, shaking my fist out as I do.

The dusty room is filled with shelves upon shelves of sealed cardboard boxes. Would the crown just be sitting in a box here, waiting to be wheeled out onstage? Shouldn't it be prepped for display tonight? It's supposed to be the most valuable, rarest, oldest piece in the collection, but everything here looks like it could belong in someone's attic. *This doesn't feel right.*

Where would I put something I couldn't touch? Something that, while valuable in its way, can't be used for magical gain by anyone else, demon or human?

There are several large, sealed wooden crates set on two long, waist-high metal worktables in the middle of the room. I could open the crates, or I could keep searching. The clock is ticking.

Then, I see it.

Another door at the back of this room, painted the exact same color of the wall surrounding it. Thin, barely visible seams outline its shape, keeping it slightly hidden in the shadows.

I dash past the shelves to grasp the handle of the far door, yanking it down and pushing at the same time until it opens—and find myself at the threshold of another room, this one nearly identical to the last, except much larger and much cleaner. Here, shiny gems and golden artifacts are separated individually within tall glass rolling cases set against the far wall, already labeled for display. The other two walls are lined with shelves holding black velvet boxes of varying sizes. There is one velvet-lined worktable in the center of the floor between the shelves with a pair of curator's gloves set atop it. I don't see the crown yet, but the glass rolling cases are sitting two layers deep and the shelves are tall.

I'll have to hunt and hunt quickly.

I take a single step toward the first case to my left—and the already dimly lit room goes completely dark.

Somewhere above me, I hear a few scattered shouts of surprise, as if the lights upstairs have gone out too. *Why would the power go out?*

Overhead, an emergency light clicks on, drenching the room in pale crimson and casting its contents in an eerie, sinister glow. Blood, watered down.

My heart thunders in my ears. *What do I do?*

Rapid footsteps in the hall interrupt my decision-making.

Audible footsteps mean a human—or another warlock.

I feel my way backward to the wall beside the open door, to the corner of the room that was empty and out of view, where the shadows are deepest.

Someone enters the outer storage room. They pause. Then move again.

Light approaches as the footsteps slow. Bright white-blue illumination stripes the floor from a handheld flashlight held in a leather-gloved fist that enters the room before the intruder does.

I hold my breath as they pace through the door, and the narrow band of light bounces off the metal and glass littered throughout the room, giving me a glimpse of the newcomer.

They are tall. Much taller than me. Broad shoulders in a black tux jacket. They have a half mask on, black covering their eyes and nose and wrapping their head in a wide band. I can't make out their hair color in the light. The intruder pops the end of the flashlight between their teeth and starts working down the shelves ducking and twisting to look at all the items.

Looking for something specific, just like I was about to do.

If they're here to steal something too, they're likely taking advantage of the distraction—or *they're* responsible for the lights going out in the first place.

Either way, they're a thief, just like me. *Well,* I think with a smirk. *Not just like me. Whoever they are, they're not the Shadow King's protégé.*

A fight in the bloodred dark might be my best bet.

The thief in the suit makes a bit of noise while they move a few of the heavier cases aside. I use the sound to cover me as I slip out of my heels to find the cold floor beneath my bare feet, breathing in and out, slowly finding my center.

When the thief bends over to look at a lower shelf, they create an opening—and I take it.

I dash forward, jump over the velvet display table, and fling myself on top of the thief's broad back. A low, masculine grunt is his only response.

He reacts faster than I expect, both hands grasping my forearm as he twists, turning parallel to the shelving unit. He's going to flip me over—I can feel it in how he positions himself, where he braces—so I wrap both legs around his waist before he can get leverage.

He groans. Twists again, this time trying to ram me into the worktable behind us.

The sharp edge digs into my back—hard—and I let it, falling, arching my own spine as I squeeze his ribs.

He gasps for air. The flashlight falls. Hits the velvet-covered metal worktable with a heavy *thunk*. White light streaks toward one wall.

He drives an elbow down into my shin. Bone on bone, whiteout pain—

My legs fall from his torso. I drop, back-first, onto the table—recover. Draw my bruised shin to my chest, and snap a hard kick into what I *think* is the back of his shoulder—

Propelling the man face-first into the shelves, rattling what sounds like priceless vases and utensils and ancient stone bowls.

His hands snap out, holding the shelves still.

We both freeze.

Wait for the fragile items to crash to the floor.

When the shelves seem to hold, I ease down from the table with my hands up. The thief's head jerks over his shoulder to watch me while his arms are raised and open, there to catch anything falling from the still-trembling shelf. Clearly, neither one of us wants to get caught, and a shattered thousand-year-old vase would do the trick.

But as soon as the shelf finally stills and the imminent threat fades, I know he'll attack again.

Or I will.

Him, or me? That tiny uncertainty sends an unexpected thrill up my spine.

A heartbeat passes.

Then—he's a blur in the darkness. Lunging, punching as he moves. I duck under his arm, make myself small against the table legs like I do when I spar with the twins. Smaller the target, harder to hit. When your opponent is fast, you've got to be faster—and this guy is fast as shit.

He withdraws and strikes again—quick like a viper, the air hissing around his fist.

But I'm already rolling, dodging, forcing him to the center of the room—punching up under his arm to strike his chin, exploding the rest of my body into the hit.

He grunts. His lower back hits the table. The flashlight rolls to the floor, clicks off, and we're plunged into unholy red darkness.

We're both breathing hard—and neither one of us can see.

But the darkness and our frozen stances make it easy to hear the voices and feet above us. People are shouting. There's still chaos upstairs, but we don't have much time. *I* don't have much time before I need to get my shoes, get out of here, back upstairs to Zoe.

My opponent uses the time I waste debating my next move to dart forward, banking on hitting me where I stand. He misses. Glances off my shoulder, stops, pivots back, and punches me hard in the jaw, below my ear.

Pain blooms bright and angry—I grunt and stumble forward, taste copper, see stars against the back of my eyes.

This guy.

Yeah.

Screw this guy.

I grit my teeth. Chaos will have to cover me. I drop low. Swing hard. Aim for his crotch—hit a thigh instead. He drops his elbow into mine, nearly snapping it. I surge up, aiming with my forehead—hit his chin hard enough to hear his teeth clack.

His arms wrap around me, too tight—as we grapple in the darkness, I send a knee up into his torso, but he takes the hit. Doesn't move. *Is he a damn tree?* Instead, he squeezes hard—breathing harder—I feel a rib bend.

Fuck this.

I call my root from within and let it flood my limbs and spine and chest where he holds me, until I am a column of purple-white flame.

My opponent is gasping, turning from the brilliant light of my root, his jaw clenched below his mask. Enough of a distraction for me to thrust both arms up, breaking his grip. He releases me, stumbling back on one foot.

My purple root is so bright, it casts shadows behind us and around us, but it shows me where *he* is, just fine.

Time to end this.

I send a fiery fist flying to his face, a deadly, root-powered right hook perfected from sparring with Elijah—

And he catches it—*God, he's fast*—grunting with the effort. Before I can jerk my fist away, he takes a deep, slow breath—

And the flames of my right hand disappear.

I jerk back, shock rattling my already ragged breath. *What the . . . what . . . ?*

I snarl and relight my power. The next seconds happen as if in slow motion.

I forge a short blade. Dart forward with it, aim for his midsection—and he sidesteps it. Skims a hand over the blade as it passes his torso—and it dissolves into shining purple fragments until the hilt is formless purple wisps. Empty-handed, I fall forward to the ground with my own momentum. Time speeds up.

My mind feels as fractured as my blade. As shattered as my construct. I pant on the ground, eyes wide. Above me, my opponent circles, fists up and loose. His silhouette limned by the red emergency light.

What the hell. What the actual . . . ?

Fury rolls me over. Revenge drives me to my feet.

If he thinks he can break my power, dissolve it, take it apart . . . then let's see if he can keep up.

Another dagger in my right hand. Thrust. He disintegrates it with his left.

But the dagger in my left hand is already moving—he dissolves it with his right.

A short flail, spinning—he raises both palms, rotates them in the opposite direction, and coaxes the weapon down from the air until it lies at his feet in sparkling ash.

A sword, lunging—he speeds around the strike, too fast.

An open palm hits me in the center of the chest and sends me skittering back, my blade flying out of my hand.

I hit the ground spine-first and watch as my dark purple weapon lies at his feet. I don't see any magic, but I catch a new scent in the air: bright cedar, ozone, petrichor.

The thief kicks my sword up into his waiting hand, then runs a hovering, open palm down the blade from guard to tip. Where his hand passes, my construct crumbles—until it falls to the floor, a glowing pile of nothing.

I spring up with a roar, throwing my body into the air—shocking us both—and he lands on his back with me straddling his waist.

I draw back to land a punch, and he bucks up, twisting. Then, *I'm* on my back, and he's kneeling over me, breath coming out in short, harsh pants. I hiss and rage against him—and the lights buzz, turning back on, blinding us both with harsh fluorescents.

"Let me go!" I grind out, still struggling to see—

"Stop!" the thief says, and his low voice echoes inside me like a bell.

I freeze, staring up into his face. Blue eyes behind a black mask, hair long and shaggy, curling beneath his ears. We blink at each other for a long moment, his mouth working open and closed as we both catch our breath.

He's younger than I thought.

The thief blinks down at me, eyes roaming over my face hidden behind my mask, his mouth open in shock.

"Bree?"

My name. He *knows my name*.

My heartbeat is so loud now that I can't hear anything at all. So loud, I wonder if it's his heart too.

When I speak, my voice comes out breathy and ragged.

"Who are you?"

PART THREE

IMPERVIOUS

32

Nick

IT'S WELL PAST two o'clock in the morning, so when the Northern Chapter archive's door clicks open, I know the person who entered did not stumble in by accident. No one would be in the archives the night before the Regents arrive, digging through the journals of the Scions of the Northern Chapter, unless they had a good reason to.

No one but me—and my guest.

"Hello, cousin."

The dim lamplight plays shadows off the face of the figure who stands in the doorway, and the sconces in the open hall behind him throw his body into silhouette.

"Donovan." I straighten behind the table. "I suppose we are cousins, yes."

The last time I saw Donovan Reynolds, he was the Scion of Lancelot, and I was the Scion of Arthur. Now we are neither.

"Mmm." Donovan hums an agreement and holds up a small piece of yellow paper between his pointer and middle finger. "Got your note."

I've kept the lights low in here on purpose so that my late-night research sessions are not immediately evident from the hallway. Luckily for me, this wing of the Keep has not been busy the past two nights; too much activity in the residential and dining areas with members of the Order's chapters acclimating to close quarters in a time of crisis.

"Close the door." I add, "Please."

Donovan shuts the door behind him, then walks into the quiet room with both hands in his pockets. "Wouldn't want someone to realize you're sneaking out of your cage, now, would we?"

"They need to think I'm still in the tower," I admit. "I leave at night and return before dawn so that nothing appears amiss."

"How *are* you getting out?" Donovan asks curiously. "When I found your note the first night of your imprisonment, I thought it was a trick. 'Meet me in the archives after two a.m.'? Could have been a booty call."

I raise a brow. "Don't let me keep you from your anonymous hookup."

"I checked, and the tower door is still latched shut—from the outside. Are you jumping down? Or climbing?"

"I'm not afraid of heights," I respond.

"It's not just the height; it's the triple-layered wards on the way back in. Each laced with truly devastating doses of terror, doubt, and dread." Donovan chuckles.

When he said the word "devastating," a small grin crossed his face. The Reynolds cruelty streak that I remember from my youth. One that I hope I haven't inherited myself.

"I can handle the wards."

"Risa could have been Kingsmage. She's powerful enough, you know. Her wards could take an experienced Mageguard to his *knees*, and Nick effing Davis simply says he can 'handle' them?" He regards me, head tilting. "How?"

I level him with a gaze. "Doesn't matter how I got past the affective wards. What matters is that no one will believe you if you claim that I did."

Donovan hears the threat. Disregards it. "I had a feeling you'd find your way here eventually." His voice holds the aristocratic drawl that I grew up hearing, first around my father and the Legendborn families, then at private schools and dinner parties and country clubs. His stride around the long study table is measured and easy, as if he has no other place to be in the middle of the night. Hands in loose designer slacks, white button-down open at the throat and untucked.

"Did you, now?" I ask, and hear the echo of my own Southern affluence rounding the vowels of my words. "If you knew I'd be here, might have been nice for you to use that knowledge to meet me one of the last two nights." I keep my voice light, amused, and dry. Keep up the game. No need to start a fight; I certainly don't feel like getting into one. I hold an arm out and gesture at the table I'm standing behind. It is strewn with heavy, thick, leather-bound journals, all handwritten, all normally kept in a locked cage at the back of the room. "There are dozens of these things."

Donovan sees through my attempt at peace and congeniality.

"Is a scrawled note slipped under a door your way of asking for *help*, Davis?" He paces toward me until we are standing over the same long study table. His eyes trail over the piles of books with recognition for their covers and their authors. "Three hundred years of journals of the past Scions of Lancelot not telling you what you wanna know?"

I grew up with boys like Donovan. I was *raised* by a man like Donovan, who grew up with other boys and men like Donovan. They—we—don't ask real questions. Not questions that have answers that could possibly knock us off our expected paths or betray our vulnerabilities.

But here I am, having snuck a note beneath Donovan's bedroom door like this is grade school, asking for his help blatantly and without hesitation. And here he is, forcing me to say it again, as if once was not enough and I need to plead—or grovel—for it to count. For it to hurt.

I don't have time to play these games. I gave them up years ago.

"The journals discuss training. They discuss life at the Keep. They discuss battles and glory and ways to properly hone an aether blade until it can cut through silk with a single stroke. They are the journals of *dead men*, Donovan. I can't ask them questions, and even if we could speak to our dead"—I press my lips together, involuntarily thinking of the girl who can speak to her ancestors, the girl who can ask her questions and have them answered—"the Reynoldses of the Line of Lancelot could have never comprehended the situation we find ourselves in today. The views of those 'founding fathers' are useless to me."

Donovan places both hands on the back of a chair to lean across the table. "And what situation is that, Davis? The one where you aren't a Davis at all?" Something hard slides in behind his gaze, spreading to his cheeks and jaw, tugging at his mouth until his teeth are bared to the light. "The one where a single bad decision created the accident that is Briana Matth—"

My hand wraps around Donovan's throat before I even realize I'm moving.

"Do *not* speak her name again." I hear the distant, quiet thunder in my own voice. "And while I have your attention, let me explain how you got here. What happened to Bree's ancestor Vera was not a 'bad decision.' It was rape. A violation Samuel Davis should have been punished for. One I'm personally happy to punish *anyone* for, really, if they try to defend him." I pause. "Which is why your spine feels particularly crushable right now. . . ."

"Okay. *Okay!*" Donovan grunts out. He swallows against my fist. "Are you going to . . . let me go? I thought you brought me here . . . because you wanted . . . to . . . talk?"

I release him, and his hands slap down against the table as he coughs once, twice, and tugs on his collar. "I do want to talk."

"You just *choked* me!" Donovan croaks. He rubs at his throat while I search internally for remorse for my own actions.

I don't find it. "I did. I even explained why. I still need your help."

He glares at me. "Would serve you right if I left you here in the dark."

"I grew up anticipating *Arthur's* powers, not Lancelot's. I've been on my own with this." I take a slow breath. "Zero preparation, no guidance. I was hoping you'd *want* to offer assistance. Just as you would have been called on to mentor the next eligible person in the Line of Lancelot as soon as your eligibility ended, like your younger brother or another cousin—"

"Except that *I* never planned on not being eligible in the first place, Davis! And I was never meant to mentor *you*." Donovan's eyes are blue daggers, cold and cruel in the lamplight.

I try another tactic. "Neither of us is in the role we've been raised to assume. Neither of us is prepared for this. We are not so different—"

"We *are* different, Davis!" Donovan takes up one of the heavier tomes—the journal of an Alexander Reynolds, 1732—and tosses it against the wall so hard, it breaks at the spine. "Because while you are no longer the Scion of Arthur, you are *still a Scion*. Second-in-command, second-ranked. As crucial to the Table as one can be without being the damn king himself. Herself. *Whatever*."

I watch Donovan recover without responding. He stares down at the broken journal, chest heaving against his own anger, and runs both hands through his hair. He paces away from me a few steps, then paces back. "Do you have any idea how many people would have to die for me to be Called?"

I have honestly not given it a single thought, but it doesn't surprise me that Donovan would. I try to comprehend the size and structure of my new family tree. Donovan is my own distant cousin, a descendant of the original Reynolds's second son. The Spell of Eternity creates warped, greedy math; I'd rather not journey down that road. "No idea," I answer. "I don't generally count how many people would have to die for me to gain something I want."

"Dozens, Davis. *Dozens*. All because your ancestor was the firstborn and mine was second. Because of the line of succession, I will *never* be eligible. I will *never* be Called." He points at me, snarling, "You and that *Onceborn-raised*—"

"I'd hate to have to choke you again, Donovan," I calmly warn.

His eyes flash, then darken at my expression. "You and the Crown Scion took my life from me."

I groan. "Jesus Christ—"

"You did!"

I throw up my hands. "No, we *didn't*. If anything, the Spell of Eternity did! The Order did! Bree and I didn't *take* anything from you. We didn't know the truth. I was there when she pulled Excalibur from the stone. Neither of us went into the ogof expecting it to go that way!" I huff out a breath. "Our lives changed that night too and, in case you haven't noticed, not for the better. Camlann is here. Multiple parties are trying to kill us, and if they don't, Abatement will. You just got your entire life back while the Regents want to *end* mine. I've bought myself time, Donovan. That's all I have. Borrowed fucking *time*. I'll die soon, one way or another."

Donovan quiets at this, jaw working as he simmers over my words. He may *feel* robbed, but his life is safe from here on out. I wonder if he even realizes that he can walk away from it all while Bree and I can't. Not really. Not truly.

"Fine," he mumbles. "What do you need?"

The knot that has lived in my chest since the moment I saw Bree collapse after the battle of the ogof loosens the merest fraction.

"Information. I'm starting from scratch."

He nods at the books. "What have you read?"

"Everything," I answer. "Some things twice." I shake my head. "There's nothing here about the inheritances. Just the same shit we were all taught about the Lines' abilities: 'The Scion of Lancelot will receive speed and vision enhanced beyond that of any man.'"

It's my turn to shove my fingers through my hair. I grimace; my hair is getting long. The sides of it rest at my cheeks instead of my temple now. When I rub my hand over my chin and mouth, pale stubble scratches at my fingers.

"Well, of course, the *experience* of the inheritances is left out," Donovan says simply. "The Lines don't keep their personal accounts lying around for any random Page to read."

"I thought each Line kept their records at the chapter that houses them. We have Line of Arthur materials in the archives back at Southern—"

"Think, Davis." Donovan raises a brow. "Do you have *every* Scion's account there? Every single personal item and artifact? Every record and detail?"

"I—" I think back to my father's collection. "My father was obsessed with the Line of Arthur. He collected a few artifacts in his private library at home."

Something several shades away from grief wraps my heart at the memory of my father sitting in his study over a book. It's not the memory of him I treasure . . . but the peace of those moments. The times when I was not his focus or his project or his weapon. When I could not disappoint him, because his attention was so wholly focused on the potential of our bloodline.

"That is one way to keep secrets. Another is to pass information down orally, father to son." Donovan dips his chin, bitterness sweeping his face briefly. "Or parent to child, rather, as we are now led by a daughter."

"Oral tradition?" I ask. "Does that mean your father *told* you things? About the inheritances?"

Donovan watches me with callous amusement. "Oh, let me think. . . ." He taps his chin, and the game is on again. "The inheritances? What could you mean? The speed?"

"Do me a favor and stop being a dick."

"Wait . . ." Donovan makes a curious sound. "Have the visions started?"

My eyes snap up to find him leaning over the back of the chair now, eyes watching me with ill intent and fascination rolled into one. "Yes."

"Oh, damn." Donovan's eyebrows rise high on his forehead. "I bet you're having a horrible time of it, aren't you, Davis? 'Enhanced vision' without a manual." He slaps his thigh, laughing. "How long?"

"A while," I reply stonily. "They're getting . . . clearer."

Curiosity sparks across his face. "Care to tell me what you've been seeing? You know, since we're cousins and all."

"I'll pass." I stare him down. "That's not what we're here for. I'm asking you—"

"This close to the curia and this far into the effects of an inheritance you were never raised to anticipate, I think you can do better than 'ask,' *cousin*," he sneers, voice dripping with venom.

I take a slow and steady breath. "All right, Donovan. I am *begging* you. Please tell me what you know about the visions of the Line of Lancelot."

Donovan crosses his arms over his chest, satisfied. "The 'enhanced vision' can't be predicted or stopped. The first thing to know is that 'vision' is a complicated word. It's both something you possess and something you receive. Something you use and something you create. What *you* see? And what you can do with that sight? No journal can tell you those answers. The best you can do is learn by experience, but as each Scion has different *kinds* of visions—"

"Wait, wait." I hold up a hand. "The visions change from Scion to Scion?"

He raises a brow, as if this were obvious. "Yes? That is, if that Scion inherits Lancelot's visions at all. Some never do."

I rock back, stunned. "That's—I've never heard of an ability that only *some* Scions of a Line inherit. Why? And why me?"

"Well, in a more typical timeline for Camlann, not one accelerated by your war-thirsty father, you would have noticed something . . . *peculiar* about your visions." Donovan's voice turns serious for the first time tonight when he recounts the story of our bloodline as his father once told it to him.

"We are taught that the bloodline Scions of the Round Table are methodically Awakened one by one in the order of the knights and magical abilities best suited to keep the demons at bay. Scions and their inheritances are Called by need, beginning with the Scion of the lowest-ranked knight and continuing up the ranks. Eligible children learn that the moment a Scion is Called, their abilities arrive instantaneously. But what the Line of Lancelot knows, and what we have kept secret for centuries, is that our bloodline—well, *your* bloodline—is the only one whose inheritances arrive staggered, rather than all at once. The speed comes first, always, but the visions, if they come at all, arrive later. And only after a very specific trigger, for a *very specific* reason." He grins.

"A trigger?" I squint in memory. "Everything happened so fast. I was Awakened, then Bree right after—"

"I'll give you a hint." He leans in, whispering, "The visions only begin once the Scion of Arthur has been Called."

A chill cascades through me. "Why would Lancelot's power be linked to Arthur's Scion?"

"Because the heirs of Arthur and Lancelot are not typical Scions. Rarely does the fighting become so dire that the Scions of Lancelot and Arthur are even Called, and rarer still that the former is Called without the latter. In many ways, Arthur and Lancelot were a court of two." His eyes widen in faux surprise. "By the way, Davis, I've heard rumors that you and the Crown Scion are your own *court of two*."

Bree's face appears in my mind, her presence ringing inside me like a bell. Resonant. Deep. Rich. As the familiar wave of her threatens to tow me under, Donovan's eager eyes scan my face, hungry for a reaction I'll never give him. "It's a good thing rumors aren't facts."

Donovan's face twists cruelly. "You know what *is* a fact, Davis? That you and our *king*, together, are illegal under Order law. The Lines cannot mix. If you and your girl get caught sparring without clothes on, the Regents will arrest you both for treason."

"If you speak about Bree 'without clothes on' again, I'll break a bone you use on a daily basis." I ignore his choked response and repeat my question. "Why are the powers linked?"

He scowls and looks away. "According to my father, Arthur and Lancelot approached Merlin in secret to ask him to connect their abilities within the Spell of Eternity, and Merlin agreed. The three of them understood that each Scion of Arthur in the Legendborn cycle would be a different kind of king. A different leader born with different needs and skills, born in different eras, fighting a different version of Camlann. So Merlin embedded within Lancelot's application of the Spell the *seed* of a power. A seed that requires the presence of Arthur's Scion to come to full fruition. But the Scions of Lancelot who inherit visions gain access to a unique, unprecedented magical ability that no one else truly knows about. They can use that power however and whenever they like," he says with a vague shrug, "even if that ability only first manifested itself in response to the king."

"Because each king requires different insight to win the war," I say, nodding.

"An optimistic guess," Donovan says with an eye roll, "but that's not what I was taught. My grandfather called the link between the Scion of Lancelot and the Scion of Arthur a type of prophecy. A promise older and deeper than an Oath. And my father says the visions are 'a holy weapon in an earthly hand.' You're new here, Davis, but the Line of Lancelot has always believed that the visions are tailored to the nature of our Awakened king for a tactical reason, not an emotional one."

I already know I won't like what Donovan is about to say. "And that reason is?"

"Lancelot was the most powerful knight of the Table, second only to Arthur Pendragon," Donovan says, his tone anything but harmless. "Perhaps Merlin knew that there could come a day when the Scion of Arthur's leadership had gone astray, and that a power should arise not to *support* the king . . . but to oppose her."

FOUR MONTHS AND ONE WEEK

AFTER BRIANA MATTHEWS DISAPPEARED

Bree

"BREE?"

My name is wrenched from the thief's mouth, a question and a declaration. A sound that is mine, but also his.

"Bree."

This time when he says it, my name is something holy.

"I . . ." What did I ask him again? The weight of him makes me forget.

Oh. *Who are you?*

Behind his mask, the blond thief's eyes dart between mine. "You don't know who I am?"

How can I be *shivering* when everything about me—the entire line of my body where it's pressed beneath his, my cheeks, my throat, my hands—feels searingly hot? I swallow, the sound loud between us, before I whisper, "No."

For a split second, the thief's expression fractures. Breaks open.

I don't know him, but he knows me. He *knows* me.

He could be *anyone*. Friend or foe. But . . . he doesn't *seem* like a foe, even as

I can feel the bruises from our fight settle into my skin. His face is so close that I could breathe fire into it and burn him away—but I don't.

Instead, my heart quietly unfurls inside my chest like it *knows* him, even if my mind can't put the pieces together. Is he the boy I longed for? And if he is, why did I feel like I couldn't have him? Why did I run?

My plan, my mission, rises in the back of my mind. "I have to go—"

"No, wait," he protests, eyes bright. "I can't believe you're here. It's been— are you all right? Are you safe? Where have you—"

Distantly, down the hall, the elevator dings. "Someone's coming," I whisper. He hears it too. *"Shit."*

The thief's demeanor shifts in a split second. He scrambles off me, pulling me up by my elbows as he goes. I don't register that he has us both moving until we reach the door. That his hand is warm against my back, guiding me forward. That I'm letting him touch me even though I have no idea who this boy is. *Why am I—*

"Those your shoes?" he asks, head halfway out into the first storage room.

I blink, uncertain what he means until I spot my heels tucked into the corner. He'd seen them in the fraction of a second before he started checking our exit.

Apparently, his mind works fast too.

Mine not so much at the moment. "Y-yes . . . ," I stammer. "Yeah—"

He ducks down and grabs my shoes, looping the straps in his gloved fingers, and pulls me past the thick metal door, through the dusty storage room, and down the long hall toward the elevator. He slips into a jog, and I follow, wordless.

"Good thing Mikael's aether sense is dull. Otherwise, he might have sensed your power by now. Still, let's hope it fades fast."

How does he know Mikael's aether sense is dull? I close my furnace up extra tightly anyway. "Yeah."

His head tips up to the security cameras, still wrapped in my purple root. "The cameras. That's you?"

"Yes."

"Can you undo it? Quickly?"

I wave my free hand at the ceiling until the root dissipates into sparkling dust.

He whistles, watching the dust fall as he tugs me forward, admiration briefly flashing across his features as he moves. "That's new."

I startle. "How would you know?"

He brings us to the elevator and punches the button for the first level. I frown. "The ballroom is on the second floor—"

"We should get caught elsewhere." He releases my hand to drive his fingers through his hair, back and forth, until it's sticking up in several directions.

"I don't want to get caught!" I hiss. "And what are you—"

"It's better if we get caught, believe me." He tugs his gloves off with his teeth, shoving them into his inner suit pocket.

"Caught doing what?"

"Forgive me." He tosses my shoes behind him. They land haphazardly—like they'd been kicked off. He turns into me, one hand firm at my waist, pressing me against the elevator wall with a rough thud.

"What—"

"Sorry." His other hand captures my jaw and cheek in a gentle claim, tipping my chin up and back—and my skin responds immediately. Turns bright, shivering-hot. My own body, shocking me into silence before I can ask why he apologized.

"No time." The only warning before he presses his mouth to mine—then, there is nothing to know, nothing to remember, nothing to earn or fight for. Only this.

The thief's lips are warm and soft, a whisper against my mouth. Another apology. Then, his head tilts, his mouth slots against mine—and I don't want his apology.

I want to chase myself through his lips. Climb into the knowledge of *us* that I'm suddenly, inexplicably certain he possesses. I want to burrow into his memories of me. Map my history using the heat of his hands against my skin.

I fall and fall.

I'm kissing a strange thief in a strange elevator, and I have no idea why except I have *every* idea why. Because he tastes like comfort and safety. Like fresh laundry from the dryer. A soft couch before a fireplace.

A *knowing* type of exposure that feels like falling, falling.

When the stranger tugs at my chin, it's a question.

I let him pull my lower lip down, an answer. In response, his mouth turns *burning*—

"Excuse me!" A woman's voice, inches from my face. The voice is sharp and pointed, but I barely hear it over the blood rushing in my ears.

The thief recovers before I do, coughing. Meanwhile, I have to blink the elevator, the world, my physical body, and my actual brain back into reality.

"Oh! Hey . . ." The thief's voice is rough and raspy, his mouth red and ripe with a smear of my lipstick. His smile spreads slow like molasses. He looks every bit a young man who was just making out with a girl in an elevator. Even his hair is still tugged up in half a dozen directions above the fabric of his mask . . . just like he'd planned. "Are we cool to go back to the auction now, or . . . ?"

"No. You are not 'cool' to go back to the auction." I recognize who that sharp voice belongs to before I see her: it's Bianca, Mikael's second-in-command and captain of his security.

She's staring at us both with suspicious eyes. Behind her stand two warlocks, both of whom are actively avoiding eye contact with me. A short, stocky man and a taller man with a buzzcut. Behind *them*, flashing emergency lights flicker overhead. There are voices milling in the foyer and Collectors crammed against the door in what looks like a mass attempt to leave the estate.

"We got a little carried away. . . ." The thief rubs his thumb at the corner of his bottom lip in a gesture that's way too obvious to be accidental, wiping away my Ruby Red Extra. He moves to extract himself from my orbit—but stops.

His megawatt smile turns on me, and I feel a tap against my thigh. I blink down at the slit in my dress and exposed leg . . . and wonder when I hooked it up and around his hip.

I flush and drop my bare foot to the floor. "Sorry."

I don't even know who I'm apologizing to. To the thief? To the elevator? Jesus Christ, Bree, to anyone in earshot?

"We'll just be on our way, if that's cool," the thief murmurs, tugging at his jacket.

"No, you won't," Bianca states. She thrusts a hand out, palm up. "Invitation?"

My stomach sinks like a stone, and every flicker of heat I just experienced fades away beneath the cold realization that I don't have my invite on me.

I'd left it in the ballroom—with Zoe.

But the thief doesn't hesitate. "Sure, no problem." He produces a black envelope.

Bianca snatches the envelope from his hand and pulls the heavy paper invite out to review it. "Lawson?" she asks. The shorter warlock moves in close to evaluate the seal. Lawson's eyes flash green, and he nods to her. His pact magic, bitter and acrid in my nose, must have granted him Sight.

Bianca presses her lips into a thin line and reads the printed text on the card herself. Then her eyes widen as she recognizes the names.

"You're Benedict Pierce?" She looks up. "The heir to the global hotel company Pierce Resorts?"

The thief—Benedict—grins. "Guilty as charged."

Bianca's eyes drop back to the invitation, then slide to me. "And you're Iris Bauer, his—"

"Yes, this is Iris," the thief says, and then, to my absolute shock, "my fiancée."

34

MY FIANCÉE.

If I weren't already standing flat on my bare feet, those two ridiculous, incorrect, *outrageous* words would have sent me to the elevator floor.

As it is, the world *still* seems to turn sideways. It takes every bit of the stability training and core strength I've earned from sparring with the twins to maintain my footing. Blood rushes in my ears. My vision tunnels to just the few feet ahead of me, the rest of the world muted and gray. Bianca is speaking, but I can't hear her. She is nodding politely, but I can't register what she could possibly be polite *about*.

Why and how could *anyone* ever look at me and this . . . this smiling, charming *thief* who knows too much, and believe we're getting *married*?

How dare *he? My* fiancée?

My head swivels to the thief, tunnel vision narrowing solely to Benedict's mild expression as he responds to Bianca's questions about—who even knows? I blink hard, like he might suddenly laugh at his silly, unbelievable joke, but he seems wholly unaffected as he takes his—our—invitation back from Bianca when she extends her hand to return the envelope.

I'm already having trouble reconciling the fact that this affable, relaxed *Benedict* is the same person I *punched* less than fifteen minutes ago. The same opponent who unraveled my constructs, countering my magic so smoothly that our fight had felt . . . easy. *Intimate,* even. Like dancing.

How is this amiable rich boy the same stranger who *apologized* to me before kissing me senseless—and the same stranger who I kissed back? This thief who knows my name is Bree but just called me *Iris*?

For a split second, I wonder if he's completely lost his mind—or if I have. Then, I see the slightest, barest twinkle in the deepest recesses of his blue eyes, and my vision snaps back into clarity. I narrow my own, chasing that twinkle down until I can capture it. Clasp it in both hands. *Squeeze* the truth out of it.

Suddenly, out of the cloud of my own confusion, I understand.

He's *playing* her. And he's roped me into whatever his scheme is, making my own fake identity more complicated—and far less likely to be believed. He could end up blowing my and Zoe's covers just to ensure his own. Not only is he playing Bianca, but he expects me to play along with him.

Screw. This. Guy.

"What did you just say?" The words erupt out of me before I can stop them.

Bianca and Benedict both look at me. While she blinks in surprise at my sudden outburst, Benedict's face grows still beneath his mask.

"You okay, honey?" When he speaks again, his voice is low and soft, like he's wrapped his deep voice in a thick, calming blanket. Exactly how one might speak to a rabid animal in the forest, soothing them before they attack. "I was just asking our host here why these alarms were set off."

Well, I won't be soothed.

"So *very many* alarms are going off, Benedict," I reply between clenched teeth. "It makes it hard to pinpoint exactly what's going on, doesn't it?"

"For sure," he says. "Everything's *super* confusing."

Benedict's eyes remain fixed on mine—and abruptly, I feel like we are back in the basement, fighting under angry red security lights. Masks on. Gloves off. My attack, his parry.

"Unexpected and *entirely* frustrating," I riposte haughtily—and watch with satisfaction as his eyelids flutter. "Not at all what I thought I'd experience tonight."

"I apologize for the confusion." Bianca interrupts us sheepishly, but neither one of us looks at her. "We've been holding these events annually for a decade now without incident, so we are, unfortunately, a bit unprepared. There was a security breach—outside the house, not inside. But it's over now. Someone tried to break a"—she pauses for just a beat before finishing her sentence—"a barrier."

When both Benedict and I turn to Bianca as one, something tells me he heard what she *didn't* say as clearly as I did: *Someone tried to breach a ward.*

Benedict responds first, his rich-boy mask firmly back in place. "Somebody tried to break into this place?" His eyes widen, and his jaw loosens in affected surprise. "Holy shit, you serious?"

Bianca eyes him. "Deadly serious, I'm afraid. We need every guest to go back to the ballroom for an announcement." Her eyes drop to my shoes on the floor. She gives them and my bare feet a pointed look. "If you don't mind . . ."

"Yeah, yeah, of course. Give us a second?" Benedict gestures down at my heels, still on the carpeted floor where he'd tossed them. "Let me give my lady back her shoes first?"

Bianca must decide we're young and harmless, because she turns her attention to the increasingly loud crowd at the door while she speaks to us. "Take the back staircase up to the ballroom and your table. The elevator is closed for the evening."

"Sure, no problem," Benedict replies while he bends down to retrieve my shoes.

Bianca gestures to the tall warlock with the buzzcut as she passes. "Santiago, you're with me." The warlock guard Bianca left behind, Lawson, stands a few feet away from the elevator, politely turned away as Benedict kneels at my feet.

Benedict clears his throat to get my attention, holding one heel up in the air.

I roll my eyes and, without thinking, grasp his shoulder for balance—startling us both with the contact. The firm muscle beneath my hand tightens, and I freeze in place. Then he's moving again, slipping the heel in his hand onto my foot while I balance on his shoulder as if nothing has happened at all. With the first heel in place, Benedict glances up at me, blue eyes that were slightly hazy and *possibly* drunk suddenly sharp and cautious—before he turns away to address my other shoe.

I already know this guy's real name isn't Benedict. But this rich, clueless, sort of bro-ish boy act is definitely *not* the same personality that nearly cracked my jaw in half down in the basement. So who *is* he?

I rub my jaw where it's tender and hope that it's only turning brownish red instead of an angry purple I might have to hide with foundation in a bathroom. I almost feel bad when I see the hint of a wince as Benedict shifts his balance; beneath his pant leg, his thigh is probably bruising nicely from my fist.

Then I remember that when he kissed me, he'd held the unbruised side of my face.

This has gone so wrong.

Zoe and I need to abort this mission. The whole night is a bust.

I eye the warlock again and try to assess how much of a fight he might put up if I attempt to evade him, get back to my table and to Zoe, and get the hell out of this place. The faster we leave, the better.

When Benedict is done with my second shoe, he sets my foot down and stands in a single smooth movement. That smile is back again—the charming, easy one that spreads slow across his face. A smile so languid, you want to follow its growth, maybe watch to see if it reaches his eyes, too. I already know that smile—and I know it's fake.

"All done." He raises his arm like a perfect gentleman. "Ready?"

"Sure, Benedict," I say tightly, and take his arm as we exit the elevator.

When his hand slips to rest gently across my lower back, I jump at that contact too, just like he did when I grabbed his shoulder for balance in the elevator. Benedict's hand stills immediately, and we both keep moving, but the warlock frowns at the two of us as we pass.

When I relax my shoulders, Benedict's hand moves again, this time up my back instead of down. It doesn't help. The sensation of his warm palm spreading wide across the bare skin between my dress straps has me fighting back a gasp. His hand is *massive*. This touch disorients me in a new way, and now I'm dizzy and confused and, suddenly, *much* too flustered.

"Everything okay, honey?" he murmurs.

Right. We're . . . engaged. And Lawson the warlock is still watching. "Just fine," I mutter, relaxing back into his palm as best I can.

Benedict presses his lips together in another fake, fuzzy smile and navigates us down the hall toward one set of spiral staircases to the ballroom. As we move closer to the empty stairs, the voices behind us grow quieter. As soon as we're out of sight of the warlock, Benedict drops his hand from my back. I'm not as steady on my borrowed heels up the stairs, and he slows his pace to match mine. The full, warm yellow glow from the sconces along the staircase finally give me a moment to take in my new companion from head to toe.

I could tell he was tall in the basement, but here in the light? Six foot three or four at least, if I were to guess. His black tuxedo jacket fits his broad shoulders and straight posture perfectly. Tailored, for sure. Still, the curves of his biceps strain the material of his sleeves in a way that might make someone's gaze linger. Not *my* gaze, per se. But someone's. Or, honestly, *everyone's*.

Good Lord.

His torso and legs are both long, and the open hand now hanging loosely at his side is as wide as I imagined, with long fingers and neat nails. I remember the feeling of his palm's rough, warm calluses on my cheek—and on my thigh. Above his mask, his hair is thick and blond, and below it, his jaw is so sharply angled and strong, it could be its own kind of weapon. This time, my gaze *does* linger, until he turns to me halfway up the stairs, and I wrench my eyes away.

"Wait." He pauses, indicating that I should do the same. We are in the middle of the staircase, standing by a window, and for the moment, we're alone and out of sight.

"What?"

He checks up and down the stairs again to make sure no one is coming before speaking. "I haven't seen you in months," he says in a low voice. "None of us have."

None of us. I feel the press of unknown faces and names and incomplete memories inside my skull, filling up the space of my mind with everything Erebus has taken. "Who is 'us'?"

"The Legendborn, your friends"—he pauses—"but also your enemies."

"And which one of those are you?" I whisper. "You attacked me, after all."

"*Pretty* sure that fight was mutual and, as it happens, more fun than I've had in months." He grins. "Wanna go again?"

"You . . . ," I sputter. "You—"

"I . . . what?" he prompts, eyes dancing. "Do tell."

"You . . . *deforged* my magic!" I don't even know if that's the right word.

He blinks. "Is that a word?"

"What else do you call it when someone *disassembles* your constructs down to *dust* with a wave of their hand?" I hiss.

Something deepens in the blue of his irises, and for a split second, I swear I see his pupils turn blue too, but the change is gone as soon as it comes. He sidesteps my question, his face serious once more. He moves closer, backing me up against the window. "I knew you were alive—we all *knew* you were alive—but we had no idea where you were, and then you just show up here? How? And why? And your memory—" He stops when a pair of voices grows closer to us from the bottom of the staircase. We hold our breaths. Wait. And then the speakers move away. "There's really no time for this. Not here."

"No time for what?" I cross my arms. "For you to interrogate someone you've just met?"

"You *know* we haven't 'just met.'"

I'm annoyed that he's right. "Maybe I do. Maybe I don't." I lift my chin. "You don't know *what* I know."

"You're right. So why don't you tell me?" he asks. "How much have you lost?"

I blink at him, stunned at both the simplicity of his question and the pain it brings. This boy, his eyes, his questions . . . He is a dagger to my heart, quick and true. So much so that I'm not prepared for my own honest answer, pulled from my chest in a hoarse rasp. "Everyone."

He holds my gaze with something like sadness—followed by swift resignation. "But you're still you, right? Your personality is the same? Your abilities?"

"Like?" I prompt.

"Can you still resist mesmer?" I don't answer, but my face must betray me, because he nods. "You can. Good. Which means whatever took this part of you away *wasn't* a mesmer."

I swallow but don't answer. Just the fact that he knows I can resist mesmer puts this masked boy in a very limited circle of possible people in my life. He is Legendborn, more likely than not. Erebus claimed that if I saw the Legendborn, my friends, and my family again, they'd be so hurt that I didn't remember them that they'd reject me. That they'd punish me for my choice to leave and that my relationships would be fractured forever. To me, I've lost knowledge. To them, I've lost memories. But Benedict doesn't seem to be angry with me. In fact, he seems to want to know more, to *understand more*. I can see the gears turning in his head and find myself curious about what he'll say next.

"What else do you think you know?" I ask.

He studies me. "Well, you don't appear to be *surprised* by whatever's affecting you. You're not shocked that you don't recognize me, which means that not only has something happened to your mind, but you already know that thing has happened—and you've known for a while." He frowns. "This is a hunch, but I don't think you know *exactly* what caused these knowledge gaps, do you?"

I lift a shoulder. "I know . . . enough."

"It's magical," he says quietly. "Isn't it?"

I wrap my arms around myself.

He leans closer. Another question. "Did someone do this to you?"

My fists ball tight, the answer pulled from my lips before I can stop it. "Yes."

His eyes flash, anger quick and bright. "And you can't reverse it." *Not* a question.

"How do you know I can't—"

"Because the girl *I* know would be fighting like *hell* to undo what someone else did to her against her consent," he says, voice low and serious. "And if you're not actively fighting it, what's happened has either *taken* that fight out of you, along with your knowledge of the people in your life or . . ."

I look up at him, heart pounding with the surety of his gaze, the confidence in what he knows—and the unnerving thrill of listening to him capture this part of me so quickly. "Or what?"

He tilts his head, the anger in his face fading. "Or you've decided that whatever this person has done to you has helped you gain more than you've lost."

Now that I've been captured, I find I don't want to be. I look away. "You can stop talking now. You don't know everything about me, *Benedict*."

A pause. Then his voice comes again, amused. "I know that you've most *definitely* already guessed that my name is *not* Benedict Pierce."

"Anyone could figure that out." I wave a hand and look at him pointedly. "You don't even look like a Benedict."

His mouth twitches, brows lifting. "Thank you?"

"You're welcome," I reply primly.

He holds my gaze and I hold his, and then I'm feeling warm and confused again. And, what's worse, it feels like he can *tell*. I shake my head to snap out of it. Change the subject. "Earlier tonight, what were you trying to . . . *acquire?*"

The only visible response to my question is a slight tightening of the skin around his eyes—smoothed out in a blink. He turns to walk up the stairs, gesturing for me to come along. "I could ask the same of you, Bree."

The sound of my name in his voice again makes me nearly miss a step. I lose balance on my heels and—in a flash of speed—his hand meets my spine, steadying me.

He'd traveled down two stairs without my noticing. "You're fast."

"I know." His eyes soften. "And . . . I'm sorry."

"For what?"

"For saying something snarky that made you trip just now, and touching you like this, and for . . . before. Hitting you like that—"

"I think I got you in the leg pretty bad," I say.

"You did. You're . . . a lot stronger than I am." Then his cheeks tinge pink. "But I'm also sorry about the elevator. Kissing you."

I blink, taken aback. "It was . . ."

"A distraction. One that just happened to work on Bianca." He shakes his head once and straightens. While I regain my balance, he removes his hand from my back to stuff it in his pocket, then continues up the stairs. "A last-minute play to avoid a situation that neither of us planned for. It won't happen again."

"Oh." I stifle the surprising surge of rebellion that rises in my chest. I don't know him. He shouldn't be kissing me. I shouldn't *want* him to kiss me. "That's fine. I'm leaving as soon as they let us go, anyway."

"Leaving? But——" He looks at me sharply. Opens his mouth, then closes it. "That's probably for the best. It's not safe here, for more reasons than one. You should get out at the first opportunity."

Indignation makes me ball my fists all over again. I glare up at him. "You can't tell me what to do."

He blinks down at me. "You've said that to me before."

"I have?" Then I recover, lifting my chin. "Well, you clearly didn't listen the first time."

"I didn't." His gaze turns almost . . . admiring. "You don't remember who I am, but you're still just as stubborn as you've always been. Just as dauntless."

My body grows warm. "Thank you?"

He grins. "You're welcome."

Parry. Riposte. Like a call and a response.

We stare at each other in the middle of Mikael's back staircase, and for a moment, I am caught by his eyes, his brow, his generous, curved mouth. Zoe and I need the crown to stop Erebus from hunting Rootcrafters, but . . . is this boy a reason to stick around? Or another reason to leave as soon as possible? What if asking more questions fills in the blanks of my mind somehow? I want to know how not-Benedict and I know each other and why he makes me feel the way I do, but I can't shake the feeling that to know more is to *risk* more. What if Erebus finds out I've run into someone from my past and makes good on the threats against people I've come to care about, like Zoe and Elijah? Or decides to hurt the people I *used* to know and care about, like my father, or the girl in a coma . . . or this handsome boy who calls me "dauntless" in a low voice that makes me shiver?

I came here ready to be impervious, and this boy—this tall, warm, *knowing* boy—is already testing that goal.

I tell myself I can ask one question, at least. Just one. "*How* do you know me?"

"It's a very long story and while we're here, it's too dangerous a story to tell." His jaw tightens as he turns again to walk up the stairs. I join him for one step. Two. A third. We're almost at the top of the staircase, in full view of everyone in the hallway outside of the ballroom. The voices above are growing louder, more agitated. "Are you safe? Wherever you've been?"

"I can't be harmed—physically, anyway," I murmur. Then, after a moment's hesitation and considering Erebus's animal constructs and sparring with the twins, I add, "Much."

He turns to me as he walks. "You do realize that's not at all reassuring?"

"It's better than the alternative," I say defiantly. "I am where I chose to be."

"Where you *chose to be*—?" He whirls back on me one step from the top. Looks as if he might press harder on that point but then decides better. In a voice that can barely qualify as a whisper, he asks, "Are you with the demon who took you from Northern?"

I don't answer that. "I don't even know your real name."

He releases his name with a strange, sad smile. "Nick."

"Nick," I repeat. "Short for Nicholas?"

When I say his whole name, a current seems to zip through him. A quiet shiver, before he closes his eyes and crests the top of the stairs to walk ahead. "Yeah."

It seems I'm not the only one who has an involuntary response to my name from the other party's mouth.

I may not know Nick, but the feelings he evokes, the sensations against my skin—those feel familiar. Feel real. Instead, I worry at my lower lip. *How can you miss something that feels like it was never really there?* I'm starting to understand how, because the idea of leaving Nick tonight makes something in my chest burn.

I want more—like I did when he kissed me—and can't tell if I should. If it's a good idea to chase more of these old feelings when I don't even know how he created them in the first place.

As I finally crest the staircase myself, I find Nick looking out over the black-and-white-checkered floor outside the ballroom doors. There is a crowd of people hovering outside in their gowns and tuxedos, some gathered in frantic clusters. Two security warlocks stand at the top of the curving grand staircase that leads down to the foyer, turning away anyone who approaches. I wonder how long they'll be able to contain this throng of powerful people without some sort of uprising.

I come to a stop beside Nick. "What are you looking for?"

"Not a 'what' but a 'who,'" he says. The skin around his eyes looks tighter than it did a moment ago.

Abruptly, my chest grows cold. I can't help but glance down at his hands. This time, his left hand is in clear view—and so is the wide silver band on his ring finger.

My fiancée.

"Oh," I murmur. "Would that 'who' be Iris?"

He glances down at me. "The thing is . . ."

Before he can answer, two figures move from the crush of standing guests and stride toward us.

I recognize Zoe immediately. She's doing everything in her power not to use cambion speed to get to me, and the forced slowness allows her to give Nick a hard look before she glances back to me with a raised brow. I shrug helplessly, not sure how to even begin to communicate the last hour to her without using words.

Hell, I don't think I'll be able to explain the last hour to her *with* words.

The second person beside Zoe is a very pretty, very angry-looking bronze-skinned girl with short dark hair, wearing a long black gown.

They get to us at the same time.

To my surprise, Nick presses his arm across my middle, pushing me behind him and out of the new girl's reach. "It's not what you think—"

"Hey," I protest, pushing his arm away. "I don't need you to protect me—"

"I know, but—"

"What is this?" the girl hisses below her breath. "Did you set me up?"

Nick is already shaking his head, his voice pitched low to avoid being heard, even though we're far away from the much louder crowd. "No, Ava. We ran into each other by accident, I swear—"

"This is a goddamn *double cross*." The girl, Ava, has to stand on her toes and twist around Nick's shoulder to try and see me. When she waves her hand in the air, I catch the diamond engagement ring on her left hand, and a completely uncalled-for zip of pain streaks through my chest. Is she his *real* fiancée? Or another fake, like me? "You really expect me to believe you just happened to run into the—"

"Chill out, rando." Zoe is around my other side, arm linking with mine. It takes her half a second to glance at my empty hands—no crown, no invite. She waves our invitation in her free hand at both Ava and Nick. "I don't know you, but this is my sister, *Vivienne*—"

"Actually," I interrupt her quietly, "I'm sort of . . . Iris now?"

Ava gapes. *"What?"*

Zoe rears back, eyes flashing red in surprise. "The hell you mean you're *Iris* now?"

"Careful!" I warn. Zoe's eyes flick back to brown. She, like me, is supposed to be on her most normal-human-girl behavior tonight. My furnace is closed tight, and she has to cover her cambion traits as much as possible so that if Mikael happens to get close to either one of us, he won't suspect that we are anything other than human guests. But it's not just Mikael I'm worried about.

I don't know this new girl, Ava, but I can tell she knows who I am—or who I *was*—and she's not happy about my presence. I don't need her spilling that info to Zoe in the middle of Mikael's event with warlocks around every corner, and she can't find out that Zoe's a cambion. "*Tamar*, we need to leave—"

"Bree?" A quiet voice interrupts us.

The Black girl behind Ava and Zoe is my height, a little older than me, with long box braids and round golden glasses over her mask. Her dress is a rich velvet red and gold, and resting on her chest is a solid black pendant on a leather cord that catches my eye—then holds it. Like Nick, she knows me, but I don't know her. As I search myself for the single clue, the single emotional remnant I might be able to associate with this new girl, I take a step toward her without noticing.

"Oh my God." The girl's brown eyes expand. "I can't believe you're *here*." She starts to close the distance between us with both arms outstretched for a hug. When I don't respond, her arms drop and she touches her mask sheepishly. "Oh, sorry. The mask." She glances over her shoulder before whispering, "It's me, *Mariah*."

"I don't . . ."

At the tone of my voice, she stiffens, then glances at Zoe, then Nick, then Ava, then back to me again. "Um . . . what's going on?"

"Good question." I groan, frustrated that I can't isolate an emotion for this girl, Mariah, even though I want to. Just like with Nick, I can't connect her to any of my other memories.

"*Great* question," Ava snaps.

"*Complicated* question." Nick pinches the bridge of his nose. "And no time to answer it."

As if proving him right, the overhead lights in the foyer and ballroom entrance hall both flash. We all look up, gazing at them with varying levels of annoyance, then down. Around us, the hall has mostly cleared—we're the only ones still lingering.

"We need to get inside the ballroom and deal with this afterward," I say.

"Hate to say it, but she's right." Ava beckons to Nick. "Come on, *Benedict*, let's get to our seats—"

"He can't." I shake my head. "'Benedict' here already told Bianca that *we're* Benedict and Iris. She saw us." I shift on my feet, face heating at the memory of Nick's mouth on mine and the warmth of his hands. "Like, *really* saw us. We need to stick with these identities for the rest of the night. Just in case."

"It's true," Nick says. "She's Iris now. She has to be."

"No way," Ava says with a scowl. "If her eyes turn even a *hint* of silver—"

My eyes? Turn silver? I swallow. There's only one reason my eyes would turn that color.

Arthur. Ava and Nick both know that I'm the Scion of Arthur and a Medium. When I glance at Mariah, she is watching me warily—and I realize that she knows both of those things, too. She knows what my possession looks like, and from her guarded expression, she has reason to be scared of it.

I don't blame her.

"I know," Nick is whispering. "But if any of us wants to walk out of here alive, we *all* have to stick with these identities through dinner. So give me the ring." He curls his fingers, a beckoning.

Ava's teeth grind back and forth until she finally twists the ring off her finger and hands it over. "Terrific. Just terrific." She turns to Mariah. "Is your name actually Mariah?"

"Er, tonight I'm Juliet, actually." Mariah pulls out a card. "Curator for a fine art gallery in SoHo."

"Did Bianca see you when you checked in?" Ava asks. "Associate your name with your face? Your clothes?"

Mariah shakes her head. "She wasn't there. The guards only checked the aether layer on the invite. Plus, I wore my mask, just like everyone else."

"And you?" Ava turns to Zoe. "Same questions."

Zoe flashes her card, smirking. "I'm just some rich girl named Tamar with a sister."

"Well, if 'Iris' is Iris, then who the hell am *I* supposed to be?" Ava demands hoarsely. Nobody answers. There *is* no answer. She can't take my place now that Bianca knows me as Iris.

I have half a second to see Zoe glance at the door and make a decision, blur between Mariah and Ava, then zoom to Mariah's side with her arm slung over the blinking girl's shoulder.

"What—" Ava begins, but is cut off when Bianca appears around a corner, calling to us from down the hall.

"I'm so sorry, everyone, but we really need you back at your seats!"

"No problem!" Nick replies with a wave. "Just a sec!"

Out of the side of my eye, I see Ava's eyes widen when she reads the card in her hand. Her face turns red as she twists around to glare at Zoe—who beams at her from beside Mariah.

"I need a fake sister." Zoe tilts her head at Mariah. "We aren't the only Black women here, but there aren't enough of us to go unnoticed. If we get asked, something tells me it'll be easier for this crowd to believe *she's* my sister instead of you."

Ava's mouth snaps closed.

That's when I realize what Zoe's done—she's given Ava Mariah's card so that Mariah is now who I was supposed to be, and Ava has taken Mariah's place as the art curator.

At least now, we're all *somebody* who's supposed to be here.

Nick, for his part, has his mouth set into that fake smile again. "Shall we, Iris?" He gestures toward the open ballroom doors.

I share one last glance with Zoe, whose eyes are glued to us both. She stares at Nick, then me, and her message is clear: *Be careful with him.*

But as I let Nick lead me to our table, I worry that her warning has come too late, because I don't feel *careful* on Nick's arm. I feel . . . reckless.

35

WHEN WE REACH our new table at the front of the room, the first thing I notice is that there's no one else seated with us, or even near us.

Nick must see the surprise on my face. "I've been to these types of things before. These are big-spender tables for the mega-rich. If you pay a little extra to the right person, you get to reap the luxury of not having to mingle with the 'common folk.'"

"So, you and your fiancée are mega-rich?"

"We are," he replies in a neutral tone.

I can't tell if he's referring to himself and Ava or himself and me, and a spark of unexpected frustration burns at the back of my throat.

"How old are you, anyway?"

"Same age as you." He pulls out my chair. "A very belated happy birthday, by the way." *So he's seventeen,* I think. *And he knows my birthday?*

I allow Nick to seat me, even though my heart is pounding with the prospect of more time alone with him. *All I have to do is get through dinner,* I tell myself.

Be impervious. Then, Zoe and I can face Erebus's disappointment—or wrath— and figure out a new plan to get the crown.

I glance around the room and stifle a small heart attack when I realize that the woman who had been seated next to me might be confused at my disappearance—and Zoe and Mariah's sudden appearance. But when I locate that first table across the room, the woman isn't even looking at Zoe or Mariah. She's sitting on the edge of her own seat, eyes darting all over the room at the increased security around its perimeter and the flashing lights overhead. At every entrance and exit, the guards have doubled.

And yet for all of that increased security, I still don't feel any demon eyes on my skin, other than the sensation of Zoe's occasional passing attention on my exposed left shoulder and cheek. When I glance at her again, her eyes are on the influx of new guards—and her nose has visibly wrinkled.

They must all be warlocks.

Ava, for her part, is seated even farther away from my and Nick's table than Zoe and Mariah are. *She's* staring at me with dark, cold eyes behind her mask, both arms crossed over her chest.

"Was that you?" Nick's voice interrupts my thoughts.

When I turn back, I wonder how long he's been studying me while wearing an expression that is somehow both guarded and disbelieving. Like he's holding something back but still shocked that I'm here.

That I'm real.

I thought that I'd become acquainted with his face, but now I wonder if that's even possible. It's not just that he's handsome; it's that, even while he's wearing a mask, his focused gaze unmoors me. Strips me bare. "Was what me?"

His blue eyes flick up to the flashing lights, to the security presence in the room. "The lights going out right before our *meeting* downstairs. Was that you and your friend?"

I blink, realizing what he's asking. "Uh, no. We didn't do that."

"Huh," Nick says, eyes scanning the room behind me as he thinks, "then someone else set off the security system, and you and I just happened to be the unfortunate beneficiaries of their failed attempt."

"Someone else?"

"A third . . . meeting attendee." Abruptly, he affects a wide smile and a slouch as he flags down a server in a tux passing our table. "Hey, what are we waiting for?"

The server stiffens at Nick's casual demeanor—one that he's simply pulled over his face as if it were yet another mask, just like before with Bianca. "Penumbra's owner—and your *esteemed* host—will be addressing his guests shortly. I'm told we are securing the premises after an incident. You shouldn't be waiting long—"

"Ugh," Nick says, slouching farther. "I bet it's gonna be some boring lawyer. Not even the real guy."

The man bristles. "I assure you that there is only one master of the estate."

"Oh," Nick perks up. "So this Mikael guy is *actually* gonna be here? I heard he doesn't even live on-site, just opens it up for parties."

The server nods. "While Mr. Di Centa does not reside on the premises full-time, he prides himself on being a good host to all guests during these special events. All welcomed guests, anyway."

Nick leans in. "Someone really tried to break into the building? Right in the middle of the gala?"

The server shifts his weight. "Not the manor proper, no."

Nick's eyebrow ticks up above his mask. "For real?"

But the server has grown tired of Nick's affected demeanor, and his face closes down. "Would you like a drink while you wait, sir?"

Nick scratches at his chin, as if thinking. "A Lagavulin 25 for me. Neat. And a . . . French 75 for my lady?"

"Of course," the server says, and pivots toward the bar.

After a beat, Nick straightens and looks at me. "What?"

My nose wrinkles. "Is that your bro face?"

Nick smirks. "You've asked me *that* before too."

"I've watched you lie before, you mean?"

His mouth tightens. "I got good at . . . pretending. When I was younger." He waves a hand toward Zoe. "You're not bad yourself."

"I'm—" I begin to say, then shake my head. "It's not just you and me. You think these black-market buyers and millionaires are using their government names while wearing masks that hide half their faces?"

"I'm not talking about their disguises, I'm talking about yours."

"I don't know what you mean."

"Sure, you don't," he drawls, looking back out over the room.

I scowl at the back of his head, suddenly feeling an urge to brawl with him again, in one way or another. "You think you're so clever."

His chin turns in my direction, even as he scans the crowd. "Someone clever told me I was clever once, so I'm going to take that as a compliment."

"I have a feeling that 'someone' was me."

"You'd be right." A beat passes before Nick turns to me again. He hesitates. "This isn't . . . how I thought I'd find you."

An ache blooms in my chest, and I don't know why. What does my body know about this boy that my mind doesn't? "How did you imagine it?"

He gives me a long look. "I don't think that matters anymore."

My heart flutters in my throat. The server returns with our drinks before I can reply. Once he sets them both down on the table, Nick pulls a wallet out of his suit pocket and passes a bill to the server. "Thanks, brah."

The moment between us is gone. The other mask Nick wears, the invisible one, has slid back in place. I shudder, then blink at the hundred-dollar bill the server pockets.

"Very good, sir," the server says, turning to go.

As soon as he is out of earshot, Nick groans quietly. "*That* will probably blow our cover before anything else will."

"Why?" I ask. "Because you tipped him well?"

"Because I tipped him at all," Nick replies. "Wealthy people don't think anyone *else* deserves to get paid for their labor. They're the worst tippers in the world."

I pause, wondering how many wealthy people he's spent time with and why he talks about them like he isn't one himself if he's, as he said, been to these types of events before. "But you did it anyway?"

Nick takes a sip of the golden liquid in his tumbler before he answers, wincing slightly at the burn as he sets it down. "I don't know if that server understands who his boss is. Lots of innocent people get caught up in magic that could get them killed."

I smirk. "So you're not that good at pretending, after all."

He flashes a quiet grin. "Not when I'm with you."

My brain skips, then scatters. In one uttered sentence, Nick has sliced the tension between us. I dive into that opening, hungry for his honesty. "What else happens when you're with me?"

Nick's brow arches. "I think we've covered some of the basics tonight already."

"Fighting?"

"I prefer to think of it as banter."

I narrow my eyes. "Combat?"

"That one was new, but I'm not complaining. Are you?"

"No. It was like you said. I had . . . fun." I surprise myself with my answer— but my answer doesn't surprise Nick.

"I noticed." He meets my annoyed gaze with an amused one of his own.

I pause, considering my next question. In the silence, Nick lightly rotates the glass tumbler on the table between his fingers. First back, then forth. He watches as I gather my own bravery. Waits as I summon my own honesty. Finally, I ask, "And what happened between us in the elevator . . . ?"

The glass stills. "We've done that before, yes. Not in an elevator."

I flush at the sense memory of heated lips and strong hands. A gravel drive-way beneath my feet in the early morning. The electric shadows of a darkened room at another gala, another time. Was that him? Was that us? "Have we done that . . . a lot?"

His mouth twitches. "You'll have to be specific."

Oh, how this boy annoys me. I lower my voice. "The kissing. The . . . touching."

Nick studies me for a moment before answering, eyes unreadable. "We've kissed enough that I know how you like to be kissed. We've touched enough that I know how you want to be touched. Which is how I know we shouldn't keep talking about kissing . . . and touching."

My breath catches. "Why?"

"Because before we had this conversation, you told me you were leaving after the gala to return to wherever you've been the last four months, and I've already decided that I won't stop you."

The finality in his voice steals any words I could generate in response. He holds my gaze while I hold his, until the volume of the ballroom around us abruptly rises, reminding me of where we are and who we're supposed to be. Not Nick and Bree, unexpectedly reunited, former maybe-lovers, but Benedict and Iris, recently engaged young Collectors. When we look away, it's just in time to see Mikael the Nightshade take the stage.

Mikael is dressed in black and green, just like his invitations. That alone tells me plenty: He likes control, and he wishes to make a certain impression. He enjoys the aesthetics of harmony, if not the truth of it.

Erebus said that Mikael likes being among humans. Values humanity for what it provides beyond the sustenance of our emotions. One look at this ancient Nightshade and even I can see that he's bought into the very human, very turn-of-the-century, very *American* appearance of wealth and power. Much more so than either Erebus or Daeza.

Mikael wears a tailored black tuxedo jacket with a basil green silk scarf hanging down the lapel around his neck, and black tuxedo pants with deep emerald stripes. His dark hair is slicked back and gelled. He's my height, but wider across the shoulders. Handsome and stately, with strong features, olive skin, and straight white teeth.

Mikael has arrived without a mask, and the statement is clear. He *wants* us to see him. Wants us to know him. Wants his followers to understand that he is so powerful he doesn't need to hide. Of course, these humans don't know that even the face he wears openly before them is yet another mask—just like Erebus and Daeza.

"A demonic great Gatsby," I murmur.

Nick hums. "An enigmatic robber baron drunk on his own mythology?"

I glance around the room at the human guests who, for all their agitation and concern a few minutes ago, seem to be suddenly and wholly thrilled at the appearance of their host. "Something like that."

Mikael doesn't bother using the microphone when he calls for our attention.

"Good evening, everyone." His voice flows across the room in a low wave. A commanding drawl laced with a Cheshire cat smile that silences the eager crowd with ease. "And welcome to Penumbra's annual Collectors' Gala."

The room applauds. But even that is not loud enough to cover the sound of the door closing, sealing us all in with a loud, ominous click.

"If we have not met in person yet, I am Mikaelaz Di Centa. But, please, call me Mikael. I confess that I usually do not make an appearance so early in the evening at these events. I must admit, security alarms, emergency lights, and unexpected disruptions do not make good entertainment when conducting business that is not *strictly* legal."

Nervous laughter skitters across the room, and the tension around us becomes palpable. A few people adjust their masks at their seats.

"However, I wanted to come before you personally to let you all know that I remain committed to the ethos of our gatherings and committed to maintaining your confidence. As a reminder: Masks that conceal the upper face are required, first names are encouraged, but inquiring as to last names and places of business is strictly banned among Collectors. What happens at Penumbra *stays* at Penumbra."

As Mikael's smile spreads, the laughter in the room shifts and lightens, but a spot at the back of my skull tingles slightly, as if I've been zapped by a tiny bolt of electricity.

"What the . . . ?" I whisper. Nick raises his brows in a silent question, but I don't have an answer for him. I don't know *what* just happened, just that something *did*.

"Thank you for complying with my security team as they not only secured the premises but ensured your safety. Tonight, we had an attempted breach of a secured outbuilding on our grounds—not wholly unexpected, given the value of the items we have gathered for our event—but perhaps more distressingly, I must share that a *second* incident has occurred. One much more violent . . . and distasteful." Mikael pauses, a small sneer pulling at his lips before he contains it. "Someone attacked one of my guards inside the building, leaving him badly injured and requiring medical attention. After a thorough sweep of the estate, my captain of security, Bianca, has determined that both the would-be thief *and* the assaulter are still here . . . among us."

The room murmurs again, and a few voices rise in alarm. I resist the urge to glance at Zoe but feel her quick look my way. Beside me, Nick emits a low hum into his Scotch that feels specifically aimed in my direction. He's gazing into his drink with far too much interest.

I scowl. I'd hoped to knock the warlock out long enough for me and Zoe to get out of here. It might have worked, too, if every other detail of our plan hadn't imploded.

But who is this other thief, this *third* culprit, who attempted to steal something from a second location? My eyes snap to Ava without hesitation, but her attention is on Mikael. Could she have been the other thief tonight? If so, why? I thought she came here with Nick.

"I understand completely if some of you are too uncomfortable to proceed with our dinner and auction. Many of you have your own security concerns to keep in mind. If you would like to forfeit your chance to bid on the auction items scheduled for tonight, you are welcome to leave now and try your luck at earning an invitation to next year's gala instead."

Mikael pauses to let his words sink in. The hesitation to take him up on his offer settles on people's faces. If they leave now, they may not be invited again.

When Elijah first explained the nature of these Collectors' Galas to us, he, too, made it clear that we were only going to get one real shot at the crown here and now. If the crown or any other item tonight is successfully auctioned, it might never again exchange hands, even somewhat privately at an event like this. We're sitting in a limited window of opportunity. And if I'm going to stop the Shadow King from being the Rootcrafter Hunter, then I can't afford to miss it. This time, I *do* glance at Zoe, and she nods once—we're on the same page. We're staying, even if we need to improvise a new plan before dessert.

"We have moved all auction items to a more secure location and have decided to reschedule tonight's auction to three days from now, on Sunday evening," Mikael continues. "Any Collectors who remain interested in these items will need to submit to an appropriate, additional level of security screening—and remain on-site, here at Penumbra, for the duration of the weekend."

Nick's drink thunks down on the table, but the sound is buried beneath the eager uproar of the formally dressed guests around us.

Everywhere I look, Mikael's Collectors are either clapping or exchanging anticipatory smiles at the prospect of staying at Penumbra for three more days. Where I only feel shock at this news, Mikael's Collectors are joyous.

Mikael speaks over the wave of excited murmurs. "I see that many of you have been a Collector long enough to remember the last time Penumbra welcomed overnight guests in communion. As in the past, we will, of course, allow you to send for the necessary items you may need. Medications, toiletries, et cetera. In keeping with the traditional atmosphere of the estate, we *will* need to provide guests with approved attire to maintain the required dress code. All expenses and meals will be covered." His comments are met with thunderous applause, as if he'd just offered everyone in the room their greatest desire.

My heart drums in my ears, but across the room, my eyes find Zoe's. She's already looking at me, inhaling slowly in acceptance.

Rules can change.

She lifts her bag slightly, reminding me that my own overnight bag is still at the table. Erebus suspected that Mikael would change the game mid-play, and he wanted us prepared. Relief floods through me at the realization that we'll have another chance at the crown—and soon.

We just need to make it through the weekend and, apparently, let Mikael dress us all up like living dolls to fit his aesthetic. I can only hope that the Rootcrafter girl from the Rat is still connected to her root. That the King won't drain her in three more days' time, and that he's consuming other sources of power.

All around us, guests are reaching under their tables to produce overnight bags of their own, and an uneasy feeling settles in my stomach.

These "Collectors" are not just an exclusive group of rare artifact admirers, not just Mikael's eager followers. They are something more than that. Erebus's voice returns to me once more: *Mikael thrives where there is both human devotion and human greed.*

But if the auction isn't happening until Sunday, then what are these humans greedy for?

As Mikael continues to speak—this time about the grounds tours and amenities guests can enjoy over the next several days—the anticipatory hunger in the room sharpens. Like the Collectors are waiting to hear about a specific event. A specific activity.

"This is weird—" I begin, but stop when I feel the table beneath my hands rattle. It only takes a moment to realize that it's Nick, his knee and thigh bouncing in agitation that matches his pensive expression. He has been so controlled and collected since I met him, or re-met him, that I'm alarmed by this open exhibit of nerves. He doesn't even seem like someone *capable* of nerves. "What's wrong?" I whisper.

"Three days," he mutters, eyes cast to the middle distance. "I can't stay here for three days."

Panic streaks through me. We're in this together now. If Nick—Benedict—leaves, does that mean "Iris" has to leave too? That won't work. Zoe and I have to stay here to find the crown. Stop Erebus. Save the kidnapped girl. Save as many girls as we can. "Why not?" I demand.

Thoughts churn behind his eyes as if I'd never spoken. "That's too much time."

I was wrong. It's not agitation I see in Nick, but desperation—and the thinnest thread of terror. What *else* does Nick know that I don't? "Too much time for what?" I reach for his arm without thinking—but he jerks back as if I'd burned him.

Behind his mask, Nick's eyes have become lightning, pinning me in his path. His face, a tortured thundercloud rolling close. "You weren't supposed to be here. An hour or two, I could handle. But three days?" He looks away, taking the storm with him. "There's no way in hell I can be around you for that long."

36

NICK'S WORDS KNIFE through me, slicing my lungs until I'm breathless. Then, indignation roars up from my gut to burn the shock away. "May I ask why I'm so horrible to be around?"

Nick's jaw works back and forth, and I watch something real move behind his eyes before he shutters it. He takes a deep, slow breath and leans back in his chair. Mikael has stepped away from the stage, but the room is still buzzing with energy. Now that the weekend stay at Penumbra has been announced, dinner service has begun.

"You can ask me anything you want," he says. "But that doesn't mean I'll answer."

"So that's how it is?" I ask hotly. "You're a whole jerk now?"

He answers without looking at me. "Very possibly."

I gape. "Were you *always* like this?"

He blows out a breath. "Depends on who you ask."

"Well, we can always switch back, you know," I say, pointing my chin to where Ava is seated. "You can go back to your real fiancée. I'm sure you'd rather spend three days with her instead."

"Bianca has seen us together. So has the server. So has Mikael now. We can't switch back. No matter how much I wish we could." His jaw tightens. "No matter how much we should."

"Wow," I whisper harshly. "I thought I wanted to know more about us and—and who we *were* before, but now, I think I might be better off not knowing anything about you at all!"

"You're lying." A quiet observation and close-lipped smile. "But I don't blame you."

The desire to throw my drink over his head seizes me so entirely that my right hand is on my glass before I know it—but Nick's hand is a blur. In a blink, his fingers catch my wrist with easy strength.

"Now, now, fiancée of mine," he murmurs, tilting his head to catch my eye, "it wouldn't do to blow *either* of our covers with a public quarrel, would it? Not when we have three more days to finish what we started in the basement."

I grit my teeth but don't let go of my glass. His left hand dwarfs my right. Veins and fine muscle engulf my wrist. I could break his grip, but it'd draw attention. My left hand, still free, slips below the table. "What *did* we start in the basement?"

"Something you know we can't continue, so why even ask?"

"Call me curious," I bite out, yanking my right hand—to no avail. His grip is iron.

"Call you *vicious*, you mean." His eyes flick down to the table, amused and knowing. "Are you *really* going for that dagger strapped to your thigh, right out here in the open?"

My left fingers have already grasped the hilt. How long has he known the dagger was there? When did he notice? In the darkened basement? When we were pressed together in the elevator, torso to torso and legs to legs? "No."

"You *are*." Wonder fills his expression. "Look at you. Incredible. You're a gorgeous, powerful, violent little enigma who would stab me in front of all these people just to make a point." He uses the tight fist around my wrist to draw himself closer, as if to see more of me. "Is that how it was?" he murmurs. "Were you always like this?"

"You know I was," I whisper cruelly. "So why even ask?"

His grin is quick. Secret. Then his eyes travel over my shoulder, expression mild, while the first course is served. "I can't let you stab me in the middle of dinner, but if you did, you'd have to make it quick. Somewhere hidden. Can't call attention to either one of us." He tilts his head, considering. "Avoid the femoral artery; too much blood. Upper outer thigh, maybe? The tablecloth would cover it."

"Now I don't even *want* to stab you," I hiss.

His mouth quirks roguishly. "Did I spoil your fun?"

"You spoiled my fun in the basement when you showed up out of nowhere."

"You do realize that, from my perspective, *you're* the one who showed up out of nowhere?"

Why am I so flustered? I growl behind my teeth. Servers wind through the room setting down salad plates, bread baskets, and fresh butter dishes in front of hungry guests. The table closest to us has just received its dinner rolls. Nick and I only have a few more minutes to ourselves before we're overheard. "What were you doing there, anyway?"

"Guess."

I glare at him while our hands are locked tight, while I squeeze the hilt of my dagger beneath the table. "You were looking for something that hadn't been prepared for public display yet."

"Correct."

I take a wild gamble. Get specific, but not *too* specific. "Are you here for something magical?"

"Yes," he answers. "I want something magical. Like you."

I don't deny it. With a very palpable effort, I release my fingers from around the stem of the glass. Nick dips his chin toward my lap. "Now the dagger." I scowl, abandoning my hidden weapon to pull my left hand back to my lap. He hums his approval. "Smart girl." Only then does he let me go.

My cheeks flame. "Why do you want it?"

He chuckles. "I have my reasons."

It feels risky to keep talking. Like I might say more embarrassing things. Or reach for something else to throw—and inadvertently invite him to grasp me again when my wrist is still practically *humming* from his touch. So I don't say anything at all.

He chuckles at *that*, too.

This boy is *infuriating*.

Mikael's voice rolls through the ballroom, settling like a blanket over the sound of clinking silverware. "If you don't mind, as dinner is served I'd like to address a bit of housekeeping." He raises a hand, waving someone to the front of the room.

Bianca and Lawson approach the stage—and guided between them is the Collector guest who got caught by the mansion's entryway ward. My stomach goes cold. Elijah didn't know what the ward was designed to catch, but it seems we're about to find out.

The man stumbles a bit as he is moved forward between tables. His frantic eyes dart around the room, but he can't escape the heavy grip on his shoulders, and no one comes to his rescue.

"We may not follow the laws of the outside world," Mikael says to the room, "but we have our own values of discretion and truth. It brings me great sadness that in addition to the two violations I have already shared tonight, we have uncovered a third. A violation of discretion."

A few gasps and whispers rumble through the seated Collectors. Nick and I exchange nervous glances. What are we about to witness?

The Collector steps forward before Lawson yanks him back. "Mikael," the man says, pleading, "I don't even know why they've been questioning me! You know I would never do anything to harm the community—"

Mikael silences the man with a look. "As soon as someone crosses my threshold, I can sense betrayal in their hearts. You know that, Eric."

"I wouldn't betray you!" Eric exclaims.

Mikael frowns. "But you came here tonight with the intent to expose us, didn't you?"

Eric's face turns the color of paper. "I . . . it was just . . . just a thought, Mikael, not a real idea. Nothing I was going to act on—"

"But our thoughts and desires are *everything*, my friend," Mikael says. "And yours have violated our code. Violations come with consequences. Consequences you have agreed to, year after year, have you not?"

Eric's shoulders drop. "I have."

"And so you accept them?"

Eric bows his head. "Yes, of course. I accept the consequences."

"In the name of discretion and truth?" Mikael prompts.

Eric's hands ball into fists. His eyes squeeze shut. "In the name of discretion . . . and truth."

There is no warning—only the dip of Mikael's chin.

Without saying a single word, Lawson slips his hand to the back of Eric's neck . . . and squeezes. Eric's body seizes. His eyes roll back in his head—and then he's gone.

Lawson bends quickly to catch his body before it falls, cradling the Collector close to his chest as if he'd only fallen asleep.

And then Nick's hand is on my knee beneath the table, pressing firmly against the bone—before acidic horror strips my insides. My body, understanding that I've just witnessed a murder before my mind has caught up. When sounds filter back into my ears, I realize the dinner service is still going. Silverware never stopped clinking against plates. Waitstaff never stopped moving. A fresh glass of wine is being poured. When Lawson and Bianca make their exit with Eric, my lungs burn against my rib cage. Nick's hand is the only thing keeping me from howling, from screaming, from bolting from the room. From becoming a violation myself.

"If you notice any other unsavory violations this weekend, my friends," Mikael says, "please do alert our staff, at any time of day. Your loyalty will be handsomely rewarded, as an insult to one of us is an insult to all of us."

The low smattering of applause shakes me to my core.

Mikael's words are those of a congenial host and gentleman, but I hear the warning: any Collector who appears to step out of line this weekend can, should, and will be reported by another Collector to Bianca and her team, where they will face Eric's same fate.

Ten minutes ago, Nick and I were worried about the few people who might see us as Benedict and Iris. Now, we need to worry about who might see us as threats. Mikael could set up another ward to surveil the mansion, but why bother? The Collectors will do his work for him.

Across the room, Zoe's arm is wrapped loosely around Mariah's shoulders, offering awkward comfort to a girl she barely knows as they both stare down at their table with wide, unseeing eyes. Next to me, Nick squeezes my knee in silent question. *Can you hold it together?*

I hate that I've met death frequently enough to understand how to survive its arrival. I answer his question with a stiff nod because I have to. If we want to make it through the next three days alive, we *all* have to hold it together.

"Please enjoy your meals." As Mikael strides away, the jazz music from earlier returns to accompany the rest of the dining service. Whatever this music is, I know I will never forget it.

Our dinner plates arrive, but neither of us can eat anything. Thankfully, we don't have to wait long before an exit strategy reveals itself. "Heads up." Nick points his chin at the group of Collectors near the ballroom doors. It seems people are forming a line to make arrangements with Mikael's small army of estate attendants.

I catch Zoe's eye. She and Mariah are murmuring together. Ava, on the other hand, seems to have disappeared.

When our server returns with a black lockbox in tow, Nick raises his brow.

The server gestures to the other waitstaff drifting around the room with similar boxes. "As part of the security process, we'll be taking devices and storing them securely." The server points to an electronic keypad embedded in the top. "You will set the code, sir."

Nick makes a sour face but reaches into his breast pocket. "Fine."

When the server looks to me, I raise my empty hands. "No phone." The server's gaze turns skeptical. "I went low-tech to fit the vintage vibes."

The server looks as if he might question me further, but decides against it.

Once Nick locks his phone in the box, the server walks away.

Nick sighs. "*That's* uncomfortable."

"I had to do the same thing once," I explain. "Handed over a necklace to get into a bar."

His expression flickers, the Benedict facade slipping momentarily. His eyes drop to my bare clavicle and sternum. "A necklace?"

"Yeah," I answer.

"What kind of necklace?" The question rakes out of him, enough so that I look up to see if his face matches the ragged sound. It does.

"A gift." And suddenly, my blood is rushing in my ears, and my breath catches in my throat. A gift. A gift. *A gift*. I see uncertainty pass over his face before his mask returns.

"We need to find the others. Talk about how we're going to handle all this."

"Right." And he *is* right. Zoe and Mariah are heading toward us, walking nearly in unison with three overnight bags in their hands, when they freeze mid-step.

I don't need to guess at what caused their reactions. Not when I can *feel* it. The demon staring at the back of my head and shoulders is very, very old. Six months ago, this attention would have sent me to the ground. The burning sensation, the scalding-hot scrape against my skin. Now, after living and training with Erebus in his Shadow King form, Mikael's attention feels more infuriating than dangerous. Like something I could crush in my hand.

I mouth a silent message to Zoe and Mariah: "Go. Find you later."

Zoe tugs on Mariah's elbow, leading the other girl toward the exit. Whoever Mariah is, she's a quick learner; she lets Zoe guide her away without risking a second look at the demon at my back. When Zoe passes our old table, she drops my overnight bag on a chair without stopping, leaving it there for me to retrieve on my own later.

As I stand, Nick rises with me. We do not turn around. Our eyes meet, and even though neither of us has turned to acknowledge our host, I can tell Nick is aware of who is watching us. Somehow, Nick *knows*.

We make it a single step.

"You must be Benedict and Iris."

We pivot together.

Nick speaks first. "That's us." He intercepts Mikael's handshake, even angling his body slightly so that Mikael can't get a full view of me. I'm relieved of Mikael's attention and grateful that Nick seems to know that demon attention is a physical sensation for me. Or maybe he just knows that, since I'm the Scion of Arthur—and the person who knocked out one of Mikael's guards—I'm the exact person that our host shouldn't spend too much time engaging with.

"Congratulations are in order," he says, "on your upcoming nuptials."

When Mikael's gaze lands on me, my skin erupts in stinging sparks. Up close, I see that his eyes are a warm honey brown instead of deep goruchel red. Contacts, maybe? When he grins, I wonder if his canines have been filed down to their nearly human length. Then, that stinging electricity from before zips down my skull. I smile, but it takes effort. "Thank you."

Nick runs a hand through his hair, appearing for all to see like a distracted mini mogul. He glances over his shoulder. "So, putting us up for a full weekend? Nice of you."

"The least I can do after putting you through a dreadful evening."

The sensation at the back of my skull rises again, zapping up and down my spine. His magic, whatever it is, is wound between his words. I step out from behind Nick. "Kind of exciting, if you ask me."

Mikael beams at me. "What a gem you are," he says. His eyes flit back to Nick. "I'm so happy that the two of you are staying. Communions will take place over the next few days, but they will be painless, I assure you."

"Communions?" Nick asks. "As in . . . a religious thing? I'm not sure we're comfortable with—"

"No, no, goodness me, nothing religious." Mikael waves a hand. "These are lowercase 'c' communions. Intimate conversations that promote fellowship and trust. Our way of ensuring that everyone present has been identified as a trustworthy participant through a guided discussion."

Nick's smile doesn't budge. "Sounds kind of like an interrogation."

"You are new to our community, so I understand your confusion. Since neither our thief nor our assailant has been captured and the premises have been secured by guards and barriers since the beginning of the evening, we can only assume that our two suspects are here at the event. Perhaps even working together." His eyes darken ever so slightly. "If I allow these insults to me *and* my property to go uninvestigated and unpunished, I'm sure you can imagine how that would tarnish not only the reputation of these exclusive events but the credibility of my business as a whole worldwide."

"Even the suggestion of weakness can spread like poison," Nick says.

"Exactly."

So this is what Erebus meant when he said that Mikael had become taken with humanity and its vices. For all that Erebus has done, he has never seemed hungry for this type of worldly power. *This* type of devotion and praise. This is a demon who wants to be king and who is clawing his way there, one mind trick and one black-market deal at a time. An aspiring king who creates a kingdom just so he can rule it. *Just like Arthur, the Order, and the Regents,* a quiet part of me whispers.

Nick turns to me. "That makes sense, doesn't it, honey?"

"Perfect sense," I say with a nod.

"I'm so glad you both understand," Mikael says. He holds an arm out to gesture toward the line at the door. "Bianca and her team will be here to ensure you have a wonderful stay."

"You won't be here to host us?" I ask innocently.

Mikael is obviously pleased that I've asked after him. "I will see you both for communions and then on Sunday evening, of course, for our rescheduled auction. Please, enjoy my property."

"Cool," Nick says. Bro face is fully on, and I'm thankful for the shield of it. For the glazed look it inspires in Mikael's eyes and the eagerness with which he walks away from us to speak to other guests lingering to meet him.

Before we approach Bianca, Nick pulls me to one of the tall windows facing the front lawn. He brings his mouth close to my ear and pitches his voice low. "Look."

I follow his gaze through the glass. There, just wrapping around the edge of the property, is a freshly cast, shimmering green ward. "No."

"Yes," he mutters. "An affective ward that looks pretty brutal from here. Mikael must have cast it while we were all figuring out which identity we wanted to play with."

"I can break it."

He looks at me. "You can break wards?"

"Yes," I say.

"He'll notice or his warlocks will," Nick replies. "Take us down before we get far. We're in the middle of nowhere, and all the taxis and rideshares have already left."

"So what do we do?" I ask.

"Nothing we *can* do. We're trapped. We need to be Benedict and Iris like our lives depend on it, because they do."

When we join Bianca's line, our masks are back in place, even though my heart is thundering in my ears with the echoes of Nick's warning. I check my root furnace again and again, even though I know it's sealed shut.

Finally, it's our turn. "Hello, Benedict and Iris," Bianca greets us, and pulls out a tablet with a map of the house.

As Nick makes small talk with Bianca, I glance over my shoulder only to see Mikael gone again and waiters removing the dirty linens from the round tables, breaking down the room for the night.

"You'll be on the third floor," Bianca's saying, swiping through what must be a hastily scribbled list on the tablet. A list that must now match the guests' names to the dozens of bedrooms across Penumbra's four floors. "In the Chambord Suite."

"Excuse me?" I ask, more sharply than I intended to.

Nick's voice is tight when he replies. "She said we'll be staying in the Chambord Suite, babe."

I glare at him, but his gaze is fixed on Bianca's tablet. No doubt imagining all the reasons he doesn't want to be forced to be in such close proximity to me—much less sleep in the same room—for the next three days. I can only imagine how much of a wrench this must be in whatever mission he and Ava came here to complete.

He's so frustrated—or disgusted—at the prospect of being attached to me that he won't even look me in the eye.

I flush, my own frustration and fury rising behind my clenched teeth. "I see." I turn back to Bianca and give her what I hope looks like a grateful smile. "Sounds lovely."

37

A WARLOCK ESCORTS us to our room, leading us up a flight of stairs until we reach the center of a long hallway lit by antique crystal chandeliers. Nick strolls in front of me with his hands in both pockets while I trail behind with my small bag.

I'm not sure how I'll find Zoe, but I know I need to speak with her, and *soon*. Then again, Erebus is the one who told us to pack bags in case the rules changed. And the rules have *definitely* changed.

When we arrive at a door with a plaque that reads THE CHAMBORD SUITE, Nick stops the warlock to ask about the clothing Mikael said he'd provide. Bianca had asked for our clothing sizes, but that doesn't mean we'll have things that fit us tonight.

"Expect garment deliveries in the morning. The basics are already inside" is all the warlock says before handing Nick an antique bronze key. When he walks away down the hall, Nick hands the key to me.

"Why are you giving me this?"

"Because there's only one key, and I don't want you to feel beholden to me."

"Oh," I mumble. "But why would I—"

Nick turns back to me. "I have to play the obnoxious, overbearing fiancé in front of our hosts. I know more about our history than you do. I shouldn't also control when and how you come and go from your only refuge over the next three days."

I take his comment in for a beat, closing my hand over the key. "Thank you. But we can share it. If you need it, I'll give it to you and vice versa."

"Okay," he says.

After I open the door, Nick searches the wall for a light switch. When he finally finds and flips it, four standing lamps around the room light up simultaneously—and I can't stifle my gasp.

Downstairs, I'd thought that the ballroom and foyer and hallways were overly ornate. The bedroom puts them all to shame.

The suite we've been assigned is large enough to include its own spacious sitting area near the door, complete with a deep-green upholstered chaise lounge, two tall-backed chairs, and a marble-inlaid coffee table on a large rug in front of a black iron fireplace. The damask-patterned wallpaper turns the enormous room with its tall ceilings and wide-planked hardwood floors into a warm red-and-brown Gilded Age cocoon. The furnishings and upholstery are all covered in soft materials like silk, chintz, and velvet.

As the warlock said, a small pile of folded pajamas with drawstrings sits on a low dresser beneath a heavy gold-framed mirror. Those clothes can't possibly be perfect fits, but I'll be glad to get out of my dress and heels.

"Great," Nick says, shaking his head. "Juuust great."

"What?" I ask—then follow the direction of his gaze.

Deeper in the room, set on a separate raised platform, is a single large, curtained four-poster king bed.

"Oh."

He assesses the chaise quickly. "Guess that'll have to do."

"What will have to do?"

He jerks his chin to the chaise. "I'll sleep there. It's fine."

"That is comically inaccurate. It's barely six feet long, and you're . . ." I look at the lounge skeptically, then gesture up and down at his—well, his all of him. "A walking tree. Like a redwood. Huge for no reason."

He turns back with a twisted frown. "I'm not that tall."

"Have you *seen* you?" I exclaim. "You're a *giant*."

"A giant."

"Enormous."

"Enormous?" He crosses his arms. "Relative to what?"

"Relative to . . . everything," I sputter. "Including that lounge."

Nick rolls his eyes and walks farther into the suite, attention fixed on the windows. "We have more critical concerns than how enormous I am. Starting with securing this room—don't say or do anything unexplainable by science until I clear it."

"Clear it for what?"

He gives me a pointed look. "Bugs. Cameras. Any recording device that might give Mikael dirt on his Collectors. This house might be over a century old and purposefully designed to appear as it did in the early 1900s when it was built, but Mikael would be foolish not to use modern security measures— especially since his guards are humans or warlocks. I know his type; they want information. Secrets. Leverage on anyone and anything." He takes his tuxedo jacket off and tosses it onto the window seat, then gets to work on his dress shirt sleeves, unbuttoning one before rolling it up over a muscled forearm. "Give me twenty or thirty minutes. . . ."

I watch Nick roll his second sleeve up for reasons I choose not to examine too closely, then turn away to let him inspect the rest of the room. His dis-carded jacket reminds me that we're both still in uncomfortable formal wear. I tug my mask up and over my curls. At this point, I have every reason to believe that Nick knows what I look like; exposing my full face to him inside this room is the least of my worries.

I take a second look at our surroundings myself, since it looks like we're going to be here awhile. The tray ceiling overhead is painted with a stormy seascape set ablaze with the bright wash of a blush-and-blue sunset, and thick, gilded crown moldings create a border where the walls meet the painting. To our right, there's a paneled door leading to what I assume is a small en suite bathroom.

I walk through the room while Nick searches for whatever he's hoping to discover and find myself touching everything, just to feel the textures beneath my fingers. Every item looks like an antique, but there's very little antique smell, very little of the dusty scent of age and wear one might find in a historic home. There are light switches everywhere, lamps that may have run on gas in the past but are electric now, and modern water pipes in the sink and shower. Mikael, it seems, likes this period of time but enjoys the updated luxuries of the twenty-first century.

Nick works through the room for a long time without speaking. I end up standing at the back windows that stretch nearly from one end of the suite to the other, bordered by twenty-foot-long floor-to-ceiling navy curtains that match the color of the seascape painting overhead. A seat stretches the full length of the window, topped by a tufted cushion.

We have a view of the maze in the rear of the property, although the hedges are so high, I'm not sure I could navigate it even visually from this angle.

As I gaze out the window, a pang of worry for Zoe—and Mariah—circles up from my stomach to my throat. Zoe can handle herself just fine, but she won't do well if she's not able to contact Elijah and tell him what's happened so her brother can report back to Erebus. Without her phone, we have no way to communicate with either Elijah or Erebus. No way to let them know that we're still in the mission, even if said mission has taken several completely unexpected turns.

On the other hand, maybe it's best that Zoe *can't* contact them. I'm not sure what Erebus would do if he found out that the very first mission he sent me on as his protégé resulted in me running—or fighting—right into the arms of a Legendborn.

I don't know how Mariah knows me, but I wonder if she's one of the Root-crafters I used to spend time with. I can't place names and faces together, but I know there were several women in my life who I trusted and who trusted me. It would be just my luck if Mariah was one of the 'Crafters who witnessed the destruction I brought to Volition . . . but the look in her eyes when she saw me in the hall outside the ballroom wasn't one of judgment or anger. It was hope— and triumph. Like she'd been looking for me. Like she'd *found* me.

A girl missing, a girl recovered. I am the first, but not the second. Just like the Rootcrafter girls the King takes. I remember the scent of root that lingered around him when he returned home and, not for the first time, imagine him feeding on one of those girls until her power snaps in half. What's the point of becoming untouchable and unstoppable and impervious if I can't use my own power to save others? After seeing Mikael and his followers use their riches for such frivolous and self-serving ends, the idea of using what I've gained solely on myself feels . . . uncomfortable. Like a shoe that doesn't fit. Dress-up doll clothes that I could never live in, given to me by a demon.

My forehead thunks against the cold glass window as I spiral deeper in thought. If Zoe and I can steal the King's crown from Mikael like we've planned, then our secret, shared mission to stop the King from hurting Rootcrafters will be one step closer to being complete. As for my personal mission, well. Killing my mentor one day will be harder if the crown eliminates his weakness. Then again, it was never going to be easy.

But now that I know just how closely we're being watched, I don't see how we *can* make another attempt to steal the crown without risking our lives. Mikael had the auction items moved to a secure location after tonight's attempts, making Elijah's maps and instructions useless.

Nick is right. I need to prioritize more "critical concerns" at the moment. The true dangers of Penumbra, the Collectors and their easy violence, could get us killed before Sunday's auction. We need to make it through the weekend. Just three days.

There's no way in hell I can be around you for that long.

"Found a camera." Nick's voice interrupts me.

When I look back, I find him standing in the center of the room holding a small round black box. As I walk closer to examine it, his hand erupts in faint silver-blue aether, coating his palm in a glove of magic. He squeezes the camera in his dimly glowing fist, crushing it into plastic dust. He brushes his palms off while talking, brow furrowed in thought. "If Mikael has one of these in every room, it's unlikely they're being monitored all at once. And, with this crowd, I doubt we're the only guests who are sweeping for bugs. He'll expect to lose some of the feeds—"

"You're a Scion," I gasp.

Nick looks up at me, and recognition sparks in his eyes as they trail over my facial features, exposed in full for the first time. He may not be a cambion or a demon, but I very nearly sense it when his gaze lingers on my mouth, my brow, my cheekbones. "So are you."

"Which one?" I ask.

Instead of answering me directly, Nick clenches his fist, sending the shining glow of aether rippling up his wrist, building gauntlets around his forearms, and streaming to his shoulders. It builds in layers upon layers, slowly, forming a breastplate and pauldrons. As I watch, he forges two shining swords into existence, their blades gleaming in the center of the suite. When I meet his gaze through the sparks and swirling smoke of his magic, I'm struck by the mixture of emotions that cross his face. Determination, focus . . . and regret.

"Lancelot," I whisper. "You're the Scion of Lancelot."

He releases his fists, and the weapons and armor fall away. Glowing bits of shining metal fall into the thick navy-and-gold woven rug at his feet. He pulls his mask away and runs a hand through his hair with a sigh. "Yes."

I'm not prepared for the moment when I finally see Nick's face in full. I find myself stumbling close to him, my feet sending the remnants of silver-blue aether swirling up and around my ankles as I go, until we are only a foot apart. He lets me study him, taking in the totality of his features and how familiar he feels even when I don't know all of him.

I know that the Scion of Lancelot of the Southern Chapter was raised to believe he was the Scion of Arthur—and that when I pulled Excalibur from its stone, I realigned not only my destiny, but his.

My hand drifts up, palm seeking his jaw and cheek—but he catches my wrist before I can make contact. "Stop."

I blink, flushing. "Sorry. I—"

"It's—" His fingers are tight around my wrist, nearly painful . . . but they're also trembling. And we both notice it at the same time. He releases me with a gasp. Drops his hands. Steps back without finishing his sentence. "Just—don't."

His mouth twists, and the cords in his neck draw tight, pulling my heart with them. I only just found him, someone from my past. But why does it feel like I've lost him all over again? Nick is standing right in front of me, whole and real and alive, but why does he feel more like the gray mist than ever? I barely recognize my own voice when I reply, "Okay."

The tension flows out of his shoulders, telling me more about his feelings toward kissing me than his words ever could. *It won't happen again.* It's not just that he won't kiss me again—he won't touch me again either. He doesn't *want* to, and I have to respect that. *You weren't supposed to be here. An hour or two, I could handle. But three days?*

I step backward—an experiment—and the rigid line of his neck loosens immediately. His breath comes easier.

And yet I could cry. I look away to hide my disappointment. I shouldn't feel rejected by someone I just met. It's ridiculous. Selfish. And devastating for no good reason.

Nick's voice draws me back. "You really don't recognize me, do you?"

"No." Still, I examine his face once more, taking each of his features in one at a time, further. Just as I go to shake my head, a faint *snap* in my mind makes my eyelids flutter in pain.

"Bree?"

The stinging pain dissipates, replaced with a single emotion: longing.

"It was you," I whisper.

"What was—?"

"*You* chased after me," I manage to say. "*You* tried to stop me from leaving."

Nick grows still. "Yes."

I shake my head. "I knew a boy had come after me, but I didn't know his name or what he looked like. Didn't know it was . . . you."

Didn't know you *were who I longed for.*

Nick swipes his tongue across his lip. "Why did you connect that boy to me now and not earlier? We touched before. We . . ."

"We did more than touch," I murmur, flushing.

"I'm aware." His eyes narrow as he looks me over. "But why now?"

"I don't know how it works. Maybe because I saw your face, fully?"

He looks down at his mask, clenching it in his hands. "Do you know anything else about me?"

How can I tell him that I missed him when I didn't know him? I can't. How do I explain the clear resonant bell of my own longing? I don't. "No."

Nick looks like he might ask me another question.

"What?"

"With so much missing," he begins cautiously, "I assume that you don't know who or where Sel is?"

My fingers spasm at my sides as I make a leap that, in truth, doesn't feel like a leap at all. "Is he the Kingsmage? Yours from . . . before?"

Before either of you knew that you weren't the Scion of Arthur, and I was.

"Yes." Nick nods. "Selwyn."

My chest tightens. "I knew there was a Merlin boy who . . ."

"A Merlin boy who what?"

"Who sacrificed himself for me." I release a rushed breath. "When I think of him, I feel guilty. So, *so* guilty."

Nick's face softens. "I don't think he'd want you to feel that way."

"That's not how guilt works," I snap.

"You're right."

"I was told that he's . . . he's gone?"

Nick shakes his head slowly. "No. He's not gone."

"How do you know?" I ask. "Through the Kingsmage bond?"

"Not the bond." He taps his chest. "I feel him. Here. Don't you?"

I close my eyes and inhale, imagining this Merlin, this Kingsmage, even if I don't know what he looks like or know his voice. I remember the hope I felt rise within me outside of Erebus's training warehouse, and how easily I'd assigned it to him. To Selwyn. When I open my eyes, Nick is watching me.

Waiting. Knowing my answer before I speak it aloud. "Yes."

I see the questions in his eyes. They're piling up every time he looks at me. "Then that's where we'll hold him until we find him."

Before I can ask him about this boy who we both know, my bloodmark pulses once—illuminating the room in bright, furious crimson. Nick's at my side in a blink, eyes wide. "Your bloodmark?"

I wince, turning my head away from the glow and the charred spice scent. The King is angry. I wonder if he's somehow found out about the rules changing at Mikael's. He'll have to adapt, just like me and Zoe. "You know about my bloodmark?"

"Yeah." Nick's eyes follow the branching shape of it across my collarbone, down my sternum and both arms. "I know an ancient demon marked your ancestor and what it does . . . but I've never seen it light up like this. Does it hurt?"

"*This* is a fun new feature," I say dryly. "It's a call. And, no, it doesn't hurt."

"A call?" His eyes snap to mine. "The way we call aether?"

I nod. "Except it's—" I break off, stopping myself before I say too much.

But Nick is quick. "It's him, isn't it? The demon who took you."

It's not my fault that the Shadow King marked my ancestor. It's not my fault that he chooses to call on my power like this, but right now, I feel ashamed about the mark in a way that I never have before. "Yes."

The mark begins to fade, the red glimmer growing smaller in Nick's watchful eyes. He is silent as it disappears and still when it leaves nothing behind but unbroken, smooth brown skin. He looks up at me then. "Can he locate you through his mark?"

I shake my head weakly. "It's his way of checking on my power. Gauging how strong I've become under his training. And . . . reminding me that my power is his to consume."

I wait for Nick's judgment about my choosing to go with the demon who marked my bloodline, for his interrogation about why I left in the first place. But instead, Nick sighs. "Well, the thing about making people like us stronger is that, given enough freedom, we'll find a way to use that strength against the very assholes who wish to control it." His eyes pin me. "Right?"

My heart blooms beneath his gaze. "Right."

Knock. Knock.

Both of us whip around at the deep sound of a knuckle against wood.

Knock. Knock.

We exchange glances. Nick sets the index finger of one hand against his lips while pointing to the wall in the corner by the four-poster bed. I roll my eyes. Obviously, I'll be quiet—I've been living with demons for the past four months. I make an effort to put every layer of my annoyance into my expression, and it must work, because he shoots me a sardonic look back before he moves closer to the bed. I nod and follow, extending my palms to my sides to call root if necessary.

Nick reaches the wall before I do, leaning closer just as a voice whispers harshly from the other side, "Iris and Benedict?"

My face breaks open into a wide smile. "Zoe."

38

A LONG, PREVIOUSLY invisible vertical line splits down the wall near the nightstand. A second later, a rectangular-shaped panel creaks open—and out steps Zoe, maskless, covered in dust, wearing a pajama set that looks a lot like the clothing left on our dresser.

"Ugh!" she grumbles. "This is nasty! Spiderwebs *everywhere*."

Nick and I step back as a plume of dust follows her into the room, sweeping across the floor and into both our faces. Nick coughs, waving his hand to clear the cloud. "I didn't know our room came with a secret passageway."

"Neither did I," I mutter. "Zoe, are you okay—"

Zoe blurs through the dust, wrapping her arms around me. "I should be asking you that. I felt your aether and followed it here through these abandoned service hallways." I squeeze her back, surprised and delighted at the show of affection—especially in front of a stranger.

"Your . . . aether?" Nick asks me.

I twist around to meet his curious gaze. He knows that's not what I call the red power that flares from my chest. I turn back to Zoe. "How'd you find this passage in the first place?"

"Elijah's map," Zoe says, shrugging as she lets me go. "It was on a slide. Did you miss that part of his presentation?"

"Probably."

She shifts gears. "Did Mikael get you earlier?"

"'Get' me?"

"Yeah," she says, wiggling her fingers. "Use his weirdo magic on you?"

"Yes!" I exclaim, grateful that someone else picked up on it. "I felt it twice in the ballroom, but couldn't figure it out."

"Same," she says. "Felt weak."

"Because it's an illusion," Nick answers. "A thin one, spread widely enough to alter the perception of a room full of humans, but not targeted enough to change a memory or go undetected by magic users."

"How do you know that?" Zoe asks suspiciously.

"Is that how he made them all watch that man die?" I whisper. "He mesmered them?"

They grow quiet. Nick doesn't reply at all, but after a moment, Zoe does.

"Demons can't mesmer," Zoe remarks. "Only Merlins can do that."

It's a swift correction—too swift. Nick looks at Zoe. "How exactly do you know what Merlins can do?"

Zoe crosses her arms. "I know things."

"That's evident," Nick replies easily, "but not what I asked."

Zoe's eyes slide to mine. "I think we're all gonna need to have a little chat here, don't you?" She jerks her chin at one of the brass candleholders on the fireplace mantel. "Grab one of those and some matches."

Ten minutes and a very dusty, dark journey through a forgotten corridor later, the three of us emerge into an even dustier space—but one that is far more beautiful, even in disuse.

"A library?" I breathe, eyes drawn upward to the enormous library and its towering shelves of ancient books. An antique grandfather clock stands in the corner, showing that it's close to midnight now.

"A hidden, *abandoned* library," a new voice says. "And Zoe already swept it for cameras and things, so we're safe to talk here."

Sitting in the middle of the room, perched on a square desk, is Mariah, holding a lit antique brass candlestick of her own. She's also changed into a set of loose gray pajamas, and her braids are pulled up and back into a ponytail. As I approach, she leans forward into a murky slant of moonlight spilling into the dusty room from the windows on our right. It's the first time I see her face without a mask covering her eyes and nose. I study her face, but recognition never comes.

"God, it's so good to see you, Bree!" She hops off the table to greet me. Her voice is so relieved and joyful that I feel desperate to know her—or know her again. I dig deep for the resonant emotion I must have retained about this girl, but unlike my moment with Nick, her face doesn't surface a distinct feeling. Not yet, anyway. When Mariah folds me in a warm, solid hug, I brace myself, but find that her embrace does not feel like judgment. Instead, it makes me feel . . . grounded. Loved. So very missed. I hug her back and she mutters into my shoulder, "We've been looking for you everywhere, Bree-Bree. You don't even know. We thought—we thought the worst."

"Bree-Bree?" I choke out a laugh. A nickname. Not only did I not know Mariah's name, but I didn't know one of my own.

"That's what I call you." Mariah passes a soft hand over my curls. "Zoe told me what happened to your mind. The missing people. Said a demon did it?"

I can imagine the story Zoe's spun—a mysterious demon who took my people away as punishment or revenge. "Yeah," I mutter.

"Was it the Hunter?" Mariah's brows pinch. "Is he the one who took you?"

That grounded love feeling is swept away by something sharper—guilt. "Not exactly."

She frowns. "But that's what he does. He takes people. Us, especially." She gives me another look. "Doesn't tend to let them go, though. What happened?"

I swallow thickly. "I . . ." *I don't know? I can't tell anymore? Where do I start?*

Mariah's eyes narrow. "Bree——"

"This library is incredible." Nick comes to stand beside me, looking past Mariah into a shadowy corner. "There's even a ladder," he says, pointing to a dusty ladder perched on a copper railing in the corner. "Old-school. How did you find it?"

I can't shake the feeling that Nick just rescued me from a conversation that he knew I wasn't ready to have.

"Again, *I* paid attention to the presentation." Zoe slides by me to perch on the table Mariah vacated and turns to the other girl. "Bree's mind wanders off half the time anyone talks to her for more than twenty minutes."

Mariah looks between us, curious. "I'm not sure I'd make it through a Power-Point about this place either."

"She's cool," Zoe says, jerking a thumb at Mariah. "Did you know she's a Rootcrafter? She figured me out right away."

Mariah and I make eye contact. Zoe doesn't know that I'm a Rootcrafter. Doesn't know I'm a Bloodcrafter. Doesn't know I'm Legendborn—and whose title I used to hold. "Oh yeah?" I ask.

Zoe nods. "Mariah spotted me quick because she knows balanced cambions."

"I know *a* balanced cambion," Mariah corrects, nervous for the first time since I've met her—or met her again. "One. And honestly, you aren't obvious," she adds, tugging absentmindedly at the necklace beneath her shirt, "I just . . . have a knack for it."

Even though she's changed out of her formal clothes, she's still wearing that piece of jewelry. I wonder if it's something meaningful to her, like my charm bracelet or my Pendragon necklace, but when she catches me staring too long, she drops her hand and looks away. Guess everyone has their secrets.

"Would this balanced cambion you know happen to be Valechaz the broker?" Nick asks Mariah.

Mariah startles. "How do you know Valec?"

Nick holds his hands up. "I only know *of* him. We've never met."

"Who's Valec?" Zoe leans closer to me, whispering, "Do *you* know Valec?"

"No."

"Yes," Nick says with a sigh, "you do."

I blink at him. "I *do?*"

Nick rubs a hand down his face. "According to William and Lark, you do."

"You know *William?*" Mariah asks Nick, wide-eyed.

"Oh my GOD! Who *are* all these people?" Zoe hops off the table, pulling me across the room, away from the others. "This was fun while it lasted, but it's legit bonkers, Bree. We need to get out of here. Now."

I hesitate. "How?"

Her eyes go to the dust-covered windows beside an empty table. "We're on the third floor. I could make that jump. So could you." She pauses. "Probably."

"There's a ward around Penumbra. Even if we could leave, Bianca has already identified us. She'll make sure Mikael knows we've left. He'll track us down. We're *in* it now, Zoe. We can't leave until this is over."

Zoe blinks. "You think we can get the crown before the auction on Sunday?"

"You heard him; it's been moved to a different location already. Somewhere more secure. The auction is the only time it's going to be exposed and ready to be moved with the winner. If we don't get it then, what're the chances we'll ever find it again?"

She gnaws at her lip. "That's three days from now in the house of a Night-shade. If something happens to you . . ." Then Elijah will lose his place with the King. *In one way or another.* My heart flips, torn between the danger to someone I know and the danger to someone I don't. I should be able to help them all. Keep them all away from harm.

"Nothing's going to happen to Bree," Nick interjects, voice traveling across the room.

Zoe's head perks up. "You sound real confident about that, white boy."

Nick's mouth quirks. "I am."

Zoe's eyes flash to glowing red in the darkness—a deliberate move, meant to intimidate.

Nick only smiles. "Nice light show. Not enough to scare *me*, unfortunately, but it might work on someone else."

Zoe steps around me, mouth open in a snarl. "Oh, I'm not trying to scare you, Boy Scout. Not yet."

Nick grins again. "You'll have to let me know when you get started; I might not notice otherwise."

Zoe growls low in her throat, and I grasp her arm. "Stop. We came here to talk, not fight."

"How do you know him, anyway?" Zoe turns to me. "He one of your missing people?"

I turn back to Nick, who's watching me closely. "Yes. He's one of mine."

Nick dips his chin. "Nice to meet you, Zoe. I'm Nick."

Zoe glares at him, but her eyes flash back to brown. "What's up with you and that angry girl, Nick? She your real fiancée?"

"No," Nick replies. "Ava and I have . . . an arrangement." He doesn't look at me when he answers, and a cold, hard stone drops in my belly. So there *is* something between them. Is that same *something* the reason he stopped me from touching him earlier? My lips tingle as I recall what Nick said about our kisses: *a distraction . . . It won't happen again.* But then, *We've kissed enough that I know how you like to be kissed.*

"'An arrangement'?" Zoe says, fingers raised in air quotes. "That sounds a lot like a bargain or a promise—and it sounds sketchy as hell."

"So does the guy you and Bree live with," Nick drawls.

"You told him who we live with?" Zoe asks me.

"He's good at guessing things. And we need to get *some* details out in the open if we're gonna make it out of here alive."

Zoe spreads her hands. "Fine. I'll follow your lead." Confusion strikes. Zoe, of all people, handing the reins over to me?

"You sure about that?"

She shrugs. "I trust you."

I look at the three of them and see the trust in me in their eyes. I don't think I deserve it, but there's no use in fighting them at the moment.

"Okay. We have three days before the auction. We're surrounded by dozens of warlock guards wielding unknown demon abilities and embedded with at least *some* of the richest, most immoral humans on the planet, in a house owned by a Nightshade with a mass-manipulation power. If we're going to make it out of this alive, we're going to need to work together. Be as honest as we can be." I look at Mariah and Nick. "I know why Zoe and I came here tonight, but I don't know why you both are here—and I'm assuming no one has seen Ava since the announcement."

Everyone shakes their head.

"Why was Ava so mad at me?" I ask.

Nick clears his throat. "Ava isn't mad at you. Ava wants to kill you."

I blink. "Oh."

"Why would Ava want to kill her?" Zoe asks.

"Ava is the leader of the Morgaines," Nick says quietly. "A sect of rogue magic users."

"So?" Zoe says. "What's that got to do with Bree?"

Nick and Mariah both turn to me, their eyes solemn. Because even though I just said we need to be honest with one another, honesty only goes so far when it comes to *my* identity, and they've both already guessed that Zoe doesn't know who I am. They know the truth—but they also know it's not their place to tell it.

Zoe looks at the three of us. "Um, anyone gonna answer my question? I thought we were gonna be all honest with each other or whatever."

My heart pounds in my chest, and Zoe tilts her head, listening. "What's wrong with you?"

I release a slow breath and meet Nick's eyes again. His face is expressionless. He has his own opinion about what I should do, but he's deferring to me. Trusting my instinct here.

I turn to Zoe, feeling my brows pinch together as I search for the words. "I remember what happened to me, but the people in those memories are gone, right?"

She nods slowly. "Yeah, I know."

"But even with all of that gone, I know myself," I say, my voice growing stronger in the silence. "I know who I am."

Zoe shakes her head. "Yeah, I know. What's the . . . ?" Her eyes narrow. Turn hard. "What are you talking about? I know who you are too—"

"No, you don't," I say, turning to pace away, then back. "The old man . . . there's a reason he bloodmarked me, Zoe."

"For your power," she says. "He told us that on day one."

"It's not just my power," I say. "It's how my powers came to be. Who . . . who one of my ancestors is."

"Who's your ancestor?"

I close my eyes, shaking my head. "I . . ."

"It's okay, Bree," Nick murmurs. When I turn to him, I see my own pain, mirrored. This burden of Arthur, shared between us. The wounds of a king. The rejection of them—and of the king himself.

But I can't keep this secret anymore. I don't want to be the girl who is missing when I am finally standing with the people who missed me.

"Bree," Zoe asks. "Who are you?"

I meet Zoe's waiting, wary eyes. "The heir to a power I never wanted." I take a breath. Release it. "I am the Scion of Arthur."

A pained expression streaks across Zoe's face for a split second—before rage takes over.

She blurs into a leap straight toward me—and I am too stunned to move.

A flash of silver-blue light—and I'm shoved to the ground. The spark and screech of nails clawing down a construct. A yowling cry—

"These blades are razor-sharp and about a quarter inch from your jugulars." Nick's voice is calm and deadly above me. "All they need is a little push."

When I look up, I find Zoe's red eyes glaring down at me from between Nick's glowing aether swords. He is on one knee between us, arms up, holding the sharp edges of his blades in a tight cross beneath her throat. "You're lying!" she shouts at me, panting with fury.

"I'm not. I mean—I *did*. I had to," I stammer. "You and Elijah would have killed me that first day if you knew!"

"You don't know that!"

"Zoe!" I cry. "You're trying to kill me *now*!"

"I'm not trying to kill you because you're the Scion of Arthur!" she shouts. "I'm trying to kill you because you're a goddamned *liar*!"

I gape at her. Nick clears his throat. "For the record, I don't care why you're trying to kill Bree. I can't let you do it either way."

Zoe bares her teeth and blurs away from his blades, back to the middle of the room. "I don't believe you," she spits at me. "You're making this up."

Nick rises to both feet, blades still extended. "Then why did you attack her?"

"Prove it!" Zoe shouts.

"How do I prove this, Zoe?" I climb to my own feet, more confused than angry now.

"Call Arthur!"

"*No*, Bree," Nick says, voice like iron. "Don't—"

"Do it!" Zoe shouts. "Make him possess you or something! The old man told me and Elijah the Scion of Arthur can be possessed."

"I can't!" I cry.

"Why not?" Mariah asks from where she's pressed herself against the window.

"Just—not right now." I shake my head, too overwhelmed to talk about ancestral streams and blood walks. "I can do something else. I can prove it."

I wave Nick away. He hesitates, then backs off to the side without releasing his blades.

I extend a palm. Turn it open. It's been months since I've called aether like this. Months of ignoring it when I feel it around me in the air, invisible and ever present, my aether sense growing sharper and more sensitive every time I train with Erebus. I can pull on my own root with ease now, close it down without thinking, and grow it to constructs the size of this room. But touching Arthur's power feels . . . risky. Like somehow agreeing to seek his inheritance out, in particular, might invite all the strife and pain back into my life that drove me to leave the Legendborn in the first place. But even though it's been ages, the power to call aether is just there beneath my skin—and a ball of spinning silver-blue flames bursts into life within my hand.

It takes barely a thought to send that sphere into a blade handle. A rounded pommel. Diamond in the center. A wrapped handle. A longsword blade, wide and silver, with a blood groove straight down the middle. In a single breath, an exact aether replica of Excalibur comes to life in my palm. My shoulder dips with the familiar weight as my fingers tighten around the shining hilt.

When I look back at Zoe, her eyes are no longer red but brown—and fixed on the blade in my hand. "You lied to us."

"Nothing I said was a lie," I say. "Everything you heard me say was the truth."

Her laugh is short and sour. "Now you *really* sound like the old man."

I wince.

She comes closer, her words for my ears and no one else's. "Are you really here for the crown?" she asks. "Or for the girls?"

"They're one and the same," I whisper back.

"No, they're not," she hisses. "If the old man gets the crown, he'll tear your little Legendborn club apart—and you'll have helped. You okay with that?"

I swallow around a thick lump in my throat. "I have to be. They won't let me lead them, anyway."

She shakes her head, walking past me toward the hidden entrance in the wall, flipping her middle finger up as she goes. "I'm outta here."

"Zoe, can we please talk?"

"I don't want to talk to you."

I catch her arm at the passageway. "Are you going to blow our cover?"

She scoffs. "No." She looks down at the glowing blade in my hand. "And I'm not gonna hurt you. You get hurt, Elijah gets hurt, remember?"

"Yeah, I remember." When I release her, she disappears down the passageway in a cloud of dust.

I turn back to Mariah and Nick. At some point, he let his blades go to dust, and now he stands empty-handed. "I don't know . . . what to . . ." I shrug, helpless.

"Well, *I* came here to find you," Mariah says in the quiet of the night.

"What?"

She walks forward, arms wrapped around herself. "You wanted us all to be honest about what we're doing here, right? If we're gonna work together? Well, me and Valec put a plan together to find you, and his contact sent us here."

"You're here for me?"

"Why does that surprise you?" She studies my face carefully. "At first, we thought Sel would be with you too, but . . ." She shakes her head. "That turned out to be a dead end."

"I see," I whisper. I debate whether to tell her that Sel is with his mother, but don't know how to explain how he got there. Not when every truth here feels like a bomb. Every secret, a regret.

Mariah's mouth pulls downward. "There are things you don't know, but there are also things you aren't ready to talk about. I can see that now. So, rather than keep pushing you, I think I'm just going to go check on Zoe. Nobody needs to be alone in a place like this. Not when death is waiting around every corner and sitting at every table."

I thank her for checking on Zoe and then watch as she walks down the passageway with her small, tapered candle in hand.

Nick waits until Mariah's steps have receded into silence before he approaches me. "You're hardening aether from a gas to a solid, nearly skipping the flame state entirely. I've only seen Merlins cast and forge that quickly."

I look back at the blade, forgotten in my hand, and move to release it, but he catches the flat end of it with the tip of his finger first. Raises it to eye level to inspect it. "You forged your swords pretty fast too," I say.

His mouth quirks. "Perks of Lancelot." His eyes drift down my blade to its hilt. "The smoke I saw you leave behind in the basement isn't Legendborn casting, though. Or Merlin casting, for that matter." He looks back at me. "This 'old man' teach you that?"

I nod.

"Huh," he says idly, still looking at my weapon. "Can you release it just as fast?"

I drop the sword—and it dusts before it hits the ground.

He whistles low. "Impressive. Quick forge, quick release. That's handy in a war."

"We're stuck in a mansion for the next three days. We aren't at war."

"Aren't we?" He walks backward, hands loose in his pockets before he pivots to take the path back to our room.

39

I WAKE THE next morning to the sound of the shower running.

Nick must have gotten up before me, letting me sleep while he gets ready. When I look over at the chaise, I find the remnants of his attempts to make it comfortable—quilts and small embroidered pillows. I frown; he *couldn't* have gotten a good night's rest. If I'd seen him do all that, I would have—I flush, looking at the empty space in my own large bed.

My belly twists in a combination of curiosity and apprehension. How much do you have to know somebody to invite them to share a mostly empty bed? I flash back to the moment at dinner when he'd jerked away from even casual contact. Accidental contact would be even worse. Sleeping in the same bed is too risky, I decide. For him and for me.

I barely remember climbing up the one-step platform and crawling into the bed myself. The mattress beneath me is soft and thick, more an oversized cushion than the firm bed I'm used to at Erebus's house. It takes two attempts to sit up, and even then, I have to fight against the mountain of embroidered pillows against the headboard just to examine my surroundings in the daylight.

Not that there's much light in the room; the long, heavy curtains around the windows are drawn closed, blocking out much of the morning sun. Odd. They were open last night, the view of the maze in the back gardens visible from our window seat. Nick must have closed the curtains on the way to the bathroom this morning, to block the light and keep the room dim.

To let me sleep.

I don't need to know every person in my past life to know, on a deep level, that this is the type of quiet, thoughtful gesture that I have come to treasure more than ever since my mother died.

I let myself wonder, for a moment, what it would be like to feel this way all the time. A slow morning in bed, hair still in my satin bonnet. The muted *shhhh* sound of a shower running in the background. Too many pillows. The luxury of safety before the day begins. A knock at the door jerks me out of my vision— and reminds me that it is a fantasy.

I climb out of the bed with my heart kicking against my ribs, my eyes trained on the collection of weapons Nick has already stashed by the door—a large, heavy candlestick; a wrought iron poker and ash pan; a letter opener; a rock-solid marble bust about the length of my arm.

Smart boy.

There is no peephole, so when I reach the door, I call out instead, "Yes?"

The voice on the other side of the door sounds preoccupied. "Clothing service."

Right. Mikael is providing costumes so we can play make-believe in his grand mansion, when in truth we're captives in his dollhouse nightmare. I reach for my masquerade mask on a nearby table and slip it on before unlocking the door. My right hand curves behind my back, palm up and open with a tiny ball of root called to its center.

Like Nick said, we're at war here. I can't afford to be complacent.

When I open the door, a young man with messy curls wearing an ill-fitting suit greets me without looking up from the phone in his hand. "Delivery from Mr. Di Centa," he mumbles. If he's one of the estate's staff members, he doesn't seem very concerned about the etiquette so prized by his boss. Behind him is a cart with a dozen black garment bags, all labeled by yellow notes pinned to the top with names and room numbers scribbled across them. He pulls the cart forward, swinging it around closer to our door. "Clothing for the weekend for the newlyweds or whatever?"

"We're not married," I begin to say, then correct myself. "I mean, not yet—"

"Perfect timing." Nick's voice, raspy from disuse, comes from behind me.

As he approaches, he brings with him the expensive scents of PENUMBRA-labeled bath products. He must have dressed quickly; his masquerade mask sits across his nose but his hair is damp, still dripping on the collar of the same white button-down dress shirt he'd worn under last night's tuxedo. The top two buttons are left open, exposing the glistening skin of his throat and Adam's apple, while the shirt falls untucked over his tux pants and bare feet.

When he steps forward, his shoulder nearly brushes mine—and I jump back to avoid our collision. He shoots me a swift look with a clear message: *Relax.*

To our visitor, Nick says, "Thanks, we've been waiting for new fits."

I open the door wider so that he can join me at the threshold, then step out of sight while he talks to the staff member.

"Thanks again," Nick is saying as he pulls our bag down from the cart. The young man mumbles something unintelligible as he drags the cart down to the next door. Nick drapes our garment bag over one arm, then shuts and locks the door behind him before removing his mask to give me a stern look.

"What?"

He looks down at my hand pointedly. "You gonna put that out?"

Oh. I follow his gaze to my still-burning ball of root and curl my fingers inward, squeezing it until it disappears. "I didn't know who it was. Mikael said he won't be around during the day, so no one can sense my root but Zoe."

"That's fair, but . . ."

"But what?"

"Lemme think about how to phrase this." He strides past me toward the bed.

"Phrase *what*?" I toss my mask back on the table near the door and follow him through the cloud of annoyingly amazing scents still lingering on his skin.

He hooks the garment bag on one of the wooden crossbars of the bed and unzips it before answering, flipping quickly through the assortment of clothes on the hangers within. "Something that might sound indelicate."

I cross my arms. "I hate it already."

His mouth curves as he pulls out individual hangers of plastic-covered clothes and inspects the items before hanging them on the makeshift rod above. "Of course you do."

"What did they send?"

"Mostly gender-neutral styles, with a few other options thrown in. Some more formal than others, suits and dresses mixed in with slacks and sweaters. All seem to be in one of the two sizes we gave Bianca last night. Everything still has the tags. And something tells me each guest gets a unique selection so that no one has to suffer the embarrassment of 'who wore it better?'" He stands back. "How does Mikael work this fast? A weekend wardrobe for a hundred people?"

"Have you seen him? All the fancy outfits and the filed-down fangs to fit in? He's demonic Gatsby, remember? It's all a show," I murmur, lifting up the plastic around a few pieces to examine the fabrics. "That Shade probably has his claws in clothing stores all over the country."

"Greed loves its pomp and circumstance," Nick mutters, rubbing at his neck and wincing.

"Let me guess, you woke up pretzel-shaped because you tried to sleep on the fancy half couch?"

He grimaces. "It wasn't . . . the most comfortable."

I gnaw at my lip. "If there's a fight, you'll be better off if you're rested. This bed is huge. You can—"

"I'll be fine," he interrupts. He turns to walk along the raised platform and, to my surprise, sits on the very end of the bed and pats the empty space beside him. "Come here."

I raise a brow. "Why?"

He rolls his eyes. "Just come here."

I walk slowly along the platform around the bed until I reach him, but stand in front of him rather than sit down.

"Stubborn girl," he mutters.

"Is this when you say the indelicate thing?"

"Yep." He sighs. "We need to practice touching each other."

I blink. "Excuse me?"

"You heard me," he says. "You leapt out of your skin at a delivery guy."

"He could be a warlock."

His expression turns wry. "Like you can't handle a warlock."

His easy praise hangs in the air between us, until I headshake it away. "Your point?"

"My point is, you didn't get startled because of him," he says. "You got startled because you thought I was going to touch you, and we can't do that this weekend. We're supposed to be engaged. We need to *act* like we're engaged if we're gonna stay off Bianca's and Mikael's and the Collectors' radars. We're new here. When it comes to violations of 'discretion and truth,' if we aren't prime suspects already, we will be." He jerks his chin at the door. "That kid *looked* distracted, but he was observing us. Taking notes on his phone. Did you see that?"

I flush. "No."

"Ava says this is a well-known community of buyers. Under the fancy masquerade masks, the Collectors are corrupt politicians, greedy CEOs, and self-serving dignitaries, just to name a few. There are killers here, Bree. I can feel it. Wicked human beings with a lot to lose who won't hesitate to do what it takes to preserve their interests and favorite pastimes. Which not only include collecting shit that doesn't belong to them, but—"

"Murdering their own, for sport and entertainment," I murmur, remembering the easy way Eric went to his own death, and the easy way his 'community' witnessed it. A part of me still hopes that Mikael's mass mesmer is somehow at the root of the Collectors' behavior before dinner, but that hope is dwindling. "You're right. But . . ."

"You don't know me," he says.

"It's not just that," I reply. "You don't *want* me to touch you, remember?"

The muscle in his jaw ticks. "Accurate enough."

I cross my arms. "So what do we do?"

He holds out his hand. "We start slow."

I extend a hesitant palm to him, but to my surprise, Nick doesn't take it—instead, he wraps his fingers around my pajama-covered forearm. Still, I jump slightly. Can't help it.

"Easy . . ."

"S-sorry," I stammer.

"You're fine." When I nod for him to continue, Nick tugs me forward until I'm standing between his knees. When he looks up at me, his hair falls into his eyes. I resist the urge to sweep it away—and breathe a silent sigh of relief when he does it himself before I can. "Okay?"

I nod. "Yeah."

His other hand finds my elbow, cupping it through the fabric with his palm—and I don't jump. "And this?"

"'M good."

Nick stands in slow increments, giving me plenty of time to move away. As he rises, his torso presses close first, brushing against me before he straightens. When he stops moving, I take a deep breath—and look up.

His damp hair is starting to dry, the ends lifting and curling. If I wasn't standing so close to him, I wouldn't have noticed the quick rise of his chest as he inhales. The rapid pulse beneath his jaw. The faint blond stubble at his throat. The pine-and-cypress scent of his shampoo, deep woods on a spring morning. An ember sparks in my belly, curious and quiet. "This?" he asks, voice low.

My eyelids flutter. "What?"

He squeezes my arms. "Is this okay?"

"Oh," I whisper. "Yes."

"You can touch me back," he says.

I hesitate. "Pretend?"

His throat bobs. "Yeah. Pretend."

I swallow, the sound loud between us, and slowly raise my hands to his chest. When I press my palm into warm muscle and rest my fingers at his collarbone, he sucks in an audible breath. My mouth quirks. "How you doin'?"

"Good," he rasps, then clears his throat. "This is why we're practicing."

"Right."

"Right." He releases a slow sigh, the tension in his body melting beneath my fingers. This close, I can see the flecks of stone in his eyes—and the sudden flicker of silver-blue across his pupils as he gazes at me. This close, I smell bright cedar, ozone, and petrichor—a scent that doesn't belong to Penumbra, but to *him*.

This is the signature I caught last night in the storage room. Magic, swift as a blade.

"Nick?" I whisper, uncertain.

His brows tighten as his face draws closer to mine, as his eyes turn searching. Piercing. As if he can see even the very corners of my mind. His voice, when it comes, is a low murmur between us. More breath than sound. "What did he do to you?"

I stiffen in Nick's arms, our spell broken. "I don't know."

When I pull away, he lets me go. When I retreat back and down from the platform, he does not follow. My mind returns to the black-haired woman working with Daeza, and the way she'd looked at me like I was something unknowable. A frustrating problem for someone to solve.

But when I look back at Nick, he's gazing at me as though I'm exactly who I should be. Like I am complete. Nick looks at me as if, no matter what's been taken from me, in this moment I am more than enough. As if I am so much that I could overwhelm him if he's not careful.

I don't want him to be careful.

I take a small step forward. "What *were* we?"

He releases a sigh, as if he expected my question. "I don't think I should answer that."

"Why?"

"Because I understand what it means to choose a different life. When I left the Order, people guilted me. Shamed me."

I release a broken laugh. "That's nothing new. Guilt me and shame me, if that's what it takes."

"No. None of that helped me figure out what I wanted to do after I left."

"What *did* help?"

His lips quirk. "Not a what. A who."

"Who——"

"*You*, Bree," he says. "You."

I take another step. "Tell me how I did it. Tell me what you felt."

He sits down on the mattress and turns to the window, silent for long enough that I worry he won't answer. Then, he does.

"The day we met, I saw you walking on the quad. Before I called your name, I watched you, just for a few minutes. You were so focused. Already on a mission. And I thought you were indescribably beautiful. Obviously. But it was more than that. I wanted to . . . experience you up close. Know your mind, watch your defiance, hear your sharp tongue. When we finally spoke, it felt like dancing, even though we were standing still. Push and pull. The first time we kissed—actually, *every* time we kissed there was an ache, a burn, a . . ." He shakes his head, shrugging helplessly. "I don't know. Kissing you feels like a reminder that . . ."

"That you're still alive." The words leave me before I know them.

His eyes snap to mine, recognition flooding them. "Yes. Like climbing a cliff at the ocean, both feet solid beneath you, and peering over the edge. Not to jump, just to—to——"

"Just to see." My heart pounds in my throat. "Just to . . ."

I can't finish—but Nick picks up where I falter. "Just to feel. To know what it's like to stand right where the world begins and ends. *Right* at the infinite." His chest rises with every breath, his blue eyes sparking into something raw and unguarded. "Kissing you is like touching the sky, like touching the horizon. God, Bree, it's even like touching the——"

"The fall," I whisper. "Not just standing at the edge, but going over. All of it."

"Yes," he says quietly. "All of it."

We hold each other's gaze for one long, lingering minute before he stands, clearing his throat. Our spell, broken again. "Right, so. That's how it was."

"Was?" I gasp.

"Yes," he says. "Was." Each step Nick takes toward me folds in a new layer of him, a new mask, a new role. By the time we stand close once more, the raw, open heart I'd glimpsed is gone, leaving only his determined focus behind. Only his drawn brows and stony voice. "Right now, I'll only kiss or touch you to help keep up the lie. And only the way we practiced. Understand?"

I hear the unspoken in Nick's words. He won't touch me in private, only when we need to put on a show and only with Mikael's dress-up doll clothes as a barrier between us. We'll only be together because of corruption and rules and blood spilled on the floor. No sky, no horizon, no fall. Our infinite is over and done, not just here at Penumbra, but outside of it too. When Zoe and I leave, all the doors I'm foolishly teasing open with Nick will close.

I answer with a silent nod.

Nick dips his chin to catch my eye. "Hey, I need words. I need to hear you say it. Can you do this for me, Bree? Can you concentrate on the here and now? On surviving?"

Not what we were or who we were, or what we could become.

"Yeah," I say. "Of course."

An hour later, we're dressed to head down to the dining hall. Nick pauses at the door to adjust his shirt collar. He's chosen a deep blue knitted sweater over dark gray slacks, and I've picked out a long-sleeved sweater-dress and flat shoes—no more heels for the rest of the weekend.

"Stick to what feels comfortable to say," he advises as he finishes fiddling with his collar. "The most realistic, truthful version of an idea rolls off the tongue more smoothly than a complete fabrication. The closer to the truth your lie is, the easier it is to remember."

"Is that what you do?" I ask, tugging at my curls.

He rolls one sleeve up, a grim smile playing across his mouth. "It's what I've learned to do." He glances at me as he rolls up the other sleeve. "And you know how to do it too. I've seen it. You did it last night with Zoe."

"I told her who I am."

"Not everything, though, right? You didn't mention that you're a Blood-crafter or a Rootcrafter like Mariah."

I huff. "One secret at a time."

"Always the mystery girl," Nick muses, eyes going soft.

"What's that mean?"

"It's what Sel calls you." He tilts his head. "Frequently, in fact."

I turn that phrase over in my mind. *Mystery girl. Mystery girl.* "I wish I knew what his voice sounds like so I could remember how he says it."

"When we find him again, I'll get him to show you. He has a"—Nick smirks—"very distinct way of speaking. To everyone, but especially to you."

I gamble on a more personal question. "What's Sel like?"

Nick considers before answering. "Mercurial. Moody like you wouldn't believe. Strong. Talented. Opinionated. Dedicated." He sighs, halfway to a groan. "Passionate. Rude. Terrifying when he wants to be, which is often."

I'm intrigued but also bewildered. "Do you like him?"

Nick's brows rise. "Like? That's . . . ah . . ." He huffs a laugh. "We don't always like each other, no." He pauses.

"After you left, the Order had no leads, no clues. I exploited a loophole, a formal protocol that would force the Regents to allow me to leave without Order supervision so I could pursue a quest of my own choosing. I used the quest to seek Ava and the Morgaines out, hoping they knew what happened to you *and* Sel. But Ava didn't know where either of you were. She had fewer leads than we did. Months of searching and it was a dead end." He sighs. "But just because someone's not fully with us doesn't mean they're gone."

I swallow, eyes suddenly pricking. Should I tell Nick that Selwyn could be with his mother? Without knowing where she is or even if her son is still with her now, four months later, I'd only be offering him another frustrating dead end. What *is* a small comfort is that, even apart, Nick and I have both landed on hope for Selwyn's return.

When I look up, Nick's already looking down at me—and I know he's not only talking about Selwyn over the past few months. He's talking about me, here and now. "Yeah."

Nick reaches for the handle to the door, but before he can open it, a slip of paper appears beneath it at our feet.

"Zoe?" he asks.

"She'd come through the passageway," I say, kneeling down to retrieve the paper. "Not really a note-writing kind of person."

I read the scrawled message aloud. *"Gardens. Twenty minutes."*

Nick takes the note from me, jaw ticking. "Ava." He pockets the note, his expression shuttering as he speaks. Like a cloud covering the sun. "I should go meet her. She may know something useful." His eyes have shifted, more stone than ocean.

"Sure, yeah. You go on. I can get to breakfast on my own."

"Are you sure? I don't want to leave you alone. . . ."

"I'll be with Zoe and Mariah." I stand straighter, fixing my face until it shows nothing, reveals nothing. Not to Nick, not to anyone. "I'm fine."

Nick sees the shift in my own demeanor and makes as if to comment on it, but instead, he closes his mouth and reaches for the door again. "Okay." When we enter the hallway, he turns left while I turn right. Before we part ways, he gives my covered elbow a squeeze. "I'll find you after."

As I watch him walk away, I can't help but want to follow. To understand what exactly is happening between Nick and Ava the Morgaine. How a search for me and Sel turned into a partnership between the Scion of Lancelot and the Order of the Round Table's sworn enemy—a girl who wants me dead.

40

BREAKFAST IS HELD in a smaller dining room. It's a less formal affair, and people seem to be drifting in and out in small groups, eating at tables that are served and quickly cleared by waitstaff for the next wave of guests.

When I enter the room, I spot Mariah and Zoe at a table by a window in the back of the room. Like me, they're both wearing their masquerade masks again. Mariah beckons me to join them, and I make my way over. Zoe glances up at me sullenly, then turns back to her plate of eggs and toast.

I slide into a seat across from them and set my elbows on the table. "Sleep okay?"

"As okay as you can in a place like this," Mariah says. She's opted for a long-sleeved sweater and a pair of fitted checkered slacks and put her braids up. Zoe's in a pair of loose-fitting trousers and a green blouse, with her hair now loose down her back. As Mariah asks me how Nick and I slept, Zoe glances up but doesn't contribute to the conversation. I let them know that he went off to meet Ava and that he'll be back later, maybe with more information about what we need to do to survive the next three days.

After a lull in the conversation, I think about what Nick said to me earlier, about not being fully honest with Zoe.

A server comes by to take my order. Her name tag says "Suzannah." Just in case Suzannah is a spy for Mikael too, we wait until she leaves before I lean forward to catch Zoe's eye. "I owe you an apology."

Her eyes snap up to mine. "You do. But tell me more."

I pause to organize my words, try to keep them true, like Nick said, but nonspecific. Nothing the waitstaff or anyone at the nearby tables could decipher as being about the Legendborn, the Order, or Rootcrafters.

"Even before the old man brought me to his house, I'd made the decision to leave a lot of stuff behind. A lot of people. Because I needed to get stronger and become what I couldn't be when I was with . . . the organization you now know I was a member of." I grimace. When I look at Mariah, she smiles encouragingly—and I'm grateful for her kindness.

Zoe frowns. "The organization I was raised to *despise*, you mean?"

"That one, yes," I say. "But that's the thing: I wasn't raised in it. I wasn't born into it, not like the other members. Not like Nick. It was a surprise that I was a member at all, and . . . I never had time to recover from that surprise. I was grieving my mom, and I wanted answers, and searching for those answers led me down a path that I never imagined was possible. I was normal before this, or, at least, I thought I was. And what I said was right; they don't want me there, not the people in charge."

Zoe snorts. "Wonder why that is."

"So, I left. As for the old man . . ." I shrug. "He knew who I was before I did. He knew my ancestor was . . . like Mariah." Mariah nods, and Zoe's eyes widen. "And he knew that my ancestor did what she could to keep her descendants safe, something that meant that I'd be born different, even from my and Mariah's folks."

Zoe sits back in her chair. "Are you saying what I think you're saying? About that furnace of yours?"

I squint. "I *think* I'm saying what you think I'm saying?"

"Well, damn."

"Mm-hmm," Mariah adds, sipping her coffee. "And what *I* think y'all are saying is that you really did go with the Hunter by choice, just like I told Valec you might've. So he owes *me* an apology."

"There's a lot of that to go around," I say, spreading my hands on the table. "I'm sorry for lying, Zoe. I've had a really hard . . . year."

"A year?"

"Lower your voice," I whisper, glancing around us. "And it's not even been a year."

"A *year* is not enough time for all *this* shit. Hell, five years isn't enough." Zoe's brows draw together. "Yeah, I forgive you."

My breath catches. "You do?"

"I'm just saying . . . ," Zoe says. "You need all the slack you can get, so I'm givin' it to you." My eyes widen, and she waves a hand. "Besides, I'm easy compared to Elijah. You know how he gets, wanting to know everything and uncover every secret. When he finds out all the stuff you and the old man have been hiding from him, he might skin you alive. Metaphorically, of course."

I wrinkle my nose but let the relief show on my face. "Delightful."

"Yeah, well." Zoe lifts a shoulder. "It's how he's always been. Jah just wants so badly to please the old man. I keep him grounded, you know? Without me, he just doesn't know how to think outside of what he wants to become."

"That . . . feels familiar," I say.

"Let's just focus on getting out of here unscathed." She leans closer. "Speaking of . . . did I see a bruise last night?"

My hand flies to my jaw, still tender from yesterday's fight. It was, blessedly, only mildly red this morning. I had to run a washcloth under freezing water half a dozen times to create a compress cold enough to bring the swelling down. Nick, however, said he has a purple bruise the shape of my fist on his upper thigh; Arthur's strength in a Bree-shaped package packs a punch. I grimace into my coffee. "Benedict and I had an . . . eventful reunion."

She grins. "Did you kick his ass?"

"He'd claim it was mutual"—I smile—"but of course I did."

"Hell of a reunion," she says.

"He asked if I wanted to go again."

"Did he now?" Mariah says, leaning in.

I wave my hand. "Not like that."

"Oh, it's *definitely* like that." Zoe plants both elbows on the table. "Y'all are way into each other."

Suzannah returns with my omelet and cheesy grits. "Thank you," I say politely. She nods. "Anything else?"

"Not right now, thanks," Zoe says.

When Suzannah leaves, I lean over to reply to Zoe. "No, we're not!"

"I mean, I can't speak for you, but that boy is down *bad*," Zoe says. "*Bad* bad."

"Not true," I correct, tugging at my mask. "He won't even touch me."

Mariah deeply *mm-hmms* into her mug again, and I glare at her. "Your contributions aren't helping."

"I'm just offering affirmations, that's all," Mariah says, pushing her glasses up against her mask. "Besides, your love life remains *unmatchedly* messy. First it's the Golden Boy, then it's Grumpy Wizard, and now it's back to the Golden Boy, but instead of a normal, happy reunion, you're *accidentally* brawling in the basement? *Girl*." She tuts as she puts her mug down. "Messy."

"You know what? Forget the other stuff," Zoe declares. "Now I'm mad you had all this drama and kept it from me."

"I didn't *know* I had all this drama!" I hiss across the table. "Can we stick to the most pressing issue, like how we're going to handle being"—I look around, lowering my voice—"trapped in this house? And these security 'communions' Mikael talked about? And maybe skip over *my* situation?"

"Her *whole* situation is confusing," Zoe says, shaking her head at Mariah. "I'm gonna need, like, a flowchart or something."

I drop my head in my hands. "Zoe. Please."

"Fine, fine," Zoe says with a laugh. When I look up, she winks, and the rest of the knot in my chest loosens as I realize she was trying to cheer me up—and show her forgiveness with more than words.

"Is Ni—Benedict coming back soon?" Mariah asks, adjusting the straps of her mask as she looks at a few of the other tables with older guests seated closer to the door.

"Don't know," I say, but I'm distracted by the groups of people at the other tables. "Don't suppose you can hear what they're saying?" I ask Zoe. Like me, she's staring at the table nearest to us—a group of white men and women in colorful masquerade masks, all wearing suits and long dresses. The most formal options available within Mikael's garment bags. Elijah said new people, particularly "new money," show up every year as the galas get bigger and bigger in size. I wonder if they're new Collectors or old ones.

Zoe squints. "Something about hedge funds. Finance stuff I don't really understand."

As we talk, Nick strides through the open doorway, brow furrowed and eyes deep in thought as he navigates the room with both hands in his pockets. He is striking even from a distance and even while wearing a dark blue mask that conceals half his features. A chiseled jaw. Thick, slightly disheveled hair. A Golden Boy, indeed. He glances up, finding us in the corner, and adjusts his path to head in our direction.

"Young man!" One of the older men from the table nearby waves a hand, beckoning Nick over.

Mild confusion ripples across Nick's face before he pauses in the middle of the room, glancing at me. I shrug, and he looks at the man, then back at me, debating. I dip my chin. A silent encouragement to go along. Play the game as Benedict would. Nick nods and turns, spilling a smile over his features as he changes course to walk over to their table.

"What's he doing?" Zoe asks.

"Pretending," I murmur.

At the other table Nick leans his elbows on the back of an empty chair as he greets the older man. I only hear snippets of the conversation, but Zoe hears it all.

"That guy who called him over doesn't even know him—he just said he saw Benedict at one of the high-roller tables during Mikael's speech and again afterward in Bianca's line. He said he asked if anyone knew who he was, then realized Benedict was new to the community," she murmurs, eyes narrowing as she listens. "The man says this is his eleventh year attending Mikael's events, and he can show Benedict around, introduce him to some of the regulars. He's introducing a few of the other people at the table."

She pauses, listening as Nick begins to speak.

"Your boy is polite as hell, I'll give him that. Thanking everyone for their kindness. No one's saying a damn thing about Benedict's whole entire *fiancée* sitting in the same room, who was the only other person seated with him at the same high-roller table last night. This isn't about being new to the galas, or else they'd have invited us over to talk too." She crosses her arms. "This is gross."

Nick stands up, chuckling at a joke Zoe doesn't bother to translate, and excuses himself to walk back over to our table. He slips into the seat beside me and very purposefully drapes his arm over the back of my chair, trailing his fingers across my shoulder.

"Hey, honey," he says loudly. When I don't jump or even shift with discomfort, he smiles.

Practice and pretend. I smile back and make sure my voice carries. "Hi. I missed you."

"Missed you too." Nick looks over my head, back at the other table, and waves, then leans in, as if kissing me on the cheek, though our skin never meets. "At least two of those old guys are turning beet red."

I grin. "Perfect." After a moment, I whisper back, "How were they?"

He lowers his voice before he answers. "Oh, they're terrible people." He reaches for the muffin basket in the middle of the table. "Snakes in suits."

"Then why'd you go over?" Zoe whispers.

Nick sits back in his seat as he chews on the muffin and swallows. "Intel."

Mariah blinks. "Intel?"

He nods. "Now I know who the insiders are. The loyal Collectors who've been to the overnight events before, who think they know how things are gonna go. Now I know their schedule for the weekend, where they'll be and when, so I can pay them a visit after breakfast to find out more about Mikael and his little"—Nick waves his muffin, smirking—"wannabe secret society he's got going on here."

Zoe looks at Nick, then me, then back at Nick. "But they're assholes. They didn't even acknowledge your fiancée. If they saw you like they said last night, they must have seen you and Bree—Iris—together, but then they didn't even ask about her? Bree walked by their table when she entered the room too. *She* didn't get invited to chitchat. They made assumptions about her."

"Yeah, they're disgusting." Nick grins. "But we can take advantage of that."

"How, exactly?" Zoe asks.

"Easy. You know this already, so I'm not saying anything new, but guys like that love a power structure." He gestures to the estate around us as he picks at his muffin. "And the power structures they wield the most—racism, misogyny, patriarchy—thrive in places like this, especially when money's involved. Let me wield their expectations of me against them. I don't need to know their names to exploit their assumptions. I can play snake-in-a-suit for a few days. Find out more about these so-called communions. Uncover what everyone else already knows so that *we* get the information we need to get out of this thing alive."

Zoe sits back in her chair, blinking. "That's . . . legit."

"It's a strategy," Nick says. "We should pool our collective resources."

"Ain't that the truth," Zoe says. "I'm in."

Beside her, Mariah nods. "Sounds good."

Nick turns to me. "What do you think?"

"Like Mariah said, sounds good."

"But it's only a good plan if you agree it's a good plan," he says, his eyes intent. "I won't leave you alone again."

I laugh. "You couldn't have been gone longer than half an hour."

"Not what I meant." He holds my gaze for a beat longer than what feels necessary. Zoe clears her throat.

I shift in my seat, certain I'm missing something. "It's a solid idea. Use the Collectors' ignorance against them so we get what we need. Plus, you made a big show of coming over here. If you get in their good graces, maybe they'll look elsewhere to find 'violations' and leave us all alone. You should wield the power you have, like you said."

"On it," Nick says with a nod. "I'll get started after breakfast."

"Speaking of intel," I say, "what did Ava want?"

Nick's eyes darken. "She said that Mikael won't be interviewing all hundred attendees. Just those invitees who he finds personally suspicious, both in their business dealings and outside interests and . . . anyone who wasn't in the ballroom when the alarms were triggered."

THE FIRST SET of communions takes place after dinner, on the other side of the estate, in a ground-floor auditorium. Unlike the ballroom, which is two stories high, wide and long, this room is set up as a proscenium-style theater, with rows of audience seats rising high in the air at an angle and a wooden stage sitting opposite. Mariah, Zoe, and I take seats closer to the top of the seating area so we can watch the Collectors seated in the rows below us—and get a better view of the activity on the stage.

Before Nick went off to gather his "intel" with the snakes in suits, he'd shared one more detail that Ava had learned in her own time gathering intel—there will only be five communions a day, and they will all be conducted by Mikael himself. Nick and I are scheduled for the last day.

My leg bounces. Nick's not back yet, and the first person is being led up to the stage under the bright golden lights.

Without warning, Mikael enters the stage from behind a curtain. The low murmurs of the masked audience disappear as soon as the houselights lower, leaving just the Shade and the masked human man in the chair at center stage. While there is a small mic stand near the seated guest, Mikael turns to the audience, projecting his voice high into the room without the need of a mic at all.

"Welcome, fellow Collectors," he says. "Today, we will reaffirm our creed of discretion and truth with offered tribute."

I stiffen in my chair—as does Zoe. We only know tributes as physical gifts. But the masked man on the stage before us is visibly trembling in his seat—and empty-handed.

Mikael sits down across from the man, opening his black suit jacket as he settles. "I will ask each of our fellow guests five questions. Nothing that will break our code of anonymity, of course, as our true identities are sacred, but these questions will help us understand whether our community member can be trusted. If someone resists their natural inclination to tell the truth of things, I will know—and there will be a punishment." Mikael turns to the audience. "Are we in agreement?"

"Discretion and truth," the audience intones.

"Truth"—Mikael turns back to the shaking man—"and discretion."

The man in the chair nods quickly. "D-discretion. And t-t-truth."

The electric snap of Mikael's illusion mesmer buzzes up the back of my skull before he even opens his mouth. Beside me, Mariah's and Zoe's eyes both narrow. We'd discussed Mikael's illusion with Mariah, who had never heard of such a thing either. This time, I'm determined to find out what the Nightshade is making his Collectors see—or what he's taking extra care to hide. I move to bite the inside of my cheek to break the mesmer, but then the communion begins.

"Did you attack and wound my guard?" When Mikael speaks, glowing green aether exits his mouth. No one else in the audience can detect the aether, much less track the way it floats and curls across the stage, because Mikael's power is only visible to those with the Sight. No one else but me, Zoe, and Mariah would know that Mikael's aether is unspooling *toward* the human man in the chair. Targeting him, even though he can't even see it himself. This spellcraft, whatever it is, is not Mikael's illusion mesmer, but something different. Something . . . invasive. Because once Mikael's aether reaches its target, it curls around the man's skull like a caress—before soaking into his eyes, his mouth, his ears, and his skin.

When the man speaks, he shudders from the effort. "No."

"Did you attempt to break into the outbuilding on the grounds of Penumbra?" Mikael asks, and again the green aether drifts toward the man, coating him until his body shakes, twisting in the chair.

With visible confusion, the man sits back up to answer. "No."

They are six feet apart, but Mikael shifts in his chair to lean closer. "Three questions remain. These three shall serve as tribute. A sign of your loyalty."

The man nods frantically. "Yes, of course."

"When did you commit your last crime?"

The man winces in his seat. "Two months ago."

Mikael lifts his nose and inhales deeply—and the glowing green smoke he laid upon the man returns to him, tinged a deep, dull emerald.

That's when I realize that the tribute is not an object . . . but a confession. And with that confession, buried, painful human emotions—rich food for a demon. Fresh from the source. Erebus's disgust for what his Nightshade has become rises in my memory: *Mikael's original demonic nature has been altered. His ability to detect humanity's worst instincts has sharpened impressively, but at great cost. Aether no longer sustains his physical form, so he must fortify himself almost entirely off human energy.*

Mikael himself shudders as he feeds before asking his next question. "And what did you do?"

"I . . . stole something."

Mikael's chin lifts. "And what was it? Be detailed. Tell us the how and the why."

The man shudders. "I altered my father's will before he died."

The audience murmurs, intrigued and pleased by this revelation.

"Go on . . . ," Mikael says, eyes lidded and voice sonorous.

"I have three siblings. My father's estate . . ." The man groans, as if dragging the truth out of himself. "It was meant to go to all four of us, equally split. I altered the will. Forged my father's handwriting. Left it all, all of it, to me. And gave my siblings nothing."

Mikael's head tips back, his mouth open and panting lightly at the consumption of the man's deepest confession. Mikael smiles as he looks back at the man across from him. "Thank you."

The Nightshade's aether rises, releasing the man from his hold. The man falls forward out of the chair, cracking his knees against the wooden floor and breaking the awed silence of the room.

Mikael crosses one knee over the other and beckons to someone offstage. "Next participant, please?"

The next four communions go much the same way, with Mikael feeding off every deep and salacious secret revealed. We hear about two attempted murders. A family betrayal. Ill-gotten profits. In the very last one, the attendee nearly resists Mikael's influence—and Mikael delivers a stark warning.

"Resistance *is* a confession, my friend," he says, standing over the struggling woman.

Finally, she reveals her truth. "I destroyed my own company . . . for the insurance money," she says, gasping. "Three hundred jobs, gone. Made it look like an accident. Some employees never recovered. They lost healthcare. Got sick. Died, destitute and in pain." The flood of deep green from her confession blankets Mikael, covering him until he cannot seem to speak.

"Guilt. Regret. Shame," he mutters, head lolling on his shoulders. "And then, deeper, your most guarded truth: pleasure. You *liked* watching their pain. Liked knowing you caused it." He shudders—and that's the moment his illusion thins enough that I can see through it. See him. *Mikaelaz* the Nightshade breaks through, if only for a fraction of a second.

Dull, emerald ichor dripping from great wings—a shadow, melting on the stage beneath his feet—red eyes in elongated sockets—fangs as long as my arm—

And then the illusion is back. Electricity along my skull. Mikael the gentleman straightens his jacket in his chair, a satisfied smile on his face as he regards the stunned executive. "Thank you for your tribute."

When Zoe and Mariah and I exit the theater, Mariah tugs on my sleeve. "There's Benedict," she whispers in a trembling voice. I'm not the only one shaken by what we've just witnessed. Zoe, for her part, seems rattled but unsurprised.

When we look up, Nick is exiting from one of the side doors alone. As most of the audience spills out around us, heading off to an open bar in one of the salons or back to their rooms, he moves between them in order to reach us.

"Where were you?" I whisper when he draws close.

"I came in late from talking with the suits," he says. "Took a seat close to the stage so I could see what Mikael's doing to get these confessions."

"What did you see?" Mariah asks.

Nick's lips press into a displeased line. "More than I wanted to." We're not the only audience members who have remained hovering in the large hall outside the auditorium. It's getting louder where we stand as the Collectors speak excitedly about all that they've just heard. The hunger in their eyes is evident, even behind their satin and lace masks. They may not be able to feed on the emotions that Mikael is eliciting or see the magic, but they are enjoying the confessions. Savoring them. Judging them. And they are eager for more. Nick looks just as disturbed by them as I feel. "We should talk. Somewhere private."

After everything we've just witnessed, the secret library, even with its dusty tomes and floating cobwebs, feels like a safe reprieve. But as soon as we enter, the dark sky outside the windows opens up, and rain pours down to lash against the forgotten windows.

"This whole thing is . . . ," Mariah says, eyes wide.

"Really, really disturbing," I say. "And confirms that Mikael's not mesmering the Collectors into supporting public executions. They do that all on their own."

"Also disturbing," she says, "just in a different way."

We take seats around the room on top of the dusty desks while Nick paces. "Mikael's illusion is only hiding his true form. The layer is thick enough to work on nonmagical eyes, but thin enough that we can See it when he loses control. It's almost like his stolen human body doesn't work like it should anymore. But the magic he's using to feed off their emotions?" He shakes his head. "I've never seen or heard of anything like it."

"That's because Mikael's a Nightshade," Zoe says, pulling one knee up on the desk. "One of the original demon knights of the Shadow Court. They're not like goruchels. They're a tier higher with their own talents. The only demon more powerful than a Shade is the King."

Nick stops pacing. "What did you just say?"

Zoe stammers. "I . . . uh, the King. The one everyone says is dead?"

"No." Nick eyes her. "You said 'the only demon more powerful than a Shade *is* the King.' 'Is,' not 'was.'"

"Did I?" Zoe says.

"You did," Nick insists. "Are you saying the Shadow King is *alive?*"

"I . . ." Zoe looks everywhere but at Nick. "No, that's just a rumor."

I notice that Mariah doesn't look surprised to hear that name or to hear about the Nightshades and the Court. I sigh. "Zoe, we may as well tell him."

Zoe leans back. "I'm not telling anyone anything!"

Nick looks at all three of us, then just at me. "The King was *destroyed* fifteen hundred years ago. We saw Arthur announce it at Camelot in a blood walk."

"He's alive," I admit quietly. "Weaker without his crown, but alive."

"His crown? Wait, *that's* what you—we—" His mouth clamps shut. "And you want his crown, why?" Nick's eyes narrow. "To give it back to him?"

I swallow. "It's not that simple. If he has it, he won't have to feed. He won't be the Hunter anymore. He can leave Rootcrafters alone—"

"Wait." Mariah stops me with a raised hand. "Did you say you can stop him from taking Rootcrafters?"

I nod. "Yes, if he doesn't need to feed anymore, he won't hunt them—us."

"There are other girls missing right now," Mariah says. "Have you seen them?"

"Just one." I share a look with Zoe, who answers for us both. "We didn't know there are others."

"There are missing girls?" Nick asks, alarmed.

"Yeah," I say. I think of the girl in the bathroom, the one who was both frightened and brave. "I saw a girl with a kidnapper, a warlock. We think the old man was behind it. He's behind a lot of things. More than we know."

"Wait, sorry." Nick shakes his head in confusion. "Is 'the old man' also the Shadow King? And is *that* the demon you ran away with?"

Tears burn at my eyes, but I refuse to shed them. "It's not what you think—"

"What exactly is it, then?" Nick demands. "Please tell me, because everything I've ever heard about the Shadow King is that he's a bloodthirsty tyrant. Something *more* than a demon, something greater. Nearly a god! The Order barely teaches us anything about him because he's so ancient, he might as well be a myth—"

"That's because the Order and the Legendborn are arrogant, self-obsessed, elitist assholes."

Nick, Zoe, and I pivot in a flash, power erupting from our palms. Silver-blue, green, and purple flames burst against the walls of the darkened library to reveal Ava emerging from the shadowed passageway. She steps forward in a long skirt and high-necked sweater, looking for all the world like a wealthy woman on vacation. "Weren't you going to invite me to your little club?"

"Applications are closed," I snap. "Sorry."

Ava's eyes flash as she stares at me. "You'd know something about that, wouldn't you, little Scion who shouldn't be?"

I grin. "I'm the Scion who chose *not* to be, thanks."

She rolls her eyes. "Keep telling yourself that." She comes to a stop in the room with her hands on her hips. "Are y'all gonna keep calling on all that power when Mikael might still be on the premises?"

Immediately, we douse our hands. Ava laughs. "So gullible. He left twenty minutes ago, and his aether sense is so dulled he can barely detect it unless it's right in front of him."

Zoe groans. "You are the least fun person I've ever met."

"Thank you." Ava looks around at the room we've taken refuge in and frowns. Outside, lightning flashes—splitting the sky open in silver and gray. "You're never going to find the crown hiding out in here."

"Where would we find the crown, Ava?" Nick says coldly. "Because I don't think it was ever in the basement, was it?"

Ava's eyes grow comically wide as she shrugs. "Oopsie. Did I point you in the wrong direction?"

"Wait," Zoe says. "We were told it was in the basement too. You saying that was wrong?"

"I don't know who told you it was there," Nick says, glaring at Ava as he speaks, "but that tip was either old or planted to get you caught. Just like mine was."

Ava waves at him, laughing. "Oh, Nickie, I didn't want to get you *caught*. I wanted to get you *killed*. That would have truly been a hat trick." She counts off her fingers one at a time. "One, create a big enough distraction that the crown in the outbuilding would be left unguarded. Two, get rid of you since you frankly know too much. And, three, hopefully escalate Camlann even further by starting a mini war between a Nightshade and the Round Table."

"You wanted a Scion to get themselves killed trying to steal something from a Shade. Of course. And you just so happened to neglect to tell me whose crown I was stealing." Nick groans between his teeth. "William and Lark were right about not trusting you."

"Don't tell me you *trusted* me?" Ava drawls. "I did try to get you killed once already, remember?"

"How could I forget?" Nick says. "And, no, I didn't trust you."

"That's right," Ava says. "You just *needed* me."

Nick's eyes turn stony. "Ava . . . don't."

Ava's eyes slide over to me as she answers Nick. "Don't worry, little Lancelot. Unlike the fools onstage today, I can keep a secret."

"What's she talking about, Nick?" I ask.

Ava smiles. "He was desperate to find you and the missing Kingsmage, you know. So desperate that I sort of wished I *did* know where you were, just so I could string him along for a little bit."

"Ava," Nick warns.

"Nicholas really is built for a mission like this, don't you think, Bree?" She lifts a hand, gesturing at Nick where he stands. "You couldn't design a better companion for a place filled with people who either believe they're kings or think they're kingmakers."

"Which one are you?" Mariah asks, crossing her arms. "You came here because you want the crown, don't you?"

"I don't want the crown," Ava says. "I want it *back*. The Morgaines have held it in our possession for over fifteen centuries, until three months ago when someone's little warlock servant *stole* it from a Morgaine stronghold. It's my duty to bring it back—it's safer with us than out in the world. We have been its caretaker from the moment Arthur took it from the fallen King's head. We have used our mistress Morgaine's spellcraft to keep it out of demon hands, and I will do everything in my power to return it to her protection."

"You speak as if Morgaine is still alive," I say.

Ava looks at me. "Aren't they all alive, little Scion?"

"But what do you get out of keeping it?" Zoe asks. "You Morgaines enchanted the crown so that no demon can sense it or touch it. And even if the crown *weren't* enchanted by y'all, it's not like the power is useful to you. The King forged it for himself. You can't bear it, and it'll obliterate anyone who tries. Mikael can auction it off this weekend and it'll just end up rusting in a dusty old gallery in some rich dude's second home!"

"Why keep anything potent close by?" Ava asks. "The same reason anyone wants anything—power. Over our enemies. Over our allies. Even over our-selves, if needed."

I frown. "That doesn't make any sense—"

"Then let me keep this simple," Ava says. "Stay out of my way."

With that, she pivots on her heel and heads back toward the corridor, illuminating her journey with a handful of blue aether and walking until she disappears into the distance. The sound of the rain outside the windows drowns out her quiet footsteps.

Nick stares after her, his fists balled tight. "She's got something up her sleeve."

"Does it have to do with whatever agreement you have with her?" I ask, shocked at the heat and irritation in my voice.

He grits his teeth. "Maybe. I don't know. Possibly."

"Each of those answers was, like, successively less helpful," Zoe says.

"You're telling me."

"What did you agree to do?" I ask.

"I told her I would help her find a crown. I didn't know the King survived,"

Nick whispers. "If I knew he could actually get his hands on it and wear it one day . . ."

"You wouldn't have helped her?" I ask.

He stares at me without answering, which is how I hear the answer anyway: *I don't know.*

I ask the next question, even though doing so makes my stomach twist. "You said you sought Ava for information on me and Sel, but she didn't have it. But you're still *with* her—"

"I'm not *with* her!" he shouts.

"You're working with her!" I insist. "You have an *arrangement*. A *bargain*. You agreed to help her steal the crown. Why? What did she offer you in return?"

Nick's jaw works back and forth. "I can't . . . explain it."

"Can't?" I say. "Or won't?"

"Both." He meets my eyes. "Even before tonight, I didn't know if I ever could, but now that you're telling me that *you* left to go work for *the Shadow King*? On *purpose*? Bree, I just—" He runs both hands through his hair, pacing away, then back. "I don't know what to say to you right now. What I *can* say. Please just . . . don't ask me."

My mouth opens and closes, confusion spearing me through. "I . . ." But then I think of all I've kept from people. All this life has demanded I keep locked away. The decisions I've made and the people I've lost—and what it means to *let* people become lost, if that's their choice. "Okay. I won't ask."

"Thank you. I know that's . . . not easy." He releases a low, ragged breath. "I'll . . . I'll be in the room."

When he leaves, I don't follow. Instead, I collapse back against the desk, fall into myself, and shut my eyes against the day. Against Ava. Against secrets and truths.

Zoe's arm slides around my shoulders first. I feel her soft curls drop against my shoulder, her heavy sigh against my cheek. Mariah's arm loops around my waist from the other side, her own sigh quiet and long. They don't speak, because they don't have to.

42

THE RAIN IS still heavy and relentless when I eventually climb into my bed. Nick is already asleep—this time on the floor, I notice, in a pile of pillows and spare linens. Apparently he'd given up on trying to make the chaise work. The white noise of the storm nearly sends me to sleep—until I hear a low, rhythmic scratch coming from the wall behind my head.

I wait a beat. Still my own breathing. Wonder if Nick's awake, if he heard—

The scratch sounds again, and then the room is blasted into illumination by two palms of mage flame, Nick's and my own. The blue and purple bounce off the mirror on the wall, then shape-shift as we each get out of our bedding. Nick's standing at the head of the bed before my feet even hit the floor.

The scratching stops. The room goes quiet.

Beside me, Nick's face is lit by blue-white light. He brings a finger to his lips to signal for quiet. Unlike last time, I don't roll my eyes. If this were Zoe, she would have pushed the door right in or called our names.

Which means whoever's in the secret passageway on the other side of our wall is *not* Zoe.

I'm tempted to whisper this to Nick when he abruptly pivots away from me—and the light catches the outline of the defined muscles along his torso beneath his fitted white T-shirt.

When he leans closer to the source of the scratching sound, I decide the ratio of his broad shoulders to the "V" taper of his waist above his sweatpants should be some sort of illegal proportion. Banned math. Criminal musculature. I suddenly don't know whether to curse our nighttime intruder or thank them. The best I can manage as I carefully slide out of bed is to drop my flaming hand by my side so my ogling won't be quite so obvious and my stunned expression won't be so embarrassingly well lit.

After a long beat without any sound, Nick turns to me with a furrowed brow. I shrug back at him. Maybe we were both spooked by a rodent in the walls? I mouth, "Mouse?" to him.

He considers but doesn't look convinced. He looks as if he might rotate his wrist to extinguish his mage flame when the wall panel he was just inspecting blows outward, sending him flying back onto the rug.

I'm already moving, backpedaling into the middle of the room, where I'll have more space to move.

The attackers that leap past the door are dressed in black, faces fully covered by dark balaclavas. But I don't need to see them to know that they're warlocks. The sour scent of pact magic fills the room—aether and ichor bonded to human flesh.

The button-down pajama top and pants I chose are easy to move in but not stretchy. If the strings come untied, the pants will be a pain. Better make this quick.

There are three of them—no, four. A large number for just two people. Or it would be if those two people weren't Scions.

Nick is up and on his feet before I block the first punch. Out of the side of my eye, I see him whirl, sending one man into the heavy bedpost with a round-house kick.

Then, I'm consumed with my own fight. Dodging one strike, then a second, in the shadowy bedroom lit only by the faint moonlight streaming in from the window. One of the warlocks mutters something in a guttural tongue—and a long, curling imp's tail emerges from behind him.

"How'd you even make that bargain? Imps don't talk much, my guy," I taunt, hoping to buy time as I consider my options. There's the heavy pewter teapot and silver serving tray at my knee on the glass coffee table. There's the glass coffee table itself. There's also just my fists.

The warlock doesn't go for my bait. Instead, he responds by sending his borrowed tail whipping out from behind him. I throw myself to the floor—and the tail strikes the teapot, sending the antique item clattering to the floor, and whizzes over my head before returning to its place behind his hips.

A glowing hoof stomps down—I roll. Another comes down on the floor beside me—catching my bonnet and tearing it free. When I pop up to a crouch, my curls flow down over my face.

Not good.

I ignite both fists as I flip my curls up and back. Command my root into two long daggers. The ends of the weapons have just finished forming when the second attacker, whose fists look like the hooves of unholy Clydesdales, comes swinging. I duck the first swing, swiping a blade at his belly before retreating. The tail sneaks into my opening, dragging its tip along my upper arm. It leaves a trail of fire behind, and I can already hear Erebus telling me to *go faster*.

I hate that with all he's taken from me, he's still so much in my head, but he is—and right now, I'm grateful for it.

Two things at once, Briana.

I drop into a low spin, kicking out with one leg and dragging my right blade through the air as I go. The leg connects with the hooved warlock, sending him tumbling. The blade drags against flesh—and a low, pained hiss tells me the strike was good.

Spiraling out and up lands me face-to-face with my first attacker. He's hurt and angry—and sloppy.

Good.

He pulls back for a punch—I duck under his arm to land an uppercut. His jaw snaps up and back—a pained grunt.

Probably bit his tongue. *Very* good.

Before I can celebrate, thick arms wrap around my forearms from behind and squeeze them hard into my chest. I'm jerked up from the floor—my back arches painfully. "Gotcha."

Second dude, with the hooved feet, is back for more. He's stronger and smarter than the first with the tail.

Imp Tail dives for my feet, catching me before I can kick. Bundling my ankles tight together with his hands.

Doesn't matter how strong I am. I don't have any leverage like this—bent back, arms pressed into my ribs, feet off the ground. I struggle and twist, using Arthur's strength to loosen their holds, but they tighten their hands, pressing into the small bones of my wrists and ankles until there's a sharp pain in both.

"Let. Go." I twist again, wiggling my torso like a fish in the air.

"Come on!" Imp Tail shouts, and then they're moving me, trying to rush me past Nick and the other two men into the opening in the wall.

Out of the corner of my eye, I see Nick take one attacker out with a heavy punch to the side of his temple.

I relax as soon as I know how close we are to the door. Let them think they have me. Stop struggling. Let them think they've succeeded.

As soon as Imp Tail shifts to lift my feet up and into the waiting, empty corridor, I twist my hips and kick a foot into his face. My heel catches his nose in a satisfying crunch, and he falls back, into the opening of the wall. My feet fall where he drops them.

Leverage.

I push off the floor, shoving myself and the warlock behind me back faster and harder than he anticipated. He stumbles and falls, hitting the floor spine-first—and I land with my head and back on his wide chest. We're both stunned for a second, then before I roll away, I take a knee by his elbow and punch him in the face before he can recover.

He's out.

The guy in the corridor looks up at me just as I look up at him—and makes a break for it into the darkness.

I jump to my feet to join Nick's fight—and quickly see I don't need to. Not at all.

His attackers are more skilled than mine, and bigger. Their footwork is more precise, more fluid—but so is Nick's. He circles them, barefoot, with both hands up and loose. If the two warlocks notice the spark of amusement in Nick's eyes or the slight, upturned tilt to the edge of his mouth, they don't take it as the warning that it so clearly is.

The first warlock darts in with quick fists—and Nick meets and deflects each blow as if the other man is moving in slow motion. Nick rotates his assailant as if he's leading the older man through ordered steps. Positioning him where he wants. Herding his opponent into his own destruction.

By the time the warlock realizes Nick has trapped him in a corner, it's too late. The man lets frustration drive his attack—a mistake.

The warlock's wild cross is met with Nick's forearm—and deflected.

A second cross flies. Nick deflects again—then answers with a viper-quick punch to the man's chin.

The warlock's head pops back. He staggers. Falls—and Nick's eyes slide to his second opponent.

The other warlock is younger. More prepared. He rushes Nick with a pact-magic-enhanced blade.

His first jab gets knocked to the side.

The second is met with the back of Nick's hand against the flat side of the blade, pushing it down.

A third attempt ends when Nick grasps the warlock's blade hand, yanking the man closer—twisting him at the elbow until the man yowls in pain and drops the knife.

Nick forces the warlock upright only to punch him into the heavy wooden bedpost.

The first attacker has recovered. As his partner falls, the older warlock leaps for Nick's turned back. I shout a warning, but it's not necessary.

Nick is a blur of motion while the man is airborne. He jumps to meet him—and knocks the man down with a quick strike to the face.

The small, wild grin tugging on Nick's mouth is short-lived. As I watch, a shadow of disappointment crosses his face instead.

This was so easy for him.

It hits me then: this was fighting, not dancing. Not like what Nick and I found with each other in the basement. To Nick Davis, every fight *could* be a dance, but only if he has the right partner. An equal one.

Nick surveys the attackers on the ground with barely a hitch in his breathing. "There's magic in them."

"Yeah, they're warlocks——"

"No, not pact magic." He kneels to examine their bodies closer. "Something else. Something faint. It's . . . fading now." He squints. "Almost like it was temporary. Set on a timer."

"A construct?" I move closer but don't see or smell anything other than the acrid smell of pact casting.

"No," he murmurs. "It's gone. I can't see it anymore."

"All warlock magic is temporary," I say. "When their bargain runs its course, their magic disappears."

He doesn't look convinced. He stands, shaking his head. "We should move them. Before somebody comes. Asks us too many questions."

Except there really isn't any place to move the unconscious warlocks . . . other than the hidden passage through which they came. Nick and I carry the three unconscious bodies into the dark corridor, then drag them through the dust with mage flame at our fingertips.

There is a main path that dips down, then up again, and spills out into a small, tight staircase with a landing. After we move the masked warlocks into a loose pile at the top of the landing, I look down the staircase—only to see more swirls of dust. "What do we do?"

"Leave them all in one place. Get back to our room. Act like none of it ever happened."

"But——"

"*Now,* Bree," Nick says, already turning. "Before they wake up and we have to knock them out all over again."

I frown at the tone of his voice but follow him back to our room. Once I'm through, he closes the door behind me. It disappears in the wall with a quiet click.

He stands back from the wall. "They won't come back."

"How do you know?"

"Would *you* come back for seconds after getting your ass beat by two teenagers in borrowed pajamas?"

"Well," I say with a shrug, "no. But——"

"Whoever sent them here wanted to abduct you. Once they find out that we didn't let that happen so easily, they'll have to think of a smarter plan. But I'm more worried someone sent these warlocks to rattle us into slipping up and exposing our real identities. If anyone was really looking at us closely the first night, they'd have already seen the calluses on both our hands, the definition in your back and arms, the way we move." He moves to one of the chairs by the fireplace and gestures for me to join him. "Help me with this?"

I lift one end while he lifts the other, and we walk the chair back over to the passageway door, setting it tight against the panel. "It's bad enough that we have to face communion. We can't draw any more attention to ourselves."

I sigh. He's right. The best thing to do is to act like this didn't happen. "What if they send more warlocks next time? A chair isn't going to stop them."

He dusts his hands off once the chair is set in place. "We sent one of their warlocks running and left the other three in a pile of twisted limbs and fresh concussions." His hair flops into his eyes as he regards me wryly. "I think they'll get the message."

"Fair point," I mutter.

He reaches for my arm—then stops himself. I follow his gaze to the scratch left by the warlock's pointed imp tail. "We need to clean that quickly, or it will get infected."

I groan, thinking of Erebus's sessions in the warehouse. "I was too slow."

Nick's eyes flick up to mine. "You were plenty fast. You fought smart. Kept the destruction of your environment to a bare minimum. I think that teakettle over there took more damage than you did."

"You're not hurt, are you?" I ask, and immediately flush at the sight of the

Adonis belt at his hips peeking out from his low-slung pants. Banned math, Bree. *Banned* math.

When he shakes his head, it sends his hair flying. "Nah." He runs a hand through it, smiling slightly at some internal memory. "I grew up fighting *Selwyn Kane* on a regular basis—and that was before my abilities manifested. I could have beaten those guys when I was twelve. On a bad day."

"You must have gotten injured?" I ask. "Back then, I mean. Merlins are so much stronger than humans. . . ."

I trail off because the slight smile has disappeared and his face has drawn tight, closed down. "The injuries Sel inflicted weren't . . ." His smile attempts to reinhabit his face, but fails. "Weren't the bad ones, believe it or not."

Before I can ask what he means by that, he bends over to pick up my satin bonnet, brushing it off as best he can. When he's done, he hands it to me. "I'll take watch. You rest."

The bonnet is a little torn and dirty, but nothing a quick round of soap and water in the sink won't fix—and it's better than nothing. "I thought you said they won't come back."

Nick's mouth quirks as he walks away to settle onto the window seat. "They won't, but Sel would draw and quarter me if he found out I went back to sleep after someone attempted to kidnap you."

"He was that protective?"

Nick studies me as though he is choosing his next words carefully. "He's a Kingsmage . . . and you're his king."

The next day greets me in slow fragments.

The slant of light stretching across the room, bouncing back at me through the dresser mirror. The muffled sound of voices drifting up from the gardens outside our window. The low creak of a door opening down the hall. The press of an errant curl slipped free from my bonnet and tangling against my forehead.

The warmth of a broad hand curled across my hip.

My breath catches. Even without looking, I recognize the weight of Nick's palm. Even through the thin layer of my pajama pants, his touch feels familiar. I hold still, memorizing the sensation of him sleeping next to me and the feelings that sensation elicits. I breathe through them one at a time, slow and steady like the heartbeat against my spine. There is curiosity. Amusement. Wonder. I feel protected. Safe.

Warm air blooms against the nape of my neck, tickling my skin until I squirm. The hand on my hip tightens—then freezes.

"Shit." Nick releases me with a gasp, rolling back and away to sit up. "Sorry!" he says in a voice hoarse with sleep.

I flip over, preparing to tell him not to worry, until I see his disheveled bed hair sticking up in every direction, the shocked, guilty expression on his face, and both of his hands hovering awkwardly in the air like he's just been caught stealing something. I try not to laugh—and immediately fail.

He watches with wide, blinking eyes as I snicker into my pillow. "Why are you laughing?"

"Because you look ridiculous," I gasp, "and I have no idea why you're apologizing."

"This—" He points helplessly at my offending, pajama-clad hip, then back at himself. Then me, then the entire bed. "This wasn't supposed to happen!" He drops his head in his hands with a deep groan. "Sel would *kill* me. I was supposed to be keeping watch."

"You couldn't have gotten good sleep on the floor, and we fought off warlock kidnappers last night," I say, shifting until I'm on my back. "You needed rest."

He shakes his head in his hands. "You're the Crown Scion of Arthur," he mumbles. "Sel wouldn't even bother killing me, actually. He'd do worse. Hang me upside down by my toes and lecture me to death."

I grin. "He sounds fun."

Nick groans again. "I should have been more careful."

"We'd have woken up if there was another intruder," I say, giggling. "I'm sure Selwyn the Kingsmage would be impressed with your *extremely* cutting-edge upholstered-chair alarm system."

"Haha." He drops his hands to stare at my pajama pants and the hip he'd grasped. "And . . . I don't just mean I should have been more careful about the warlocks."

Oh.

I cross my arms over myself. He means waking up curled around me. Touching me. "You were asleep. We both were. It's fine."

"It's risky."

"What's risky?" I exclaim. "I don't understand——" The next words are ripped away from me in a gasp, because Erebus chooses this exact moment to call my bloodmark.

It's my turn to groan as the glowing red branches erupt along my skin beneath my button-down shirt, pulsing bright crimson beneath the thin fabric. The familiar aroma of Erebus's power fills my nose and mouth. Rich and ancient and *suffocating*. I scowl at the light.

To my surprise, Nick crawls closer, brows furrowed as he studies the mark growing brighter, then dimming, then brightening again. "It's your magic, but it's . . . it's his, too. Wound together."

"As if I can forget," I mutter.

He leans over me, careful to keep our skin from touching, as his eyes trace the thinner branches that extend down my shoulders, dip into my elbows, and wrap around my forearms. "It's not sitting on your skin the way a tattoo would. It's deeper than that. Embedded. Like it's following your veins."

"You can see all that?"

His eyes flick to mine—and I see the deep blue flash across his irises. "Yes."

"How?"

He squints, making a decision. "The Line of Lancelot inherits . . . enhanced vision."

"Enhanced how?"

His jaw works back and forth as he shifts his focus back to my bloodmark. "It's never the same. The inherited sight manifests differently with each Scion who receives it. I don't know what the previous Scion of Lancelot before me saw, but I see the inner workings of magic. How it's put together. How it was constructed. Aether is an element, but like any element, it has its constituent parts. Its molecules, for lack of a better phrase." He nods at the mark. "I can see how a construct was made, and sometimes, I can see how to . . . unmake it."

I push up to sit across from him. "That's how you—"

"Deforged your constructs?" He smirks. "Yes. Although, with other constructs I've tried, it's taken a lot of work. A lot of focused study of the crafting before I can attempt to take it apart. Like your magic? It's rich. Layered. Anything that complex is usually difficult to unravel, but with you, it was . . . instinct. Like breathing."

I feel my brows draw tighter. "I don't know if I like that you can unmake what I create so easily."

"I'm not sure I like it either." His eyes drop back down to my bloodmark, more exposed now with the shifting of my collar. "I definitely don't like that he can do this to you. Not just here, where it'd be dangerous for anyone who happens to see it, but anywhere. You're a king too. Just because the Shadow King bloodmarked your family doesn't mean he gets to terrorize you whenever he pleases."

I gape at him. Nick speaks the complexity of my life into simplicity so easily, so frequently. The conclusions I fumble around to find he just . . . states out loud. And he speaks those truths half to himself and half to me, as if this perspective on my bloodmark is obvious and easy, and not an elusive clarity that I keep chasing and chasing.

Suddenly, I can't tolerate keeping this secret from him.

"It's Erebus," I blurt out.

He blinks. "What's Erebus?"

"The King," I say quickly. "Erebus Varelian is the Shadow King, in disguise."

43

NICK GOES VERY, very still. "How long?"

"A long time," I say. "Decades."

"Why?"

"To . . . to unmake the Order," I whisper, "from the inside out. To get revenge on Arthur and destroy his legacy. To find me when the time came, and to consume my power when I die."

Nick sits back on his haunches, eyes darting back and forth. "The Shadow King controls the Guard. Controls the Merlins. Erebus assigned Sel to be my Kingsmage, for God's sake. He's been in my *home*. Sat at my family's table. He was there when they took my mother. His Mageguard *killed* my father and nearly killed *me*, under his orders. He would have killed—"

He stops himself short. Focuses on me again. His eyes grow cold, sharpening to steel.

"William told me what Erebus and the Regents did to you at the Institute. How they tortured you, drugged you. Wanted to experiment on you to find out how your Bloodcraft worked. Erebus *let* the Regents lock you away when he had the power to stop them. Why? Just to keep his own identity hidden? Or because he wanted to see how much you could take?"

I remember the Institute. Remember the repeated mesmers. The fear I'd felt—the hopelessness. Of that entire experience, the only face I can see in my mind's eye is Erebus's.

"I think"—I pick at the comforter, speaking aloud something I've never said before—"he wanted to do both. Preserve his identity, and then, when he could, fake my death and take me away. Hide me until he could use my power."

"And let you suffer in the meantime?" Nick says, outraged. "Let the Regents brutalize his prized weapon?"

"Yes. And Erebus let *you* suffer too," I say. "He watched you grow up, knowing all along that you weren't the Scion of Arthur. The Order treats its Scions with cruelty. Turns them into child soldiers."

"Oh, I know." Nick's eyelids flutter, lost in his own history. "There are some memories I wish I could forget. Then again, maybe I'll get my chance to tell Erebus exactly what his manipulations have cost us all."

"He said someone would be a nuisance to him," I say, recalling my and Erebus's conversation at the museum. "Maybe it was you."

"Oh, I *hope* it was me." A coiled, eager expression shifts across Nick's features. "I'd love nothing more than to be a nuisance to Erebus Varelian, the Shadow King of Annwfyn."

"Annwfyn?"

Nick nods. "The stories say that is where the King came from. Not the demon dimension but another place. An otherworld."

I chew on my lip, thinking. "He's never mentioned Annwfyn. Only the demon plane."

Nick's voice is a distant murmur. "Legends are born from a kernel of truth, but myths create meaning because people *treat* them like truth. A being that old could be one or the other—or something in between."

As he finishes speaking, we watch my bloodmark darken and dim. When it disappears back into my skin, Nick's gaze turns inward. "My father told me so many tales about Arthur and his great foes. At first, I believed them all. Then, I saw how much he lied and understood how those lies served him. It's gonna take me a while to wrap my head around at least some of those stories being true."

"Do you want to talk about him?" I ask tentatively. "Your father?"

He focuses on me. "No. But thank you for asking."

"I mean it."

"I know you do."

A beat later, Nick inhales sharply, shaking his head as if to clear it. "We should get dressed. There's another communion today."

"Are you sure?" I ask, uncertain. "It's okay if you need a minute to—"

He smiles. "I'm fine. I should head down anyway. I want to spend some time with the suits, see what other details I can squeeze out of them with my bro face."

Half an hour later, we're ready to head down to breakfast. Today, Nick's dressed in a charcoal sweater and wool dress pants. I've pulled out an emerald-green pleated skirt and tights and a peach sweater, finishing it off with a green-and-cream plaid silk scarf around my neck and shoulders and pulling my hair into a high ponytail.

I don't miss Nick's appreciative once-over of my ensemble; I was hoping for it, honestly. He clears his throat as he meets me at the door. "Ready?"

"Ready."

But before he can turn the knob, he pitches forward against the door with a gasp.

"Nick!" My heart kicks into a sprint. I scan the room, looking for the evidence of a warlock attack, scenting the air for pact magic—or, worse, Mikael.

His eyes squeeze shut as he presses both palms against the wood. "I'm fine!"

"But—" I reach for his shoulder.

"Don't!" he snaps, as if he can sense my nearness.

I withdraw my hand, but panic is a living thing in my throat. "What's happening?"

"It's Sel." He grimaces, dipping his chin against his chest. "*Sel's* happening."

The facts of the Kingsmage Oath pour into me. "He's . . . angry?"

"Murderous," Nick clarifies between panting breaths. "Very, *very* murderous." He drops his forehead against the solid door, gritting his teeth to hold back a deep, pained groan.

I remember, then, the way he'd asked if Erebus's call to my bloodmark hurt me. I'd waved his concern away because it never had—but now I know why he asked. "Can you do anything to stop him?"

Nick shakes his head against the door. "Doesn't work that way."

"He can feel your mortal fear—"

"Not if I don't feel any fear."

"But—"

"Wherever Sel is, he's got plenty . . . of things . . . to worry about," Nick grits out. "I refuse to be one of them. Not anymore."

It takes everything in me not to reach out. Not to hold him. "How can you control your fear?"

His hands ball into fists on the wood. "With lots . . . of practice."

"That's—"

"*God*, he's pissed." His face twists into a half smile, half grimace. "Furious."

I wince. "Does this . . . does this happen a lot?"

Nick peers at me from one eye. "Daily."

"*Daily?!*"

"I'm usually a lot better . . . at . . ." He groans, pressing his forehead even harder into the wood. "Hiding it."

Then, as soon as Sel's anger has come, it begins to fade.

I watch the effort of containing it drain from Nick's body one muscle, one breath, at a time. It's all I can do—be there, watch, and wait. A minute passes, then two, until finally, he releases a long, shaky breath and flips himself over to slide down the door. He lands in an exhausted heap with his arms draped over his knees, his chin tucked against his chest. When he eventually uncurls his clenched fingers from their fists, the joints crack and pop, echoing in my ears.

After a few more moments, the only evidence that anything out of the ordinary had even happened is the faint moisture curling the hair at Nick's temples, at the nape of his neck. His breathing has evened out before I can even come up with something to say. Then, the only words I have are: "That was horrifying."

Nick chuckles, the sound muffled beneath his arms. "They've been worse."

"How much worse?"

He tips his head back against the door. "Sometimes they last longer. A few hours, one night. I think William thought I was having nightmares," he says with a weak smile. "Nightmares would be much more pleasant, that's for sure."

I shake my head. "How long have you been hiding these?"

Nick tilts his head back and forth, stretching his neck. "Since Northern."

I suck in a breath. "That's been four months! And you've had them *daily*?"

"They didn't start out that bad," Nick admits. He takes a deep breath, swiping a tongue over his dry lower lip. "They were short. Mild. Then . . . they got more severe. It's the demonia, I think. We're taught that all of a Merlin's emotions become more extreme, even the positive ones. Heightened. It's not his fault that I can feel it too."

I study him and see the circles beneath his eyes. Have they always been there? Or has being here in Mikael's house broken down his defenses? "Is that why . . . ?" He looks at me. "You have your masks?"

He huffs a breath. "Nah. Sel's not the reason I wear those. He sees *through* my masks, actually. Always has."

I hug my knees to my chest, considering their history and Nick's decision to hold Sel's rage. To be a vessel for it, without complaint or blame . . . and still have faith that Sel will return from his demonia.

That Sel's not gone, just absent.

I prop my chin on my knees. Nick feels me watching him. Turns to look at me. "Sorry you had to see that."

"I'm not." I hug my knees tighter. "Something about this place is making it harder to . . . hide."

"Yeah."

After a long moment, I shrug. "Guess we all have our demons."

He frowns—then releases a bark of warm laughter. "That is an *excellent* joke."

"You like that?" I smile. "Just came up with it."

"Please tell Sel when we find him." He grins. "He'll hate it."

When we enter the dining room, Zoe and Mariah beckon us over to join them at a table tucked in a corner of the already nearly empty space.

A server comes by to take our orders, and we wait until she leaves before I fill them in. "We had some visitors last night," I whisper.

"The kind that rhymes with the words 'four' and 'clock,'" Nick says, grabbing a muffin.

Zoe's eyes widen. "Are y'all okay?"

"We got rid of them," I say.

A worried expression crosses her face. "Were you injured?"

"A tiny scratch," I assure her. "He won't hurt Elijah over a scratch."

She gives me a look. "The old man can't be trusted when it comes to you, sorry."

"Did you see their faces?" Mariah asks.

"No," I say. "They wore ski masks."

"So they could be any warlock here?" Zoe asks. "Like Bianca's favorites, Lawson and Santiago?"

"Whoever they are, they were enchanted somehow," Nick says. "On top of their pact magic. We got rid of them, but that doesn't mean we're safe. We need to be more careful than ever now." He looks at the clock in the dining room. "I've got to go. Time to catch up with the snakes before the communion."

I lean back in my chair to watch the same group of wealthy, masked guests hovering at the door with to-go coffees in paper cups. "I sort of hate that you running off and leaving your fiancée behind with the womenfolk is actually a great cover in this situation."

Nick squeezes my shoulder. "Agreed. But it'll be worth it if I can come back with info we can use about our own communions tomorrow. I'll meet y'all later." He heads off with his hands in his pockets, his mask firmly back in place.

I shake my head, a new worry making itself known. "I don't know if I can play along well enough for Mikael. What if he notices something's different about me?"

Instead of responding right away, Mariah surprises me by calling the server back to ask if we can get our meals to go. Then she says, "I hope Nick finds out something we can use, but we should talk about a backup plan to protect you from Mikael tomorrow. Privately."

We carry our meals carefully through the hidden corridor that leads from Zoe and Mariah's room to the sanctuary of the abandoned library. After we finish eating, Mariah claps her hands together.

"No other way to say this, I suppose, but what's wrong with your branch?"

I blink. "My root's fine—"

"No, it's not," Mariah says. "First of all, it's the wrong color, but that's your Bloodcraft. I'm talking about you being a Medium. Something's off." She pulls her necklace out from beneath her shirt collar, holding the black stone in front of us. "This is the Heart of a Grand Dame. It enhances the wearer's natural branch of root. In my case, it enhances my Medium abilities. And I can see that your connection to the dead is broken."

I freeze like she's accused me of something. Like I've been caught.

Mariah steps forward, covering my hands with her own. "What happened? You know I'll help if I can."

Her support hurts to hear, for some reason. Maybe because it's just so . . . simple?

I'd believed Erebus when he told me that my loved ones would reject me when they realized that I no longer knew them. I shouldn't have.

I feel a sudden urge to share every bit of knowledge I *do* possess so that I'm not as alone as he wanted me to be.

"I . . . tried to save the world," I whisper. "Tried to be everything to everyone. Do everything my ancestors asked me to do, even when I didn't understand it. Even when it didn't make sense. I wanted to be like my mom, or like I thought she was, or how she'd want me to . . ."

Mariah squeezes my hand. "No one person can save the world, Bree. Not even you."

"I know, but I want you to know what I tried to do . . . and what I did when I failed."

And then, I tell her and Zoe everything. About believing that I could handle Arthur—and how he took advantage of me. How I remember hurting people because of it. How Erebus told me that Sel sacrificed himself for me—and now Sel's angry and hurting Nick at the same time. How I know that I have a father, but I don't know what he looks like. How the only people who still live inside me are the dead . . . even though I can no longer speak to them.

By the end, Zoe is seated cross-legged on top of a desk across from us, jaw completely slack.

Mariah has long since let go of my hands, growing stiller and more somber by the minute. Apprehension churns low in my gut before she asks the question I know is coming. "Bree," she says, "what did you do to your ancestral plane?"

I look between her and Zoe, and think of this bubble of safety the three of us have built. How limited it is, and what's on the other side of the doors waiting for us when we leave.

"I burned it. Scorched it with my root. Cut myself off from Arthur, from Vera, from . . . everyone. Even my mother."

Mariah sucks in a breath. "How could you?" She stumbles back, distancing herself from me. "Bree, how *could* you?"

And suddenly, there it is. The afterimage feeling, the deep gut echo, the single resonant emotion that my mind has assigned to Mariah: shame.

Deep, world-stopping, blanketing shame. Shame that slices. That makes one feel impossibly small and permanently suspended, in space, in time, in life. That makes me wonder if I'm worth other people's worry. Shame so consuming, it paralyzes my heart, my voice, my mouth. It takes a few attempts to start talking again, for thoughts to become words, for words to become sound.

"After the revival at Volition, I felt so . . . so abandoned. My mom was gone, and my ancestors couldn't help me, and I—" My eyes prick, turn hot with unshed tears. "I know it's not their fault they couldn't help me harness my root. Some didn't use it, didn't know how, or were too scared to expose themselves and risk the little they had. By the time Vera appeared, I thought she'd be the one, you know? The one who could help me. But she couldn't."

"She made a desperate decision during an impossible time, Bree," Mariah cries. "If she hadn't made the choices she did, you wouldn't *exist*. You owe her *respect*."

"I don't blame her for her choices."

"Then how could you—" She shakes her head. "You were their chosen one!"

"I never asked to be chosen! Being open to everyone meant being vulnerable to Arthur!" I say, pulling on the silver curl at my temple.

"You were the most powerful Medium I'd ever met!" Mariah says. "You were the culmination of it all. The answer. The plan."

My heart crumples inside my chest. "But I'm just one person, Mariah. I can't be everyone's answer. I can't be everyone's plan."

She shakes her head again, like my story isn't enough. And maybe it isn't, but it's what I have and I know it's true.

They let me gather myself, but even then, the words are hard.

"Vera had no idea that the Hunter, the Shadow King, had piggybacked on her bargain and marked her Line. When I told her what her descendants had been through carrying this power and this mark . . . it just felt like she didn't *care*. Like she didn't care that we had *all* lost our mothers because of this gift that we didn't ask for. That we haven't been able to stop running for our lives long enough, or even *live* long enough, to try and stop our own deaths. That we can't even save *ourselves*. If I have a daughter, she'll die young just like I'll die young and just like my mom died young—" My breath is a ragged, tearing thing from my lungs. "Our Bloodcraft, our weapon, kills us. Steals time. Steals life."

Mariah and Zoe sit and watch me breathe and cry. The sun passes behind a cloud, dimming the late-morning light in the library, turning its far corners into deep shadows. Mariah speaks in the silence. "I didn't realize. Didn't know your deaths are . . . a cycle."

"I *wanted* to become what they asked. The tip of the spear, the point of the arrow. The wound turned weapon," I say, voice catching on my clogged throat. "I still *want* to be their chosen one, but I just . . . I don't know how."

"Maybe . . . ," Mariah begins slowly, tentatively, her fingers twining around the leather cord of the Heart, "maybe it's not that Vera *didn't* care. Maybe she also just . . . didn't know how."

The shame bubbles up again. "I shouldn't have yelled at her."

"Why *wouldn't* you?" Zoe demands, jolting us both. "You'd been tortured and hunted like prey."

"No, I . . . I could have taken a beat—"

"I don't get it." Zoe says, shaking her head. "Y'all are both trying to be picture-perfect descendants, even though *you've* only ever lived your life once. And that life has only just gotten started. Talk about an impossible standard."

Mariah hedges. "As Rootcrafters, we're taught to defer—"

"No, you're not," Zoe says abruptly. "Or at least the ones I know aren't. We've got Rootcrafters in our family too, me and Elijah. They're taught to commune with the dead, not worship them. Truly commune, not that crap Mikael's doing with the Collectors."

Mariah's mouth snaps shut.

Zoe points at me. "Fix your ancestral-plane thingy and apologize to Vera for yelling if you want, but, goddamn, are you gonna punish yourself forever?" Then she looks at us both. "Who does that benefit, huh? Who?"

Mariah blinks, clearly as taken aback as I am by Zoe's clarity.

Zoe pulls her knees to her chest on the desk. "Look, Bree. You lost all your people, right? Well, in the middle of living with that, you made *me* realize the crown could be more than just the King's prize. That night at the Rat, you reminded me that the crown could be a way to stop him from hurting Rootcrafters. A way to stop other folks from losing *their* people. We're trapped in this nightmare mansion where we might slip up and get murdered, sure, but we're here because you cared about a girl you'd never even met before! About Rootcrafter girls that other people might forget about. That the news might forget about. That may not be Vera's mission for you or whatever, but I think it counts for somethin'." She shrugs. "Vera mighta had a vision for your life, but don't you deserve a chance to update her on the *reality* of your life? And petition for her help with *that*?"

Mariah's eyes widen at us both. "That . . . makes a ton of sense."

"I'm just saying, Vera never coulda known what Bree would be up against." Zoe lifts a shoulder. "I don't expect or need all of my ancestors to understand my life, but I think I deserve to live it. I deserve to figure it out."

Mariah considers Zoe, then turns back to me, nodding slowly. "Zoe's right. Vera couldn't have known, but neither could I. I haven't been through what you've been through, Bree. No one has. You've been *alone* in so much of this."

My eyes burn when she steps closer to me again. Takes my hands again.

"I don't think I want to be," I admit. "Not anymore."

"What *do* you want to be?"

It's only six words. One single question. But it feels impossible to answer.

We hear Nick's steps coming down the corridor before we see him. He walks in preoccupied, then pauses when he senses the energy in the room. His eyes take in each of us in a single scan, then land on me—and the tears on my cheeks.

He's at my side in a blink. "What's wrong?"

I wipe at my face. "Noth—"

"Don't say 'nothing.'"

"Um—"

"Bree just told us all about how she burned her ancestral plane," Zoe says, hopping down from her desk.

Mariah frowns at her. "That's not your story to share."

Zoe shrugs. Nick examines my face. "What does that mean, exactly?"

"I destroyed my own Medium powers." I sigh, puffing my cheeks out. "I can't speak to any of my ancestors anymore. Can't sense the dead. Can't blood walk. Can't be possessed."

Nick's brows rise. "You can't be possessed?"

"No. Not by Arthur. Not by anyone."

His eyes unfocus briefly, a strange expression passing over his face before it disappears. "Do you . . . want to reverse it?"

I look at him, then Mariah, then Zoe. Think about the silence in my heart and mind, not just from the people I've missed but from the people who have departed. My own mother. The ability to speak with her—something most human beings can never do, no matter how much they want to. I swallow around the lump in my throat. "Yes."

Nick's face is a mixture of emotions—affection and sadness. Pride. "Then you will."

"'Course she will," Zoe says. She turns to Nick. "Did you find anything else out about today's communion?"

Nick's eyes sharpen, back to the task at hand. "Yes. And we need to go, now."

"What's the urgency?" I ask.

"They think they've found the third thief."

44

THIS TIME, WE all sit together in the auditorium. We take four seats half-way up from the stage as the Collector audience continues to file in.

Nick leans in close to whisper into my ear. "Ava's here. Down on the left."

I follow his directions and find Ava seated by herself in the first row, one leg crossed primly over the other in a designer dress. "Up close and personal."

"She's up to something," Nick says.

I don't doubt it. She doesn't look our way or even seem to have noticed that we've arrived. Instead, her dark eyes are focused on the empty chairs onstage.

When Mikael enters, the crowd quiets just as it did before, but there is something silent and electric in the room today. Word must have spread that today's communion would include a confession to one of the weekend's scandals, and every guest in the audience seems to lean forward. Eager to see what secrets Mikael will rip from his five victims today.

"Welcome, Collectors," Mikael booms from the stage. "Once again, today we will reaffirm our discretion and truth with offered tribute."

The first guest walks out onstage. A tall woman with long black hair, red nails, and a heavy robe over a velvet dress and heels. Mikael gestures for her to take a seat, but she tips her chin up. "I'll stand, thank you."

Mikael flashes her a grin. "As you wish." He settles in the chair across from her, unbothered by her height or his position below her eye level.

I don't know if this woman feels more powerful standing—I would—but I know that Mikael's form of magic won't care whether she is seated or standing. He will feed from her truths no matter what.

"I will ask each of our guests five questions," Mikael repeats, "to help us understand if our community member can be trusted. If someone resists their natural inclination to tell the truth of things, I will know—and there will be a punishment." Mikael turns to the audience. "Are we in agreement?"

"Discretion and truth," the audience intones.

"Truth"—Mikael turns back to the tall woman—"and discretion."

Again, Mikael's illusion strikes at the back of my skull. But at least now I know why he reinforces it right before he feeds. It's a precaution, in case he overindulges and loses control over his human costume.

"Did you attack and wound my guard?" Mikael asks. The glowing green smoke of his talent rises to the woman's face, circling her mouth and nose.

Like the people Mikael interrogated yesterday, she shudders from its effects. "No."

"Did you attempt to break into the outbuilding on the grounds of Penumbra?"

She dips her chin to her chest, fists squeezed tight at her sides. "No."

"She's not resisting," I murmur.

"A strategy," Nick says.

Mikael leans forward. "Three questions remain and serve as tribute. A sign of your loyalty."

The woman nods. "I am ready."

Mikael hums. "When did you commit your last crime?"

The woman tilts her head. "Five days ago."

Mikael lifts his nose and inhales deeply—frowning. "And what was it?"

"Fraud."

"She's not ashamed," Nick whispers. "Not feeling tormented or guilty. Not feeding him."

"Lucky her," I mutter.

Nick shakes his head, eyes narrowing at the stage. "No. He's frustrated."

Mikael's jaw tightens. Instead of pursuing the same line of questioning he did with the five communions yesterday, he switches gears for his final inquiry. "By whom were you last betrayed?"

The woman flinches. Mikael grins. This time, the smoke around her face loops around her eyes and ears, filling her mouth as she inhales, scooping out her truth. "My sister. She . . . she seduced my husband. Lied to my children about me. Stole my grandmother's wedding ring from my bedside table."

"The closest betrayals deliver the richest wounds." Mikael tips his head back, smiling. "Your pain. Your anger. Your sadness. Thank you."

The woman blinks as if waking from a dream and staggers offstage.

The next three communions proceed much like the ones yesterday. An executive ignores product safety reports. Another inflates the prices of life-saving drugs. A judge accepts bribes for convictions. They leave the stage spent and confused, as if they never expected their secrets to be collected too.

Then, the last communion begins, and even at this distance, I can see Mikael's eyes flash with hunger.

This is the third thief.

The man walks out onstage stiffly, as if his own elbows and knees are fighting him—and he drops into the chair as if pressed down by a pair of invisible hands.

Zoe nudges me. "Something's up."

I nod. The man is not moving easily, but there is no magic around him. No green smoke. Nothing to make him seem as off as he is.

But Mikael's sharp eyes notice every movement, every twitch of the man's fingers on his designer slacks, every pulse of the muscles in his jaw.

"Did you attack and wound my guard?" Mikael asks, unspooling his power around the man's eyes and throat.

When the man answers, his voice comes out strained. "No."

Mikael makes a low humming sound in the back of his throat. "Did you attempt to break into the outbuilding on the grounds of Penumbra?"

For this answer, the man visibly bears down on his back teeth, molars grinding. The audience murmurs around us in the darkness.

"Resistance is a confession," Mikael reminds him.

The man's jaw snaps open. "Yes."

Several gasps erupt from the audience. Behind, below, and beside us. Whispers break the silence, threatening to disrupt the calm manner in which Mikael has conducted the communions thus far. Mikael rises slowly, withdrawing his magic from the man's face. "Why did you commit this crime?"

The man struggles once more—until finally he seems to break whatever has been holding him back. "She made me!"

More gasps from the crowd. My eyes dart to Ava, who has not moved a muscle. She sits placidly, hands in her lap, eyes straight ahead.

"Who is 'she'?"

The man's eyes roll in their sockets.

"He's been mesmered," Nick whispers in my ear. "I *see* a spell woven into his body, and it's not Mikael's." Nick's eyes dart to Ava, who has not moved. "It's the same magic that was on the warlocks who attacked us."

I stiffen in my seat. "Ava sent them."

"She timed the mesmer to fade before it could be connected to her or anyone else."

I lean closer. "If she can mesmer, why wouldn't she have just mesmered you?"

"She would have if she could, so maybe she can't."

Mikael's magic focuses on the man, churning around his face. "Who is 'she'?" he demands again. "Answer me!"

Tears stream down the man's face. I can't tell if he's resisting Mikael or resisting Ava. In the end, he shakes his head so violently that spittle flies from his mouth. "No one. Nevermind. That was a lie!"

"You lied to me?" Mikael roars.

"Yes," the man gasps. "Yes!"

Mikael's patience snaps. His illusion flickers—red eyes burning bright.

Quick as a snake, his hand darts out—and a dagger embeds itself into the man's chest.

The stage lights go dark before the first drop of blood spills. The houselights rise—and down at the front, Ava is walking swiftly to the end of her aisle while most of the audience remains glued to their seats.

"We have to—" I start.

But Nick's already moving. "Come on."

And then we are pushing past people toward the exit, not bothering to apologize as we shuffle around the knees of the other seated guests in our row. The audience around us is gathering up their coats and talking among themselves, like this was a show and they'd gotten their money's worth. But some are staring at us like we're the strange ones.

"Slow down," I whisper to Nick, and he slows his pace.

I feel a spike of worry for Mariah. For Zoe. For anyone who hasn't seen this much death up close or caused it themselves. But Nick and I have to find Ava and quickly, before she disappears.

When Nick hits the outer aisle, he visibly forces himself to take even steps. To not clamber down the stairs two at a time to the first-level exit. To not sprint as fast as I know he can to the double doors. He turns to me with a strained smile, holding his hand out to help me down the stairs like a good partner would—and I know it's killing him to do this. To pretend like we aren't who we are, like we don't want to fight Ava for what she's done. I reach for his hand, and his grip squeezes tight; I find I don't mind the pain. I squeeze him back too.

We walk down the stairs hand in hand, holding each other tight, our hearts pounding in our chests. When we finally hit the exit doors, the hall is empty—every other guest is still in the auditorium—and we break into a sprint after a shadow slipping around a corner.

Nick is a blur of gray down the hall, speeding after Ava. I don't shout for him to slow down now because I am sprinting behind him, arms pumping, my skirt flying in the air behind me.

By the time I round the first corner, I don't even see him. All I can do is follow the sound of his feet. I race to the end of a long hallway, trying to recall the map of Penumbra that Elijah showed us.

I round another corner, nearly skidding into a wall, then another. By then, I've lost Nick's path, lost the sound of his feet. I keep running anyway, straining to hear them, taking deep breaths in case I catch an aether signature. I pass a dozen rooms on the ground floor, two salons, and a gift shop before I finally stop running.

I stand panting in the hallway, chest heaving. I don't dare cry out for him, but I don't know where he's gone. Don't know where Ava's gone.

I've lost them.

Two security guards spot me before I recover my breath. "Ma'am?" one of them says.

I can smell his pact magic slowly creeping out from his skin—a warlock, readying himself. I smile demurely and smooth my hands down my skirt. "Oh, hello," I say, using every breathing technique Erebus ever taught me to control my panting breaths, tame my frantic heart rate.

The best lies are close to the truth.

I tug at my scarf and wave a hand. "Whew, it's hot in here!"

The guards frown as they approach. "Can we help you?" The one who spoke to me looks at his watch. "The communion just finished, but you're a long ways from the auditorium—"

"Oh, I know!" I say. "I was looking for the kitchen and got lost in this big old place."

"The kitchen?"

I nod, pivoting on one heel, then the other. I rest my palm against my forehead. "I got outta there a little early because I got so overheated in my seat. It's my first time at Penumbra, you know," I say, letting my drawl have its way with my vowels, and smile. "I thought I'd get myself a cold glass of water or some tea . . . something to cool myself off before dinner."

The warlocks exchange glances, uncertain. But after a moment, the scent of pact magic begins to dissipate.

"We can escort you to the dining room, if you'd like?" the second warlock says. "They'll have any beverage you like available there."

"Oh, would ya? I just got so turned around."

"No problem. We're walking that way now."

I smile. "Please. Lead the way."

Dinner is a nightmare. When I make it back to our usual table in the dining room, only Zoe and Mariah greet me. Nick is nowhere to be seen.

It's another formal affair with bustling waitstaff in a busy room. While we could probably communicate without hushed whispers, no one feels like talking. I have no idea what I order, just that what arrives doesn't look very appetizing.

We don't bother keeping up appearances by being chatty. Mostly, Zoe and I exchange worried glances over Mariah when she's not looking. She picks at her food, offering little commentary.

I don't blame her.

One execution was too many, and now we've seen two.

"Did Benedict find . . . ?" Zoe finally asks when it's clear no one is really eating.

"I don't know," I respond, pushing a vegetable around on my plate. "I lost them. Couldn't keep up."

"I didn't know she could do that. To someone."

"I think it was rumored but not confirmed."

"Well, we've confirmed it," Mariah mumbles.

"Yeah," I say.

As dinner closes down, Zoe turns to me as Mariah walks down the hall ahead of us, in the opposite direction of my and Nick's room. "We're gonna turn in," she says. "I'll take care of her. Go find him."

She nods and squeezes my shoulder before jogging off after Mariah.

The energy at Penumbra is busy tonight—Collectors energized by what they've seen onstage and eager to talk about it, to mingle. I pass two wood-paneled drawing rooms staffed with bartenders serving cocktails to chattering guests. I drift down the hallway without being noticed much, slipping in and out of salons, hoping to catch a glimpse of Nick or Ava. I could go back to our room, but something tells me that he's not there. If he had found Ava—he'd be confronting her. If he lost her, he'd have come back to the dining room to join us and keep up appearances. Make sure I was okay.

I give it another half an hour of moving around on the lower floor before turning down a more dimly lit hallway that leads to the indoor pool. When I round a corner, I feel a blast of warm, humid air, and my nose burns with the smell of chlorine. A steady dripping noise greets me as I peer down the hall. I take a few more steps—then freeze as I hear a pair of low voices and heavy footsteps heading in my direction.

I back up swiftly, reversing my path—until a hand clasps me over the mouth, dragging me sideways before I get a chance to scream.

45

MY CAPTOR SHOVES me into a tight space. Pitch-black. The sharp stench of cleaning supplies leaks through their fingers over my nose.

I wrench their hand away from my face and pivot, fist raised—

"*It's me,*" whispers a familiar, low voice in the darkness.

Shock turns to anger. "Where have you been?"

Nick smacks a hand over my mouth again just as the voices outside the hall grow louder, echoing against the walls and tall ceilings. The sound of approaching footsteps—expensive shoes on marble floors—stops me from speaking more thoroughly than Nick's hand ever could. I shove his hand away and shuffle past him to the door, pressing my ear against it before the voices get too close. He leans over me to do the same.

"Some of the guests knew the gentleman who failed the communion." Bianca. "They are uncomfortable with his confession."

"They aren't the only ones." Another voice. Lawson the warlock. "Did Mikael really have to off him in front of everyone?"

"His strength would have been contested if he hadn't," Bianca says. "Maintaining the community's trust is a delicate balance. Which is why new players are not admitted midway through. We wouldn't accept that in a normal year, and this one has exceeded our norms several times over already."

"Yeah, I know. But this player brings cash. Lots of it." A shuffling of fabric. "Says there's more where this came from if he can join the auction tomorrow."

"Mikael will need to vet him personally."

"The guy says he'll do what it takes. He's outside the gates right now, waiting."

A pause. They've stopped walking.

"Boss?" Lawson prompts.

"I'll speak with Mikael," Bianca replies. "Prep our visitor. Bring him in through the garden gate, *not* the front door. If Mikael agrees to let him stay, he'll need to be masked. Keep him separate from other guests to safeguard against anyone noticing a newcomer and late admittance. No meals in the dining room, no tours, no attendance at tomorrow's communion. He can attend the auction and *only* the auction."

"Understood."

Their footsteps pass by the closet door, receding down the hall.

"A new—" I begin.

"Shh," Nick whispers. "Not yet."

We wait until the footsteps grow muffled. When they finally go silent, I feel more than hear Nick counting the seconds under his breath. Thirty. Forty. Fifty. At sixty, he releases a long sigh. "Okay."

"A new player?" I ask. "Someone wants in on the auction?"

"Someone who wasn't invited in the first place," Nick murmurs. "Could it be Erebus? Coming to retrieve you, his 'investment'?"

"No. He checks on my bloodmark once a day, so he already knows I'm alive. Knows I'm strong enough to fight. This mission was a test, for me and Zoe both. If he was going to show up and crash Mikael's party, he would have done it the first night when we didn't go home; he's the one who told us to pack overnight bags just in case. He's too patient to rush in like this."

"But he wants his crown."

"Not just the crown. He won't attack Mikael to get it, because he wants his Court back too. Wants Mikael and the other Nightshades to join him again. And even if he did come here, he can't touch the crown himself. The Morgaines made sure of that when they bewitched it."

"So this new player is someone new who just so *happens* to be in the market for rare artifacts during a weekend when at least three other people are here to steal one? I don't buy it."

"Neither do I, but it's not like we can confront Mikael or Bianca about it. We'll have to wait and find out tomorrow."

"Waiting isn't my strong suit."

"Mine either."

"I'm aware."

I huff. Pause. "Where were you?"

"Chasing Ava." Nick sighs above me, a rush of breath over the top of my curls. "I thought I had her in the gardens. Didn't think she'd risk using aether while Mikael was still on the property, but her power—Morgaine power—is so subtle, it's nearly impossible to detect. She blasted me back—stunned me. Knocked me out."

I inhale sharply. "Did she hurt you?"

"My pride, maybe," he whispers. "I'm more mad at myself. When I woke up, she was gone. I went to our room, and you were gone too. Went to Zoe and Mariah's, and they said you'd gone looking for me, so I asked around until someone said they'd seen you walk this way." He makes a sound of frustration at the back of his throat. "I shouldn't have left you alone. I should have stayed back."

"We were both chasing Ava down. You're faster."

"Something could have happened to you."

"We won't tell Sel—"

"It's not about *Sel*," Nick whispers, voice harsh. "It's about *me*. And not leaving you behind again."

We fall silent. I listen to his breathing slow. Hear him swallow.

"You keep saying you left me," I murmur. "I don't *remember* you leaving me—"

"But *I* do—"

"I only remember *me* leaving you."

Another pause. A sigh. "You had your reasons."

"And you didn't?"

"You're a king." I feel his forehead drop down against the back of my curls. Feel his hands fall to my waist, fingers light. "The only decisions kings make are the hard ones."

"I know a man named Martin Davis died," I whisper. "I remember someone else nearly died right after. And that person defended themselves against an enemy. If that was you—"

"We've all witnessed horrible things." He sighs. "Sometimes we're the ones who commit them."

"Sometimes we attempt great things too."

"Not like you. You're looking for the crown to stop Erebus from going after the girls."

I shake my head against him. "But Zoe's right. If I give the crown back to Erebus, he'll destroy the Order. It's a shortsighted plan—"

Nick squeezes my hips. "It's a plan that *saves* people. Those plans are always worthy. And the Order can't go on as it is, anyway. It will fall. The cycle has to stop."

"It'll only stop if I die."

"You won't die," he whispers. "The Order doesn't deserve your life—and it will *never* deserve your death."

I swallow tightly. Feel my eyes burning at their corners. "Because I'm its king?"

"No. Because you're Bree." Nick's breath blows warm against my neck, intimate. "Brilliant, beautiful, brave Bree."

I shiver at his closeness—and the memory of his kiss. Then I realize, belatedly, that the moment he pulled me into this closet, he'd touched me. Not over the layer of my clothes, but skin against skin.

I hesitate—then take a chance. Lean back against his chest. Fold deeper into his arms.

At first, his fingers loosen around my hips, and I worry that he might release me—or, worse, push me away. Open the door to invite the harsh, bright, terrifying world of Penumbra into our cocoon of stolen time. But then, Nick's hands settle, firmer this time, until his heart beats steady against my spine.

Still, I wait for him to pull back. Wait for him to remind me that he shouldn't touch me, even through my clothes. But Nick doesn't pull back. Instead, he smooths one palm slowly forward along the curve of my hip.

His hand pauses, as if he's making a decision.

Then, his finger slips under the hem of my sweater to slide across the narrow, exposed strip of my waist. I hold my breath. He doesn't move to caress me further—doesn't need to. Here in the darkness, this single point of contact, where his forefinger rests against my bare skin, consumes all of my attention.

I don't know what's changed. Why he's touching me like this. What decision he's made. But I find I don't care, I don't care. All I know is that Nick feels like . . .

"Cliffside at the ocean. Touching the sky." His voice is a quiet ache. "Touching the horizon."

I tip my head back against his shoulder. "And the fall?"

In answer, a gentle tug at the scarf around my neck.

Nick's fingers, pulling the silk loose. It slips free. Drifts down to our feet, baring my throat and collarbone. Fingers lift my curls, pulling them back and to one side.

Warm lips press against the juncture of my neck and shoulder. Softly. Briefly. And then they're gone.

"The coast should be clear." Nick whispers. "We should get back."

My eyelids flutter. "You'll have to . . . lead the way. I got pretty lost earlier." He chuckles. "I got you."

Nick lets me shower first. The hot water loosens the muscles in my shoulders, but every time I close my eyes, I think of the man struggling in the chair. Ava sitting calmly, watching her spellcraft at work. Mikael—and the dagger I never saw coming.

By the time I'm back in my bed, wrapped in my pajamas, I've replayed the scene over and over again. And come to some dire conclusions.

As Nick leaves the en suite in his T-shirt and pants, rubbing a towel over his head, I speak up. "We should have run the first night."

Nick tosses his towel onto the window seat. "Huh?"

"We should have run," I say, hopping off the bed to pace. "You'll be able to pass the communion without lying, but who knows what you'll have to reveal in the meantime? I might be able to pass *while* lying, but Mikael won't accept that *no one* is guilty of the second crime—Bianca made that clear earlier. We should have just made a break for it."

"Running would have been an admission of guilt, and he'd have killed us both."

"We might have had a chance—"

"And leave Zoe and Mariah behind?"

I stop pacing. He's right. I drop my head in my hands. "We're never gonna even make it to the auction. The communion takes place right beforehand."

"Hey, hey." Nick strides over to me, grasping my arms through my sleeves. "We'll figure it out. We're gonna be fine."

"How do you know that?"

"Because it's you and me."

I blink at him, gaping. "Why do you say that like it's . . . like that's an answer?"

"Because it *is* an answer."

I bat his hands away. "Don't change the subject."

"I'd forgotten how prickly you get when I say sweet things."

I scowl. "You're not allowed to say sweet things."

"Why's that?"

"Because . . ." I throw my hands up. "We're missing parts of our history, and you don't want to touch me, but then you *do* touch me, and one of us might die tomorrow, and there's still a war going on, and—"

"Hey." Nick grasps my arms again, laughing. "Everything you said just now is true—except one."

"Which one?"

He sighs, smile falling away. "I do want to touch you."

"Then why do you keep saying you don't? Why'd you touch me tonight?"

"I never said I don't want to," he murmurs. "But we have to stop."

"Why?"

"It's not a good idea."

"Over it." I turn to walk away—and he darts forward, catching my shoulder.

"Wait," he says. "Please."

I let him turn me back around. "Don't mess with my head."

"I don't want to, I promise—"

"Then what *do* you want?"

"I . . ." Nick steps closer. He searches my face, torment pulling at his features. His gaze claims my brows, my eyes, my lips. When he finally answers, his voice is a desperate rasp. "I'm drowning in you, Bree. I shouldn't want to. I should fight it. But I can't."

My eyes flutter closed, then open. I inhale a ragged breath. Exhale an answer. "So drown."

He groans—and we break against each other, mouths crashing. A wave of heat, lips, teeth. His palms capture my jaw, pulling me closer. A lifeline. An anchor. Skin to blessed skin.

When we part, I surface before he does. "You said you wouldn't kiss me again," I gasp. He is so still, I wonder if I'd thought the words instead of spoken them out loud. "You said—"

"I know what I said." Then, his mouth surges to meet mine—and we collide.

Nick grips my thighs, lifting me up, walking me back, tipping me over until I'm pressed into the mattress beneath him. Heat, weight, and nothing that feels close enough.

The kiss in the elevator felt like fierce longing, but his words afterward still echo: *A distraction. A strategy.*

Now, when Nick grasps my chin, tilting it so he can kiss me more deeply, so our mouths meet more fully, those words become hollow. When Nick's lips coax mine open, the elevator becomes a trick, one of his quiet lies.

I moan in response to his questing mouth—on my jaw, across my throat— and he answers with a deep, hungry sound. He drags my shirt down one shoulder, teeth grazing my collarbone—but when my leg hitches up around his hip, he pauses, pulls away.

"Wait, wait—" Nick pushes back to his knees, hand warm against my leg, stilling it against his lower ribs. "I didn't . . . I didn't say all that just to"—he runs a hand down his face—"just to get you in bed."

I devour his breathless voice, the red flush on his cheeks. Collect them as if they're mine. "Congratulations?" I say, grinning.

He breathes out in frustration, glaring at me over his fingers. "You know what I mean."

"I do." I tug at the hem of his shirt, pulling him down until he falls with both hands on either side of my head.

He lets me kiss him again until he fists the quilt. Until he uncurls a hand to gently grip my shoulder, breath catching in his throat. "Bree . . ."

"Yes, Nick?" I drag my fingers through his hair, against his scalp.

He groans at the sensation, eyes closing in pleasure. "That feels—" The hand on my shoulder rises to my own, stilling it in his hair.

"One night," I whisper, my own voice breathy.

"What?" His eyes snap open.

"One night, before tomorrow," I say quietly. "That's all we have for certain."

His eyes soften. He pulls my palm down to kiss it with a hot, open mouth. "I know."

Anticipation zips through me, my breath turns shallow with want.

"And . . . ," he murmurs, "I'm sorry."

I freeze, realizing what he's said without saying it. I withdraw my hand from his lips, flush with embarrassment. I wish I could shrink, become tiny and invisible. Slip out from under him without either of us noticing.

His eyes widen. "No, that's not—"

"No, it's okay. I, um . . . I can . . ." I reach for the blanket, even though I'm already dressed. As if covering myself up with another layer might protect me further, hide me better—

"Hey." He dips his head to catch my eye, squeezing my knee. "Look at me?" A request.

I look everywhere *but* him. "Nope." I shake my head. "Can't—"

"Bree, look at me."

When I finally meet his eyes, they strike me deep—a mixture of banked heat, fond amusement, remorse. His thumb presses into my bare shoulder, a warm stamp against my skin. "You understand why I can't be with you like that, don't you? At least a little?"

"Because you don't," I whisper, *"want—"*

"No, B, no." His pleading sigh sends his hair floating above his brow. "I can't be with you because you're not yourself in full yet, and I know you want to be. This isn't about missing people or missing memories. You're still *you*, and if you have to, you'll make new memories. I'm talking about what's been *done* to you. What Erebus took. Your quest—your *real* quest—isn't complete."

I gnaw on my lip, feeling as fragile as old glass. As breakable. Especially because I know he's right. "I know," I admit.

But it still feels like there's something he's not saying.

Another thought occurs to me. "If this is because it's my first time . . ."

"It's not." Nick presses a lingering kiss against my forehead. "But thank you for letting me know. That's information I want to have."

I flush beneath him. "But there *is* something else, isn't there?"

He looks up and around, at the room, the mansion, all of it. "*This* is not how I want you. I don't want masks and artifice. Where we have to be Benedict and Iris because if we're Nick and Bree, we could be killed. When there's risk if we don't . . . pretend."

I purse my lips together. Consider what he's saying. I want to rebel against his reasoning, but in the end, I can't. Still . . .

"How *would* you want me?" I ask. "If we weren't pretending?"

Nick's eyes flash, pupils widening as my question sweeps through him. He leans close until our mouths are nearly touching, until our breaths mingle and my face heats.

"If we weren't pretending, I would want *all* of you, Bree Matthews." His voice rumbles low enough to carry through my body, from the tips of my ears, across my hips, down to my toes. When he shifts against me, I gasp. "I want you whole." His next kiss is a promise that leaves me trembling. "I want you *entire*."

Nothing about that felt hypothetical. It feels so real that it takes a few attempts to speak. The first sound that leaves my mouth is definitely not a word. After another struggling moment and ragged breath, I finally manage something verbal. "Oh."

He grins against my cheek. Chuckles low beneath my jaw. Traces soft kisses around my chin, to the edge of my mouth.

"Can we . . . ?" I whisper against his mouth as it glances over mine. I run my hand down his side until he's the one shuddering. "Can we pretend to be . . . Nick and Bree?"

He draws back. "B . . ."

"Just while we sleep?"

He lifts my chin with a finger. Studies me. The connection between us flickers like a candle, then holds. "Okay. We can pretend to be Nick and Bree."

When he pulls the covers over us and wraps me in his arms, neither of us pulls away.

46

WE WAKE UP tangled in each other. Nick's palm has captured my belly beneath my top, his fingers spread across my skin. His shoulder curves over mine, a heavy shield against the sunrise. One of his pajama-clad legs is slung over my thigh, pressing my hips down into the too-soft mattress. My lungs might be crushed from the weight of his rib cage, but I find that I don't care.

Who needs air, anyway?

The cramp in my calf, however, is lodging a complaint. I'm debating how long I can ignore it when Nick mumbles against my neck, "If we don't get out of bed, maybe Mikael will leave us alone."

I grin into his bicep. "I don't think we'll make it long without food."

"I have a confession," he murmurs, pulling me closer until his mouth is a secret whisper at my ear. "I've been sneaking muffins into the room every day after breakfast."

I burst into laughter. "They're not even that good!"

"But they're *lemon pound cake* muffins. That amount of butter alone could keep us alive for a *week*."

I collapse into a giggle, and he grips me tighter. I feel his smile against my neck, my hair. It feels good to laugh . . . until it doesn't. Until it hurts, because I know it can't last.

Because today's our last day. And because no matter what happens at the communion—or the auction, if we make it that far—we're leaving Penumbra tonight.

Nick swallows hard in the silence between us. Presses a kiss against my shoulder. Speaks my fears into existence in a low voice. "We could run, like you said."

"And go where?"

Neither one of us has an answer to that, and he knows it.

"If I don't go back to Erebus, he'll come find me. If I leave with you or Mariah, I'll bring the Shadow King right to your doorsteps." I gnaw at my lip, my own confession burning in my chest, along with a terrible guess. "I haven't told you about the bargain I made with him."

His grip tightens. "Tell me."

"I asked Erebus to train me, to make me stronger in a way that no one else could . . . but I also asked Erebus to take Sel to his mother to see if she could stop his demonia. I don't know where they are, or if she could even help him, or if I just made everything worse—"

"William told me about Natasia. If what he said about her is true, then no one else on the planet could help Sel better than his mother right now." Nick's arms tighten around me, his voice forgiving and soft. "Thank you for sending him to her. You did the right thing."

"Not if he's this angry—"

"Sel's always angry. His mother won't be able to stop that." Nick sighs heavily. "But I'm glad he's safe. Relieved that he's with someone who cares about him. Sel's not good on his own. He shouldn't be alone."

I fall silent. Wait for him to demand my reason for not sharing all of this earlier. It doesn't come. Instead, Nick taps my stomach. "Hey, what's going on in your head?"

I swallow. "There's more. More to the bargain."

"I'm listening."

"I asked Erebus to grant me two demands, and he agreed to both, but he only claimed one trade in exchange: my offer to go with him. I still owe him a debt. He can call it in at any moment and has threatened everyone I care about—everyone I love—if I refuse."

Nick doesn't speak, but I hear him breathing. Feel the pace of his heart pick up where it rests against my back.

I feel my neck heat with shame. "Say something."

"I'm thinking too many things to say just one."

"What kind of things?"

"Dangerous things. Violent things." His voice deepens. "How to kill a god."

"No." I twist around to find that shadowed darkness in his eyes and clutch his face between my palms. "He'll destroy you."

"If he dies first, I won't mind."

"Nick, no. Mikael *plays* with his food—Erebus is beyond that. He waits and watches. Traps people when they think they're safe, lures them in when they ask for help, finds weaknesses you don't even know you have. He's the *real* snake, the viper—"

"If it means you'll be free," Nick says, voice tight, "that you can rest—"

"I don't *want* to rest," I say. "I want to stop him. I want my mind back. I don't want anyone else to die."

He studies me, the shadow leaving his face until it softens at my fingertips. He slides one hand over mine. Pulls it gently away to kiss my palm. "I know."

Today's communion takes place after breakfast, to give Penumbra's guests free time to themselves before the auction in the evening.

"Glad to see we all look like we're considering escape plans." Zoe stands with her arms crossed, in a vintage blazer, slacks, and low boots, gazing at the crowd around us in their masks and formal wear. Waitstaff drift between groups of people, balancing black trays in one hand, offering drinks to anyone who looks their way. "Wouldn't want to be the only one not smiling and drinking Bellinis."

"I don't know how they can drink right now." Mariah is beside me with her arms wrapped around herself, shifting her weight from side to side. "I just want this to be over."

"Benedict and Iris." Bianca's voice draws our attention.

We turn as a group to see her and her warlock lieutenant, Lawson, walking toward us.

"That's us," Nick says.

Bianca waves a hand behind her. "You've seen the communions. You know how these go?"

Nick nods. "We do."

She beckons her lieutenant forward. "Lawson and I will escort you to your seats."

"You mean you're here to make sure we don't run," I say.

Bianca's smile is tight. "Why would you run?"

Lights flicker once, twice, overhead, urging the audience to enter the auditorium and find their seats for today's show. My stomach tumbles. My breakfast choosing now to fight my nerves.

I give a final nod to Zoe and Mariah and begin to walk forward, but Nick reaches Bianca first. "I need to make a pit stop."

Bianca frowns. "If you try anything—"

Nick smiles reassuringly. "Nah. Me and Iris are in this together. You can escort me to the bathroom and back if you want."

Bianca purses her lips, then waves Lawson over. "Take Iris. I'll watch Benedict."

Before I can say a word, Nick steps closer to brush his lips across my cheek. "See you inside. I'll be right there."

I watch Bianca lead him toward the restrooms down the hall, to the left side of the theater doors.

When I turn back, Lawson clears his throat.

I bite back a wince at the acrid magic scent rising off his skin. "I'm ready."

"This way."

Lawson escorts the three of us to the front row, pointing out the open seat assigned to Nick. This time, Zoe sits on the far end with Mariah between us. As the auditorium fills around us, I start to get worried.

"Where is he?" Mariah asks.

I gnaw on my lip. "He'll be here. Better question is how am I supposed to know when to go onstage?"

"Bianca or Lawson will signal, I bet," Zoe says.

But then the houselights lower, and the stage lights rise to reveal two empty chairs, and Nick isn't back yet.

Mikael walks out in a bloodred tuxedo, eyes bright and smile wide.

As if he hadn't just killed a man on this same stage in front of everyone less than twenty-four hours ago.

"Welcome, Collectors," Mikael calls to the audience. "This morning, we will reaffirm our discretion and truth with offered tribute. And, I hope, find our final culprit. As we have already uncovered the attempted thief, today we will pursue the individual who harmed my loyal guard."

The audience boos and stomps in response, more active—and eager—today after yesterday's bloodshed.

"But I bring news! Because one suspect has been eliminated, today we'll have *four* questions dedicated to tribute instead of three."

The audience cheers and claps. Hungry for more horrible truths, just like their demon leader. Even though they can't feed on the anguish of the confessors, they desire the anguish all the same.

Mikael makes a motion toward the far end of the stage, and the first guest walks out. A short, brown-skinned woman with blond hair, wearing a dark blue mask and matching pantsuit.

I look for Nick again and don't see him in the shadows or near the entrance. Worry creeps into my nervous stomach. What if he spotted Ava? What if they're fighting again? But, no, Bianca is with him and he said he wouldn't leave me.

He said that . . . but where is he now?

I'm so preoccupied with Nick's absence that the woman's confession goes by in a blur. I'm too busy sweating beneath my cardigan and thin dress. Mikael's illusion prickles at the back of my skull, stronger today. As if he's already antici-pating losing control of his human form.

By the time the third guest walks out onto the stage, my heart is thundering in my chest in apprehension. I remind myself that when I sit across from Mikael, he won't know who I am or what I can do—Erebus has made sure of that, and here, in the midst of all this horror, I can't help but be grateful. My furnace is sealed up so tight, it may as well be welded shut. Mikael won't discover that I'm the Scion of Arthur.

I've already planned to lie about attacking his guard, but with Mikael's acute sense for human secrets, my lies might not be enough. And even if I pass *that* test, there's still the tribute questions. Mikael wants my pain, and I've got plenty to give him, but sharing any of those truths will get me killed here. My every anguish and heartbreak and regret is tangled up with magic. With the Order, with Arthur, and with the rogue Nightshade's own former king. Nothing I can say is something a sheltered human rich girl should know anything about, and resistance is a confession.

And yet it's Nick I'm most worried about. My bloodmark may protect me if it comes to that, but it won't protect him. If Mikael can't punish Iris, an example must still be made—and Benedict is his next closest target.

The third guest's confession, whatever it was, must have energized Mikael, because he stands from his seat smiling through a heavy swarm of deep green aether while that person staggers away.

Nick's still not here, so I'm next. Mariah squeezes my hand, sending her encouragement. *I can do this.*

But as I begin to rise from my seat, Mikael calls to someone hidden by the heavy curtains to the right of the stage. "Come forward."

And Nick walks out onstage.

Zoe leans over. "What's happening?"

"I don't know. I guess . . . Bianca took him backstage instead?"

Nick crosses the stage in his crimson dress shirt and black slacks in easy, measured strides.

"Welcome, friend," Mikael says.

Nick nods curtly and drops elegantly into his seat, posture loose.

I try to catch his eye, but he won't look at me—and that's how I know something's wrong.

Nick's masks are up—all of them. The nonchalant heir. The unflappable thief. The impervious liar. The boy without fear. And when Mikael's grin grows wide, then wider, I know the Nightshade demon can see right through every one.

Mikael takes his seat across from Nick but turns to his audience to speak. "Today, I received an intriguing and unusual proposal. As you all know, we typically present five guests for communion who each answer five questions, but Benedict here has requested a change."

The audience boos loudly, stomping their feet in protest. Mikael uses both hands to gesture them down and put them at ease. "Let me finish, friends. Let me finish! Benedict's proposal is one I think you will enjoy! He has suggested that, instead of using the final two slots of the weekend for him and his fiancée in which they answer five questions each, he will take on the burden for them both—and answer ten!"

The audience cheers at this, clapping loudly.

My stomach drops like a stone. Onstage, Nick's face is unreadable. Neutral and open, as if he has retreated somewhere inside of himself and is letting his disguises run the show.

"What the hell is he doing?" Zoe hisses across Mariah. "Ten?"

I shake my head, the words to respond stolen from my mouth. Why would he do this? I would've found a way to dodge the minefields of five of Mikael's questions, in one way or another. But ten? If Nick resists at any point, Mikael will kill him in front of everyone.

I move to my feet—and Mariah's arm shoots out to lower me back down.

She shakes her head. "Let him do this."

"But—"

She presses me back. "Look at them. The crowd and Mikael are already on board. If you stop them now, they'll turn on you."

She's right. It takes twice as long for Mikael to calm the room. By the end, I feel the sharp, electric wave of his talent flowing up my spine, a clue to the effort it's taking for him to keep his illusion in place.

Nick's face remains placid as he waits for the communion to begin.

Mikael turns to him, sitting back with one knee resting on the other. "I will ask you ten questions to help us understand if you can be trusted. If you resist your natural inclination to tell the truth of things, I will know—and there will be punishment." Mikael smiles. "Are we in agreement?"

"Discretion and truth," Nick replies evenly.

"Truth," Mikael says, "and discretion."

Mikael's power strikes—stronger than I've ever seen it.

Thin, near-translucent wisps of green aether encircle Nick's chest and flow up his throat like water.

I watch him swallow, but his eyes remain fixed on Mikael's. Waiting.

"Did you attack and wound my guard?" Mikael asks. The glowing smoke of his talent pours over Nick's shoulders.

"No."

Mikael's eyes narrow. Nick is neither resisting nor struggling. Mikael's eyes flash to me in the audience, lingering long enough for his gaze to burn against my skin. Then they snap back to Nick.

Mikael knows that I could be the culprit—or that someone else here is—but he's out of options to question anyone else. His only course is to press Nick, if not for answers to the crime committed in his house, then for food. For pain, guilt, shame, and torment.

"Do you *know* who attacked and wounded my guard?" Mikael asks.

Nick's voice is clear. "No."

I freeze in my chair. Nick knows it was me. But maybe after a weekend at Penumbra, I'm not the same girl I was when I entered.

Lies are easiest when they are close to the truth.

Mikael's question required a simple yes-or-no answer, and Nick answered but did not elaborate. For Mikael's purposes, he spoke the truth—and did not flinch or resist.

Mikael's lips purse together, frustration evident on his face. "It seems that the mystery of who wounded my guard may go unanswered."

"Sorry to disappoint you," Nick says.

"I don't appreciate mysteries, but that's because I much prefer truths," Mikael says, eyes glinting. "Eight questions remain and serve as tribute. A sign of your loyalty."

"I'm ready."

"We'll see," Mikael says with a hum. His eyes find me in the audience once again, then return to Nick.

"Why did you offer to take your fiancée's communion?"

Nick shifts in his chair, the first sign of discomfort since he sat down. Mikael pounces on it, and his magic grows thicker and more opaque around Nick's chest and shoulders, soaking into his skin, mouth, and eyes.

"Resistance will not serve you," Mikael reminds him. "I will ask again: Why did you offer to take your fiancée's communion?"

"Because . . ." Nick inhales, steadying himself. "I don't deserve her."

Mikael's eyes widen, and the audience murmurs. Somewhere, several voices offer *awws* at Nick's answer.

"Well," Mikael says, "that was unexpectedly romantic, Benedict. But romance is not all hearts and roses, as we know. Why don't you deserve her?"

The muscles in Nick's jaw work for a second, but his answer comes faster, like he anticipated it. "Because when she needed me most, I ran."

The smoke around him drifts back to Mikael, flowing up to the demon's open, smiling mouth. Nick has given him an emotion he can savor. Two. Guilt and shame, wrapped together?

The most realistic, truthful version of an idea rolls off the tongue more smoothly than a complete fabrication. . . . It's what I've learned to do.

Understanding strikes me.

Nick isn't giving up easy lies; he knows Mikael won't tolerate that. Knows the demon is hungry for the hard truths, the secrets that hurt. And in these first two answers, Nick has purposefully directed Mikael down the path that will hit closest to the bone. Nick has chosen the shape of his own suffering and the wound he's willing to expose.

It's me. How he feels about *me*.

And the audience loves it.

I shut my eyes against the sound of their delighted laughs and curious murmurs. It takes every ounce of me not to twist around in my seat and tell them to turn away. To cover their hungry ears and greedy gazes.

But when I turn back to Nick, his eyes are already on me, their message clear: *I don't care about them. I want you to know. Want you to see.*

Mikael leans forward, pulling Nick's attention away from me. "Why did you run from her? Details, please, Benedict. We need more than these brief answers."

Nick takes short breaths against the circle of aether around his chest when it tightens. "I didn't just run from her, but our—our friend, too. I ran because I saw something they couldn't."

"What did you see?"

"Death."

Nick pitches forward as Mikael draws his anguish from him, inhaling and savoring it like a fine wine.

Mikael gestures with his hand. "More. We all see your lovely Iris sitting here in the front row. We know that she did not die. You must explain your answer—and why it pains you so."

Nick catches his breath in quick, short gasps. Sweat drips down his brow as Mikael's magic flows up to his skull, his ears. "There was someone else there. A man who wanted to kill me but wanted Iris more. To hurt her—" Nick winces, pressing his hands to his thighs to push back up while Mikael feeds. "I didn't understand what I was seeing, how I was seeing it, but I understood what that man was capable of . . . and he was death incarnate."

I hear what he's not saying, what he can't say. That he saw Erebus's magic that day at the cabin, saw that it was more than a Merlin's. Nick saw the Shadow King's magic—and saw through Erebus's disguise—but he had no explanation for the depth or source of that power.

Even I didn't know Erebus's true nature then. No one did.

"Our friend would have defended Iris with his life—and lost it. He would have sacrificed himself to protect her, and if not to protect her, then me," Nick mutters. He shakes his head once, the next words ripping from him in a single rush. "I ran because I saw that if I went with Iris and our friend, death would follow. Our friend would die. Iris would suffer. And it would be my fault. My choice."

Mikael curls his fingers in the air, and I already know what he's pulling. Guilt and shame, yes, but also grief. Grief for Sel, who did not die that day . . . but who sacrificed himself in the end anyway.

When Mikael's head jerks in my direction, his eyes flicker red for the briefest second. .

My own grief for Sel, calling to the Nightshade before I can seal it away.

Zoe's fingers reach me from across the back of Mariah's seat, squeezing my shoulder until the pain stuns me back into the moment. I seal my despair away, sending silent thanks to her with my eyes.

Mikael's eyes narrow at us both, then turn back to Nick. "I must say, Benedict . . . I wonder if there is something in this tale that you are not divulging. Something you are holding back. Tell me about this 'friend' and your Iris. Do you think there exists between them something *other* than friendship?"

Nick's head jerks up, his own eyes flashing with anger. Mikael scoops that up too, folding it between an open palm. "Answer the question."

"I don't *think* it." Nick's chin twists to the side. He fights another answer before it erupts from between his clenched teeth. "I know it."

The audience gasps behind me. Mariah's hand clenches my thigh. My heart thunders in my ears.

For months now, all I've known of Selwyn Kane is what others have told me. I guessed that Sel and I had shared something . . . but I didn't know. Assumed no one did. That whatever we shared, there were no witnesses.

But when I see Nick's face, the hard line of his jaw and the stone certainty of his gaze—I know that whatever Sel and I shared *had* been witnessed. *Had* been known. Maybe earlier and more clearly than either of us realized.

"Do share more, Benedict," Mikael urges. "How do you know this?"

"I know it because I know them," Nick rasps. "And I know why there would be . . . intimacy . . . between them."

"I see." Mikael leans forward. "And how does that make you feel?"

Nick blows out a shallow laugh. "A lot of things."

Mikael frowns. "You must name one—no, two—and why."

Nick hesitates, his eyes searching for an answer that will give the demon what he wants. An answer he can give without resisting or lying—without risking a dagger to the chest. He turns to me. Holds my gaze. "Relief. Our lives are hard. Short. They both deserve happiness where they find it."

"And?"

Nick's throat bobs. I watch a flurry of emotions cross his features, so quickly that I can't identify them all. Without looking at Mikael, he finally answers.

"Heartache. Because I don't know what or how I'll feel if . . . if their happiness is found with each other."

While the audience *oooohs*, I feel my heart break.

Mikael tuts sympathetically, even as he draws Nick's pain closer to him, inhaling it in steady streams. "Tragic, Benedict. Truly a tragic tale." He sits back with a thoughtful expression on his face. "Next question."

Nick turns back to him, eyes hard. "Ask it."

"Oh, I intend to." Mikael grins. "Before this communion, I dare say that everyone in attendance believed you and Iris to be a happy couple, deeply in love, and ready to begin your lives together. Now you reveal that she has had a dalliance with your trusted friend. You must have been angry with her?"

Nick's answer is immediate, if breathless. "Never."

Mikael's brow lifts. That answer was honest—and it did not elicit one of demonkind's most prized emotions. Nick's anger did not rise.

All humor drains from Mikael's face. "Final question—"

"You've asked ten already," Nick states, shaking his head as if to clear it. "We're done here."

He's been counting? I can barely breathe watching him endure this, and he's been counting the entire time?

If Mikael is as surprised as I am, he doesn't show it. "Call this a bonus round."

"Changing the rules?" Nick gasps.

Mikael smiles. "Rules *can* change."

"Convenient." Nick huffs, fists tightening, but he does not fight Mikael. Knows he cannot. "Ask your question."

Mikael searches his face. "You say you aren't angry with Iris. Why not?"

Nick pauses before he replies. Then he raises his chin, casting his voice clear to the room. "Because she is worthy." Nick's eyes seek mine one final time. "And while I have lost my faith in the world . . . I never lose faith in her."

As his statement settles across the audience, the room fills with silence.

When Mikael drops his enchantment, Nick shoots to his feet so abruptly, the chair clatters to the stage behind him. Mikael calls to the crowd, "What a show, what a show, my friends. In the name of truth—"

"And discretion," the audience responds.

"Please give our friend Benedict your appreciation!"

The audience bursts into applause, but my eyes are only for Nick.

He glances at me, throat working—and stumbles off the stage before anyone can stop him.

47

MARIAH AND ZOE help clear the way for me to run after Nick. They shout at the other guests, not caring how they appear, so that I can rush to the exit. When I burst through the doors, he's gone—but I don't care if he's running. Not anymore.

I push past the guests who have started to flow out of the auditorium and race across the estate and down long hallways, nearly tripping on my dress as I go. The morning sun streaks across the carpeted stairs where we stood the first night at Penumbra, challenging each other in hushed whispers, parried with words and smiles. I round the landing where he'd found me when I was lost and reminded me who I've always been. Where he'd been Benedict and I'd been Iris, but we were always Nick and Bree.

I'm down the hall, sprinting, breathless, when I skid around a corner—and run face-first into someone walking in the opposite direction.

"Excuse me," a deep voice says. A pair of hands lands on my shoulders, steadying me where I might have stumbled.

"Apologies," I mumble, and step back—expecting the hands at my shoulders to release.

When they do not, I wrench backward only to find that the stranger I have bumped into is staring down at me, mouth slightly ajar. Even behind his satin mask, I can see that his eyes have widened. And he still has not let me go.

"How . . . ?" he murmurs, eyes searching my face. I blink up at him. He is a middle-aged white man with dark blond hair and a beard; sharp, light eyes; and a well-groomed appearance. "How are you here?"

Alarms ringing in my mind, I jerk back until he finally releases me, and yet his hands hover for a moment—as if he might reach for me again.

I slide back another step. "Who are you?"

At a short distance now, the man takes in my pastel blue cardigan, honey-gold floor-length dress, and short boots. My curls twisted up in a bun at the back of my neck, the bit of makeup on my face. "You . . . ," he whispers, "don't know who I am?"

My body is screaming at me now, some primordial area of my brain yelling at me to run from this man. That I *do* know him, or I used to, and what I know of him is enough to send me racing away—or should be. He recognizes me, even with my mask on, and seems to think I should be able to recognize him . . . but I don't.

It's not the mask that's blocking my ability to identify him; it's my mind.

I wrap my arms around myself and take another step back. "I need to go."

He steps toward me, eyes glinting with a dark fascination. "You don't know who I am." This time, it's not a question. It's a statement, a fact he finds both wondrous and amusing—and powerful.

"Of course I do," I say, swallowing.

"Then what is my name?" he demands quickly.

I open my mouth, clamp it shut. Swallow hard. My eyelids flutter as the mist returns. I don't know this man, but my body is shouting at me that he is *dangerous.*

When I don't respond, the man's face curls up in a satisfied grin. "What else do you not know, I wonder?" His head tilts. "What else have you lost?"

My heart thunders in my ears, and this time, I do run. I hear his laughter in the hall behind me, bouncing off the walls and through my mind.

I don't even remember navigating to the third floor and the Chambord Suite. When I reach the door, it is unlocked. I twist the knob open and slam it shut behind me, pressing my forehead to the wood—half expecting the strange man to be right on my heels.

My thundering heart eventually slows. When it is clear that the man has not followed me, I release a long, slow breath. It takes a few minutes to realize that the shower is going in the en suite behind me, and that that's the reason Nick has not greeted me.

I flip around and brace my spine against the door. Sunlight stripes the rug at my feet, casting a warm glow over the still-rumpled sheets on the bed where we'd woken together only a few hours ago.

The door to the bathroom is shut, the sound of water muffled.

He'd run straight here and gotten in the shower . . . to hide? To delay facing me?

It seems so silly after everything he's just shown me. Everything he's just exposed about us and himself and Sel . . . to a roomful of strangers. After all that, how can he hide from me again?

Or is that why he was hiding in the first place?

I need to tell Nick about meeting the man in the hall. About my instinct that he is the "new player" that Bianca mentioned. But that can wait.

Nick and I can't.

I walk toward the bathroom and pause at the door, finding my courage waiting for me just beneath the surface of my skin.

"Nick?"

Silence.

I shut my eyes. "Nick, please open the door."

Silence.

"We need to talk," I say.

"I think I've said plenty." Nick's voice is muffled behind the door, but it doesn't sound like he's actually taking a shower. There's no interruption in the flowing water hitting the tile floor. No sound of movement. I imagine him standing under the water, hands against the tile, letting the stream take away the lingering sensation of Mikael's magic. It's what I'd do.

"Can we talk about it?" I ask.

Silence, aside from the flowing water. Then, he says, "You were right."

"About what?"

"About this place making it harder to hide."

"Mikael feeds on it," I remind him. "The confessions. The secrets. It isn't . . . You shouldn't have had to do that. In front of everyone. All those thieves and murderers and frauds. You don't have anything to be ashamed of."

I hear him sigh. "I *am* a murderer, if you recall."

"You were defending yourself."

A long pause. "I could have gone for Zhao's arm or leg, you know. I didn't."

I recall how quickly he'd stopped Zoe with his swords at her neck—and how he'd stopped short. "Zhao was going to kill you, and if he hadn't, Erebus would have. I know him, remember? The *real* him. The King is ruthless and you were right to run. He'd have killed Sel without blinking. Killed you, too, if you'd gotten in his way."

I listen, waiting for a response. Eventually, I hear the shower faucet squeak and turn. I step back from the door and wait while he towels off. I hear the clink of his belt buckle. The shuffling of cloth and material as he gets dressed.

When the door opens, steam flows out of the room in a thick cloud.

It's only when it clears that I can see that he's standing in front of me, shirtless. Waiting.

I get a split second to note the width of his shoulders, the curve of his biceps, before my eyes are drawn to the center of his muscled chest.

Then, I see it.

There, right at his breastbone, lies a small black fragment of metal no more than two inches long. Surrounding it is a layer of blue crosshatched magic.

Aether, bright and clear, but not from a weapon. Not from Nick's palm or glinting off his armor, but from encasing something deeply embedded in the center of his chest.

"Nick," I breathe. "What is that?"

I look up to find Nick watching me with sad eyes. "You were never supposed to know. At least, that was my plan."

"That magic, I can't sense it or smell it—"

"By design. It's been rendered undetectable, and so has the fragment it's surrounding."

"Nick," I repeat, eyes filling with tears. "Whose magic is that?"

"Ava's," Nick whispers. "Her casting. Her construct. Her enchantment."

The fragment of metal is so dark, it swallows light. "And what is it?"

"I think you know."

A half sob claws its way up my throat. "Tell me it's not—"

"A piece of the Shadow King's crown?" Nick says. "It is."

"I'll kill her myself," I growl, vision red with rage. "Why would she do this to you—"

"Because," Nick replies quietly, "I asked her to."

Blood rushes in my ears. The floor tilts beneath my feet. "What?"

"This is the reason I agreed to come here with her. In exchange for"—he gestures at his chest—"this, I'd help her get the crown. That was our bargain."

"Nick, this is . . ." I shake my head. *"Why?"*

"I thought I could hide it." He inhales slowly. "At least until after it was done."

"After *what* was done?"

He gestures toward the window seat. "Let's sit?"

I follow him numbly to the seat but keep staring at the shard of the King's crown in his chest like it's something I could pluck out with my bare hands. It's so small, the magic a type of cage, the cage a type of ward—

"If you try to take it out by force, it will kill me."

Nick's calm voice snaps me out of my daze. I curl my fingers against my thighs, and he smiles softly. "I recognize that look. A classic Bree Matthews fighting face. The look you get when you sense a grave injustice has been done."

"I don't have a face like that," I bite out. "Now talk."

"It's not just you who can't take it out safely. No one but a Morgaine can. It's . . ." He gestures at his chest, where the blue-silver light glows against his skin. "It's how this type of magic works. They infuse their workings with a type of magical lock that even I can't unmake, or, at least, I'm too scared to try when it's in my own body. This magic is something that requires one of *them* to undo."

"Just like the crown itself." My fingers still itch to claw it out of him, but his matter-of-fact reminder about the power of Morgaine magic helps me focus when all I want to do is scream.

"Yes. The shard is held in place by a similar enchantment, but I wouldn't want an unpracticed hand to make an attempt to remove it, because it's tied to my heart." He pauses, glancing up at me. "People are complicated. Magic attached to people is even more complicated. Difficult to unravel."

I grimace. "Nick . . ."

"I know how it sounds. How it looks." He sighs. "I thought that when I explained this to you, if I ever did, it would be to you and Sel both. At the same time. So you'd have time to prepare." He tips his head back against the window. "Although, if Sel were here, he probably would have already tried to remove it by force, so maybe it's good I only have to deal with one of you being head-strong, impulsive, overly ambitious—"

"Nick. Keep explaining why you did this or I'm going to let the impulses win."

He sighs again. Looks away. "I told you about my visions. What I can see and do. I have visions because the original Lancelot had visions, but his were more . . . traditional. He could see his near future. Nothing far, but far enough. Last year, when you blood walked me into his memories, sometimes he would . . . linger. Show me things."

"Arthur lingered too," I whisper, remembering my visits with the king on my ancestral plane. The things he'd say. "I didn't realize it was happening with you and Lancelot. I didn't—"

"I know," Nick says gently. "I didn't tell you it was happening. When would I have? How? I didn't understand what I was seeing and hearing. Didn't know anything about Lancelot. When he came to me, he shared his memories. He showed me that the original Morgaine studied the Shadow King's crown against her brother and Merlin's wishes. It was Morgaine who discovered that the crown allowed the King to walk the living world without needing to feed. Not only that, but she realized that when the King wears it, he can choose to share that ability with his Court members. So she enchanted the crown to ensure that, if the King ever returned to power, he would not be able to find it and no other demon could touch it."

"Insurance," I say. "To make sure that the Court could not rise again."

Nick nods solemnly. "Then Lancelot showed me his visions and what he'd seen of Morgaine's future ambitions. He showed me that Morgaine would eventually desire more than just insurance. She wanted to fight."

"Morgaine wished to be like her mentor," I murmur, remembering the girl with dark hair who was so eager to please. The apprentice to the original Merlin, from my own time in Arthur's memories. A long-dead girl I'd met in a dream that wasn't my own and whose memory I'd retained.

"Yes," Nick says. "She also wished to be like her brother, Arthur, and find a way to live on forever through her own descendants and fight by his side. Morgaine was . . . creative. Experimental. She knew her descendants wouldn't have the benefit of the Spell of Eternity, nor would they be part Shadowborn like all Merlins. She needed another solution. Her experiments with the King's crown gave her one. She theorized that she could alter one of the inherent qualities of the crown—its ability to share the bearer's powers with chosen recipients—to create her own version of the Spell of Eternity. She thought it might be possible to pass on her own acquired magical abilities to her descendants if they bore a shard within their bodies. Morgaine hid this theory from Merlin and her brother, knowing it was risky and that they'd never approve. It was only on her deathbed that she convinced her daughter to try it. Morgaine's daughter embedded a shard of the crown into her own chest and touched her mother as she died, expecting to receive her mother's abilities—but Morgaine's *spirit* transferred instead. It was not a full possession . . . but a sharing. Morgaine lived on within her daughter, and that's how her daughter was able to wield her powers."

My stomach turns and twists as I think of Arthur, layered beneath my skin. "I've shared my body with a spirit; it's not simple or easy. It feels awful. Like you don't own yourself."

Nick's eyes harden. "Morgaine's daughter pushed the experiment further. Her daughter discovered that if she touched another human sorceress who bore a shard of the crown, even if they weren't related by blood, her mother's spirit and magical abilities transferred again to the new recipient—while a sort of 'copy' of her mother's abilities remained with her. The embedded shard acted like a receiver as well as a conduit, mimicking the way Merlin's Spell of Eternity uses blood. But unlike the Spell, Morgaine's spirit was *forced* from one body to the next, by shard and by contact. Morgaine's daughter called this process 'Enthralling.' Lancelot showed me that Enthralling continued in secret for centuries without the Order ever finding out, with the original Morgaine's spirit being passed from one shard bearer to another, all of whom called themselves Morgaines."

I shudder at the image, all of those possessions. All of those shards. "Is that why the Morgaines splintered off?"

He shrugs. "That I don't know for certain. Lancelot's visions didn't go that far. But I do know that the original Morgaine was only trying to help, in her own way, and the Order was likely looking for a reason to remove a sect of mostly women sorceresses from their ranks."

The knot in my stomach twists. "Did you search for Ava to become one of them?"

"No." His mouth lifts at an edge as he leans forward from the window to rest his elbows on his knees. "After I found Ava, I caught her off guard when I told her what Lancelot and your blood walking had shown me. I was the first Legendborn member in six hundred years who knew Morgaine's story and the true source of their power, and who didn't condemn their namesake for her efforts. But I didn't join them. Once I realized that Ava didn't know where you or Sel were, I asked her if their technique could help me do something . . . else."

I frown—then cold and horrible clarity comes. "Nick—"

"I have never in my life felt more helpless than when Arthur possessed you. Not when my mother was taken. Not when my father"—he grits his teeth—"sent Liege after Liege to train and break me."

"Please don't tell me you did this . . . for Arthur," I whisper in horror.

He twists on the bench to grasp both my hands. "When Arthur took over your body in the ogof, I felt like I was *dying* inside watching him ruin another life." Nick dips his head to catch my gaze, pleading with me to understand. "And he did it again, at Volition and the Keep. Sel and I got there right before the Morgaines were going to *kill* you for being *him*. We couldn't get you back. We tried everything. Sel and I—" He breaks off, looking away. "We didn't know if our blood walk would even work."

I try to imagine what they'd seen. Watching Arthur use my body to fight a battle I hadn't agreed to. Watching Arthur wield my flesh and bones like a weapon, speak from my mouth . . . when they both knew how much I hated it.

How much of a violation it is.

Nick's eyes turn fiery. "Arthur took you away, Bree. Not just from me, or your father, or your friends, but *yourself*. I saw him in your dreamworld. I recognized the look on his face—the look of a powerful man desperate to remain powerful. Arthur may be lost to you now, but he's not gone. He wants nothing else but to return to the living—and he didn't and *won't* care when you suffer the consequences. If he possesses you again, he won't ever let you go."

"No—"

"*If Arthur takes you again*," Nick says, voice like steel, "I will take *him* from you. For good."

I pull my hands from his. "That's why you wouldn't touch me," I whisper in horror, rising from the window seat. "*Arthur.*"

"No—"

"It was him. He was the real reason. The only reason." I back away, then turn away, embarrassment sending me across the room. "You didn't know I'd burned my ancestral stream. You thought he could possess me at any second—"

Nick's hand is at my elbow, tugging me around to face him. "That wasn't the only reason I couldn't touch you, Bree. You know that!" He pulls me close, pulls me tight. "And if you don't, then I'll remind you for as long as I have breath: I will *never* be careless when it comes to you. I will never be thoughtless about what you deserve. And I will never let Arthur Pendragon keep us from who we are together."

My eyes blur all over again, this time from an ache so deep I can't speak.

"I chose the shard so Arthur couldn't choose himself. Even if . . ." As he gazes down at me, his expression turns pained. "Even if that meant I couldn't touch you again. Or didn't get a chance to explain before it happened."

"Explain it now, then," I whisper. "What will happen if I find a way to restore my ancestral plane, but I can't stop Arthur from possessing me? What will happen if he takes over and you take his spirit?"

"If that were to happen and I'm killed by a Shadowborn while I have his spirit," he says with a quiet sigh, "the Legendborn cycle can stop . . . without killing you."

"By killing you instead?" This time when I pull away, he lets me go. "No!"

"Cestra might have me murdered any day as it is. This quest was only buying me time. I could fall in battle, anyway. That's the life of a Scion; even Sel had to prepare for it to happen—"

"That's all a gamble!" I cry. "What about before then? If you touch me and *don't* die? You have no idea what it could do to have two spirits within you at once. The Order forbids Scions from crossing the Lines because they're assholes, but there could be a good reason for that! You're no Medium. You don't know how Merlin's spell works. Holding both Arthur and Lancelot could *kill* you. The Abatement could . . . could accelerate!"

"Those are chances I'm willing to take," Nick says, closing the distance between us in a single step. "The Order was built on a scale of abuse I can't even begin to comprehend, the weight of which *you* bear without your consent. *Arthur* is a weight you bear without your consent. Being his Scion, hiding the truth everywhere you go. If the Order wanted to punish us for being together, we both know they'd take most of that out on you, not me. And Samuel Davis? What he did to Vera . . . ?" He pauses. Clenches his jaw. "He's not my ancestor, but my family benefited from his sins." Nick takes a deep breath in, and exhales a declaration. "I was born to thrive in this machine, Bree. It was built with me in mind. It's my responsibility to take it apart."

"But it's not your responsibility to die," I whisper through tears. "If you do this, you could die."

Nick pulls me into his arms. "And if you keep Arthur, you won't?"

I try to argue, but no argument comes. "I just got you back. . . ."

He presses a kiss to my temple. "I could say the same."

"If Sel—"

"If Sel feels me fall now, he can recover quickly. The more his humanity fades, the easier it will be to survive me . . . being gone."

I ball my fists against his chest and meet his gaze straight on. Ask the question I must ask. "Do you want to take Arthur from me because you *want* to die?"

"I don't want to die, I promise." He cradles my face. "But I also don't want *you* to die. Let me take Arthur from you, so he'll never be the reason you do."

"But—"

"I'm not scared, B." He leans back, mouth curved in a sad smile. "Not anymore. I'm already cursed, after all. Arthur and the Order have taken my mother, my family, my friends—" His breath leaves him in a rush. "My Kingsmage. The only good thing Arthur Pendragon has ever done for me was bring you into my life."

I sob.

"Let me do this." His thumb brushes my cheek, wiping a tear away. "Let me end it."

I shake my head. "No."

"Yes." He taps his forehead to mine.

"No . . . ," I whimper. "We're . . . we're you and me, like you said."

He presses me to his chest, squeezing me tight. "Not for this."

48

NICK AND I spend the rest of the day wrapped up in each other. There are no more words to say. He drifts to sleep, but I can't rest. Everything feels urgent, but I can't figure out how to fix it or what to do.

We meet Mariah and Zoe in their room to discuss our plan for the final hours at Penumbra. While we talk, I trade my cardigan for a leather jacket from Mariah's closet. I keep the honey-gold dress, but step into their bathroom to strap my hidden dagger and holster to my thigh.

When we eventually head downstairs to the ballroom for the auction, the difference in the room's setup is immediate. The ballroom seating has been changed from round dining tables to long rows of wooden pews. There are more warlocks present than I have seen before. Many of them stand near a platform with a long row of black velvet cloth–covered boxes on pedestals.

There must be at least thirty warlocks scattered around the room in suits and fitted with earpieces. I wonder if any of them are the masked warlocks that Nick and I dispatched in our rooms, and if they are, if they even remember attacking us after Ava's mesmer.

One of the warlocks we met the first night, Santiago, appears to check our invites. After a quick scan, he gestures to some open seats at the back of the room.

Santiago hands each pair of us a numbered white card on a wooden stick. "If you win your item, you'll be asked to approach the stage to coordinate immediate payment via wire transfer."

Mariah and Zoe stay close to me and to each other. We stuff our overnight bags beneath the pew in front of us as we settle in. Just as Nick and I take our seats, we see Ava enter the room. She tips her head in our direction before sitting in a row closer to the front.

I want to climb over the rows and tackle her with my bare hands. Force her to take the magic out of Nick's chest. Threaten her at the end of my dagger until she does it. Until she fixes what she's broken. But that's not the plan.

We'll let Ava bid for the crown, as that's the likeliest way she'll try to acquire it at this point. If she loses for any reason, Nick thinks she'll follow and attack the winning bidder once they leave the estate grounds to steal it back. Morgaines, he said, are very persistent. The crown was in their possession for a long time.

I have no doubt that Ava has backup Morgaines outside the ward of the estate grounds, ready to assist her in her attack—or escape.

Zoe and I will have to move fast if we're going to stop Ava, faster still if she's chasing someone. We have our bags with us for just that reason. A *quick* exit is the only exit we'll be making tonight.

As I scan the crowd, a door in the corner opens to reveal the man I'd seen in the hallway. I'd described him to Nick earlier in our room, but without knowing the man's name or how he knew me, Nick couldn't identify him any better than I could.

But Nick must recognize him now, because he shifts abruptly, turning in my direction to speak into my shoulder. "Shit."

"What?" I whisper.

"The man you saw in the hall, the one you couldn't remember—did he just walk in?"

"Yes."

Nick's fist clenches. "Gabriel."

"Who's—"

"A Regent."

My eyes widen, and I sink down too. The man, fortunately, seems to be caught in a conversation with a warlock and not looking our way at all. Before I can panic further, Zoe and Mariah lean forward on the pews in front of us, resting their arms on the back and helping to hide us where we've ducked. Then, the man sits down to face the front of the room.

"This isn't good," Nick says.

"Why is he here?"

Nick meets my eyes. "I don't know. Did he see us?"

"I don't think so." I peek around Zoe's hair.

"But he recognized you this morning?"

"Yes."

"He'll recognize me, too," Nick mutters, shaking his head. "He knows both our faces too well."

"What do we do?"

Zoe, who's been listening, mutters under her breath, just loud enough for us to hear. "Wait it out. Avoid him. Hopefully he leaves in the opposite direction of the crown."

Mariah speaks next. "We can't do anything here until the auction items are won—too many opponents in one room, too many warlocks, too dangerous. Wait until the auction is over, the winners are confirmed, *then* we move. That's the plan."

"Right." Nick nods.

I grind my teeth, and Zoe glares at me. "Bree. That's the plan."

I look up to find all three of them staring at me. "What?"

"You don't *follow* plans," Zoe mutters.

I glare at each person in turn. "I can follow a plan."

Nick bumps his head softly against mine, voice strained but fond. "You have your strengths, B. This isn't one of them. We're outnumbered and overpowered here. . . ."

Indignation feels like a bright, living thing in my chest. "Fine."

All three of them breathe sighs of relief and visibly relax in a way that honestly feels rude.

A bell chimes once, twice, three times. The auction is about to begin.

The lights dim in the room as balcony-mounted lights buzz onto the stage. Mikael appears in a full tuxedo and top hat with tails while the auctioneer takes a seat behind him. The room erupts in a steady, respectful applause that does nothing but twist the knot of anxiety in my stomach even tighter.

"Welcome, Collectors," Mikael says, tipping his hat dramatically. "Tonight concludes our weekend festivities with an auction of fifteen rare items for your appreciation, your admiration, and, of course"—he pauses—"your *wallets.*"

Low amused chuckles whisper through the room. Beside me, the fingers on Nick's left hand begin an agitated tap on his knee.

"Without further ado, the first item for tonight."

A warlock pulls the black velvet drape off the leftmost pedestal to reveal a piece of ancient papyrus behind a glass cube. Mikael begins to describe the origins of the document and how it survived a flooded chamber from ancient Rome. When the bidding begins, it starts in the low six figures.

"The crown will be one of the last items," Nick reminds us. "Mikael knows it has magical properties, even if the humans here don't. He'll build up to it, make a show of it, to get the highest price."

Waiting feels like torture. My eyes glaze over at the bidding as each item is unveiled. Unlike Daeza's tributes, the items here don't need to be soaked in humanity. Instead, they only need to prove their rare provenance. And unlike Daeza, Mikael does not seem to care how the items and artifacts were acquired—and whom they belonged to first.

Nick's fingers are tapping so quickly against his knee that by the time we reach the thirteenth item—a scepter uncovered in a recent excavation—I have to cover his hand with my own so that *I* don't get nervous too.

Then, a warlock wheels in the fourteenth box, and the energy in the room shifts perceptibly. The most eager Collectors lean forward, silent and focused as they wait for their cue to bid. Mikael's eyes sparkle as he pauses before removing the velvet cover, ever the showman.

He whips the drape away—and reveals the Shadow King's crown.

The crown I'd seen had tall spires circling the gnarled black metal like daggers reaching for the sky. The crown before us now has uneven obsidian spikes, torn and twisted in varying lengths. Still a nightmare, but tortured under centuries of arcane, experimental spellcraft.

Mikael has let us look our fill. "Behold the ancient crown of Arawn, a truly ageless and priceless piece said to have originated in Annwfyn, the Welsh otherworld."

Arawn?

Mikael circles the crown, explaining its appearance for the Collectors' edification. "The crown was once circled by tall black spires, but, alas, these have been worn down over time."

I can't help but glance at Ava and wonder what she's thinking. Based on what Nick shared, one fragment of the crown is embedded in her chest even now, just like one is embedded in Nick's.

I look up to see Nick's lips drawn tight, his fingertips resting lightly over his sternum. When I open my mouth to ask why, he shakes his head once, eyes straight ahead. A dismissal. A question I'll have to reserve for later.

"There are rumors about this piece, of course. That if a demon were to even touch it, they would turn to dust." Mikael smiles apologetically. "Thus, in the spirit of keeping these rumors alive, a human intermediary is not only recommended but required."

The room's quiet laughter rises again, and Mikael grins, pleased at his own joke at the expense of human ignorance. "As I said, priceless." Mikael turns to the room. "Of course, tonight we seek the impossible. To name a price for such an artifact. Let the bidding begin!" Mikael claps his hands together and steps to the side as the auctioneer stands up.

"The bidding begins at one million," the auctioneer drawls.

The next five minutes go by in a blur. Ava raises her bid card no fewer than seven times, but she is in competition with at least three other people—including a few of the suits Nick has been meeting with. The bidding slows down as people drop out, until it is only Ava and another man going back and forth.

In the end, the man drops out before Ava does. The auctioneer calls it. "To the young woman in red, for nine point eight million."

Zoe whistles low. I have to agree.

Ava's smug smile is visible even beneath her mask. My muscles tense for action, though I know we have to wait. She walks to the front of the room and begins to converse with the warlock who has been retrieving the winners' lock-boxes and phones to coordinate payment.

"And now for our final item." Mikael takes the stage again. "Or should I say 'items'?"

The room shifts, another wave of low, knowing laughter.

Mikael approaches the last pedestal.

"These items are unique in that their power is not solely in what they are, here in this room, but what they represent—or, rather, whom they represent."

The velvet-draped box on top of the pedestal is larger than the rest, five by five feet at least. But what "items" represent a "whom"?

No. It can't be.

The reasons Mikael can't possibly be auctioning off Rootcrafter girls flow through my head, down my veins, turn desperate. Turn flashing. Like broken lightbulbs exploding beneath my skin.

Those reasons are so good and so strong and so logical and humane that I can almost convince myself to believe them.

That is, until Mikael unveils the final box—revealing four clear, decorative three-foot-tall crystal vials filled with glowing gold smoke.

Root, stoppered and captured, on display before our eyes.

The root in each of the four vials shifts and churns within its glass. Living power in slightly different hues.

Deep butter yellow, rich and smooth.

Brilliant honey gold, sparkling.

Canary, flickering with streaks of shiny chrome.

And a shade I saw a month ago in a dingy bar bathroom—reddish-gold root the color of a sunset.

49

I'M ON MY feet in an instant—and Zoe and Nick both yank me back down.

My ears are ringing. A high-pitched whine, blood rushing through my head. My brain, in all of its diminishing function, idly recognizes that Mikael's eyes have found us in the back of the room as he continues to speak—and that I'm calling far too much attention to myself.

"Bree!" Zoe hisses, looking past me to the rest of the security warlocks at the end of our pews, who are looking at us with curious eyes.

The rest of the room—and the pews in front of us—never even noticed me standing. They murmur to one another, gasping, as Mikael continues speaking, and I realize that he never really stopped.

"This is the vivid power of so-called magical Rootcrafters." The Collectors lean forward in their pews as he speaks, trying to get a better look. "Mind you, there are special treatments applied to these crystal vases that make this kind of power source visible to the average human eye. In addition, of course, this root must be captured from a living human 'Crafter, which these are. Magic like this must also be captured from a powerful 'Crafter mid-casting, while they are actually in *active* contact with their ancestral guides. A truly fascinating phenomenon to behold."

Beside me, Mariah lowers her hand. She fingers the cord of the Heart of the Dame around her neck as we exchange glances.

Four Rootcrafter girls are still alive—and Mikael or someone working through him—has held them captive long enough to capture their power and put it on display.

"Tonight, you are not solely bidding on these vials," Mikael continues, "but bidding on access to the living sources behind these powers as well, so that you may refresh the magical displays for your enjoyment once they wane. It is a bit uncouth to present these four young women in this setting, but, rest assured, they are being safely held and have been treated with respect and care by the seller. We will promptly provide coordinates for pickup to the winning bidder. We do request that you do not cause these young ladies damage or lasting harm, or, at least, do not do so in a setting that can connect such activity back to our community. Remember, only a *living* Rootcrafter can supply a lasting power source. In all things, please maintain discretion and truth."

Respect and care? Discretion and truth? For the second time tonight, I want to launch myself over the pews. This time, to take on Mikael directly and rip the Southern genteelness out of his lying mouth.

I don't realize that I'm vibrating with the effort of restraining myself until Mariah presses her hand to my knee. "We have to stick to the plan."

"The plan?" I hiss. "Screw the crown. We have to—"

"We can't," Mariah urges. "We don't know where they are, Bree. *We don't know where they are.*"

At that, I freeze. She's right. We could take the vials, release the power, but that doesn't help us find the girls. They're selling access to the girls, too, so that a Collector can "refresh the magical displays" for their enjoyment.

Mariah looks just as rattled as I do. She glances at the warlocks down the aisle, keeping her voice low as she talks. "It's the same plan as before. Wait for the winner, but . . ."

Follow the winner. Find the girls.

I release a broken, rattling breath. Mariah nods, and that's when I know that she's right. I glance at Zoe, who is peering back at me with wide, waiting eyes. She nods once. She's on board. Then, I feel Nick's thumb at my bicep, a slow and steady pressure. I glance up at him, and his face is twisted with emotions—distress, worry, anger—but determined.

None of us cares about the crown any longer. They're ready to find the girls, just like I am.

But every time a card is raised, I commit that face to memory. Every time the price goes up, I grind my teeth to near breaking. I don't know how long the bidding lasts. All I know is that it feels like an eternity and the *numbers* aren't enough.

Mikael can disguise it all he likes, but they're bidding on people. Human beings. Whole lives, just like mine. Whole dreams. Girls with minds and hearts.

Their families must miss them so much.

Tears make my eyes blur.

Beside me, on my left, Zoe trembles. A fine tremor from her feet, to her torso, to her lips. On my right, Mariah has clasped my other hand—and her body is vibrating too. With rage and pain or both. She's taken Nick's place, and I don't remember him moving.

I look up to find that Nick has shifted down the pew to face one group of the warlocks, his spine a rigid line of tension, his palms open for battle. He is protecting us as best he can as we wait.

When it's over, our heads snap up to see who the winner is.

The only man with his bid card still raised.

Gabriel.

Nick twists to catch my eye, and I know we're thinking the same thing. Gabriel wants the Rootcrafter girls; does that mean the Regents do too?

I swallow and glance at Zoe, and she shakes her head, confusion on her face. If the girls are being kidnapped by Mikael's contacts, by people who have hired warlocks, then trafficked to the highest bidder—in this case, the Regents, or at least Gabriel—then Erebus isn't their customer. Which means he's likely not feeding from these girls, after all. The Regents don't know that Erebus is the Shadow King who needs to feed on power to survive.

"Congratulations," Mikael is saying to Gabriel, who is now standing and buttoning his suit jacket. "The seller will contact you directly after your wire has cleared. We can provide an escort to you tomorrow so that you may retrieve your winnings safely."

"That won't be needed," Gabriel says. "My own transport will be waiting outside in just a few moments." He tips his head in acknowledgment and walks toward the waiting warlock to retrieve his phone and enter his credentials.

But behind him, there is unrest in the pews. A few of the other guests who have been here all weekend are murmuring among themselves, the tones of their voices pitched low—and angry.

"Why was a newcomer allowed to join the auction at the last minute?" The tall woman from the second day of the communions rises to her feet. "The rest of us have been vetted. Some of us have waited *years* to attend. How has this person skipped the procedures?"

Mikael raises his hands for peace. "I understand the confusion. In this case, I allowed a single exception—"

"But he didn't even have to endure communion, as we did!" The man from the first day shoots to his feet.

Nick slides back, closer to us now that the warlocks who have been eyeing our group have shifted their attention to the upset Collectors.

Mikael frowns. "Truth and discretion are always—"

"We cannot risk a new player!" the tall woman shouts. "You have broken our trust, Mikael!"

Mikael's human face slips as his lips draw back. His power sparks at the base of my skull, and then his face is human once again. "You will apologize. And you will leave."

Three dozen Collectors are on their feet now, moving from their seats to advance on Mikael—and the row of priceless artifacts still on display.

At Bianca's signal, the warlocks begin shifting. Their borrowed powers bloom to life, expanding their heights, their arms and legs, even sprouting tails.

Lawson grows a pair of long tusks. Santiago, elk horns. Even Bianca changes, with a ripple of green scales rising along her cheek and down her neck. The smell of pact magic fills the room—and the humans scream, tumbling over one another to get out.

Our row stands as one. "*This* is bad," Zoe says, gathering our bags.

"Yeah, no kidding," I say, tugging my leather jacket off to free my arms.

Mariah shifts beside me. "I think we need to go."

"I think we need to follow him!" I say, pointing to the back corner door where Gabriel is being quickly ushered away.

"Where's Ava?" Mariah says.

When we all look to her seat, we see it empty. Nick curses. "Gone for the crown. Let's go."

The four of us climb over the pews rather than running down them, but the fight between the warlocks and the panicking humans has escalated, and a pew comes whistling down in front of us, breaking another into splintered pieces.

We all fall back, and Mariah scampers to my side. "I'm not quite as durable as you three. . . ."

I glance at her. She's right. We can't wade through a warlock fight with her in tow—not without worrying she'll get hurt. "Mariah—"

"But," she says, eyes twinkling, "I think I can still help."

"How?"

She is busy looking over my shoulder and around the room. "I need to be higher." She points to the balcony. "Can somebody get me up there?"

Zoe is already crouching down. "Get on."

Mariah climbs onto Zoe's back, wrapping her legs and arms around the taller girl. "Be back soon," Zoe says, and then she's a blur, running in the opposite direction of the brawl.

"Duck!" Nick's shout distracts me from watching Zoe and Mariah's departure, just in time for him to tackle me to the floor, throwing an aether shield over both our heads as a piece of the balcony comes crashing down.

He winces, bracing against the impact. I feel the weight of the piece rattle through his body, and through him, mine. He heaves upward to shove the piece off near our feet but doesn't move. "You okay?"

Sawdust floats overhead like strange dust through his sparkling aether shield. "Fine."

"Then let's go." He's already up and moving, pulling me to my feet. "Gabriel's getting away." He grasps my hand and runs me down the aisle.

Shouts and growls fill the space, echoing up to the balcony. I hear something—or someone—tear open, flesh ripping in a way that makes my stomach turn. Mikael's imitation dollhouse falling apart.

I feel the wave of power before I see it. A hot golden surge of power that hits me and Nick before it passes over us harmlessly.

We both look up just as it strikes the warlocks—and their bodies freeze entirely in place where they stand.

"Holy shit," Nick mutters.

Even Mikael has frozen, eyes wide and teeth bared. Only his eyes move, and they shift overhead and up to the balcony behind us.

We follow his gaze to see Mariah standing on the balcony with her arms outstretched and eyes filled with root, fingertips lit with glowing light. Her brows are knit with the effort, but she's holding the warlocks in her grip—all of them. Whatever body part they've transformed with undead demon power seemingly pulling them to the ground while the rest of their human bodies struggle to get away.

She groans and curves her fingers downward, and the warlocks' bodies hit the floor all at once. She flattens her palms, pressing, and a chorus of groans and growls tells us that she's holding them in place wherever they've fallen.

"Go!" Mariah shouts down at us. "I can't hold them forever . . . !"

Nick and I don't hesitate. We leap over the pews and bodies, heading toward the door where Gabriel had been guided out.

"Stop!" Mikael's voice reaches us at the last second, ragged and angry. Unlike the others, he is slowly, slowly peeling himself up off the ground, fighting Mariah's power. He glares at me, jaw opening in a too-wide snarl.

Nick pulls me forward. We race down a hall, but I can tell he's holding back—so I push him ahead. "Go! You're faster!"

Nick gives me one last look before blurring forward. I run as fast as I can to keep up, bursting out a door into the courtyard—then see the trail of blue aether he's left behind, faint but visible enough to guide me.

Smart boy.

Following the trail before it fades takes me through another building, to an exit that spills out onto the massive back lawn. At the very edge of the lawn is the barrier—and just outside of it is Gabriel getting into a waiting helicopter, its blades already whirring.

Nick is speeding to the outer ward of Penumbra—a bright silver-blue bullet directly toward Gabriel—when he is thrown back by a dark green shadow.

Nick flies across the lawn, hits the ground with a deep thud, and skids another twenty feet. "Nick!"

My shout is lost in the sound of the blades. I pivot, running toward his body where it lies still and crumpled on the ground, his aether armor gone dark and dusted.

He's not moving.

Nick's not *moving*.

I fall to his side where he's landed, tentatively touching his shoulder. His eyes are closed, and his hair is stringy and wet across his forehead, mixed with blades of dewy grass. I check his breathing—he's alive. Alive, but bruised or with broken bones—

"Next time, Crown Scion!" a voice calls. I turn to see Gabriel waving from the edge of the helicopter, a grin splitting his face open.

I stand, ready to run after him—and immediately get knocked back down to the ground. The dark green aether scent that hits me is old, ancient. Thick and rich.

The last thing I see is a pair of heavy boots walking slowly toward me across the damp grass. The last thing I hear is a low, amused chuckle.

Then, darkness.

50

"BREE . . . WAKE UP, please."

I gasp awake—and immediately close my eyes against the swimming, murky vision overhead.

A trio of relieved sighs echoes in my ears.

"Thank God."

"Is she okay?"

A warm palm at my chin. A deeper voice. Nick's whispered kiss on my brow. "I'm right here, Bree." *Nick's here. I'm okay. Not safe, but okay.*

Then I'm shifted, adjusted, my head lolling to the side. The voices fade.

When I open my eyes again, I see Mariah's face bent over mine, delicate brows pressed tight together behind her wide-rimmed golden glasses. "Hey, Bree-Bree," she whispers. "Awake for real now?"

"Maybe," I croak, then wince at a clanging sound. "What is . . . ?"

"They're trying to get us out."

I blink again, my eyes dry as sandpaper, and follow her eyes to the source of the clanging.

We are in a small, dark room with dirt floors lined with concrete blocks stained with damp, and on the opposite wall is a row of iron floor-to-ceiling bars. Bars that both Zoe and Nick appear to be attacking vigorously.

"We're—" I begin.

"Underground," Mariah says with a sigh. "Imprisoned. The warlocks caught me and Zoe pretty quickly after I ran out of gas, and by then, you and Nick had already been knocked out by Lawson."

I push at the dirt floor beneath my hands, and Mariah's legs shift beneath me as she moves to help me sit up. Beside my knee are my and Zoe's small overnight bags, straps still drawn tight from when we'd secured them before the auction. I don't care about our dirty clothes, but I'm relieved that Zoe still has access to her meds.

"How long was I out?"

"Half an hour," Mariah answers. She leaves a hand steady at my spine as I curl forward. "Slowly . . . ," she advises. "You've got a goose egg."

My fingertips float up to my temple, where a tender lump has sprouted at my hairline.

"We were outside, away from the warlocks and Collectors, and chasing Gabriel," I say. "Why would Lawson attack us?"

"Because rules change," a low voice says from beyond the bars.

Nick and Zoe back up simultaneously, speeding to the center of the room to stand in front of me and Mariah. Beyond them, in the corridor outside the prison cell, a figure shrouded in dark green aether appears.

"Lawson," Zoe snarls. "You rotten warlock. Did Bianca send you to gloat?"

"So quick to judge, Zoelle," Lawson says.

Zoe and I both freeze. She helps me rise to my feet before we peer closer at the figure. "What did you just call me?" she asks.

"Your name, Shadeling." The voice in the shadows shifts from Lawson's low baritone—to one more familiar. The dark green aether transforms into a crackling black cloud, and out of that cloud steps Erebus Varelian. "*Zoelle.*"

⚡

Zoe snarls, blurring to the bars to clench them between tight fists. "You did this!" she shouts. "You were that warlock this entire time?"

I understand her fury, but I don't share it. Instead, my eyes fall shut, every moment of the past three days rushing behind my lids like a nightmare. The ward, trapping us in Penumbra. The worry about what Erebus might do to us. The mistaken identities, then the claimed ones. The library. The communions. The confessions. All of it, while the Shadow King watched.

"Did you really think I would let you and Briana completely out of my sight?"

"Goddamn you, old man!" Zoe shouts. "We thought we might die in there. We came here for you—"

"No, Zoelle," Erebus says. When I open my eyes, he's surveying each of us, one at a time, until his gaze lands on me. "You came here to try to free Root-crafter girls whom you believed I was devouring."

"Did you spy on us?" I ask, stunned by the calm and measured tone of my own voice. "Listen in on what we were saying? Watch us struggle and strategize and . . . worry we'll get caught?"

"No." He shakes his head. "Believe it or not, not everything revolves around a group of exhausting, tortured teenagers. Not even when one of those teenagers is you, Briana."

"So what did you do?" Nick says, crossing his arms over his chest. "While we were *tormenting* ourselves for your amusement?"

"I was needed as Erebus much of the time, Nicholas." A bit of Lawson's smile bleeds into Erebus's face, spreading his mouth wide as he surveys Nick. "And I did not find your torment amusing, Scion of Lancelot. I found it exquisite."

Nick flushes. "Glad I could entertain."

"Even now, your hidden rage is palpable and rich," Erebus says. "I won't need to feed for weeks."

"Why?" I demand. *"Why?"*

"Quests within quests. Secrets within secrets." Erebus sighs.

"No more riddles," I snap. "Tell me why, right now."

"Demands even here, Briana?" he says. "I'd be careful with those."

"Answer her," Nick says. He gestures around the cell. "You have us imprisoned. You watched us become trapped in this estate. You can't tell me you did all of that and never anticipated your grand reveal. You are a chaos creature after all, Arawn."

Erebus's eyes narrow. "Careful with names, Scion. You know not of what you speak."

"Well, now I see how your name gets under your skin," Nick says, eyebrow quirking. "So that's one thing I know."

Erebus eyes him for a moment longer, fingers twitching at his side. "Merlins have been killed at an increasing rate over the past several months. The Council had no leads, much to everyone's frustration, including my own. When young Nicholas here suggested at his curia that the Morgaines were likely suspects, it was something we had not, in truth, considered. After he, the Scion of Gawain, and Guard Douglas departed, the Regents—Aldrich, Gabriel, and Cestra—began meeting in undisclosed locations at odd hours, refusing to share their whereabouts with their Seneschals." He sneers. "Silly, short-lived creatures scurrying off in their private jets to preserve their triumvirate of human power."

"That must have annoyed you to no end," Nick says, "seeing as you had to keep up appearances as the subservient mage."

Erebus glares at him, ignoring his jab. "I suspected that the three Regents may have created a plan to pursue the Morgaines themselves, not trusting a Merlin or a child"—he smiles pointedly at Nick—"to do the job. But I had no proof, and Morgaines are notoriously difficult to find. I did not trust them to be successful. 'Lawson' began to investigate back channels."

His gaze falls to me. "But then, one day, Briana questioned me about hiring warlock mercenaries and kidnapping Rootcrafters—an odd inquiry. The next day, I was informed that my ward Elijah had heard a rumor from a desperate goruchel that my crown had been stolen by a warlock from the very Morgaines who had hidden it from me for fifteen centuries. Warlocks stealing Rootcrafters, warlocks stealing the crown, Morgaines undoubtedly seeking their stolen trophy . . . It was all too much to be coincidence." He paces away, humming in thought. "All it took was an order from me barring the twins and Briana from seeking Daeza out to motivate them into doing just that. I knew that they, with Briana's impulsive displays of power, could interrogate and persuade my Shade to share what she knew much more easily than I. After Daeza connected the crown to Mikael and one of his distasteful Collectors' Galas, it was simple work to use 'Lawson' to help monitor and move things along."

"So what I'm hearing," Nick mocks, "is that you're not really having any luck getting your Shadow Court back together."

Erebus grits his teeth. "You are, somehow, more infuriating than your Kingsmage."

"How is Sel, by the way?" Nick asks.

"I wouldn't know," Erebus replies. "I have considered that *he* may be behind the Merlin deaths, but, again . . . no proof."

Nick's jaw works back and forth.

"No clever retort to that, Scion?" Erebus says, smiling. "Where is that shining, sanctimonious Lancelot faith now?"

I cross my arms. "Sel's not a murderer."

"You have no idea who Selwyn Kane is, and yet you defend his integrity?" Erebus tuts. "I taught you better than to trust a demon."

"You can turn into a warlock, who are exactly the type of magic users you told us you 'despise,' by the way," Zoe mutters. "Why didn't you just go after the crown yourself?"

"Because while I can mimic many things, I cannot trick a Morgaine enchantment." Erebus sighs. "And simply recovering my crown is not enough for me to reclaim it."

Zoe nods in annoyed understanding. "You needed a Morgaine to remove the lock they placed on it."

"Exactly," Erebus says.

Zoe scowls. "So you waited until Mikael threw one of his fancy auctions—"

"Yes, and?" Erebus prompts. Like he's teaching us again.

"And you used the auction to flush out a Morgaine who could undo the demon-proof ward," I say.

"Correct," he says. "If you set your bait strategically and be patient, the mice will come to you from beneath the floorboards and behind the walls, even if it means they are crawling to their own destruction."

Zoe groans, pacing away. "That's why you sent me and Bree, isn't it? So we could retrieve the crown ourselves, just in case a Morgaine never showed."

"When you live as long as I do, you create plans within plans. Sending two of my own agents who could touch the crown when I cannot, and who have bonded over their shared interest in seeing the crown in my hands, was a safeguard in case a Morgaine never made an appearance—or ran before I could force them to undo their magic."

"If you're still here, that means you lost Ava," I say. "Let me guess, you were so busy playing 'Lawson' that she bolted before you could catch her?"

"Unfortunately," Erebus says. "She scampered away before I could trap her, leaving the crown in its case behind. I convinced poor Santiago to secure it on my behalf."

"So you retrieved your crown but lost your Morgaine?" Nick says. "Pity."

"Not ideal," Erebus replies to Nick. "But also not a total loss. As I said, plans within plans. Over time, I have discovered that the true prize in any war is *information*. Information—about you, for instance, Scion of Lancelot. Your abilities and skills. What you are capable of when pushed. What you can see and do, as it is always a surprise with the Scions of your Line." He spreads his hands. "And I have gained insight about the Regents and what they have been whispering about in places where I cannot overhear. I did not expect to witness a visit from Gabriel at Penumbra, and I certainly did not anticipate discovering that the Regents are not only pursuing Morgaines, as I first thought, but Rootcrafters as well. It is an unexpected change in their strategy. The Order has long been too self-obsessed and foolish to understand what demonkind has always inherently known."

"And what knowledge is that?" I ask.

His eyes flash. "That *true* ancestral power lies in the hands of those who craft root, not within the silver-spoon-fed Scions the Regents ply with praise and false honor. Goruchel know that Rootcrafter prey are far more valuable alive than dead, but taking a Rootcrafter *captive* instead of killing them outright is nearly unprecedented in Order history."

"We're not prey," I spit. "We're people."

"Perspective," Erebus says, then his eyes turn to me and Zoe, eyes warming. "It was a bonus that I was able to test the loyalty of my most powerful protégés along the way. Well done, both of you. I could not be more proud."

I turn away in disgust as Zoe pounces. "What about Elijah? Everything he does is for you! You tricked him. Used him."

Erebus's fangs flash. "Elijah's desire to please me limits his growth. I do not wish to be pleased. I wish to be *strengthened*!"

"You aren't strengthened by me and Zoe," I say. I step closer to the bars, tipping my chin up to meet his ruby gaze. "Even if Ava had gotten your crown, we decided not to pursue it once we saw the vials of root. We may have come for the crown, but it wasn't for you. It was for the missing girls."

"No, I don't think so. You did it for yourself." Erebus's voice turns dark and taunting. "Did you become impervious, Briana? Are you ready for your next lesson?"

"What's my next lesson?"

He smiles. "To become ruthless."

A desperation to defy him rises in my chest. "I'll never be what you are."

"No," he says. "You will become something much more fascinating."

When I stumble back from the bars at his statement, Erebus only laughs.

Shadows begin to creep in around his ankles, filling the space outside our prison cell. "I must attend to this matter of the Regents and the Rootcrafters with urgency, as I do not know what Gabriel is planning, whether he is working in secret with any of my Mageguard, or where the seller sent his helicopter. As I must pursue the matter as Erebus, the situation requires some . . . bureaucracy."

"You can't just leave us here!" Zoe shouts.

"Oh, but I can. This prison is designed to hold demons. You won't be able to break out of it, but," the King says, as the shadows close around him, leaving only two glowing red eyes behind, "I do invite you to try."

PART FOUR

RUTHLESS

Natasia

THE THREE LIEGES guarding the Matthews home are well-meaning but sloppy.

They have no idea that they're surrounded. No clue that there are four Mageguard forming a loose circle around the split-level house, and that those Guards must have been deployed to the Matthews residence by none other than the Mage Seneschal Erebus Varelian himself.

After a week of searching, I lost Selwyn's trail. I rushed to Bentonville to secure Edwin in the event Selwyn sought Briana here at her childhood home. When I arrived, my son was nowhere in sight, but instead, I find myself bearing witness to a stark display of the Order's factions and competing missions:

Lieges, former *Legendborn*, seemingly protecting the Crown Scion's Onceborn father from her demon and human enemies while the very Mageguard sworn to protect that same Crown Scion seek to rob her of her sole surviving parent, either through kidnapping or murder.

There are simply no other explanations for a unit of Mageguard to exist in a quiet suburban neighborhood. No other reason for trained soldiers to move like silent water between the twilight shadows of quiet streets lined by white oak trees and plastic trash bins awaiting their morning pickup. The soundproof ward cast around the property and the deadly intent in the Guards' gazes only offer further confirmation that their intent here is not to protect, but to attack.

Something must have gone very wrong, very recently for Erebus to have sent his elite soldiers to Briana Matthews's father's home. Did she defy the Regents in some way? Does Erebus seek to punish her by threatening her father? Or does he wish to eliminate a tie to her former Onceborn life, further isolating her from her own humanity?

Selwyn craves Briana. If Erebus sent his Guard here, he seeks to *control* her. There is a critical difference.

But there *is* no controlling a Matthews girl. If Erebus hasn't caught on to this truth yet, I will do my part to ensure that he does.

I have been watching the Guards for over an hour now, and they have yet to detect me; they'll likely wait until the sun finally rests to move in on the Lieges and Edwin. Human neighbors still walk the streets with their dogs, chatting about the school year, the rising gas prices, the weather. In the time the Mageguard and I have spent waiting for their moment, I have been able to heal most of the damage my son dealt me.

I am the last person in the world who should have underestimated Selwyn Kane . . . and yet I did just that. In the four months Selwyn stayed with me, the most magic I saw him wield was the handfuls of aether he would call into visibility within the boundaries of his palm. I saw him test that aether, prod it, claw it, then release it more times than I can count.

But what I saw him do in my cabin, the way that he fought, his speed, his strength—and the dark joy I saw in his eyes as he attacked—was like nothing I'd ever witnessed, not even in a goruchel.

All of that very visible, very *repetitive* testing of his power back at the cabin, done in the most nonthreatening manner possible? All those little bursts of magic in my son's palm? Perhaps they *started* as genuine experiments, but I see them now for what they became: a strategic ploy to deceive his grieving, guilty mother into believing that he was weaker than he was—and I fell for it.

Use your enemy's assumptions against them. Lean on their ignorance to customize their downfall. Not a lesson the Merlin academy taught him but a lesson *I* taught him at the age of five.

There is undeniable poetic justice in my son using my own teachings against me. Enough to make me smile in the dark shadows of my hiding place—and wince immediately at the sharp ache in my face. With one expertly aimed blow toward the end of our fight, Sel dislocated my jaw and broke my first and second premolars. I stifle a grimace, not at the pain from broken teeth—I pulled those out myself on the drive over—but at the itchy, uncomfortable sensation of those two teeth growing *back*.

I swear . . . when I see that boy again, we're going to have some *serious* words about honesty and deception and rebuilding our estranged relationship. Maybe after I show him what a *real* ward can do.

The sun is closer to the horizon now. The Mageguard have another twenty minutes until they can use the night as an accomplice. While I wait, I test the other injuries I earned in my battle with Selwyn: My left shoulder is still healing at the joint, but it will hold. The left kneecap he kicked out of place was moved back into position before I ever got into the car, and stopped aching about ten minutes ago. Sel knocked me out with a roundhouse to the face that sent me flying into my kitchen cabinets. I woke up in a pile of broken boards and bloody metal cabinet pulls with a searing headache.

And my car was missing.

That fucking kid. Chagrin and pride bloom together in my chest. At least I won't have to worry about a goruchel overpowering him in the wild.

What I do have to worry about is what Selwyn is willing to do to get to Bree. Now that I know it was Bree's root that tipped my son into demonia, I am even more desperate to prevent them from reuniting. A Bloodcrafted Matthews girl in her full power is too dangerous for any cambion to consume once, much less twice.

And I have no idea how he will react if she does not remember him, as she could not with me. Something isn't fully *connected* within Bree, some core component loosened and fractured, but what *is* there is power unheard of.

Faye would be so proud. Terrified for her daughter's safety, but proud.

If Faye were here, we could have shared in these emotions. Seen ourselves as mothers . . . and laughed at the impossible absurdity of it all. Pain slices me deep at what we both lost.

I shake my head. I need to focus on the here and *now*.

After I procured another vehicle, I didn't bother driving to the Lodge because I know Bree's with those twins in Asheville—or at least I hope she is. Selwyn, however, has no leads on Bree's whereabouts. I can only hope he returned to the Lodge first to locate her, as that gives me enough of a head start to remove Edwin from my son's path.

Four Mageguard and three Lieges were *not* variables in my calculus. I didn't expect them.

Then again, they didn't expect me, either.

I've just knocked out the last Mageguard and tucked her behind a dormant hosta when the first of the Lieges finds me.

"Hey!"

I freeze.

"Turn around!" the Liege shouts. "Now!"

I cast the glamour mesmer before I turn around, hoping that the Liege's Sight isn't strong enough to see through it before it takes effect.

The tall white woman has short dark hair and bears the sigil of Geraint. She was a Scion, once, and is a hardened warrior who has earned a smattering of silver Liege hair for her time served. I won't enjoy knocking her out.

"I . . ." Her eyelids flutter as she takes in what is probably quite confusing. The thin, older woman she saw standing by a low shrub has transformed into a tall, broad-shouldered police officer with bushy eyebrows and blue eyes.

"Evenin'," I say, and cringe inwardly. My Southern accent is rusty.

She frowns as the mesmer settles in. "What are you . . . what are you doing here, Officer?"

"Heard some reports of break-ins in the neighborhood."

She frowns again. Her Sight starts to win out over my hastily cast mesmer—and her apprehension must be enough to call over her bonded. I curse silently. The Warrior's Oath means that her emotions are transmitting over to her former Squire—and I don't have the time or energy to cast a mesmer over them, too.

"Ophelia?" a voice calls, and a shorter white woman Liege with shiny bronze hair rounds the corner.

"Yeah, Lyss, this officer here—"

Lyss spots me. "Get back! She's a Merlin!"

I groan silently but apologize out loud: "Sorry."

They're both pulling weapons—stun batons designed to take down a demon—when I strike.

I blur to Ophelia first, tapping her as lightly as I can on the forehead with an open palm.

Her eyes roll back. She crumples. *One down.*

Lyss is quick for a human. Her baton is lit, and she jabs, but I'm already moving—ducking the crackling end and backhanding it out of her grip.

Her eyes widen—I dart to the side, punching her in the temple with a quick right hook.

She falls in my arms. I set her down easily, rolling her on her side, just in case.

"What the—" Another voice. *Damnit.*

No point in keeping up the mesmer now. It's useless against the third and final Liege and draining to keep up, so I drop it, let it melt—that visual alone confuses the man who is sprinting toward me from the other side of the garage. Makes him hesitate.

I meet him halfway with a clothesline to the Adam's apple—and cradle his head on the way down before it strikes the pavement.

"That could have gone better," I mutter apologetically to his unconscious form. I check his pin—Liege of Lamorak. Glad I caught him as a Liege and not an active Legendborn; the Line of Lamorak might have given me some run for my money.

I turn him onto his side quickly, then dart back toward the front shrubs to do the same to Ophelia.

It's only been ten minutes, but I'm breathing a little harder and my shoulder aches.

I take a deep breath and stand up, brushing off my pants, then raise my fist to knock on the front door. Before I can rap more than once, however, the door opens to reveal Edwin Matthews in a tattered blue robe and slippers. He meets my gaze with a stern one of his own. "Did you just knock out those nice people?"

"Uh . . ." I blink, momentarily stunned, arm still raised in the air. I follow his gaze to Ophelia behind me, Lyss by the hydrangeas, and the Liege of Lamorak by his dormant butterfly bushes. "Well . . ."

"I like them," he says pointedly, looking over me as he talks. Without the mesmer, I appear as what I am: a slightly winded, middle-aged white woman he's never met before with gold eyes and a bit of blood at her temple, wearing a sweater and loose pants. "They do good work down at the shop, then come around to make sure I'm safe . . . for some reason they won't explain." He crosses his arms over his chest. "They're good people. You better not have done them any permanent damage."

My mouth closes, then opens again. I drop my hand. I am so stunned and disarmed by his calm, disapproving demeanor that all I can do is answer his questions. "No . . . no permanent damage. They'll be fine."

"Hmph." Edwin regards the drying blood smeared across my cheek with an unimpressed eye, then the bruise on my jaw from Selwyn's kick, the blood on my bare knuckles from two of the Mageguard, and the odd way I'm standing— still favoring the left knee. "They do all that to you?"

I shake my head. "No, sir. That was . . . my son, actually."

"Your *son*?" Edwin's eyes widen. "What kinda relationship you got with your son?"

I start to tell him, in no uncertain terms, "A bad one, but we're working on it." But no words come. Instead, a wave of dizziness sweeps over me, nearly taking me to my knees.

Guess I got hit in the head one too many times today.

Edwin's arms swoop beneath my armpits before I fall, holding me up. "What the hell, lady?"

"'M fine," I mumble. "The black spots are . . ." I wave a hand in front of my face, slurring slightly. "Goin' . . . n'away. Been a rough . . . months. Day."

"You got a concussion?" he asks, voice alarmed.

"Probably."

"From your *son?*"

"Eh."

"Goddamnit." He shifts his weight, positioning his hip so that he can half carry me inside. "Well, come on, you need help—"

"No," I cry, digging my feet in before he can go farther. I paw at my bloody shirt, at the necklace hidden beneath it. Will my mind to sharpen, to stay awake, to meet this moment. "Wait, don't call the police—"

"I'm already outta my mind tryna help a random, tore-up white woman on my doorstep, but I sure as *hell* ain't callin' the cops. They'll say *I* did all this mess. And now you say you don't want my help?" he says, pulling against me. But I've got my feet planted, and he can't budge me an inch. "What the—"

I push against his chest gently until I can stand on my own two feet, wobbling a bit in the process. The dizziness is passing. "No, wait. Please."

He releases me to stand back. I glance at the warm home behind him. The living room with ESPN on on the large TV mounted above the fireplace. The tidy kitchen where, occasionally, Faye and I would meet on one of our too-rare check-ins, when Edwin was out of the house for work and when I wanted to make sure the Order hadn't sent anyone else to observe her. I glimpse the table where she'd make me tea and ask me how my research was going. I see the photos of elementary-aged Bree with missing teeth. Bree with rainbow-colored ball hair ties in her thick dark hair for picture day at school. Bree with her friend Alice grinning at each other over ice cream at the zoo.

I see Bree's childhood and Faye's entire universe in the home behind Edwin . . . and it breaks my heart to know what I have to do next.

"Well?" Edwin asks, and his heart rate is finally matching the terror his human instincts are creating. Within his concerned brown eyes, his pupils are expanding. His brows are knitted close. Fight or flight, setting in. His body is readying him for something that no Onceborn can ever truly be ready for.

Good.

"This isn't going to make any sense," I say, voice heavy with grief and sadness both, "but there's no time to explain. Your life is in danger, and a long time ago, I made a promise to protect it."

Fear streaks across his features, rightly so. "My life?"

"And," I say with a grimace, "my son might be on his way, looking for your daughter."

His gaze sharpens. "The son who gave his own mother a concussion is looking for *my* daughter? What for, exactly?"

"Well." I squint. "He doesn't want to *hurt* her, if that helps."

"It doesn't." Edwin crosses his arms. "What the hell does he want with her?"

"That is a very . . . nuanced question. With a long, complicated, awkward answer."

I glance over my shoulder. The Mageguard will likely wake at any moment. I fish out the necklace beneath my shirt and yank the chain to break it. He watches as I pull a heavy golden engraved ring off the loose links and hold it between my forefinger and thumb. I raise it between us at eye level so that he can get a good look.

"I thought I lost that ring . . . ," he murmurs, "*years* ago."

"You didn't," I say. "Your wife took it, in secret, and gave it to me."

"Faye?" he says, voice cracking. "Why would she give you my ring?"

"I'll tell you everything I can, I swear it," I say, "but right now I really, *really* need you to put this on."

52

PRESENT DAY

Bree

HOURS PASS. ENOUGH that we start to ask questions about options for using the bathroom. Enough that the dungeon lives up to its name in every way. It is only dimly lit by sconces down the hall outside our cell. It is damp. Bone-chillingly cold. Silent, save for a dripping sound that echoes against the stone walls. If I had to guess, I'd say that it was early morning now. Before dawn.

The King said he needed to confront Gabriel "as Erebus" and that it would require bureaucracy. That could take at least a day, maybe two, before he even bothers to come back. Maybe more. I doubt that he'd send warlocks to check in on us; Zoe and I could likely overpower them, even through the demon-proof bars. No, he's going to leave us here until he's ready to return and the more pressing matter of the Regents' subterfuge is resolved.

At some point in the night, Nick wrapped me in the cocoon of his body. His broad chest warms my back and his arms enclose my shoulders enough that he can lace his fingers over my bent knees. Every once in a while he tugs me closer and dips his chin into my shoulder, shuddering in the cold. When I ask if he's okay, he mutters, "'M fine."

Zoe does something similar to Mariah, holding the shorter girl tight around her shoulder while they sit side by side so that Mariah can take advantage of Zoe's cambion body heat.

I'm just working up the courage to tell everyone that I might need to use a corner and embarrass myself for life when we hear a rumbling noise from the rear wall of the cell.

Nick tugs me up, forcing my stiff joints to move, yanking me toward the cell bars as Zoe does the same with Mariah.

The rumbling grows louder.

Zoe, Nick, and I thrust our palms out simultaneously, calling power to our hands in a rush of green, blue, and purple flames.

Nick's voice is a hoarse whisper. "Don't suppose there's any chance you'll let me greet our guests first?"

"Why would I let you greet the . . . giant moles that seem to be burrowing straight for us first?" I whisper. "I don't think the code of chivalry says anything about giant burrowing moles."

"That's the old code," he says slowly, eyes narrowing at the wall. "The new edition has a whole chapter on oversized rodents; didn't you see? Completely different species."

"You two are *really* annoying me right now," Zoe snaps.

"I'd rather be annoyed than eaten," Mariah mutters.

"I second that," I say.

"Third," Nick murmurs. The rumbling becomes a high-pitched grind. Nick slides forward. Humor leaves him. "It's getting closer."

It is. The floor beneath our feet vibrates to an urgent rhythm. "Strong moles," I murmur.

Nick's armor rises to life along his skin. He rubs at his chest, shuddering as if chilled. "Bree—"

"If you tell me to stand back, Davis, I swear to *God*—"

His mouth quirks. "Just gonna ask you to start sending your root to the floor, my king. Let's extend a friendly hello."

"Flaming welcome mat," I say. "I like it."

I do as he suggests, releasing low, rolling streams of mage flame from both fists. It floods the floor in a heavy whoosh, covering the dirt with a roiling layer of bright purple. My root licks up the corners of the walls, climbing the edges of our enclosure.

A second later, the concrete wall starts to shake. Mortar crumbles and spills in quarter-size chunks that spark as they hit the flames below. Larger chunks fall, cracking apart when they strike the ground. We press into the bars in a single line. Beside me, Mariah's breath picks up, turns to shallow pants.

When the first crack forms, it races from the center of the wall upward. When the concrete blocks begin to bend, Nick's chin dips to his chest, his eyes focused and intent.

"Get ready—"

The wall breaks inward, concrete falling in fist-size chunks that create plumes of dust when they land. I shut my eyes and turn away, holding my breath as a wave of stone dust surges into our faces.

If the giant moles attack us, we'll be sitting ducks. Beside me, I hear Zoe coughing. Nick is the only person who has moved—I see his blue-white aether armor shimmering among the cloud of gray particles. His blade blooms in the billowing dark—and is met with another. This one a shining golden-white.

I know that color. That root. I've seen it before. I piece the memory together based on what Nick has told me—an attack in the woods. Two cambions fighting with me, fighting *for* me, one with blue-white aether and another with golden weapons in his hands. One was Sel, the other must have been . . .

"Valec!" Mariah cries.

A beat as the two blades hold against each other, then withdraw.

"I told you this was it," a low voice drawls.

Someone grumbles beside him. "This was the third tunnel, man. *Third!*"

As the dust begins to settle, Nick appears in front of me, blocking me from the newcomers' view with his body. In the slight tilt of his head is a silent question just for me: *Do we trust them?* I extinguish my flames and wrap a hand around his gauntlet and blade arm, lowering it to get a better look.

A figure materializes, waving his hand over his face as the smoke clears around him. I don't know what I was expecting, but it wasn't a tall Black boy wearing a gray-and-red pinstripe vest, shirt, and pants with a golden pocket watch chain gleaming at his chest. At first glance, he looks like he'd be more at ease in one of Penumbra's smoking salons than emerging out of the wall of an underground prison cell. Then, his eyes flash red, and his mouth pulls back in a wide grin, fangs low and visible on his bottom lip—and I realize that this cambion could make himself look at home pretty much anywhere.

"Anyone order a rescue?" he asks. Mariah runs forward, and he swings her into a hug. "Word got around everything went to hell up at Penumbra last night, and I knew it was time to get you out."

The taller figure behind him must be the owner of the second voice. He's an older Black man with wide shoulders, wearing a jacket, jeans, and far more appropriate footwear for burrowing through a wall. Mariah turns to him and laughs. "Emil?"

Emil steps in, clapping a hand on her back and pressing his cheek to her forehead. "Hey, cousin. Heard you needed some earth moved."

It's only now that the rest of the dust has cleared that I see that the tunnel behind them is perfectly round and supported by what looks like wide, glowing golden bands of light. A trail of smoky gold magic connects the root in the tunnel to Emil's fingertips, and by the tight knit of his brows, he's using not a small amount of focus to keep the tunnel intact.

"Holy shit." Zoe steps forward beside me, inspecting the use of root with the same wonder as me. "Is that . . . root?"

Emil regards her. "You didn't think it was all healing herbs and tea, did you?"

Zoe smirks. "You're cool."

"Powerhouse?" Valec peers around Nick's shoulder. He steps over the rubble, nearly tripping on a few broken pieces in his rush to reach me, his arms extended. "Goddamn, it's good to see you!"

I step around Nick with a small smile pulling at my lips, but my body language must give my hesitation away. Valec's arms drop and he stops short a few feet away. "Hi, Valec," I murmur.

"'Hi, Valec'?" His dark eyebrows rise in confusion. "We strangers now?"

"I . . ."

Nick collapses his blade and steps forward. "We haven't met."

Valec's eyes flicker as he takes in Nick's armor. "No, Scion, we have not."

"Can we have this conversation back at the Lounge?" Emil asks, gritting his teeth. "I can't hold this all day."

"Yeah, Emil, we're coming," Valec calls. He studies me for a moment longer. "Y'all ready to go?"

I am already nodding when my bloodmark flares to life in my chest—a bright pulse of red light that floods the room. Valec is the only one who doesn't shield his eyes. He stares at the mark as it glows above the neckline of my dress, following the branching crimson streaks as they reveal themselves across my collarbones and down my arms. "You doing that, Bree?"

"No. *He* is."

Valec's jaw tenses. "He know where you are?"

"He's the one who put us here," Zoe says, voice acrid. "But he can't trace her. Won't be able to find her when we leave. Which I'd like to do as soon as possible. I need to call my brother when we get somewhere safe."

"Only place safe is the Lounge, and we ain't there yet." Valec's jaw works to one side. Then, his eyes slide to Nick. "What's wrong with you?"

Nick's hand is at his chest, rubbing over his sternum and the hidden shard beneath Ava's spellcraft. "Nick?" I ask.

"I don't know," Nick says. "It's so cold, Bree." When he shudders again, I realize that the cold he'd been feeling wasn't just coming from the dungeon.

"It was the shard, wasn't it?" I whisper. "All night?"

Nick blinks, nodding. "Must have been, but it's never done that before."

I step closer. "Does it hurt?"

He winces. "No." A lie. "Maybe if I focus on it, I can . . ." His gaze turns inward, and I can tell that he's searching Ava's magic with his own, trying to understand what's changed.

Valec looks between us, gaze scrutinizing, studying. But I know that if the King isn't able to sense Ava's spellcraft and Nick's shard, then Valec won't be able to either. Frustration flickers across his face. "Y'all gonna explain whatever's going on?"

"Not here," I say.

"Mmnh." Valec's face turns stony. "We're gonna need to have a long talk when we get back to the Lounge, you and I."

"Understood," I reply. "Let's go."

"Yes," Emil calls. "Let's *go*!"

"We're *coming*, Emil!" Valec says.

"Wait," Nick says, turning as if he's heard something, his fingers pressing on his chest. "I can feel . . . an echo. Another"—he taps his own chest—"like this."

Valec and I exchange glances, and Zoe walks over. "Another like what?"

"You all don't—" Nick stumbles back to the bars, pressing his face to them, eyes shut tight. "You don't feel that? See that?"

"Feel what, Nick?" I ask. Whatever he's "seeing" is beyond my Sight. Existing on a spectrum that only he can perceive with the inheritance of Lancelot.

Nick turns back to me, eyes opening wide. "I think . . . I think the crown is still here."

In the end, it takes my, Zoe's, and Valec's strength combined to budge the bars. Together, we bend three back to create enough space for Nick to crawl through and for me and Valec to follow.

Nick moves as if pulled by the fragment in his chest, down a long, winding path of empty cells that look like ours, all the way to a smaller, warded alcove embedded at the end of the stone-lined hall at shoulder height.

Inside the ward sits a cloth-covered, circular lump, marked at regular intervals by protruding jagged points.

The crown.

"Why would the King leave it here unattended?" Valec taps at the glowing ward around the small alcove. "This is a simple barrier. A human couldn't get past it, but a powerful enough demon could."

"But a demon can't touch the crown," I say, "so this is as safe a place as any."

"He didn't know that I'd be able to sense the crown when I'm close," Nick murmurs, peering into the alcove. "Didn't know about the shard. Not as all-knowing as he thinks he is, is he?" Nick reaches in for the crown, but I grasp his hand. He turns back to me. "It won't hurt me, Bree."

"I know," I say, "but we don't know what will happen if you touch it either. You're human, but you've got a piece of it inside your chest. If the crown can call to its broken shards, who knows what it will do when your body is all that's separating it from its lost pieces?"

Nick withdraws his hand. "Good thinking."

Valec doesn't say a word as we talk, taking all of it in silently. When I glance at him, his calculating gaze tells me that our "talk" might not be the most pleasant conversation. "Later," I say.

"Soon," he corrects.

In the end, I take the crown myself but wrap it so that it doesn't make contact with my skin. I'm not sure I want to touch it either. "Let's get out of here."

We run back toward the cell and Emil, but just as we pause at the bent cell bars for Nick to crawl through, I stop and look at Valec again. "Wait. You're *Valec*."

Valec stares at me like I've grown two heads. "I know who I am. What the hell is wrong with you—"

"You know *William*," I interrupt.

He looks at Mariah inside the cell, then back to me. "Yes and? You *know* I know William—"

"No, she doesn't," Mariah says.

"Can you call him?" I ask, heart pounding in my chest. "And tell him to get to the Institute?"

Valec's pulling his phone out, but it's Nick who asks me a question. "Why the Institute?"

I shake my free hand, brain turning. "Because I think that's where the missing Rootcrafter girls are being held."

"How do you know that?" Valec demands.

"What time is it?" I ask, ignoring him.

Valec clicks his phone awake. "Quarter after four a.m."

"Call William *now!*" I shout, urgency stripping away my patience.

Valec doesn't argue. "Got it." He's already dialing, racing away to find a signal.

"Why the Institute?" Nick repeats.

"Gabriel and the other Regents kept the girls a secret from Erebus, right?" I ask, the idea forming in my mind quickly—but also much too slowly. I should have figured this out sooner. "If Gabriel retrieved them from the seller's location and needed to hide them somewhere overnight, somewhere secure where he could study them or experiment on them or whatever they want them for . . . the Institute's where he'd take them. There are labs there. Doctors. The staff are loyal to the Regents and would keep his secret, even from Erebus."

"Got William on the phone," Valec says, blurring back. "Told him to head to the Institute, but he says he and Douglas tried to get in a couple of days ago and couldn't get past security."

I don't know who Douglas is, but I assume I'll meet him again soon.

"Tell them to go back," I order. "Tell them to say Regent Gabriel sent them. There are hotel-looking residential rooms on the other side of the building, across a bridge. A suite on the sixth floor. They have to go there, and they have to go now, while it's still early, before daylight, before Erebus figures it out—"

"What's Erebus got to do with it?" Valec asks.

"No time!" Mariah shouts.

"Okay, okay," Valec says, pacing away to speak into the phone. "Did ya get that?"

Nick shakes his head, eyes bright with awe. "Brilliant girl."

"Only if I'm right," I caution.

"You're right. I can feel it."

53

WE DON'T HEAR from William right away, and the adrenaline in my veins makes it hard to wait. I pester Valec to check his texts so frequently that he ends up tossing the phone in my lap just so he can focus on the road and I can watch for William's call myself.

The trip from Penumbra back to the Lounge takes long enough that Mariah and Zoe fall asleep in the back of Valec's SUV, but I'm too anxious to rest.

If I'm wrong about the girls, then I'm out of ideas. If Gabriel has taken them somewhere else, then I'm almost certain we'll never find them. They might be missing forever. Reduced to statistics in a news report. It's not guilt that floods me now, but desperation.

A hunger to set things right, from one missing girl to four others.

After the first half hour of the drive, Nick urges me to rest with gentle words. I don't remember agreeing with him, but my body must have had other ideas. I fall asleep with Valec's phone clenched in my fist.

Nick nudges me awake as Valec pulls into the Crossroads parking lot, but my brain takes longer than usual to come back online. When my eyes open, I can just glimpse the layer of magic visible over the building.

"That your ward?" Nick asks. "It's nice work."

"Yep, that's mine." Valec nods as he parks the car. "Layered so thick the Crossroads could withstand a siege even from a Shade. As soon as we found out the Hunter had taken Bree, I cut the Lounge's business hours in half and stopped doing contracts so I could retain enough energy to cast the wards. Started taking house calls so I could chase leads outside my territory." He cuts the engine. "Figured if we found Bree, we could bring her back here. Hide her from the Legendborn and the Hunter, least for a little while. If y'all hadn't told me, I'd have never guessed the Hunter was in the Order, much less a damn Mage Seneschal. He might return to Penumbra, find y'all gone, and trace us to the area, but the wards prevent magic performed inside the Lounge from being detected on the outside. That'll slow him down. So will coming up with a new strategy. We've got a day or two to regroup, I suspect."

"You've been searching for her," Nick observes. "Trying to find her this whole time."

"And Kane, too, though that turned into a dead end real quick. But yes, I have." Valec catches Nick's eye in the rearview. Holds it. "You ain't the only one who wants to see the powerhouse safe, Scion. You ain't the only one who wants to keep her that way."

Nick returns the cambion's gaze with a steady one of his own. "I'm aware."

The door opens, letting the cold night air in. Emil takes the crown from me then helps me step down from the SUV. My legs are shaky after the drive, and he lets me lean on him while I regain my balance.

"Thanks," I say to him quietly. "For rescuing us and helping—"

Emil smiles. "Nothing to it."

"Nothing to holding up literally *tons* of earth?" I ask. Behind us, Nick steps down, followed by Zoe and Mariah. Now that we're in sight of the Lounge's ward, Zoe's got Valec's phone at her ear, trying to reach Elijah.

"Well," Emil says with a small smile as we begin to walk, "that part's impressive, but I can't claim all the credit. Ancestors, y'know?"

"Yeah, I know."

He chuckles. "Bet you do. Bloodcrafter, huh?"

I nod. "Inherited."

He whistles. I expect him to make a comment about the sin of Bloodcraft, but he doesn't. As we approach the Lounge, he squeezes my arm. "If your ancestor made that choice, then I'd say you're doing a mighty fine job of making it count."

My eyes prick. "You don't know me well enough to say that."

"You're fighting to save four 'Crafter girls you don't even know," Emil says. "I think I know enough."

When we pass under the ward surrounding the building, I shiver from the sensation of Valec's magic. It's not an affective ward, not harsh and violent the way that Erebus's was, but it's solid. Secure.

As soon as we emerge through the heavy curtains in the entryway into the empty main room of the Lounge, the feelings that wash over me are enough to make my knees buckle. The last time I was here, I was with people I cared for deeply. And when I left, things were different. *I* was different.

I wonder if, when I leave this place again, I'll have changed again.

Emil taps my arm. "You okay to stand here? I'm gonna go check on the others." He hands the covered crown back to me before he goes.

"Thanks, yeah."

Just as Emil moves away, a new person approaches. "There she is, thank every goddess!" A middle-aged Black woman with gray braids steps into my field of vision. Her voice brings with it a wave of apprehension that swamps my chest. But care, too, and respect.

"Hello," I say as the woman grasps me in a hug.

"That's Aunt Lucille." Mariah is at my elbow, lifting the crown gently out of my grasp behind her aunt's back.

"She knows who I am, Mariah!" Lucille swats at her niece's shoulder but then pulls her in with us too. "And we are gonna have a talk about you taking that Heart and putting yourself in harm's way behind my back!"

"No, she don't," Mariah mutters. "And do we have to?"

Lucille turns back to me with wide brown eyes. "What's she talking about, Bree?"

"Um . . . ," I say.

Mariah untangles us both. "Aunt Lu, Bree's under a type of spell—"

"A spell?" Aunt Lu's eyes widen.

"Bree?" A shorter Black woman wearing a shawl walks toward us. "Oh, thank God." She wraps me in a hug too, folding me into her chest. I stiffen in her arms, if only because I don't know her name. But her voice and face—and this hug, oh my *God*, this hug—send warmth deep into my bones.

"Hi," I greet her, voice muffled.

The woman releases me immediately. Her eyes are alert—and darting all over my face, my body. "Something's not right with you. Are you injured?"

"No, I . . ."

"Hazel, she's been hurt," Lu says. "A spell."

"Whose spell?" Hazel asks me. "What do you need?"

"She needs sleep and a warm meal, but she's going to put up a fight on both fronts until we hear the girls are safe," Nick informs the woman, saving me from having to explain when he steps beside me. "I'm Nick, by the way." He extends his hand.

"Of course you are," the woman says. She stares up at him. "Who else *could* you be but Nick Davis?"

Nick flushes. "Ma'am?"

"Call me Hazel." She looks over her shoulder back toward one of three darkened hallways made of shipping containers attached to the building. Each hall is labeled above by a glowing neon sign: RESPITE. DESIRES. DELIGHT. "We have a spare bed where Bree can rest."

"Not yet." Valec moves to stand next to Hazel. "While we wait to hear from William, I think Bree and I should have our little chat."

"Why can't your 'little chat' wait?" Hazel demands.

Valec looks down at me. "You got an answer for that, powerhouse?"

I don't. I'm not tired, as much as I know I should be.

"What's going on, Bree?" Concern is written in the fine lines of Hazel's brown face.

"I . . ." My chest tightens at the thought of disappointing her. "I *feel* that you're someone I know and trust, but our interactions, our conversations . . ."

Nick steps in when Hazel looks alarmed. "I can explain."

"I'd like to hear an explanation myself," Valec says, "but from *Bree*, not you."

"I don't like your tone," Nick says sharply to the cambion. "Something on your mind?"

"A lot of things," Valec shoots back. "Thanks for asking."

"I'm not sure I like your tone either, *Valechaz*." Zoe steps in closer to the circle. She's got Valec's phone in her hand, but the anxious way her nail taps the plastic case tells me that Elijah must not have picked up when she called. On the car ride over, we guessed that he's got at least a day before Erebus returns to his home, but I know she'd rather talk to her brother now.

"Oh, what is *this*?" Valec turns to her, eyes amused. "Don't tell me a cambion pup thinks she can talk down to me in my own domain? Within the boundaries of *my* ward?"

Zoe smirks. "This *pup* doesn't really care whose domain it is. What's your problem, *Grandpa*?"

"Something's not right with the powerhouse. We can all feel it." Valec's eyes flash red in anger and his voice dips an octave. "And my patience is finite. So *somebody* better—"

"I don't know you!" I shout, stopping him short.

His eyes widen, then sharpen. Before he can ask for more, I speak again. Push everything out in a shaking rush. "I don't know who you are! I don't know my own father. My own friends. I could pass them on the street and—I don't even know people's names, their faces. Why I like them, why I *love* them." I swallow audibly, eyes burning. "How and why they like or love me."

The room quiets as I speak, until I can hear my own rattling breath.

"He *did* this to me," I state. "*Stole* something from me. And I don't know how to get it back."

A beat of silence. Valec crosses his arms. "Do you want it back?"

I answer without hesitation. "Yes."

A smile spreads over Valec's face. "That's all I need to hear."

Forty-five minutes later, after Hazel insists we eat a full meal and after *I* insist that the crown be secured in a warded safe behind Valec's bar, I find myself sitting on a stool under the bright lights of the empty Crossroads Lounge stage while Valec circles me with a hand on his chin.

"Is it going to hurt her?" Mariah asks. She, Nick, Hazel, Zoe, Lucille, and Emil are standing in a row at the bottom of the stage.

"Nah." Valec comes to a stop across from me. "Just gonna take a little tour inside our powerhouse's metaphysical body."

I startle. "Metaphysical—"

"Believe it or not, we've done this before." Valec gives me a cheeky grin. "It's how I discovered your bloodmark. What I do is like taking a peek at your magical inventory."

"Like reading my aura?" I ask.

"Aura is somethin' folks *emit*, not somethin' they carry within. I can sense a few elements *inside* somebody, including the abilities and magic they were born with, and I can also find magic they've taken in over time. Like an Oath or bargain"—he pauses, a haunted expression rippling across his fingers before passing—"or a mesmer laid in someone's mind without their knowledge or consent."

There's more to this comment about nonconsensual mesmers than Valec's revealing. I can see it in his eyes. I want to ask more, dig into *him* the way he wants to dig into me, but when his dark brown eyes refocus on mine, they are shuttered tight. The message is clear: the intimacy of this moment goes one way and one way only. He can see me, but he won't let me see him.

That doesn't seem fair. My lips tighten into a frown.

Valec senses my protest before I voice it. "We gotta stay focused, yeah?"

I release my questions—for now. "Yeah, okay," I concede. "Well, I can already tell you this isn't a mesmer."

"I haven't taken a look yet, but I suspect you're right."

"If you find what the King did"—I glance to Nick, remembering the constructs and spellcraft he can See and undo—"can you figure out how the magic works?"

Valec shakes his head. "Just because I can read the ingredients on a box of cake mix doesn't mean I can tell ya how to bake the thing."

Nick's lips press into a frustrated line, and I'm sure he's thinking the same thing I am. Valec can't do to magic what Nick can; he can't See the deeper layers of magic, its inner workings, and attempt to deconstruct it, but he can sense and locate magical elements in ways that Nick can't.

I shift on the stool. If Valec can't uncover and undo what Erebus has done, will letting him sift through my metaphysical insides really get me any closer to restoring the part of me that's been taken? Or will I just know more . . . and not be able to do a damn thing about it?

Sensing my discomfort, Nick steps close to the stage and lowers his voice. "Bree, you don't have to do this."

"I know," I say weakly.

His jaw tenses at the uncertainty in my voice. "Maybe it's better if we take a beat."

I straighten in the chair, drawing confidence up for him and for myself. "I want to do this, Nick."

"Yeah, Scion," Valec calls to him. "She wants to do it. I say let's go."

Nick's eyes are only for me. His fists clench on the stage, a silent signal that he'll back me up if I walk away.

"I'm ready," I say to him, to myself, to Valec.

"So am I," Valec murmurs, stepping closer. "Maybe this time, don't blow me across the room?"

I raise a brow. "No promises."

Valec smirks. "Noted." He steps closer again, his palm open. "Same warning. This won't hurt but it ain't gonna feel *great* either."

I brace for not great—then there's a heavy bang on the door.

"They're here!" Lucille says.

Valec's head whips over his shoulder, eyes narrowing as his hand falls. He calls to Emil, "Get ready, in case they brought company." Emil nods and jogs to the door. Nick follows, asking the older man for information as he matches his longer stride.

"We're gonna have to postpone this." Valec steps back, then makes eye contact with Zoe. "By her side, pup."

"I know what to do!" Zoe snarls and snaps at him, red eyes flashing. "And stop calling me that." She blurs up the stairs to stand next to me just as Valec leaps down to follow Emil and Nick.

There's silence as the three of them step into the entryway, and Zoe hugs closer to me. A second later, Valec calls out, "All clear!" Both of our shoulders drop. "Need several hands, though!"

Zoe checks in with me, then runs to the door. Mariah and I follow her just in time to see the rustling curtains part. "Bree! Mariah! Come here!" Zoe calls, and Mariah and I jog faster to meet her and the new faces at the door. "They found them! They found the girls!"

Emil enters first, aiding a thin Black girl in loose jeans and a T-shirt as she walks hesitantly into the Lounge, her eyes glowing bright. A Rootcrafter, mid-casting.

The soft magic flowing from the girl's hands and eyes is canary yellow, flickering with streaks of shiny chrome. One of the four root colors in the vials the Regent Gabriel sought with his winning bid. Her round cheeks are light brown with red splotches from the winter air. As the crowd parts between us and Mariah rushes through the curtains, the girl catches my shocked expression and waves weakly, full lips around silver braces. "Hi."

She is *so* young. Barely a teenager. My eyes burn. "Hi."

At her side, Emil looks up. "Hazel? She's shaking. We need to get her new clothes, a blanket . . ."

Hazel is already bustling close to us. "We have the rooms ready, Emil, right down this hall."

Emil follows her down one of the metal hallways, and the young girl looks back over her shoulder at the tall, empty bar and lit stage before she's escorted away.

Zoe comes next, guiding an older girl with deep brown skin. The girl's hair is in long braids that start out dark at her roots before flowing into loose brown and blond strands that land at her hips. Her gaze is sharp, darting around the new environment of the Lounge even as exhaustion pulls at the circles beneath her wide glowing eyes. The root within them also flows from her face and fingertips. It's another color I recognize: a sparkling honey gold. By the time they pass me, I am crying in full but trying to hide it. Lucille swoops in and helps the taller girl walk when her knees buckle. "We need to close down your casting," the older woman whispers. "Then you'll feel better. We'll get some food on your stomach, something warm to drink . . ."

Mariah walks inside with her arm wrapped around a third Rootcrafter girl. This girl's root is rich yellow, the color of home-churned butter. She leans heavily on Mariah, eyes only open to thin slivers of light. Her hair is cropped close to her temple in tight black coils. The girl's fingernails dig deep, desperate circles into Mariah's forearms—something I doubt she even realizes she's doing—but Mariah doesn't complain or ask her to let go. When Mariah offers her a quiet word, the girl's face opens up into a brilliant smile, revealing a sweet gap between her two front teeth and too many dimples to count. As they pass me by, I make eye contact with her, and the girl smiles at me, too.

The rescued girl's smile spurs me into movement. I rush to the door to help with the last girl—hoping I recognize her too. Not just by her magic, but by her face. Praying that she is safe, that I didn't fail her—

Then, just as I pull back the curtains, I come face-to-face with the girl who's lived in my mind for weeks now. The girl I first saw on the floor of a dirty dive-bar bathroom. The root swimming in her eyes is golden, nearly the color of a sunset. She gasps. "It's you!"

"I—" We step toward each other, and before I can ask her if she's all right, she wraps her arms around me.

My vision blurs. Her shoulders shake. I hold her tighter. "I'm sorry," I mutter at the same time that she says, "Thank you."

I gape, stepping back. "I didn't . . . I didn't do anything."

The girl shakes her head, wiping at her eyes before she answers. "Yes, you did. They told us a Rootcrafter girl sent them to find us, and I wondered if it was you." She squeezes my hands in hers. "You didn't forget me."

I don't have an answer for that. How could I have forgotten her? With every person who has gone missing in my own mind, with parts of myself going missing too, holding on to her felt easy . . . because it was right.

"Of course not." I swallow, my voice cracking. "I should have gotten to you faster. Should have chased you down."

She shakes her head again, a weak smile shining through her tears. "I told you not to." She laughs. And I laugh. And I can tell that it's been too long for both of us.

"I don't even know your name," I say.

"Nora." She smiles again. "Nora Green. What's yours?"

"Bree," I say. "I'm Bree Matthews."

"The other three are Joy, the little girl who came in first. Then Melanie and Amber."

Nora. Joy. Melanie. Amber. I commit their names to memory.

I wrap an arm around Nora's waist, and together, we take slow steps into the Lounge. Mariah exits one of the hallways lit by neon signs and shakes her head when she sees us. "Neither one of you is fit to walk on your own; what are you doing?" She steps in beside Nora and wraps her arm around the other girl's waist. "Let's get you to a room, help you get out of your working."

"Can we sit first?" Nora asks. "Everything happened so fast. I just need a minute."

We pause at the bar. Mariah makes sure Nora is comfortable before excusing herself to go help her aunts with the others.

"I suppose you want to know what happened?" Nora asks.

I nod. "If you don't mind telling."

"We were all taken at different times, but every one of us was taken by a warlock while in the middle of a working," she says, swallowing thickly. "They fed us, didn't hurt us, but wouldn't let us leave or contact our families or shut down our connections to our ancestors. They wanted the channel between us and the dead active and open. *Insisted* on it. Nearly killed Joy. She's so new to the craft, you know? So young." Her dark brows knit in memory. "They, uh, kept us on the move in motels. Then, late last night, a man in a suit showed up. We were blindfolded. The warlocks and the man walked us outside to a field and put us into a helicopter. Maybe an hour or two passed in the air? I couldn't tell. But we landed outside some sort of compound. Almost a nice hotel vibe, but creepy? I heard the pilot talking. He called it the . . . the . . ."

A chill runs down my spine. "The Institute."

She nods quickly. "Yeah, that was it! Weird people delivered food. The man in the suit and a doctor came to the room and"—she rotates her arm upward to show me a small bandage at the bend of her elbow—"they took our blood."

"It was Gabriel," a new voice says. A white Merlin boy I don't recognize stands at the doorway behind us. He is tall with an auburn undercut, a hairstyle that I recognize as part of the Mageguard uniform. "Gabriel hid them at the Institute, Bree, just like you said."

I don't know what this boy wore when I last recognized him, but today he's in a dark navy peacoat. A pair of gloves peeks out of one pocket. Below the long coat he wears loose black pants and worn leather boots.

"I don't know . . . ," I begin apologetically.

"Who I am?" the boy says, his Scottish accent thick even in just these few sentences. He smiles. "Aye, I know. Nick explained outside. It's all right. I'm Lark. And we can catch up soon." The Merlin steps closer to Nora, offering his arm. "Will and Hazel would like to make sure you're okay, if you're still up for being looked over? I think there's a homecooked meal waiting for you, as well?"

Nora takes his arm. "That sounds excellent."

Lark guides her away. "Valec's calling your folks. They'll be here soon."

Nora's smile widens. "Thanks." She waves over her shoulder. "Thanks again, Bree."

I wave back, but it takes every ounce of strength not to collapse in agony when I do so.

The Regents wanted the girls' blood, but Erebus said that hunting Root-crafters to take them alive is unprecedented in Order history. The implication being that the Order had never held any interest in Rootcrafter power the way that demons do. The Regents didn't think Rootcrafters were a threat *valuable enough* to capture alive, much less study in a lab somewhere. Erebus didn't know why the Regents would turn their attention to Rootcrafters now, after dismissing them for so long.

But I do.

I know exactly why the Regents want Rootcrafters now when they never have before.

Me. They want them because of me.

54

I'M STILL STANDING in the middle of the Lounge floor, swimming in my own dread and anger, when Nick and another white boy push past the heavy curtains to enter the building, deep in conversation. The new boy is tall with a gentle face, wearing a heavy coat, jeans, and boots.

I know without asking that this is William.

Nick meets my eyes from across the room, the smile falling from his face when he sees my expression. Before his penetrative gaze can examine me further, William spots me.

"Bree!" William's shaggy light-brown hair lifts as he jogs toward me, grinning wide. He skids to a stop where I stand, eyes bright and cheeks pink from the wind.

A layer of my anger bleeds away at William's eager expression, then the rest nearly fades as deep worry overtakes his features. He looks me over from head to toe, as if scanning for injuries. "Nick told me about your knowledge loss," he says, voice breathless. "I know you don't know who I am, but I'm just so, so glad you're all right."

I notice right away that he says "knowledge loss" rather than "memory loss." That he's being precise with his language and that means Nick must have been too. "You're William," I murmur. "Scion of Gawain. A healer. You chased after me the day I left the Keep too."

"Yes." He nods encouragingly, smile widening. "All of that is true. I'm also your friend who is currently *very* valiantly resisting the urge to hug you."

A weak smile tugs at my mouth. "Actually, I could use a hug from a friend right now."

William folds me into his arms so quickly, air escapes me in a single breath. He swings me around in a circle, laughing low in my ear in a voice so filled with relief and joy that an answering laugh erupts out of me unbidden.

It's a quick embrace, only a few seconds, but I let that hug coat me like a warm blanket. Let it ground me before the next blow comes.

When William pulls back, he looks at me again, eyes retracing the same path from my head, to my face, to my torso, down my legs. "*Are* you okay? No injuries?"

"Nothing physical." I gnaw at my lip, the despair from earlier rising again even amid William's light. "I just heard from Nora what happened to her and the other girls."

His eyes darken. "I'm glad you had Valec call us. We were able to get to the Institute quickly because we were already at the Lodge. We'd tried to get into the Institute a few days ago, after Nick left with Ava in Georgia, but the security guards wouldn't admit us. There aren't enough Merlins to spare to protect a mostly empty building, so the guards are all human Vassals. We considered fighting them, forcing our way in, but there was a chance they'd alert the Council, and I couldn't risk being taken captive again and . . ." William hesitates, breathing out slowly through his nose. "We needed a better plan."

"They tortured us there, William. That I *do* know," I say. "You were right not to risk it."

"That's what I said." Lark strolls back into the room. He stops at William's side, offering a gentle press from his shoulder before turning to me. "Your idea to use Gabriel's name worked perfectly, Bree. The Vassals on-site operate strictly under

Gabriel's authority. There are rumors Tacitus has even mesmered some of them to alert him if any other Merlin tampers with their memories, so I couldn't risk a mesmer either. But as soon as we told them we were there under *Regent Gabriel's* orders to move his new 'guests,' they led William right to the girls."

"While Lark used cambion speed to search the labs," William adds in a pleased voice.

Lark flushes. "Just following yer hunch, Will."

"What hunch?" Nick asks as he walks forward to join us. "Last time I saw you, you were on the road when I left with Ava."

William nods. "We found syringes on Thompson. Instead of heading back to the Keep or the Lodge, we went to the Institute."

He and Lark exchange glances. "We should show her the photos," Lark says.

"What photos?" I ask.

"Parked your car out back, Mageguard." Valec reenters the bar and tosses a pair of keys to Lark, who snatches them neatly out of the air. "Nice ride. Never took you for a minivan guy."

"Welllll"—Lark flushes for the second time tonight—"I wouldn't exactly call it *my* car. We needed something to get here quick, so . . ."

Valec's brows lift in amusement. "Don't tell me you *stole a vehicle*, Mr. Law and Order?"

William snickers, and Lark glares at him. "That was just for the last few miles. The Lounge is a five-hour drive from the Institute, so I maybe, perhaps, *possibly* . . ."—he winces—"also stole Regent Gabriel's helicopter from the hangar nearby?"

"Grand theft auto *and* grand theft 'copter? All in one night?" Valec beams. "There's hope for you yet, Guard Douglas."

"What photos were you talking about?" I redirect, impatient.

Lark's expression turns serious as he pulls a phone out of his inner coat pocket. "Like Will said, while he got the girls, I searched the labs to follow up on the vials we nabbed from Thompson. Only had enough time to take a handful of pictures, so we don't know for certain what they're planning, but . . ." He hands me the phone, and Nick and Valec crowd closer to me.

There are five photos in an album. A couple are blurry, like they were taken hastily, but I can make out what I'm seeing well enough. A long black laboratory counter with test tubes and beakers and vials. I swipe to the second picture. An open notebook with equations I don't understand. Swipe again. Four vials labeled only with letters A through D. A centrifuge. Then finally, another set of five vials this time marked with nearly identical labels scrawled in neat black ink: *BM1. BM2. BM3. BM4. BM5.*

Nick catches the phone before I drop it. "What is this shit, Will?"

"'BM' is fairly obvious." William looks apologetic, although he has nothing to apologize for. "It's Bree's blood. They're experimenting with Bree's blood."

"And the blood of actively working Rootcrafters," Valec says, voice low and dangerous. "For what?"

William swallows. "If I had already been experimenting with controlling magical properties in the human body, turning abilities on and off with a serum, trying to isolate the power of the Cycle somehow . . . and if I had come across someone like Bree, who can access her ancestors' abilities in a new, more powerful way . . ."

The room grows quiet. But the King's words about greed and weakness ring in my ears even now. *A man who is both will attempt to recreate that which is beyond his comprehension, obliterating the original in the process.*

"They can't find me. They can't control me. So they're trying to recreate me instead?"

William blows out a breath. "Replicating your power, or at least learning how to neutralize it, might be possible. It's been months since you were last seen. If they gave up on tracing your family tree to locate the next Scion of Arthur, then they'd want to use what they have to control the Table and maintain their supremacy in the Order and in the war. It seems they've pivoted to tracking down rogue magic users with powers like yours to study them and try to regain the upper hand."

"It won't work." Valec walks away, teeth bared. "There *are* no random, rogue magic users with powers like hers! Bree's a once-in-a-lifetime intersection of power. Unique."

"*We* know that," William says, "but the Council doesn't. And they don't need to recreate even *half* of Bree's power to wreak havoc in the war. And beyond it."

"Where did they even *get* vials of Bree's blood?" Nick exclaims.

"From when I was at the Institute," I answer. "They mesmered me so much, I lost days there. *Days.*"

"Never thought I'd say this." Valec rubs at his jaw. "But this might be worse than the Hunter feeding off the girls' magic." He paces back to William. "What can they do with what they have?"

"I don't know," William says. "Maybe nothing. It depends on what they already know, the research they've already completed. . . . As far as I understand it, Bree is an anomaly, like you said. It's possible they'll use the girls' blood and Bree's blood and come to a dead end. Most of science is dead ends, honestly."

"But we know they're trying to do *something*," I say. "They're getting creative."

"And desperate," Nick says. "Gabriel spent a small fortune last night. Who knows what other resources they're throwing at the situation?"

"The situation *I* created, you mean," I say, "when I left."

"No." Nick grasps my shoulders. "Don't blame yourself. They could have been on this path before you left. They already had your blood stored. The Order has been disappearing people for decades. They could have been taking rogue magic users' blood before murdering them this whole time."

"But if I hadn't left, they would have just studied *me*." I raise a trembling hand to my mouth. "And Nora, Amber, Joy, and Melanie wouldn't have been captured."

"You don't know that," Valec says. "Davis is right."

"I can *guess it*," I snap. "Even if the girls would have been taken anyway, it doesn't change how much the Regents have to be stopped. They can't do this!"

"They've *been* doing this," Valec says hoarsely. "Messing with bodies and people who don't belong to them. It's why you're here in the first place, powerhouse. It's why you left—and I don't even blame you for that, except for some additional stress lines that I'm fairly certain are your fault."

I pace away. "No. I don't accept this. I don't."

"What do you want to do?" Nick asks.

I look at Valec. "First things first. Get my missing people back."

This time, Valec doesn't give me a warning. He thrusts his palm to my sternum—and then I'm lost. Drawn down and churned by his crimson eyes, his deep voice. "Just breathe."

When he stops his tour, he is left standing—and puzzled.

I come back to the stage blinking, dizzy on my chair, with his hand resting on my collarbone. "Did it work?"

"No," he says, voice confused.

"What happened?" I ask. "I felt you."

He shakes his head. "I don't know. I saw your mark, saw your Bloodcraft, your root, even saw bits of that Spell of Eternity, but it's like . . . there's a piece of you missin'—" He pulls his hand back.

"What does that mean?" William calls. "Did something go wrong?" He, Lark, Zoe, Mariah, and Nick are standing at the end of the stage looking on this time. Emil, Lucille, and Hazel are in the back tending to the girls while we wait for their parents to arrive.

"Not wrong, just unexpected. Need to take a closer look." Valec steps closer to me, expression tight and focused. His hot hands wrap my jaw, fingers gripping my temple and thrust into my hair—and his brown eyes pull me down once more. *"Look at me,"* he intones, and I unspool beneath his gaze.

All my edges peel back, tear open. The heavy swoop of his power tugs deeply at my chest and mind, then tosses parts of me away as if he's rustling through my very being, my component parts. A tug, then a release. A deep pull, then a push, like an ocean wave.

After a moment, he gasps back, dropping his hands from my face as if he's been burned. "Shit."

"What?" I ask drowsily. "What'd you see?"

"More like what I *didn't* see. What's been broken." His handsome features twist in horror. He blinks rapidly, fingers twitching at his sides as he mumbles.

"I've never . . . Didn't know it was even *possible*. Didn't even know I *could* see it, but now that it's gone, now that it's fractured, it's plain as day. Visible only in the absence—"

"What's wrong with me?" I ask, mind sharpening. "Why do you look so scared?"

"Not scared," Valec whispers, eyes distant. "Shocked. Yeah. That's what we'll call it."

"Valec!" Mariah calls. "What is it?"

Valec's gaze floats to his cousin at the sound of her voice. "Why?"

At first, I think Valec is talking to Mariah, but then he turns to me, and his question is the same. "*Why*, powerhouse? Why'd you do it?"

"Do what?"

To my surprise, his gaze crystallizes into angry red rubies and his voice turns accusing. "Why'd you give part of your soul away?"

I blink, startled. "I didn't."

His upper lip curls in disgust. "Don't lie to me. I deserve better than that. And so do you."

"No, I—" I sputter. I look down at my friends' shocked faces and back to Valec's furious one. "I'm not *lying*!"

"Do you have any idea what you've done?" Valec snaps. "How *irreversible* this is?"

I spring backward, away from the gust of heat rising from his skin. The stool clatters to the stage behind me. "I don't know what you're talking about, I swear."

"Valec!" Mariah calls. "Explain!"

He swallows roughly, eyes darkening to brown. "As much as we brokers like to mess with folks' heads about the devil in the crossroads trading souls for talent and the like, it's not something we actually have the power to tamper with. It's a legend for us, too. A fiction that there could be a demon *so* powerful that he can take possession of a human soul." A frustrated breath leaves him as he paces back and forth across the stage. "It's a fable because a soul isn't a physical object someone can hold in their hand. It's an amorphous, mutable, ungraspable thing. Even though every human possesses a soul, each and every single soul is unique. The soul is the engine that drives a person forward, the thing in life they can't live without, and as such it can be composed of anything you can imagine. It's an unknowable metaphysical core that cannot exist outside its bearer. But in the stories about this demon who *can* hold a soul, there's a catch. A big one. That demon can't take a living person's soul away unless they offer it up." He looks at me. Stops pacing. "A soul can't be removed without the bearer being willing to part from it."

"But I . . ." I look down at my friends' faces again, shaking my head. "I would never choose to forget my friends, my dad, my . . . ," I stammer. "When I got to Erebus's home, he said I was *fractured*. He did something to me then, maybe broke my soul somehow—"

"Oh, Bree . . ." Mariah's eyes shimmer, dread driving the blood from her face. "Your ancestral stream."

"What about her ancestral stream?" Valec demands.

Every nerve in my body turns raw. A white-hot pain beneath my skin. "I . . . burned it. . . ."

Valec's eyes widen. "You did *what?*"

I flush, the shame rising quick. To my surprise, it's Mariah who steps in. "You don't get to judge her on this, Valechaz."

Valec blinks down at his cousin. "Like hell I won't—"

"No!" Mariah says, raising a finger. "She's still Bree. And she's the only one who's had to deal with everything. From every angle."

"And *this* is how she dealt with it?" Valec seethes.

"Back off, man!" Zoe calls from the floor.

Valec whirls on me. "Decisions like that have *consequences*, powerhouse! When you burned your ancestral stream, you fractured your *own* soul. Broke off a piece and left it free for the taking!"

"She didn't know," William counters firmly. "And yelling at her is *not* helping."

Valec scoffs. "Don't you get it? The King didn't even *need* a contract; all he had to do was take what was offered!"

"It wasn't offered!" I'm shouting before I can stop myself. "I didn't know my soul was connected to the people in my life. How could I? Don't blame me for the King's theft!"

"That I won't do, because you're right. Theft is theft," Valec says tightly. "But you *did* willingly give up part of yourself. Not just the ancestors but us, too."

Anger and guilt burn into a dangerous combination in my chest. "That's *not* fair—"

"What's not fair are the things we had to do to find you!" Valec releases a hollow laugh. "The things we risked . . ."

"I didn't ask you to take risks for me."

"And you'll never have to." Valec's eyes are hard—and only for me. "A soul like yours is something to kill and die for, Briana Matthews. Your soul is the engine behind a power that could change the *world*. Unparalleled, in this dimension or the next. Beyond priceless. And you *gave* it away like it was *nothing*." He growls low in his throat, snarling in outrage—and I flinch.

In a blink, Nick stands between me and Valec, bright aether sparking in warning at his fingertips. "Enough."

The room goes silent at the deadly simmer of Nick's voice.

In response, a hot wave of fury rolls off Valec's body, billowing against our faces. Forcing the others, even Zoe, to turn away.

But when Valec's anger touches Nick, it only hardens his resolve. "You need to walk away, Valechaz. Now."

"That so"—Valec's chin tips up, exposing glinting fangs beneath the stage lights—"Nicholas?"

Lightning flashes in Nick's eyes. "A soul to kill and die for, right?"

One beat. Two. We all hold our breaths for the fight to come. Then Valec curses, turning to walk away, rage falling from him like water.

I leap after him, running to grasp his shoulder. "Valec, wait—"

"No, the kid's right." He shakes me off. "I need to step out."

Panic fills me. "But I need your help to fix this!"

He whips around, eyes shining. "I *can't* fix this, Bree!"

"It's my *soul*," I argue. "I need that missing piece back."

He shrugs helplessly. "If there's even a piece to recover."

I blink, knocked to my heels. "What are you saying?"

He sighs heavily. "A demon powerful enough to remove a fragment of your soul is powerful enough to destroy it. We don't know the King's long game. You need to prepare yourself for the possibility that this is *it*. In fact, go on ahead and plan for that fragment not coming back. Probably smarter that way, 'stead of getting your hopes up."

My eyes burn. "That's cruel, Valec."

"You're tellin' me," he murmurs. "I can fix a lot of things, powerhouse, but some things you just gotta live with."

And with that, he stalks out of the room, leaving me behind in stunned silence.

55

AFTER THE REVELATION of my fractured soul and Valec's disappearance, Hazel successfully persuaded Mariah, Zoe, Lark, and William to rest in the back rooms of the Lounge for the day. Zoe took Valec's phone to her room, still hoping to hear back from Elijah. They were offered hot showers and warm clothes, and after I waved them all away, my friends finally relented.

Nick took much more convincing to leave my side, but I pressed him backward down the hallway with my own two hands against his chest, our gazes locked in equal determination and care. He only left after I promised to rest once I saw the girls off safely.

In truth, it was me who did not wish to be seen.

I spend the rest of the morning with Lucille and Emil, listening to them talk not about souls or Regents or Rootcraft, but about the repairs at Volition. Family gossip. Rumors about a restaurant opening across the street from Emil's. They let me wander behind them as they clean up some of the mess from our early breakfast and prep food for a late lunch. None of the others emerges from their rooms looking for food, so Hazel joins us and the four of us eat quietly while we wait.

By the time the first family arrives at the Lounge, it is late afternoon. We hear a car rolling up the unmarked gravel driveway outside the building and Emil texts Valec to alert him. A few moments later, he receives a text back. "All clear," Emil rumbles with a smile. The next cars arrive over the course of a few hours.

Lucille and Emil greet each set of parents outside the door and welcome them in through an eight-foot-wide gap in Valec's ward. I stand out of the way in a shadowed corner behind the bar as they enter. If any of the family members notice the dragon-shaped skull over the neon sign outside the Lounge, they don't pay it any mind at all; their eyes are only for their recovered daughters, their spirits pointing only toward reunion.

I watch as Joy is folded into her weeping mother's arms and as the both of them become enclosed by her father's body. An hour later, I see a bespectacled little brother collide with Melanie's legs after darting ahead of her father's eager jog. Next, Amber and her parents and three siblings collapse into a tearful, laughing heap just inside the curtains, not even making it as far as the main room. Finally, Nora's mother and grandmother arrive, weaving their wide brown arms around her in a tight braid.

Each time the girls embrace the members of their family, and every time I see a face contort with emotion, I feel the relief of something lost being returned. A heart, back where it belongs. A soul, in its right place.

I'll never be able to hug my mother again, but I'm glad that the girls can. As for my father? I'll have to be satisfied knowing that he's safe. Even if I saw him again, I don't know how I could let myself hug him knowing that, on some level, I'm part of the reason he lost me in the first place.

Even here, Erebus's voice finds me: *How do you think they'll feel when you remember everything about yourself, but not them?*

Valec might hate that his reaction to me was predicted by one of his enemies, but Erebus has been right about so many things that I can't say that I am surprised. I knew an explosion was coming. I just didn't know from whom, or realize how much damage had already been done. How much could never be undone.

Nora is the last to leave, late in the evening. She spies me hidden in the corner and, after asking her mother and grandmother to give her a moment, calls me over. We meet in the middle of the Lounge, just as we had earlier this morning. The gold in her gaze is gone now, her ancestors' connection closed safely. She studies me with soft brown eyes.

"You take care of yourself, Bree." When she hugs me, my arms rise around her instinctively. After a moment, she steps away to take a last look at the Lounge. The empty tables with chairs overturned on top. The aether swirling in bottles behind the bar. The second-level loft shrouded in odd-shaped shadows beneath the skylights. "You got a nice crew. Don't know what y'all're up to, but be safe, okay?"

"Yeah, I . . . I do have a nice crew."

Nora gives my hand a final squeeze then leaves to join her family. Emil had offered to open his restaurant up and cook everyone a nice dinner, and the families were more than glad to take him up on it. I'm sure that's where she'll be headed now. I don't know for certain if Emil's offer had an ulterior motive, but my gut tells me that Emil and Valec had conspired to get the girls and their families as far away from the Lounge as possible, as quickly as possible, in case Erebus or the Order found their way back to us. I don't think I'll see Emil again anytime soon, and for that I'm relieved. One less person in harm's way.

I promised Nick that I would seek him out as soon as the girls departed. I know which hall will lead me to his warm bed and even warmer body. I also know that I would lose myself in him, seeking solace from my own thoughts, and, for some reason, I'm not quite sure I deserve that.

I'm not ready to let him take my misery away.

With my emotions swirling, I turn away from the three hallways and the strange echoes of an empty nightclub. I grab a heavy winter coat from the pile of clothes Lucille left on the bar for the taking and climb the stairs to the second floor, pausing at the locked door of Valec's office. A shaft of light shifts beneath the doorway, like someone has moved across the room, then stopped. I swallow and walk past it down the hall.

When I emerge from the rickety elevator onto the empty roof, the moon greets me through Valec's ward from behind softly bloated clouds. I slip on the coat, throwing the hood up over my curls to protect my ears, and aim myself toward an old wooden garden bench facing the low wall perimeter of the roof's edge. As soon as I collapse onto it, the dark country night folds over me like a heavy blanket, and I fall into a deep, dreamless sleep.

I sense another presence on the rooftop before I hear the soft steps. My eyes snap open to find winter stars still shining overhead, but now they are accompanied by the thin amethyst and navy streaks of dawn playing tricks on my eyes from the horizon. I jerk upright, yanking my hands from the deep pockets where I'd buried them—and a warm hand rests heavy on my shoulder in response.

"You're safe."

My chest loosens immediately. I relax against the carved back of the bench, turning my head up to meet Nick's soft gaze. He releases my shoulder to press a steaming mug into my hands. "From William."

While I cradle the mug, he rounds the bench to settle beside me, stretching his long legs out on the gravel. I notice he's taken a coat from the available pile too, and changed into jeans and a heavy sweater. Just seeing the warm clothes on him makes me acutely aware of the frigid air. My cheeks sting from exposure, and the thin dress under my coat feels laughably inadequate.

But the hot tea is perfectly timed and more than welcome, and so is the company. The tea along with Nick's quiet reserve tells me that he didn't come up here to pull me away from my rooftop respite, and for that I am grateful. A whiff of the mug tells me something of William's intentions, too. "Chamomile."

"My nonprofessyst prescription," Nick murmurs, "but William agreed."

We sit in silence for a beat, until I look at him. "Did you know?"

He knows what I mean without my having to elaborate. "I knew something had been taken from you, but I didn't know what it was." Frustration pulls at his mouth. "Souls are, apparently, a different kind of magic. I can't see them. Wish I could."

I consider his answer. Consider the ease with which Nick found me here on the roof. The ease of sitting with him now, even when it's so cold out that my teeth might start to chatter.

"You . . . see *me*, don't you?" I whisper. "And I don't mean with your powers."

He turns to look at me. "I think we see each other. Now, and before all of this." A pause. "And I don't mean with my powers."

"Probably better that you can't see souls with your magic vision." I chuckle softly into the mug, sipping. "If you'd told me at Penumbra that the Shadow King of Annwfyn possessed part of my soul, and that I might not ever get it back, I probably would have run screaming into the woods, Mikael's affective ward be damned."

He stares up at the sky. "Literal woods or metaphorical woods?"

I huff into the tea. Let the steam blow against my nose. "Either."

A pause. Then: "Would that be so bad?"

I expect to hear amusement in his tone, see it on his face, but when I look at him, it never comes. "What do you mean?"

He turns to me, attention sharpening. "I used to think that the Order as a society was broken, but watching you navigate it, knowing what they've done to you because of it, being away from it myself, showed me that it's not *broken*. It's working exactly as designed. A wheel, drenched in hate and control, churning. Every time you wield your power, every time you own the right to speak, the Regents make *you* the lightning rod for their evil." He hesitates, then reaches a hand to my face, pushing past my lined hood to hold my cheek in his blessedly warm palm. "Listen to me. You don't owe them anything, Bree. *No one* deserves your suffering."

I close my eyes, letting his words wash over me. Feeling found, even when all I want to do is hide. "What if my soul is fractured forever?"

"Then you have already begun to live your new forever, and live it well," he says quietly. "Which is more than many with fully intact souls can claim."

I open my eyes to meet his patient gaze and swallow around a lump in my throat. "So if I ran off screaming into the woods . . . ? Literal, not metaphorical."

A smile tugs at his mouth. "I'd point them in the opposite direction."

My eyes sting. "And if I chose to just . . . *not* be the Scion of Arthur and decided to live as a normal human girl?"

"Mm." His hand slides down my cheek, circling, until he gently cups my nape, massaging the muscles there with heated fingers. "I'm listening." I shiver, then, but not at the cold. I feel the quiet strength in his grip and see the invitation in his patient gaze, both there for me to accept.

In a single long breath, I let go.

I relax the tension in my neck until my skull rests in the support of his warm hand. My eyes fall shut, breath leaving me in a silent shudder.

I didn't realize how much I'd been holding until he offered to take it.

He hums, satisfied, and presses deeper into the tight cords beneath my ears.

"Would you forget me?" I murmur, voice drunk with pleasure.

"I could lose my entire soul . . . and still never forget you."

"Please don't," I whisper. "I can't recommend it. In part or in whole."

His lips brush across mine, soft and too brief, before he leans closer to rub his cheek lightly against my own. With my eyes closed, the warm stubble at his jaw is comforting and electrifying all at once. "I'll take that into consideration."

I take bravery from the darkness. Pull the most frightening question up from my depths to breathe it into existence, because Nick makes it safe to do so.

"Do you think I made a mistake?"

He holds my face in both his hands until my eyes open. "No." His gaze searches mine, soft yet sharp. "Your choices save *lives*. And often, your own. Your existence, in whole or in part, helps people. Makes the world around you better. I could see that before you were Awakened by Arthur. Now when I look at you . . . If I could offer you even a *fraction* of the life you deserve . . ."

Tears fill my eyes at his words.

He uses a thumb to swipe a tear away. "If you need to go, I won't force you to stay."

Another dip into my well of bravery. An impossible question and a wish, cast into his waiting gaze. "And if I wanted you to go with me?"

"I'd go." He tilts my chin to press a lingering kiss to my mouth. "And never look back."

"Never look back?" I breathe.

"Never."

"And if I want . . . ?" My breath turns shallow, my skin burning beneath the winter coat.

His brows lift in question. "If you want . . . ?"

"Actually," I murmur, "that might be the end of the sentence."

His eyes darken. "I see." Without breaking our gaze, Nick slips the cup of tea from my hands. He studies me silently, turning those too-perceptive eyes to every tiny betrayal written on my skin. My parted lips, the rapid pulse in my neck, the rise of my chest. Then, he moves to set the mug on the low wall, body twisting away, pausing. He sets the mug down and turns back to give me his full attention. "If you . . . *want.*"

"Yes." I nod quickly. Pleading without words.

His mouth quirks. "Bree . . ."

My name in Nick's mouth is intoxicating—I want him to say it again. "Yes?"

But this time, he says it differently. "Bree."

If Nick has ever uttered my name like that before—breathy, low, a warning—then I'm glad to have forgotten it. I shudder at the sound, and at the open desire on his face as he watches that same shudder travel down my body. His hands find my waist, as if to catch my reaction between his palms. Trap it. Feel it for himself. When I swallow, his gaze drops to track the motion at my throat, then drags its way back up to my face again. Something heady and hungry prowls behind his features, and I'm suddenly, irrepressibly, eager to set it free.

"Our enemies are still out there," he murmurs.

"Out there," I whisper. "Not here."

Nick's expression flickers. His fingers tighten at my sides until I gasp at the pressure. Until I squirm in my seat. He absorbs my responses, appreciative. Knowing. "Your quest—"

"Is what I make it."

"I'm not your fiancé anymore." The low timbre of his voice ripples across my skin. "You don't have to pretend."

"I know," I rasp. "Neither do you."

Nick's jaw tenses. We hold each other's gazes for a sharp, burning second. A match, struck. The storm in his eyes, gathering between us.

Until it breaks.

A low curse erupts from him and he dives forward, capturing my lips with his, igniting us both. Our kisses at Penumbra felt like clouds gathering, like thunder in the distance. This is an unleashing.

"We weren't pretending," he groans.

"No," I pant. "We weren't." His mouth works down my jaw to my throat, searing my skin until my eyelids flutter. "Even then, when I didn't know you and we were lying to everyone else, it was . . . we were . . ."

"What were we, B?" Nick murmurs, voice strained as he pulls back to meet my eyes. My heart thumps under my chin, at the bruised places where he'd kissed me. "Even then?"

The grip of his broad hands wrapped around my thighs frays my mind at the edges, but still . . . a phrase surfaces. A clear resonance pulling us together.

"You and me," I breathe, smiling.

"Yes," he says, voice rough, "you and me."

Those words—*our* words—settle in my stomach and burn like embers. I let Nick pull me into his lap and guide my legs to either side of him. In turn, he lets me explore his mouth, his jaw with my lips. When a low hum becomes a moan, we both chase the sound, seeking its source—

Nick pulls away with a gasp, silver-blue mage flame flashing in his irises. It radiates from both eyes, smoky and electric, before dimming. As if he's reining it back. Shuttering his vision as he looks away.

That won't do.

"What do you see," I urge, gently turning his chin, "when you look at me?"

When he faces me again, the magic in his eyes flickers . . . then flares.

Lightning between us, summer rain in winter.

"I'll tell you." Words fall from him, then. Nick paints reverence across my throat and seals wonder to my mouth. He whispers my own magic into my skin. His hands slip down and down past the edge of my coat to grasp the long skirt of my dress. He tugs the thin fabric up and up until his fingers find my waiting skin, my arched spine, my rolling hips. His molten voice floods my veins, cascading through me, until I am heat itself. A sun in a body. "I'll show you."

Letting go and holding tight.

Falling and climbing.

Forgetting and remembering.

All at once.

Long moments later, I pull away, gasping. Nick's head tips back against the chair, a languid, pleased smile stretched across his face. His thick hair is a mess of deep tunnels from my desperate fingers, while his eyes reflect the sunrise behind me as their glow fades. My borrowed coat lies unzipped and forgotten somewhere on the roof—a joint effort, I think. Winter air meets my exposed hips and thighs, but my body is too feverish from Nick's clever hands to care.

We stare at each other, chests rising and falling in sync with our ragged breaths. I gently tug at his ripe, shiny lower lip; he nips at my thumb. I graze my knuckles across the square shape of his jaw, exploring; he responds with a low, satisfied rumble. I hook my fingers into the belt loops of his jeans; he holds me tight as I lean backward to watch the sky over us turn pink, then orange, then a rich, glowing amber. Our breathing slows. Nick's hands flex at my rib cage, fingers still hot on the skin beneath my dress, but he does not pull me closer or ask me to speak.

Nick lets me think. Lets me become who I need to be in the circle of his arms. Around us, the forest begins to wake. And still, he watches and waits.

Until I know what I want to ask next.

The thought sends me down to him again—and he surges to meet me. As the world dawns, we claim each other's mouths. Call and response.

When I finally whisper, "And if I want to burn it all to the ground?"

His answer is a quick grin against my lips. "My blade is yours."

56

WE FIND VALEC at the outer border of his ward and pause to watch him work. His fingers glide up the translucent golden surface of the ward, leaving a thicker layer behind that melts, then solidifies before our eyes.

Nick's arms circle my waist from behind, and he drops a kiss on my shoulder. "I'll look into breakfast."

I nod and squeeze his wrists before he lets me go.

"Hazel invited us to her place for breakfast," Valec calls to us without turning away from his barrier, having heard Nick's comment even at a distance. "And the Lounge is out of food, so Sir Lancelot's gonna have to eat bar peanuts for now."

I hear Nick chuckle as he walks inside, leaving me and Valec alone.

"He'll survive." I walk closer to the cambion, admiring the ward as I approach.

"You sure 'bout that? That boy looks like he needs at *least* four protein shakes a day. Mebbe five."

I roll my eyes but smile. If Valec is joking with me, then maybe he's not too mad to talk.

I stride up beside him but keep a safe distance as he continues to work. When he doesn't speak, I decide I won't either. Instead, I shuffle along behind him as he patches the ward, occasionally murmuring something I can't quite make out.

Finally, he speaks. "I was raised thinking that cambions like me couldn't cast wards."

That surprises me. "Said who?"

He shrugs. "Well-meaning folk."

"But why would the Merlins be able to, and you couldn't?"

"Merlins are descended from a great sorcerer and their wards are, allegedly, protective." A pause. "I am the crossroads child of a Shade."

My eyes widen, remembering a scene from a memory walk long ago. A scene that appears clearly in my mind, because the women within it are long dead. A young woman named Pearl and her newborn baby with amber eyes that glowed like the sun. "Your father was . . ."

He turns, dusting his hands off. "A Nightshade of the Shadow Court."

"Wow."

A wry expression overtakes his face. "I just told you that my father is not only evil but one of the world's most *ancient* evils, in service to the being that devoured part of your soul, and all you've got is 'wow'?" He shakes his head. "This generation is doomed, I swear."

"Okay, I can say more than 'wow,'" I protest. "I can say, 'Holy shit, Valec, that seems like a really messed-up legacy to walk around with. How are you holding up?'"

"You could say that; you're right."

"Not gonna, though," I say, turning back to the ward. "In case that's rude."

He blinks. "You're truly something else, Briana Matthews."

I peer at him out of the side of my eye. "Does what you did to try and find me have to do with your father?"

He takes a slow, deep breath. "Put myself back on the radar of one of his fellow Court members when I've done everything I could in the last hundred years to distance myself from each and every Shade on this plane. When the only reason I can do this"—he nods toward the ward—"is because I cut contact with the Court entirely."

I consider this. "How do you know that's the only reason you can use root?"

"Because root is about uplifting life not death," Valec says. "Even though we walk beside death to access it and honor the ones who came before, the workings are for the living. Not the undead. I'm lucky the ancestors even let me do this much, and forge the occasional weapon for defense. Not like I'm really built for 'good,' so to speak."

"Ah."

He narrows his eyes. "You don't believe me."

I smile. "Nah."

He huffs in frustration. "I've been around quite a bit longer than you, powerhouse."

"True," I admit, then shrug. "But someone once told me that while we know ourselves best, we don't always know what we're capable of doing or becoming. And I think that's a pretty nice way to look at it."

"Since when did you get wise?"

"Since a demon ate part of my soul, I guess."

A laugh bursts out of him. He shakes his head, smiling. "Whew . . . shit."

I smile back at him, happy to have made him laugh even for a moment, before I sober. "I'm sorry for putting y'all out like I did."

He waves a hand. "You didn't do that. *We* did that. Because we care. And I shouldn't have made you feel guilty about it."

"But I made a choice, and I have to live with it, like you said."

"If I trust you, and I do, then I gotta trust you to make your own calls. I'm not living your life, *you* are." He crosses his arms, tucking his chin into his chest. "I put you up on a pedestal, Bree. Saw you as someone who can walk between worlds, you know? Do the impossible thing I've been chasing my whole life. And that's not fair. That's the stuff that got you all mixed up in the first place. I'm sorry."

My throat tightens. "I didn't come out here expecting an apology."

"But I owe you one anyway." His shoulders rise and fall in a heavy sigh. "And if I may, I'd like to amend your little saying."

I glance up. "How so?"

"While we know ourselves best, we don't always know what we're capable of doing or becoming"—he pauses, thinking—"*and* we can always choose new paths if we need to."

I swallow around a lump. "Rules can change."

His eyes flash red. "Picked up a little demon talk on your walk 'round the dark side?"

"Seems so."

He studies me. "I turned my back on my people once too. Gave in. Why I did it is my business and a story for another day, but why did you? Why'd you burn your ancestral stream, *really*?"

"I failed. I was . . . failing," I say. "Everyone. Everywhere. At everything I did. I tried to do what my ancestors asked me to do, tried to be what they needed me to be . . . tried to be what the Legendborn told me I could be, tried to defy the Regents, tried to harness Arthur, and look what it all got me? My best friend is in a coma, Selwyn is gone, my dad doesn't even know where I am—"

"Slow down, slow down," Valec says, holding his hands out to grasp my shoulders. "You *had* to fail, Bree. You had to fall."

"Why?" I exclaim.

"Because you had to *rise*." He steps closer. "A true leader has to know every side of her battle: the wins, the losses, the enemies, the allies, the good, and the bad. And she has to know who has her back, without the titles and legacies."

"Do you have my back?"

He smirks. "Always, powerhouse."

The tension in my shoulders breaks apart, crumbles, and it feels like I can breathe again. Like every minute with these people who were looking for me gives me back a bit of myself.

Valec's arms drop and his smile turns sly. "How about that boy who just went inside?"

I frown. "What about him?"

"I like him." Valec shrugs. "*He's* got your back."

"Probably some other parts of you too," a new voice says, "if you let him."

Valec laughs. I look over his shoulder to see Zoe leaning against the exterior door with a wide grin on her face. "How long you been standing there?" I demand.

"Just a couple seconds." She blurs over to us and tosses a handful of peanuts in her mouth and waggles her eyebrows. "Long enough to call you out for not going to bed last night."

Valec crosses his arms, smirking. "See, I wasn't gonna say anything."

"Why not?" Zoe asks. "*Somebody* has to keep Bree on her toes."

"You're right," Valec agrees solemnly. "I lied. I *was* gonna say *something*."

"See?" Zoe says to Valec. "You should have seen them at Penumbra——"

"No." I point between the two of them. "You two getting along is a *cursed* combination. Make it stop."

Valec snickers. "Nah." He regards Zoe, who looks up at him with wide, hesitant eyes. "Besides, I have a feeling we have a lot we could talk about, huh, kid?"

Zoe wrinkles her nose but nods. "Yeah, I guess."

"When you're ready," Valec adds.

She shrugs and looks away. "Yeah."

Valec turns back to me. "After we're done giving the powerhouse here a hard time about her white boys, that is," he says—and they both collapse with laughter.

I roll my eyes, but don't fight the amused smile curling my lips. "Cursed. Combination."

"Honestly, Davis seems all right," Valec says as he recovers. "But he's bonded to the Kingsmage, and that Oath ain't nothing to play with. Ain't no way to break it either. Question is, what's *Kane* think about you and his bonded canoodling like teenagers?"

"What——" I sputter. "We *are* teenagers!"

Zoe butts in. "So you *admit* to the canoodling!"

I am saved from responding by the pulse of my bloodmark. The loose laughter leaves their bodies in simultaneous whooshes as both cambions' eyes drop to my chest and the blazing red branches. I rub at my sternum in frustration.

Valec's humor disappears. "Bloodmark botherin' ya?"

"Yeah," I reply. "That's what I came out here to talk to you about, actually."

"Can't do anything about that mark," Valec warns.

"No, I know, but"—I shift my weight—"I want you to take another look at what the King did to me. I'm not done fighting. And I need you to not be done fighting either, Valec."

He rubs a hand over his jaw. "Take another look, huh?"

"I need to know everything I can about what he did to my soul, even if there's a chance I can't restore it to whole," I say. "We have his crown. We know his true identity." I throw my hands up. "I *have* to believe that *something* can still help us. It can't end like this. I won't stand for it."

Valec sighs. "There is *one* thing we could try—no promises. Something Hazel might be able to do, but it's gonna take both of us." He eyes me warily. "And it might not work, because of . . . of what I told you about me."

I put all my confidence in my gaze. "Let's do the impossible."

Valec exhales. "Well, when you put it that way . . ."

I take a hot shower and change clothes while the others get ready to leave. An hour later, when we pull up as a caravan to Hazel's house, she and Lucille greet all seven of us at the porch: me, Valec, Zoe, Nick, William, Lark, and Mariah.

William whispers to me that he had been with me the last time I was here. That Alice is here now, safe from the Order.

Alice.

I freeze at the name. My best friend, close to death—before I left her behind. A new fear flashes in my mind: What if I see her and don't feel what I should?

Hazel doesn't let my stricken expression set in. Quickly, she invites me to walk with her to the back room where Alice is resting. I hesitate for only a moment, because it reminds me of another day, *another* moment, when someone I loved with my entire being was lying alone and still in an otherwise empty room. Except that time, the person was my mother, and she was dead . . . and I wasn't allowed to see her body.

Hazel and Mariah step beside me, taking my hands in each of theirs. "It's all right, Bree," Mariah says. "Let us be brave with you."

I swallow around a hard lump in my throat. "Okay."

They walk me into the room together, and then I see her. The fear that held me back dissipates as soon as I see her sleeping face, and I am at her side in two strides, holding her hand.

"Alice . . . ," I whisper. There is something tight in her expression. "What's happening to her?"

Mariah comes around to the other side of the bed. "She's in a type of purgatory, as far as we can tell. Not quite dead, not quite alive." She frowns. "I visited her there. She's fighting her own death. If I were to guess, I'd say that she's replaying the moment she thinks she failed you. The moment when she could have made a different choice to help you . . . and to help herself."

"She didn't fail me," I whisper, voice cracking. "I failed her. . . ."

"None of that," Hazel murmurs. "The ones we love don't think in those terms. They give us grace when we fall. . . ."

"So that we can rise," I whisper.

She nods. "Seems you and Ms. Chen are cut from a similar cloth."

"We grew up together."

"Same high standards, same sense of justice," Hazel says. "Same love for each other. The kind of sisterhood that has you throwing yourself in the way of a demon, just to protect the other person from more harm."

"I didn't—"

"Didn't you?" Hazel asks. She comes closer and presses her lips to my temple. "I'm gonna finish making breakfast with Lu. You sit with her as long as you like."

Mariah watches her aunt leave. "I can go—"

"No," I murmur. "I . . . could use a little of that extra bravery . . . if it's still on offer?"

Mariah grins. "You got it."

Thirty minutes later, Mariah and I emerge from Alice's room together. She rubs my back and excuses herself to go help her aunts cook. When I look up, I see William has already made himself available in the kitchen—and so has Nick.

"You cook?" I call.

Nick flashes me a grin. "I can cook." He glances back at Hazel over a deep dish of sausage gravy. "But not like this."

"I know that's right," Lu mutters behind him.

"You make *food* is what I'm hearing," Valec drawls. "There's a difference."

The room bursts into warm laughter—until suddenly the cambions stiffen, tilting their ears to the door.

"You expecting somebody else, Haze?" Valec asks.

She shakes her head.

Valec, Lark, and Zoe blur out to the porch and the gravel drive beyond it, leaving the porch door swinging.

Nick is at my side in a blink, hand wrapped around my wrist. "If there's a fight, we need to get you out of here."

"No," I say. "Not running."

He bites back a response and nods once. "Then we need to be prepared." He looks to the others in the room just as I do. William is already ushering both Hazel and Lucille into their bedroom, armor rippling into place over his forearms, while Mariah walks to stand beside us, her hand on the Heart at her chest. I open up the root furnace in my chest, let the flames lick down my biceps and elbows.

If Erebus wants to take me back, I'm not going to make it easy.

"Bree!" Zoe calls. "You better get out here."

Nick's fingers tense around my wrist. "Let me look first." Not a question, but I nod anyway.

He dashes to the porch door, opening it slowly to exit. It swings shut behind him. Then, a moment later: "Bree, it's . . ."

"Is it safe?" I call.

He hesitates before answering. I blink at Mariah. What could be out there that has rendered all three cambions *and* Nick totally speechless?

"It's safe," Nick finally shouts. "Just . . . come outside."

I draw my flames back but keep them simmering behind my sternum. Mariah and I approach together, and I ease the front door open, unsure of what I'm going to find on the other side.

Nick is blocking the doorway, his broad shoulders filling my view. "What is it?"

He glances back at me, then steps away to reveal the new car that has pulled into the driveway—and its new occupants. "That's Sel's mom."

I take in the tall, black-haired woman in tactical gear standing with her hands up by the driver's side of an SUV. I freeze. The same woman had been at Eclipse when Elijah and Zoe took me to meet Daeza. She'd spoken to me oddly, as if she'd recognized *me* even as I didn't recognize her. *She's* Selwyn's mother?

"And I've never met him before, but," Nick continues, nodding to the passenger side, "I think . . . I think that's your dad."

The middle-aged Black man standing by the passenger side of the car is gripping the top of the door as he eyes the cambions around him. Then, he looks up, and our eyes meet—and my heart stutters in my chest when he smiles and offers a weak wave. "Hey, kiddo."

57

I CAN SEE why Nick assumed the man standing in front of me is my father. We have similar features—the same dimples, if not the same smile, the same mouth and nose.

The flood of emotions that rushes into me when I meet my father's gaze makes me burst into tears on the porch—near-violent, shoulder-wracking sobs that probably startle everyone with their abrupt appearance. Then, I feel warm arms around me, smell a comforting, sharp cologne, and I'm being guided back into Hazel's house and onto her couch.

I don't know how long I sob against my father's chest.

I come back to the room slowly, to his arms rocking me, the sound of his low hum against my ear, and little rhythmic squeezes of my shoulder that remind me that I am loved.

In the end, it's the smell of hot breakfast that brings me fully back to myself. Griddle cakes, hot syrup, homemade biscuits and gravy fill my nose. The sounds of clinking silverware and low voices reach me from Hazel's screened-in porch.

I peek through teary eyes to see that a folding picnic table has been set up outside and that my friends are gathered together to eat, leaving me and my father inside to our reunion.

I sniff—and cringe at the wet sound. My father hands me a tissue before I can ask for one. "Thanks," I mutter.

"I've been helping you wipe your nose for seventeen years," his low voice mumbles, amused and warm. "Don't expect that'll stop anytime soon, even if you don't remember who I am."

I push up to sitting, and he loosens his arms around me. "I know who you are," I protest, even as I take in his features. His bushy brows and thinning hair. His athletic shirt and tracksuit pants. His single, thin golden chain necklace peeking out from his collar and the old leather watch he wears on his left wrist.

My father smiles. "Natasia filled me in on what's been going on." He raises a hand to show off the gold ring around his right ring finger. "And your mom told me the rest."

My jaw drops. "Mom . . . how?"

He tugs at my wrist. "Same way she told you, I gather."

I remember. The bracelet. Her voice. Her message to me right when I was filled with despair and too many unanswered questions. I shake my head. "How is she helping us even now?"

He smiles softly. "She's eternal like that, kiddo. And"—he shrugs—"she was always ten steps ahead. Prepared for any scenario." He looks outside. "Natasia told me what things have probably been like for you since you inherited your mom's . . . abilities. I understand why your mom didn't tell us what might happen if there was a chance it might not happen at all. Neither one of us would have been better prepared with all that knowledge in our heads, knowing that she might die early and leave you to face this world on your own."

"I'm not . . . ," He tilts his chin as if challenging the lie before I state it. "I'm not always alone," I say quietly.

"But a lot of the time, it feels like you are," he murmurs, "doesn't it?"

I sniff again, and he hands me the whole box this time. "Yeah."

He regards me for a moment. "We're with you. You're never truly alone."

"But I miss her. I don't want to lose anyone else, but I think . . . loving folks hurts too."

"I know." He sits back against the couch, and together, we watch my friends as they pass another plate down the table. "Loving other people and losing them hurts. And loving them when they're gone? Opens up the wound again. Now, I'm no expert, but I think the only way to live with grief is to seek its antidote. For me, that's learning how to live my life without your mom in it and figuring out how to be your dad without her beside me, while remembering how she made me feel about myself. If I don't do that, I'm pretty sure I'll forget how to love other people altogether, not because I *can't*, but because I won't remember *how*. Loving folks is a practice, baby."

I sit with that for a moment. If I restore my soul, it won't just be the people that come back, but the everyday practice of *being* with those people too. The relationships.

I look at him with a frown. "Are you always like this?"

He grins, clapping me on the shoulder. "I've been known to say a thing or two, yeah."

I shake my head. "I can't wait to remember everything else you've said, then. That was like rocket fuel."

He chuckles, his laugh loud and warm. "Natasia told me what she and your mom got up to back in the day. She told me the stuff you've already had to face down at Carolina. You're Bree Matthews, baby. You can do anything."

When we step outside, there are two seats waiting for us. My father urges me to the seat next to Natasia Kane while he sits closer to the head of the table with Lu and Hazel. He seems to sense my eagerness to speak with her, now that my head has cleared.

Hazel cooked for an army. Everyone's plate is full, and there's still more food waiting in colorful serving dishes and chafing dishes above warming candles. As I move around the table, Lark gives me an update. "Valec's out casting new wards. Crown is secured. We should be safe here for the day, if you're comfort-able staying."

"Sounds good," I say. "I want us to have time to eat. Fuel up for what's next."

When I sit in the open chair beside Natasia Kane, she offers me a warm smile. Nick and Lark cast expectant gazes between us that don't go unnoticed. But Nick's eyes are curious *and* concerned, and Lark's are just . . . concerned.

"He's a Kingsmage," Natasia says quietly to me. "Or was trained to be. If he didn't keep an eye on you, he wouldn't be worth the title."

I study her features up close as she studies mine. Black hair like a raven, golden eyes, a strong jaw. She knew my mother, knew her power. I wish I could ask her more questions. *Every* question. But for now, there is only one. "Where is Sel?"

The table quiets.

Natasia doesn't seem surprised by my question. "I don't know."

Nick and I make eye contact. If the taut expression on his face is any indica-tion, he has already asked the same question of Natasia—and received the same inadequate answer.

"But Erebus took him to you," I insist.

That surprises her. "How do you know that?"

"Because I told him to."

Natasia blinks. "What?"

William and Lark exchange glances, this information new to them as well.

"*You* told him to?" she asks.

"Why don't you know where he is?" Nick presses. "Why are you hesitant to say more?"

Her hands flatten on the tablecloth. She draws a slow breath. "Because you are his friends, but you aren't cambions. You aren't Merlins. You can't under-stand—"

"I'm a Merlin," Lark interrupts. "And I *do* understand. He escaped, didn't he?"

Natasia stiffens, locking eyes with him. "Demonia is not what you've been taught—"

"Is Sel the reason you're injured?" Nick asks. "Why do you have those bruises?"

To my surprise, Natasia and my father share a look across the table. Some understanding passes between them. "You lost him?" I ask.

"For now," she admits. "I tried to help him, but my methods didn't work. I don't know why. They're all experimental as it is, but his emotional state is so different than mine was. His *anger* is——" She looks up at me, at the concern on my face for her son. "I used the ring Faye had me mesmer to bring Edwin's memory back so he could understand the risks, and I brought him here, to the home of the Grand Dame, to keep him out of harm's way. I had no idea I'd find you here too, Bree."

"Why would my *father* be in harm's way?"

"It's just a precaution," she says hurriedly. "I don't truly think Selwyn would harm Edwin. Nor does he wish to harm you, not directly. It's just . . ." Natasia's brows draw tight. "Demonia makes us hungry. Selwyn wants your power, in particular."

"Why's that?" Valec's voice is tight as a wire. He leans against the doorway, arms crossed over his chest. "Exactly?"

Heat floods my face. Natasia frowns. "I was told he consumed it at some point."

"Devouring Bree's root when he saved her from Arthur's dreamscape is what tipped him over," Lark explains. "Although Kane was already succumbing. Well on his way to his descent. If he's anything like other demons——"

"It's not a descent," Natasia interjects. "And he *isn't* like any other demon."

Lark raises a brow. "If he's tasted Bree's root, then he won't stop until he finds her."

"Not only that, but if he's consumed her power, he'll be more attuned to her root signature than he would be otherwise." Valec curses low, eyes flashing. "Kane's on the hunt right now, I expect. Tracking Bree down by her magic from *miles* away."

"Yes, but she's safe here," Natasia insists. "Selwyn can't find her in this house."

The table goes still. William speaks first. "Why not?"

"Because," Natasia says with a relieved smile, "Selwyn doesn't know Bree's been to Hazel's house before. He won't even know to look in this region, much less the state of Georgia."

William's fork clangs onto his plate. Mariah drops her head into her hands with a groan. And Lucille stands, tossing her napkin on the table with a low curse. "We got a problem, then."

"What's the problem?" Natasia asks. "Why's everyone upset?"

"Selwyn *definitely* knows Bree's been to this house," Lucille says sharply, "because they were *both* here together not five months ago!"

Natasia's on her feet in a blur. "I thought . . ." She looks down at me. "I didn't realize. Bree, I'm so sorry. I thought it was just the once, with your mother—"

"My mother brought me here?" I exclaim.

"Yes, she—" Natasia makes eye contact with Hazel, whose own face is stricken with some new understanding. Natasia's head whips back to mine. "That's not urgent. What's urgent is that Sel could be on his way—at any moment."

"Would he come straight here?" Nick asks, coming around to stand by Natasia. "He was with Bree a lot of places—"

"Like my bar!" Valec adds. "I swear, if he destroys the Lounge—"

"He scented Bree on my clothes from Daeza's, but that wasn't her root. Not a strong enough trail to follow. He'd start where he last saw her use magic." Natasia runs her hand through her hair. "Retrace his steps. Where were they last together?"

"The Keep," I say, heart thrumming in my chest.

"Where would he go after that?" Nick asks.

Natasia steps in front of me. "Where did you go after the Keep? The next place you used your magic?"

"The house in Asheville," I say, eyeing Zoe.

"That's good," Natasia says, nodding. "Asheville's a long way from the Keep. Even with an aether sense primed to detect Bree, distance *will* slow him down—"

"That's *not* good," Zoe corrects. "My brother is there! And he hasn't been answering his phone!"

"Bree was just at Penumbra," Lark points out. "Any trail she left behind at that other house is *days* old. Kane's aether sense is sharp but not *that* sharp."

"You'll be dismayed to hear that it's gotten better," Natasia says wryly. She turns to me. "How much aether——er, root—did you use at the Asheville location?"

My eyes widen. The barn, the house, the backyard—the ward *around* the barn. "A lot."

She raises a brow. "How much? How often?"

"A *lot*," I repeat. "And daily. For months."

"She's all over that house," Zoe says, voice strained as she walks away with her arms crossed over her head. "Elijah's a good fighter, but . . ."

"I don't feel murderous intent through the bond, and Sel won't hurt someone who doesn't threaten him," Nick says, then pales as he registers that he doesn't know what Sel would do right now. That none of us does. "Right?"

Natasia seesaws her head back and forth. "He's not his most *human* self right now. He is instincts, precision, and hunger. He hasn't fed for months, that I know of. He escaped several times when we were together, attacked . . . some people. Merlins and demons . . . I think."

"How do you know he won't attack humans?" my dad asks from his spot at my shoulder. "No offense, but he kicked your ass, and you're his own mother!"

"I was trying to keep him from what he really wanted. What he's craving. Sel doesn't *want* anyone else's power or emotions." She looks at me. "He wants Bree."

58

BREAKFAST SITS FORGOTTEN on Hazel's back porch. After Natasia's declaration, everyone moved inside to debate our options.

The debate was quick; there isn't much time.

I watch the cambions shift Hazel's furniture around, placing things gently out of the way after Natasia asked to make an open circle in the middle of the room.

My father stands at my side, eyes wide at the ease with which Zoe and Lark lift Hazel's heavy dining table. But some evidence of my churning emotions must show on my face, because after a moment he loops his arm around mine. I offer him a tight smile.

Old emotions batter my heart. Frustration, that a quiet moment, in what was meant to be a safe place, has already been interrupted by a new threat. Guilt, that Selwyn's sacrifice to save me has led to this. Worry, that we won't be able to help him. That he, like Lark, has followed the story of demonia that the Order has declared to be true—a path that Natasia so firmly disavows as false. Shame, that it will always be this way for those around me. A piercing voice within tells me that my friends and father don't deserve to be caught up in another one of my messes.

But when Zoe blurs by to sneak another biscuit before going back to work, her question from Penumbra finds me again. *Who does that benefit?* And when Valec pulls Nick aside to debate tactics for neutralizing Sel without harming him, I hear his words, too. *You had to fall . . . because you had to rise.* And when my father squeezes me close, immovable determination in his features even in the face of a situation he can't fully understand, he reminds me that this room of people are enacting his wisdom in real time.

Loving folks is a practice.

Guilt and shame won't help me here. They arrest motion, and now is the time to *act*.

"Wait," Valec says, and the room stops. "We need to take a second look at Bree's soul. It's why we came here in the first place—"

"Let me do this first," Natasia says. "Please. I'll buy you some time, in case Sel's on his way."

Valec steps back, shrugging. "Do your thing."

Natasia beckons me into the circle and puts her hands on my shoulders. "I need you to forge a construct, Bree."

I blink. "What kind of construct?"

"Something hard and strong. A construct that'll persist, even when you're not maintaining it." Her golden eyes look over my features. "You're powerful enough. *I* can feel it. Can you?"

I nod quickly. "Yeah. Yes."

"You sure?" Lark asks skeptically. Half the room shoots him a glare. "What? I'm not, like, *doubting* doubting. I just mean, you've never had to make one that, you know, lasts. That takes a lot of focus and precision. Years of training for most Merlins."

"Bree's not a Merlin, *Merlin*," Zoe shoots back. "She's got this."

"Zoe's right. Before . . ." I glance up at Valec, then Nick. "Before my soul piece was taken, I couldn't have done something like this. Now I can. I'm sure of it."

Natasia squeezes my shoulder. "I believe you." She steps back, giving me about eight feet of clearance. "Something big but not spherical. Protrusions are best."

I hold my hands out wide. "Big, not spherical . . . protrusions." I close my eyes and envision the space around me as the void from Erebus's early lesson. In it are two things: my power and myself.

I inhale slowly, and when I release the breath, I open the furnace in my chest. Distantly, I hear the others react at the sight of it, and I imagine what they see.

A roiling, purple eruption all over my arms and skin, licking up my throat, flowing down my legs, engulfing me in my own power. It writhes around my legs like snakes, curls around my body like living smoke, lifting my hair and tickling along my spine.

I don't need to use words for most workings anymore, but I find they help. So, for this one, I choose . . . *Grow.*

The power rushes outward into a swirling pool at my feet. I churn it into a round, smooth bud tall enough to meet my shoulder. Wide at the base, coiling into a pointed tip at the top.

Once the bud settles, I give it another push. *Bloom.*

Without much effort, the bud expands.

I open my eyes to watch the bright purple-white light of my root sparking and flowing, part flame, part liquid, as it blossoms open into a half dozen wide petals the length of my arm, with a set of secondary stems beneath them. When the petals open to reveal a crystalline center, I tell the bloom to stop.

The glowing flower shifts and floats in the air, breathing as it waits for my next command.

Valec whistles into the silent room. "Yeah, I'd say she learned a thing or two."

The concentration of root in my construct is so substantial that even my father can see it. When I look back at him, his eyes are filled with shiny pride—and my heart blossoms too.

Hazel shifts closer to me, clutching my arm. "Do you know what plant that is?"

I shake my head. "No. It just seemed right."

"Your mom grew these," my father says, "before you were born."

"What are they?" I ask.

"*Epiphyllum oxypetalum.*" Hazel's eyes have gone teary. "More commonly known as queen of the night. These flowers require regular sunlight to flourish and yet they only bloom in darkness, only one night a year. A Wildcrafter like your mother would have known exactly how to care for one of these plants. Sensed its blossom in time to watch it open and wilt before dawn." She wraps an arm around my shoulder. "These flowers take faith, Bree. Even when we can't see their progress, even when we forget they're growing, they bloom. And they are worth the wait."

I swallow around a lump in my throat.

"Faye would have loved this." Natasia looks to Hazel. "Tell Bree——"

"I will." Hazel nods.

"Okay," Natasia says. When she steps closer, the purple leaves of the plant sway toward her and illuminate her face in a deep lavender glow. "Believe me when I say that I think this is incredible work, Bree. Truly stellar. But"——she reaches up to a petal——"we're gonna have to destroy it."

She grimaces, wrapping her hand around the petal and yanking down—hard—until it snaps off in her hand. To my satisfaction, the petal holds its shape. A gleaming crystal in her palm.

Natasia turns and does a quick head count of the room. "How many cars?"

"Four, including yours," Valec answers.

She tosses the first petal to him and he catches it easily. "Take this one with you."

She breaks another off, then throws it to Lark. "That's two."

"You're using the petals as decoys," Nick says, stepping closer. "Splitting us off so that Sel will take the bait while we get Bree clear."

"Yup," she says. She crosses her arms over her chest and addresses all the cambions at once, a general before her troops. "Four cars, four different routes, one cambion per car. Valec and Lark will each take a piece of Bree's construct as bait, and I'll take one, too. Bree will ride with Zoe in the final car while she keeps her power secured and *hidden*. He should go for one of our cars before he picks up on hers. As cambions, you'll sense his presence faster than a human would and, with any luck, you'll be able to slow him down while Bree goes undetected."

Valec flexes his free hand, root sparking in his palm. "I can stop Kane just fine, Merlin."

Natasia regards him. "Noted. *You* might hold your own, but he won't make it easy. He'll be territorial. Any cambion who stands in his way will be considered a threat."

"What are you gonna do?" I ask. "You only broke off two pieces."

Natasia claps her hands together and forges a sprawling silver-blue net, then tosses it over the remaining core and petals of the flower. "I'll take the biggest bait with me. Leave first to try and head him off entirely. The two other Bree decoys will be backups while you head in the opposite direction." She collects the rest of my construct and hefts it onto her shoulder to walk through the sliding door to the porch outside.

"Wait!" I run after her. "How will we know if he takes the bait?"

Natasia shrugs. "You won't know unless you get somewhere safe and successfully take transportation he can't track as easily. A train or plane, maybe. This isn't a solution; it's a stall until you get where you need to go, and we get a handle on Selwyn."

"If I end up facing him, I don't want to do it without my memories," I protest.

"We'll tackle that next," Valec says, setting down his piece of the bloom for a moment. "Natasia, you go. Lark and William, y'all get going too."

Lark begins to complain, but William shushes him.

Valec continues. "We'll make this quick here with Bree, and then she, Zoe, and Nick can hit the road. I'll set an extra ward so that Hazel, Lu, Mariah, Alice, and Bree's pops are good and protected, then take off on my own."

"Mariah's with me," I say.

"My thoughts exactly," Mariah says, crossing her arms.

"Riah—" Valec starts.

"You didn't see her at Penumbra," I say. "With the Heart on she can take a cambion or a demon out if she has to, without getting hurt. I want her with me."

Valec looks like he might argue again, but this time it's Lu who stares him down. He groans, but gives up. "Fine."

Natasia is gone before I can say much of a goodbye. William and Lark leave next, and say they'll call us if they encounter Sel. They take William's phone, but leave Lark's with me so I'll have one to call the others just in case.

Everyone else watches as Hazel draws me and Valec into the now empty circle in the center of the room.

"Did you meet me as a kid, Miss Hazel?" I ask as she draws a salt circle over her carpet. "What Natasia said . . ."

She looks up. "Yes. But I didn't know it was you, or I woulda told you earlier. And, of course, when I worked with you, your power didn't surface." She finishes the circle and dusts her hands off. "When a Rootcrafter wants to get a handle on their child's likelihood of becoming a 'Crafter, of having a branch of power, they bring them to me. Sometimes, not all the time, but sometimes, they put a mask on the child so that no one can identify them later. Safety precaution, when they don't know me."

Lu frowns. "Which explains why I don't remember it. I step out when folks ask for privacy, even as the Grand Dame."

"How folks handle their magic is their business. We don't force people to disclose. You never know what they've experienced—or who they're running from," Hazel says.

"Faye was always careful about bringing new folks around the house," my dad says slowly, eyes distant with memory. "I just thought she didn't like company, but . . ."

Lu sighs. "It makes sense Faye didn't want her daughter to be identifiable to anyone, in the event that Bree inherited the Bloodcraft. A power like that needs to be hidden, protected, until it can be properly claimed."

"Hate to say it, but plenty of Rootcrafters would have been suspicious of Bree and her mother's Bloodcraft, given how folks feel about binding power from the dead to the living." Mariah sighs heavily. "So protecting Bree wasn't just about keeping her away from demons and the Legendborn, but her own community too."

"She took so many precautions," I murmur. "Plans within plans, for every possibility."

"Ten steps ahead," my dad says fondly. "Always."

"Now," Hazel says, her hands on her hips. "My branch of root allows me to petition the ancestors to strengthen folks' connection to their own life force. If I am working with an individual who possesses a dormant or suppressed vitality, or a hidden Rootcraft power, then I can ask the ancestors to help them surface it temporarily. If that individual's abilities have already presented themselves, however, like Valec's have, then I help them petition for greater control."

I beam. "That's great!"

"Not so fast." Valec's arms cross his chest. "What Hazel's not saying is that my ability to take stock of someone's magical luggage isn't a Rootcrafter power inherited from my Rootcrafter ancestors. That's a party trick gifted to me by my father. So, Hazel will be petitioning my *human* ancestors to help boost a power that came from a Shade."

"Is that why you don't think it's going to work?" I ask.

Valec sucks his teeth. "I said it *might* not work. As far as I know, it's never been tried."

"We can't control what the ancestors will do," Hazel adds. "But we can ask."

She walks over to her counter and comes back with a strong-smelling tea. "Ancestral magic of any type requires an open connection in both directions. In this case, we're opening the way using a mixture of dandelion, wormwood, bergamot, bladder wrack, and bay. My intention is woven into this tea already, Valec, so all you have to do is drink it."

"I think we have a cocktail like this at the Lounge." Valec takes the drink and sniffs it, wincing. "Nope, nevermind. That would never sell."

He tips the whole thing back and sticks his tongue out, shuddering as he hands the cup over the salt line and back to Hazel. "Gahtdamn, that's nasty."

I can't help but snicker. "Better you than me."

He shoots me a glare. "Get over here. Let's do this."

I step closer. He places his hand on my sternum—and nothing happens. "Valec?"

He grits his teeth, twisting his head to the side. "Gimme a minute."

We wait a second more, then he turns back to me again. "Look at me."

We fall.

The world turns red and redder, until it nears black. As if a thundercloud has passed over us all, stealing the sunlight from its journey to the earth before it reaches us.

Wherever we go, Valec is at my side. His fingers curl, turning to claws against my skin.

Someone shouts—but I can't move. Green smoke erupts between us and seeps from beneath his black-veined fingertips. Hands try to pull us apart, but we are seared together.

I hear voices.

The bright summer storm scent of Nick's aether swords reaches me from afar.

My eyes snap open.

Valec's eyes are a furious bloodred. His fangs rest long on his lip.

I had forgotten that part of him is so inhuman.

He snarls, yanking his arm back and pulling me with him—and then freezes.

His eyes begin to change. No pupil, no iris, no brown or red—just the bright, blazing golden color of root.

The room returns to me in bits and pieces. Daylight finds us through the windows. The others surround us in a tight, shocked circle. But all I can see is Valec, blinking.

"Well, that's different." When he speaks, his voice resonates and booms around the room, deep and grating.

"Can you see my soul?" I whisper.

He tilts his head as he stares at me. "Clear as day."

My breath catches. "And?"

Valec's brows tighten. "What did the King say, exactly, when you realized you'd lost people?"

That first morning comes back to me quickly. "He seemed curious that they were missing at all. Like he hadn't been certain what to expect from his own spell."

"So even the King of Shadows can only guess at the true essence of a human soul before he tampers with it," Valec muses. "Like I said, souls are unknowable. What else did he say?"

"That no one could reverse it."

Valec frowns. "Then why are the cuts so clean?"

"What do you—"

"This isn't the work of an amateur, or a demon out of control with hunger. No jagged edges. No tearing or shreds." He tilts his head the other way, eyes narrowing. "This is a precision cut by a steady hand who understands his craft. You make cuts like this when you want to *preserve* something, not destroy it."

My heart leaps in my throat. "Valec, please tell me good news."

He licks his lips. "I think . . . I think the King left things tidy so that he could make your soul whole again, if he wanted to."

"So it was a lie?" My eyes widen. "He said he can't restore it. That no one could—"

"Wordplay. Oldest trick in the book." Valec bares his teeth. "'No one' *can* reverse it. If the stories are true, that two parties are required to sever a soul, then the reverse could be true, as well. No one *single* person can fuse the two pieces. Only two. You both have to agree to return it whole, together."

Distantly, I hear Zoe curse. Something that starts with an "M" and ends, well, rudely.

"He'll never agree to that," I say.

"Not unless you give him a real good reason to reconsider." He squints. "But there's something else . . . something I couldn't see before. Didn't have the power." He steps closer, voice low with awe. "This ain't just a break. It's an injury. There's scar tissue here, and that's not on the King. That's all you."

"What does that mean?" I ask, suddenly frantic that I'll always have gaps.

"You lost an *aspect* of your soul." Valec murmurs a quick thank-you to his listening ancestors, and his eyes return to their usual brown. "Your soul is an engine, remember? Engines have critical components to help them run."

I shake my head. "I don't understand."

Valec smiles softly. "No matter where you are or what power you have, you choose to help, powerhouse. To fight. To save people. It's what you did with the missing Rootcrafter girls, isn't it?"

"Fighting?" I blink through sudden tears. "My soul can't *just* be about fighting . . . I won't survive that. I can't *live* at war—"

"It's not just about being at war. It's more than that," Valec says, stepping closer to take my hands. "When the King took part of your soul, he took the part of you that holds on to the folks in your life. *That's* what made them disappear. But that scar tissue proves that those missing people and the conflicts they bring to your doorstep are not *all* that drives you. Even in your own grief, even without your community, you healed over the raw break the King left behind, patched it up, and kept going. You used your soul again, risking reinjury, for a group of girls you didn't know, when nobody else was watching, just so you could sleep at night." When tears drip down my face, he wraps his arms around me, holding me tight. "You pushed me to try something today that I never even thought was possible, just because you wouldn't give up on yourself and you *refused* to give up on me. Even when you choose yourself, you turn hope into something tangible for the rest of us. Even when you choose *not* to fight, you turn the tides. If you ask me, that right there is the soul of a king."

"Soul of a leader," my father adds.

"A hero," says Nick, eyes fond.

"An icon!" Zoe shouts, grinning.

The room laughs, but I blink through tears, shaking my head. "I didn't . . ."

"Yes, you did." Valec draws back to look at me. "That's the point. What you chose, yeah?"

I nod. "Yeah." He lets me go with a squeeze.

"So, what's the move?" Mariah asks. She glances at the still-glowing petal. "We gotta leave here as soon as possible. Where we headed?"

They all look to me, waiting, and for once, I don't feel like their expectations, their hopes, are a burden. They're . . . an honor. And one I won't take for granted.

"I have an idea."

Two minutes later, I'm on the back porch, pacing while my friends and family watch. The phone rings once, twice, then the line picks up.

The voice on the other end is low and even. Far too calm. "Would I be correct in assuming that you are not, in fact, Larkin Douglas?"

I wait a beat before I reply. "You'd be correct."

Silence.

"Have the rules changed, Briana?"

I look at my friends. My father. Nick. And think of everyone who's still missing. Of Alice. "They have."

Another beat.

"I see."

"We need to meet."

"Why is that?"

"Because you have something of mine." My eyes slide to the brown cloth—covered crown on Hazel's counter. "And I have something of yours."

He chuckles. "All right. Meet me at Mikael's estate, tonight in the back grounds. If you aren't here on the property by the time the sun sets, then I will pay a visit to the home of the Dame. I heard your father went missing—would I find him there?"

I grip the phone but remain calm. "No need for threats. I'll be there."

"You are a very clever, very resourceful girl. Before you come up with a scheme to cross me, may I remind you, I hold an unmet bargain over your head?"

"I think you'll listen to what I have to say."

"And why is that, Briana?" His voice is hard and unforgiving. "What would I gain from giving up my advantage? I could simply order you to give my crown to me as soon as you arrive."

I expected that question, and so my answer is ready.

"You could," I say. "But if you do not, and you hear me out, you'll receive something from *me* that I will never offer you again."

"Oh?" he says. "And that is?"

"My mercy, Erebus," I say. "My mercy."

59

EVEN THOUGH HAZEL and my father both insist that I eat a full meal, we set out for Penumbra in Valec's nice SUV with more than enough time to spare.

But we're racing against time on not one count, but two: the clock Erebus has set in motion and the one driven by Sel.

Everyone in our car is silent with tension.

Zoe insisted on driving, citing her nerves, and Nick took the passenger seat beside her. Mariah and I are in the back with the wrapped crown sitting on the floorboard at our feet. I've never been so thankful that the Morgaine enchantment around the crown—and around the crown shard in Nick's chest—is still in place. We're already hoping to avoid Sel's attention. We can't afford any extra trouble from demons we might meet on the road.

About halfway to the estate, Mariah clears her throat and turns to me. "Wild to think that your mom brought you to Hazel when you were a kid."

I tap my knee nervously. "Every time I think I know what that woman was all about, she finds some way to surprise me."

"Sounds like a fun lady."

I smirk. "The best."

"Slow down." Nick's voice sets us all on edge. "There's something in the road."

Zoe slows the car. "I see it too."

"Could be a boulder," Mariah says. "The mountains around here get rock-slides. . . ."

"Could be a trap." Nick says what we're all thinking.

The car rolls to a stop, but nobody gets out.

We're still about a hundred yards away, but even I can see the object in the road now. "It does look like a boulder," I say, "but why is there only one? If it were a rockslide, wouldn't there be others?"

"Maybe." Mariah checks the phone her aunts let us borrow. "No texts from anyone else."

"Do you even get reception out here?" I ask.

She looks chagrined. "Depends."

Zoe scoffs and puts the car into park. "We gotta move it, so we may as well get out." When she opens her door, the world sends cold wind rushing to meet our faces, driving away the warmth of the car's interior. We're on an empty, two-lane mountain road, with a rocky cliff face high on our right, a steep drop-off into a wide valley to the left, and a deeply packed forest beyond.

I move to open my own door, and Nick shoots me a glare over the back of his seat. "Any chance you'd stay in the car?"

"Nope," I say.

"Right." He nods to himself as he unlocks his door. "Why do I even ask?"

"Hope is good for the spirit," I say brightly, and get out.

Mariah hesitates, but then I hear her door open too. The four of us stand in a line in front of the still-running car. The sun is still visible between the clouds in the sky over the valley, but it's definitely starting its trek to the horizon. Up ahead, the road climbs up before it curves right to disappear behind the mountain. Road signs warn about oncoming traffic, falling rocks, and treacherously reduced visibility around the tight bend. We gave ourselves a couple of hours to get to Penumbra, and while we built in an extra hour of buffer, this boulder is already eating into it.

"I can help Zoe move it," I offer.

Nick's watchful gaze searches past the boulder, up to the cliffside on our right, back down the empty road behind us. "Make it quick?"

"Quick as we can," I reply. Zoe and I stride forward together, both of our eyes scanning the boulder and the road ahead—and the curve, where another car could appear at any moment.

Zoe squats down near the boulder, and I mirror her on the other side. "Lift with your legs."

I roll my eyes, finding awkward handholds around the hard surface. "Mm-hmm. On one?"

"Two."

"Three." We get it up in the air by about a foot before we have to drop it. It's too smooth to grip securely. "Roll it?"

"Yep."

This time, we both get on the same side, ready to push—until a hot, searing line of attention strokes down my cheek. I stand up abruptly, clapping a hand to my face.

"What are you—"

"Shh." I cast my gaze around the road. "Someone's here."

Nick rushes to my side. "Which direction?"

The burning attention on my skin shifts to the back of my neck, to the other side, to my forehead. "I don't know. We need to—"

The three of us turn our backs against the boulder as one, arms spread wide. Armor ripples up Nick's body in a fluid wave. Zoe snaps a long, angry-looking mace into her right hand. I don't dare call my root, just in case . . . It's not *him*.

"Zoe!" a familiar voice shouts, and we all turn back toward the car—to find Elijah standing by the car with one hand wrapped around Mariah's arm and the other clasped across her terrified face.

"Elijah?" Zoe calls.

"Let my sister go!" Elijah yells, fangs bared at me and Nick. "Let her go or I'll hurt your friend!"

The three of us freeze in shock. At the violence in Elijah's red eyes. The desperation in his ragged voice. The tight grip he has on the delicate joint of Mariah's elbow.

"Elijah," I murmur. "What are you doing?"

"Making sure my sister is safe!" By the look on Mariah's face, Elijah must have snuck up on her without making a single sound. She lets out a muffled scream, and he twists her closer to his body, snarling in her ear, "Shut up!"

I lunge forward—and Nick pulls me back. "Wait."

"Let her go, Elijah!" Zoe drops her weapon, letting it spark to dust on the road, and blurs toward her brother. She stops halfway between us. "Nick and Bree aren't hurting me!"

Elijah's flashing eyes dart between me and Nick. "But your voicemails, your texts—"

"Why didn't you call me back?" Zoe shouts.

"Penumbra was blocked off, so I was in the mountains looking for you! The messages all came through at once when I got home. In the last one, you said you were heading back to Penumbra!" Elijah yells, face uncertain. "The old man wasn't home, I knew something went sideways with Mikael, and . . . you sounded scared."

Something like embarrassment colors Zoe's features. "Just let Mariah go, Elijah."

Elijah hesitates for only a moment before releasing Mariah. He speeds to the middle of the road to meet Zoe, and the siblings wrap each other in a tight hug.

I breathe a sigh of relief while Nick shouts to Mariah, "Get in the car!"

"Don't have to tell me twice!" she yells back, and climbs into the SUV, slamming the door shut and locking it behind her.

We're standing just close enough to hear Elijah mutter into his sister's shoulder, "The old man left and didn't come back, didn't tell me where he was going. I lost contact with you and Bree, and then . . . there were rumors of a new player," he says. "Someone too dangerous to do business with. Someone on the hunt, willing to hurt cambions. I thought the Merlin you called about might be going after you—"

"Kane's not after me," Zoe says. She pulls away from her brother, tipping her head in my direction. "He wants Bree. It's just like the old man said. An unbalanced cambion that sent himself over the edge."

Elijah eyes me, then Nick, then looks back at his sister. "The old man—"

"Can't be trusted," Zoe says sternly. "He *lied*. To us. To you."

Elijah's brows draw together in confusion. "No, he . . ."

"He *lied*, Elijah!" Zoe snaps. "We're on our own now. It's you and it's me, and that's it."

Elijah looks as if he wants to argue, but before he can, both of their heads snap to the far side of the road—and to the shadowed curve that disappears around the mountain cliff.

"What is it?" I step closer. "What do you hear?"

Fear returns to Elijah's eyes until it makes them flash back and forth between crimson and brown. "Zoe . . . ," he whispers.

Zoe tucks her chin to her chest. "I hear it."

"But *we* can't," Nick says, shifting his stance until his back faces the long drop-off into the valley and he can more easily see the road in either direction. We both turn to check on Mariah—she's in the car, eyes wide, a hundred feet away—before peering back into the darkness, where the cambions have sent their full attention. "Tell us what's going on, please?"

Zoe listens for a moment, focusing, then her eyes widen. She and Elijah go stock-still.

Heart pounding in my chest, I reach for her arm. "Zoe, what's—"

Without moving her head, her eyes find mine. "He's warning us."

My heart stutters still in my chest. Then begins again—faster.

Selwyn.

"What's he saying?" Nick asks, voice low.

Zoe listens for a moment longer, then turns back to her brother. The twins unite in a long look that I can't decipher. A look that isn't meant for me or Nick or anyone else.

Then, Zoe's eyes fall shut. "I'm sorry, Bree."

I know what she's going to do, what they're both going to do, before they do it.

I hazard a guess anyway. "He won't hurt you if you go?"

Zoe nods stiffly.

"You're cambions," Nick mutters, eyes filling with understanding, "so you're a threat."

Zoe nods again. When she turns to me, her eyes glisten under the moonlight. "It's just . . . it's just me and Elijah now, so—"

"Go." I meet Nick's gaze. "He won't hurt me and Nick."

Elijah and Zoe both jolt where they stand, as if electrified by an invisible circuit.

"You sure about that?" Elijah asks, looking between us. "Because he can hear you. And he just said, 'That remains to be seen.'"

Nick's jaw tightens. "Go. Both of you. We'll be fine."

Elijah has to pull Zoe away. He salutes me, face apologetic, as he draws his sister back toward the car. "Bree, I'm sorry about—"

"We'll be fine," I say to them both with a soft smile. "See you 'round, Elijah."

I don't know if either statement is true. But they feel much better than goodbye.

Zoe gives me one last look filled with remorse and worry, frustration and fear.

And then they're both gone, speeding down the road toward a vehicle I assume Elijah parked far out of sight.

Nick and I circle the boulder and turn to the empty road ahead of us—and wait.

The winter wind slices through my coat, lifting the loose curls on the top of my head up and away from my face. The scent of a summer storm fills my nose right before Nick's aether armor brightens, then darkens into a deeper blue. Without needing to recast it, he manipulates his armor into a more solid, thin construct that will make it easier for him to be agile. To move and run and dodge. But I don't get the feeling that he plans to do any of that. Not really.

My heartbeat is a living thing in my throat while my root pulses like an echo beneath my breastbone. I could call it to my upturned palms in an instant.

Harden a protective dome around us with a thought. But I don't plan to do any of that either.

The clouds shift overhead to reveal the bright crescent moon hanging low in the sky.

And still we wait.

Selwyn was close enough to hear our conversation with the twins—which means that now he is simply toying with our senses. Withholding his presence, on purpose. Watching us as we watch for him. Studying us. Letting our adrenaline build until it overflows, bleeding out on the dark asphalt like a carpet unrolled for a king.

Then—a cheery whistle splits the silence.

With the cliff on one side and the vertical stretch of mountains on the other, there's no way of knowing where it's coming from. It bounces from one side of us to the other. Nick shifts his weight, dipping his chin low against his chest.

In the distance, a dark figure appears around the curve.

Selwyn ambles toward us, whistling, in a long dark coat. Glowing green aether writhes around his hands and arms where they sway loose at his sides.

"That's new," Nick murmurs.

The figure's pace does not slow, although Sel must have heard Nick's voice in the night. The sensation of his gaze scalds my skin, and my shoulders draw up to my ears without my permission. I have to force them back down. That level of intensity in his gaze must be new, too. I can't imagine ever getting used to it, but then again, maybe I did?

"Sel," Nick says, voice even and quiet at my shoulder. "We should talk."

Sel doesn't stop walking, but he stops whistling. He tilts his head to the left, as if considering, but then the bright cheerful melody resumes as he continues to close the distance between us in even, leisurely steps.

"You don't want to hurt Bree," Nick continues, voice calm. "I know you don't."

The whistle rises until it pierces the air.

"Let her go," Nick urges. "Let's talk, just you and me. Bree has to be somewhere important, and there isn't much time."

Sel doesn't stop. With every step he takes, the sensation of his eyes against my skin grows hotter, brighter. "Please, Sel . . . let us go. Just for right now."

At my voice, he stops. Then, without warning, he is a dark blur against the shadows of the rocks, coming to a stop mere inches away.

This person is like nothing I imagined when I thought of "the Merlin boy who made me feel guilty." He is . . . all fire and anger, from the curling grin and long fangs to the glowing hands and black-tipped claws. His magic is a sour, burning wave against my face, so sharp that I have to shut my eyes tight against it. Terrifying and beautiful, all together, all at once, and everything inside me tells me to run—but I can't.

"Hello, Briana."

Nick's aether blade erupts to life between us, a thin, sharp divide separating Sel's chest from mine. The silver-blue light of Nick's sword illuminates Sel's smiling face and the dark veins spreading from his glowing red eyes.

"Hello, Nicholas," Sel purrs without looking away. "Thanks for the light. I do want to get a good look at her."

Nick's blade hand is steady. "Selwyn—"

Sel's eyes flick to Nick. "Your hair is too long."

Nick fires back, "No time to get it cut."

"The stubble?" Sel asks. "Really?"

"It's been a long few months."

"You have no idea." Sel's eyes snap back to me. "Drop the sword, Nicholas, or I'll break it."

"I don't want a fight," I say.

"There will be plenty of time for us to fight later." Sel's eyes trail over my face, my cheeks, my brow. "Why fight now, when you are as glorious as I remember? As powerful? More, even. I would rather enjoy simply . . . perceiving you."

"You can try to consume my root a second time," I warn, raising my chin, "but you should know that I won't make it easy."

He leans closer infinitesimally—throat pressing against Nick's blade—and I suck in a breath. Black blood beads along the silver sword where it cuts into his pale skin, but he doesn't seem to notice or care. "Please *never* make it easy."

Our gazes lock together. His, a hot blaze against my face and my lips, sends a shudder down my spine without my permission. My mouth works open and closed.

He grins. "Got you."

"Got who?" I whisper.

His grin widens, recognition and satisfaction sparking across his face. "I will never forget our first meeting." He edges closer, voice pitched like a low wave. A rush against my ears and chest and legs that threatens to tow me under. "The wildness in you. The fury. The *indignance*."

"She doesn't *know* your first meeting," Nick says in the quiet space between us. "She doesn't know you."

Sel rears back, alarm skipping over his features. "Is this a trick? Briana can't be mesmered."

"Not a trick and not a mesmer," Nick says. "This is why you need to let us go."

Sel growls, lip curling. "Is this what my mother meant when she said that I could not give Briana what she needs?"

I flush—and so does Nick.

Sel ignores us both as he searches my face. "You are missing part of your life? Unacceptable." He eyes the sword between us. "Remove your weapon, Nicholas."

"He's angry," Nick informs me in a careful voice. "But I don't feel murder in him. Your call."

I weigh my options. "Drop the sword."

The sword dissipates between us, bright silver dust falling to our feet. Nick rises out of his fighting stance but stays put beside me. "Did you throw that boulder into the road?"

"No. That cambion from Asheville did." Sel looks over my shoulder. "It was a helpful obstacle. Now we have time to chat."

"We *really* don't," I say.

"How did you find us?" Nick asks.

"Again, the cambion." Sel sighs as if bored. "I tracked Bree's root signature to a home and thought I might surveil it from the woods. Listen in from the outside. But then he played a voicemail that included your name and drove off in a rush. I followed."

My stomach sinks. Zoe's calls to Elijah led Sel right to us.

Sel's mouth turns down in mock concern. "Good thing Elijah's very worried sister called and left that final extremely frantic message. If she hadn't, I might not have found you for another day. Maybe two."

I cross my arms. "Your mother said you haven't fed."

The mockery leaves him, gone as if it had never been. "Came to see you, did she?"

"Yes."

His head drops back with a groan. "Always protecting a *Matthews girl*," he drawls, voice turning biting. "It seems that mission is her eternal fate—and her eternal failure."

"I don't need her protection," I say.

His head snaps forward. "You used to need mine."

"I was a different girl then."

Sel's voice turns raw, a brief unmasking. *"And I was a different boy."*

"You are still a Kingsmage," Nick says quietly, unfazed.

Sel blurs in front of him in a blink, eyes flashing up at the taller boy. He bares his fangs, words spiking between them in a hiss. "And what good is that? A Kingsmage without a king."

Nick's gaze is steady. "I was never your king, Sel."

Sel sneers. "A bonded brother, then? Trapped with a monster?"

"You were never a monster," Nick replies evenly. "And we were never brothers."

"What was I, then? And what does that make me now?" The register of Sel's voice slips lower and lower until it becomes a rumbling growl. "If not a willing and unwilling sacrifice on a *false god's altar?*"

"You are a Kingsmage. You can still *be* a Kingsmage"—Nick's eyes travel to me, then back to his bonded—"if you want to be."

"In name only!" Sel roars. "Never to be tied to my duty in truth *or* in magic! No. There are so many things that I can never be, things I never was, things I cannot become, even now in the wake of yet another one of my mother's glorious failures."

"You *aren't* a failure!" I say.

He smiles, harsh and slow. "And how would you know that, gorgeous girl? How could you ever understand what failure looks like? What it means to *fall*?"

I inhale a shaky breath. Swallow. "I know what it means."

"Oh?" he says. "In your time away from the Order, do you now comprehend how much of a *problem* I am? Especially when they find out my mother couldn't fix me."

"You aren't a problem to be fixed," I grind out.

Sel steps back a few paces. "Nicholas thought I was."

"No, I didn't." Nick shakes his head. "The Oath between us wasn't—isn't— *right*. It shouldn't have been forced on either of us. The Oath, my father, the Order, the Regents." Nick groans, eyes imploring Sel to understand. "All of *it* is the problem, Sel! I'm sorry if I ever made you feel like that problem was you."

Something unreadable passes over Sel's expression. "Did you ever wonder why the Kingsmage Oath binds us by our fear and by our rage? Those two emotions, specifically?"

Nick does not answer.

"I have given the question long hours of contemplation," Sel continues. "And I have concluded that fear and rage are not so different. The passage between them, so very slippery. We both held much of each, didn't we? Even before we were bonded." Sel turns to me, raising his hand to his mouth. "Can I tell you a secret, Bree?"

Nick and I share a glance before I answer. "Yes?"

He continues in a stage whisper. "Nicholas is not as tooth-achingly sweet and good as everyone thinks he is. He has his own demons. Pun intended."

Nick's eyes grow stony. "I've never claimed to be sweet or good."

"You never had to!" Sel straightens, spreading his hands wide, sending small streams of green aether through the air. "It was just . . . assumed. A benefit you were given. A benefit I myself gave you, even though I knew better."

"Sel, listen," Nick says exasperatedly, glancing at the moon overhead, "Bree and I have to go. We need to get to Penumbra. It's critical—"

"Nicholas Davis and Selwyn Kane." Sel ignores Nick's attempt to redirect him. "The sun and the moon. You are the warmth and the light and I am the bitter deep cold, or so it has always appeared. But we know the truth, don't we, Nicholas?"

Nick and I both go still as Sel approaches us. He comes to a stop where we stand shoulder to shoulder and leans in until his head hovers between ours. But as Sel brings his mouth close to Nick's ear, his crimson gaze slides to mine. In a low whisper, meant for the both of us, he asks, "Does she know that the moon lives in you, too?"

As Sel draws back with a satisfied smirk, he reveals Nick's shuttered expression. I don't think either Sel or I expect Nick to respond to the taunting question, but he surprises us both.

"She does," Nick whispers. "Just like she knows the sun lives within you."

Sel's seething anger sends him into terrifying stillness.

But not for long.

A sly grin reveals the dark tips of his fangs. He speaks to me this time, while his words are for Nick. "Did Briana tell you that she kissed me?"

Breath leaves me in a rush, my face flaming. I know that Nick is aware of what happened between me and his Kingsmage, but to me, this news is still fresh. Still information that I don't possess. It is, however, a memory that Sel does not mind sharing.

"No?" When Nick doesn't answer him, Sel's expression turns triumphant. "Well, she did. Pulled my face right down to hers, and I let her. . . . *Oh*, how I *let her*—"

"Stop," Nick commands. "I know what you're doing. It won't work—"

"She tastes like heat and danger and honey and"—Sel shudders—"*power*. Addictive, even without her root."

When Nick doesn't reply, Sel's brows lift. He looks between us, eyes narrowing, until he finds what he's searching for.

"I see. You two have become . . . reacquainted. And recently, too." He pounces on the idea of it, claws out and gleeful. "Does it make you jealous, Nicholas? That Briana kissed me while you were so very absent?"

Nick surveys him. "Do you *want* me to be jealous, Sel?"

Sel rears back, his laughter a breaking sound against the mountain. "All I am *made of* is want, now. I find I am insatiable—and I find I do not mind it."

"What *do* you want?" I step forward. "It's not just me."

He lets me come to him. "Haven't you figured it out yet, mystery girl?"

"No."

"I want what every demon wants, Briana." When he reaches for my hair, pausing to give me enough time to pull away, I don't move. He tugs on one of my black-brown curls, drawing it down only to release it and watch the recoil. "Chaos."

"Chaos will have to wait," I grit out.

Root flares along my wrist and up to his elbow, and his eyes widen in delight. "An aperitif?"

Quick as a snake, he catches a hint of the flame and brings it to his nose. His eyes fall shut as he takes a slow, savoring breath of my magic—and frowns. His eyes snap open. He looks back at me accusingly, sniffs again. "Something's wrong."

I glare back. "I'm aware."

His eyes flick to Nicholas. "Her magic is altered. *She* has been altered."

"That's what we've been trying to tell you," Nick says with a sigh. "We need to get to Penumbra."

"What will you do at this *Penumbra?*" Sel asks.

"Reverse it, if we can," I say.

Selwyn regards us both, then casts a long gaze at Nick. "Don't let me stop you."

"This conversation isn't done," Nick says. "We're not finished."

"No, we're not done," Sel agrees. He inhales again, seeming to brighten from the inside. "But this conversation *has* been . . . delicious."

"You're just going to let us go?" I ask warily.

He shrugs. "For now."

"And what will you do when we're gone?"

"Maybe you're right, Briana Matthews, and I am not a problem to be fixed." His eyes flare, red flame leaking from their corners. "But perhaps I should become one."

Before we can say another word, he turns on his heel, whistling an easy tune as he strolls back up the road and into the night.

60

WE ARRIVE AT Penumbra with only a few minutes to spare, still rattled from what happened with Elijah and Zoe—and stunned by our encounter with Sel. Nick cuts the engine in the empty driveway and peers up at the mansion through the windshield.

"Windows are dark," he mutters. "Every light inside, off. Looks like no one's home."

"I got used to it being busy," Mariah murmurs, leaning forward to gaze up at the darkened fourth floor and the starlit sky overhead. "Full of awful people but still . . . full."

"Did you message the others about Sel?" I ask.

Mariah nods. "Told them y'all had . . . an encounter."

Nick's hands grip the wheel. I shift in my seat. Neither of us has spoken about our meeting with Selwyn, but I can tell we're both still shaken from the hurricane of emotions he surfaced within and between us with only a few easy words.

"We need to focus," Nick says. "Let's go."

When Mariah, Nick, and I make our way around the back of the building by the light of the still-lit iron lampposts that line the brick-laid path, we do so as one, our steps aligning. But before we enter the gardens, I stop.

They pause ahead of me and turn back.

"What is it?" Nick asks.

I look at them both. "Mariah, if it's a fight, a physical one—"

"I'll run," she says. "But I'm not going back to the car. I took Mikael down."

"The King is not Mikael. He's who Mikael used to kneel to," I say.

She nods. "If he transforms, or I can't hold him, I'll tell you."

I turn to Nick. "And if you can't—"

"I can do it."

"But if you *can't*—"

"Trust me?" Nick says, stepping forward to squeeze my hand.

Love. Trust. Both a practice, I decide. "Okay."

When we reach the gardens at the back of the estate, Erebus is alone. He sits on a stone bench on the patio that overlooks the maze, one knee crossed over the other.

"You know what they say," he says as he stands. "Ten minutes early is on time, and on time is too late."

I stride toward him, scowling. "Spare me."

His eyes flick to my right, where Nick walks with me, then to my left, where Mariah has hung back as planned. "Bringing a human to a mage fight? Her tricks won't work on me."

I come to a stop before him with the cloth-covered crown resting at my hip. "'Unsettle your opponent early, so they never feel that they have the upper hand.' You taught me that in our second week of training."

He beams. "You *do* listen."

"Let's keep this simple," I say. "Give me back my soul fragment."

He claps slowly. "You uncovered the mystery."

I ignore that and hold the crown forward. "If you return my fragment, we'll return your crown—and remove its enchantment so that you can wear it once more."

Erebus's expression turns skeptical. "And how do you expect to do that? The Morgaines have gone to ground again."

Nick steps forward. "I can remove it."

Erebus narrows his eyes. "I've never met a Scion of Lancelot who could undo magic."

"And they say you can't teach an old dog new tricks," Nick says with a smirk.

With a sigh, Erebus turns back to me. "If Nicholas can indeed remove the enchantment, then you will return the crown to me . . . and I will consider our original, unfinished bargain completed."

I suck in a breath. "That's not what I offered."

He spreads his hands. "But it's the bargain before you. I find that owning a piece of your soul is much too beneficial to give it up this easily."

"So you're keeping it for your own amusement?" I ask. "You can't need it for yourself!"

He walks closer. "Do you know that most humans with broken souls never find their way back to their original path? They falter. Stray. Become people they never wished to be as they subconsciously guard what has been wounded. But you, Briana Matthews . . ." He tilts his head as he gazes deep inside me. "You risked irrevocable injury to pursue your life's mission. Perhaps risked losing even more of yourself for your troubles."

"I know about the scar tissue," I interject.

"Then you know what fascinates me. It is a rare being who keeps wading into the war of life with a fractured weapon. I find I am curious to see how much more powerful you might become with one hand tied behind your back. Perhaps I will only return the missing fragment of your soul when you are nearing your full potential. Then we shall see what heights you may still reach."

Nick steps forward. "That's not what we came here for—"

"You are not welcome in this bargain, *boy*," Erebus snaps. "This conversation is between kings."

"You say that, but I have *excellent* eyesight and when I look around"—Nick casts his gaze wide across the empty stone patio, voice wry—"the only king I see here is Bree."

Erebus's face pulls away from human, stretching briefly into an angry shadow.

"Unlike you, she stands with a court," Nick continues, "and unlike you, she could wear the crown in her hands without it burning her into a pile of ancient, feeble, forgotten dust."

The King's mouth snarls, a black abyss of claw-like fangs. *"Silence."*

"I accept," I say.

Nick's head whips around. "Bree!"

"I can't, *won't* let him hold this over my head any longer," I say to Nick. "He could ask for anything at any time. I won't give him open access to the rest of my life. No one is owed that, remember? No one deserves my suffering."

Nick's lips press into a line as he looks between me and Erebus. After a moment, he nods.

"Then we are in agreement." Erebus claps his hands together. "Now let us see if the arrogant Scion of Lancelot can be the second that his king requires."

Nick eyes him before turning back to me. "I'm ready."

I pull back the cover on the crown, then set it down on the bricks between us. A hint of blue crosshatched aether sparkles over the black metal in the lamplight. The old relic looks almost innocent here, but the open hunger in Erebus's eyes reminds me that it is anything but. Like him, the crown has not been harmless for the past fifteen centuries but dormant. Never powerless, but always hidden. Protected. The crown's true power has been locked away for so long, it might be easy to mistake it for something other than what it can be. Something less than what it can do.

Suddenly I feel an unexpected kinship with the ancient artifact—and wonder what we might both become after this moment of claiming.

Nick circles the crown, his eyes narrowing, then flashing a deep, deep blue. He kneels with both hands extended over its broken spires.

I hold my breath, hoping that this will work. Unsure what we'll do if it doesn't.

Then, one strip of aether at a time, the Morgaines' crosshatched glowing enchantment begins to peel away.

Erebus's eyes widen, grow redder with every passing moment. "Incredible."

Nick grunts softly with the effort, his shoulders riding up to his ears as his fingers curl down.

As the layered lines of Morgaine magic pull back, the black color of the crown seems to deepen. Lightning flickers across Nick's eyes, seeping from the edges in jagged sparks as he pulls the near final strip of power away.

There are only two glowing blue bands left, each stretching from one edge of the crown's circle to the other, forming a glowing X.

Nick glances up at me. The signal.

Then, in a burst of speed, Nick blurs twenty feet away to the far side of the patio.

"It's not finished!" Erebus shouts after him.

"I'm aware." Nick grins.

"Now!" I shout.

In an instant, black-and-gray shadows lift from Erebus's skin. He snarls at Mariah over my shoulder, "I told you, this won't work—"

I ignore him, clapping my hands together. *Contain.*

A shimmering purple sphere encloses me, the crown, and Erebus.

"Your barrier can't hold me either, Briana." Mariah's magic pulls shadows from his skin and clothing, lifting them away from his hair and from his cheeks until it looks like he is bleeding black swirls of air. "Neither of you is strong enough."

"Not trying to hold you," I whisper. "Just want to remind you what you've taken."

I hear Mariah's final gasp of effort—and the curling black wisps tugging at Erebus's body explode all at once around him, filling my sphere with a thousand ghostly bodies. Erebus's victims. Apparitions of his violence.

The crowd is churning, hovering on transparent legs, mouths snarling at the demon in the center of my sphere. I recognize some of the faces from my ancestors' blood walks: a young white man wearing fifties clothing and a Black man

Emmeline saw in New Orleans in the thirties. The thin man from the British Museum, Bianca's warlock lieutenant, Lawson, and so, so many others.

A multitude of genders, of races, people of different heights and shapes, people wearing modern clothes and dated clothes from across the country— no, across the *world*. And their glowing red eyes are filled with anger—but not toward me.

"You killed all these people . . . ," I gasp.

"Yessss," the Shadow King growls from a mouth of smoke. His crimson eyes burn in his true form—a winged creature with curved claws and black limbs made of darkness and mist. He is Erebus no more, because the ghost of the real Erebus stands a foot away from him, a young boy tethered to the King's body by a thick thread of smoke.

"And there are many, many more missing, Briana. Nearly twenty centuries of bodies I have devoured and consumed until I could walk in their skin, live in their lives, see as they saw, and experience all the ugly, sour, selfish flavors of humanity. And do you know what I have learned about humans in that time? In all your messiness and your striving, in all your choices and truths and lies?"

My voice comes out in a breathy tremble. "No."

"I have learned that you are *nothing* without your desires. Any power you have is driven not by what is right, or what is fair, or what your neighbor wishes, but what you *want*. What your will and intention make manifest."

"That may be true," I say, "but you need us, don't you?"

"A comforting lie," the King whispers, "but a lie nonetheless."

I meet his furious eyes. "You can't be *you* without all of *our* messy humanity. And I think you know that. You know it—and you hate it."

He snarls, his mouth of fangs wide and snapping.

Behind me, Mariah moans, and the King clacks in satisfaction. "She is tiring. She can't hold me forever."

He extends a clawed hand toward me—and my bloodmark flares to life. The scent of it fills my sphere—oud and sap, myrrh and incense. *Erebus's* scent, not the King's charred spice and embers. "Looks like you're getting tired too."

He snarls again, and the bloodmark flares, rippling across my skin and turning bright and burning. It takes me to my knees. I shut my eyes against the light—and remember my mission. Remember who *I* am. Who I can become, if I want.

I see Vera in my mind's eye. Her white dress and bare feet. Her smile and wry expression. I can't tell if it's a fantasy or if she's real. But I reach out for her, raise my arm so that it stretches between me and the demon who haunts us—and feel a thick thread form between my fingers.

My eyes snap open to find my arm extended toward the Shadow King, but my hand is empty.

Except it doesn't *feel* empty. It feels like I'm holding something hot and pulsing. Something that belongs to me.

"Bree!" Mariah calls. "I can't—" Her grip on the King's ghosts fails.

But the ghosts around me have their eyes on my hand, smiles filling their faces. They look at me as one—and then, they're gone.

I curl my fingers around the invisible thread—and the Shadow King jerks forward, falling onto bent limbs until we are both on the ground. Both leveled to our knees.

We stare at each other with wide eyes, mouths gaping.

Hazel's words ring clear in my mind: *Ancestral magic of any type requires an open connection in both directions.*

Two parties tied together by blood.

I squeeze my hand again, and the Shadow King lurches in response.

"What are you . . . doing?" the King gasps.

I could say I don't know, but as soon as I start to, I know that's wrong. Because I *do* know.

"I'm calling you." I push from my knees to my feet, holding the invisible thread tight, and as I rise, so does he. "An open channel runs both ways."

Alone in my sphere now, without the distraction of his ghosts, I see the fear in his eyes. It strikes quick, like his lightning, but instead of fading—it lingers. Grows. His black fangs widen.

"Let me go."

"Make my soul whole."

He chuckles. "You won't ever be the same again. Scar tissue, remember? Your soul fragments will never fit together the same way. You will be forever altered, Briana Matthews."

I grit my teeth. "I can live with that."

His wings flare wide. "You think you hold all the cards when there are still cards to play."

"What do you mean?"

He laughs again, the sound of boulders cracking and glass shattering. "Before I was Erebus, before I was the Shadow King, before *Arthur*, I was Arawn of Annwfyn—shepherd of souls to the otherworld. If you force me to return your soul . . . I will ensure Alice Chen *never* wakes."

My stomach drops. "What did you do to Alice?"

"I did not send her to purgatory, Briana. You did." He grins wide. "But my hounds tell me that she is there. Stuck. Unable to die, unable to live."

I chance a look back at Mariah, who kneels on the ground, panting from her effort. She looks as if she might pass out at any moment—something she warned me could happen—but she nods frantically. "There are hounds—I've heard them. They're . . . circling her. Hunting her."

My head jerks back to the smiling King. "I have not seen my realm in centuries, but my hounds still hear my voice. I retain some power yet. So choose, Briana Irene. Your innocent friend's life . . . or the reunion of your fractured soul?"

My head whips to the other side, to find Nick at the outside edge of my sphere, face torn. He holds my gaze, and I see every ounce of his faith in me there. That I can make this decision. That I *will* make this decision. Nick has faith in me . . . but I don't know if that's enough. If faith can make this choice easy or clear. Nick presses an aether-enveloped hand to my barrier, the collision of our powers sparking blue and purple at his fingertips.

"Your choice will be right," he says. "Either way."

I hang my head. Tears burn at the edges of my eyes. My fingers tense around the cord that binds me to a god. I feel my own scream before I hear it. My agony rips the silence in half.

"Decide, Briana."

My answer leaves me in a hoarse whisper. "Make my soul whole."

"As you wish."

It happens in an instant.

As Erebus returns my missing soul piece, the missing people return too.

And along with them, a flood of a million tiny memories fitting back into their places along the skein of my life. Faces around the table on birthdays. New people on the first days of school. My father at his shop. The guests at my mother's funeral. Nick on the quad at Carolina. The Legendborn at their trials. Meeting Mariah and Patricia on campus. William showing me the Wall of Ages. Partygoers at the Eno Quarry. Selwyn's wry smile and sarcastic voice. Alice hanging a poster in our dorm room.

The people, I expected. The full memories, I hoped for. But that's not all that returns.

It's as if my world had faded and I hadn't noticed its dimness, because surrounding those tiny million memories is deeper joy and sharper anticipation and richer humor—and so, so much love. Or perhaps my world had grown too bright and I had forgotten its shadows, because also surrounding these returned people is fear with more clarity, confusion with more severity, and fear. So much *fear*.

I inhale a shaky breath. Exhale a shuddering sigh.

I breathe through it all. Then do it again.

When I open my eyes, my sphere has turned root red—but I am too filled with anguish to appreciate its return. My magic greets me like an old friend, but its price was the loss of another.

"We'll—we'll get her back, Bree. We will." Mariah's voice calls to me, and I twist toward her where she kneels.

But I hear the crack of doubt in her words. Know that they're not a guarantee. Our eyes meet, and she nods once before collapsing to the ground in an exhausted heap.

When I turn, Nick meets my eyes through my red barrier. As I gaze at him, every feeling I'd started to nurture between us at Penumbra blossoms fully in my heart. I feel him in my heartbeat. Feel him in my hope. Call and response, deeper and richer. When Nick takes in my expression, he presses both hands to my barrier to bring himself closer, as if he can tell that our shared history is complete for me now, as it has always been for him. Then, I see what Nick had kept hidden from me until this moment. What he would have never revealed if I hadn't made my own decision to restore my soul. There, in the face of the boy whose eyes see so much, is an open, unfettered ache. While I had longed for Nick, he had *yearned* for me.

My heart breaks, and my barrier falls.

When I let the King go, he collapses back into Erebus's body on the ground. Blood streaks run down the sides of his mouth. His hand rises to his head, coming away streaked with blood.

His burning eyes focus on me where I stand. "And thus . . . ends . . . our lesson," he pants, then grins through bloodied teeth.

"What lesson?"

"You have become . . . ruthless, after all."

61

WHEN EREBUS CRAWLS to his crown, reaching for it even though it's still enchanted, I am too dazed to stop him. Too stunned that he's willing to risk touching it at all.

Nick shouts, running in a blur—

But Erebus is closer, hand outstretched—until a bolt of green aether slices through his bloodied wrist, severing his hand to the ground.

Nick skids to a stop and I freeze, while Erebus stares, stunned, at the bleeding end of his forearm.

A second bolt strikes him, blasting a hole through his opposite shoulder.

"I have always wanted to do that."

The voice comes from above me. I look up to find Selwyn staring down at his former mentor, fangs flashing in a grin, with both hands in his pockets. When Sel returns my gaze, our history floods me in a rush. In a split second, his face and voice and presence fill in the waiting gaps of our every shared moment. The emotions he's inspired tumble through me like dominoes, stealing my breath where they land. Guilt is there in my throat, but then frustration arrives. Indignation, not far after. When affection spreads through me like melted metal, heating everything it touches and leaving something even more molten behind, my eyes widen and my chest flushes—and he arches a single, amused brow. "Hello, Briana."

"Selwyn!" Erebus's fury snatches our attention. He is back on his feet, snarling—but then he sways, tipping forward onto both knees and his remaining limb. Blood pools beneath him, soaking his pants.

"You don't seem to be healing very quickly," Selwyn drawls. "All those bodies to draw from, twenty centuries and all that, and a little hole in the chest is slowing you down?" He scoffs. "Pathetic. Maybe you should go back to being a Seneschal."

Erebus's teeth pull back. "Nice to see you, Kingsmage."

"Can't say the same."

"It appears your mother failed you," Erebus sneers. "Or did *you* fail *her?*"

"Oh, I think there is plenty of failure to go around," Sel says. He stalks forward toward his former mentor. "So *you* were the snake in our midst the whole time. You commanded the legion of foxes at the Lodge. You planted the uchel attack on the road. You attempted to capture Briana before she underwent the Rite of Kings. And yet you had *me* arrested."

Erebus wavers on his knees, but his mouth kicks up. "Clever Kane."

The green aether in Sel's palm crackles. "You let the Order name me a traitor."

"Does it haunt you that the blame was so easily shifted?" Erebus straightens. "It should."

"Few things haunt me these days," Sel says. "Enough talk. Shall I finish you off?" Erebus eyes the crown—and Sel wags a finger. "Nuh-uh. You get to die, or you get to run. Two choices—take your pick. This dusty old piece of metal isn't one of them."

"That *dusty old piece of metal* was your ancestor's greatest prize. Merlin paid for it in pain and *blood.*" Erebus's eyes drag up to Selwyn. "You don't know the enemy you're making."

Sel grins. "Neither do you."

Erebus stares at me once more. "We've only just gotten started, Briana

Matthews. You still bear my mark. You are a king without a sword. A Pen-dragon, poisoned. Your own pain and blood await."

I lower my chin to level my gaze at the tormentor of both my bloodlines, my former mentor, my opponent—and my enemy, bleeding out on his knees. "Goodbye, Arawn."

He smirks—and a churning cloud of dark shadows sweeps him away.

When the King is gone, Selwyn peers down at me from one crimson eye. "You are yourself in full."

I gape at him. "I . . . what?"

He nods at the sparkling red root still glowing on the ground around us. "Your magic. Your scent. You." He looks down at me again. "I like you better this way."

I blink, shaking my head. "Thank you?"

"And you're quite fast, Nicholas." He turns to Nick. "That's new."

Nick comes to stand with us, his armor fading. "Sel, your powers are—"

"Much improved," Sel sneers. "Thank you for noticing."

He studies the crown where it lies on the stone pavers, lit by a single glow-ing line of magical protection. "We saw this crown in your blood walk, just after the original Merlin acquired it."

"Yes." I rise to my knees, ignoring the wave of dizziness and the answering weakness in my limbs. The memory of that blood walk appears easily. "The Table thought taking it from Arawn would be enough to weaken him. They were right, but it didn't last."

Sel tilts his head. "Merlin attempted to keep the crown from his apprentice, the original Morgaine. It seems his efforts were unsuccessful."

"The Morgaines' enchantment kept the crown cloaked from demon senses for centuries." When I glance at Nick, I think of the hidden shard in his chest—the one that neither Erebus nor Sel can detect due to that same Morgaine cloaking magic. "But now that Arawn knows we have it *and* he knows that Nick can remove the enchantment for good, he'll definitely be back to take what's his. We'll have to hide it too, like the Morgaines did."

Sel lowers to his heels to get a closer look. "I see."

A small pinprick of apprehension draws my stomach tight.

Nick must feel it too. "Don't touch it."

"Why not?"

"It could kill you," Nick says.

Sel frowns. "Less than ideal."

"The Morgaine enchantment also makes it so that no demon can touch the crown without dying, and well"——I hesitate——"you aren't a typical cambion right now. You're more . . ."

"Demonic?" Sel's lip curls. "You can say it, Briana. I won't be offended."

"Yes, demonic!" I say quickly. "You might die! Just . . . let me grab the wrapping—"

"'Could' and 'might,'" Sel muses, low voice singsongy. "'Might' and 'could.'"

"Selwyn . . . ," Nick cautions. *Don't.*

Sel's eyes gleam. "But those odds are *fun*." Sel extends a long-fingered hand—but before his fingers can touch a single black spire, the crown disappears in a blur of speed.

Sel's hand remains hovered in the air, arm outstretched, as confusion strikes him. Then, we both turn to see Nick standing ten feet away, one hand clutching the crown.

"No!" I scramble to my feet.

Sel can't touch the crown, but Nick shouldn't either. We don't know what the King's living creation will do if its broken pieces are reunited, even for a second. The crown already calls to itself as if it wants to be whole—and Nick's heart is bound to one of its shards. A wicked conduit quietly burning inside his body.

"Nicholas, that was very rude," Sel states, bewildered as I run past him.

"Drop it!" I skid to a stop an arm's length from Nick. "It's too dangerous!"

"Sorry," Nick mumbles. He sways on his feet, but when the crown falls from his hand, clattering to the ground, his balance returns. He shakes his head as if to clear it from a fog. "Had to. Had to stop him."

I start toward Nick, but he halts me with a look. "I'm fine."

"I have no clue what's happening with you two"—Sel stands, dusting off his pants—"but I do love a chase."

Sel moves toward Nick and the crown on the patio, but stumbles. His eyes fall to his left leg where it extends behind him—caught by a band of smoking red root coiled around his ankle. He follows the root to its source to find my glowing and curled fingers.

He makes a pleased sound. "You have new tricks too."

"More where that came from," I mutter, straining to hold him.

"Excellent. Keep them coming." He summons a dagger from the air, swiping it through my root in an instant. As he stalks toward Nick again, he extends a hand, curling his palm upward until bright green sparks appear in his palm.

I call root to both palms, preparing for a fight. Nick calls a blade to life in his fist.

As he pivots to face us both, Sel widens his fingers, then squeezes them closed—

And I gasp, my hand flying to my chest.

Sel stops to stare at my bloodmark as it flares bright.

"Calling you already?" he asks. "That old man really is pathetic."

But the scent of my flaring bloodmark isn't the same as it had been moments ago with Erebus. It's not the earthy fragrances of oud and incense and myrrh . . . but the charred spice I've grown accustomed to over the past few months.

This scent—warm resin turned to ash—has become as familiar as my own face.

A signature once rich and full, now burnt to embers.

I stare down at my bloodmark—and then back at Sel's hand as his fingers curl around the sparkling green flames in his palm.

I thought it was always the King calling me, his signature sometimes that of Erebus and sometimes that of his true form, but . . .

When Sel's fingers open, my mark pulses.

When Sel's hands contract, my mark dulls.

Nick speeds to my side. He watches the rise and fall of the bright light, his sharp gaze following the rhythm as understanding dawns in him, too. "Holy . . ."

"What?" Sel demands. "If you're trying to distract me—"

"Sel," I say.

He looks at me, annoyance incarnate. "Yes, Briana?"

"Your magic."

He rolls his eyes. "Is different now, I am aware. Do keep up."

"No—"

"Excuse me?"

"Selwyn!" Nick snaps. He points to his Kingsmage's hand and then to my mark. "Look."

Sel's eyes fall to the glow of my mark beneath my shirt, then travel back to his own palm. He opens his fingers wide, sending the aether flames high—and my mark blooms high with it.

His eyes widen, then narrow.

He repeats the motion, and my mark follows along.

His face and body go still. "When I woke up in my mother's cabin I felt a fathomless well of power but did not know where it was or how to find it. I pursued it as best I could, alone in my room, by calling out to it. Not once did I consider that that well might belong to you. Or that the power I craved and the power that felt so eternal . . . both belonged to you."

"How are you doing this?" Nick whispers.

Sel squeezes his hand shut, then opens it wide. "How, indeed."

But I know. "Bloodmarks can be . . . inherited."

Sel's hand stills. His flame falls.

The three of us stare at one another in silence. Waiting for someone to speak. To fill the empty patio with the impossible, *possible* truth. Sel's eyes fall to the crown on the stone between us.

Before Nick and I can stop him again, Sel waves a hand—and wide glowing green bands snap in place around us, pinning our arms to our sides.

"Stop!" Nick shouts, struggling. "Even if it is true . . . !"

Sel stares at the black metal crown and its uneven spires. "Yes, Nicholas?"

I groan, red root flaming from my arms. "Even if you touch it and survive the Morgaine enchantment, Arawn forged his crown to be its sole bearer! It's a living weapon, just like Excalibur, except if you aren't its true wielder, the crown could kill you!"

"There's that word again," Sel murmurs. *"Could."* His bands wrap our mouths shut.

Sel extends black-veined fingers to the crown, grinning at our muffled, desperate screams. When his fingers grip the thick black metal, the grin falls—as if he hadn't really expected to make contact with it.

A deep, ear-popping boom—and shadows explode beneath Sel's hand. They race up his wrist, ravenous for his skin. He hisses as the dark shapes twist around his forearm to his elbow, shooting to his feet with a grimace.

I use Arthur's strength to tear through one of Sel's constructs while Nick's arm is a blur, eroding a band at his elbow. But when we each snap a snare, the broken bands grow back in an instant—stronger than before. Crimson root burns bright and brighter at my fingertips. Nick's eyes flash deep blue and shining silver as he strains to unravel the ancient power consuming Sel—a power no one has seen in over a millennium. But our attempts to fight back make no difference; we cannot escape and we cannot stop the King's crown. The deadly shadows climb Sel's throat, forcing us to witness his destruction in helpless horror.

When the writhing, grasping streams of ink reach his cheekbones, Sel's head snaps back—violently. In a crack. In a snarl. His spine arches. Death slithers beneath his eyelids, slips between his teeth, then flows from his ears in raging black rivers.

The end comes quickly.

As Sel loses consciousness, he loses control. His glowing aether bands wither around us. A Merlin's decaying constructs, dimming beneath the starlight.

As our bodies are finally freed from Sel's waning magic, his body goes rigid—then lax.

As we hold our terrified breaths, Sel releases a single breath of his own—ragged, clawing, final.

Then, there is only silence and shock and heart-shattering agony . . . because Selwyn Kane is dead.

62

NO. NO. A howling scream builds in my throat, a choked gasp leaves Nick's—and Sel's body begins to fall. His head lolls back on his shoulders, lifeless. . . .

"No!" My voice, Nick's, I can't tell—

Before either of us can scream again, a thick gurgling sound emerges from Sel's chest.

The deep sound rises, expands, then pours from him in sharp, crackling waves. Greedy gasps, inhuman.

Then . . . his spine straightens, his head snaps forward—

And his eyes open—bright, boiling red chasing away the whites. His black-tipped fangs grow longer, gleaming in the moonlight, until his mouth is a hungry, vicious shape. The gasping breaths stop, become a low chuckle, become sinister in the night.

The weapon forged by death incarnate did not deliver death as promised. The King's living crown may destroy all false bearers, but it did not destroy Selwyn Kane . . . it transformed him.

Only then does the truth rise in full between us, like an unknown, unknowable silent secret now spoken aloud: like Excalibur, the crown recognizes its rightful heir . . . and Selwyn Kane is the Shadow King's son.

A hoarse, dazed laugh breaks past Sel's lips when he surveys the darkly pulsing metal in his hand. As if compelled, he raises the crown up . . . and places it atop his head.

"Looks like my father dropped this."

"Oh my God," I breathe.

"How, Sel?" Nick whispers. "How is this possible?"

"I have no idea." Sel's crimson gaze drags leisurely between us, both satisfied and ravenous. *"But here we stand and here we are. A king, a knight . . . and a prince."* Sel's smile spreads slow across his face, like thick blood flowing from a wound. *"What . . . shall . . . we . . . do?"*

THE LINE OF VERA

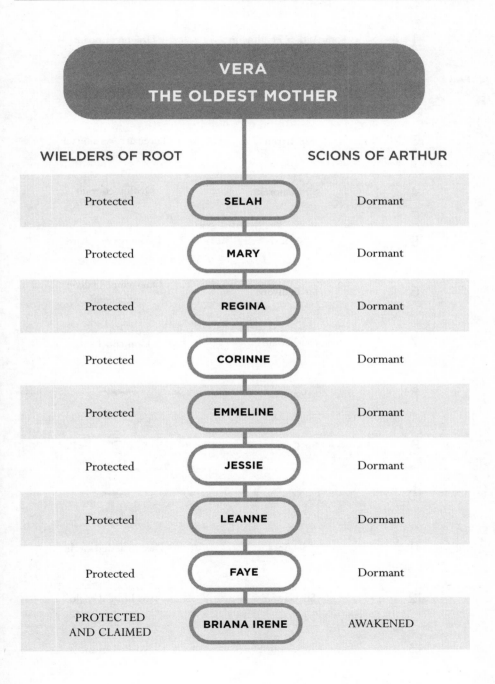

WIELDERS OF ROOT | VERA THE OLDEST MOTHER | SCIONS OF ARTHUR

Protected — SELAH — Dormant
Protected — MARY — Dormant
Protected — REGINA — Dormant
Protected — CORINNE — Dormant
Protected — EMMELINE — Dormant
Protected — JESSIE — Dormant
Protected — LEANNE — Dormant
Protected — FAYE — Dormant
PROTECTED AND CLAIMED — BRIANA IRENE — AWAKENED

RANK	BLOODLINE	SIGIL
1	King Arthur Pendragon	Dragon rampant
2	Sir Lancelot	Stag at gaze
3	Sir Tristan	Three arrows sinister
4	Sir Lamorak	Griffon courant
5	Sir Kay	Two keys in saltire
6	Sir Bedivere	One-winged falcon expanded
7	Sir Owain	Lion couchant
8	Sir Erec	
9	Sir Caradoc	
10	Sir Mordred	
11	Sir Bors	Three-banded circle
12	Sir Gawain	Two-headed eagle
13	Sir Geraint	Wolf courant

COLOR	INHERITANCE	WEAPON(S)
Gold	The King's Wisdom and Strength	Longsword
Storm Cloud Blue	Speed and Enhanced Vision	Dual Longsword
Azure Blue	Marksmanship and Speed	Bow and Arrow
Carmine Red	Preternatural strength (enduring)	Axe
Burnt Umber	—✳—	—✳—
Amethyst Purple	—✳—	—✳—
Tawny Yellow	Aether lion familiar	Quarterstaff
Aquamarine	—✳—	—✳—
Currant Wine Red	—✳—	—✳—
Midnight Black	—✳—	—✳—
Burnt Orange	Agility and Dexterity	Longsword
Emerald Green	Enhanced healer abilities; preternatural strength at midday and midnight	Dual Daggers
Stone Gray	—✳—	—✳—

ACKNOWLEDGMENTS

OATHBOUND IS THE book the Legendborn Cycle series needed, but not a book I originally planned to write. Many people helped make this book a reality, and many people helped me become the author who could write it; thank you, all. Special thanks to my readers on this epic journey.

Thank you to my parents: I miss you and hear you still. Thank you to my given and chosen families for supporting both my spirit and my long absences as I pursue this work.

Joanna Volpe: My gratitude for you as my agent grows with every book. Thank you for advocating for: my instincts, a career longer than any one book, and the trope turducken.

Kendra Levin: Thank you for tackling this impossible feat. We were spinning plates while juggling cupcakes inside a plot hurricane. *Oathbound* simply wouldn't exist without you.

Jenica Nasworthy, you are the only dragon tamer (i.e., production editor) who could take on this epic quest. I am so grateful for your endurance, patience, and commitment. Thank you.

Enduring thanks to everyone at Simon & Schuster, and especially the teams at Simon & Schuster Books for Young Readers. In particular, I am grateful to Justin Chanda, Anne Zafian, Tionne Townsend, Kaitlyn San Miguel, Sara Berko,

Chava Wolin, Hilary Zarycky, Chrissy Noh, Caitlin Sweeny, Alissa Rashid, Bezi Yohannes, Shannon Pender, James Akinaka, Amy Lavigne, and Saleena Nival; Michelle Leo, Nicole Benevento, Amy Beaudoin, and the entire education and library team; and Morgan Maple, Tara Shanahan, Lisa Moraleda, and the entire publicity team. Thank you also to Penina Lopez and Lynn Kavanaugh. Huge, endless gratitude to Laura Eckes for your artistic vision and to Laura and Hillary Wilson for this *powerhouse* of a cover!

Thank you to the incredible team at New Leaf Literary & Media, including but not limited to Jenniea Carter, Lindsay Howard, Hilary Pecheone, Eileen Lalley, Tracy Williams, and Keifer Ludwig. Special thanks to additional folks in the "Team Legendborn" community: Joniece Abbott-Pratt, Ashley Mitchell, Emily Ritter, Andrea Barzvi, and Dani Pendergast.

Enormous gratitude to my research consultants and readers: Dr. Gwilym Morus-Baird, Dr. Chanda Prescod-Weinstein, Lillie Lainoff, D. Ann Williams, Juno Baker, and David Taylor.

There are so many authors and creatives to thank for their support and advice, including Karen Strong, Olivie Blake, Daniel José Older, Brittany N. Williams, Leigh Bardugo, Roseanne A. Brown, Bethany C. Morrow, L.L. McKinney, Sabaa Tahir, Adam Silvera, Victoria Aveyard, Veronica Roth, Chloe Gong, Alex Aster, Victoria Lee, Ayana Gray, and Sarah Rogers.

To Mage of Space: Thank you for being our dream artistic champion.

To Annalise and Alyssa: Our spells are objectively the best.

To Kathy Hampton: Your magic is everything.

To Adele: Thank you for being both blade and shield for me and Bree. You're an army.

To Walter: You stand by my side to challenge the mountains, and when those mountains turn out to be volcanoes, you engineer a plan to conquer those, too. Thank you and I love you.